DURHAM PUBLIC LIBRARY

5/17

W9-CUQ-048

RISE
THE COMPLETE NEWSFLESH COLLECTION

BY MIRA GRANT

Parasitology

Parasite
Symbiont
Chimera

Newsflesh

Feed
Deadline
Blackout
Feedback
Rise: The Complete Newsflesh Collection

Apocalypse Scenario #683: The Box (ebook novella)

Writing as Seanan McGuire

Rosemary and Rue
A Local Habitation
An Artificial Night
Late Eclipses
One Salt Sea
Ashes of Honor
Chimes at Midnight
The Winter Long
A Red-Rose Chain
Once Broken Faith

Discount Armageddon
Midnight Blue-Light Special
Half-Off Ragnarok
Pocket Apocalypse
Chaos Choreography

Sparrow Hill Road

RISE

THE COMPLETE NEWSFLESH COLLECTION

NEW YORK TIMES BESTSELLING AUTHOR

MIRA GRANT

www.orbitbooks.net

This book is a work of fiction. Names, characters, places, and incidents are the product of the author's imagination or are used fictitiously. Any resemblance to actual events, locales, or persons, living or dead, is coincidental.

Copyright © 2016 by Seanan McGuire
Countdown copyright © 2011 by Seanan McGuire
San Diego 2014: The Last Stand of the California Browncoats copyright © 2012 by Seanan McGuire
How Green This Land, How Blue This Sea copyright © 2013 by Seanan McGuire
The Day the Dead Came to Show and Tell copyright © 2014 by Seanan McGuire
Please Do Not Taunt the Octopus copyright © 2015 by Seanan McGuire
"Everglades" copyright © 2015 by Seanan McGuire
All the Pretty Horses copyright © 2016 by Seanan McGuire
Coming to You Live copyright © 2016 by Seanan McGuire

Jacket design by Lauren Panepinto
Jacket images © Shutterstock
Cover copyright © 2016 by Hachette Book Group, Inc.

Hachette Book Group supports the right to free expression and the value of copyright. The purpose of copyright is to encourage writers and artists to produce the creative works that enrich our culture.

The scanning, uploading, and distribution of this book without permission is a theft of the author's intellectual property. If you would like permission to use material from the book (other than for review purposes), please contact permissions@hbgusa.com. Thank you for your support of the author's rights.

Orbit
Hachette Book Group
1290 Avenue of the Americas
New York, NY 10104
orbitbooks.net

First Edition: June 2016

Orbit is an imprint of Hachette Book Group.
The Orbit name and logo are trademarks of Little, Brown Book Group Limited.

The publisher is not responsible for websites (or their content) that are not owned by the publisher.

The Hachette Speakers Bureau provides a wide range of authors for speaking events. To find out more, go to www.hachettespeakersbureau.com or call (866) 376-6591.

Library of Congress Control Number: 2016904482

ISBNs: 978-0-316-30958-5 (hardcover), 978-0-316-30956-1 (ebook)

Printed in the United States of America

RRD-C

10 9 8 7 6 5 4 3 2 1

For those who choose to rise.
I am forever proud of you.

Contents

Introduction

The book you are holding in your hands right now is the culmination of a lifelong dream: my very own short fiction collection. It's my personal Frankenstein's monster, assembled one piece at a time and now brought to beautiful, terrible life by the combined efforts of my publisher, my editor, and you, the reader, whose willingness to follow me into this house of horrors has made everything possible. It may sound sappy, but I am grateful to you, down to the bottom of my heart, for this incredible gift. I hope it will mean as much to you as it has meant to me.

If you're here looking for a new full-length Newsflesh novel, I'm afraid you're going to be disappointed: This is not a novel. This is, as I mentioned above, a collection, a trip through the various side streets and territories of the greater narrative. You may have been to some of these places before. This volume contains every piece of formally published Newsflesh fiction, from *Countdown* and "Everglades" through to *Please Do Not Taunt the Octopus*. It also contains two new novella-length adventures, showcasing old favorites in places and situations where we've never seen them before. I hope those two novellas will be enough to tempt you into picking up the book, if you haven't done so already. (If you have, thank you. I, and my hungry cats, appreciate it.)

Because this is my first formal introduction for a piece in the Newsflesh world, I want to take a moment to talk about where it all started: with a series of dinners. My friend Michael used to live in Berkeley, California. Every Wednesday night, I and our mutual friend Jeanne would head over there for a home-cooked meal, a movie, and long, sprawling conversations about anything and everything that struck our fancy.

One night, while I was walking to the house, a bush shook suspiciously. Being me, I asked myself, "What if that was a zombie raccoon? What if we lived in a world where raccoons could be zombies? What if we lived a world where the zombie apocalypse happened and we didn't lose?"

I spent the next two years talking endlessly about this setting, mostly over those Wednesday night dinners. It was a thought experiment masquerading as a world, and I loved poking it from every angle I could find. My friends were...well, they were marginally less tolerant. Finally one night, Michael said, "Write the book."

"There's no story," I said.

"Find it," he said. "Or no dinner next week."

One week later, I had four chapters, a plot, a setting, and a cast of characters with whom I had fallen fully and immediately in love. What came after that was a lot of hard work and a lot of long nights, and I don't regret a moment of it. I am forever grateful to Michael for threatening to take away my access to his cooking, which turns out to be an excellent way to motivate me to write a novel. I am forever grateful to everyone who had to listen to me talk during the two years I spent slow-cooking this setting (with special thanks to Tony Fabris, for the loan of his kitchen table during the last three chapters of *Feed*). Most of all, I am forever grateful to each and every one of you. Thank you for reading. Thank you for following me this far.

Thank you for following me just a little bit further. There are monsters in these trees; there are dangers waiting for the unwary. But I'll show you the way, if you'll let me. Only trust me, follow me, and when I tell you that the rustling in the bushes is only the wind, believe me. That's all you have to do.

Now come on. We've got work to do.

RISE

Countdown

Introduction

When I first finished writing *Feed*, I thought it was a stand-alone novel. I was quickly disabused of this notion by, oh, anyone who had ever met me, and by the time it was approaching release, I was living 24/7 in the post-Rising world, sticking my nose into every nook and cranny—and there were a lot of them. I wrote book two. I wrote book three. I started writing short fiction set in the same universe. I started really figuring out the pieces that had previously been obscured by fences, or walls, or piles of corpses. And, as is my wont, I started getting twitchy.

When I am twitchy I generate words.

Thirty days from the release of *Deadline*, I went on my blog and posted the first in a series of entries chronicling the lead-up to the single most important in-universe event in the world of Newsflesh: the Rising. I began with the roots of both Marburg Amberlee and the so-called Kellis cure, a tailored strain of the common cold that was intended to protect against its virological cousins. I followed them through their release, and through their inevitable spread across the world. For thirty days, I posted something new every day, tracing not only the viruses that would trigger the Rising, but the people who would shape its course.

I'm not going to lie. It was pretty damn exhilarating.

Those thirty posts, collected and revised, became *Countdown*, the very first Newsflesh novella. It went on to be picked up by the Orbit Short Fiction Program, was nominated for a Hugo Award, and now it's leading off my very first collection.

Not too bad for a whim.

Countdown

"The Rising is ultimately a story of humanity at both its very best, and at its very worst. If a single event were needed to represent all of human history, we could do worse than selecting the Rising."

—MAHIR GOWDA

"People blame science. Shit, man, people shouldn't blame science. People should blame people."

—SHAUN MASON

May 15, 2014: Denver, Colorado

"How are you feeling today, Amanda?" Dr. Wells checked the readout on the blood pressure monitor, his attention only half on his bored-looking teenage patient. This was old hat by now, to the both of them. "Any pain, weakness, unexplained bleeding, blurriness of vision . . . ?"

"Nope. All systems normal, no danger signs here." Amanda Amberlee let her head loll back, staring up at the colorful mural of clouds and balloons that covered most of the ceiling. She remembered when the staff had painted that for her. She'd been thirteen, and they'd wanted her to feel at ease as they pumped her veins full of a deadly disease designed to kill the disease that was already inside her. "Are we almost done? I have a fitting to get to."

"Ah." Dr. Wells, who had two teenage girls of his own, smiled. "Prom?"

"Prom," Amanda confirmed.

"I'll see what I can do." Dr. Wells took impatience and surliness as insults from most patients. Amanda was a special case. When he'd first started treating her, her leukemia had been so advanced that she had no energy for complaining or talking back. She'd submitted to every test and examination willingly, although she had a tendency to fall asleep in the middle of them. From her, every snippy comment and teenage eye roll was a miracle, one that could be attributed entirely to science.

Marburg EX19—what the published studies were starting to refer to as "Marburg Amberlee," after the index case, rather than "Marburg Denver," which implied an outbreak and would be bad for tourism—was that miracle. The first effective cancer cure in the world, tailored from one of the most destructive viruses known to man. At thirteen, Amanda Amberlee had been given at most six months to live. Now, at eighteen, she was going to live to see her grandchildren...and none of them would ever need to be afraid of cancer. Like smallpox before it, cancer was on the verge of extinction.

Amanda lifted her head to watch him draw blood from the crook of her elbow. Any fear of needles she may have had as a child had died during the course of her cancer treatments. "How's my virus doing?" she asked.

"I haven't tested this sample yet, but if it's anything like the last one, your virus should be fat and sleepy. It'll be entirely dormant within another year." Dr. Wells gave her an encouraging look. "After that, I'll only need to see you every six months."

"Not to seem ungrateful or anything, but that'll be awesome." The kids at her high school had mostly stopped calling her "bubble girl" once she was healthy enough to join the soccer team, but the twice-monthly appointments were a real drain on her social calendar.

"I understand." Dr. Wells withdrew the needle, taping a piece of gauze down over the small puncture. Only a drop of blood managed to escape. "All done. And have a wonderful time at prom."

Amanda slid out of the chair, stretching the kinks out of her back and legs. "Thanks, Dr. Wells. I'll see you in two weeks."

Daniel Wells smiled as he watched the girl who might well represent the future of mankind walk out of his office. A world without cancer. What a beautiful thing that would be.

* * *

Dr. Daniel Wells of the Colorado Cancer Research Center admitted in an interview this week that he was "guardedly optimistic" about having a universal cure for cancer by the end of the decade. His protocol was approved for human testing five years ago, and thus far, all subjects have shown improvement in their conditions...

May 15, 2014: Reston, Virginia

The misters nested in the ceiling above the feeding cages went off promptly at three, filling the air in the hot room with an aerosolized mixture of water and six different strains of rhinovirus. The feeding cages were full of rhesus monkeys and guinea pigs that had entered five minutes earlier, when the food was poured. They ignored the thin mist drifting down on them, their attention remaining focused entirely on the food. Dr. Alexander Kellis watched them eat, making notes on his tablet with quick swipes of his index finger. He didn't look down.

"How's it looking?"

"This is their seventh exposure. So far, none of them have shown any symptoms. Appetites are good, eyes are clear; no runny noses, no coughing. There was some sneezing, but it appears that Subject 11c has allergies."

The man standing next to America's premier expert in genetically engineered rhino- and coronaviruses raised an eyebrow. "Allergies?"

"Yes." Dr. Kellis indicated one of the rhesus monkeys. She was sitting on her haunches, shoving grapes into her mouth with single-minded dedication to the task of eating as many of them as possible before one of the other monkeys took them away. "I'm pretty sure that she's allergic to guinea pigs, poor thing."

His companion laughed. "Yes, poor thing," he agreed, before leaning in and kissing Dr. Kellis on the cheek. "As you may recall, you gave me permission yesterday to demand that you leave the lab for lunch. I have a note. Signed and everything."

"John, I really—"

"You also gave me permission to make you sleep on the couch for the rest of the month if you turned me down for anything short of one of the animals getting sick, and you know what that does to your back." John Kellis stepped away, folding his arms and looking levelly at his husband. "Now, which is it going to be? A lovely lunch and continued marital bliss, or night after night with that broken spring digging into your side, wishing you'd been willing to listen to me when you had the chance?"

Alexander sighed. "You don't play fair."

"You haven't left this lab during the day for almost a month," John countered. "How is wanting you to be healthy not playing fair? As funny as it would be if you got sick while you were trying to save mankind from the tyranny of the flu, it would make you crazy, and you know it."

"You're right."

"At last the genius starts to comprehend the text. Now put down that computer and get your coat. The world can stay unsaved for a few more hours while we get something nutritious into you that didn't come out of a vending machine."

This time, Alexander smiled. John smiled back. It was reflex, and relief, and love, all tangled up together. It was impossible for him to look at that smile and not remember why he'd fallen in love in the first place, and why he'd been willing to spend the last ten years of his life with this wonderful, magical, infuriating man.

"We're going to be famous for what we're doing here, you know," Alexander said. "People are going to remember the name 'Kellis' forever."

"Won't that be a nice thing to remember you by after you've died of starvation?" John took his arm firmly. "Come along, genius. I'd like to have you to myself for a little while before you go down in history as the savior of mankind."

Behind them in the hot room, the misters went off again, and the monkeys shrieked.

* * *

Dr. Alexander Kellis called a private press conference yesterday to announce the latest developments in his oft-maligned "fight against the common cold." Dr. Kellis holds multiple degrees in virology and molecular biology, and has been focusing his efforts on prevention for the past decade...

May 29, 2014: Denver, Colorado

"Dr. Wells? Are you all right?"

Daniel Wells turned to his administrative assistant, smiling wanly. "This was supposed to be Amanda's follow-up appointment," he said. "She was going to tell me about her prom."

"I know." Janice Barton held out his coat. "It's time to go."

"I know." He took the coat, shaking his head. "She was so young."

"At least she died quickly, and she died knowing she had five more years because of you."

Between them, unsaid: *And at least the Marburg didn't kill her.* Marburg Amberlee was a helper of man, not an enemy.

"Yes." He sighed. "All right. Let's go. The funeral begins in half an hour."

* * *

Amanda Amberlee, age eighteen, was killed in an automobile accident following the Lost Pines Senior Prom. It is believed the driver of the vehicle in which Amanda and her friends left the dance had been drinking, and lost control while attempting to make a turn. No other cars were involved in the collision...

June 9, 2014: Manhattan, New York

The video clip of Dr. Kellis's press conference was grainy, largely due to it having been recorded on a cellular phone—and not, Robert Stalnaker noted with a scowl, one of the better models. Not that it mattered on anything more than a cosmetic level; Dr. Kellis's pompous, self-aggrandizing speech had been captured in its entirety. "Intellectual mumbo jumbo" was how Robert had described the speech after the first time he heard it, and how he'd characterized it yet again while he was talking to his editor about taking this little nugget of second-string news and turning it into a real story.

"This guy thinks he can eat textbooks and shit miracles," was the pitch. "He doesn't want people to understand what he's really talking about, because he knows America would be pissed off if he spoke English long enough to tell us how we're all about to get screwed." It was pure bullshit, designed to prey on a fear of science. And just as he'd expected, his editor jumped at it.

The instructions were simple: no libel, no direct insults, nothing that was already known to be provably untrue. Insinuation, interpretation, and questioning the science were all perfectly fine, and might turn a relatively uninteresting story into something that would actually sell a few papers. In today's world, whatever sold a few papers was worth pursuing. Bloggers and internet news were cutting far, far too deeply into the paper's already weak profit margin.

"Time to do my part to fix that," muttered Stalnaker, and started the video again.

He struck gold on the fifth viewing. Pausing the clip, he wound it back six seconds and hit "play." Dr. Kellis's scratchy voice resumed, saying, "—distribution channels will need to be sorted out before we can go beyond basic lab testing, but so far, all results have been—"

Rewind. Again. "—distribution channels—"

Rewind. Again. "—distribution—"

Robert Stalnaker smiled.

Half an hour later, his research had confirmed that no standard insurance program in the country would cover a nonvaccination preventative measure (and Dr. Kellis had been very firm about stating that his "cure" was *not* a vaccination). Even most of the upper-level insurance policies would balk at adding a new treatment for something considered to be of little concern to the average citizen—not to mention the money that the big pharmaceutical companies stood to lose if a true cure for the common cold were actually distributed at a reasonable cost to the common man. Insurance companies and drug companies went hand in hand so far as he was concerned, and neither was going to do anything to undermine the other.

This was all a scam. A big, disgusting, money-grubbing scam. Even if the science was good, even if the "cure" did exactly what its arrogant geek-boy creator said it did, who would get it? The rich and the powerful, the ones who didn't need to worry about losing their jobs if the kids brought home the sniffles from school. The ones who could afford the immune boosters and ground-up rhino dick or whatever else was the hot new thing right now, so that they'd never get sick in the *first* place. Sure, Dr. Kellis never *said* that, but Stalnaker was a journalist. He knew how to read between the lines.

Robert Stalnaker put his hands to the keys and prepared to make the news.

* * *

Robert Stalnaker's stirring editorial on the stranglehold of the rich on public health met with criticism from the medical establishment, who called it "irresponsible" and "sensationalist." Mr. Stalnaker has yet to reply to their comments, but has been heard to say, in response to a similar but unrelated issue, that the story can speak for itself...

June 11, 2014: Allentown, Pennsylvania

Hazel Allen was well and truly baked. Not just a little buzzed, oh, no; she was baked like a cake. The fact that this rhymed delighted her, and she started to giggle, listing slowly over to one side until her head landed against her boyfriend's shoulder with a soft "bonk."

Brandon Majors, self-proclaimed savior of mankind, ignored his pharmaceutically impaired girlfriend. He was too busy explaining to a rapt (and only slightly less stoned) audience exactly how it was that they, the Mayday Army, were going to bring down The Man, humble him before the masses and rise up as the guiding light of a new generation of enlightened, compassionate, totally bitchin' human beings.

Had anyone bothered to ask Brandon what he thought of the idea that, one day, the meek would inherit the Earth, he would have been completely unable to see the irony.

"Greed is the real disease killing this country," he said, slamming his fist against his own leg to punctuate his statement. Nods and muttered statements of agreement rose up from the others in the room (although not from Hazel, who was busy trying to braid her fingers together). "Man, we've got so much science and so many natural resources, you think anybody should be hungry? You think anybody should be homeless? You think anybody should be eating animals? We should be eating genetically engineered magic fruit that tastes like anything you want, because we're supposed to be the *dominant species*."

"Like Willy Wonka and the snotberries?" asked one of the men, sounding perplexed. He was a bio-chem graduate student; he'd come to the meeting because he'd heard there would be good weed. No one had mentioned anything about a political tirade from a man who thought metaphors were like cocktails: better when mixed thoroughly.

"Snozberries," corrected Hazel dreamily.

Brandon barely noticed the exchange. "And now they're saying that there's a *cure* for the *common cold*. Only you know who's going to get it? Not me. Not you. Not our parents. Not our kids. Only the people who can *afford* it. Paris Hilton's never going to have the sniffles again, but you and me and everybody we care about, we're screwed. Just like everybody who hasn't been working for The Man since this current corrupt society came to power. It's time to change that! It's time to take the future out of the hands of The Man and put it back where it belongs—in the hands of the people!"

General cheering greeted this proclamation. Hazel, remembering her cue even through the haze of pot smoke and drowsiness, sat up and asked, "But how are we going to do that?"

"We're going to break into that government-funded money machine of a lab, and we're going to give the people of the world what's rightfully theirs." Brandon smiled, pushing Hazel gently away from him as he stood. "We're going to drive to Virginia, and we're going to snatch that cure right out from under the establishment's nose. And then we're going to give it to the world, the way it should have been handled in the first place! Who's with me?"

Any misgivings that might have been present in the room were overcome by the lingering marijuana smoke and the overwhelming feeling of revolution. They were going to change the world! They were going to save mankind!

They were going to Virginia.

* * *

A statement was issued today by a group calling themselves "The Mayday Army," taking credit for the break-in at the lab of Dr. Alexander Kellis. Dr. Kellis, a virologist working with genetically tailored diseases, recently revealed that he was working on a cure for the common cold, although he was not yet at the stage of human trials...

June 11, 2014: Berkeley, California

"Phillip! Time to come in for lunch!" Stacy Mason stood framed by the back door of their little Berkeley professor's home (soon to be fully paid off, and wouldn't that be a day for the record books?), wiping her hands with a dishrag and scanning the yard for her wayward son. Phillip didn't mean to be naughty, not exactly, but he had the attention span of a small boy, which was to say, not much of an attention span at all. "*Phillip!*"

Giggling from the fence alerted her to his location. With a sigh that was half love, half exasperation, Stacy turned to toss the dishrag onto the counter before heading out into the yard. "Where are you, Mr. Man?" she called.

More giggling. She pushed through the tall tomato plants—noting idly that they needed to be watered before the weekend if they wanted to have any fruit before the end of the month—and found her son squatting in the middle of the baby lettuce, laughing as one of the Golden Retrievers from next door calmly washed his face with her tongue. Stacy stopped, biting back her own laughter at the scene.

"A conspiracy of misbehavior is what we're facing here," she said.

Phillip turned to face her, all grins, and said, "Ma!"

Stacy nodded obligingly. Phillip was a late talker. The doctors had been assuring her for over a year that he was still within the normal range for a boy his age. Privately, she was becoming less and less sure—but she was also becoming less and less certain that it mattered. Phillip was Phillip, and she'd love him regardless. "Yes."

"Oggie!"

"Again, yes. Hello, Marigold. Shouldn't you be in your own yard?"

The Golden Retriever thumped her tail sheepishly against the dirt, as if to say that yes, she was a very naughty dog, but in her defense, there had been a small boy with a face in need of washing.

Stacy sighed, shaking her head in good-natured exasperation. She'd talked to the Connors family about their dogs dozens of times, and they tried, but Marigold and Maize simply refused to be confined by any fence or gate that either family had been able to put together. It would have been more of a problem if they hadn't been such sweet, sweet dogs. Since both Marigold and her brother adored Phillip, it was more like having convenient canine babysitters right next door. She just wished they wouldn't make their unscheduled visits so reliably at lunchtime.

"All right, you. Phillip, it's time for lunch. Time to say good-bye to Marigold."

Phillip nodded before turning and throwing his arms around Marigold's neck, burying his face in her fur. His voice, muffled but audible, said, "Bye-time, oggie." Marigold wuffed once, for all the world like she was accepting his farewell. Duty thus done, Phillip let her go, stood, and ran to his mother, who caught him in a sweeping hug that left streaks of mud on the front of her cotton shirt. "Ma!"

"I just can't get one past you today, can I?" she asked, and kissed his cheek noisily, making him giggle. "You go home now, Marigold. Your people are going to worry. Go home!"

Tail wagging amiably, the Golden Retriever stood and went trotting off down the side yard. She probably had another loose board there somewhere; something to have Michael fix when he got home from school and could be sweet-talked into doing his share of the garden chores. In the meantime, the dogs weren't hurting anything, and Phillip *did* love them.

"Come on, Mr. Man. Let's go fill you up with peanut butter and jelly, shall we?" She kissed him again before putting him down. His giggles provided sweet accompaniment to their walk back to the house. Maybe it was time to talk about getting him a dog of his own.

Maybe when he was older.

* * *

Professor Michael Mason is the current head of our biology department. Prior to joining the staff here at Berkeley, he was at the University of Redmond for six years. His lovely wife, Stacy, is a horticulture fan, while his son, Phillip, is a fan of cartoons and of chasing pigeons...

June 12, 2014: The lower stratosphere

Freed from its secure lab environment, Alpha-RC007 floated serene and unaware on the air currents of the stratosphere. It did not enjoy freedom; it did not abhor freedom; it did not feel anything, not even the cool breezes holding it aloft. In the absence of a living host, the hybrid virus was inert, waiting for something to come along and shock it into a semblance of life.

On the ground, far away, Dr. Alexander Kellis was weeping without shame over the destruction of his lab, and making dire predictions about what could happen now that his creation was loose in the world. Like Dr. Frankenstein before him, he had created with only the best of intentions and now found himself facing an uncertain future. His lover tried to soothe him and was rebuffed by a grief too vast and raw to be put into words.

Alpha-RC007—colloquially known as "the Kellis cure"—did not grieve, or love, or worry about the future. Alpha-RC007 only drifted.

The capsid structure of Alpha-RC007 was superficially identical to the structure of the common rhinovirus, being composed of viral proteins locking together to form an icosahedron. The binding proteins, however, were more closely related to the coronavirus ancestors of the hybrid, creating a series of keys against which no natural immune system could lock itself. The five viral proteins forming the capsid structure were equally mismatched: two from one family, two from the other, and the fifth...

The fifth was purely a credit to the man who constructed it, and had nothing of Nature's handiwork in its construction. It was a tiny protein, smaller even than the diminutive VP4, which made the rhinovirus so infectious, and formed a ring of Velcro-like hooks around the outside of the icosahedron. That little hook was the key to Alpha-RC007's universal infection rate. By latching on and refusing to be dislodged, the virus could take as much time as it needed to find a way to properly colonize its host. Once inside, the other specially tailored traits would have their opportunity to shine. All the man-made protein had to do was buy the time to make it past the walls.

The wind currents eddied around the tiny viral particles, allowing them to drop somewhat lower in the stratosphere. Here, a flock of geese was taking advantage of the air currents at the very edge of the atmospheric layer, their honks sounding through the thin air like car alarms. One, banking to adjust her course, raised a wing just a few inches higher, tilting herself hard to the right and letting her feathers brush through the upper currents.

As her feathers swept through the air, they collected dust and pollen—and a few opportunistically drifting particles of Alpha-RC007. The hooks on the outside of the virus promptly latched on to the goose's wing, not aware, only reacting to the change in their environment. This was not a suitable host, and so the bulk of the virus remained inert, waiting, letting itself be carried along by its unwitting escort back down to the planet's surface.

Honking loudly, the geese flew on. In the air currents above them, the rest of the viral particles freed from Dr. Alexander Kellis's lab drifted, waiting for their own escorts to come along, scoop them up, and allow them to freely roam the waiting Earth. There is nothing so patient, in this world or any other, as a virus searching for a host.

* * *

We're looking at clear skies here in the Midwest, with temperatures spiking to a new high for this summer. So grab your sunscreen and plan to spend another lazy weekend staying out of the sun! Pollen counts are projected to be low...

June 13, 2014: Denver, Colorado

Suzanne Amberlee had been waiting to box up her daughter's room almost since the day Amanda was first diagnosed with leukemia. Her therapist said it was a "coping mechanism" for her, and that it was completely healthy for her to spend hours thinking about boxes and storage and what to do with things too precious to be given to Goodwill. As the parent of a sick child, she'd been all too willing to believe that, grasping at any comfort that her frightened mind could offer her. She had made her lists long ago. These were the things she would keep; these were the things she would send to family members; these were the things she would give to Amanda's friends. Simple lines, drawn in ink on the ledger of her heart.

That was thought. The reality of standing in her little girl's bedroom and imagining it empty, stripped of all the things that made it Amanda's, was almost more than she could bear. After weeks of struggling with herself, she had finally been able to close her hand on the doorknob and open the bedroom door. She still wasn't able to force herself across the threshold.

This room contained all Amanda's things—all the things she'd ever have the opportunity to own. The stuffed toys she had steadfastly refused to admit to outgrowing, saying they had been her only friends when she was sick and she wouldn't abandon them now. Her bookshelves, cluttered with knickknacks and soccer trophies as much as books. Her framed poster showing the structure of Marburg EX19, given to her by Dr. Wells after the first clinical trials began showing positive results. Suzanne could picture that day when she closed her eyes. Amanda, looking so weak and pale, and Dr. Wells, their savior, smiling like the sun.

"This little fellow is your best friend now, Amanda." That was what he'd said on that beautiful afternoon where having a future suddenly seemed possible again. "Take good care of it and it will take good care of you."

Rage swept over Suzanne in a sudden hot wave. She opened her eyes, glaring across the room at the photographic disease. Where was it when her little girl was dying? Marburg EX19 was supposed to save her baby's life, and in the end, it had let her down; it had let Amanda die. What was the good of all this—the pain, the endless hours spent in hospital beds, the promises they never got to keep—if the damn disease couldn't save Amanda's life?

Never mind that Amanda died in a car crash. Never mind that cancer had nothing to do with it. Marburg EX19 was supposed to save her, and it had failed.

"I hate you," Suzanne whispered, and turned away. She couldn't deal with the bedroom; not today, maybe not ever. Maybe she would just sell the house, leave Amanda's things where they were, and let them be dealt with by the new owners. They could filter through the spindrift of Amanda's life without seeing her face, without hearing her voice talking about college plans and careers. They could put things in boxes without breaking their hearts.

If there was anything more terrible for a parent than burying a child, Suzanne Amberlee couldn't imagine what it would be. Her internal battle over for another day—over, and lost—she turned away, heading down the stairs. Maybe tomorrow she could empty out that room. Maybe tomorrow she could start boxing things away. Maybe tomorrow she could start the process of letting Amanda go.

Maybe tomorrow. But probably not.

Suzanne Amberlee walked away, unaware of the small viral colony living in her own body, nested deep in the tissue of her lungs. Content in its accidental home, Marburg EX19 slept, waiting for the trigger that would startle it into wakefulness. It was patient; it had all the time in the world.

* * *

Amanda Amberlee is survived by her mother, Suzanne Amberlee. In lieu of flowers, the family asks that donations be sent to the Colorado Cancer Research Center...

June 15, 2014: Reston, Virginia

"Alex?"

The lights were off in the main lab, leaving it in claustrophobic darkness. Most of the staff had long since gone home for the night. That made sense; it had been past eleven when John Kellis pulled into the parking lot, and the only car parked in front of the building was his husband's familiar bottle-green Ford. He hadn't bothered to call before coming over. Maybe some men strayed to bars or strip clubs. Not Alex. When Alex went running to his other lover, he was always running to the lab.

John paused before pushing open the door leading into the inner office. The last thing he wanted to do was upset Alex further when he was already so delicate. "Sweetheart? Are you in here?"

There was still no answer. John's heart started beating a little faster, spurred on by fear. The pressure had been immense since the break-in. Years of research gone; millions of dollars in private funding lost; and perhaps worst of all, Alex's sense of certainty that the world would somehow start playing fair, shattered. John wasn't sure that Alex could recover from that, and if Alex couldn't recover, then John didn't think he could recover, either.

This lab had been their life for so long. Vacations had been planned around ongoing research; even the question of whether or not to have a baby had been put off, again and again, by the demands of Alex's work. They had both believed it was worth it for so long. Was one act of eco-terrorism going to change all that?

John was suddenly very afraid that it was.

"I'm back here, John," said Alex's voice. It was soft, dull...dead. Heart still hammering, John turned his walk into a half jog, rounding the corner to find himself looking at the glass window onto the former hot room. Alex was standing in front of it, just like he had so many times before, but his shoulders were stooped. He looked defeated.

"Alex, you have to stop doing this to yourself." John's heartbeat slowed as he saw that his husband was unharmed. He walked the rest of the distance between them, stopping behind Alex and sliding his arms around the other man's shoulders. "Come on. Come home with me."

"I can't." Alex indicated the window. "Look."

The hot room had been resealed after the break-in; maybe they couldn't stop their home-brewed pathogens from getting out, but they could stop anything new from getting in. The rhesus monkeys and guinea pigs were back in their cages. Some were eating, some were sleeping; others were just going about their business, oblivious to the humans watching over them.

"I don't understand." John squinted, frowning at the glass. "What am I supposed to be seeing? They all look perfectly normal."

"I've bathed them in every cold sample I could find, along with half a dozen flus and an airborne form of syphilis. One of the guinea pigs died, but the necropsy didn't show any sign that it was either an infection or the cure that killed it. Sometimes guinea pigs just die."

"I'm sorry. I don't understand the problem. What's wrong with your lab animals being healthy?"

Alexander Kellis pulled away from his husband, expression anguished as he turned to face him. "I can't tell which ones have caught the cure and which haven't. It's undetectable in a living subject. After the break-in, we're probably infected, too. And *I don't know what it will do in a human host.* We weren't ready." He started to cry, looking very young and very old at the same time. "I may have just killed us all."

"Oh, honey, no." John gathered him close, making soothing noises... but his eyes were on the animals behind the glass. The perfectly healthy, perfectly normal animals. Suddenly, it seemed like he couldn't look away.

* * *

Dr. Alexander Kellis has thus far refused to comment on the potential risks posed by his untested "cure for the common cold," released three days ago by a group calling itself "The Mayday Army"...

June 18, 2014: Atlanta, Georgia

The best description for the atmosphere at the Centers for Disease Control in Atlanta, Georgia, was "tense." Everyone was waiting for the other shoe to drop, and had been waiting since reports first came in describing the so-called Mayday Army's release of an experimental pathogen into the atmosphere. The tension only intensified when Dr. Alexander Kellis responded to requests for more information on the pathogen by supplying his research, which detailed, at length, the infectious nature of his hybridized creation.

One of the administrative assistants had probably put it best when she looked at the projected infection maps in horror and said, "If he'd been working with rabies or something, he would have just killed us all."

If he was being completely honest with himself, Dr. William Matras wasn't entirely sure that Alexander Kellis *hadn't* just killed them all, entirely without intending to, entirely with the best of intentions. The proteins composing the capsid shell on Alpha-RC007 were ingeniously engineered, something that had been a good thing—increased stability, increased predictability in behavior—right up until the moment when the idiots in the Mayday Army broke the seals keeping the world and the virus apart. Now those same proteins made Alpha-RC007 extremely virulent, extremely contagious, and, worst of all, extremely difficult to detect in a living host. The lab animals they'd requested from Dr. Kellis's lab in Reston were known to be infected, but showed almost no signs of illness; four out of five blood tests would come up negative for the presence of Alpha-RC007, only to have the fifth show a thriving infection. Alpha-RC007 *hid*. It could be spurred to reveal itself by introducing another infection into the host...and that was when Alpha-RC007 became truly terrifying.

Alpha-RC007 was engineered to cure the common cold, something it accomplished by setting itself up as a competing, and superior, infection. Once it was in the body, it simply never went away. The specific structure of its capsid shell somehow tricked the human immune system into believing that Alpha-RC007 was another form of helper cell—and, in a way, it was. Alpha-RC007 wanted to help. Watching it attack and envelop other viruses that entered the body was a chilling demonstration of perfect biological efficiency. Alpha-RC007 saw; Alpha-RC007 killed. Alpha-RC007 tolerated no other infections in the body.

What was going to happen the first time Alpha-RC007 decided the human immune system counted as an infection? No one knew, and the virus had thus far resisted any and all attempts to remove it from a living host. Unless a treatment could be found before Kellis's creation decided to become hostile, Dr. Matras was very afraid that the entire world was going to learn just how vicious Alpha-RC007 could be.

He sat at his desk, watching the infection models as they spread out across North America and the world, and wondered how long they really had before they found out whether or not the Mayday Army had managed to destroy mankind—with the help of Dr. Alexander Kellis, of course.

"Cheer up, Will!" called one of his colleagues, passing by on the way to the break room. "A pandemic disease that makes you healthy isn't exactly the worst thing we've ever had to deal with."

"And what's it going to do to us in a year, Chris?" Dr. Matras shot back.

Dr. Chris Sinclair grinned. "Raise the dead, of course," he said. "Don't you ever go to the movies?" Then he walked away, leaving Dr. Matras alone to brood.

* * *

The Centers for Disease Control have issued a statement asking that people remain calm in the wake of the release of an unidentified pathogen from the Virginia-based lab of Dr. Alexander Kellis. "We do not, as yet, have any indication that this disease is harmful to humans," said Dr. Chris Sinclair. A seven-year veteran of the Epidemic Intelligence Service, Dr. Sinclair graduated from Princeton...

July 2, 2014: Denver, Colorado

Janice Barton knocked twice on the door to Dr. Wells's office before opening it and stepping inside, expression drawn. "Do you think you can see three more patients today?" she asked, without preamble.

"What?" Dr. Wells looked up from his paperwork, fingers clenching involuntarily on his pen. "I've already seen nine patients since four! I've barely finished filing the insurance information for Mrs. Bridge. How am I supposed to see three more before we close?"

"Because if you'll agree to see three more, I can probably convince the other nineteen to come back tomorrow," Janice replied. For the first time, Dr. Wells realized how harried his normally composed administrative assistant looked. Her nails were chipped. Somehow, that seemed like the biggest danger sign of all. A man-made virus was on the loose, Marburg Amberlee was doing...something...and Janice had allowed her manicure to fray.

"I'll see the three most in need of attention, and then I have to close for the night," he said, putting down his pen as he stood. "If I don't get some sleep, I won't be of any use to anyone."

"They're all in need of attention. I can't choose. But thank you," said Janice, and withdrew.

She was gone by the time he emerged from his office, retreating to wherever it was she went when she was tired of dealing with the madhouse of the waiting room. On the days when it *was* a madhouse, anyway. This was definitely one of those days. The gathered patients set up a clamor as soon as he appeared, all of them waving for his attention, some of them even shouting. Dr. Wells stopped, looking at the crowd, and wondered if the other doctors involved in the Marburg Amberlee tests were having the same experience.

He was deeply afraid that they were.

The trouble wasn't the patients themselves; they looked as hale and healthy as ever, which explained how they were able to yell so loudly for his attention. Their cancers were gone, or under control, constantly besieged by their defensive Marburg Amberlee infections. It was the people they had brought to the office with them that presented the truly alarming problem. Husbands and wives, parents and children, they sat next to their previously ill relatives with glazed eyes, taking shallow, painful-sounding breaths. Some of them were bleeding from the nose or tear ducts—just a trickle, nothing life-threatening, but that little trickle was enough to terrify Dr. Wells, making his bowels feel loose and his stomach crawl.

They were manifesting the early signs of a Marburg Amberlee infection, during the brief phase where the body's immune system attempted to treat the helper virus as an invasion. That was the one stage of infection that could be truly harmful; when Marburg Amberlee was hit, it hit back, and it was more interested in defeating the opposition than it was in preserving the host. These people were infected, all of them.

And that simply wasn't possible. Marburg Amberlee wasn't transmissible through casual contact—or at least, it wasn't supposed to be, and if the trials had been wrong about that, what else could they have been wrong about? Pointing almost at random, he said, "You, you, and you. I can see you before we close. Everyone else, I'm very sorry, but you're going to have to come back tomorrow. See Janice before you leave, she'll set you up with an appointment."

Groans and shouts of protest spread through the room. "My baby's sick!" shouted one woman. A year before, she'd been dying of lung cancer. She'd called him a miracle worker. Now she was glaring at him like he was the devil incarnate. "What are you going to do about it?"

"I'm going to see you tomorrow," said Dr. Wells firmly, and waved for the chosen three to step through the door between the reception area and the examination rooms. He retreated with relief, the feeling of dread growing stronger.

He honestly had no idea what he was going to do.

* * *

Rumors of an outbreak of hemorrhagic fever in and around the Colorado Cancer Research Center are currently unsubstantiated. The center's head doctor, Daniel Wells, is unavailable for comment at this time.

July 4, 2014: Allentown, Pennsylvania

The streets of Allentown were decked in patriotic red, white, and blue, symbolizing freedom from oppression—symbolizing independence. That word had never seemed so relevant. Brandon Majors walked along, smiling at every red streamer and blue rosette, wishing he could jump up on a bench and tell everyone in earshot how *he* was responsible for their *true* independence. How *he*, working in the best interests of mankind, had granted them independence from illness, freedom from the flu, and the liberty to use their sick days sitting on the beach, sipping soft drinks and enjoying their liberty from The Man! They'd probably give him a medal, or at least carry him around the city on their shoulders.

Sadly, their triumphant march would probably be interrupted by the local police. The Man had his dogs looking for the brave members of the Mayday Army, calling them "ecoterrorists" and making dire statements about how they'd endangered the public health. Endangered it how? By setting the people free from the tyranny of Big Pharma? If that was endangerment, then maybe it was time for *everything* to be endangered. Even The Man would have to admit that, once he saw how much better the world was thanks to Brandon and his brave compatriots.

Brandon walked toward home, lost in thoughts of glories to come once the Mayday Army could come out of the shadows and announce themselves to the world as saviors of the common man. What was the statute of limitations on ecoterrorism, anyway? Would it be reduced—at least in their case—once people started realizing what a gift they had been given? Maybe—

He turned the corner, and saw the police cars surrounding the house. Brandon stopped dead, watching wide-eyed as men in uniform carried a kicking, weeping Hazel down the front porch steps and toward a black-and-white police van. The back doors opened as they approached, and three more officers reached out to pull Hazel inside. He could hear her sobbing, protesting, demanding to know what they thought she'd done wrong.

There was nothing he could do.

He repeated that to himself over and over again as he took two steps backward, turned, and began to run. The Man had found them out. Somehow, impossibly, The Man had found them out, and now Hazel was going to be a martyr to the cause. There was nothing he could do. The pigs already had her. They were already taking her away, and this wasn't some big Hollywood blockbuster action movie; he couldn't charge in there and somehow rescue her right out from under their noses. Her parents had money. They would find a way to buy her freedom. In the meantime, there was nothing, nothing, *nothing* he could do. Hazel wouldn't want him to give himself up for her. He was absolutely certain of that. One of them had to get away. One of them had to escape The Man.

Brandon was still repeating that to himself when the sirens started behind him and the bullhorn-distorted voice blared forth, saying, "Mr. Majors, please stop running, or we will be forced to shoot." The owner of the voice didn't sound like she'd particularly mind.

Brandon stopped. Without turning, he raised his hands in the air and shouted, "I am an American citizen! I am being unfairly detained!" His voice quaked on the last word, somewhat ruining the brave revolutionary image he was trying to project.

Heavy footsteps on the street behind him announced the approach of the cop seconds before Brandon's hands were grabbed and wrenched behind his back. "You call this unfair detention? You should feel lucky we're arresting you at all, and not just publishing your name and address in the paper, you idiot," hissed the officer, her voice harsh and close to his ear. "You think this country loves terrorists?"

"We were doing it for you!" he wailed.

"Tell it to the judge," she said, and turned him forcefully around before leading him away.

* * *

The ringleaders of the so-called Mayday Army were arrested today following a tip from one of their former followers. His name has not been released at this time.

Brandon Majors, 25, and Hazel Allen, 23, are residents of Allentown, Pennsylvania. Drug paraphernalia was recovered at the scene...

July 4, 2014: Berkeley, California

The Berkeley Marina was packed with parents, children, college students on summer break, dog walkers, senior citizens, and members of every other social group in the Bay Area. A Great Dane ran by, towing his bikini-clad owner on a pair of roller skates. A group of teens walked in the opposite direction, dressed in such bright colors that they resembled a flock of exotic birds. They were chattering in the rapid-fire patois specific to their generation, that transitory form of language developed by every group of teens since language began. Stacy Mason paused in watching her husband chase her son around the dock to watch the group go past, their laughter bright as bells in the summer afternoon.

She'd been one of those girls, once, all sunshine and serenity, absolutely confident that the world would give her whatever she asked it for. Wouldn't they be surprised when they realized that, sometimes, what you asked for wasn't really what you wanted?

"Where are you right now?" Michael stepped up behind her, slipping his arms around her waist and planting a kiss against the side of her neck. "It's a beautiful summer day here in sunny Berkeley, California, and the laser show will be starting soon. You might want to come back."

"Just watching the crowd." Stacy twisted around to face her husband, smiling up at him with amusement. "Aren't *you* supposed to be watching something? Namely, our son?"

"I have been discarded in favor of a more desirable babysitter," said Michael gravely. His tone was solemn, but his eyes were amused.

"Oh? And who would that be?"

Behind her, Phillip shouted jubilantly, "*Oggie!*"

"Ahhhh. I see." Stacy turned to see Phillip chasing Maize in an unsteady circle while Marigold sat nearby, calmly watching the action. Mr. Connors was holding Marigold's leash; Maize's leash was being allowed to drag on the ground behind him while the Golden Retriever fled gleefully from his playmate. "Hello, Mr. Connors! Where's Marla?"

"Hello, Stacy!" Mr. Connors turned to wave, one eye still on the fast-moving pair. "She went down the dock to get us some lemonades. Hope you don't mind my absconding with your boy."

"Not at all. It'll do both of us some good if our respective charges can run off a little of their excess energy." Stacy leaned up against Michael, watching as Maize and Phillip chased each other, one laughing, the other with tail wagging madly. "Maybe they can wear each other out."

Michael snorted. "That'll be the day. I think that boy is powered by plutonium."

"And whose fault would that be, hmm? I just *had* to go and marry a scientist. I could have held out for a rock star, but no, I wanted the glamour and romance of being a professor's wife."

This time, Michael laughed out loud. "Believe me, I count my blessings every day when I remember that you could have held out for a rock star."

Stacy smiled at him warmly before looking around at the crowd, the sky, the water. Phillip was laughing, his sound blending with the cries of seagulls and the barking of overexcited dogs to form just one more part of the great noise that was the voice of humanity. She had never heard anything so beautiful in her life.

"I think we should all be counting our blessings every day," she said finally. "Life doesn't get any better than this."

"Life can always get better." Michael kissed her one more time, his lips lingering lightly against her cheek. "Just you wait and see. This time next year, we won't be able to imagine looking back on this summer without thinking 'Oh, you had no idea; just you wait and see.' "

"I hope you're right," said Stacy, and kissed him back.

* * *

The annual Fourth of July laser show at the Berkeley Marina was a huge success this year, drawing record crowds. The laser show, which replaced the traditional firework displays as of 2012, has become a showpiece of the year's calendar, and this year was no different. With designs programmed by the UC Berkeley Computer Science Department . . .

July 7, 2014: Manhattan, New York

In the month since his report on the so-called Kellis cure had first appeared, Robert Stalnaker had received a level of attention and adulation—and yes, vitriol and hatred—that he had previously only dreamed of. His inbox was packed every morning with people both applauding and condemning his decision to reveal Dr. Alexander Kellis's scientific violation of the American public. Was *he* the one who told the Mayday Army to break into Kellis's lab, doing thousands of dollars of damage and unleashing millions of dollars of research into the open air? No, he was not. He was simply a concerned member of the American free press, doing his job and reporting the news.

The fact that he had essentially fabricated the story had stopped bothering him after the third interview request he received. By the Monday following the Fourth of July, he would have been honestly shocked if someone had asked him about the truth behind his lies. As far as he was concerned, he'd been telling the truth. Maybe it wasn't the truth that Dr. Kellis had intended, but it was the one he'd created. All Stalnaker did was report it to the world.

Best of all, he hadn't seen anyone sneezing or coughing in almost two weeks. Whatever craziness Kellis had been cooking up in that lab of his, it did what it was supposed to do. Throw out the Kleenex and cancel that order for chicken soup, can I hear an amen from the congregation?

"Amen," murmured Stalnaker, pushing open the door to his paper's New York office. A cool blast of climate-controlled air flowed out into the hall, chasing away the stickiness of the New York summer. He stepped into the room, letting the door swing shut behind him, and waited for the applause that inevitably followed his arrival. He was, after all, the one who had single-handedly increased circulation almost fifteen percent in under a week.

The applause didn't come. Instead, an uneasy silence fell as people stopped their work and turned to stare. Bemused, he looked around the room and saw his editor bearing down on him with a grim expression on his face and a toothpick bouncing between his lips as he frantically chewed it into splinters. The toothpicks had been intended as an aid when he'd quit smoking the year before. Somehow, they'd just never gone away.

"Stalnaker!" he growled, shoving the toothpick off to one side of his mouth as he demanded, "Where the hell have you been? Don't you check your e-mail?"

"Not during breakfast," said Stalnaker, taken aback by his editor's tone. Don never talked to him like that. Harshly, sure, and sometimes coldly, but never like he'd done something too wrong to be articulated; never like he was a puppy who'd made a mess on the carpet. "Why? Did I miss a political scandal or something while I was having a bagel?"

Don Nutick paused, forcing himself to take a deep, slow breath before he said, "No. You missed the Pennsylvania police department announcing that the ringleaders of the Mayday Army were taken into custody Friday afternoon."

"What?" Stalnaker stared at him, suddenly fully alert. "You're telling me they actually *caught* the guys? How the hell did they manage that?"

"One of their own decided to rat them out. Said that it wasn't right for them to get away with what they'd done." Don shook his head. "They're not releasing the guy's name yet. Still, whoever managed to get an exclusive interview with him, why I bet that person could write his or her own ticket. Maybe even convince a sympathetic editor not to fire his ass over faking a report that's getting the paper threatened with a lawsuit."

"Lawsuit?"

"I told you you needed to check your e-mail more."

Stalnaker scoffed. "They'll never get it to stick."

"You sure of that?"

There was a moment of silence before Stalnaker said, reluctantly, "I guess I'm going to Pennsylvania."

"Yes," Don agreed. "I guess you are."

* * *

While the identity of the Mayday Army's deserter has been protected thus far, it must be asked: Why did this man decide to turn on his compatriots? What did he see in that lab that caused him to change his ways? We don't know, but we're going to find out...

July 7, 2014: Somewhere in North America

The location doesn't matter: What happened, when it happened, happened all over North America at the same time. There was no single index case. It all began, and ended, too fast for that sort of record keeping to endure.

On migratory bird and weather balloon, on drifting debris and anchored in tiny gusts of wind, Alpha-RC007 made its way down from the stratosphere to the world below. When it encountered a suitable mammalian host, it latched on with its tiny man-made protein hooks, holding itself in place while it found a way to invade, colonize, and spread. The newborn infections were invisible to the naked eye, and their only symptom was a total lack of symptoms. Their hosts enjoyed a level of health that was remarkable mostly because none of them noticed, or realized how lucky they were. It was a viral golden age.

It lasted less than a month. Say July 7th, for lack of a precise date; say Columbus, Ohio, for lack of a precise location. July 7, 2014, Columbus: The end of the world begins.

The only carrier of Marburg Amberlee in Columbus was Lauren Morris, a thirty-eight-year-old woman celebrating her second lease on life by taking a road trip across the United States. She had begun her Marburg Amberlee treatments almost exactly a year before, and had seen a terminal diagnosis dwindle into nothing. If you'd asked her, she would have called it a miracle of science. She would have been correct.

Lauren's first encounter with Alpha-RC007 occurred at an open-air farmer's market. She picked up a jar of homemade jam, examining the label with a curious eye before deciding, finally, not to make the purchase. The jam remained behind, but the virus that had collected on her fingers did not. It clung, waiting for an opportunity—an opportunity it got less than five minutes later, when Lauren wiped a piece of dust away from her eye. Alpha-RC007 transferred from her fingers to the vulnerable mucus membrane inside her eyelid, and from there made its entrance to the body.

The initial stages of the Alpha-RC007 infection followed the now-familiar pattern, invading the body's cells like a common virus, only to slip quietly out again, leaving copies of itself behind. The only cells to be actually destroyed in the process were the other infections Alpha-RC007 encountered in the host body. These were turned into tiny virus factories, farming on a microscopic scale. Several minor ailments Lauren was not even aware of were found brewing in her body, and summarily destroyed in Alpha-RC007's quest for sole dominion.

Then, deep in the tissue of Lauren's lungs, Alpha-RC007 encountered something new, something that was confusing to the virus, inasmuch as anything can ever confuse a virus. This strange new thing had a structure as alien to the world as Alpha-RC007's own: half natural, half reconfigured and transformed to suit a new purpose.

Behaving according to the protocols that were the whole of its existence, Alpha-RC007 approached the stranger, using its delicate protein hooks to attempt infiltration. The stranger responded in kind, their protein hooks tangling together until they were like so much viral thread, too intertwined to tell where one ended and the next began. This happened a thousand times in the body of Lauren Morris. Many of those joinings ended with the destruction of one or both viral bodies, their structures unable to correctly lock together.

The rest found an unexpected kinship in the locks and controls their human creators had installed, and began, without releasing each other, to exchange genetic material in a beautiful dance that had begun when life on this world was born, and would last until that life was completely gone. Oblivious to the second miracle of science that was now happening inside her, Lauren Morris went about her day. She had never been a mother before. Before the sun went down, she would be one of the many mothers to give birth to Kellis-Amberlee.

* * *

It's a beautiful summer here in Ohio, and we have a great many events planned for these sweet summer nights. Visit the downtown Columbus Farmers Market, where you can sample new delights from our local farms. Who knows what you might discover? Meanwhile, the summer concert series kicks off...

July 8, 2014: Atlanta, Georgia

Chris Sinclair's time at the CDC had been characterized by an almost pathological degree of calm. He remained completely relaxed even during outbreaks of unknown origin, calling on his EIS training and his natural tendency to "not sweat the small stuff" in order to keep his head while everyone around him was losing theirs. When asked, he attributed his attitude to growing up in Santa Cruz, California, where the local surf culture taught everyone to chill out already.

Chris Sinclair wasn't chilling out anymore. Chris Sinclair was terrified.

They still had no reliable test for the Kellis cure. Instead of charting the path of the infection, they were falling back on an old EIS trick and charting the absence of infection. Any place where the normal chain of summer colds and flu had been broken, they marked on the maps as a possible outbreak of the Kellis cure. It wasn't a surefire method of detection—sometimes people were just healthy, without any genetically engineered virus to explain the reasons why. Still. If only half the people showing up as potential Kellis cure infections were sick...

If only half the people showing up as potential Kellis cure infections were sick with this sickness that wasn't a sickness at all, then that meant that this stuff was spreading like wildfire and there was no way they could stop it. If they put out a health advisory recommending people avoid close contact with anyone who looked excessively healthy, they'd have "cure parties" springing up nationwide. It was the only possible result. Before the chicken pox vaccine was commonly available, parents used to have chicken pox parties, choosing sickness now to guarantee health later. They'd do it again. And then, if the Kellis cure had a second stage—something that would have shown up in the human trials Alexander Kellis never had the opportunity to conduct—they would be in for a world of trouble.

Assuming, of course, that they weren't already.

"Still think we shouldn't be too worried about a pandemic that just makes everybody well?"

"William." Chris raised his head, giving a half-ashamed shrug as he said, "I didn't hear you come in."

"You were pretty engrossed in those papers. Are those the updated maps of the projected spread?"

"They are." Chris chuckled mirthlessly. "You'll be happy to know that our last North American holdouts have succumbed to the mysterious good health that's been going around. We have infection patterns in Newfoundland and Alaska. In both cases, I was able to find records showing that the pattern manifested shortly after someone from another of the suspected infection zones came to town. It's spreading. If it's not already everywhere in the world, it will be soon."

"Have there been any reported symptoms? Anything that might point to a mutation?" William Matras filled his mug from the half-full coffeepot sitting on the department hot plate, grimacing at the taste even as he kept on drinking. It was bitter but strong. That was what he needed to get through this catastrophe.

"I was wondering when you'd get to asking about the bad part."

"There was a good part?"

Chris ignored him, shuffling through the papers on his desk until he found a red folder. Flipping it open, he read, "Sudden increased salivation in the trial subjects for the McKenzie-Beatts TB treatment. That was the one using genetically modified yellow fever? Three deaths in a modified malaria test group. We're still waiting for the last body to arrive, but in the two we have, it looks like their man-made malaria suddenly started attacking their red blood cells. Wiped them out faster than their bone marrow could rebuild them."

"The Kellis cure doesn't play nicely with the other children," observed William.

"No, it doesn't." Chris looked up, expression grim. "The rest of these are dealing with subjects from the Colorado cancer trials. The ones that used the live version of the modified Marburg virus. They're expressing the same symptoms as everyone else... but their families are starting to show signs of the Marburg variant. Somehow, interaction with the Kellis cure is teaching it how to *spread*. That, or it was already spreading on a subclinical level, and now the Kellis cure is waking it up."

William stared at him, coffee forgotten. "Oh, Jesus."

"I'm pretty sure he's not listening, but you can call him if it makes you feel better," said Chris. He handed his colleague the folder and the two of them turned back to their work. They were trying to prevent the inevitable. They both knew that. But that didn't mean they didn't have to try.

* * *

Effective immediately, all human clinical trials utilizing live strains of any genetically modified virus have been suspended. All records and patient lists for these trials must be submitted to the CDC office in Atlanta, Georgia, by noon EST on July 10th. Failure to comply may result in federal charges...

July 10, 2014: Reston, Virginia

The sound of the front door slamming brought Alexander Kellis out of his light doze. He'd managed to drift off on the couch while he was waiting for John to come home with dinner—the first time he'd slept in days. His first feeling, once the disorientation passed, was irritation. Couldn't John be a little more careful? Didn't he know how exhausted he was?

Then he realized that he wasn't hearing any footsteps. Annoyance faded into concern. "John?" Alex stood, nudging his glasses back into place as he started, warily, toward the foyer.

Jonathan and Alexander Kellis lived in a sprawling house that was really too big for just the two of them, something they'd been intending to fix once Alex's research paid off and early retirement became a viable option. Neither of them really wanted to have children without knowing that one parent, at the very least, would be able to be home for the first few years—and whether they adopted or found a surrogate, they'd always known that one day, they'd fill that empty house with children.

At the moment, however, all that filled the house was silence. And the silence was somehow terrifying. "John?" he repeated, and stepped into the darkened foyer, fumbling for the light switch with one hand. He found it and clicked it on, illuminating the room... and then he froze, eyes going wide, mouth going dry as he tried to process what he was seeing.

How John had managed to make it into the house under his own power was a mystery that might never be solved. Into the house, and no farther. He was collapsed across the hardwood floor, limp and boneless. A smear of blood on the wall showed where he had tried to grab hold as he was falling.

"*John!*" Alex broke out of his fugue, closing the distance between them in three long steps. He barely even felt the pain when his knees slammed into the ground. Fumbling for a pulse with one hand, he said, "John? Sweetheart? Can you hear me?"

John moaned. It was a soft, hollow sound, like the kind made by ghosts in bad horror movies, and it made Alex's blood run cold. "Alex?"

"I'm here, honey. Be still. I'm going to call 911. You just... you just keep still."

"They beat me, Alex." John Kellis managed, somehow, to roll over enough to look up at the man he'd loved since college, when they were both so damn young, and so wonderfully full of optimistic fantasies. "Line at the Chinese place was too long. I went for Indian. Drove past the lab... lights were on. I thought you'd gone out again. I thought you were choosing those *damn* monkeys over me." The venom in his voice made Alex jump. Oblivious, John continued. "Stopped the car. Went in to get you... found them. They let them out, Alex. They let them all out." John closed his eyes. "I'm sorry. I couldn't stop them."

"Stop who?" asked Alex, frozen.

"Said you were... experimenting on animals. Said it was unethical. They said... we deserved what we got." John sighed. "They said we deserved... everything we got."

"Stay with me, sweetheart. Stay awake. Stay with me." Alex fumbled his cell phone out of his pocket, dialing as he raised it to his ear. "Hello, 911? This is Alexander Kellis. My husband has been badly beaten. We're located at..." He took John's hand in his as he gave the address, and held it until the ambulance arrived, waiting for John to say something—anything—to let him know that it would be all right. To let him know that this wasn't how it ended.

John didn't say a word. The ambulance arrived, and the EMTs loaded John into the back, leaving Alex to follow in his car. If John woke up on the way to the hospital, no one noticed; no one heard whatever he might have said. Jonathan Kellis was pronounced dead on arrival at 9:53 P.M. on July 10, 2014. If there was any mercy in this—and there was no mercy to be seen, not then—it was that he died early enough to stay that way.

* * *

Jonathan Kellis, husband of infamous genetic engineer Dr. Alexander Kellis, died last night following a beating at the hands of unidentified assailants. Mr. Kellis had apparently surprised them in the act of vandalizing Dr. Kellis's lab. No suspects have been identified at this time...

July 13, 2014: Allentown, Pennsylvania

After six days of snooping, bribery, and the occasional outright lie, Robert Stalnaker had finally achieved his goal: a meeting with the college student who had blown the whistle on the leaders of the Mayday Army. It had been more difficult than he'd expected. Since the death of Dr. Kellis's husband—something that was *not* his fault; not only did his article not say "break into the lab and free the experimental virus," it certainly never said "beat the man's lover to a bloody pulp if you get the chance"—the security had closed in tighter around the man who was regarded as the state's star, and really only, witness to the actions of the Mayday Army. Robert carefully got out his pocket recorder, checking to be sure the memory buffer was clear. He was only going to get one shot at this.

The door opened, and a skinny, anxious-looking college boy stepped into the room, followed by a pair of visibly armed police officers. Stalnaker would have attempted to convince them to leave, but frankly, after what had happened to John Kellis... these were unsettled times. Having a few authority figures present might be good for everyone involved. Especially since they were authority figures with guns.

"Thank you for meeting with me, Matthew," he said, standing and extending his hand to be shaken. The college boy had a light grip, like he was afraid of breaking something. Stalnaker made a note of that, even as he kept on smiling. "I'm Robert Stalnaker, with the *Clarion News* in New York. I really do appreciate it."

"You're the one who wrote that article," said Matt, pulling his hand away and sitting down on the other side of the table. His eyes darted from side to side like a cornered dog's, assessing the exit routes. "They would never have done it if you hadn't done that first."

"Done what, exactly?" Stalnaker produced a notepad and pencil from his pocket, making sure Matt saw him getting ready to take notes. The recorder was already running, but somehow, it never caused the Pavlovian need to speak that he could trigger with a carefully poised pencil. "I just want to know your side of the story, son."

Matt took a shaky breath. "Look. I didn't—nobody told me this was going to be a whole thing, you know? This girl I know just told me that Brandon and Hazel could hook me up with some good weed. I was coming off finals, I was tense, I needed to relax a little. That was all."

"I understand," said Stalnaker encouragingly. "When I was in college, I heard the siren song of good weed more than a few times. Was the weed good?"

"Aw, man, it was *awesome*." Matt's eyes lit up. Only for a moment;

the light quickly dimmed, and he continued more cautiously. "Anyway, everybody started talking about revolution and sticking it to The Man and how this dude Kellis was going to screw us all by only giving his cold cure to the people who could afford it. I should have done the research, you know? I should have looked it up. It's *contagious*, see? Even if we'd left it alone, let Dr. Kellis finish his testing, we would have all been able to get it in the end. If it worked."

Something about the haunted tone in Matt's voice made Stalnaker sit up a little bit straighter. "Do you think it doesn't work? Can you support that?"

"Oh, it works. Nobody's had a cold in weeks. We're the killers of the common cold. Heigh-ho, give somebody a medal." Matt shook his head, glancing around for exits one more time. "But he didn't finish testing it. Man, we created an *invasive species* that can live inside our bodies. Remember when all those pythons got into the Everglades? Remember how it fucked up the alligators? This time *we're* the alligators, and we've got somebody's pet store python slithering around inside us. And we don't know what it eats, and we don't know how big it's going to get."

"What are you saying?"

Matt looked at Robert Stalnaker and smiled a bitter death's-head grin as he said, "I'm saying that we're screwed, Mr. Stalnaker, and I'm saying that it's all your fucking fault."

* * *

The trial of Brandon Majors and Hazel Allen, the ringleaders of the so-called Mayday Army, has been delayed indefinitely while the precise extent of their crimes is determined. Breaking and entering and willful destruction of property are easy; the sudden demand by the World Health Organization that they also be charged with biological terrorism and global pollution is somewhat more complex...

July 17, 2014: Atlanta, Georgia

"We have a problem."

William Matras looked up from his computer screen and blanched, barely recognizing his colleague. Chris looked like he'd lost fifteen pounds in five days. His complexion was waxen, and the circles under his eyes were almost dark enough to make it seem like he'd been punched. "Christ, Chris, what the hell happened to you?"

"The Kellis cure." Chris Sinclair shook his head, rubbing one stubbly cheek as he said, "I don't have it. I mean, I don't think. We still can't test for it, and we can't afford to have me get sick right now just to find out. But the Kellis cure is what happened. It's what's happening right now."

"What are you talking about?"

"There's been a development in one of the research studies we've been monitoring."

"The McKenzie-Beatts TB treatment." It wasn't a question, because it didn't need to be. William was abruptly glad that he hadn't bothered to stand. He would have just fallen back into his chair.

"Got it in one." Chris nodded, expression grim. "The patients involved in the trial died, William. Every one of them."

"When?"

"About an hour and a half ago. Dr. Li was on-site to monitor their symptoms. The first to start seizing was a twenty-seven-year-old male. He began bleeding from the mouth, eyes, nose, and rectum; when they performed the autopsy, they found that he was also bleeding internally, most heavily into his intestines and lungs. It's a coin toss whether he suffocated or bled out." Chris looked away, toward the blank white wall. He'd never wanted to see the ocean so badly in his life. "The rest started seizing within fifteen minutes. An eleven-year-old girl who'd been accepted into the trials a week before the Kellis cure was released was the last to die. Dr. Li says she was asking for her parents right up until she stopped breathing."

"Oh my God..." whispered William.

"I'm telling you, man, I don't think he's here." Chris rubbed his cheek again, hard. "You ready for the bad part?"

Numbly, William asked, "You mean that *wasn't* the bad part?"

"Not by a long shot." Chris laughed darkly. "Everyone who had direct contact with the patients—the medical staff, their families, hell, *our* medical staff—has started to experience increased salivation, even though the trial virus was certified as noncontagious. Whatever this stuff is turning into, it's catching. They're sealing the building. Dr. Li's called for an L-4 quarantine. If they don't figure out what's going on, they're going to die in there."

William said nothing.

"The malaria folks? We don't know what's going on there. They stopped transmitting an hour before the complex blew sky-high. From what little we've been able to piece together, the charges were set inside the main lab. They, too, decided that they needed a strict quarantine. They just wanted to be absolutely sure that no one was going to have the chance to break it."

There was still a piece missing. Slowly, almost terrified of what the answer would be—no, not almost; *absolutely* terrified of what the answer would be—William asked, "What about the Marburg trials in Colorado?"

"They're all fine."

William stared at him. "What? But you said—"

"It was spreading, and it was. As far as I know, it still is. Half of Denver's had a nosebleed they couldn't stop. And nobody's died. The bleeding lasts three days, and then it clears up on its own, and the victims feel better than they've felt in years. We have a contagious cure for cancer to go with our contagious cure for the common cold." Chris laughed again. This time, there was a sharp edge of hysteria under the sound. "It's not going to end there. We don't get this lucky. We *can't* get this lucky."

"Maybe this is as bad as it gets." William knew how bad the words sounded as soon as they left his mouth, but he couldn't call them back, and he wouldn't have done it even if he could. Someone had to calm Cassandra when she predicted the fall of Troy. Someone had to say "the symptoms aren't that bad" when the predictions called for the fall of man.

Chris gave him a withering look. "Say that like you mean it, or I'm going home to Santa Cruz."

He couldn't, and so he said nothing at all, and the two of them looked at each other, waiting for the end of the world.

* * *

The CDC has no comment on the tragic deaths in San Antonio, Texas. Drs. Lauren McKenzie and Taylor Beatts were conducting a series of clinical trials aimed at combating drug-resistant strains of tuberculosis...

July 18, 2014: The Rising

It began nowhere. It began everywhere. It began without warning; it began with all the warning in the world. It could have been prevented a thousand times over. There was nothing that anyone could have done.

It began on July 18, 2014.

At 6:42 A.M., EST, in a hotel in Columbus, Ohio, Lauren Morris rolled over in her sleep and sighed. That was all; the starting bell of the apocalypse was a simple exhale by a sleeping woman unaware of the transformation going on inside her body. Marburg Amberlee and the Kellis cure fell dormant as their children, their beautiful, terrible children, swarmed through Lauren's blood and into her organs, taking over every function and claiming every nerve. At 6:48 A.M., Lauren's body opened its eyes, and the virus looked out upon the world, and found that it was hungry. She would be found clawing at the door three hours later when the maids came to clean her room. The room did not get cleaned.

At 9:53 A.M., CDT, in the city of Peoria, Illinois, Michael Dowell was hit by a car while crossing the street at a busy intersection. Despite flying more than three yards through the air and hitting the ground with a bone-shattering degree of force, Michael climbed back to his feet almost immediately, to the great relief of bystanders and drivers alike. This relief turned quickly to bewilderment and terror as he lunged at the crowd, biting four people before he could be subdued.

At 10:15 A.M., PDT, in the town of Lodi, California, Debbie Goldman left her home and began jogging along her usual route, despite the already record-breaking heat and the recent warnings of her physician. Her explosive cardiac event struck at 11:03 A.M. Death was almost instantaneous. Her collapse went unwitnessed, as did her subsequent revival. She staggered to her feet, no longer moving at anything resembling a jog. As she made her way along the road, she encountered a group of teenagers walking to the neighborhood *ampm*; three of the six were bitten in the struggle that followed.

At 11:31 A.M., MDT, at the Colorado Cancer Research Center in Denver, Colorado, two of the patients from the Marburg Amberlee cancer trials went into spontaneous viral amplification as the live viral bodies already active in their systems were pushed into a form of slumber by the encroaching Kellis-Amberlee infection. The primary physician's administrative assistant, Janice Barton, was able to trigger the alarm before she was overtaken by the infected. The details of this outbreak remain almost entirely unknown, as the lab was successfully sealed and burned to the ground before the infection could spread.

Ironically, Denver was the source point for one of the two viruses responsible for ending the world, and yet it was spared the worst ravages of the Rising until the second wave began on July 26th. Some say that the tragedy that followed came about only because of that temporary reprieve; they weren't prepared. Those people are not entirely wrong.

And so it went, over and over, all throughout North America. Some of the infected suffered nosebleeds before amplification began, signaling an elevated level of the Marburg Amberlee virus; others did not. Some of the infected would find themselves trapped in cars or hotel rooms, thwarted by stairs or doorknobs; others would not. The Rising had begun.

At 6:18 A.M., GMT, on July 19th, in the city of London, England, Lawrence Whitaker was waiting for the Central Line tube to arrive and take him to work when he felt a warm wetness on his upper lip. He touched it lightly, and frowned at the blood covering his fingertips. He hadn't had a nosebleed since he was a boy. Then he shrugged, produced a tissue, and wiped the blood away. Nothing to be done.

At 3:47 P.M., IST, in the city of Mumbai, India, Sanjiv Gupta was answering calls for the American company whose customers he supported when he realized that his eyes were no longer quite focusing on the screen. Pleading exhaustion, he excused himself for his afternoon break, retreating to the employee restroom. He rinsed his eyes three times, but the blurriness in his vision didn't go away. Then his nose began to bleed, and an inability to see became the least of his problems.

And so it went, over and over, all throughout the world. The end was beginning at last.

* * *

Reports of unusually violent behavior are coming in from across the Midwest, leading some to speculate that the little brown bat, which has been known to migrate during warm weather, may have triggered a rabies epidemic of previously unseen scope...

July 19, 2014: Berkeley, California

"In looking at the biological structure of the screwfly, the real question isn't 'What was evolution thinking,' it's 'Are any of you paying attention to me, or should I just stop talking and put all of this on your final exam?' " Professor Michael Mason picked up one of the books on his desk and dropped it without ceremony. The resulting boom made half the students jump, and made almost all of them guiltily focus their attention on the front of the lecture hall. Michael folded his arms. "Since you're all clearly sharing with the rest of the class, does anybody feel like sharing with *me*?"

Silence fell over the lecture hall. Michael cocked his head slightly to the side, watching them, and waited. Finally, one of the students cleared her throat and said, "It's just there are these crazy stories going around campus, you know? So we're a little on edge."

"Crazy stories? Crazy stories like what?"

One of the football players who was taking the class for science credit said, "Like dead dudes getting up and walking around and eating living dudes."

"We're living in a Romero movie!" shouted someone at the back of the room, drawing nervous laughter from the rest of the students.

"All right, now, settle down. Let's approach this like scientists—if it's important enough to distract you all from the important business of biology, we should do it the honor of thinking about it like rational people. You mentioned Romero movies. Does that mean you're positing zombies?"

There was another flurry of laughter. It ended quickly, replaced by dead seriousness. "I think we are, Professor," said the herpetology major in the front row. She shook her head. "It's the only thing that makes sense."

Another student rolled his eyes. "Because zombies *always* make sense."

She glared at him. "Shut up."

"Make me."

"Now that we have demonstrated once again that no human being is ever more than a few steps away from pulling pigtails on the playground, who wants to posit a reason that we'd have zombies now, rather than, oh, six weeks ago?" Michael looked around the room. "Come on. I'm playing along with you. Now one of you needs to play along with me."

"That Mayday Army thing." The words came from a tiny bio-chem major who almost never spoke during class; she just sat there taking notes with a single-minded dedication that was more frightening than admirable. It was like she thought the bottom of the bell curve would be shot after every exam. She wasn't taking notes now. She was looking at Professor Mason with wide, serious eyes, pencil finally down. "They released an experimental, genetically engineered pathogen into the atmosphere. Dr. Kellis hadn't reached human trials yet. If there were going to be side effects, he didn't have time to find out what they were."

She sounded utterly serene, like she'd finally found a test that she was certain she could pass. Michael Mason paused. "That's an interesting theory, Michelle."

"The CDC has shut down half a dozen clinical trials in the last week, and they won't say why," she replied, as if that had some bearing on the conversation.

Maybe it did. Michael Mason straightened. "All right. I'm going to humor you, because it's not every day that one gets a zombie apocalypse as an excuse for canceling class. You're all dismissed, on one condition."

"What's that, Professor?" asked a student.

"I want you all to stay together. Check your phones for news; check your Twitter feeds. See if anything strange is going on before you go anywhere." He forced a smile, wishing he wasn't starting to feel so uneasy. "If we're having a zombie apocalypse, let's make it a minor one, and all be back here on Monday, all right?"

Laughter and applause greeted his words. He stayed at the front of the room until the last of the students had streamed out; then he grabbed his coat and started for the exit himself. He needed to cancel classes for the rest of the day. He needed to call Stacy and tell her to get Phillip from his kindergarten. If there was one thing science had taught him, it was that safe was always better than sorry, and some things were never on the final exam.

* * *

Professor Michael Mason has announced the cancellation of class for the rest of the week. His podcast will be posted tomorrow night, as scheduled. All students are given a one-week extension on their summer term papers.

July 20, 2014: Manhattan, New York

The anchorman had built his reputation on looking sleek and well-groomed even when broadcasting from the middle of a hurricane. His smile was a carefully honed weapon of reassurance, meant to be deployed when bad news might otherwise whip the populace into a frenzy. He was smiling steadily. He had been smiling since the beginning of his report.

He was beginning to wonder if he would ever stop smiling again.

"Again, ladies and gentlemen, there is nothing to be concerned about. We have two particularly virulent strains of flu sweeping across the country. One, in the Midwest, seems to be a variant of our old friend, H1N1, coming back to get revenge for all those bacon, lettuce, and tomato sandwiches. Symptoms include nausea, dizziness, disorientation, and of course, our old friend, the stuffy nose. This particular flu also carries a risk of high fevers, which can lead to erratic behavior and even violence. So please, take care of yourself and your loved ones."

He shuffled the papers in front of him, trying to give the impression that he was reading off them and not off the prompter. Audiences liked to see a little hard copy. It made them feel like the news was more legitimate. "The second strain is milder but a bit more alarming. Thus far, it's stayed on the West Coast—maybe it likes the beach. This one doesn't involve high fevers, for which we can all be grateful, but it does include some pretty nasty nosebleeds, and those can make people seem a lot sicker than they really are. If your nose starts bleeding, simply grab a tissue and head for your local hospital. They'll be able to fix you right up."

He was still smiling. He was never going to not be smiling. He was going to *die* smiling. He knew it, and still the news rolled on. "Now, ladies and gentlemen, I have to beg you to indulge me for a moment. Some individuals are trying to spin this as a global pandemic, and I wish to assure you that it is nothing more than a nasty pair of summer flus. Please do not listen to reports from unreliable sources. Stick with the news outlets that have served you well, and remember, we're here to make sure you know the *real* story."

"And...we're clear!" said one of the production assistants, as the cheery strains of the station break music began to play. The anchor kept smiling. "Great job, Dave. You're doing fantastic. Can I get you anything?"

"I'm good," said the anchor, and kept smiling. No one seemed to have noticed that they had no footage, no reports from experts or comments from the man on the street. All they had was a press release from the governor's office and strict orders to read it as written, with no deviation or side commentary. They were being managed, and no one seemed to care, and so he kept on smiling and waited for the commercial break to end.

There was no footage. There was *always* footage. Even when good taste and human decency said not to air it, there was footage. Humanity liked to slow down and look at the car crash by the side of the road, and it was the job of the news to give them all the wrecks that they could stomach. So where was the wreck? Where was the twisted metal and the sorrowful human-interest story? Why did they have nothing but words on a teleprompter and silence from the editing room?

"And we're back in five... four... three..." The production assistant stopped in mid-countdown, eyes going terribly wide. "Dave? Do you feel all right?"

"I'm fine. Why?" He kept smiling.

"You're bleeding."

The news anchor—Dave Ramsey, who had done his job, and done it well, for fifteen years—became suddenly aware of a warm wetness on his upper lip. He raised his fingers to touch it, and looked wide-eyed at the blood covering them when he pulled away again. His smile didn't falter. "Oh," he said. "Perhaps I should go clean up."

When the broadcast resumed, his co-anchor was sitting there, a cheerful smile on her face. "We have an update from the Centers for Disease Control, who want us to reassure you that a vaccine will be available soon—"

* * *

News anchor Dave Ramsey passed away last night of complications from a sudden illness. He was forty-eight years old. A fifteen-year veteran of Channel 51, Dave Ramsey is survived by his wife and three children...

July 26, 2014: Denver, Colorado

Suzanne Amberlee's nose had been bleeding for most of the morning. It had ceased to bother her after the first hour; in a way, it had even proven itself a blessing. The blood loss seemed to blunt the hard edges of the world around her, blurring things into a comfortable gray that allowed her to finally face some of the hard tasks she'd been allowing herself to avoid. She paused in the process of boxing Amanda's books, wiping the sweat from her forehead with one hand and the blood from her chin with the other. Bloody handprints marred every box and wall in the room, but she didn't really see them anymore. She just saw the bitter absence of Amanda, who was never coming home to her again.

In Suzanne Amberlee's body, a battle was raging between the remaining traces of Marburg Amberlee and the newborn Kellis-Amberlee virus. There is no loyalty among viruses; as soon as they were fully conceived, the child virus turned against its parents, trying to drive them from the body as it would any other infection. This forced the Marburg into a heightened state of activity, which forced the body to respond to the perceived illness. Marburg Amberlee was not designed to fight the human body's immune system, and responded by launching a full-on assault. The resulting chaos was tearing Suzanne apart from the inside out.

For her part, Suzanne Amberlee neither knew nor cared about what was happening inside her body. She was one of the first to be infected with Marburg Amberlee, which had been tailored to be nontransmissible between humans... but nothing's perfect, and all those kisses she'd given her little girl had, in time, passed something more tangible than comfort between them. Marburg Amberlee had had plenty of time to establish itself inside her, and paradoxically, that made her more resistant to conversion than those with more recent infections. Her body knew how to handle the sleeping virus.

And yet bit by bit, inch by crucial inch, Kellis-Amberlee was winning. Suzanne was not aware, but she was already losing crucial brain functions. Her tear ducts had ceased to function, and much of her body's moisture was being channeled toward the production of mucus and saliva—two reliable mechanisms for passing the infection along. She was being rewired, cell by cell, and even if someone had explained to her what was happening, she wouldn't have cared. Suzanne Amberlee had lost everything she ever loved. Losing herself was simply giving in to the inevitable.

Suzanne's last conscious thought was of her daughter, and how much she missed her. Then the stuffed bear she was holding slipped from her hands, and all thoughts slipped from her mind as she straightened and walked toward the open bedroom door. The back door was propped open, allowing a cool breeze to blow in from outside; she walked through it, and from there, made her way out of the backyard to the street.

The disaster that had been averted when the Colorado Cancer Research Center burned began with a woman, widowed and bereft of her only child, walking barefoot onto the sun-baked surface of the road. She looked dully to either side, not really tracking what she saw—not by any human definition of the term—before turning to walk toward the distant shouts of children playing in the neighborhood park. It would take her the better part of an hour to get there, moving slowly, with the jerky confusion of the infected when not actively pursuing visible prey.

It would take less than ten minutes after her arrival for the dying to begin. The Rising had come to Denver; the Rising had come home.

* * *

Please return to your homes. Please remain calm. This is not a drill. If you have been infected, please contact authorities immediately. If you have not been infected, please remain calm. This is not a drill. Please return to your homes...

July 26, 2014: Allentown, Pennsylvania

The people outside the prison could pretend that the dead weren't walking if they wanted to. That sort of bullshit was the province of the free. Once you were behind bars, counting on other people to bring you food, water, hell, to let you go to the bathroom like a human being...you couldn't lie to yourself. And the dead *were* walking.

So far, there hadn't been any outbreaks in Brandon's wing of the prison, but he knew better than to attribute that to anything beyond pure dumb luck. Whatever caused some people to get sick and die and then get up again without being bitten just hadn't found a way inside the building. It would. All it needed was a little more time, and it would.

Brandon was sitting on his bed and staring at his hands, wondering if he'd ever see Hazel again, when the door of his cell slid open. He raised his head, and found himself looking at one of the prison guards—one of the only guards who was still bothering to show up for work.

"You've got a visitor, Majors," said the guard, and gestured roughly for him to stand. Brandon had learned the virtue of obedience. It was practically the first lesson that prison taught. He stood, moving quickly to avoid a reprimand.

There had been other lessons since then. None of them had been pleasant ones.

The guard led Brandon through the halls without a word. Some of the prisoners shouted threats or profanity as they passed; Brandon's role in the Mayday Army was well known, and was the reason he was placed in solitary. As the situation got worse, his future looked more and more bleak. Outside the prison, he would probably have already been lynched. As if it was his fault somehow? That bastard Kellis was the one who built the bug. He should be the one getting the blame, not Brandon—

The guard led him around the corner to the visiting room. There were only two men standing there. One was the warden. The other was a slim, dark-haired man Brandon felt like he should recognize. Something about him was familiar.

"Brandon Majors?" asked the man.

"Yes?" Maybe he was from the governor. Maybe he had come to pardon Brandon and take him away from all this; maybe he understood that it wasn't his fault—

"My name is Alexander Kellis."

Hope died. Brandon stared at him. "I . . . you . . . oh, God."

Alexander looked at Brandon—the little ringleader who had managed to bring about the end of the world, the one whose name was already dropping out of the news, to be replaced by Alexander's own—and said, very quietly, "I wanted to meet you. I wanted to look you in the eye while I told you that this is all your fault. History may blame it on me, but neither of us is going to be there to see it, and right here, right now, today, this is all your fault. You destroyed my life's work. You killed the man I loved. You may very well have brought about the end of the world. So I have just one question for you."

"What?" whispered Brandon.

"Was it worth it?"

After five minutes passed with no answer, Dr. Kellis turned to the warden. "Thank you. I'd like to go now." They walked away, leaving Brandon standing frozen next to the guard.

That night, Brandon's cell was somehow left unlocked. He was found dead in the hall the next morning, having been stabbed more than a dozen times. None of the other inmates saw what happened. At least, that's what they said, and this one time, the warden chose to believe them. It wasn't his fault, after all.

* * *

If you have not been infected, please remain calm. This is not a drill. Please return to your homes. Please remain calm. This is not a drill. If you have been infected, please contact authorities immediately...

July 27, 2014: Berkeley, California

"Get those walls up! Cathy, I want to see that chicken wire hugging those planks, don't argue with me, just *get it done.*" Stacy Mason rushed to help a group of neighborhood teens who staggered under the weight of the planks they'd "liberated" from an undisclosed location. At this point, she didn't care where the building materials came from; she cared only that they were going to reinforce the neighborhood fences and doors and road checkpoints. As long as what was inside their makeshift walls was going to make those walls stronger, they could start tearing down houses and she honestly wouldn't give a fuck.

Berkeley, being a university town in Northern California, had two major problems: not enough guns, and too many idiots who thought they could fight off zombies with medieval weapons they'd stolen from the history department. It also had two major advantages: most of the roads were already half blocked to prevent campus traffic from disturbing the residents, and most of those residents were slightly insane by any normal societal measurement.

The nice lesbian collective down the block had contributed eighty feet of chicken wire left over from an urban farming project they'd managed the year before. The robotics engineer who lived across the street was an avid Burner, and had been happy to contribute the fire-breathing whale he'd constructed for the previous year's Burning Man. Not the most immediately useful contribution in the world, but it was sufficiently heavy to make an excellent roadblock...and Stacy had to admit that having a fire-breathing roadblock certainly gave the neighborhood character.

"Louise! If you're going to break the glass, break it clean—we don't want anyone getting cut!" They really, *really* didn't want anyone getting cut. The transmission mechanisms for the zombie virus were still being charted, but fluid exchange was definitely on the list, and anything getting into an open wound seemed like a bad idea. "We gave you a hammer for a reason! Now *smash* things!"

The distant shrieks of children brought her head whipping around, the hairs on the back of her neck standing on end. Then the shrieks mellowed into laughter, and she relaxed—not entirely, but enough. "Damn dogs," she muttered, a smile tugging at her lips. "Exciting the children and stopping my heart."

"Mrs. Mason? I can't figure out how to make the staple gun work." The plaintive cry came from a young woman who had been Phillip's babysitter several times over the summer. She was standing next to a sheet of plywood with a staple gun in her hand, shaking it helplessly. It wasn't spewing staples at the moment—a small mercy, since the last thing they needed was for anyone to get hit by friendly fire.

Stacy shook off her brief fugue, starting toward the girl. "That's because you're holding it wrong, Marie. Now, please, point the staple gun *away* from your body..."

The comfortable chaos of a neighborhood protecting itself against the dangerous outside continued, with everyone doing the best that they could to shore up their defenses and walls. They'd lost people on supply runs and rescue trips, but so far everyone who'd stayed on the block had been fine. They were clinging to that, as the power got intermittent and the supply runs got less fruitful. Help was coming. Help had to be coming. And when help arrived, it would find them ready, healthy, and waiting to be saved.

Stacy Mason might be living through the zombie apocalypse, but by God, the important word there was "living." She was going to make it through, and so was everyone she cared about. There was just no other way that this could end.

* * *

If you are receiving this broadcast, you are within the range of the UC Berkeley radio station. Please follow these directions to reach a safe location. You will be expected to surrender all weapons and disrobe for physical examination upon arrival. We have food. We have water. We have shelter...

July 27, 2014: Denver, Colorado

Denver was burning. From where Dr. Wells sat, in the front room of his mountain home, it looked like the entire city was on fire. That couldn't possibly be true—Denver was too large to burn that easily—but oh, it looked that way.

In the house behind him he could hear the sound of shuffling, uncertain footsteps as his wife and children made their way down the stairs to the hallway. He didn't move. Not even to shut the door connecting the living room with the rest of the house. He was lonely. His city was burning, his research was over, and he was lonely. Couldn't a man be lonely, when he was sitting at the end of the world and watching Denver burn?

Daniel Wells lifted his scotch, took a sip, and lowered it again. His eyes never left the flames. They were alive. Even if nothing else in the city he called home was alive, the flames were thriving. There was something comforting in that. Life, as a wise man once said, would always find a way.

A low moan sounded from the hallway right outside the front room. Daniel took another sip of scotch. "Hello, darling," he said, without turning. "It's a beautiful day, don't you think? All this smoke is going to make for an amazing sunset..."

Then his wife and children, who had finished amplification some time before, fell upon him, and the man responsible for Marburg Amberlee knew nothing but the tearing of teeth and the quiet surrender to the dark. When he opened his eyes again, he wasn't Daniel Wells anymore. Had he still possessed the capacity for gratitude, it is very likely that he would have been grateful.

* * *

This is not a drill. If you have been infected, please contact authorities immediately. If you have not been infected, please remain calm. This is not a drill. Please return to your homes. Please remain calm. This is not a drill...

July 30, 2014: Reston, Virginia

It had taken six of the Valium pills John kept hidden at the back of the medicine cabinet, but Alexander Kellis was finally ready. He checked the knot on his rope one more time. It was good; it would hold. Maybe it wasn't elegant, but he didn't deserve elegant, did he? He'd destroyed the world. Children would curse his name for generations, assuming there were any generations to come. John was gone forever. It was over.

"I'll see you soon, sweetheart," he whispered, and stepped off the edge of his desk. No one would find his body for weeks. If he reanimated, he starved without harming anyone. Alexander Kellis never harmed anyone.

Not on purpose.

* * *

Please return to your homes. Please remain calm. This is not a drill. If you have been infected, please contact authorities immediately. If you have not been infected, please remain calm. This is not a drill. Please return to your homes...

July 30, 2014: Atlanta, Georgia

The bedroom walls were painted a cheery shade of rose-petal pink that showed up almost neon in the lens of the web camera. Unicorns and rainbows decorated the page where the video was embedded; even the YouTube mirrors that quickly started appearing had unicorns and rainbows, providing a set of safe search words that were too widespread to be wiped off the Internet, no matter how many copies of the video were taken down. The man sitting in front of the webcam was all wrong for the blog. Too old, too haggard, too afraid. His once-pristine lab coat was spattered with coffee stains, and he looked like he hadn't shaved in more than a week.

"My name is Dr. William Matras," he said in a calm, clear voice that was entirely at odds with his appearance. "I am—I was; I suppose I'm not anymore—an epidemic researcher for the Centers for Disease Control. I have been working on the issue of the Kellis cure since it was first allowed into the atmosphere. I have been tracking the development of the epidemic, along with my colleague, Dr. Christopher Sinclair." His breath hitched, voice threatening to break. He got himself back under control, and continued. "Chris wouldn't sanction what I'm going to say next. Good thing he isn't around to tell me not to say it, right?

"The news has been lying to you. This is not a virulent summer cold; this is not a new strain of the swine flu. This is, and has always been, a man-made pandemic whose effects were previously unknown in higher mammals. Put bluntly, the Kellis cure has mutated, becoming conjoined with an experimental Marburg-based cure for cancer. It is airborne. It is highly contagious. And it raises the dead.

"Almost everyone who breathes air is now infected with this virus. Transmission is apparently universal, and does not come with any initial symptoms. The virus will change forms under certain conditions, going from the passive 'helper' form to the active 'killer' form of what we've been calling Kellis-Amberlee. Once this process begins, there is nothing that can stop it. Anyone whose virus has begun to change forms is going to become one of the mindless cannibals now shambling around our streets. Why? We don't know. What we do know is that fluid transmission seems to trigger the active form of the virus—bites, scratches, even getting something in your eye. Some people may seroconvert spontaneously. We believe these people were involved with the Marburg trials in Colorado, but following the destruction of the facility where those trials were conducted, we have no way of being absolutely sure.

"Let me repeat: We have been lying to you. The government is not allowing us to spread any knowledge about the walking plague, saying that we would trigger a mass panic. Well, the masses are panicking, and I don't think keeping secrets is doing anybody any favors. Not at this stage.

"Once someone has converted into the... hell, once somebody's a zombie, there's no coming back. They are no longer the people you have known all your life. Head shots seem to work best. Severe damage to the body will eventually cause them to bleed out, but it can take time, and it will create a massive hot zone that can't be sterilized with anything but fire or bleach. We have... God, we have..." He stopped for a moment, dropping his forehead into the palm of his hand. Finally, dully, he said, "We have lied to you. We have withheld information. What follows is everything we know about this disease, and the simple fact of it is, we know there isn't any cure. We know we can't stop it.

"Early signs of amplification include dilated pupils, blurred vision, dry mouth, difficulty breathing, loss of coordination, unexplained mood swings, personality changes, apparent lapses in memory, aphasia..."

* * *

If you have been infected, please contact authorities immediately. If you have not been infected, please remain calm. This is not a drill. Please return to your homes. Please remain calm. This is not a drill. If you have been infected...

July 31, 2014: Berkeley, California

Marigold felt bad.

There had been a raccoon in the yard. She liked when raccoons came to the yard, they puffed up big so big, but they ran ran ran when you chased them, and the noises they made were like birds or squirrels but bigger and more exhilarating. She had chased the raccoon, but the raccoon didn't run. Instead, it held its ground, and when she came close enough, it bit her on the shoulder, hard, teeth tearing skin and flesh and leaving only pain pain pain behind. Then she ran, *she* ran from the raccoon, and she had rolled in the dirt until the bleeding stopped, mud clotting the wound, pain pain pain muted a little behind the haze of her confusion. Then had come shame. Shame, because she would be called bad dog for chasing raccoons; bad dog for getting bitten when there were so many people in the house and yard and everything was strange.

So Marigold did what any good dog in fear of being termed a bad dog would do; she had gone to the hole in the back of the fence, the hole she and her brother worked and worried so long at, and slunk into the yard next door, where the boy lived. The boy laughed and pulled her ears sometimes, but it never hurt. The boy loved her. She knew the boy loved her, even as she knew that the man and the woman fed her and that she was a good dog, really, all the way to the heart of her. She was a good dog.

She was a good dog, but she felt so bad. So very bad. The badness had started with the bite, but it had spread since then, and now she could barely swallow, and the light was hurting her eyes so much, so very much. She lay huddled under the bushes, wishing she could find her feet, wishing she knew why she felt bad. So very bad.

Marigold felt hungry.

The hunger was a new thing, a strong thing, stronger even than the bad feeling that was spreading through her. She considered the hunger, as much as she could. She had never been the smartest of dogs, and her mind was getting fuzzy, thought and impulse giving way to alien instinct. She was a good dog. She just felt bad. She was a good dog. She was... she was... she was hungry. Marigold was hungry. Then she was only hunger, and no more Marigold. No more Marigold at all.

Something rustled through the bushes. The dog that had been a good dog, that had been Marigold, and that was now just hungry, rose slowly, legs unsteady but willing to support the body if there might be something coming that could end the hunger. The dog that had been a good dog, that had been Marigold, looked without recognition at the figure that parted the greenery and peered down at it with wide-eyed curiosity. The dog, which had always been ready with a welcoming bark, made a sound that was close to a moan.

"Oggie?"

* * *

We are experiencing technical difficulties. Please stand by.

August 1, 2014

Kellis-Amberlee unified the world in a way that nothing had ever unified it before, or ever would again. Cities burned. Nations died. Tokyo, Manhattan, Mumbai, London, all of them fell before an enemy that could not be stopped, because it came from within; because it was already inside. Some escaped. Some lived. All carried the infection deep inside their bodies, tucked away where it could never be excised. They carried it with them, and it lived, too.

The Rising was finally, fully underway. Mothers mourned their children. Orphans wailed alone in the night. Death ruled over all, horrible and undying. And nothing, it seemed, would ever make it end.

But on the Internet, Dr. Matras's message repeated, over and over again, and others began repeating it with him. The future was arriving. All they had to do was live to see it. So the world asked itself a question:

When will you Rise?

And the world gave itself an answer:
Now.
Welcome to the aftermath.

"In telling the stories of the Rising, we must remember this above all else: We did what everyone claimed mankind could never do. We survived. Now it is up to us to prove that we deserved this second chance."

—Mahir Gowda

Everglades

Introduction

The most personalized, professional rejection I ever received came from John Joseph Adams. I still have it. I treasure it. I especially treasure the part where it starts "Dear Mr. McGuire . . ." because sometimes I have a strange sense of humor.

When he sent me that rejection, John was the assistant editor of *The Magazine of Fantasy and Science Fiction*, a publication I've loved fiercely since I was a child. He went on to become a prolific anthologist, editing some of my favorite anthologies of the last ten years. As a consequence, when I was offered the chance to submit to *The Living Dead 2*, his second anthology of original zombie fiction, I was absolutely overjoyed.

And then I was stumped. Because I needed a short story that said something new and interesting about the zombie apocalypse, and I wasn't finding it. Everyone had unleashed the virus; everyone had devoured the world. Everyone had *survived.*

That was the key. Everyone had survived. But what about the people who didn't? What about the people who looked at the face of the changing world—the world that was never going to be the same, even if they made it out the other side—and decided to say, "You know what, thanks but no thanks; I'd rather be a statistic"? Any disaster is going to come with a certain soft cost: a certain number of suicides and accidents surrounding the deaths that come as an immediate consequence of the event. I wanted to focus on one of those people.

"Everglades" is, at the time of this writing, the only piece of Newsflesh fiction not to have originally been published by Orbit in some form. I am so glad to have it in this collection, joining its siblings, finally coming home.

Everglades

The smell hanging over the broken corpse of the campus is rich, ripe, and green—the heavy reptile smell of swamplands and of secrets. It teases its way past sealed windows and in through cracks, permeating everything it touches. Across the empty expanse of the quad, the green flag suspended from the top window of the Physics Building flutters in the wind. It marks the location of survivors, waiting for a rescue that may never come. I wonder if they smell the swamp as clearly there, tucked inside their classrooms full of quiet air, where the search for the secrets of the universe has been replaced by the search for simple survival.

Something darts across the pathway leading toward Shattuck Avenue. I twitch the telescope in that direction quickly enough to see a large black cat disappearing under the Kissing Bridge. I haven't seen anything larger than a stray dog in the two hours of my watch. That doesn't mean it's safe to stop looking. Alligators are invisible until they strike, a perfect match for their surroundings. In this dead world, the zombies are even harder to see. From A to Z in the predator's alphabet.

This is California, a world away from Florida, but that makes no difference now; the Everglades are here. I lean back against the windowsill, scanning the campus, and breathe in the timeless, tireless smell of the swamp.

* * *

I was eight and Wes was twelve the last time we went to visit our grandparents in Florida. True to family form, Grandma and Wes promptly vanished to spend their time on the sunny beaches, exchanging hours for sandy shoes and broken seashells, while I dove straight for Grandpa's tobacco-scented arms. Grandpa was my secret conspirator, the man who didn't think a passion for snakes and reptiles was unusual for a tow-headed little girl from Ohio. Our visits were wonderful things, filled with trips to zoos, alligator farms, and the cluttered, somehow sinister homes of private collectors, who kept their tanks of snakes and lizards in climate-controlled rooms where the sunlight never touched them. My parents saw my affections as some sort of phase, something that would pass. Grandpa saw them for what they were: a calling.

Grandpa died five years ago, less than a month after seeing me graduate from high school. Grandma didn't last much longer. That's good. I haven't seen any reports out of Florida in days, and I haven't seen any reports from anywhere that say people who've been dead that long have started getting back up again. Only the fresh dead walk. My grandparents get to rest in peace.

That summer, though, the summer when I was eight and Wes was twelve, that was the perfect summer, the one everything else gets to be measured against, forever. Our second day there, Grandpa woke me up at four-thirty in the morning, shaking me awake with a secret agent's sly grin and whispering, "Get dressed, now, Debbie. I've got something to show you." He rolled me out of bed, waited in the hall for me to dress, and half-carried me out of their cluttered retiree condo to drop me into the front seat of his ancient pickup truck. The air smelled like flowers I couldn't name, and even hours before sunrise, the humidity was enough to twist my hair into fat ringlets. In the distance, a dog barked twice and was still. With that bark, I came fully awake, realizing at last that this wasn't a dream; that we were going on an adventure.

We drove an hour to a narrow, unpaved road, where the rocks and gravel made the truck bounce uncontrollably. Grandpa cursed at the suspension while I giggled, clinging to the open window as I tried to work out just what sort of an adventure this was. He parked next to a crumbling little dock, pilings stained green with decades of moss. A man in jeans and an orange parka stood on the dock, his face a seamed mass of wrinkles. He never spoke. I remember that, even though most of that night seems like a dream to me now. He just held out his hand, palm upward, and when Grandpa slapped a wad of bills down into it, he pointed us toward the boat anchored at the end of the dock, bobbing ceaselessly up and down amongst the waterweeds and scum.

There were lifejackets in the bottom of the boat. Grandpa pulled mine over my head before he put his own on, picked up the oars, and pushed away from the dock. I didn't say anything. With Grandpa it was best to bide your time and let him start the lesson when he was ready. It might take a while, but he always got there in the end. Trees loomed up around us as he rowed, their branches velvet-draped with hanging moss. Most seemed to stretch straight out of the water, independent of the tiny clots of solid ground around them. And Grandpa began to speak.

I couldn't have written exactly what he said to me even then, without fifteen years between the hearing and the recollection. It was never the exact words that mattered. He introduced me to the Everglades like he was bringing me to meet a treasured family friend. Maybe that's what he was doing. We moved deeper and deeper into that verdant-scented darkness, mosquitoes buzzing around us, his voice narrating all the while. Finally, he brought us to a slow halt in the middle of the largest patch of open water I'd seen since we left the dock. "Here, Debbie," he said, voice low. "What do you see?"

"It's beautiful," I said.

He bent forward, picking up a rock from the bottom of the boat. "Watch," he said, and threw the rock. It hit the water with a splash that echoed through the towering trees. All around us, logs began opening their eyes, pieces of earth began to shift toward the water. In a matter of seconds, six swamp gators—the huge kind that I'd only ever seen before in zoos—had appeared and disappeared again, sliding under the surface of the swamp like they'd never existed at all.

"Always remember that Nature can be cruel, little girl," said Grandpa. "Sometimes it's what looks most harmless that hurts you the most. You want to go back?"

"No," I said, and I meant it. We spent the next three hours in our little boat, watching the gators as they slowly returned, and being eaten alive by mosquitoes. I have never been that content with the world before or since.

I'm so glad my grandparents died when they did.

* * *

The slice of campus I can see through the window is perfectly still, deserted and at peace. The few bodies in view have been still for the entire time that I've been watching. I don't trust their stillness; alligators, all. Corpses aside, I've never seen the quad so clean. The wind has had time to whisk away the debris and even the birds are gone. They don't seem to get sick the way that mammals do, but without the student body dropping easy-to-scavenge meals, there's nothing for them here. I miss the birds. I miss the rest of the student body more—although we could find them if we tried. It wouldn't be that hard. All we need to do is go outside, and wait for them to follow the scent of blood.

A loudspeaker crackles to life on the far side of the quad. "This is Professor Mason," it announces. "We have lost contact with the library. Repeat, we have lost contact with the library. Do not attempt to gather supplies from that area until we have reestablished communications. We have established contact with Durant Hall—" The list continues seemingly without end, giving status updates for all the groups we're in contact with, either on or off the campus. I try to make myself listen and, when that doesn't work, begin trying to make myself feel anything beyond a vague irritation over possibly losing the library. They have the best vending machines.

The broadcast ends, and the speaker crackles again, marking time, before a nervous voice says, "This is Susan Wright from the Drama Department. I'll be working the campus radio for the next hour. Please call in if you have anything to report. And, um, go Bears." This feeble attempt at normalcy concluded, her voice clicks out, replaced by a Death Cab for Cutie song. The sound confuses the dead. It isn't enough to save you if they've already caught your scent, but if the radio went offline we wouldn't be able to move around at all. I doubt we'd last long after that. A prey species that can't run is destined to become extinct.

Footsteps behind me. I turn. Andrei—big, brave Andrei, who broke the chain on the Life Science Hall door when we needed a place to run—stands in the doorway, face pale, the shaking in his hands almost imperceptible. "I think Eva's worse," he says, and I follow him away from the window, out of the well-lit classroom, and back into the darkness of the halls.

* * *

A school the size of ours never really shuts down, although there are times when it edges toward dormant. The summer semester is always sparsely-attended when compared to fall or spring, cutting the population down to less than half. I'd been enjoying the quiet. The professor I was working for was nice enough and he didn't ask me to do much, leaving my time free for hikes in the local hills and live observation of the native rattlesnakes. They have a hot, dry reptile smell, nothing like the swampy green smell that rises from an alligator's skin. Such polite snakes, warning you before they strike. Rattlesnakes are a lot like people, although that's probably not a comparison that most people would appreciate.

Monday, some aspiring comedian did a mock news report on the school radio station. "This just in: Romero was right! The dead walk! Signs of life even spotted in the Math Department!"

Tuesday, half my mailing lists were going off-topic to talk about strange events, disappearances, attacks. Some people suggested that it was zombies. Everybody laughed.

Wednesday, the laughter stopped.

Thursday, the zombies came.

Some people fought, some people ran, and some people hid. On Saturday, there were twenty-six of us here in the Life Sciences Building, half of us grad students who'd been checking on our projects when chaos broke out on the campus. By Monday, that number had been more than cut in half. We were down to nine, and if Eva was worse, we might be looking at eight before much longer. That's bad. That's very bad. Because out of all of us, Eva is the one who has a clue.

Andrei leads me down the hall, through the atrium where the reconstructed Tyrannosaurus Rex stands skeletal judgment over us all, and into the lecture hall that we've converted, temporarily, into a sickroom. Eva is inside, reclining on the couch we brought down from the indefensible teacher's lounge. She has her laptop open on her knees, typing with a ferocious intensity that frightens me. How long does it take to transcribe a lifetime? Is it longer than she has?

In the lecture hall, the smell of the Everglades hangs over everything, hot and ancient and green. The smell of sickness, burning its way through human flesh, eating as it goes. Eva hears our footsteps and lifts her head, eyes chips of burning ice against the sickroom pallor of her complexion. Acne stands out at her temples and on her chin, reminders that she's barely out of her teens, the youngest of us left here in the hall. Her hair is the color of dried corn husks, and that's what she looks like—a girl somehow woven out of corn husks that have been drenched with that hot swampy smell. She barely looks like Eva at all.

"It's viral." That's the first thing she says in her reedy little voice, the words delivered with matter-of-fact calm. "Danny's team over at the med school managed to isolate a sample and get some pictures. It looks sort of like Ebola, and sort of like the end of the fucking world. They're online now." She smiles, the heartbreaking smile of a corn husk angel. "They've been trying all the common anti-virals. Nothing's making any difference in the progression of the infection."

"Hello to you, too, Eva," I say. A duct tape circle on the floor around the couch marks the edge of the "safe" area; any closer puts us at risk of infection. I walk to the circle's edge and stop, uncertain what else to say. I settle for, "Professor Mason just gave an update. We've lost contact with the library."

"That isn't a surprise," says Eva. "They had Jorge over there."

"So?" asks Andrei.

"He updated his Facebook status about three hours ago to say that he'd been bitten, but they washed the wound out with bleach. Bleach won't save you from Ebola, so it's definitely not going to save you from Ebola's bitchy big sister." She coughs into her hand before saying, almost cheerfully, "Good news for you: the structure of the virus means it's not droplet-based. So you don't need to worry about sharing my air. Bad news for me: If Jorge took three hours to turn after being bitten, I'd say I have another hour—maybe two—before I go."

"Don't say that." There's no strength in Andrei's command. He lost that when Eva got the blood in her eyes, when it became clear that she was going to get sick. She was the one who told him we needed to run. Losing her is proof that all of this is really happening.

Eva continues like she doesn't hear him: "I've been collecting everyone's data and reposting it. The campus network is still holding. That's the advantage to everything happening as fast as it has. Professor Mason has a pretty decent file sharing hub in place. If you can keep trading data, keep track of where the biters are, you can probably maintain control of the campus until help arrives." Matter-of-factly, she adds, "You'll have to shoot me soon."

Andrei is still arguing with her when I turn and leave the room. The smell of the swamp travels with me, hot decay and predators in hiding.

* * *

Minutes trickle by. Susan from the Drama Department gives way to Andy from Computer Science; Death Cab is replaced by Billy Ray Cyrus. There are no gunshots from inside. Professor Mason gives the afternoon update. Contact with the library has been reestablished. Six survivors, none of them bitten. There are no gunshots from inside. The hot smell of the swamp is everywhere, clinging to every inch of the campus, of the city, of the world. I wonder if the alligators have noticed that the world is ending, or if they have continued on as they always have... if they observe our extinction as they observed the extinction of the dinosaurs: with silence, and with infinite patience.

The risen dead have more in common with the alligators than they do with us, the living. That's why the smell of the Everglades has followed them here, hanging sweet and shroudlike over everything. The swamp is coming home, draped across the shoulders of things that once were men. Was that how it began for the dinosaurs? With the bodies of their own rising up and coming home? Did they bring it on themselves, or did the dead simply rise and wash them from the world? The alligators might remember, if there was any way to ask them. But the alligators have no place here. Here there is only the rising of the dead.

Professor Mason is on the campus radio again, this time with an update from the CDC. They're finally willing to admit that the zombie plague is real. Details are given, but the gunshots from inside drown them out. The smell of the swamp. The smell of blood and gunpowder. The smell of death.

My grandfather's hand throwing the rock. The sound of the rock hitting the water. *"Always remember that Nature can be cruel."*

"I never forgot," I whisper, and open the door.

The campus stretches out in front of me, majestic in its stillness, the smell of swamp water and the dead holding sway over everything. The door swings shut behind me, the latch engaging with a click. No going back. There is never any going back for those who walk into the swamp alone. This is cleaner. This is the end as it was meant to be—for dinosaurs, for humans, for us all.

The rock fits easily in my hand, sized precisely to the span of my fingers. I look up at the speaker that broadcasts Professor Mason's update, the masking sound that confuses the reality of my presence. Let the survivors cling to their petty hopes. I choose my window with care, making certain not to select one that shelters the living. I pull back my arm, remembering my grandfather's face, my brother's voice on the phone when his wife was bitten, the golden eyes of alligators in the Everglades. My aim is true; the sound of shattering glass is alien here. All I need to do is wait.

I close my eyes, and spread my hands, and I am eight years old. I am safe beside my grandfather, and the smell of the swamp is strong and green and sweet. The sound of water running in my memory is enough to block the sound of footsteps, the sound of distant moaning on the wind. I am eight years old in Florida, I am twenty-three in California, and I am temporary. Nature can be cruel, but the alligators, the Everglades, and the dead are eternal.

San Diego 2014: The Last Stand of the California Browncoats

Introduction

The San Diego International Comic Convention is a world entirely unto itself.

I've been attending since I was sixteen years old. I've missed a few years—mostly in my early twenties, when time and money were both tight—but on the whole, I've been a constant feature on the floor. I've seen the convention go from manageable to massive around me. The crowds are . . . well, they're virtually impossible to describe. They can only be experienced.

(The closest comparison I have to trying to move across the San Diego Comic-Con floor on a Saturday afternoon is trying to cut through Times Square on New Year's Eve, or across the plaza in front of Cinderella's Castle at Disney World just before the fireworks show. If you have ever done any of these things, I'm sorry. If you haven't, well, I have done all three of them, which means you don't have to.)

It's sort of inevitable that someone with a morbid turn of mind will eventually look at San Diego Comic-Con and think "if the zombie apocalypse happened here, we'd be massively fucked." It's a lot of people crammed into a small space; many of them are in costume, some covered in fake blood; because there's so much noise and so much going on, even emergencies tend to go overlooked by people who are not immediately effected. Up until recently, the Wi-Fi and cellular signals inside the convention center were mind-numbingly terrible, which meant that people who were *inside* the hall were essentially isolated from people *outside* the hall.

What a perfect recipe for chaos.

On a parallel track: Some years ago, Joss Whedon made a television show called *Firefly*. It aired for a season on Fox before it was canceled, inspiring a devoted fan base, including the nonprofit organization known as the California Browncoats. They appear annually at Comic-Con, raising money for charity and keeping the signal going. Several good friends of mine, including Shawn Tutt, are involved with the California Browncoats. I knew when I decided to write my Comic-Con story that I wanted the Browncoats to be involved.

Not only are several of the characters in *San Diego 2014* based on real people—including Shawn and Lynn Tutt, and their daughter, Lorelei—but the California Browncoats were given the opportunity to auction off several Tuckerizations for charity. "Tuckerizations" are a literary tradition of long standing, in which individuals are written into a fictional universe, whether as heroes or villains, with their full and informed consent. Kelly Nakata and Lesley Smith (and Lesley's service dog) were written into this story because they won the auction. I remain grateful for the support of the California Browncoats, and of the Trevor Project, which was the recipient of their donations.

During the writing of this story, I fell a little bit in love with Elle Riley and her fictional show, *Space Crime Continuum.* I was disappointed when the Canadian science fiction drama, *Continuum*, premiered—I had been looking forward to writing lots and lots of fanfic for a show that didn't exist.

Oh, well.

San Diego 2014:
The Last Stand of the California Browncoats

Prologue: Chasing the Story

The Rising is not a single narrative; there is no one true story that unifies that entire bloody summer, no one event which exemplifies the human experience. It is a piece of history like any other, a tapestry of lives which, viewed in total, may someday give us that rarest of commodities: We may, by looking at them all, someday discover the truth.

—MAHIR GOWDA

When I was a kid, people used to talk about living in the future. Well, I live in the future. I want to go back to living in the past.

—LORELEI TUTT
CAPTAIN, UNITED STATES COAST GUARD

LORELEI TUTT'S APARTMENT, LONDON, ENGLAND, JUNE 1, 2044

Lorelei Tutt is a harshly attractive woman in her forties, tall and lean, with scars from her combat gear on her hands and elbows. Her naturally brown hair is streaked with natural gray and sterilization blonde, and she wears it in a short-cropped, almost military style that does nothing to soften the lines of her face. She walks with a subtle limp, the result of learning to walk on a prosthetic right leg at the age of twenty-five. Her left eye is shaped normally but filmed with cataract white from an old war injury. She moves with studied precision, and it is clear from her expression that she is not happy to see me.

The front room of her London flat is at odds with her appearance: The time she spent in the United States Coast Guard has left her seeming businesslike and cool, but her decor is that of a teenage member of the science fiction and fantasy subculture that thrived before the Rising. Books and assorted forms of recorded media pack her shelves, and the walls are covered in posters advertising long-canceled television shows, long-forgotten movies.

She indicates that I should sit. She does not do the same. Her accent is American: She may have left the country of her birth after she left the Coast Guard, but some things are not so easily forgotten.

LORELEI: You know, I don't know why you people keep coming looking for me, sniffing around the graves like this. San Diego was thirty years ago. There's no reason to keep dredging up what happened.

MAHIR: Actually, ma'am, that's precisely why people are becoming interested again. Thirty years... that's long enough for terror to fade and nostalgia to start taking over. Did you hear that there's been talk of doing another convention? The city of San Diego has expressed a willingness to host it. They think it might help restore the tourist trade.

Lorelei freezes. I have never seen this happen so literally before: One moment I am speaking to a living, if cold, woman, and the next, I am sharing a room with a statue made of flesh. When she speaks again, what little human warmth her voice contained is gone.

LORELEI: This interview is over. Get out.

MAHIR: You never intended to speak with me today, did you? [silence from Lorelei] That's your right, of course, but I have to ask you... why? Why did you let me come here if you weren't intending to actually have a conversation about what happened?

LORELEI: You people have wasted so much of my time over the last thirty years—all you damn bloggers acting like you're heroes because you stayed in your rooms and told each other about the zombie apocalypse. You people had been doing that since long before the zombies came. You weren't heroes.

MAHIR: But your parents were. [again, silence from Lorelei] Isn't that why you're angry? Because your parents were true heroes of the Rising, and almost no one knows their names? It was very hard to track you down, Miss Tutt. You have no idea.

LORELEI: I thought I told you to leave.

MAHIR: Miss Tutt... I've lost people, too. Maybe not as many as you have, maybe not the way that you did, but I've lost them, and I can't have them back. And I know that the only thing that would have made it even harder for me—the only thing that could have made the worst thing that ever happened to me even worse—would have been knowing that someone else was telling their stories, and telling them wrong. This story is going to be told. I can't stop it. Neither can you. But what I can do, what I have the power to do, is to ask you if you'll let me tell it the way you want it told. If you'll let me tell the truth.

There is a long silence. I begin to think that I've lost her—and then Lorelei gestures for me to stand, beckoning me deeper into the flat.

LORELEI: I need to put the kettle on. If I'm going to tell you what happened, I'm going to want a cup of tea in front of me.

I nod, rise, and follow the last known survivor of the 2014 San Diego International Comic Convention out of the front room. She leads me to the kitchen, where she fills the electric kettle and sets the water to boil. She moves with nervous efficiency. She does not look at me. The time for looking at me is done.

LORELEI: I was just a kid when the Rising started. I didn't think of myself that way—I was eighteen, I was a grown woman, I was not a child—but I was still just a kid. I had no idea how ugly the world could be, or how bad things could get. We'd heard the news. I mean, who hadn't? But we didn't think it was really happening, and even if it was, it wasn't happening where we lived. We did the con every year. It was one of the things we all looked forward to as a family. Me, and Mom, and Dad, rolling into San Diego like we were going home...

Preview Night

The trouble with saying "I would have done it differently" is that we're always speaking from a position of knowing exactly what is about to go horribly wrong. The truth is, we'd be lucky to do half so well if the Rising began again today.

—Mahir Gowda

Get it in, get it up, get it done.

—Shawn Tutt,
Lt. Commander, United States Coast Guard (d. 2014)

The San Diego International Comic Convention was an annual event which drew hundreds of thousands of comic book, science fiction, fantasy, and horror enthusiasts from around the world. For a week every year, San Diego's Gaslight District would be transformed into a strange new country, one with its own traditions, rules, and hazards. It was a golden age for what those enthusiasts called "fandom," and as with all golden ages, it was not properly recognized until it was over.

It's easy to look back on July of 2014 from our modern perspective, with our full knowledge of what was already happening to the world, and condemn the people who chose to attend that year's comic book convention, or "Comic-Con." We tell ourselves that they should have known better. But why should they have known better? It was a different time. It was a more innocent era. And the fans of the world were descending, as they always did, on San Diego, California.

The following narrative has been assembled from eyewitness accounts, security footage, social media updates, and various other sources that I am not currently at liberty to disclose. Some of the events described may not have happened in this exact fashion, but for once, I have put aside the goal of absolute truth in favor of a greater goal: understanding. To truly understand what it was like for those brave souls who died in the first major San Diego outbreak, we must first understand what it meant to be them...

—From *San Diego 2014* by Mahir Gowda,
June 11, 2044

Wednesday, July 23, 2014: 10:24 A.M.

The sky over San Diego was a beautifully pristine shade of blue, the sort of thing that triggered a thousand tourist snapshots and seemed impossible to anyone who hadn't seen it with their own eyes. The streets were already beginning to fill with the early arrivals, the people who had come to town for whatever reason before the official start of the convention. Some were there to wait for the doors to open on Preview Night, hoping to snag early bargains or rare collectibles. Others were there to settle into their hotel rooms and prepare for the chaos to come. And still others—such as the California Browncoats, a nonprofit fan organization modeled around the protagonists of a canceled science fiction Western called *Firefly*—were there to set up their official booths.

"I know you don't have much respect for authority, Dwight, but around here we respect the laws of physics," said Rebecca, a petite brunette with a clipboard in one hand. She looked from her paperwork to the former Marine, who was trying, somewhat vainly, to hang the awning from their booth's precarious piping-and-plywood frame. "That means that if you're not careful, you're going to plummet and crack your skull open on this lovely concrete floor. Can we try to not have any major injuries *before* the show opens this year? It would be a fantastic improvement over last year."

"I'm not the one who injured myself last year," Dwight shot back as he continued tinkering with the bolts that were supposed to hold the awning in place. "That honor goes to Leita, who doesn't understand that you're not supposed to pick up knives by the pointy end."

"Hey!" Leita's head popped up over the edge of the display case. She pouted prettily at Dwight, the studs beneath her lower lip poking upward at an angle. "It's not my fault."

"It never is," Dwight said, and kept working.

Rebecca sighed. "Just please try not to fall and die before we're finished setting up? I am begging you. This is my begging-you voice."

"Do you need me to whip these heathens into shape?" demanded a voice from behind her, loud enough to command attention without shouting, the kind of voice that made cadets jump and crowds clear out of the way.

"Oh, thank God." Rebecca turned, shoulders sagging in relief. "I thought you were never going to get here."

"Traffic was worse than we expected. This year is going to be crazy." Shawn Tutt—United States Coast Guard and designated booth organizer—walked over and gathered Rebecca into a firm hug. He was tall enough to tower over her, something that didn't seem to bother either of them.

Shawn's wife, Lynn, and teenage daughter, Lorelei, followed him to the booth, slowed by the large plastic tub that they carried between them. It was packed to capacity with T-shirts and rolled posters.

Lorelei cleared her throat. "Is there someplace we can set this down? My arms are getting tired." She was almost as tall as her father, and her naturally brown hair was streaked with bright green.

"Let me." Vanessa—a quietly pretty woman in a black T-shirt—put down her iPad and hurried to relieve Lynn and Lorelei of their burden. Before they had a chance to thank her she was gone, carrying the tub off to put it with the rest of the merchandise.

"The van's stuffed," said Lynn. She was shorter than Lorelei and taller than Rebecca, with short brown hair. "If we can get some people to help us unload it, we'll be able to help set things up in here."

"Of course." Rebecca pulled away from Shawn. "Dwight . . ."

"I know, I know. Strong back, weak mind." Dwight climbed down from the stepladder, putting the hammer he'd been using down on the nearest stack of boxes. "I'm on it."

"Take some of the others with you. Anyone who looks like they're not doing something absolutely vital is fair game."

"I'll start unpacking shirts," said Lorelei.

"No, you won't, but that was a nice try," said Shawn. "You'll empty the van with the rest of us."

Lorelei sighed, managing to express in a simple exhale just how frustrated she was with the entire situation. "I've been cooped up in that van for *hours*, Dad. Why do I have to help you unload it?"

"Because everybody pitches in during setup," said Shawn. "Come on. The faster we get started, the faster we'll be finished." He turned and walked back the way he'd come. Half the booth followed him, most of them looking relieved to have something else to do.

"Finally," said Rebecca, and reached for the hammer. "Now we can get things *done* around here." She climbed up on the stepladder, humming the theme from *Doctor Who* under her breath, and got to work.

11:00 A.M.

The parking garage attached to the San Diego Convention Center was reserved for "official vehicles" during the convention itself—people who were affiliated with one of the vendors or fan groups in the main exhibit hall, core convention staffers, and attending celebrities of sufficient importance that they couldn't be expected to walk more than a few hundred yards out in the open, where enthusiastic fans might catch them. It was still early enough on Wednesday afternoon that almost a third of the spaces were empty. That wouldn't last. Long before the convention really got underway, the garage would be full to the point of becoming a fire hazard, and the parking attendants would be on the prowl, looking for vehicles that didn't belong. Anyone found without the appropriate tags and permits would be towed, no questions asked or warnings given.

The Tutts had traveled down the California coast from the Bay Area in a large white-panel van. The space that hadn't been carved out for passengers was packed to the gills with the bins, boxes, and plastic tubs that contained the supplies for the booth. They weren't the only people bringing items for the convention—that would have required three vans, and left no room for either driver or passengers—but they were definitely the most important, apart from Rebecca, who had driven down with a trailer that contained the actual booth structure. Without their stores of merchandise, decorations, and most important, snacks, the convention would have been a grim place for the Browncoats.

Shawn handed Robert—Leita's skinny, long-limbed older brother—a flat of Coke. He stacked a flat of Diet Coke on top of it a few seconds later. "Think you can take two more, or is that your limit?"

Robert whistled. "First, I can take four more, but I won't, because I don't feel like showing you up. Second, are we preparing for a convention or a siege?"

"You weren't here last year, were you?" asked Dwight. He clapped Robert on the shoulder, sending the slimmer man staggering forward a step and nearly causing him to drop the soda. Robert shot him a wounded look. "The only difference between a Comic-Con and a siege is whether or not they're actually trying to kill you. And sometimes these ones try to kill you anyway, just to keep things interesting."

"Don't scare him away before his shift, Dwight," said Shawn.

Lorelei scowled as she dug a plastic bin out of the back of the van and hefted it in front of her, her knuckles going white from the strain. "What if we all tried doing our jobs and getting this over with before they open the doors?" she asked sourly. "I know it's not the fun, free-wheeling party that we're having right now, but it might make for an interesting change."

"Lorelei—" Lynn began.

She was too late: Her teenage daughter had already turned on her heel and was stalking away, back toward the entrance to the show floor. She sighed.

"I know she loves Comic-Con, but her attitude is going to be the death of me," she said.

"She's been in the car since this morning," said Shawn. "Let's get the van unloaded, and then I'll talk to her."

"She always listens to you," said Lynn. She didn't sound happy about that.

Shawn kissed the top of her head and went back to unloading the van.

The other Browncoats looked uneasily at anything but the Tutts while all this was going on. They might regard themselves as one big family—a crew of people joined by common interests and uncommon hobbies—but there was something about seeing a mother getting angry with her child that reminded them all of their own childhoods. Some experiences are nearly universal, and no more pleasant when viewed from the outside.

The easy camaraderie was gone as they finished unpacking the van, loading boxes and crates onto a pallet loader that Dwight requisitioned from the custodial staff. Then they went trudging back into the increasingly crowded hall. Fun was fun, but it was time to get to work.

2:00 P.M.

The damn Browncoats were nearly done setting up their booth, which was a relief to anyone who had to set up near them. It wasn't that they were bad neighbors—they weren't, and they always had plenty of supplies, which could be a godsend when things got really crazy. But they were also loud, and enthusiastic, and had a tendency to break into song with little to no provocation. Sometimes Marty suspected that oxygen was all the provocation they needed. It wouldn't be so bad once the convention got underway. Once the halls were crammed with fans, the Browncoats could host a live concert in their booth and it wouldn't make a dent in the overall noise levels. Hell, at previous conventions, the Browncoats *had* hosted live concerts, and Marty had been aware of them only after the fact.

"How's that shelving coming, Eric?" he called, forcing himself to stop glaring at the plywood wall behind him. The noise of the laughing Browncoats drifted through from the other side. At least someone was having fun.

After ten years of Comic-Con, fun was no longer Marty's top priority, if it ever had been. He was here to work. He wiped a smear of chalk off his dark brown skin, waiting for Eric's response.

Eric held up a wire basket. "I'm almost done. I just need to get the plush hangers in place, and then we can start unboxing the merchandise." Eric had been Marty's assistant for three years. He was a tall, skinny man, with gawky good looks that seemed to pull the women toward the booth. It was good for profits, even if Eric wasn't for sale.

"We have four hours before those doors open and the hordes descend," said Marty. He picked up a box of graphic novels, beginning to stack them neatly on one of the already constructed bookshelves. God bless IKEA in all its many forms. "Where's Pris?"

"She's on the lunch run," Eric replied. "I figured we should get some actual food before the insanity begins."

"Trust me. By the end of this weekend, you're going to be ranking food well under sleep and alcohol on your personal scale." Marty continued stacking graphic novels. "Did you give her money?"

"I told her you'd reimburse her when she got back."

"Of course you did." Another burst of raucous laughter came from the direction of the Browncoats. Marty grimaced. "Do you think she'll be smart and bring back beer?"

"Probably not this early in the convention."

"No, probably not. She'll learn. Now finish getting those shelves up."

Eric grinned and snapped off a quick salute. "Aye-aye, Skipper."

All around them, other merchants, artists, and exhibitors were in the process of finalizing their booths, getting their walls up and their artwork hung as they turned the convention center floor into a labyrinth of tiny, temporary spaces. Some not so tiny: The movie studios, television networks, and larger comic companies had booths that were easily the size of large retail stores, each one flashier than the last. The network that produced *Space Crime Continuum* had even constructed a full-sized replica of the precinct headquarters where their intrepid Time Police did their jobs and smiled for the cameras. Banners with row numbers dangled from the ceiling to help people figure out where they were actually going. Thanks to the annually shifting design of the booths, even old hands could get lost during the first few days of Comic-Con.

By day three, the floor would be so jammed with bodies that getting lost wouldn't be nearly as much of a concern as getting crushed, or being swept three rows past your destination by people who were packed together too tightly for you to fight your way free. It hadn't always been that way, but since Hollywood had discovered Comic-Con, the people had come in increasing numbers every year. Tickets had been sold out for months. Only the lucky would be getting through those doors, and the lucky would number in the thousands.

"Another day, another battle for survival," Marty muttered.

4:30 P.M.

"I can't believe we're actually here! This is going to be so much *fun*!" Patty flung herself backward onto the hotel bed, arms and legs splayed like she was going to start making snow angels on the industrial-grade duvet. "My first Comic-Con! I've wanted to go since I was twelve. Did I tell you that?"

"Yes, you did," said Matthew, unpacking his duffel bag into the top drawer of the room's small dresser. "Five times during the ride from the airport alone. Also, you need to stop using so many exclamation points when you speak. That can't be healthy."

"You just say that because you're British," said Patty.

Matthew paused in the process of tucking a shirt into the drawer, squinting at her. "What does that even *mean*?"

"I don't know. I just figured it would make you stop ragging on me about the way I talk." Patty sat up and stuck her tongue out at him. "We're at Comic-Con. We're newlyweds. This is a time for geek love and geekier lust. Now stop putting your clothes away and come take some of my clothing off of me."

"I wish I could do that, you poorly punctuated enchantress, but all it will do is make you angry." Matthew continued unpacking.

"What? Why would you ravishing me make me angry? I'm pretty sure that being ravished is in my newlywed contract."

"Because the doors will open for Preview Night in a little over an hour, and you wanted to be on the show floor first thing. I assure you, while I'm able to resist your allure by staying over here and dealing with my trousers, if I begin the ravishing process, I won't be finished after a mere *hour*."

Patty folded her arms. "I hate it when you make sense."

"If you hate it when I make sense, you should have married a politician, not a scientist. Scientists make sense because we can't imagine a world where there would be any point to doing anything else."

"I think you enjoy it."

"That, too." Matthew gestured toward Patty's suitcase. "Why don't you unpack? You'll feel better if you're doing something, and as soon as you're done, we can head for the convention center and queue up to get our badges."

"Comic-Con." Patty heaved a happy sigh, her sulk already forgotten. "Can you believe we're really here?"

This was a familiar loop: They'd been around it dozens of times since the plane that carried them from London to San Diego began its initial descent. Matthew smiled. "Yes," he said. "I rather do believe I can."

5:30 P.M.

Elle Riley, star of the moderately well-rated science fiction drama *Space Crime Continuum*, waited not-so-patiently for the man who was supposed to be escorting her around the convention to get his goddamn act together already. He'd been arguing with the convention center security for the better part of twenty minutes—no, twenty-five minutes, according to her phone—about whether they could use the service tunnels. If he didn't work things out soon, she was going to be late for her first panel. Not that *SCC* was that big of a deal, or it wouldn't have been one of the first shows presenting at the convention. Still, they had two panels this weekend, one on Preview Night and one on Sunday afternoon, and she didn't want to mess things up for the rest of her cast. She was already going to make the panel a living hell. She could at least be on time.

Some actors were chosen because of raw talent, or because of the kind of drive that could be used to power the time ships her franchise was built around. Elle was smart enough to know that she hadn't been cast for either of those reasons. She could read a script, she could give a reasonably nuanced performance, and she could deliver technobabble explanations of hackneyed plot twists with the best of them. But none of those things were responsible for her continued employment. No matter what the blogs sometimes implied about her, Elle Riley was too smart to think that she got work when better actresses didn't because she was somehow more deserving.

She got work when better actresses didn't because she was pretty, and because she had big green eyes that she could widen with the right degree of confusion and awe when someone told her she was looking at a time anomaly on the green screen, and most of all, because the ratings went up every time the writers found a good reason for her character—the fetching chronoforensic analyst Indiction "Indy" Rivers—to take a deep breath. And all of this meant that when she sat on a panel, at least half the questions from the audience would be thinly veiled excuses to tell her how pretty she was.

At least the convention-supplied moderators managed to block the marriage proposals and offers of private dinners. Mostly. When they didn't stop the questions from being asked, the moderators hurried the questioner away before he—or sometimes she, although that was rarer, which was amusing, all things considered—could expect an answer. And all of that was secondary to the fact that they were about to be late.

Elle cleared her throat, trying to be polite about it, and aware that no matter how polite she was, there was a good chance she would be interpreted as another spoiled starlet trying to throw her weight around. "Um, excuse me?" The two men continued arguing. "Excuse me?" They still gave no sign that they'd noticed her. Elle sighed before stepping forward and tapping her handler on the shoulder. "Hello?"

"Ms. Riley?" The handler turned to face her. He'd been doing this job long enough to be very good at hiding his irritation, but Elle had been doing *her* job long enough to catch it anyway, reading his displeasure in the way the muscles tensed around his eyes. Still, his tone was completely professional as he asked, "Is there a problem?"

"I'm sorry to interrupt, and I really appreciate the way you're trying to take care of me, but we're going to miss my panel if we don't start moving about five minutes ago." Elle grimaced apologetically. "I think they sort of want me to be there."

Her handler's eyes widened as he looked down at his own watch. Then he swore—too softly for her to make out the exact words, but the tone was enough to make his meaning clear—and said, "Ms. Riley, if you don't mind, I think we need to start moving if we want to get you to your panel on time."

Elle bit back several caustic responses before settling on a neutral "Yes, that's probably a good idea. Are we taking the service halls?"

Her handler nodded. The convention center security guard shook his head. Her handler frowned, but appeared to realize that it was long past the time to stop arguing and start moving. "No, ma'am, we're not. It's late enough that we need to cut through the convention center floor. If you'd just follow me, I'll get you to your panel before they even start seating your costars."

Privately, Elle doubted that this was physically possible, especially if they were taking the route through the middle of the main floor. It might be Preview Night, but if the doors had opened while her handler was arguing with the security guard, there would be literally thousands of comic book and television aficionados crammed into the single cavernous room. Once upon a time, before *Space Crime Continuum* had come into her life, a girl named Elle Riley would have been out there with the rest of them. And given how her teenage self would have reacted to a real live television star suddenly popping into view, this would be like trying to play through the final boss level of a modern-day version of *Frogger*. Only this game would have autograph chasers in place of alligators, and large clots of fans taking pictures of a woman dressed like slave-girl Princess Leia in place of trucks.

And there was absolutely no point in arguing about it, because they were out of time. Elle put on a sunny smile. "Well, then," she said. "Let's get moving."

5:45 P.M.

"Ladies and gentlemen—and Browncoats who refuse to tie themselves down to a single option—I declare the 2014 California Browncoats booth open for business!" Rebecca flung her arms open in a gesture that would probably have been more triumphant than threatening if she hadn't still been holding a hammer. Dwight swore and ducked. Shawn laughed. Rebecca blinked at them before turning to look at the tool clutched in her hand. With a sigh, she put it down on the nearest flat surface. "As I was saying . . ."

"Time to get to work!" said Shawn. This elicited cheers and nervous laughter from the members of the group who were just glad that Rebecca wasn't waving the hammer around anymore.

Only Lorelei didn't cheer *or* chuckle. She folded her arms, scowling at the ground. Her mother tapped her on the shoulder.

"What's your problem?" Lynn asked. "I thought your father spoke to you."

"About my 'attitude'? Yeah." Lorelei rolled her shoulder away, taking a step to the side at the same time. "I'm being a team player. See? I'm here."

"What I see is that you're being dead weight. You need to do your part for this crew."

Lorelei turned her glare on her mother. "I've been working all day. My head hurts. Don't you make it sound like I haven't done anything to help this crew."

"Hey." Shawn was suddenly there, stepping up and putting himself between them. "Don't talk to your mother like that."

"She started it!"

"Someone has to. Lorelei, if you're so tired, why don't you go back to the room and take a nap until your head feels better? We can hold things together here until you feel up to coming back."

"Shawn—" Lynn began. She stopped as she realized that Lorelei was nodding, a relieved expression on her face.

"Okay, Daddy. I'm sure I'll feel better after I just lie down."

"Make sure you take your phone charger. I want to be able to reach you." The cell coverage inside the hall was notoriously spotty, but the Tutts, like many others, had found a way to work around it. Their phones were also designed to function as walkie-talkies, tuned to other phones on the same plan, with a range that was good up to a mile. The technology involved using short-wave radio, rather than strictly sticking to wireless or cell towers, and meant they could communicate even through the thick concrete walls of the convention center.

"Okay," said Lorelei again. "I'll call as soon as I get to the room."

"Good girl. Love you."

"Love you, too," said Lorelei, and hugged him impulsively. She paused long enough to hug her mother in turn, and then she was gone, running through the growing crowd to get to the outside door before the waiting throngs came pouring in and all hell came busting loose.

6:00 P.M.

Somewhere between fifteen and twenty thousand people were waiting outside the sprawling convention center complex by six o'clock on Wednesday afternoon. Another thirteen hundred were already inside, getting their booths and fan tables ready for the onslaught.

According to security footage of the convention center lobby and front sidewalk—what was recovered from the remains of the disaster, which wasn't much; the destruction was too complete, and the recovery had to wait for quite some time, given the events that followed—the last person to leave before the doors opened was Lorelei Tutt, a member of the

California Browncoats fan organization. Preview Night officially began six minutes later.

The first events of Preview Night were mostly small: announcements from minor comic companies and interviews with the convention's lower-profile guests. One television program was presenting their sneak preview of the season to come at six thirty: *Space Crime Continuum*, which ceased production permanently following the convention. Four thousand people packed themselves into a midsized ballroom to see their favorite stars up close and personal.

We may never know which of those four thousand was infected, or how the outbreak began. Perhaps the outbreak's Patient Zero had been bitten by something—human or animal, it doesn't matter in the grand scheme of the Rising—on the way to the convention and had chosen good seats over seeking medical care. Perhaps a heart attack or stroke claimed a life and left a husk for the virus to reanimate and control. Perhaps it was a case of spontaneous amplification, rare in the modern day, but substantially more common during the Rising, when the human body was still adapting to the infection that would become known as "Kellis-Amberlee." However the infection entered the building, it entered, and once it was inside, there was no way it could be forced to leave.

At 6:30 P.M., July 23, 2014, the first major panel of the convention began. The cast of *Space Crime Continuum*—minus their leading lady, the lovely Elle Riley, who was mysteriously absent from the greenroom—began filing onto the stage. Convention security staff waved more and more people into the hall, until there were no seats left empty. That was when the doors swung closed, and what happened from there, in that room, in that dark, empty space, is lost to history.

Given the nature of the things we did not lose, perhaps this is a mercy.

6:43 P.M.

Elle Riley struggled to keep up with her handler as he shoved his way through the convention center, fighting against the tides of eager fans rushing for the delights of the booths against the back wall. There were less congested routes, but she hadn't realized her handler meant it literally when he said they'd be going through the middle of the floor, and by the time she understood that he was planning to go the worst way possible, it was too late for her to tell him it was a bad idea. Not that he would have listened if she'd tried. No matter how many interviews she gave where she mentioned her past as a rabid fan of shows like *Star Trek*, *Buffy*, and *Doctor Who*—which was the reason she'd auditioned for a time-travel procedural in the first place—people kept assuming she was another pretty face who didn't know a damn thing about the way the geek world functioned. Even though it was her knowledge of the geek world that told her *not* to try cutting between the Marvel and DC booths in order to exit the main hall at Comic-Con.

"We're almost there, Ms. Riley," announced her handler, loudly enough that another half-dozen heads turned in their direction. Elle bit back a groan and forced herself to keep on smiling. This was her public, after all; she couldn't afford to look ungracious.

Great, more autographs and pictures and questions, she thought. *Just what I needed.* Maybe if she was lucky, they'd make it to the panel in time for the question-and-answer session. Or maybe she'd be even luckier, and they wouldn't make it to the panel at all. She'd look flaky but not inconsiderate if she missed the panel because she was signing autographs. She'd look like a stuck-up diva extraordinaire if she waltzed in for the last fifteen minutes and forced everyone else to listen to the inevitable stream of comments about her appearance masquerading as questions. As if she could possibly enjoy that sort of thing. As if *anyone* could possibly enjoy it.

Now they weren't even moving, forced into a holding pattern by the people shoving past in front of them. That meant there was no good reason for the fans to stay away, since it wasn't like she was trying to get anywhere. Sure enough, a timid voice at her elbow said, "Excuse me, are you Elle Riley?"

Elle's smile remained fixed in place as she turned toward the speaker, a sweet-faced woman with a slight Kentucky drawl and hair that cascaded to her shoulders in a series of artificially copper curls. She was wearing a shirt that proclaimed her to be a member of the Time Police. That didn't necessarily make her a fan—lots of shows and stories about time travel had time police in them—but it definitely shifted the odds toward fandom.

"I am," she said. "And you are...?"

"Patty! I mean...I'm Patricia Meigs. This is my husband, Matthew." She took the arm of the man beside her, who was more mundanely dressed in a sweater vest and gray slacks. He was wearing a bow tie, at least, which was a nod to the geekier elements in the wardrobes around him. That, or he was one of those poor, misguided souls who actually believed that bow ties were "cool."

"Hello," said Matthew. He had a mild British accent. Elle amended her assessment of his bow tie: It probably marked him as a *Doctor Who* fan, which meant that the tie was most definitely cool. "It's an honor to meet you, Miss Riley."

"Thanks," Elle said. "I'm supposed to be on a panel right now, but I guess we judged the traffic wrong, and..." She shrugged a little.

Matthew's eyebrows went up. "You're trying to get to a panel by going right down the middle of the hall? Was that entirely wise?"

"Hey, *I* wanted to cut down the back to Artist's Alley and make our escape that way, but I'm not the one calling the shots here." Elle gestured toward her handler's unmoving back. "He's supposed to deliver me where I'm going, and I think he's planning to tackle anything that gets in our way."

"That's going to be quite a lot of tackling," said Matthew.

"I can hear you, you know," said the handler.

"You really *have* been here before!" said Patty. The other three turned to face her, even the handler, who put his back to the crowd in order to stare at Patty. She reddened, shrugging. "I read a lot of blogs. There's a whole debate about you saying that...um..." She stopped, apparently realizing that what she was about to say could be construed as insulting.

Elle sighed. "I know. There's a whole debate between the people who say I'm being coached on what to say in order to build up my 'fandom street cred' and the people who remember seeing me haunting the fan tables back when I was an awkward teenager trying to convince the cast members from *Buffy the Vampire Slayer* to give me acting tips. One side says I'm a liar; the other side says I'm part of the family. I'm with the second side, naturally. This would be my sixteenth Comic-Con, if I were actually allowed to attend at all. But since this is probably as much as I'm going to see of the show floor, I'm trying not to think about it too hard."

"Wow," said Patty, in a voice that was suddenly very small. "Love of fandom got you into the business, and now the business is keeping you away from the thing you love. That's so *sad*."

Privately, Elle thought the girl was being melodramatic, but that didn't make her wrong. "I guess that's one way of looking at it," she said. She glanced at the crowd, which was still forbidding forward movement—more than she would have expected, actually. Something must have been going on toward the front of the hall. "What brings the two of you to San Diego?"

"It's our honeymoon," said Matthew. He smiled fondly at Patty. "We got married in London and hopped onto the next flight to San Diego. We landed about four hours ago."

"No window for jet lag at all?" asked Elle.

"'Jet lag is just another lie time tells, and I can't stand liars,'" said Patty. Then she paused, cheeks reddening again. "Uh. I bet it's considered gauche to quote your character's lines at you, huh?"

"Not really," said Elle, and was surprised to realize that she meant it. "I mean, people quote Indy at me all the time, but it's usually the catchphrases, not the actual dialog. It's not like I get a lot of that. It's sort of flattering."

"Geeky but flattering," said Matthew, and grinned. "I'd take it if I were you, Patty. That's a good way to be viewed."

Patty opened her mouth to respond, and stopped as someone at the front of the convention center screamed. It wasn't a playful scream. A playful scream wouldn't have been able to cut through the rest of the ambient noise. All of them turned instinctively toward the sound, their shoulders going tense as they tried to calculate the respective virtues of fighting and fleeing. None of them were aware of those calculations: They were carried out by a part of the brain older and more focused on survival than anything conscious could be.

"What's going on?" asked Elle. "Did someone get hurt?"

"Ms. Riley, I'm afraid I'm going to need to ask you to wait here," said her handler—but his brisk words couldn't conceal the fear in his eyes, and somehow, that just made everything worse.

"What? No! You're not supposed to leave me alone on the show floor!"

"Stay with your friends, and stay in this immediate vicinity," said her handler. "I'll be back for you as soon as I've assessed the situation." Then he was gone, plunging into the suddenly unmoving crowd, heading toward the sound of screams.

Elle stared numbly after him. "But I just met them..." she said weakly.

"This strikes me as one of those 'can't possibly be good' situations," said Matthew.

Patty worried her lip between her teeth, and for once, she didn't say anything. The three of them stood, looking out into the crowd, and waited for someone to come on the intercom and tell them what was going on.

6:52 P.M.

Kelly Nakata was near the doors when the screaming started. She'd been studying a booth display of replica weapons, some of which looked impressively sturdy. Her head whipped around at the first sound of trouble. She didn't see everything, but she saw enough that she was immediately convinced of the danger, even if she wouldn't understand the true scope of it until it was far too late for anything to be done. If she'd seen a little more, maybe she would have run for the lobby before the doors closed; maybe Kelly Nakata would have joined Lorelei Tutt among the survivors of the San Diego outbreak, rather than joining so many others among the lists of the dead.

What Kelly saw:

The doors were propped open for Preview Night, allowing throngs of fans to stream past the already visibly bored security guards hired by the convention center. The crowd ranged from people in T-shirts and jeans to others in full-body costumes, all of them wearing the little laminated badges that marked them as attendees. Superheroes and monsters, characters from movies and books, all walked side by side through Comic-Con's welcoming doors. Amidst all that color and variety, the man in the blood-soaked shirt didn't stand out at all—at least not until he turned, grabbed a half-naked woman dressed as a character from a popular horror comic, and bit a chunk out of her shoulder. The woman screamed. The man bit her again.

That was when the other people in bloody clothing began staggering through the doors. Some of them were missing chunks from their arms, hands, or even necks, although those were rare; most of them looked like they'd been wounded only superficially. And all of them were biting.

Kelly reached behind her, grabbing the first thing her hands hit—a large staff with a decorative spearhead on the end. She assumed a fighting stance, holding the staff out in front of her. The owner of the stall, who had been considering objecting to having her grab things she hadn't paid for, quickly changed his mind; if the crazy girl wanted to defend him from the crazier biting people, he wasn't going to tell her to stop.

"What the fuck, man?" demanded Kelly, of no one in particular.

"It's that zombie virus thing that was on the news!" shouted a man in a Starfleet uniform. It was *Next Generation* command red, but he was running *away* from the danger, not toward it. Maybe that was how the command crew stayed alive. "They'll eat you if you stay here!"

"They can try," said Kelly grimly, and braced her feet. She felt like some sort of modern-day warrior princess standing there with her staff and her steely determination, like she was Buffy, or Xena, or Indy Rivers. As long as she kept thinking of the situation like that—like it was a story, something she was watching on television, and not something that was actually happening around her—she'd be fine. She hoped.

It wasn't like she had a choice. At this point, running wasn't an option.

The stall's owner screamed, adding his own little bit of noise to the din, and cowered behind his register. Kelly was privately starting to think that this might be a good idea. Then the people in the bloody clothes were on top of her, and there wasn't time to think about anything but fighting for her life. She swung her staff first with military precision and then with wild panic, hitting bodies that barely seemed to notice the impact.

It wasn't until their greedy, grasping hands bore her to the floor that she added her own voice to the screams around her, and by then, it was too late for anyone to come to her defense. For Kelly Nakata, the convention seemed to be over before it properly began.

7:01 P.M.

The California Browncoats were set up toward the back of the hall, far from the open doors and the sound of screaming. Still, the commotion eventually filtered back to them. Dwight jumped onto a stack of boxes so he could peer over the booths, which were mostly the same height. "Some sort of commotion near the doors," he reported. "Security's moving in."

"Actual security or our security?" asked Rebecca. It was an important distinction. The actual convention center security would be dressed in the normal rent-a-cop array, and wouldn't do much to quell a fannish riot. The con's private security force, on the other hand, was a mixture of Dorsai Irregulars and people in full-body armor dressed as Imperial stormtroopers. They could stop a bunch of pissed-off fans with a stern look and a waggled finger.

"Both," said Dwight. He paled, still staring at the doors. "The people who're coming in from outside don't look good."

"Don't look good how?" asked Shawn.

"Bloody. Biting." Dwight turned to face the other Browncoats. "I don't really feel like describing what's happening right now. But I think maybe we should start looking for another door."

That was when the lights went out on the convention center floor and the screaming began in earnest. The Rising had come to San Diego.

LORELEI TUTT'S APARTMENT, LONDON, ENGLAND, JUNE 1, 2044

Lorelei's voice is a soft monotone as she recites the events of July 23, 2014; she does not look up from her teacup.

LORELEI: The lights were a mistake. Some stupid rent-a-cop thought it was just an ordinary riot, and decided people would calm down if they couldn't see anything. I wish I knew his name. I'd like to go and spit on his grave.

MAHIR: Who turned them back on?

LORELEI: The Klingons. One of them saw him do it, and they were fighting to hold the lobby, so he went after the guy. Do you even have Klingons anymore?

MAHIR: They were the villains of a pre-Rising science fiction drama, weren't they? One of the Star Trek spinoffs.

LORELEI: Not quite, but I guess that's close enough. The Klingons I'm talking about weren't aliens; they were people wearing heavy costumes and silly latex heads, and somehow they figured out what was going on. I don't know how; maybe one of them knew someone who'd already encountered Kellis-Amberlee outside of San Diego. They were the ones who realized that most of the infected weren't in the main hall yet. If they closed the doors, the people inside might have a chance.

MAHIR: So they closed the doors?

LORELEI [*nodding*]**:** Yeah, and then they got the lights back on. There were already some zombies inside, but they were figuring that the people in the hall would find a way to hold them off until help arrived.

MAHIR: The people inside? What about the Klingons?

LORELEI: They stayed in the lobby. It was the only way they could get the doors to close. They even barricaded them, to keep the other infected from breaking through. They must have held out for a while. They managed to lock almost all the doors between the convention center and the street before they weren't in a position to keep fighting. There's this thing they used to say, about good days to die. I guess that day was a good one for them. Because they all died, every last one of them. The worst part is, they thought they were doing the right thing...

Lorelei Tutt, last survivor of the 2014 San Diego outbreak, begins to cry into her tea. There is nothing for me to say, and so I say nothing at all.

The Siege Begins

We have lost a great deal since the Rising. Perhaps the deepest of these losses is one that we barely notice today: our innocence. We are incapable of imagining a return to a world where we could abandon all care and spend a week living in a fantasy. But that's exactly where these people died.

—Mahir Gowda

Time is a tool. Once you learn how to use it properly, you'll find that paradox is no more problematic than a broken pipe—and you're the one with the wrench.

—Chronoforensic Analyst Indiction Rivers,
Space Crime Continuum, season two, episode five

It is difficult to grasp the sheer variety of the fan groups that existed in realspace before the events of the Rising pushed such activities into a primarily virtual setting. Hundreds of "fandoms" met in person, their adherents dressing in everything from normal street clothing to full battle armor. Some of their costumes were practical, easy to move in or even fight in, while others... weren't. The outbreak in San Diego began on the first night of the convention, when most attendees were wearing street clothes, rather than the more elaborate attire they had packed for later in the weekend. This may have saved many of them when the outbreak began, as they were able to run from their attackers. Even so, the few surviving images we have of the San Diego outbreak show men in medieval gear and teenage girls with rainbow-streaked hair and bloodstained wings strapped to their backs. Whatever fandom held their allegiances before the dead rose, they all fought the same battle in the end.

—From *San Diego 2014* by Mahir Gowda,
June 11, 2044

Wednesday, July 23, 2014: 7:08 P.M.

"What the *fuck* was that?" demanded Vanessa, jabbing a finger toward the front of the hall. The Browncoats had reacted with instinctive speed when the lights cut out, all of them forming a circle inside the boundaries of their booth. Dwight was still standing on his lookout point when the lights came back on. Shawn was standing so as to block the one access point from the aisle, a two-by-four in his hands and a menacing expression in his eyes. Even Lynn didn't like to cross him when he looked like that. Maybe it was that look—like he knew exactly what was going to come next and was willing to do it, no matter how little he liked it—but all the others turned to him, waiting to hear what they were going to do next.

All except for Dwight. He kept watching the front of the hall. There was still screaming, but it was dying down, losing its immediacy; this sounded less like people who were wounded and more like people who were scared, confused, and being set off by the screams of those around them.

"Dwight?" said Shawn sharply. "Report."

"The doors are closed," Dwight said. "The biting seems to have stopped—the ones who were doing the biting have pulled back. They're blocking access to the doors and snapping at people who approach them, but otherwise, they're not moving."

"What the *fuck*?" repeated Vanessa.

It was a sentiment the rest of the Browncoats not-so-secretly shared. Shawn pulled out his phone, checking for service. As he'd expected, there were no cell bars. He'd have to hope the radio signal would get through. "Start securing the booth," he commanded. "Assume that if we're not under attack right now, we will be soon. I'm going to see if I can call for help."

"The police?" asked Rebecca.

"The Marines?" asked Dwight.

"My daughter," said Shawn.

7:15 P.M.

Eric and Marty stood at the doorway to their booth, waiting for whatever was going to happen next. Eric held the crowbar he'd used to open the heftier book boxes, keeping it loose, ready to swing. Marty held a baseball bat. Neither Eric nor Pris had asked him where he'd gotten it; at the moment, neither of them was inclined to look a gift horse in the mouth. They'd all heard the doors slam shut after the screaming began, and what little they'd been able to learn from people fleeing for the back of the hall was . . . not good. That was putting it mildly.

It might not have been so bad if the screams had stopped, or if they'd been continuous. But there were patches of silence long enough to let them think that the worst had passed, and then the screaming would start up again, as loud and terrified as ever. It made it impossible to stop jumping, waiting for the screams to be their own. Maybe paranoid fear was the right emotion when locked in a huge building filled with dangerous strangers. That didn't mean that it was easy on the heart.

Marty could hear the Browncoats—he could always hear the Browncoats, and for once, he found that comforting. They were hammering on something, probably shoring up the walls of their booth, and using call-and-response games to keep track of each other whenever they had to move out of direct sight. "Marco" and "Polo" seemed to map to moving forward or backward in the hall, while "Hidey" and "Ho" mapped to movement to the left or right. They were an organized group. He'd have to congratulate them on that, if they survived.

"How's it looking back there, Pris?" Marty asked, as loudly as he dared. He might admire the Browncoats for their organization, but he was also concerned about all the noise that they were making. If they attracted the attention of whatever was attacking the convention, he didn't want it coming after his crew, too.

"Whoever killed the lights took out the wireless signal at the same time, and they didn't come back up. I've got no cellular signal. The best I can do is an emergency convention center service band that has about a thousand warnings on it telling me I'm not allowed to log in under penalty of being escorted from the premises and never allowed to come back for as long as I live."

Marty snorted. "Right now, kid, I'd take that as a blessing from God. Go ahead and log on. We need help, and we need it about fifteen minutes ago."

"On it," said Pris, and began typing again.

In the distance, people screamed, and the Browncoats continued whatever strange things they were doing. Eric glanced anxiously at Marty.

"I've been hearing things on the Internet, you know," he said. "Like people saying that the flu everybody says is going around isn't flu at all—it's something we made in a lab. Something to do with that cure for the common cold thing that was on the news a couple of weeks ago."

"That was a hoax," said Marty. "You can't cure the common cold. You'd need something that could take out a million different germs in order to do its job, and that would be a superbug. No one's stupid enough to make a superbug."

"I don't know," said Eric. "People do some pretty stupid things because they want to see what will happen."

Marty paused. His employee sounded pretty shaken up, and who wouldn't be? They were apparently under some sort of attack. Crazy locals looking for fat geek wallets, most likely, but whatever it was, they couldn't get out of the hall. All they could do was stand their ground. "All right, I'll humor you for a second," he said. "If it's not the flu, what is it?"

"Zombies," said Eric grimly.

Marty stared at him and didn't say anything. It should have been funny. It should have been an excuse to laugh out loud. But somehow, with the sound of screaming coming from the front of the hall and Pris typing frantically away behind him, it wasn't funny at all.

Pris got up, moving to stand between the two men. She kept her tablet clutched to her chest. "I spammed every port I could find asking for help," she said. "Now what do we do?"

"We wait," said Marty grimly. "That's about the only choice we have."

7:15 P.M.

At the same time, on the far end of the hall, Kelly Nakata was beginning to believe that she had somehow offended God.

The people who'd attacked her were disorganized, unlike the mob of men in Jedi robes who'd come to haul them off of her. She'd been able to roll under the nearest table in the confusion, scrambling to get herself as far away from danger as she possibly could. And then the lights had gone out—only for a few minutes, but long enough that when they came back on again, nothing was the same.

The Jedi were gone, or mostly; some of them were in pieces on the convention center floor. Others staggered, wounded, and were ignored by the people who'd been attacking them before. It was like they didn't care about their targets anymore, not once they'd been bitten. It didn't make any sense.

Bitten... Kelly paled, beginning to do a quick inventory of her limbs. No bite marks. The mob had come at her from all sides at once, and they'd managed to block one another from getting a really good shot at her. She was bruised, and her back felt like it was seriously rug-burned from where she'd hit the floor, but she wasn't bitten. Kelly had no real idea what was going on around her. She still knew enough to know that when people who were acting like they had some kind of rabies tried to bite you, your best move was to not get bitten.

"Miss? Are you all—"

Kelly whirled, slapping her hand over the stall owner's mouth before she could really consider the inanity of a move like that immediately after she'd been thinking about teeth. Luckily, the scared little man who was now staring at her didn't seem inclined to attack. Faint, maybe. "Shhh," she hissed. "Don't attract attention." She glanced over her shoulder, in case even that much noise might have reminded her former attackers that she existed.

Once again, luck was on her side. The convention hall presented a target-rich environment, and with so many people screaming and running madly from place to place, there was little chance of a whispered conversation standing out. As Kelly watched the chaos, a chilling new factor introduced itself: One of the Jedi who had previously been sprawled on the carpet, eyes open, unblinking, and staring into nothingness, was back on his feet. That wasn't a bad thing... except that he had the same slack expression as the people who'd attacked her. His eyes still seemed empty—until a screaming girl dressed as Rainbow Dash from *My Little Pony* ran too close. Then he reached out with surprising speed, grabbing the girl and dragging her into biting range.

"I gotta get out of here," whispered Kelly. She turned back to the stall owner. "I'll take you with me if you let me take whatever I think we'll need."

"It's a deal," said the stall owner, eyes flicking to the girl in the Pony costume. The Jedi was gnawing on her throat now, and she was twitching helplessly. "Just get me the hell away from these freaks."

"All right," said Kelly. "Here's the plan..."

7:20 P.M.

"Are they gone?" whimpered Patty.

"Where are we?" asked Matthew. He looked around the shabby little room in confusion, trying to figure out how they'd gone from the madness of the convention center floor to this... this office. There were desks and everything. It made no sense.

Elle mirrored his glance. Then, much to his surprise and dismay, she started to giggle.

"Do you mind telling me what's so funny?" he asked.

Her giggles turned into full-blown laughter, which she did her best to smother against the heel of her hand. Finally, shaking her head, she managed, "We're in my precinct."

"She's right!" said Patty. Her fear was gone, replaced by sudden delight. It was remarkable how quickly that woman could bounce back. Then again, that was part of what had attracted him to her in the first place. "We're in the Time Police Paradox Control Unit headquarters! Oh my gosh, that's Indy's desk! I mean, your desk. I mean..."

"The network built a full-scale replica for fans to tour and have their pictures taken in," said Elle. "We're supposed to do some video interviews here with bloggers later in the weekend. I just ran for the nearest door."

"Well, let's see. On the plus side, we now have four walls between us and the crazy people," said Matthew.

"On the minus side, those walls are made of plywood," Elle shot back. "At least the shades are closed. As long as we keep those down and don't make too much noise, they may not realize that we're in here. If they do, we're sitting ducks. There's nowhere left for us to run."

"Come on, Elle," said Patty. She smiled hopefully at the actress, every line of her body broadcasting the message that they were friends now, good friends even, since they were going through adversity together. "Indy would find a way out of this."

Elle bit back her first response, which would have been far harsher than the other woman deserved. "I know," she said. "But Indy has script-writers and a director to help her out. We don't have that."

"We have each other," said Matthew. "We're going to be fine."

Outside their artificial shelter, someone screamed.

7:20 P.M.

In her family's room at the small hotel reserved for visiting military personnel and their families, Lorelei Tutt slept and dreamt of the perfect convention. Every fan was enthusiastic and wide-eyed with wonder, not rude and shoving other people out of their way. The exclusives were plentiful, and freebies and swag flowed like water. It was wonderful. It was the kind of convention that could never exist in the real world but that a fan could spend her whole life dreaming of. It was...

It was...

It was slipping away as consciousness came oozing around the edges of her mind. Lorelei scowled, trying to force herself to stay asleep. It was no use; she was on the downhill side of waking up now, and momentum was taking over.

"—respond. I repeat, Lorelei, if you can hear me, please respond."

"Daddy?" Lorelei opened her eyes, squinting groggily into the dim hotel room as she tried to reconcile the dream she'd been having with the note of panic in her father's voice. He wasn't in the room; she was alone.

Lorelei sagged back into the mattress. "Stupid dream," she mumbled, and closed her eyes, getting ready to go back to her perfect convention.

"Lorelei Jezebelle Tutt, if you are anywhere near your phone, you will pick it up *right now*."

Lorelei's eyes snapped open. This time, there was no mistaking her father's voice for part of the dream: It was too loud and too tense to be anything but reality. And it was coming from her jeans, which she'd left discarded on the floor when she crawled into bed.

"Daddy?" Lorelei lunged for her jeans, forgetting the blankets that were tangled around her legs. They pulled tight and she went sprawling, smacking her elbow in the process. She yelped, pausing for a few seconds to rub her injury before she grabbed her pants and fumbled her phone out of the front pocket. She had no missed calls, but several missed walkie-talkie connections. A feeling of inexplicable dread built in her chest as she raised the receiver to her mouth, pressed the walkie-talkie button, and said, "This is Lorelei Tutt. Mom? Dad? Are you there?"

There was no pause before she got her answer. As soon as she released the "transmit" button her father's voice was there, demanding, "Lorelei? Are you all right? Where are you? Are you hurt?"

"What?" Lorelei sat on the floor of her hotel room and blinked at the phone, utterly puzzled. "What are you talking about? I'm in our hotel room. I was taking a nap."

When she released the button, she thought she heard her mother sobbing in the background. Her father took a shaky breath and said, "I don't want you to worry too much, sweetheart, but we have a bit of a situation over here at the convention center."

"What kind of situation?" Lorelei finally boosted herself up onto the bed, grabbing her jeans at the same time. "Do you need me to come over there?"

"No!" The answer came from both her parents at the same time and was delivered with such immediate vehemence that Lorelei nearly dropped her phone. There was a pause while her father took another shaky breath. Then he said, "This isn't the kind of situation that gets

better by adding you. It would get worse, because then your mother and I would be worrying about you when we need to be worrying about the entire crew."

The dread was solidifying now, turning into something concrete and real. "Daddy, what are you talking about?"

"I need you to be brave for me now, Lorelei. Can you do that? You've always been one of the strongest people I know—you'll never understand how proud of you I am for being so strong—and right now I need that strength more than ever. So can you be brave for me?"

"Daddy, you're scaring me."

Her father laughed unsteadily. That just scared her worse. Her father might say that she was strong, but she'd learned it from him. He had always been the rock in her life, and right now he sounded like he was on the verge of crumbling.

"I'm scared, too, Lorelei," he said. "Remember those blog posts you tried to make me read? The ones about the people going rabid and attacking each other?"

"You mean the ones about the zombies?" whispered Lorelei.

"I'm not quite ready to use the *Z* word, but yes, those are the ones. Honey, something like that is going on here. Some people managed to lock the doors to the exhibit hall before too many sick folks could get inside, but we're sort of stuck now, and we don't know how much trouble we're in. I want you to do me a huge favor. It's going to mean keeping it together and staying calm for me. Can you do that?"

"Yes, Daddy." Lorelei was still whispering. She couldn't seem to make her voice get any louder.

"I need you to go down to the base office and tell them that we have a situation here at the convention center. I'm not in any position to contain it; I have to worry about our people. If they ask why I didn't call this in myself, tell them that some idiot tried to play hero and shut off our wireless. None of us have a signal. If we hadn't paid for the walkie-talkie feature, I wouldn't be talking to you now."

Shawn sounded totally calm. Somehow, all that did was make Lorelei feel even worse. She licked suddenly dry lips before asking, "Is—is Mom okay?"

"Your mother's fine, or as close to fine as any of us can be right now. She's currently helping Leita and Robert get the edges of our booth secured. The people next to us hadn't shown up when the doors locked, so we're expanding into their space for the time being, getting things settled while we're relatively calm."

Lorelei took a sharp breath. She knew what it sounded like when her father was getting ready to go on a dangerous mission; there was a certain tension in his voice that spoke of knowing that he might be just a man doing a job, but that job could still turn deadly. "Daddy..."

"We're going to be fine, Lorelei. I promise. Now just go tell base that we need assistance here, and then get back to your room. I want you to stay put until all this is taken care of. You understand me?"

"But I could—"

"*Stay away from the convention center.* That is an *order*, Lorelei. Do I make myself perfectly clear?"

"Yes, sir," she said. She finally pulled on her jeans. "I'll get your message to base. Be careful. I don't want to pay for this hotel room out of my allowance." The comment was made jokingly, but there was an air of desperation behind it, as much a part of the conversation as Shawn's tension.

"We'll be fine," said Shawn. "Call me as soon as you've spoken with base. I need to go help Rebecca."

"Daddy—"

But it was too late. He was already gone.

7:27 P.M.

Shawn lowered his phone, looking at it with a stomach-churning mixture of panic and pride. Thank God she was already outside the hall when things went bad. Thank God she was going to be okay. Even if the rest of them wound up stuck inside for days—and at the moment, that was the worst scenario he was willing to entertain—Lorelei would be safe at the hotel, running up a big room service bill and getting mad about being left out. She'd be *fine.*

"Shawn..." He turned to see the tears streaming down Lynn's normally calm face. "Did I hear that right? She made it back to the hotel? She's okay?"

Lynn's worst fear—Shawn's too, although Lynn had been more vocal about it—had been Lorelei getting distracted on her way out and somehow winding up trapped in the lobby. She would have had no way to get back into the exhibit hall, and if those doors were locked, the doors to the street were probably locked as well.

But they didn't need to worry about that. Lorelei was safe. They could worry about everything else, like how to keep themselves safe, now that they knew they didn't have to worry about her. "She's in her room," Shawn said. He put a hand on Lynn's shoulder, trying to block out the distant sounds of screaming. "She's *fine*. She didn't even know we were having problems over here. She was taking a nap when I called."

"Oh, thank God," whispered Lynn.

"Lorelei is on her way to the base office now to notify them of the issue here. Assuming local law enforcement isn't already on the way, it may help if they know that we have some military personnel inside."

"Did you tell her to stay on the base?" Lynn's eyes widened. "Please tell me you told her to stay on the base. Please tell me she isn't going to try coming *back* here."

"I told her to stay put, but that doesn't mean she's going to do it."

Lynn sighed. "I know."

Shawn squeezed her shoulder before pulling his hand away. "It's going to be okay, Lynn. She's a smart girl. She won't come back here unless it's safe, and we'll all be back at the hotel getting on each other's nerves before you know it."

"Maybe faster than that," said Dwight from behind him. Shawn turned. The ex-Marine was holding a heavy Maglite-brand flashlight, the sort that could be used just as easily as a club when the situation demanded it. He smirked a bit at the look on Shawn's face. "It's not the size that counts; it's how hard you're willing to swing it."

"What are you talking about?" asked Lynn.

"Rebecca and I are going to go check the parking garage. All the locks here are manual, and whatever shit's going down started at the front of the hall. We may be able to get out the back if we're real careful about it."

Shawn straightened. "That's a great idea. I'll get Robert and—"

"No, boss. This is a scouting mission. We don't know whether the garage has been compromised, or what might be going on back there. It's best if we don't risk the entire crew on something that might not pan out." Dwight's smirk faded into something much grimmer. "You know shit in here is going to get worse before it gets better."

Someone in the distance screamed, punctuating his words. The screams seemed to be getting less frequent. None of them knew whether this was a good thing. None of them wanted to be the one who guessed wrong.

"All right," said Shawn finally. They all knew that his consent was just a formality—his leadership was always conditional on the other members of the group wanting to do what he told them to do, and getting a bunch of fans to do anything was a lot like herding cats—but formalities can help a lot, when you let them. "Take Rebecca and anything you think you might need. Report back here."

"All right. And, boss?"

"Yeah?"

"If we don't come back in half an hour, don't send anyone looking for us. Either we've made it out and we're coming back with help, or we didn't make it and we're not coming back at all. There's no sense in you throwing good people into a meat grinder for our sakes."

For a long moment, Shawn didn't say anything. Then he nodded and saluted the other man. "Good luck, soldier."

"Oorah," replied Dwight solemnly as he returned the salute. Somehow, the strangeness of the moment did nothing to rob the traditional battle cry of the United States Marines of its efficacy. Then he turned and walked away, off to find Rebecca.

Lynn Tutt stepped up next to her husband, watching Dwight go. "Is it silly of me to be afraid that we're never going to see him again?" she asked.

"No," said Shawn. "You're not the only one."

"Oh, good. I'd hate to be silly right now."

Shawn took her hand, and the two of them stood there for a moment, and neither of them felt silly in the least.

7:30 P.M.

"The worst of it is, Unis, I don't even know how we got up here." Lesley Smith, British journalist and sudden shut-in, gave the chair she was perched on a little kick. It spun in another lazy circle, carrying her with it. Her view of the room remained the same: almost total blackness, broken here and there by smears of light. "It's a bloody joke." Her chair drifted to a stop. She didn't kick it again.

Unis lifted her head off her paws, ears cocked inquisitively upward. The Woman was speaking. The Woman was using her name. Perhaps that meant that something was about to be requested of her—but no, The Woman had returned to scowling at the big flat place. As long as The Woman wasn't scowling at Unis, all was right with the world. Unis yawned and put her head back down.

The big flat place that Lesley was scowling at was a control panel of some kind. She'd been able to work that much out by feel, running her fingers over the dials and buttons with labels she couldn't read. As for what it controlled... no one had thought to label anything in braille. Why would they? It wasn't like there was any chance a woman with severely impaired vision would ever be locked in their little control room, unable to figure out how to turn the damn lights on. That would just be *silly*.

The room they were in had two large glass windows looking out over the convention center's main exhibit hall. Thousands of people were locked in down there, and Lesley was locked in up here, along with her guide dog, half a bottle of water, and a granola bar. And no bathroom. And no lights.

"I'm so glad I came to Comic-Con," Lesley muttered bitterly, giving the control panel another spiteful glare. She could still hear the madmen who'd chased her up the stairs milling about in the convention center outside. The door between them was thick enough that she wasn't worried about anyone breaking in—well, she wasn't worried much, and that was the best she could say at the moment.

Unis thumped her tail once against the floor, acknowledging that she'd heard The Woman speaking, but didn't otherwise move. Unis was resting. Unis had already had a long day.

If Unis had been able to speak, she could have told The Woman how they reached the small, safe room with no other people in it, the one with the door that could be shut, and locked, to make safety where there had been only danger. She could have told The Woman that when she'd been given the command to get away from the bad people who smelled like blood and sick—and "Unis, away!" was such a rare command, a danger command, that she obeyed it even more fervently than she obeyed all the others—when she'd been given that command, she had followed it to the letter. She had led The Woman to this safe place, this good place, because she, Unis, was a Good Dog.

Unis let her tail smack the floor again. Lesley glanced over toward the flat-coated retriever and smiled despite her anxiety.

"Silly dog," she said. Then she went back to glaring at the control board.

8:03 P.M.

It had taken longer for Dwight and Rebecca to reach the back of the hall than they had expected. Preview Night had barely begun when the doors closed, but thousands of people had still managed to cram themselves inside, and many of them had fled for the walls when the chaos began. Several of the display booths looked more like armed encampments now. The jokingly named "webcomic district"—three half aisles of semi-affiliated booths manned by the teams from popular online comic strips—was already completely shut off to outside traffic. A surprising number of webcomic artists turned out to be pretty good with tools; they had constructed barriers over the mouths of the aisles in record time and were in the process of shoring them up with chairs and sheets of plywood scavenged from the booths at the center of their territory. It would have been impossible for anyone to get in without a crowbar. Anyone who wanted to use a crowbar would find themselves facing some stringent resistance from the assembled artists and their respective staffs, all of whom watched passersby with wary, narrowed eyes.

"It's starting to look like a Mad Max film in here," said Rebecca, as they finally reached the wall. Between the detour around the sealed-off webcomics district and the detour around the seating area in front of the snack bar—which had turned into an impromptu babysitting crèche and gathering place for the wounded—they had already been gone longer than either one of them wanted to be.

Dwight nodded grimly. "It's just going to get worse from here, you know. If we don't find a way out...how many of these people do you think remembered to bring food or water? How many people with medical conditions didn't bring an extra dose of their medication?" He hooked a thumb toward the snack bar, still being manned by anxious-looking employees. "If those people had a brain in their heads, they'd lock up and run. There's going to be a riot when folks start getting hungry, and this place is going to be the epicenter."

"We have food," said Rebecca, looking shaken.

"We also have a lot of people who've got each other's backs. Besides, Leita and Shawn have got everybody continuing the fortifications while we're away. We're going to come back to an impenetrable fortress. Just you watch."

Rebecca sighed. "I'd just like it if we made it back."

Dwight smiled, nudging her in the ribs with his elbow. "Come on. This is Comic-Con. How dangerous can it be?"

In the distance, someone screamed. Rebecca raised an eyebrow, and just looked at him. They kept walking.

"Do you really think it's the zombie apocalypse?" asked Rebecca, after they'd traveled another fifteen yards or so through the crowded hall. At least most of the people near the wall were relatively nonviolent unless approached too quickly, and very few of them had visible injuries. Rebecca paled every time she saw someone with blood on their shirt, but managed not to keel over. There were times when a fear of blood became a genuine inconvenience, and this was one of them.

"I don't know." Dwight shook his head. "There's been some really weird stuff on the Internet lately. I just wish we could get online from in here."

"The wireless will come back eventually. It has to." The exhibit hall security officers who were supposed to be flanking the door to the garage were gone. Fortunately, it looked just like every other locked door in the center.

Unfortunately, it was just as locked as the rest of them.

Dwight gave the bar one last, futile shove. "This is hopeless," he said. "We should get back to the others and tell them we're stuck in here."

Rebecca smiled. "Oh, ye of little faith." She dug her hand into her messenger bag, coming up with a Swiss Army Knife. "My dad didn't believe in leaving a key under the mat. He said it was a security risk, even if I was supernaturally skilled in the area of losing my keys." She pushed Dwight to the side, crouching down in front of the lock.

Dwight blinked, watching her. "I take it you decided to find other avenues for getting into the house after you'd been locked out."

"If by 'other avenues,' you mean 'taught myself to pick locks out of an old Boy Scout manual I found at the library,' you're totally right."

Rebecca carefully inserted the thinnest blade on her Swiss Army Knife into the keyhole and began to twist. "Dad was actually really proud of me for that. He said it showed initiative. And then he grounded me for a month for picking locks without permission."

"You have a weird family, Rebecca," said Dwight.

"Oh, you have no idea." There was a soft click as the lock turned. Rebecca withdrew her knife and turned to beam up at Dwight as she straightened. "But my weird family just got us into the parking garage. Let's go."

"Ladies first," said Dwight, and clicked his Maglite on.

8:05 P.M.

The lights were off inside the parking garage, but that didn't matter as much as it could have. It was summer in San Diego. The sun had only recently gone down, and every light outside the convention center was turned on full-watt, as if that could make up for the hour. Even so, Dwight's Maglite provided much-needed extra illumination as the pair began walking carefully through the maze of close-packed cars. It seemed even more deserted after the chaos inside the convention center.

"We should cut around the marina," whispered Rebecca. "That way, we get cell signal and can call for help, but we don't get caught up in the crowds out front."

"Agreed," whispered Dwight. The doors had closed early enough that there were probably almost as many people outside as there were inside. Thousands of them, crammed onto the sidewalks, trying to get into a sealed convention center. Even if the riots had spread, new fans would have been arriving almost constantly. Why—

Dwight stopped walking, heart sinking as he fully thought through the possible ramifications of the Comic-Con crowd. Rebecca kept going for a few more steps. Then she stopped as well, turning back and frowning at him.

"Dwight? What's wrong?"

"What if this is the zombie apocalypse?" he asked, voice still kept low. "Do you really think we managed to lock them all inside?"

Rebecca's eyes widened, visible even through the gloom. Then she nodded. Just once; once was enough. Dwight turned, and together they ran for the door back into the exhibit hall.

They didn't run fast enough.

There weren't many infected in the garage. Maybe a dozen, all fully amplified and demonstrating the common infected tropism toward dark, shadowy places. They were well fed and had left the pursuit of food to other, hungrier individuals. But Dwight and Rebecca had come too close and had triggered the need to hunt. As they ran, the infected pursued, moving with the graceless speed of the freshly seroconverted.

The infected caught Dwight first, bearing the former Marine down to the garage floor with the weight of their bodies. The Maglite flew from his fingers and went skittering across the concrete. *"Rebecca!"* he shouted, all efforts at subtlety forgotten. *"Keep running!"*

Rebecca looked back and screamed. The infected were already tearing into Dwight. Blood spurted across the concrete like oil. A wave of dizziness washed over her, costing her a few precious steps. She managed to swallow it, fighting it back, and resumed her flight toward the door.

She knew before she got there that she was never going to make it. The infected were too close, and she was outnumbered. All she could do was lead them into the unprotected rear of the convention center, where a bunch of scared people were trying to hide. It wouldn't be a fair fight. It wouldn't be the right thing to do. So Rebecca Safier became one of the first heroes of the Rising with one simple gesture: When she reached the door, she stopped running.

And she turned the dead bolt, locking both herself and the infected out of the convention center. "I'm sorry," she whispered. Then they were upon her, and she didn't say anything else. After that, there was only screaming . . . and eventually, silence.

8:24 P.M.

"They're not coming back, are they?" asked Vanessa. "They should have been back by now. They're not coming back."

"Shawn?" asked Lynn.

Shawn didn't have an answer. He put his arm around Lynn's shoulders and looked away, out over an exhibit hall that had gone from familiar ground to enemy territory in a single evening. There was nothing left for any of them to say, and so, for once, none of them said anything.

LORELEI TUTT'S APARTMENT, LONDON, ENGLAND, JUNE 1, 2044

We have finished our first cups of tea. Lorelei is preparing another round, less out of thirst than from the simple need for something to do. It is an understandable impulse. I wish I had something to do with my hands as well.

LORELEI: We know more about what actually happened to Dwight and Rebecca than we do almost anyone else. It's all supposition with the inside of the exhibit hall, but there were cameras running in the garage. I've seen her locking the door a thousand times. She didn't have any other choice. There was nothing they could have done.

MAHIR: She was very brave. She could have sacrificed a lot of lives in the effort to save her own, and she didn't.

LORELEI: No, she couldn't have. Not Rebecca, and not Dwight, either. They were my friends. They were good people. They were heroes.

MAHIR: Yes, they were.

LORELEI: I was down at the base office while all of this was happening, trying to get somebody to listen to me. It turns out that teenage girls trying to report secondhand riots aren't at the top of anyone's priority list. I did get them to listen, eventually. It was too late by then—but I mean really, it was too late when Dad called me. It was probably too late by the time I left the convention center.

MAHIR: Everyone was doing the best they could with their understanding of the situation.

LORELEI: I wish they'd understood the situation just a little bit faster. More of my friends might have managed to get out alive. Or any of them.

The Second Act

Science fiction and fantasy literature has always been defined by tales of heroism. It is meant to represent humanity at our very best, willing to oppose all odds in order to protect the side of good. The Rising gave all people the opportunity to become heroes. Only a few rose to the challenge. Sadly, even fewer are remembered by name.

—Mahir Gowda

I always knew my father was a hero. I never needed him to prove it.

—Lorelei Tutt, Captain, United States Coast Guard

8:37 P.M.

No one paid attention to the time. The people who were locked inside the hall had other things to worry about—like why the people who'd started the emergency by attacking their fellow attendees had stopped fighting and retreated to the doors. Anyone who tried to approach them was likely to find themselves bitten, or worse; but if the blank-eyed, bloody-garbed aggressors were left alone, they didn't bother anyone.

Kelly Nakata didn't know much about what was going on, but she knew that once a dog starts biting for no good reason, it doesn't tend to stop. She made her way quickly away from the front of the exhibit hall, the owner of the booth where she'd originally taken shelter sticking close by her side. She didn't know his name. She didn't want to. With as quickly as things had gone sour, she wasn't willing to go forging any lasting bonds. He was a good guy, and he'd equipped her pretty well for the fight she was sure they were walking into. She was still going to leave him behind if he turned into dead weight. It wasn't the compassionate thing to do. Screw compassion. People in the middle of the zombie apocalypse couldn't afford it.

"Zombie" wasn't a word she would have brought into things on her own. It was a cliché, dead things and girls in lingerie and Elvira on a velvet love seat making cracks about impractical shoes. Still, it was an unavoidable idea, especially here, where every other person seemed to be a self-proclaimed expert on zombie culture. There were booths boasting every possible kind of zombie-themed goodie, from books and movies to artwork and couture. There was even a magazine called *Chicks with Corpses* that had decided to focus on the lingerie and impractical shoes over the carnage and destruction of mankind. The word "zombie" was everywhere, and it was as good a label as any for the psychos who were clustered at the front of the hall.

What some people didn't seem to be taking into account was that zombies made more zombies. Kelly had seen it happen with her own eyes when the zombies turned on her Jedi-costumed rescuer. He wasn't the only one who'd been bitten, and unless the zombie virus was selectively transferrable—which never seemed to be the case with zombie viruses, so it was a little too much to hope for in this situation—a whole lot of people were going to go rabid in the next few hours. Kelly was grimly sure that was why the first wave of zombies had withdrawn. They were waiting for their reinforcements to get hungry.

"Where are we going?" asked the booth owner.

"Back of the hall," said Kelly. "Where there are exits. They usually have security mooks guarding them, but I figure a bunch of psychopaths biting people at the front doors takes priority. We may be able to get out that way." And if they couldn't, they would at least put some ground between themselves and the next big bite-a-thon.

"What if we can't?"

"We start looking for a fire door. There's bound to be *some* sort of an emergency exit in this place. We just have to find it." Find it, and pray that it wasn't already a solid wall of impassable meat thanks to other people with the same idea.

Giving up wouldn't do either of them any good. Kelly tightened her grip on her borrowed staff and kept on walking. Maybe they could find someone who was selling armor—Kevlar would be best, but she'd take leather, or even hardened canvas, if that was what she could get—and convince them to join their merry band. Like *The Wizard of Oz*, only with zombies instead of flying monkeys.

"I didn't catch your name."

"Keep walking."

"My name's Stuart."

Kelly winced. "Oh."

"What's your name?"

If she told him, she'd be admitting that he was a person, too; she'd be making him real. In a way, she'd be making this whole crazy situation real, because real people didn't show up in dreams. She'd definitely be making it harder to turn her back on him when the time came—and the time was *going* to come; she was absolutely sure of that. This was a zombie apocalypse. The time always came.

Kelly sighed. "My name's Kelly," she said. "Now keep walking."

They kept walking.

8:45 P.M.

Exhaustion and panic had finally carried the day: Patty was asleep. She was draped half-over the authentic reproduction of Indiction Rivers's desk, her head propped up on one arm, snoring softly. Elle paused in her attempts to peer through the blinds at the exhibit hall outside, shaking her head.

"How is she *doing* that?" she asked. "I can't imagine sleeping before someone comes to get us out of here." At least the screams had stopped, or at least faded back into the greater noise of the crowd. Even that seemed more subdued, as if people were getting quieter as they realized they couldn't escape. That would change soon, she was sure: Panic would make a reappearance, and then their hidey-hole would become even more essential.

Matthew smiled. "It's a fairly impressive skill, I admit. She actually fell asleep on me the very first time we met. It was at a *Doctor Who* convention in Chicago. I'd flown out for the con. We wound up standing next to each other in the autograph line, and got to chatting. From there, we took our conversation to the bar, and I thought, 'This is splendid; this is a splendid girl.' Only next thing I knew, she was snoring on her stool, and it was, well, 'Right, then. You've blown another one.' "

Elle smiled a little. "And you hadn't blown it at all."

"Not a bit. My Pat just sleeps when she's tired, that's all. It's like convenient narcolepsy. I envy her a bit. We'll all want to be well rested come tomorrow, and she's going to be the only one standing up straight."

"As long as we have a tomorrow, I'm happy." Elle took another peek out the window. "I admit, I was wishing I'd have an excuse to spend some time in the exhibit hall without being rushed along by a handler, but this isn't what I meant."

"So you miss it, then? The convention scene?"

"It's different when you're a professional. Even when you wish it weren't." Elle stepped away from the window. "I can't really tell what's going on out there, but I don't think going out to check would be a good idea."

"In that, we are agreed."

"That's a relief." Elle put her hands on her hips and studied the room. It both was and wasn't like the set where she spent her workdays: For one thing, it had all four walls, rather than being an open sound stage. They had a complete precinct room, but they very rarely filmed there. Too hard to get all the cameras inside.

Working together, the three of them had managed to shift the filing cabinets up against the room's single door, effectively locking it, and three of the four windows were completely covered with leaning sheets of plywood that Matthew had discovered being used to prop up the "chrono monitor" behind Indy's desk. Leaving the fourth window uncovered was a calculated risk. It left them vulnerable to attack, but covering it would have meant cutting off all contact with the main room. For the moment, the window was more valuable as it was.

"Patty's quite excited to have met you, you know," said Matthew. "I hope it's not too forward to say this, but *Space Crime Continuum* is one of our favorite shows. We watch it together, and we both enjoy it quite a bit."

Elle blinked at him. Then, slowly, she said, "We've been fortifying a replica of my fictional office against attack together because we're afraid of I don't even know what, and you're worried about me deciding you're being forward because you like my work?"

Matthew paused. "When you put it that way, it does sound a bit silly, doesn't it?"

"Yeah, just a bit." Elle leaned up against the nearest desk. "I just wish there was something else we could be *doing*. I don't like just standing around."

"It's too bad Patty left her knitting back at the hotel, then."

Elle blinked at him before she snorted laughter, and said, "Even if I *could* knit, which I can't, I don't think I'd feel right knitting while I was potentially in mortal danger. It would just seem a little weird."

"Has anything about this day *not* been a little weird?" asked Matthew.

"Fair enough." Elle sighed. "I'm sorry. I'm just tense. I wish we had cell service in here. I was supposed to be back at the hotel as soon as my panel ended."

"Have you got someone waiting?" Matthew blanched almost as soon as the words were out. "I'm sorry. That's none of my business. I was just making conversation."

"No, it's all right—I brought up the hotel; it's a reasonable question." Elle shrugged. "I do have someone waiting, and I hate being inconsiderate like this." She was hedging, she knew she was hedging, but she'd been doing it for so long that it was almost second nature. Pretense came with the job.

"Ah," said Matthew. "Well, I'm sure he'll understand."

Screw pretense. "I'm sure she will," Elle agreed. Sigrid had always been so very understanding. Understanding when the producers said she couldn't show up on set, as their viewership was made up almost entirely of heterosexual males and Indy Rivers was supposed to be their newest geek sex goddess. Understanding when Elle took her male costar to the Spike Awards. Understanding when she didn't get to come to Comic-Con to see Elle's panels.

Then again, maybe that last bit of understanding was enough to balance out some of the others, because Sigrid was safely back at the hotel, far away from all the chaos at the convention center, while Elle was trapped inside the building while all hell was breaking loose. Maybe the universe had been testing them, and Sigrid had passed while Elle hadn't.

Matthew, meanwhile, was looking at her with that wide-eyed expression of sudden comprehension that she'd been seeing on the faces of straight men since the first time she explained that no, she really wasn't interested, ever. "Sister?"

"No."

"Friend?"

"Significant other. Six years. We're going to get married as soon as I'm well established enough that it won't kill my career." Elle crossed her arms defensively, and hated herself for it. This wasn't supposed to be an issue anymore. It wasn't her fault that she'd been called to a profession where people still cared, at least if you were a woman new enough to be trading on tits and ass. "Are we going to have a problem?"

"Not a bit of it. I'm just surprised is all."

"Why? Because I'm gay?"

"Because you've managed to hide the existence of a significant other from the blogs. I don't care if you're involved with a man, a woman, or a sapient pear tree. You ought to go into international espionage. I never even heard a rumor."

Elle blinked at him before laughing again. "I'll have to tell Sigrid you said that."

"You do that," he said, and smiled.

"Heck, if we get out of here soon, you can tell her yourself. I figure this is the sort of experience that justifies buying you dinner, if anything will."

Matthew nodded. "I'd like that. I think that will elevate you to some form of godhood in my lovely wife's eyes."

"I've always wanted to be a god," said Elle.

Patty sighed a little in her sleep, snuggling up against the replica of Indiction Rivers's stapler. For the moment, everything seemed to be calm. There was no way the moment was going to last.

9:16 P.M.

Terror makes you tired. Marty and the others were taking turns sleeping, one of them retreating to the back of the booth and curling up in a makeshift bed of plush toys and wadded-up newspaper while the other two stood watch. They'd decided on three-hour shifts as the most efficient, allowing them to get through one deep REM cycle—maybe; it was Eric's idea, and he wasn't totally clear on the science—before they had to get up and let someone else have a turn. At the moment, it was Eric curled up in the back, while Marty watched the aisles for signs of trouble.

Pris, who was supposedly standing guard with him, was actually seated at the register, tapping madly away at her tablet. She didn't look like she was even remotely aware of her surroundings. Marty found himself envying her, and he didn't interrupt. What she was trying to do was just as important as what he was doing—maybe more. After all, he might be keeping them alive, but she was going to be the one who got them out.

The sounds of humanity had grown softer as the minutes ticked by and rescue didn't come. Marty could see people sleeping in the aisles, pressed up against the edges of the booths. The lucky ones who'd remembered to bring a sweater or coat into the convention center were hugging them around themselves, as much to be sure that they wouldn't be stolen as for warmth. They had nowhere else to go. Marty felt bad for them, even as he patrolled the edges of his own booth every fifteen minutes or so, shooing away squatters. No matter how bad he felt, he wasn't going to compromise his already fragile security by allowing people to get too close.

He had people of his own to protect. Pris and Eric were his responsibility, and by God, he was going to get them out of here in one piece.

"Marty?"

"What is it, Pris?"

There was a note of excitement in her voice that he wasn't expecting. It seemed almost obscene, given the rest of the situation. "I got an answer."

"What?" Marty actually took his eyes off the aisle as he turned to face her. "From who?"

"Convention center management. They finally noticed that I was pinging their private channels, and they decided to answer me."

"Well? What did they say? Is someone coming to get us the hell out of here?"

Pris grimaced. "Not quite. They say there's a problem outside. Some sort of riot is blocking the doors—they can't get in to let us out."

"Fuck."

"They say that it's pretty ugly. We should be glad that we're in here." Somewhere in the distance, someone screamed. Pris grimaced more. "I think they wouldn't be saying that if they were actually *in* here."

"Did they have anything useful to say?"

"Yes." Pris held up her tablet, and smiled. "They told me how we can get the wireless back on. That's something, right?"

Marty frowned. No food, no water, no exit... but they could get the Internet back on. Somehow, that didn't seem quite as valuable. On the other hand, they were in a convention center full of geeks. Maybe getting the Internet back up would distract everyone else, keep them from making things worse—and maybe they would be able to find a way out once they had access to the outside world. "What do we need to do?" he asked.

"There's a control room on the main concourse," said Pris. "All we have to do is get to one of the house phones, call up, and tell whoever's in there which switches to press."

"How do we even know that there's someone inside?"

Pris gestured with her free hand, indicating the convention center. "Look around. There's no way someone had the opportunity to get into a secure room with a lock on the door and didn't do it."

Marty looked at her. She looked back, a challenge in the tilt of her chin. Pris wasn't a girl who enjoyed sitting idle; once she had a thing that could be done, she wanted to do it. Getting the wireless back on was something she could do, and that meant that she wanted to be doing it.

As bad as things were, they could get a lot worse. This wasn't the time to start trouble with the people he needed watching his back. "Wake Eric up," Marty said gruffly. "We're going to get the wireless back on."

9:25 P.M.

Shawn's phone beeped softly, snapping him out of his light doze and into a state of almost instant awareness. The phone beeped again. He hit the button to activate the walkie-talkie function, and Lorelei's voice said uncertainly, "Dad? Are you there?"

"Lorelei?" He smiled as he raised the phone to his mouth. "I'm here, honey. What's going on?" Around him, the convention center slept, or tried to. Dwight and Rebecca had never come back from their trip to the parking garage. Their absence had created an uneasy divide among the Browncoats. Half of them were firmly convinced that Dwight and Rebecca had managed to find a way out and would be coming back with emergency services. The other half believed that Dwight and Rebecca were never coming back at all.

After spending most of his adult life in the Coast Guard, Shawn knew better than to pin all his hopes on empty wishes. Dwight was a Marine. If he'd been able to come back, he would have done so, leaving Rebecca to organize a rescue party while he told everyone else what was going on. He hadn't come back. That meant he *couldn't* come back . . . and anything that could stop a Marine who didn't want to be stopped was probably stopping that Marine permanently.

"I finally got them to listen to me at the office. Lieutenant Farago said to let you know that he's working on getting cell service into the hall, but nobody would tell me what was actually *happening*." There was a note of panic in Lorelei's voice that Shawn didn't like. At the end of the day, she was his daughter, and she shared his tendency to go running toward danger as fast as her legs could carry her when she felt like the people she loved were at risk. "Are you okay?"

"Well, honey, we've had to redefine the local standards for 'okay,' but none of us is hurt right now." Not unless you included Dwight and Rebecca, and that was just a possibility, not a definite fact. "So they think they can get our phones to start working? That's a good thing." It would have been better if it had happened faster. Most of the people in the convention center probably weren't carrying chargers. Shawn could see outlets and universal connectors becoming the start of the next big fight.

"Yes. But getting the phones working won't get you out right now."

"I understand that, honey."

Lorelei paused for a long moment before she asked, "Doesn't that worry you?"

"Yes," admitted Shawn. He couldn't think of any good reason for the relative peace that had settled over the hall. After the screaming and hysterics that had accompanied the beginning of the siege, he was expecting all-out chaos, not this strange and sudden lull. "But worrying about what we can't change won't do us any good. You tell Lieutenant Farago that we need an exit strategy as soon as he can get us one. Things are calm right now. I don't know how long that's going to last."

"Okay, Daddy," said Lorelei. "I love you."

"I love you, too, sweetheart. Just keep flying, okay? Everything's going to be just fine. You'll see."

Lorelei didn't answer him.

LORELEI TUTT'S APARTMENT, LONDON, ENGLAND, JUNE 1, 2044

Our tea is cold. Lorelei doesn't seem to notice, and I don't feel that pointing it out to her would be beneficial. Her gaze is far away. Sometime during the most recent part of her story, she left the present behind and slipped into a time and place that I have never seen. She is back in San Diego, back in the first summer of the Rising, and I begin to understand why she never wanted to tell her story.

LORELEI: We didn't know how the infected behaved yet. Fuck. We didn't even know for sure that they were infected. Maybe if we'd had more information... [she stops for a long moment; when she speaks again, her voice is even more distant] It wouldn't have made any difference at all. Those doors were already locked. What was going to happen was already a foregone conclusion. All that could have changed is the details.

MAHIR: Sometimes, it's the details that matter the most of all.

LORELEI: The people who'd been infected were skulking around the edges of the hall, waiting for the lights to dim. They weren't hungry yet. They had enough to eat, and they were in the incubation phase. Once in a while they'd grab someone from the edges of a group, but my dad didn't know that.

MAHIR: Kellis-Amberlee had a longer incubation in the early days of the Rising. Today, it's all through our bodies even before we begin to amplify. One bite triggers a cataclysmic chain reaction. For them, back then... how quickly they lost control would have been determined by a dozen factors. Prior exposure, general health, height, weight... It's simpler now.

LORELEI: Yeah. If you can ever call the zombie apocalypse "simple." Anyway, our booth was set up toward the back of the hall, and the infection was self-containing at that stage. I think sometimes that it would have been kinder if it had been like the movies, you know? One zombie gets in, everyone's bitten or dead inside of an hour.

MAHIR: Life rarely concerns itself with being kind, I'm afraid. If it did, we would all be much more content.

LORELEI: Ain't that the truth?

She appears to notice her tea for the first time in almost an hour. She pushes the cup aside, and stands.

LORELEI: I'm going to need something stronger for what comes next. You game?

MAHIR: All things considered, yes. I believe that I am.

10:06 P.M.

It shouldn't have taken an hour and a half to reach the back of the hall. Not with the amount of space available and the relatively small number of people who had been able to cram themselves inside for Preview Night before the doors were closed. But that was a reflection of Comic-Con B.E.—Before Emergency—and this was travel through Comic-Con now. Walkways that should have been open were barricaded, some with as little as caution tape and "Keep Out" signs, others with full-on walls that had been constructed from cannibalized booth displays. Of the people Kelly and Stuart encountered outside the barriers, it seemed like everyone knew someone who had been attacked.

One girl had confessed in a whisper that she and her boyfriend had been right up front when things turned ugly, probably right near where Kelly herself had been attacked. "He got bit by this guy who ran away right after, like it didn't even matter," she said. "He seemed fine for like, *ages*, and then he started getting sort of shaky. And then he flipped out and bit *me* and ran away. Just like that other guy. Just like the guy by the door."

Kelly and Stuart hadn't said anything as the girl rolled up her sleeve and showed them the bite marks scored deep into her lower arm. Her boyfriend's teeth had clearly broken the skin.

The girl had looked calmly between them as she rolled her sleeve back down. "I know what this is," she'd said. "It's the zombie apocalypse. We're all going to die in here, because this is the zombie apocalypse. I'll die before you do. I've already been bitten." Then she'd turned and wandered away, like they didn't matter anymore.

The barriers made a lot more sense as Kelly and Stuart resumed their slow passage toward the back of the hall.

They were almost through the last of the truly congested areas when three people came around a blind corner and stopped in the middle of the aisle, eyeing Kelly and Stuart warily. Kelly and Stuart stopped in turn, eyeing the trio right back. It was two men—one older, one in his mid-twenties—and a woman, clutching a tablet to her chest like it was the only handle she had left on reality.

"You don't want to go that way," said Kelly, breaking their small bubble of silence. "There's nothing that way but scared people building cardboard walls and talking about the zombie apocalypse."

"Which may be actually happening," added Stuart.

"Which may be actually happening," allowed Kelly, in a resigned tone. "Anyway. It's not safe that way."

"Maybe not, but we think we have a way to get the wireless turned back on," said the woman.

Leave it to the geeks of the world to prioritize Internet access over staying alive. "The convention center is full of zombies, victims, and proto-zombies," said Kelly slowly. "Maybe you should go for option number four, and walk away from the carnage, not toward it."

"Or maybe we should make it easier for emergency personnel to coordinate with people inside the hall and keep everyone a little bit calmer by enabling their Facebook updates," countered the younger of the two men. "Who are you, anyway? We're not stopping you from going anywhere you want to go."

"I'm Stuart; this is Kelly," said Stuart helpfully.

Kelly groaned. "You just love introducing yourself to people, don't you? You have to stop that."

"I'm Pris," said the woman with the tablet. "This is Marty and Eric. We appreciate the warning, but we really do need to get the wireless working again. It may be the best shot we have at getting out of here."

For a brief moment, all Kelly could think of was the pale-faced girl with the bite on her arm and the resignation in her eyes. That girl had known what the real score in the convention center was. She had known that the time for hope was long over.

Somehow, Kelly couldn't bring herself to make the same leap. "Fine," she said. "You've convinced me—and since we just came from the front of the center, we can show you which way not to go. Let's go turn the Internet back on."

The older of the two men, the one Pris had identified as Marty, eyed Kelly suspiciously. "Not to sound like I'm looking a gift horse in the mouth, but why should we trust you, young lady?"

"Because I have a spear and you don't, and right now, that means I'm a lot more likely to stay alive than you are," said Kelly, in what she hoped was a reasonable tone of voice. She wanted to yell. She just wasn't quite sure at whom. "Look, listen to me, don't listen to me, it's no skin off my nose. But if you really want to fix the wireless, you probably shouldn't go sneering at anybody who's actually willing to help you."

"Besides, she hasn't stabbed me or anything yet," said Stuart, in what was probably intended as a helpful tone. "She sort of saved me, actually, when those freaks first came breaking into the hall. You know. Before we realized that they were zombies."

"We still don't know that 'zombie' is the right word to use here," said Kelly.

Eric rolled his eyes. "You're not one of those people who calls it 'the *Z* word' and refuses to say it, are you? Look: If what we're dealing with here is that disease people have been whispering about in the blogosphere for the last few weeks, then 'zombie' is the best word there is. Are they alive? Yeah. But they weren't at one point, and if they get hold of you, you won't be for long. That's zombie enough for me."

"Semantic arguments won't turn the wireless on," said Marty.

"Then let's go," said Pris, and started walking. Marty and Eric followed her.

Kelly and Stuart exchanged one last look. Then they fell into step beside the trio, starting back the way they'd come.

10:10 P.M.

Patty was still asleep, slumped against the replica of Indy Rivers's desk. Matthew had joined her, slipping reluctantly into a light doze. Only Elle remained awake, sitting with her back to the room's thin plywood door and listening to the sounds of the convention center outside. Lacking anything better to do, she had her phone out and was using the memo function to type out a message.

Sigrid—

If you have this, it's because someone has given you my personal effects. (That may be wrong. I can never remember the difference between "effect" and "affect." That's your job.) I'm sorry. I'm sorry I left you alone. I'm sorry I didn't come home. But I'm not sorry that you aren't with me, because I'm scared, Sig. I'm scared enough that having you here would just scare me more. I'd be so afraid of losing you that I wouldn't be able to breathe. It's better this way. Really.

You're probably watching this on the news by now. Comic-Con is a pretty big deal, and something like this happening to it has got to be a headline. I'm sorry if you're scared for me. If it helps at all, I'm scared for me, too. That probably doesn't help. I wouldn't want to know that you were scared. I'd want to be there to hold you, and to take the fear away.

Patty stirred in her sleep, making a small protesting noise as she rolled over. Elle looked up, eyes narrowed. Patty didn't move again, and Elle went back to tapping laboriously away.

I love you, Sigrid. I haven't always been as good at showing that as I should have been, but it's true. If I make it out of here, everything's going to change. No more letting agents or focus groups run my life—run our life. I promise you. I am so scared, but I have never seen things as clearly as I do right now.

Yours always, Elle.

Elle hit "save" and put her phone back into her pocket, slumping against the door. She felt better for having written the letter, even if the odds were good that Sigrid would never see it. It was the sort of thing people did in horror movies, usually right before they got eaten. She'd always thought they were idiots for attracting the attention of whatever force controlled the narrative. Now, though, she finally understood why they did it.

They did it because it felt like closure, and when you already felt like you were going to die, closure was just about the only thing left to aspire to. She closed her eyes, picturing Sigrid's face, tight with concentration or lit up from within as she laughed. Elle smiled a little. Sigrid was always beautiful, even when she was angry.

Holding the image of Sigrid's face firmly in her head, Elle relaxed against the door and finally let herself drift into sleep.

11:11 P.M.

It took only an hour to get back to the front of the hall. It was faster partially because Kelly and Stuart knew the lay of the land now—where the blocked halls were, where the clusters of scared or wounded people had built up—and partially because they were going against the flow of traffic. Almost everyone was heading for the back, where the bathrooms and the food court were, and where there weren't any bloodstains on the carpet.

Yet.

Kelly found herself eyeing the shadows with her hands clenched tight around her spear, waiting for the other shoe to drop. Pris and Eric walked almost carelessly, not seeming to realize how much danger they were in. Even Stuart seemed more relaxed now that they were in a larger group, like that was going to make any difference to people crazy enough to attack with their teeth. Only Marty seemed to understand how dire the situation really was. He walked quietly, with his bat swinging ready at his side.

It was hard to really focus on watching for an attack. Even with most of the people in the hall busy moving toward the rear, there were enough of them around to make it difficult to know whether something was dangerous or not. Some enterprising souls had turned to looting, either through smash-and-grabs, or simply by strolling up to booths that had been abandoned and starting to fill their complimentary Comic-Con bags. Stuart grimaced every time they passed a looter, probably thinking of his own unguarded wares. His life was worth more than all the weapons on his table, and he seemed to know that, because he didn't say anything about going back. Privately, Kelly hoped he *did* get looted. Maybe if a few more people had been armed when all this started, they wouldn't be locked inside now.

When they reached the last broad open space before entering the maze of narrower aisles leading to the locked doors at the front of the hall, Kelly stopped. "All right," she said. "Where, *exactly*, are we going?"

"There." Pris pointed up to the large glass windows that overlooked the convention center floor. "There's supposed to be an access panel on the wall under them. We can use that to see whether anyone's in the control room, and if not, we can try to do this manually from down here."

"Why can't we do that anyway?" asked Stuart.

"Because if there *is* somebody up there, we don't want them to start hitting switches randomly when the alarms go off. And trying to turn the wireless on manually will trigger a *bunch* of alarms, at least according to the instructions I have."

Kelly looked at their destination and sighed. "Right."

From an architectural standpoint, Pris's goal made perfect sense. It was a natural recess between two of the large doors leading to the lobby. There were usually trash cans and small kiosks set up there, reducing the chances of people wandering over and prying open the access panel out of simple curiosity. It was a great place to put a backup system. It was also shadowed, providing no clear line of sight, and close enough to the doors that the biting people had probably taken refuge there.

"It looks dark and stupid," said Stuart dubiously. "I'm not really sure we should be going anywhere near there."

"We probably shouldn't, but we have to if we want to get the wireless on," said Pris. She straightened up, mouth set in a thin, hard line of determination. "People need to be able to communicate with the outside world. As bad as things are, they could get worse. We need to have hope."

Hope. What a funny idea that was. Kelly looked from Pris, so determined, so convinced that this was worth whatever it cost her, to Stuart, so scared, so ready to run back to his booth and hide from whatever was coming. Dammit. This was Comic-Con. It wasn't supposed to be *hard* on anything except her bank account. "Supposed to" never changed anything. This was how things were, and what came next was up to her.

Kelly Nakata had always wondered what it felt like to truly understand that she was going to die. But here and now, in this place...

If this was the zombie apocalypse, no one was coming to let them out. They were already compromised, already potentially infected, and no sane person would open those doors ever again. If this wasn't the zombie apocalypse—but ah, that was the problem, wasn't it? There was nothing else that this could really be. It made too much sense. It fit the facts too well, and that meant that everyone inside the building was going to die there. They could die scared and hiding, doing nothing. Or they could try to make things a little better in whatever way they possibly could.

Kelly gave her spear an experimental twirl. "I can't believe I'm doing this," she muttered, before saying, more loudly, "All right. Marty and I are the best-armed, so we should go in first, in case of trouble. Pris, you're next. Eric and Stuart, you bring up the rear, make sure nothing comes up from behind us to try getting in the way."

"What do we do if something *does* come up behind us?" asked Stuart.

"Hit it until it stops coming," said Kelly. "Pris, you do whatever it is you need to do to get the wireless back online." The few people who were in earshot were turning toward them, suddenly interested in what they were hearing. It figured that mentions of a working Internet would be enough to get people's attention, no matter what other crap was going on at the time. "This is where we start moving, or we're going to get mobbed."

"Who died and put you in charge?" asked Marty, sounding half-amused.

"My Jedi master," said Kelly dryly. Then she started walking, heading toward the shadowy nook where Pris claimed the wireless access panel was located. The rest of the group followed her. At this point, what else were they supposed to do?

11:13 P.M.

The first bloody-lipped man came lunging out of the darkness as soon as Kelly and Marty stepped off the carpet and out of the protection of the overhead lights. Kelly didn't make a sound. She just swung her borrowed spear low and hard, hitting the man across the stomach. He moaned, a sound that was chillingly familiar, thanks to a hundred zombie movies. Kelly froze.

And Marty brought his baseball bat down solidly on the man's skull, which caved in with a horrific crunching sound. The man stopped lunging for Kelly and fell, leaving chunks of bloody gore on Marty's bat. For a moment, everyone was silent, each of them trying to wrap his or her mind around what had just happened. Either zombies were real, or Marty had just killed a man. Either Marty was a murderer, or he was a savior.

The contradiction was too big to be absorbed, and so without saying a word, they all dismissed it.

"Let's move," said Kelly.

They were almost to the wall when the second pair came charging out of the dark, just as silently as the first one—but unlike the first one, they started moaning before they were hit. One grabbed for Pris, who screamed, a short, startled sound. The other went for Kelly.

Moving fast, Kelly whirled and slammed the butt of her spear into the man who was reaching for Pris. He staggered back a step, but otherwise didn't seem to notice. That was when Kelly flipped the spear around and thrust the point into the man's throat, pinning him in place long enough for Eric to slam his crowbar into the back of the man's head.

That was when the third man sank his teeth into Kelly's shoulder. Kelly screamed and swore at the same time, trying to wrench herself free. She succeeded, briefly, but that was long enough for Marty to close the distance and beat the man off her with his baseball bat. Kelly clamped her hand over her wounded shoulder, staggering a few feet away before she turned to look back at the carnage.

The man kept moaning even as he died. It wasn't until his skull cracked that the sound stopped, replaced by limpness and eerie silence.

"Kelly?" Stuart hesitantly touched her uninjured shoulder. "Are you okay?"

No, you asshole. I'm bitten, and we both know what that means; we're not idiots *here.* Kelly forced herself to look toward him, smile wanly, and lie. "Fine," she said. "It's just a flesh wound."

Not one of them believed what she was saying. But Stuart nodded with quiet resignation, like he understood why she needed to lie, and that seemed to speak for the whole group. "Good. Let's get moving. I think we're almost there."

Nothing else attacked them as they finished crossing the distance to the wall. Kelly was half-expecting there to be no access panel at all, and was quietly relieved when she saw it, industrial gray steel creating a patch of darker shadow on the wall.

Pris walked to the hatch and pried it open with her fingernails. There was a red emergency phone inside. She lifted the receiver, checked her tablet one last time, and hit the "0."

All that was left to do after that was wait.

11:16 P.M.

Lesley jumped when the phone rang, nearly toppling out of the office chair where she'd been dozing. On the floor, Unis lifted her head off her paws before climbing to her feet, tail wagging cautiously. Sometimes the phone meant it was time to go Out. Unis thought that Out would be a lovely idea. The Woman had been still for too long, and the smells from outside were not the comforting kind, not grass or food or home. Outside the door smelled like blood and fear and peeing, and Unis wanted to get The Woman away from here if she could.

"What in the world . . . ?" said Lesley. She fumbled around the large control board until her hand hit what felt like a phone receiver. The ringing stopped when she picked it up. She brought it to her ear. "Hello?"

"Hello!" said a female voice, half-laughing with relief. The voice grew distant for a moment as it said, "Guys! Guys, I got somebody! There's somebody there!"

"Thank God," said a male voice. "Tell them we're stuck in here."

"I'm stuck, too, and I can hear you," said Lesley. "Who's this?"

"My name is Pris Garrison. I'm here with some of my friends in the hall. Please, do you work for the convention center? We're locked in. Can you let us out?"

"I'm afraid not, Ms. Garrison. My name's Lesley Smith. I'm a journalist from the UK. I flew out to cover the convention, and when things went pear-shaped, I somehow found myself locked up in here. I was sort of hoping you'd called because you were about to rescue me."

A soft choking sound came through the receiver. After a moment, Lesley realized that it was Pris, laughing.

"What?" she asked sharply. "I assure you, this isn't funny."

"I know! I know. That's why I'm laughing. Look, I'm sorry we can't save you, but maybe you can still help us. Do you see a big gray button labeled 'wireless controls'? It should be on the left side of the main control panel."

Lesley abruptly understood why Pris had been laughing. Sometimes the universe was so cruel as to become comic. "I'm afraid I won't be able to help you with that, Ms. Garrison."

"What? Why not?"

"Because I'm legally blind. I can see well enough to get myself around, with the help of my dog—she's here with me—but I can't read a label on a switch in this light, and I don't think you want me to start flipping things at random."

There was a moment of silence before Pris said, "Okay. That's... okay. I can get things back online from down here, but I need you to not touch anything, no matter what starts beeping or flashing. Can you do that? We're hoping that if we can get the wireless back on, we might be able to call for help."

"I'm blind, not stupid," said Lesley. "I can manage to keep my hands to myself while you do whatever needs to be done."

"Sorry," said Pris, sounding abashed. "I didn't mean... anyway, thank you. It'll just take me a second. Thanks for your time."

Suddenly, the thought of being left alone in the little locked room was unbearable. "Is there anyone else with you?" asked Lesley. "I'd like to talk to them, please. If you don't mind."

"Um, sure. Hang on." Pris's voice got distant for a moment as she said, "She wants to talk to somebody else."

There was a scuffling sound, and a male voice came on the line, saying, "Hello?"

"Hello. My name's Lesley. I'm locked in the control room at the moment, although I'm afraid I won't be able to help Ms. Garrison with getting the wireless back on. What's your name?"

"Marty," said the man. "There are three other people here, besides me and Pris. Stuart is helping Kelly bandage her shoulder. Eric's keeping watch."

"One of you has been hurt, then?"

"Yeah. Kelly got bit pretty bad getting to this phone. She's not bleeding as much as she was, but even a little bleeding is too much when you're trapped in a big-ass convention center with no medical supplies."

It was ironic. Lesley's tour of the convention center had included the locations of all the first aid and disability assistance checkpoints... and they were all outside the central hall. With the doors locked, everyone was stuck. "I hope she's all right."

"Ma'am, not to be rude, but I don't think *any* of us is all right at this point."

"I'm afraid that might be true." Something started beeping. Lesley turned toward the sound and saw that a large red light had snapped on in the middle of the center control panel. "Whatever Ms. Garrison is doing, it appears to be having some effect. There's a red light on up here—no, wait. It's just gone yellow, and now it's flashing."

"That's a good sign."

"I hope so. What were you hoping for this Comic-Con, Marty? If I may be so bold."

"I'm a vendor. I was hoping for some good sales, and maybe a bargain or two if I got time to do any shopping for myself." Marty chuckled darkly. "Well, the stores are open. Too bad there's nobody to take my money."

"No one taking money at Comic-Con? Truly, it *is* the end of the world." It was meant to be a lighthearted joke. Somehow, it didn't quite come out that way. Lesley cleared her throat. "The light's gone green now, if that helps anything."

"It might. Pris! Try the Wi-Fi."

There was a pause, and then Lesley heard the voice from before, whooping in triumph. Someone else laughed. Whatever Pris had done, it must have worked, then. Not that it did her any good at all. She was still alone with her dog, sitting in the dark, and feeling increasingly unsure that any rescue was coming.

"Marty? Are you still there?"

"I am, yeah. Thanks for all your help, Lesley."

Don't hang up; don't leave me alone up here in the silence, thought Lesley frantically. Clearing her throat, she said only, "It was nothing, really. All I had to do was sit still and not touch anything. Fortunately for you, that happens to be a talent of mine."

"Still, we appreciate it. If this gets taken care of before the end of the convention, come look me up. I'm at Marty's Comics and Games, in row 2100. I'd like to meet you in person."

"I'd like that, too," said Lesley quietly. Good-byes would have felt too final—and given the circumstances, they probably would have been. So she said nothing more as she took the phone from her ear and dropped it back into the cradle, cutting off their conversation.

Alone in the silence once more, Lesley Smith put her hands over her face and wondered when it was going to end. If it was ever going to end.

11:30 P.M.

"How's your shoulder feeling?" Stuart took a step backward, wiping his bloody palms against the seat of his pants. There'd been so *much* blood. He wasn't sure how much blood was safe for a person to lose. He was deathly afraid that he was about to find out.

Kelly offered him a small smile. She could feel the bloody fabric of her shirt sticking to her skin, and she knew the situation wasn't good. "It hurts like hell," she said. "I'm glad we got the wireless back on."

"Me, too. I'd hate to have waded back into this mess for nothing."

Kelly's smile strengthened. It was good, she decided, that he'd introduced himself without being prompted; it was good that she'd gotten to know him, even if it was only a little, before things went all the way wrong. "Hope's not nothing. Remember that, okay?"

"What?" Stuart blinked, expression turning alarmed. "Why are you talking like that?"

"I got bit, Stuart. You remember what that girl said. I'm as good as dead."

"No, you're not. The real world doesn't work like that. The real world—"

"She's not wrong." Pris's voice was very soft. Kelly looked past Stuart to the other woman, realizing as she did that she hadn't even noticed when the cheering stopped. Pris was pale, and the hand that held her tablet was shaking. "It's all over Facebook and Twitter. People are calling this the zombie apocalypse. Actual people, who aren't trapped inside here. They're saying it's an outbreak. The government didn't lock the doors, but they're not going to let anybody unlock them because we're all already written off as dead. Infected."

"See? It's the zombie apocalypse, and in the zombie apocalypse, once somebody gets bitten, they're not your friend anymore." Kelly held out her spear, waiting for Stuart to take it. "Go. Find a back door, find a way out of here, and *go*. Tell people we got the Internet up. Maybe if we make enough noise from inside, they'll have to open the doors."

"Kelly, we're not leaving you."

"Yes, we are." Marty stepped up behind Pris, who shot him a relieved look. "I'm sorry as hell that you got bit helping us out. I'd take it back if I could."

"Would you take my place?" asked Kelly.

Marty looked away. They should kill her; all the zombie movies he'd ever seen told him that they should kill her. And he couldn't. That would be the final step toward making this all real, and he couldn't.

"I didn't think so." Kelly sighed. "Stuart, please. You saved my ass by setting up shop where you did, even if you don't have a damn clue how to use the weapons you were selling. Let me save yours. Get the hell out of here."

"I don't want to go without you," said Stuart quietly. He reached out as he spoke, and took the spear gently from her hand.

Kelly smiled. "I don't give a fuck what you want." Somehow, the words sounded like an endearment. Her attention swung to Marty. "Look out for Stuart. He needs a lot of looking after."

"I'll do my best," said Marty.

Pris sniffled, wiped her nose with the back of her hand, and said, "I'll make sure everybody knows what you did. How brave you were."

"You do that," said Kelly. "Now go."

She stayed where she was, tucked into the shadowy nook off the main wall, and watched as the other four turned and walked away. Stuart glanced back at her several times. She forced herself to keep watching until they vanished around a corner and were gone. Then she sighed, all the straightness going out of her spine as she sank, cross-legged, to the floor. Her shoulder ached. Her feet hurt. She was so tired. So, so tired. Maybe she'd just stay there forever, she thought. Maybe that would be for the best.

Kelly Nakata closed her eyes, letting her head list forward, and waited to stop caring about what was going to happen next. She was small. She'd lost a lot of blood.

It didn't take as long as she might have thought.

LORELEI TUTT'S APARTMENT, LONDON, ENGLAND, JUNE 1, 2044

The rum is sweet and burning at the same time. It makes it a little easier to discuss the events inside the convention center. Kelly Nakata and the others restored the record of what happened during the siege of Comic-Con; without their attempts to turn the wireless back on, we might never have known as much as we do. Lorelei was right when she said she'd need something stronger for what came next. So did I.

LORELEI: It's funny. I mean, there's this whole story that has nothing to do with my family, happening at the same time that my family was fighting to survive. But without it, I'd never have known what happened to them. Was the whole Rising like that, do you think? Just layers and layers of tangle, so that you can never really tell where one thing ends and the next one begins?

She seems more human now, and more lost. I put my cup down and push it carefully away. I need to be sober for the remainder of this interview. No matter how much I want not to be.

MAHIR: I believe so, yes. Everyone has his or her own story to tell. The San Diego Outbreak was unique only in that so many people were confined in such a small space. Their stories were almost forced to overlap.

LORELEI: I spent a lot of time after the Rising going through all the social media feeds from that outbreak, looking for... something. I don't know. Something that would make it all start making sense. Not linear sense. Just...

MAHIR: You wanted something to make it fair.

LORELEI: Yeah. That's it, exactly. I wanted something that would make it fair for my parents to have died in there. I wanted something that would make it fair for me to have lived when they didn't. I know—I know—that they were both glad I made it out of the hall before the doors closed. But that doesn't make it right. And it doesn't make it fair.

MAHIR: I don't think "fair" ever entered into it.

LORELEI: Yeah, I guess not. That was never part of the equation. You know, I met Kelly Nakata's brother a couple years ago. He came to one of the Equality Now film screenings that I helped put together. He was a really nice guy. He wanted to meet me.

MAHIR: I can understand why.

LORELEI: We're almost to the end. Do you think we can get through this tonight?

MAHIR: I would like that.

LORELEI: Yeah. So would I. Let's finish this.

Everything Must Go

The heroes of the Rising took many forms. Some of them fought. Some of them hid. Some of them just left artifacts for us to find after they were gone. But all of them died, and all of them, whether they knew it or not, were mourned.

—Mahir Gowda

Me? Oh, I'm just your ordinary time-traveling badass with a badge. Now freeze, dirtbag. You're going to Paradox Prison for a long, long time.

—Chronoforensic Analyst Indiction Rivers,
Space Crime Continuum, season one, episode three

11:30 P.M.

"Holy crap—Shawn! The wireless just came back on!" Robert waved his phone like it would illustrate the point. "I've got connection!"

"Me, too," said Leita, holding up her own phone. "Maybe this means they're finally getting ready to break us out of here."

"Maybe," said Shawn, with an utter lack of conviction. He didn't want to discourage the others in their hoping—at this point, hope was about the only thing they had going for them, and he'd rather it lasted—but he couldn't work up any excitement for something as small as the Internet coming on. Not unless it was accompanied by an announcement that the National Guard was on the way. He paused. The National Guard . . . "Shit."

"What is it?" asked Vanessa. She was holding her iPad again, fiddling nervously with her new video-editing software. Maybe later, she could edit together a video about their Comic-Con adventure. Assuming they all survived.

"We need to get back to work on the barricades. Break time's over." Shawn grabbed a hammer. "I want this place so fortified that we could live in it."

"What?" Vanessa's eyes widened. "Why? Didn't you hear Robbie? They're going to come and rescue us soon!"

"No, they're not." Shawn shook his own phone at her. "You hear that? Silence. Lorelei's at the Coast Guard *right now*, and what I've got is silence.

That means she hasn't managed to get them moving yet, and if the Coast Guard isn't moving, neither is anybody else. We're not being saved just because we can check our e-mail again. And when people realize that, they're going to lose what little serenity they had left. The shit's about to hit the fan in here, and all that's standing between us and the chaos is the hull on this ship."

"It's a booth, Shawn," said Lynn quietly, stepping up next to her husband.

"Right now, it's our ship, and it's the only way we're flying safely out of this." Shawn thrust the hammer at her. She took it. "Get to work, all of you. We don't have much time."

"I hope you're wrong, Shawn," said Lynn, and leaned up to kiss his cheek before walking briskly toward the other side of the booth.

Shawn sighed. "So do I." He glanced around at the others, finally settling on Robert. "Hey. I need you to do something for me."

"What?" asked Robert, putting down the box that he'd been lifting.

"Come here." Shawn beckoned him closer. Robert came, and when he was close enough, Shawn murmured, "I want you to get online and start looking for anyone who has outside eyes on this place. We need to know what's going on. We need to know how bad things are going to get. Can you do that?"

"Sure," said Robert. He had to fight to ignore the sudden churning in his stomach. This wasn't how his Comic-Con was supposed to go. Not a bit of it. "Is there anything I should be watching for, in specific?"

"Yeah," said Shawn. "Look for people talking about the zombie apocalypse. I need to know whether this is the end of the world."

Wisely, Robert didn't say anything else. He just moved to one of the booth's folding chairs, sat down, and started to search. Shawn watched him go. Then he picked up another hammer, and turned to his work.

11:30 P.M.

Elle's phone pinged, signaling that her e-mail had successfully been sent. It was a familiar enough sound that it didn't wake her. Sleeping sitting up with her back braced against a door wasn't the most comfortable thing in the world, but she was tired enough and wrung-out enough from her day that she didn't care anymore. On the other side of the replica office, Matthew and Patty slept sunk deep into their own respective dreamlands. Patty seemed almost entirely boneless, a limp puddle across the model of Indiction Rivers's desk. Matthew was slightly more upright, but only slightly, with one arm curved protectively around her back.

Then the phone rang, and all three of them snapped awake. Matthew was on his feet before his brain and his body fully caught up with each other. Patty sat up, blinking bemusedly. And Elle, who knew that ring tone better than she knew almost anything else in the world, was simply reaching for the phone. It was reflex. If she'd been awake and able to think about what she was doing, she might not have answered... but she was half-asleep, and sleep can make you careless. The phone was almost to her ear before she realized what she was doing, and by then it was too late.

"Sig?"

"Elle?" The edge of panic on her girlfriend's voice was painful. Elle winced.

Sigrid demanded, "What the hell is this e-mail I just got? What's going on in there?"

"I'm sorry. I set my memo function to auto-send, and someone must have managed to turn the wireless in here back on. You weren't supposed to see that." *Not while I was still breathing, anyway.*

"The police have cleared and cordoned off the Gaslight District. The hotels were evacuated almost an hour ago."

"Where are you?"

"I'm still in our room. I tried to go down to the convention center when I realized you were stuck there, but there are police blocking all the access roads. They're not letting anyone near." Common sense dictated that "the talent" stay as close to the convention center as possible, to make sure that they could get to and from their panels quickly and easily. Sigrid and Elle were staying at a very nice B&B almost two miles off-site. If Sigrid couldn't enjoy the convention, she could at least enjoy their accommodations—and it made it less likely that there would be a public slip where one of Elle's fans might see.

Elle had never been so grateful for her paranoia. "I'm glad," she said quietly. "I don't want you anywhere near here."

"Are you hurt?" The edge of panic was spreading, saturating Sigrid's tone. "Elle, are you alone in there?"

"No, no, honey, I'm *fine*. I'm here with two friends, Matthew and Patty. We managed to get to cover before the lights went out. None of us is hurt. We're all fine."

"I kinda need to pee," said Patty, and promptly blushed a brilliant red, adding, in a mutter, "I don't believe I just said that in front of Elle Riley."

"Where's your handler?" asked Sigrid. "Isn't there someone who can get you out of there?"

"No, there's not. I lost him when the screaming started, and I haven't seen him since. Maybe he made it out of the hall." Or maybe he got caught up in the riot at the front, and was out there somewhere, looking for her. Elle couldn't manage to muster any compassion for his possible plight. He was the one who'd run away and left her with two strangers in the middle of the exhibit hall.

"That letter—"

"I meant it. I meant every word of it. I'm done pretending."

"Why would you write that if you thought you were coming home? What would make you do that?"

Elle sighed, shoulders slumping. "Sigrid . . ."

"Are you coming home to me?"

Elle looked across the room to Matthew and Patty, who were watching her, not saying a word. She couldn't see through the blocked-off windows, but she didn't need to; she knew what the exhibit hall looked like. There would have been screaming if things had already started going downhill. It was probably only a matter of time.

"Yes," said Elle calmly. She was an excellent actress, no matter what the critics said; she'd gotten her job because she knew how to do it, not just because she looked good in a bikini. "I'm coming home. I promise."

"Elle—"

"I have to go, Sigrid. I love you. I'll see you soon. I promise."

"I love you," Sigrid whispered.

Elle lowered her phone, hitting the button to disconnect the call at the same time. Then she just sat there, staring at it. Minutes ticked by.

Finally, hesitantly, Patty asked, "Are you okay?"

"I never lied to her before." Elle raised her head, smiling sadly. "I'm not sure I want to make it out of here. I never wanted to know that I could lie to her."

Outside the plywood walls of their room, someone screamed.

11:43 P.M.

Kelly Nakata opened her eyes.

Slowly, with none of her former grace, she clambered to her feet. She used both arms to push herself upright, not shying away from putting pressure on her wounded arm. Anyone looking into her eyes would have found a curious absence of pain, considering how much blood covered her skin and drenched her clothing. When she stood, she left behind a broad dark splotch on the carpet. But Kelly Nakata didn't care. She was back on her feet, and unlike the zombies who had entered when the siege began—the ones who were well fed and seeking to expand the size of the pack—she was freshly risen, weak from blood loss, and hungry.

So *hungry*.

The exact mechanics of the Kellis-Amberlee virus were not yet known on that hot July night, but that did nothing to stop them from working as nature and genetic engineering had intended. Kelly Nakata was no longer in her right mind, and the virus controlling her body knew what it needed to do. It needed to spread. It needed to nourish itself. It needed to feed.

As Kelly began walking toward the sound of living food—moving not with the characteristic lurch of the long-infected, but with a smooth, almost fluid gracelessness, like all her joints had lost their tension—other infected emerged from the shadows and followed her. It was as if she had provided some final tipping point to their number, taking them from the need to grow and leading them into the need to hunt.

Somewhere in the middle of the slowly expanding pack, one of the infected began to moan. The rest echoed it, until the entire mass of stiff-limbed people with glazed eyes and bloody hands was moaning in near-unison. Together, they half-shambled, half-walked down the aisle, heading for the unmistakable sounds of the living.

11:45 P.M.

"We shouldn't have left her," said Stuart, shifting Kelly's spear from one hand to the other. "This is just crazy. Things like this don't really happen."

They weren't moving as fast as Marty wanted them to be. Pris was distracted by poking at her tablet, and Stuart had been dragging his feet ever since they walked away from Kelly. Only Eric seemed to understand how important it was that they make it back to the fortified safety of the booth, where they might have a chance in hell of keeping themselves alive until rescue came. "It's happening, and we need to deal with it," Marty snapped. "Kelly knew the score. She's the one who *told* us to leave her behind. Now keep on moving. We have a long way to go before we get back to where we need to be."

"Facebook is going *nuts*," said Pris, eyes still glued to her screen. "There's a lady over in Artist's Alley who says her best friend flipped out and ate her husband. Like, actually *ate* him. And there's a bunch of interns holed up in one of the big toy company booths using boxes of action figures as barricades. They're freaking out because people keep stealing pieces of their walls." She snorted. "I guess it's never too bad for people to want their exclusive swag."

"Is anyone saying anything about a rescue?"

"Lots of rumors on the inside—jeez, it's like half the convention was just waiting for the chance to get online and start screaming—and some people on Twitter are talking about the military moving in around the convention center. Maybe they're coming to break us out of here."

"Yeah," said Marty gruffly. "Maybe that's what they're doing. Just keep moving, okay? I want us all back where we know the territory as fast as possible."

"What's that sound?" Much to Marty's disgust, Eric stopped walking and turned to look back in the direction they had just come from. "Do you hear that?"

"All I hear is a convention center full of geeks who finally have their e-mail back, which means this is our best shot at getting back to the booth without anyone stopping us," said Marty. "Now *move*."

"It sounds like someone's hurt or something. They're moaning."

"We are in the middle of what looks increasingly like the *zombie apocalypse*," said Marty, stressing his last two words as hard as he could. "Moaning people don't need help. Moaning people are intending to *eat* us."

To illustrate his point, Kelly came around the corner of the aisle they had just walked down, with half a dozen more blood-drenched people shambling along behind her. Kelly was leading the others straight for her former companions.

"Kelly?" said Stuart uncertainly.

"Kelly's dead," said Marty. Any doubts he'd had about the nature of their predicament vanished when he saw Kelly's blank face, mouth half-open as she moaned with the others. He grabbed Stuart's arm before the other man could do anything they were all going to regret. "That's not Kelly anymore. Now *move*."

Much to his surprise, the other man moved. Hauling Stuart along with him, Marty ran. Eric and Pris followed... and the zombies, as one, followed them.

After hours of waiting, the chase was finally on.

11:51 P.M.

The screaming was getting louder and more frequent. Patty pressed herself against Matthew, moaning slightly with fear. It was a living, vital sound, very different than the soft, insistent moans that Elle could hear under the panicking crowd outside their hidey-hole. She slid off the desk where she'd been sitting, taking a long step backward.

"I don't think that's the cavalry," she said.

"Matthew, I'm scared," wailed Patty.

"I know, love." He put his arms around her, looking grimly at the door. In that moment, he wished he'd never heard of the San Diego Comic Convention, or allowed himself to consider it as a location for his honeymoon. He held his wife as tightly as he could, and wondered whether he was ever going to see England, or his family, again. "Just hold fast. Rescue is coming."

"We're as secure in here as we're going to get," said Elle. "We—" Her words dissolved into a yelp of fear as someone started banging on the door, sending it shuddering. It wasn't constructed to stand up to any sort of pressure, after all; it was only intended as a replica.

"Let us in!" shouted a male voice, very real, and very much alive. "We can hear you in there!"

"Please!" added a second voice—female this time, and very clearly terrified.

Matthew and Elle exchanged a look. They didn't say anything. In a moment like this, there was nothing to be said. Matthew let go of Patty, pressing a kiss to the top of her head as he stood to help Elle move the filing cabinets. As soon as they were out of the way, Elle stepped forward and opened the door.

"Get in here," she said to the small group of people clustered in the aisle outside. "Now."

"Thank you," said their leader, an older African-American man with a death grip on an aluminum baseball bat. He turned and started gesturing for his people to get into the building: two other men, both younger than he was, one Asian, one white, and a pale-faced woman with a mop of wild, uncombed curls. Once all three of them were in, he followed, and Elle slammed the door behind him.

"Matthew, the filing cabinets," she said.

"On it," he replied. To his surprise and mild relief, the newcomers hastened to help him. With all of them working together, they had the door blocked in a matter of seconds.

"Good," said Elle. The moaning outside was getting louder. "I guess this means help isn't on the way, huh?"

"Not quite yet," said the older man.

"That's what I was afraid of."

The wild-haired girl was staring at Elle. "Aren't you . . ."

"I used to be," Elle replied. "Hi. I'm Elle. This is Matthew, and Patty. They're on their honeymoon. I have no idea why I thought it was important to tell you that, but I did, so there you go. The censors are officially off duty for the duration of this convention."

"I'm Marty," said the older man. "These two are Pris and Eric."

"I'm Stuart," said the Asian man. He was holding a spear like he didn't really know what to do with it but was terrified of what would happen if he put it down.

"Nice to meet you all," said Elle briskly. "Now, what sort of danger did you people lead to our door?" She realized she was falling into the speech patterns she used for Indiction Rivers—and well, so what if she was? Indy Rivers got things *done*. Maybe she was a fictional character, but they were in a fictional place, in a fictional situation. There were worse things to be than fictional.

Fictional people cried only when the story told them to.

"Well, ma'am, I don't know how to break this to you, exactly, but I'm afraid we're in the middle of the zombie apocalypse here," said Marty. "One of our friends got bitten. She's outside now, leading a whole mob of them after us."

"And you came *here*?" cried Patty, standing. "Why would you do that? We were doing just fine before you came crashing in here! Now we're probably going to die, and it's going to be all your fault!"

"Patty." Matthew put his hand on her shoulder. "Patty, sweetheart, hush. It's not their fault. It's not anyone's fault."

"That asshole who decided to cure the common cold, maybe," said Eric.

"Or maybe not," said Elle. "I don't think 'blame' is what we should be looking for here. Survival is. If those zombies are behind you, this is where we start shoring up the walls, and we get ready to make our last stand. Are you with me?"

Marty nodded. "Just tell us what to do."

Elle told them.

11:57 P.M.

"Daddy!" Lorelei's voice came through the phone in a wail, terror and heartbreak warring with fury for dominance.

Shawn snatched his phone from his belt and depressed the walkie-talkie button as he raised it to his mouth. "Lorelei, what's wrong?"

She was crying; he could hear it even before she spoke again. Little hitching sobs that she was trying, and failing, to hold back. She'd cried that way since she was a little girl. "D-Daddy, they're . . . I just heard them saying . . ."

"Slow down. Breathe. Are you all right?"

"They're going to blow up the convention center!" This was less a wail, and more a scream. Shawn went cold, his fingers clenching on the phone as she continued: "They didn't know I could hear them when they started talking about it. They said there was no safe way to do an extraction. There are too many z-z—" She broke down and started crying in earnest before she could even get the word out.

"Zombies," said Vanessa quietly, stepping up next to Shawn. "There are too many zombies for them to get us out."

"Damn," whispered Shawn. Then he raised his phone again and said, "Okay, honey. I need you to breathe deep and stay calm, and listen to me. *Do not* try to get off the base. *Do not* try to get over here. Whatever's going to happen, I don't want you in the middle of it. Do you hear me? You stay where you are. Your mother and I need to know that you're safe."

"Didn't you hear me?" Lorelei wasn't screaming anymore. She was barely even whispering. "They're going to blow it up. The whole thing. They're going to *kill* you."

"And I wish that wasn't going to happen, but, sweetheart, what matters here is that you're safe. You're not in this building. You're going to be fine." Shawn closed his eyes. He didn't want to risk seeing his wife's face. Once she started crying, there was no way he'd be able to keep from doing the same. "It's going to be hard. Everything's changing. But you got out. That means we won."

Someone was crying; he could hear them, even with the screaming that was starting to get closer and closer to their position, even with the sound of distant moans. It didn't matter. What mattered was Lorelei's whispered reply: "I don't want you to die."

"I don't want to leave you. We all have to do things we don't want to do. Can you keep flying for me, baby girl? Please? Because all I need to know right now is that you can do that."

"I'll try," whispered Lorelei.

"That's all I'll ever ask of you." Shawn opened his eyes and turned to his right, where he knew Lynn would be waiting. The tears were running down her cheeks, but her expression was calm. She knew what was coming next. "Honey, I'm going to give the phone to your mother now. You need to talk to her before we lose connection. I love you, Lorelei. Don't ever forget. Promise me that you won't."

"I won't, Daddy. I love you."

"Good," said Shawn. He handed the phone to Lynn before he could say anything else—before he could stretch it out any further, before he could insist that she keep talking to him until it was too late to say anything else. He'd said what needed saying. Everything else would just be self-indulgent, and they were past the time for things like that. He had work to do.

Vanessa and Robert followed him to the far side of the booth. "Tell us what to do, and we'll do it," said Vanessa.

"If they're going to blow this place to Kingdom Come, we've got two choices," said Shawn. "First, we sit here and wait for the boom. Odds are we wouldn't feel anything. That sort of thing tends to happen pretty damn fast."

"And our second choice?" asked Robert.

Shawn smiled grimly. "We get the fuck out of here."

Vanessa nodded. "Sounds good to me. Lead the way."

12:02 A.M.

Unis lifted her head off her paws, attention fixing on the door. Her ears pricked forward and her nostrils flared. The smell coming through the door wasn't a good smell. It was Bad. It was a Bad Smell, bad enough to stand out against all the other smells in the world. A low growl started in her chest, shaking her body as she got slowly to her feet. The Bad Smell was getting stronger. But she was a Good Dog. She wouldn't let the Bad Smell reach The Woman. No. That wouldn't happen while *she* was standing guard.

"Unis? What's wrong?"

Unis kept growling. She knew that her duty was to The Woman—and yes, usually that meant answering to her name, because The Woman might need something. But Unis knew that The Woman's nose wasn't as good as hers. The Woman didn't know that there was a Bad Smell. It was up to Unis to protect her.

"Unis." This time, Lesley's voice cracked with command. Unis's growl wavered, losing focus for a moment as instinct warred with training. In the end, instinct and loyalty won: No amount of training could have pulled her attention away from that door.

For her part, Lesley was becoming alarmed. She knew her dog. Unis was the best service dog she'd ever had, and if Unis was ignoring her, that meant that something was seriously wrong.

"This isn't good," she whispered, and wished, not for the first time, that she wasn't locked in alone with her dog, who might be excellent company but had never quite mastered the art of conversation.

Unis continued growling. It was getting louder now. It still couldn't quite block out the new sound that was coming from the other side of the door: human voices, moaning.

"Here!" said Lesley, sitting up a little straighter. "Whoever you are, you can just go away! You're frightening my dog! We don't want any!"

The moaning didn't stop. If anything, it increased, and someone began banging on the door. Several someones, from the sound of it.

"Go away!" shouted Lesley.

They didn't go away.

Unis stopped growling and began barking wildly when the door started caving inward. By then, it was too late to do anything about the infected who were smashing their way into the control room—but really, it had been too late since they were locked in. Lesley screamed.

Unis, who was a very Good Dog, fought to the end to defend her mistress, and died knowing that The Woman was safer because she had been there. Out of everyone who fell during the siege of San Diego, she may well be the only one who died at peace, knowing that she'd done her best.

The same cannot be said of Lesley Smith. Her last thought was of Unis, whose frenzied barking had stopped a few seconds before. Worrying about her dog made it a little easier to endure the teeth biting into her flesh—and then there was only pain, and darkness, and then there was nothing at all.

No one on the convention floor noticed what was happening in the control room. By that point, they all had problems of their own.

12:09 A.M.

Lynn came to join the group as they were preparing to move. Shawn's phone was in her hand. She offered it to him, saying quietly, "The battery died. She said to tell you that she loves you."

"Thank you," said Shawn, and took the phone, clipping it to his belt.

Lynn nodded and looked around at the remains of their group. The screaming from the front of the hall was getting louder, but it wasn't quite on top of them. Yet. "Where are we going?"

"The food court," said Shawn. "The parking garage clearly isn't a viable exit, or Dwight and Rebecca would have contacted us by now. That means we need another way. There might be an employee door at the back of their little café—and if not, there's the freezer. It could survive the bombing."

"And it's better than sitting here waiting to be blown up," said Leita.

"Leita's right," said Lynn. "But if we're going to move, it needs to be now. If we stand here too long, we're not going anywhere."

"Then let's go," said Shawn.

The five of them left the booth together, holding what weapons they could improvise or scrounge from the toolbox. Each of them knew that they would never be coming back, and carried what they thought was important: a backpack, a tote bag filled with merchandise, the cash box, the signed picture of Joss Whedon from the charity drawing. Shawn knew that some of the things people had chosen to carry would slow them down, but he didn't say anything about it. There would have been no point. They were more likely to die trying to escape than they were to make it out of the building. If people felt better because they died holding their laptops or their favorite shirts, he wasn't going to be the one who told them no.

As for Shawn himself, he brought his phone, the hammer he'd been holding off and on since arriving at the convention center, and his wife. His daughter was already safe. Nothing else could possibly have mattered to him in that moment.

Together, the last of the California Browncoats walked deeper into the hall, heading for the food court, hoping for a miracle.

They weren't going to get one.

12:11 A.M.

The moaning outside was getting softer as the zombies moved away, pursuing easier prey along the aisles of the convention center. Elle realized she was giggling under her breath. She clapped a hand over her mouth. That just made it worse. She folded double, laughing and crying at the same time, struggling with the need to do both as quietly as possible.

"What's so funny?" asked Marty. He didn't sound belligerent, just tired. They were all tired.

"A friend of mine has—" Elle caught herself. If the lying was going to stop, the lying was going to stop right here and now. "My girlfriend has this shirt that says, 'In the event of a zombie apocalypse, I don't have to run faster than the zombies. I just have to run faster than you.' I guess it's more accurate than we ever thought."

Marty chuckled once, eyes narrowed. "I guess that's true. But it doesn't tell us what we're going to do next."

"How bad is it out there?" asked Matthew. "We've been shut in here since the lights went out. We don't really know what's happening on the floor."

"It's bad," said Stuart unsteadily. "It's really bad. Kelly . . ."

"One of our friends got bitten, and then she became one of those things," said Pris, a little unsteadily. She was still clutching her tablet. She looked down at it, blinking. She hadn't realized that she still had it; she'd assumed it was lost during their flight down the aisles. Then she realized that she didn't remember much about what happened when the zombies came. First Kelly was coming around the corner, and then the rest of them were running through the open door of the makeshift little house.

"So we know it's contagious," said Elle. "What does that mean for us? Do we stay in here and keep hoping for rescue, or do we start trying to get the hell out of here?"

The others started talking, some of them on top of one another, all trying to put forth the best idea for what came next. Matthew and Stuart were both in favor of staying put, since there was no way they could be locked inside forever, and at least they had a door that shut. Eric and Patty were in favor of getting the hell out. Elle and Marty were doing their best to get everyone to discuss things calmly.

No one was looking at Pris.

She put her tablet down on the nearest desk—realizing only in that moment that they were in a replica of the precinct office from *Space Crime*

Continuum—and took a step toward the wall, turning her back to the group. Then she rolled up her sleeves and looked at her arms. There were no bite marks. She relaxed marginally.

"Oh thank God," she muttered, and turned back to the others.

They were all watching her. "Pris? Was there something you needed to tell us?" Marty's tone was gentle, almost sad.

She shook her head. "I'm not bit. I blacked out a little bit during the run, but I'm not bit."

"Thank God," said Eric.

Pris smiled. "My sentiments exactly."

"I don't feel so good," said Stuart, and sat down on the edge of a nearby desk, bloody hands tightening around his borrowed spear. "And no, I'm not bit, either. I just don't like blood and dying and running for my life."

"No one does," said the little British man—Matthew, that was his name. Matthew. "Can we get back to the business of sorting out what happens next?"

"I think we should stay here," said Pris. "We have the wireless back on. We can keep transmitting our position to the authorities, and you guys are right; having walls between us and the rest of the hall is a luxury we can't afford to give up."

The argument resumed. This time, it was Stuart who didn't join in. He let his head loll forward, trying to figure out why he felt so dizzy. It had been coming on in waves since they left Kelly alone by the front wall, and the dizziness was just getting worse as time passed.

None of them understood the Kellis-Amberlee virus: Understanding was something for the future, for the survivors of the Rising and the heroes at the CDC who would begin their multi-decade fight against an elegant work of accidental genetic engineering. But they understood zombies, and they knew that a bite, under these circumstances, could very well mean death.

None of them considered that bloody hands carelessly touching the face, brushing against the mucus membranes of the nose and mouth, wiping tears away from vulnerable eyes, could be just as dangerous as a bite, if slightly slower-acting. They were smart people. By the standards of their time, they were well equipped to survive. But none of them had the knowledge they needed to understand what was going on inside Stuart's body. Kellis-Amberlee was already with them in their little sanctuary; it had entered via the front door, and it was not leaving.

Stuart clutched his spear a little tighter, and waited for the room to stop spinning.

LORELEI TUTT'S APARTMENT, LONDON, ENGLAND, JUNE 1, 2044

The rum is gone. Lorelei stopped drinking shortly after I did, and now stares into her empty cup like she expects it to start offering answers. I have barely needed to prompt her through the last segment of her story. Now that the floodgates are open, it is all rushing out.

LORELEI: Vanessa had this program on her iPad. It was a little video recorder thing. She had it set to transmit everything to the server, so that even if she lost the physical tablet, she'd still have the recordings. I think it was supposed to be some sort of crime-prevention thing. Like if the iPad got stolen and the thief hit the wrong button, he'd find himself on *Candid Camera*. She turned it on when they left the booth. Everything recorded. Everything uploaded. And I watched it all.

MAHIR: Do you still have the footage?

LORELEI: I've tried to delete it a thousand times. I can't. It's my parents. It's the last time they were alive anywhere in the world. They were less than ten miles away from me, and they were on camera, and I wasn't there. I should have been there. I should have stayed. But I had to be a pissy little bitch and get myself sent to the hotel. I—

MAHIR: Do you really think they would have held things together any better if you'd been in danger with them? My daughter is very young, Ms. Tutt. She's not even walking yet, much less sulking off because she's tired of me. And I'd sooner die than see her in danger. As a parent, I can assure you that your absence was the greatest gift you could possibly have given them.

Lorelei looks at me, startled. Her eyes are very wide, and for a moment—only a moment, but it's real—I can see the teenager she must have been, innocent enough to enjoy a weekend at a comic book convention with her parents, naive enough to think that nothing bad would ever happen to her. My heart breaks a little in that moment. Not for Captain Lorelei J. Tutt, United States Coast Guard, but for the Lorelei who might have been, the girl who was on that hot summer day at the beginning of the Rising. She died there as surely as her parents did, in everything but flesh.

Finally, she speaks.

LORELEI: Would you like to see the footage?

MAHIR: Yes. I very much would. If you don't think it would be too difficult for you.

LORELEI: It will be. But it's something I need to do. Come with me.

She rises and leads me back to the living room, where she opens a cabinet beneath the television to reveal a stack of old-style DVD cases. She doesn't need to look for what she wants: It's right at the top. Without saying another word, Lorelei opens the case, extracts the disk, and slips it into the DVD player. The press of a single button turns on the television, and the video begins to play.

The tall, bald man with the hammer in his hand and the broad shoulders must be her father, Shawn Tutt. A glance at Lorelei's face confirms this; there are tears in her eyes, and when he says, "Come on, people. We need to pick up the pace," her lips move along with the words.

The other people with him both do and do not look like I pictured them. The short brunette woman with the determined eyes must be Lynn Tutt, Lorelei's mother. I thought she'd be taller; Lorelei must get her height from her father's side of the family. Leita is younger than I expected, with pale skin and dyed black hair. Her brother is younger still, clearly afraid, just as clearly determined that he will not be the first to break. Only Vanessa herself walks unseen, the woman behind the camera.

I have friends who would have appreciated that role.

"Are we sure this is the right way?" Leita is asking, a ragged edge of exhaustion and fear in her voice. "I don't want—"

12:15 A.M.

"—to get stranded down a blind alley because nobody had a damn map."

"We get to the back wall, and then we walk toward the far end of the hall until we come to the food court," said Shawn grimly. "Once we're there, we deal with whatever gets in our way."

"What do you mean 'deal with'?" asked Robert. He sounded nervous. They were all terrified; he was just the only one who couldn't seem to stop himself from showing it.

"I mean we deal with it," said Shawn, hand tightening on the handle of his hammer.

Leita put a hand on her brother's arm. "Let it go," she murmured. "This isn't the time to start questioning the chain of command."

"I should have stayed home and played video games all weekend," Robert muttered, and kept walking.

"Vanessa? Are you all right back there?" Lynn twisted around to look at Vanessa, who was bringing up the rear.

"I'm fine," said Vanessa. "I'm just checking the news sites. I want to see if there's anyone talking about the bombing. Maybe we can find out how long we have."

"Just watch your step," said Shawn, after a very brief pause. He wanted her paying attention. He wanted information even more.

"I'm watching," said Vanessa, and kept tapping.

Lynn paced alongside her husband, her own makeshift weapon—a length of timber that was intended to be part of the booth's main structure—clutched tightly in her hands. She didn't say anything at all. At this point, she didn't want to tell lies, and she didn't want to hear them, either. All the pretty reassurances and mealymouthed platitudes in the world wouldn't change their situation. So they just walked on.

The blockades around the webcomic district stopped them. "Now what?" asked Robert. "Do we go around?"

"Not if we can help it." Shawn stepped forward, rapping his hammer against the nearest makeshift wall. "Hey. We're clean. We need to get to the wall. Let us through."

Silence answered.

Shawn rapped again, a little harder. "Hey! We need to get to the back wall, and we don't have time to go around you! Let us through!"

This time, there was an answer from the other side: a single soft moan that made the hairs on the back of Lynn's neck stand on end. She grabbed Shawn's elbow before he could rap a third time, pulling him backward.

"Shawn," she hissed. "They're not going to let us in, and I don't think we want them coming out."

Shawn hesitated. Then, slowly, he nodded. "All right," he said. "We go around."

The zombies trapped inside the carefully constructed borders of the webcomics district gathered by the barrier and moaned as the Browncoats turned and walked away. But they didn't break through, and for the moment, it seemed like escape might still be possible.

12:37 A.M.

A consensus had finally been reached, after a great deal of argument and some uncalled-for swearing: They would stay put, monitor the social media feeds, and wait for rescue. Looking quietly relieved, Matthew sank down into one of the desk chairs, with Patty standing somewhat sulkily next to him. Elle sat back down on the replica of the precinct captain's desk, head bowed in a combination of resignation and simple exhaustion. None of them had eaten, visited a bathroom, or really slept for hours. Pris, Eric, and Marty gathered together near one of the other desks, unconsciously illustrating the ongoing divide between the two groups.

Only Stuart didn't move. Stuart hadn't moved for a while, sitting on the edge of a desk, resting most of his weight on the spear he'd taken from Kelly.

Stuart didn't feel good. And by that point, he knew that something was seriously wrong. He made a small sound, somewhere between a grunt and a moan. It had been long enough since he'd made any sounds at all that the others turned toward him, somehow hearing him above the screaming from outside.

"Stuart?" said Eric. "You okay, buddy?"

"You need . . . to go," said Stuart. Forcing out the words seemed like more work than it should have been. He raised his head. That was even harder than speaking had been.

Patty's eyes widened. "Your nose is bleeding."

"You need . . . to go," repeated Stuart. "What Kelly had. Think she gave it . . . to me. You can't. Stay."

"Oh, God," whimpered Patty, and plastered herself against Matthew.

"Please," said Stuart. *"Please."*

"But she didn't bite him!" said Eric. "How the fuck did he get sick, huh?"

"Does it matter?" asked Matthew. He got to his feet, tugging Patty along with him. "Come on, sweetheart. We need to go."

"There are more out there than there are in here," said Marty. "I think the odds are still better if we stay put."

"And get blood everywhere, when we've just shown that the damn stuff is indirectly transmissible?" snapped Matthew. "No. If we're going to be fucked no matter what we do, I'd rather be fucked running than sitting still."

Stuart moaned, the spear falling from his hands. And then he lunged.

Maybe it was the setting. The precinct was the office of the Time Police, after all; it was the place where Indiction Rivers fought the forces of evil, prevented paradoxes, and always had perfect hair, even in the middle of a firefight. Maybe it was instinct. Or maybe it was simply that Elle had put herself in charge of her little accidental group of refugees, and when they were put in danger, she had to react. Whatever the reason, she flung herself from the desk where she'd been seated and grabbed Stuart by the back of the neck before he could reach the shrilly screaming Patty.

Whirling, Elle slammed Stuart against the nearest wall, using every technique she'd learned in her self-defense courses and in training for her role with the show to keep him pinned. "Go!" she shouted. "Get moving!"

"We're not leaving you!" said Marty.

"You won't have to! I'll let him go when I have a clear shot at the door—but I'm not doing it before! Now move it!"

The others moved.

Stuart squirmed. Elle shoved him harder against the wall. "You seemed like a nice guy," she said. "I'm sorry this happened to you."

The techniques Elle had learned were designed to restrain people without harming them, and worked partially because most people would not hurt themselves to get loose. They were never intended for use on people who no longer cared about pain. She was still holding Stuart in place when he twisted himself at an angle that dislocated his shoulder with an audible popping sound and sank his teeth into her upper arm.

Elle screamed. Matthew, who had been escorting the others out the door, turned and stared at her in horror.

"Go!" she shouted. "Just *go*!"

Matthew hesitated. Only for a second. Then he nodded, mouthed the words "Thank you," and stepped out of the room, pulling the door shut behind him.

Elle Riley, who would be remembered by most of history for her portrayal of Indiction Rivers, Time Police, and by a woman named Sigrid Robinson for everything else, closed her eyes. And then she let the zombie go.

If she screamed, no one heard it. Elle Riley died bravely, and when she died, she died alone.

Outside, the others moved into the aisles, heading away from the sound of screaming, heading toward the unknown dangers lurking in the darkness along the back wall.

1:09 A.M.

"We don't have long," said Vanessa, scrolling through Twitter as she walked. "People outside are reporting that they're being moved even farther from the convention center. It looks like there's a half-mile perimeter being established."

"If it's only a half-mile, they're not using anything radioactive," said Shawn, walking a little faster. The rest of the group matched his pace. "That's good. That means we have a much better chance of getting the hell out of here."

"How much farther?" asked Robert.

"I don't know," said Shawn. "Those damn barricades..."

"Just keep moving," said Lynn. "That's all we can do. Keep moving."

They hadn't been attacked yet, but they all knew that it was coming. So when a single blood-encrusted figure stepped from behind a nearby booth, Shawn nearly bashed his head in with the hammer. Only the figure's quick backward stumble and cry of, "No, don't! I'm not gone yet!" held his swing.

"Who are you?" demanded Lynn, raising her board into a defensive position.

"Matthew. Matthew Meigs. Are you clean?"

"For the moment," said Shawn, lowering his hammer. "You're covered in blood."

"None of it's mine." Most of it was Patty's. Dear, sweet Patty, who had only ever wanted to be married, and to go to the San Diego Comic-Con, and to love him... Matthew shook his head, willing the thought away. "The back wall's no better than the main floor, and in some ways, it's worse. A lot of people fled there. My group among them." All those hands, grasping, and all those *teeth*...

"That's where the exit is, and we have to get out of here," said Robert. "We don't have a choice."

"We're all infected." Matthew's tone was soft, even resigned. "It's in the blood."

"You're the only one with blood on you," said Leita.

"For now. But if you fight your way back to that wall, even if you make it there, you won't be clean anymore. You may not be bitten, but you won't be clean. And then what? If you make it out, then what? You spread this? You take it out into the world?"

"It had to come from somewhere," said Vanessa.

"That doesn't mean we have to take it back there." Matthew shook his head. "You'll never walk away. You'll just find yourself on the business end of a sniper rifle instead of dying in here with the rest of us. You've no cause to believe me. I know that. But you can save yourselves a great deal of pain by staying away from that wall." He looked at his bloody fingers. "As for me, I got a drop in my eye when the bastards took my wife, before I turned and ran. I haven't long. I'm going back to where I left a friend of mine, in a little room with a door that shuts. I think I'll go inside and shut the door behind me. Elle deserves the company. It was nice to meet you all."

With that, the blood-covered little British man turned and walked away, vanishing quickly into the maze of aisles.

"What a crock of shit," said Robert. "Come on. Let's move."

None of the others moved at all. Shawn and Lynn were looking at each other.

"Do you think he was telling the truth?" asked Lynn.

"It's possible," said Shawn. "It seems probable, even, given the reaction we've seen so far."

"So what do we do?"

"Lorelei," said Shawn quietly. It was all he had to say. They couldn't take this out of the convention center, not when their daughter was out there, not when she would run to them at the first chance she got. He turned and looked to the others. "I can't tell you what to do. It's not my place. But Lynn and I won't be carrying this infection out into the world. We're going back to the booth. Seems a fitting place to wait for what comes next."

Leita reached over and took her brother's hand. Robert looked down at the floor. "We'll come with you."

"Me, too," said Vanessa. She smiled, just a little. "Never leave a man behind. That's what it means to be part of a crew, right? Never, ever leave a man behind."

"It was an honor," said Shawn.

"Same, Captain," replied Vanessa.

They turned, five people in a convention center given, now, mostly to the dead, and slowly made their way back to where they'd started.

1:24 A.M.

The dizziness was coming in waves by the time Matthew reached the precinct. He'd passed a few of the fully infected on the way—not many; most were at the back wall, but enough—and none of them had troubled him. They knew their own.

No sounds were coming from inside. Either Stuart had killed her after he turned or they were both in there waiting, silently, for escape. It didn't matter. Nothing mattered at this point.

"Hello, Elle. I came back to keep you company," said Matthew, and opened the door.

LORELEI TUTT'S APARTMENT, LONDON, ENGLAND, JUNE 1, 2044

The Browncoats on Lorelei's recording are singing. They began shortly after they reached their booth, and have continued since, asserting over and over that they're still free. Lorelei is singing with them, tears running down her face, and she keeps singing when the white flash of the bombs hitting the convention center wipes the image away. She knows the words they never had the chance to say. There's something beautiful in that, a sort of immortality for the people who died that day.

The screen goes from white to black. Lorelei goes silent. I keep watching the screen, giving her a chance to compose herself as we both pretend that I didn't see her cry. Finally, when she's ready, she speaks again.

LORELEI: So that's what happened. That's everything I know about what happened.

MAHIR: I have other pieces of the story. I was able to interview Sigrid Robinson. She knew more about what happened with that poor man who warned your parents off going to the rear.

LORELEI: I've always wondered. If they hadn't met him... would they have made it out? The Rising happened. A few more people wouldn't have changed anything.

I've seen the blueprints of the convention center as it was before it fell. I know the answer. I do not hesitate.

MAHIR: No. They would simply have died in a different place, and without making the right decision.

LORELEI: That's good. That's... good.

She turns to look at the poster behind the television set. It looks almost like a comic book cover, lovingly drawn: a group of people, some of whom I now recognize, standing against a field of stars. Their clothing looks something like the American West, something like what they wore in the video. They are looking off into the distance, staring forever toward a future they died before seeing.

Beneath them is written a simple epigram:

SAN DIEGO, CALIFORNIA, 2014

KEEP FLYING

MAHIR: Thank you for speaking with me today.

LORELEI: I miss them.

For once in my life, I have nothing to say, and so I don't say anything at all.

Remember, when you talk about the Rising: The story you know is not the only one that contains the truth. We may never find all the pieces, and some of them may be broken beyond understanding. But we must all, in the words of a doomed man to his child, keep flying.

It is the only way left for us to honor the dead.

—Mahir Gowda

How Green This Land, How Blue This Sea

Introduction

Between this and *San Diego 2014*, I'm starting to feel like the recipe for me writing a Newsflesh story is really loving something, and wanting to fill it to the absolute brim with zombies just to see what happens. I love Australia. I love the island ecosystem. I love the snakes. And I love the passionate Australian conservationists who I have had the pleasure of meeting, listening to, and learning from. So bringing the Rising to Australia was inevitable.

But more than that...for me, one of the beauties of the Newsflesh world is that what happened, happened globally. It wasn't just an American apocalypse. The fact that the books have, thus far, been based in America, doesn't change the fact that the Rising happened everywhere, all over the world. I wanted the opportunity to show its effects on a continent as removed from North America as I could manage.

Plus, zombie wombats. I mean, come *on*. How could I resist?

How Green This Land, How Blue This Sea

Part I

Around the World in Eighty Permits, Seventy-three Blood Tests, and More Trouble than the World Is Really Worth

People used to travel for fun before the Rising. Can you believe that?

—Alaric Kwong

No.

—Mahir Gowda

1.

My flight left London at six o'clock on Friday morning. We made a stop in Hong Kong twelve hours later to change planes, at which point everyone had to go through the entire security and boarding process again, complete with medical screening. It's something of a miracle that I was permitted to return to business class—same seat number, virtually identical seat, for all that it was on a different airplane—given that I was half asleep the whole time. After you've been pursued across the United States by a global conspiracy, it's rather difficult for airports to disturb you. All the same, my lack of response and glazed demeanor should have singled me out for additional security measures. There's little that can spoil a trip more than being trapped inside a flying metal tube with someone who has just undergone amplification.

Being in coach might well have done it. I reclined in my spacious seat, sipping my complimentary cup of hot tea—if you can call something "complimentary" when it requires buying a ticket that costs several thousand quid before they'll give it to you—and watched the other passengers being herded back to their seats. Each group of five was escorted by two flight attendants who made no effort to conceal their firearms. Before the Rising, guns were verboten on airplanes, carried only by government agents and representatives of local law enforcement. Now most passengers flew armed, and the flight attendants carried more weapons than your average Irwin. It's funny how the world can change when no one's looking.

The business class flight attendants were a slightly less menacing breed, although they still possessed the warmth and personal charm of cobras considering whether or not you were worth biting. The attendant on my side of the cabin stopped by long enough to collect my cup and check the lock on my seat belt. It would release only after a clean blood test from me and a keyed-in okay from the flight attendant. I smiled at him through the fog of my exhaustion. Staying on his good side would be extremely helpful for my bladder in a few hours.

"State your name," he said.

"Mahir Gowda," I replied. I'd been through this routine before. There was nothing personal about it.

"Place of origin."

"London, England. I flew out of Heathrow."

"Destination."

"Melbourne, Australia."

"Will you be having the fish or the chicken for this evening's supper?"

"The chicken, please."

"Very good. Welcome aboard, Mr. Gowda." He continued on with a perfunctory nod, already keying up the next passenger on his datapad.

I saluted him silently before setting my head against the thin airplane pillow. No matter how plush they make the upper tiers of flying, they'll always have those same thin, lifeless pillows. Hong Kong was a blur of lights and motion outside the window, all of it set back at a respectful distance, which blurred it even more. One more place I hadn't been, not really; one more example of "just passing through."

Sometimes I feel like it's my job in this life to be a tourist, forever visiting, never coming home. I was mulling over that thought, and what it meant for my marriage, when consciousness slipped away from me, and I fell back into the deep, unrejuvenating sleep of the traveler.

2.

I woke twice during the remainder of my flight: once to eat a bowl of some of the most tasteless chicken curry it has ever been my sorrow to encounter and once to connect to the plane's free Wi-Fi and set my phone to download all my e-mail. There was a time when I would have worked through the flight, ignoring my body's increasingly desperate pleas for rest; an airplane is a foreign environment, and the combination of changing cabin pressure and changing time zones makes it hard on even the strongest systems. I used to fight through the urge to close my eyes, refusing to admit that I could be felled by something as petty as biology.

I have matured since then, if maturity means losing a few hours of work to the Great God Sleep. Still, as head of After the End Times, one of the Internet's premier news destinations, it was my job to have all of the world's information at my fingertips. So I set my phone to download and closed my eyes again. It wasn't as if I could do anything to *change* the news from where I was.

The first sign that we were approaching Australia came when the flight attendants walked through the plane, leaving breakfast trays in front of us and pressing the small buttons over our seats that would sound our personalized alarm tones. The myriad small, familiar noises were intended to wake us with a minimum of trauma, thus reducing the chances that a passenger, distressed by the unfamiliar environment, would turn violent. My alarm was the sound of my one-year-old daughter, Sanjukta, laughing. In all my experience with the world, I had never encountered any sweeter sound, or any laugh that more made me want to smile.

"Good morning, Mr. Gowda," said the attendant. He was still smiling the same plastic smile. It had been—I glanced at my watch—twelve hours. The fact that he was still smiling was either a testament to his training or an argument in favor of stimulants.

"Good morning," I managed, and reached for the tea that was already waiting, enticingly hot, on my tray. "What time is it?"

"The local time in Melbourne is half-past five o'clock in the afternoon." The flight attendant smirked slightly as he glanced at my plate of turkey bacon, scrambled egg, and reheated croissant. It was the first sign I'd seen that he might be human after all, and not just a very convincing robot. "I'm afraid we're serving you breakfast for dinner. Such are the trials of international travel."

"It's quite all right," I assured him. "My mother always said that eggs were appropriate no matter the time of day." That was a filthy lie: My mother was a traditional woman who would have died before she'd fed me breakfast this late in the day. Still, there was no need to tell him that, and he looked quite pleased.

"We'll be landing in about twenty minutes," he said. "Please eat quickly, and signal if you need to use the restroom." Then he was gone, moving on to the next passenger on his list.

I turned my attention to the food. It was palatable, as airplane food went; it didn't taste of much of anything, but as taste can go either way, I was content to eat my variously textured bits of tastelessness and call it a successful meal. The other passengers were stirring, reacquainting themselves with the world as they woke. Grumbles and half-formed complaints filled the cabin, providing a discordant accompaniment to breakfast. One passenger got a bit too aggressive in his complaining. The flight attendant produced a sedative patch, slapped it against the side of the passenger's neck, and moved on. The passenger's complaints did not resume.

Many of the security precautions humanity has embraced since the Rising are silly, useless things, more about what my old colleague Georgia Mason always called "security theater" than actual security. The safety regulations that have been added to air travel, however, make perfect sense to me. If someone is going to be belligerent, I would much prefer they be confined to their seat and handled by the in-flight crew, who have been trained for this sort of thing.

I picked up my phone, pleased to see that my e-mail had finished downloading, but less pleased to see that more than five hundred messages had arrived since we left Hong Kong. At least half were flagged "urgent." My staff is good about using "urgent" only when something actually is, but given my current situation, I wasn't sure how much good I was going to be.

I stowed my phone and pulled my tablet out of the seatback pocket, entering my password with a few quick swipes of my thumb. The home screen came up, and I pressed the icon that would grant me immediate access to the After the End Times management chat room. Half archaic IM protocols, half homebrew system devised by the late, lamented Georgette Meissonier, it was the most secure chat relay I had ever encountered, and quite probably the most secure relay I ever *will* encounter. We could exchange nuclear launch codes over that thing, and no one would ever know.

Well, except for the part where we're a news site, and if we had nuclear launch codes, *everyone* would know in short order, as Alaric set half the Factual News Division on writing a scathing exposé of the weaknesses inherent in the national defense system. Reporters are excellent at ferreting out a story. We're not so good at keeping secrets.

As I had hoped, Alaric was online. It was—I did some quick math in my head—ten A.M. in California. He must have just gotten out of bed. That, or he'd pulled another all-nighter and was about five minutes away from passing out on his keyboard.

ALARIC, NEED YOUR ATTENTION. Typing on a tablet computer while on a moving airplane wasn't the easiest thing I'd ever done, but it was no harder than anything else would have been, under the circumstances.

While I waited for his reply, I pulled up the forums in another window, skimming their titles to see whether anything important had managed to catch fire while I wasn't looking. It was the usual mix of serious news, frivolous rumor, and wild conjecture that would never make it past the first-tier review board. One of the newer Irwins was proposing an expedition up into Canada to try to locate the Masons. I opened the thread, scrolled to the bottom, and added a quick one-word reply: NO.

Shaun and Georgia Mason were two of the three founders of After the End Times. The third founder, Georgette "Buffy" Meissonier, died during the Ryman/Cousins presidential campaign. Georgia herself died not long after. Shaun was the only survivor of the original trio, much to his chagrin, and he had spent quite some time after Georgia's death trying to join her through whatever means were necessary. He stopped trying to get himself killed only when he found something to live for: an illegal clone of Georgia, created by the Centers for Disease Control. It was a terrible situation, made worse by the fact that no one knew who to trust until it was over—and for some of us, trust didn't come easy, even then.

Shaun and the new version of Georgia celebrated our successful discovery of a massive government conspiracy by vanishing into the wilds of Canada. There were very few people living there, and most of the people who chose that life had no interest in helping the government. It had been almost two years. No one had seen them since. Maybe someday they would tire of their privacy and come back to civilization. Until that day arrived, I was not going to have any member of the site that they had helped to create go after them. They had earned their retirement, if retirement it truly was.

Sometimes I worried. I won't lie about that. Cloning is a strange science, restricted by morality laws and jealously guarded by the few organizations that know its secrets. So far as I was aware, the second Georgia was the first clone ever released into the wild without medical oversight. She could collapse at any moment, killed by some previously unknown glitch in the process that made her, and the rest of us might never know.

Shaun Mason was a good man, and he held himself together far longer than the rest of us had any real right to ask him to. If I worried about him—if I worried about *her*—well, so what? He'd earned a little worry. They both had.

My chat window flashed, signaling a reply. I tapped the icon, bringing the chat back to the front of my screen.

HI BOSS, read Alaric's reply. HOW'S AUSTRALIA? HAVE YOU TRIED VEGEMITE YET?

STILL ON THE PLANE, HAVEN'T LANDED YET. WHY IS MY E-MAIL FULL OF URGENT FLAGS?

NOT FEELING MUCH LIKE SMALL TALK, HUH?

I HAVE BEEN IN TRANSIT FOR TWENTY-FOUR HOURS. MY MOUTH TASTES LIKE THE BAD END OF A ZOMBIE'S DIGESTIVE SYSTEM. WHY IS MY E-MAIL FULL OF URGENT FLAGS? Alaric was a good Newsie, but he had somehow managed to lead a very sheltered life for someone who'd been through hell alongside the rest of us. Sometimes he didn't understand that brevity meant "explain yourself before I am forced to become cross with you." Still, he was loyal to a fault, and I respected that.

MINOR KA-I OUTBREAK IN ALABAMA, Alaric replied. HAD TO SCRAMBLE A FIELD TEAM TO GO OUT AND GET THE GOODS. GEO GOT A LITTLE OVERENTHUSIASTIC WITH HIS EQUIPMENT REQUESTS. MAGGIE AND I MANAGED TO REIN HIM IN. SORRY YOU GOT ALL THE CCS.

IT'S NO PROBLEM. AT LEAST I KNOW. The head of the Action News Division—more commonly known as "the Irwins," named in honor of the late Australian conservationist and crocodile enthusiast, Steve Irwin—was a very earnest young man named George Freeman, who went by "Geo" to avoid confusion with Georgia Mason. He'd been hired after Shaun left, and we'd never met in person, but he seemed like a good sort. OUTBREAK CONTAINED?

LOOKS THAT WAY.

GOOD. I'M SIGNING OFF FOR LANDING. WILL TRY TO CHECK IN AFTER I GET SITUATED WITH THE LOCAL TEAM.

MAGGIE SENDS HER LOVE.

TELL MAGGIE THANK YOU. I closed the chat window. I rarely say good-bye anymore; it feels too much like an invitation to disaster. Instead, I try to approach everything as if it were simply an ongoing sequence. Conversations didn't end. I merely had to pause them every once in a while.

Tucking my tablet back into its pocket, I relaxed in my seat and waited for the wheels to touch the ground.

3.

The Rising was a global event. It began with two American research projects, thus permanently cementing the so-very-American idea that they were the center of the world—after all, who but the center of all things could bring about the end of days?—but once the Kellis-Amberlee virus was loose in the atmosphere, it went around the world in under a week. Some places were hit harder than others when the dead began to walk. India was completely evacuated, as were parts of Japan, China, and the United States. But given time, the world recovered. That's what the world does.

Australia has always been isolated by geography. That didn't keep Kellis-Amberlee out, but it did change the landscape that the virus had to deal with. Instead of cattle and horses, Kellis-Amberlee found kangaroos and wombats. There were densely packed urban population centers, but they tended to be closer to the wilderness than similar cities in other nations. Video footage of zombie kangaroos laying siege to Sydney was one of the last things to escape Australia during that first long, brutal summer of the Rising. Then the networks went down, and there were other things for people to worry about. Unbelievable as it sounds today, there was a time when the rest of the world genuinely expected the entire continent to be lost.

There was one thing no one considered, however: Australia was populated by Australians. While the rest of us were trying to adapt to a world that suddenly seemed bent on eradicating the human race, the Australians had been dealing with a hostile environment for centuries. They looked upon our zombie apocalypse, and they were not impressed.

After the Rising was over, life for Australians went on much as it had before. They went to work, went to the pub, and endeavored not to die while living in a country that contained the lion's share of the world's venomous snakes, deadly spiders, and other such vermin. The addition of zombie kangaroos—and worse, zombie wombats—did nothing to change the essential character of the nation. If anything, global response to the Rising only confirmed something that many Australians had quietly believed for quite some time: If forced to live in Australia for a year, most of the world's population would simply curl up in a fetal ball and die of terror.

Still, some things had to change, and those changes had been, by and large, ignored by the world media. They weren't sensational enough to make good headlines; they were too practical and too easy on the nerves. Add in the fact that several governments had been devoted to a campaign intended to keep us all cowering in our beds, and it was no wonder that Australia's unique approach to animal husbandry and handling had gone mostly ignored by anyone who didn't live in Australia.

A pleasant chime sounded through the cabin, signaling that it was time to stow any loose items that might have been taken out of their containers during the flight. The attendants made one last quick pass through the cabin, helping the less-prepared travelers to get their personal items secured before we began our final descent. Then, with no additional fanfare, the nose of our plane titled sharply downward, and we broke through the clouds over Melbourne, giving me my very first glimpse of Australian soil.

To be entirely honest, it wasn't that impressive. From my small window, I could see a coastal city that looked just like every other coastal city I'd had the misfortune to visit. I am a homebody at heart, and this was my third continent, as I worked my way through an unwanted checklist. Fourth continent, if I wanted to count Asia, which I didn't particularly. I'd have been perfectly happy counting nothing but London, and London alone, until the day that I died.

I was still dwelling on that thought as the city outside my window grew rapidly closer, until finally the wheels were touching smoothly down on the runway, executing a perfect landing. Applause rose from the other passengers. Apparently, they didn't know how much modern air travel depends on autopilot systems, or how unlikely it was that our pilot had done anything to aid that seamless landing.

Ah, well. Let them have their little illusions. I joined the rest of the cabin in applauding. Sometimes it's the veils that you draw over things that make them worth looking at. Not as honest, perhaps, but certainly more palatable.

Deplaning was a straightforward, if slow, process: The flight attendants unlocked our belts one row at a time, allowing us to leisurely stand, collect our belongings, and head for the jet bridge. No one grumbled about the wait. Some of the people toward the back of the plane were probably seething silently, but there was no point in voicing that sort of thing aloud. All it would do was cause problems, and when the flight attendants are authorized to use deadly force in subduing a "problem passenger," no one wants to make a fuss.

My bag was a sturdy duffel that had seen stranger trips than this one. I slung it over my shoulder as I exited the jet bridge and started scanning around for signs that would lead me to Customs. Ah, Customs, the first trial of every international traveler.

Large, pleasant signs provided directions, accompanied by helpfully animated arrows that drew lines down the wall, just in case the addled, time-shifted tourists had lost the ability to read. I staggered in the indicated direction, followed by most of the population of my flight. I am quite sure that, in that moment, there was very little to differentiate us from your average zombie mob. No one was moaning, but all the rest of the characteristic signs were there: the slack-jawed expressions, the shambling gaits, and the absolute lack of apparent intelligence.

Eventually, we found ourselves funneled through baggage claim, where I retrieved my suitcase, and into the cattle chutes of Australian Customs and Immigration. As a visitor, I was funneled one way, while returning Australian citizens were funneled another. Their line was more than three times the length of mine. Statistically, Australians make up sixty to eighty percent of the world's international travel, and Australian nationals are in perpetual demand with multinational corporations in need of mobile executives. An Australian with half my schooling could easily get a job making three times my annual salary, simply because people are willing to pay for an accent that has become associated with survival. It would be irritating, if it wasn't so comic.

In due time, I reached the front of the line and was confronted by a bored-looking Australian woman whose hair appeared to have been the victim of an unfortunate home perm kit. A piece of clear Plexi separated us. "Please place your passport in the slot, place your hand against the indicated panel, and state your name," she said.

"Mahir Gowda," I replied, following her directions. A needle bit into the heel of my hand, followed by a soothing burst of disinfectant spray. No lights came on anywhere that I could see. This was a test that I was going to be taking blind.

"What is the purpose of your visit, Mr. Gowda?"

"I'm a registered Internet journalist, associated with After the End Times," I said. "I am a British citizen, and have filed the necessary papers to continue my work while visiting Australia. I'm joining some of my colleagues for a tour of the State Barrier Fence."

That was enough to elicit a spark of interest from the customs officer. "You're touring the rabbit-proof fence?" she asked. "You *do* understand that it's not in a nicely secured, well-populated area, yes?"

"Yes, ma'am, I do, and I think you'll find that all my clearances are in order." Assuming I'd filed the correct forms; assuming that Jack and Olivia hadn't been pulling my leg when they told me this was possible. If I'd just flown to Australia for a prank, well. Looking for a new job was going to be the least of their problems.

"They are," she admitted, with something that sounded like grudging respect. She pressed a button; my passport emerged from the slot where I'd placed it. "Welcome to Australia, Mr. Gowda. I hope you have a pleasant stay."

"So do I, ma'am," I said. "Have a nice day." Then I was past her gate and walking down the corridor toward freedom, released onto Australian soil at last.

God, did I need a toilet.

4.

There were lavatories situated outside the corridor connecting new arrivals to the exterior concourse. I had one last reunion with the denizens of my plane as I stopped to deal with certain necessary business and then turned myself to the next pressing matter on my agenda: finding my local guides.

The concourse was a dizzying whirl of activity, especially when compared to similar locations in Europe or America. People had actually come into the airport to collect their friends and loved ones. Everywhere I looked, joyous reunions were unfolding, often accompanied by the sound of one or more returning Australians complaining loudly about the condition of the rest of the world. There was something almost self-congratulatory about it. *See?* it said. *We may not be the biggest continent, and we may not have the most people, but we're the best. We're the most reasonable. Let everyone else be eaten alive in their beds. Australia will endure.*

I stopped in a clear space, turning a slow circle as I tried to get my bearings in this new place. People walked closer than I was comfortable with, some of them actually bumping against my suitcase as they passed me. The Australian idea of personal space was clearly less draconian than it was in the rest of the world.

Halfway through my second turn, I spotted two people hustling toward me across the concourse. Both were clearly Australian, given the way they were navigating through the crowd, squeezing themselves between people without an apparent concern about accidental contact. The man was tall and thin, holding a sign that read GOWDA in one hand as he ran. The woman was shorter, curvy, and had given up holding her sign in a readable position in favor of keeping her iconic Australian slouch hat on her head as she ran.

They stopped about five feet in front of me, both of them plastering broad smiles across their faces and holding their signs out in my direction. I raised an eyebrow.

"Your sign's backward," I said to the woman.

"...bugger," she muttered, and flipped the sign around, adding the message WELCOME, BOSS! to the man's GOWDA.

"Sorry we're late," said the man. "There was a bit of a traffic snarl on the way into the airport. You know how it is when you have to be somewhere in a hurry."

"Yes, I leave early," I said, and took a beat to study him. He was about my age, with dark skin and short, dark brown hair cropped close to his scalp. There was a certain indefinable tension about him, like he could do virtually anything at any moment. It was a trait he shared with most of the Irwins I knew. "Jack, I presume?"

A wide grin split his face. "In the flesh. It's a real honor to finally meet you."

"I'm not feeling particularly honorable right now. More exhausted, jet-lagged, and in need of a very long shower." I turned to the woman. Her hair was a shade of blue that occurs naturally only in certain kinds of very toxic frog, although it went well with her eyes. "That means you must be Olivia."

"Yessir," she said, pronouncing it as a single word. Her cheeks flushed red. "I mean, er, yes, hello, sir, it's very nice to meet you, I didn't mean—"

"It's all right." I grabbed the handle of my suitcase. "I assume if you're both here, the car's here, too? I'm ready to be out of the limbo of air travel and back among the lands of the living."

"Right this way," said Jack. At the same time, Olivia said, "Let me get that," and stepped forward to make an awkward grab for the handle of my suitcase, resulting in my losing my grip and letting the whole thing tumble to the floor. The three of us stood frozen for a moment, looking at my fallen suitcase. The noise of the concourse continued around us, but where we were, there was silence.

Then, without quite realizing that I was going to do it, I started to laugh.

Jack and Olivia exchanged a nervous look, like they weren't quite sure how they were supposed to respond to this clear breach of protocol. Then, softly, Olivia giggled. It turned into open laughter. Jack joined in, and the three of us stood there, suddenly at ease, surrounded by weary travelers, and laughed the nerves of a botched first meeting away. I was miles from home, in a place I had never been before, but I was among my people. I was going to be just fine.

5.

Jack Ward, Irwin, and Olivia Mebberson, Newsie, were part of the five-person team that covered Australia—and the only part of that team to live geographically close together. Olivia shared a home outside Melbourne with her husband and wife, while Jack lived near the city center and often used Olivia's home as a base of operations when he wanted to take trips out into the You Yangs, a nearby series of granite ridges that had been the subject of a yearlong series he'd done for the site. The two had been friends before they ever started working for After the End Times, and while they hadn't applied as a unit, we had received their applications within minutes of each other.

They were good, hard workers, and their credentials had been above reproach. Still were, which was why, when they'd proposed a piece on the impact of the so-called rabbit-proof fence on Australia both before and after the Rising, I'd been willing to fly out for a look. All of us were hoping that this would bring some more attention to our resident Australians, and maybe bring their page hits a little higher in the rankings. For all that many people viewed Australia as the last wild frontier, it was surprisingly difficult to get those same people to pay attention to Australian media. It was like trying to make them care about what was happening on Mars. Sure, it was interesting and all, but it was happening in a place that most of them would never visit or see, and there were more interesting things happening at home.

Jack carried my suitcase out to the car while Olivia chattered on like she was afraid that her license to produce words might be yanked at any moment. I tried responding a few times before I realized my participation wasn't required. I started merely nodding, and that worked much better for the both of us. We cleared the blood test to exit the concourse, and a second blood test to enter the parking structure. Jack led the way to his car, a sturdy pickup truck with an extended cab capable of seating four. I took the back and was asleep before he could start the engine.

Perhaps sleeping through my first exposure to the city of Melbourne was irresponsible of me, but in my defense, my body—fickle thing that it was—really didn't give me much of a choice. One minute, we were parked at the airport, and the next, the car was rolling to a stop and Jack was announcing cheerfully, "We're here. All out for the Mebberson-Yamaguchi residence."

I mumbled something unintelligible before pushing myself up with one hand and rubbing the other across my face, trying in vain to wipe away the exhaustion and grime of twenty-four hours of constant travel. "How long was I out?"

"About an hour. You're lucky this isn't America, mate, or we'd have had to wake you six times for blood tests." Jack grinned again as he bounded from the driver's seat, slammed his door, and opened mine. He was far too awake for my tastes, and I couldn't decide whether to hate him or simply go back to sleep.

"Well, then, all hail Australia." I sat up, my back protesting every movement. "Ah, damn, I'm getting too old for this shit. Where's Olivia?"

"She's inside, getting Zane and Hotaru ready for us. Probably shooing cats off counters and such, so they can make a good impression on you." Jack stepped away from my open door, crossing to the back of the car.

By the time I convinced my clumsy fingers to unfasten my seat belt and grabbed my duffel from the seat beside me, Jack had retrieved my suitcase from the back of the truck and was halfway to the house. I trudged after him, trying to study the landscape without actually waking up enough to appreciate it. It wasn't as difficult as it might sound; *nothing* was going to wake me up enough to appreciate Australia.

It was fall in London, a season of mists and turning leaves, but here, in this strange and distant land, it was the very heart of spring. A thin scrim of green covered the ground, only an inch or so high and still the color of fresh, new growth. Some of the trees on the property were eucalyptus—I recognized them, ironically enough, from the time I'd spent in California with the After the End Times team—but others were entirely new to me. Birds chirped and whistled from their branches, colored in a dizzying array of eye-burning shades.

I stopped walking. "Is that a *parrot?*" I demanded, unsure whether to be amazed or scandalized by the bird that was eyeing me with avian interest.

Jack called back, "Yup, it's a parrot. We'll see more when we hit the road. Now come on. You don't want to miss the house security system."

Mention of the security system made me start walking again, now paying attention to the man-made features of my surroundings. A high fence surrounded the house and yard on all sides, and the house itself was a long, low construct, only a single story in height, with surprisingly large windows.

"Don't let all the glass bother you," said Jack, as I caught up to him. "There's automated shutters and retractable bars that automatically descend at night. You're safe as houses. Olivia and her lot just weren't willing to sacrifice their view on the off chance that a mob could take out the fence before they got the shutters down."

"Don't scare him, Jack," said Olivia, opening the front door. She didn't step over the threshold. "The blood test plate is to your right, boss. Once you've checked in, you can come and go as you like, unless you're trying to enter with someone who hasn't been tested clean within the last six hours. If you leave the property or go over six hours, of course, you have to check clean again."

"Sensible," I said, and slapped my hand down against the testing plate. Needles bit into the base of my palm, and a moment later, a small green light clicked on inside the doorframe.

"Come on in," said Olivia. "Zane and Hotaru are very excited to meet you."

"I'm terribly sorry for them, then," I said, smothering another yawn. "I'm not exactly at my best right now."

"We understand jet lag," said a tall, barrel-chested man whose bushy red mustache had been the subject of more than a few cheerful meme explosions started by Olivia. He offered me his hand, and I noted dispassionately that he was almost a foot taller than I was. "Zane Mebberson-Yamaguchi. It's a real pleasure to finally meet you."

"Mahir Gowda," I said, slipping my hand into his, where it was engulfed by his fingers. "Thank you for your hospitality."

"That's on Olivia," he said, shaking once before letting me go. "She said her boss was coming to the country, and she couldn't exactly ask him to stay at a hotel, so would we mind? As if we could tell her no."

"You could, but you'd wake up with spiders in your bed," said Olivia, walking by and leaning up onto her absolute tiptoes. Zane ducked his head, allowing her to kiss his cheek.

"I already wake up with spiders in my bed," he said. "Find a better threat."

Rather than pay attention to their banter—which had the long-practiced feel of a call and response, the sort of private patter that partners tended to develop over long periods of time—I turned and studied the living room. It was surprisingly normal; except for the windows, it could have been placed in any American or British home and fit right in. There was a large entertainment center in one corner, with a stationary bike discreetly folded and tucked off to one side. About a third of the room had been sectioned off with a metal bookshelf, forming a private workspace.

"That's mine," said an unfamiliar female voice. I turned from my consideration of the workspace. A slim young Japanese-Australian woman had entered the living room, a pillow under one arm. She had red and blue streaks dyed in her shoulder-length black hair; the blue matched Olivia's closely enough that it was doubtless from the same bottle. "You must be Mr. Gowda. Olivia's told us so much about you."

"And you must be Hotaru."

"Exactly." Her smile was wide and warm. "Your room's ready for you, except for the pillow, which is here." She held it out to me. "Welcome to Australia."

"I'm thrilled to be here," I said, taking the pillow. "Now, if someone would show me where I'm meant to be sleeping, I'd like to go pass out until I feel secure in my ability to remember any of this."

Olivia laughed. "Come on," she said. "It's this way."

"Oh, thank God," I muttered, and followed her down the hall, away from the already-chattering cluster of people, until we reached a small, blessedly dark room. There was a single twin bed pressed up against the wall, and in that moment, it seemed larger and more welcoming than any bed that I had ever seen. My suitcase was already there, next to the nightstand. Jack must have moved it while I wasn't looking.

"Do you need anything?" Olivia asked.

"Just sleep," I said.

"I'll leave you to it, then," she said, and shut the door behind herself as she left the room.

Improbable as it seems, I truly believe that I was asleep before my head hit the pillow, and I celebrated my arrival in Australia by falling into a deep, dreamless unconsciousness.

Part II

A Fantastic Voyage into the Land of Venomous Snakes, Improbably Large Spiders, and Marsupials

People make Australia out to be some dangerous, horrifying wilderness, but it's not. It's a country like any other, and for the people who live here, it's home. You can get a little tired of people acting like your home is some sort of Murderland.

—Olivia Mebberson

Whoever authorized the evolution of the spiders of Australia should be summarily dragged out into the street and shot.

—Mahir Gowda

1.

When I awoke, the inside of my mouth tasted like a public toilet, every inch of my body ached, and the light oozing into the room around the edges of the single closed blind was somehow indefinably wrong, like it had been designed by someone who had never seen proper sunlight. I heaved myself into a sitting position, wondering if I could somehow convince myself to go back to sleep, when my nose caught another whiff of the aroma that had awakened me. Somewhere in this house, someone was frying sausages.

My stomach, which had otherwise offered very few opinions since leaving home, stirred and announced that going back to sleep was not an option—not when there might be sausages to be had. I groaned and climbed out of the bed.

There was no shower in the guest room, but I had tidy wipes in my travel kit. I cleaned myself up as best I could, changed into clean clothes, and made my way out of the room. Voices drifted down the empty hall. I walked toward them, following the smell of sausage until I found the kitchen, where Jack, Olivia, and Hotaru were clustered around a table. Zane was at the stove, a spatula in his hand and a frying pan in front of him.

"He lives!" Zane roared, and broke out in a deep, belly-shaking laugh.

"Good morning!" said Jack, turning from his plate and beckoning me toward the table. "We were just arguing about who was going to get the duty of coming and waking you up for breakfast. Have a seat, there's more than plenty."

"But is there tea?" I asked, with more of an air of desperation than I had actually intended. I half walked, half stumbled to an open place at the table, collapsing into the chair. "Please tell me that there's tea."

"There's tea," said Hotaru, and stood. "I'll start the kettle. Is English breakfast all right?"

"English breakfast will qualify you for sainthood," I said. A plate appeared in front of me: scrambled eggs, toast, fried mushrooms, fried tomatoes, and two links of the sausage that had coaxed me out the bed. I took the fork Olivia offered me and fell to, barely remembering the manners my mother had taken such unending pains to teach me.

When I was somewhere in the middle of the eggs, tea appeared. I nodded thanks to Hotaru and kept on eating.

Jack waited until I was done with my second cup before he said, "It's about nine now—you slept clean through the night—and we're set to strike off at noon. We'll be driving to Adelaide, via the Western Highway. That's about eight hours and should give us plenty of time to review the material that we've gathered for you about the fence. When we get there, we've got friends with a private plane who'll be transporting us to Nullarbor. From there—"

"I'm sorry; this is probably a stupid foreigner question, but why can't we fly out from here?" I put down my mug. "Wouldn't that make more sense?"

"It *would*, but the travel restrictions between here and Adelaide made it a bear. We're in Victoria right now. This is one of the more restrictive states. Adelaide is in South Australia. It's easier to fly out of there. Nullarbor is a good refueling spot." Jack shrugged. "It may seem a little odd, but it really is the best way."

"We're about three thousand miles from the fence," said Olivia. She smiled a little at the look on my face. "Australia's really big, remember? We're a country and a continent at the same time, and that means getting places can be a bit tricky."

"As for why we're starting from Melbourne instead of meeting up in Perth or thereabouts, it's easier for us to take a trip of this magnitude when we're doing it with a visiting journalist." Jack made a face. "Travel permits can be hard to get unless you can demonstrate that your report would be good for tourism."

I raised an eyebrow. "Australia *has* tourism?"

"Mostly in the form of attractive singles from around the world coming here hoping to marry a native and get permission to stay," said Hotaru. She sounded amused. "That's what they assume I am, until they hear my voice, and then they want to know if I'm in the market for a spouse."

"But..." I looked around the open, airy kitchen, with its windows looking out on the backyard. "Most of the people I know would be intensely uncomfortable living like this."

"Sure, they would, but they're thinking of their kids," said Olivia, with a shrug. "Marry an Australian and know that your children will have the best life they could possibly have, or spend your life locked in your room and waiting for the sky to fall. It makes us tempting. Trouble is, we don't want to be the world's solution to cowardice. We want people to come here, pump their dollars into our economy, and go the hell home."

"I can't promise that our report will have that sort of effect," I said carefully. "To be quite honest, my work tends to *discourage* casual tourism more than it encourages it."

"That's all right, that's what we're expecting," said Jack. "I'd rather people never came here in the first place. We've got a quite sufficient human population, and expanding the cities would mean going up against the wildlife. Not a plan for the faint of heart. I'm more interested in telling the licensing board what they want to hear in order to get us to the fence and get our numbers up."

"Maybe you don't need the money, mate, but we do," said Zane, appearing behind Olivia and putting a hand on the smaller woman's shoulder. She leaned back against him, apparently quite comfortable with her position. "If our Liv can just go up a few notches in the ratings, it'll make a big difference for us as a household."

"I can understand that," I said, remembering my own days as a struggling beta, back when a single reprinted article could make the difference between pot noodles and proper meals for the remainder of a week. "Let's see what we can't do to make you stars, all right?"

Everyone around the breakfast table beamed.

2.

Of course, there was the small wrinkle of travel to be accounted for. In order to reach the fence, I would first have to spend eight hours in a car, rocketing through the Australian countryside. Not precisely how I had planned to start my stay. I eyed Jack's car sadly as he and Zane packed our equipment and my luggage into the back.

"Are you quite sure we'll be safe outside of the city?"

"No, but the odds are in our favor." Jack grinned. "Calm down a little. You're in Australia now. We do things differently here."

"I'm starting to see that," I said, and went inside to get myself another cup of tea. I needed to settle my nerves before we got on the road and I was subjected to the Australian highway system while conscious for the first time.

Most countries, England and the United States among them, have adopted an infrastructure-based approach to security. Highways are heavily guarded, with walls separating them from the surrounding countryside, blood tests required at many access points, and even manned guard booths staffed by highly trained marksmen. Any signs of amplification will be met with immediate and lethal force. I had plenty of opportunities to see the American highway system in action during my time with the Masons, and while I freely admit that it has its flaws, those flaws did not include a lack of fail-safe measures.

The Australian highway system, on the other hand, approached things in a way that fit what the world had come to recognize as the Australian aesthetic. Instead of building walls and manning guard towers, they had reinforced their cars and trained their drivers to keep a close eye on the surrounding wilderness. "The highways cut through a lot of important wildlife habitats" had been Jack's explanation, when I asked him. "Sure, you're going to get some roadkill no matter what you do, but we can at least make sure that we're not cutting off all access."

"Half the wildlife in Australia wants to kill us."

His answer had been a wide grin. "Sure, but the other half needs all the help that it can get."

By the time I returned from the kitchen, Jack had the last of our gear loaded into the car, and Olivia was involved in a complicated three-way embrace with her husband and wife. Feeling as if I were intruding, I turned my back on them and asked Jack, "Is there anything I need to know before we get on the road?"

"Nothing I can't explain once we're rolling," he said. "We've got a pretty clear route and some alternates programmed into the GPS in case of road closure. I checked in with Forestry this morning, and there's no reported mobs in this area, so we should have smooth sailing for a good long while. We'll gas up when we stop for lunch, and get to Adelaide by nightfall."

"Mob" was the word for a group of the infected. It was also the word for a large gathering of kangaroos. Glancing nervously at the fence, I asked, "Do you, ah, have kangaroos in this part of Australia?"

"Not as many as we used to, sad to say. Most of them are fenced in up in the You Yangs, where we can monitor them for signs of infection and clear out any that amplify before things get out of hand. It helps that they're good about knowing when one of them is sick. When someone sees a mob moving away from a solitary roo, that's a good sign that something's wrong."

I blinked at him. "You sound almost sorry that they're not here anymore."

"Kangaroos are beautiful animals, mate, and they belong here. Australia's theirs as much as it's ours. We're just the ones who evolved into fence makers."

"You'll forgive me if I'm somewhat dubious."

"It's all right. Just don't go taking potshots at anything that moves, and enjoy the view." Jack clapped me on the back with one hand. "This drive's going to be an education for you. I guarantee it."

Try as I might, I couldn't come up with any reason that he might be wrong.

3.

An hour later, we were finally on the road, leaving Melbourne, Zane, and Hotaru behind us. Olivia was driving, while Jack took the shotgun position—in more ways than one, as he had produced a hunting rifle before getting into the car and was riding with it propped between his knees.

I was in the backseat, along with the cooler that held our lunch, a folder containing hard copy of all our travel permits, and a book on the history of the rabbit-proof fence. I began flipping through the folder, frowning a little at the variously colored slips of paper. "I think I have most of these saved on my phone," I said.

"Yes, but you're foreign, and we're journalists, and worst of all, you're a foreign journalist," said Olivia. "For everyone who's going to be delighted to see you as a potential bridge to future tax revenue, there's someone who'll see you as a threat to Australian independence, trying to infect us with the fear that grips the rest of the known world, et cetera, et cetera, and then we're held up at a checkpoint for six hours while someone tries to prove that the files in your phone were faked."

"Hard copy's just as easy to fake if you're really determined, but a lot of folks still trust it more," said Jack. "Most of the networks went down during the Rising, and it took a few years to get Internet access back to absolutely everywhere."

"It's sort of exactly the opposite of the way it worked out in America," said Olivia. "There, no one trusts paper anymore. Here, no one's quite sure you didn't invent whatever's on your screen."

"Given how many Americans think Australia was invented by a bunch of kids in their garage with a green screen, that's not unreasonable." I stopped, squinting at a piece of bright pink paper. "Hang on—why do we need a waiver clearing us from prosecution in the event that we're forced to injure an attacking koala? Isn't the word 'attacking' enough in that sentence?"

"Not in Australia," said Jack cheerfully. "There are millions of humans and not nearly that many koalas. Most of them are too small to amplify, and they tend to live pretty high up in the trees. A big old male actually manages to get sick, he isn't going to find very many targets. Most of the other koalas are more coordinated than he is once the infection really sets in, and so all he does by biting at them is piss them off and get himself shoved out of the tree. Infected koalas go after easier targets. Like humans."

"Only you can't necessarily tell infected-and-shot from startled-you-and-shot," said Olivia. "Since humans can outrun koalas on level ground, people are encouraged to avoid koala habitat and wear good running shoes, rather than risk reducing the koala population further."

I stared at the back of her head. "You're serious?"

"Serious as a zombie outbreak in a public mall," said Jack. "We want our citizens to be comfortable and happy and we're as interested in the survival of mankind as anyone else, but at the end of the day, we can always get more people. It's all our immigration restrictions can do to keep us from getting more people than we can handle. But we can't get more koalas."

I sat back in my seat, mulling this over. Australia's conservation efforts had been well known before the Rising, and unlike most of the world—where wildlife conservation had been dismissed as a luxury of existing in a time before zombie tigers—they hadn't abandoned those efforts after the dead got up and walked. Instead, they'd doubled down, treating the existence of infected mammals of all sizes as some sort of challenge. Zombie kangaroos? Bring them on, we'll find a way to deal. This new bit of information about the koalas shouldn't have been surprising. And yet...

"Why hadn't I heard about this legislation before? It wasn't in any of the travel information I received from your government."

"We *do* want people to come visit occasionally, and you're a journalist, not a biologist," said Olivia. "Their documents are a lot more terrifying. Not that most of them care. I thought Irwins were fearless to the point of stupidity until I met my first field biologist."

"By which, of course, she means Zane," said Jack.

"At least he just studies spiders," said Olivia serenely. "Much safer."

"There is no contribution for me to make to this conversation," I said. "How far to Adelaide?"

"Another six hours, give or take a road closure," said Jack. "Settle back and enjoy the ride, mate. We've got a ways to go."

"Charming," I said, and reached for the reading material.

My purpose in visiting Australia was twofold: to increase page hits for our Australian correspondents, who needed the income, and to examine the infamous rabbit-proof fence, which no longer had much of anything to do with rabbits. Originally constructed in 1907, the fence was intended to keep imported animals from destroying Australia's unique ecology. It blocked not only rabbits, but dingoes and foxes. "The" fence is something of a misnomer in this context, as there were originally three of them, stretching across a great swath of Western Australia.

In the 1950s, the government began controlling the rabbits with disease, and the fence became much less important. Parts of it fell into disrepair; the rest of the world treated the entire concept of a rabbit-proof fence as one more sign that Australia was an alien continent, full of people they could never understand. Who builds a fence to keep out a digging animal? People smart enough to run wire netting underground, that's who. The rabbit-proof fence was an effective deterrent in its day, and the people who built it were justly proud of it—proud enough, in fact, to maintain the bulk of its length.

That would eventually be what saved them.

When the Rising reached Australia, the Kellis-Amberlee virus did what it had done everywhere else, attacking every mammal it could find with equal ferocity. The keepers of the rabbit-proof fence reacted to this new threat by reinforcing the existing structure, building it higher than it had ever been, and herding the infected animals through. The modern fence was a combination of the original No. 1 Fence and the smaller No. 3 Fence, carving off a vast chunk of upper Western Australia as the sole domain of the infected. It was, in effect, the world's largest cage, and it was our destination.

Much of the land the modern fence enclosed had belonged to the indigenous people of Australia, who had been working on reclamation since the 1970s. Their communities were triumphs of perseverance and justice, and too many of them were lost during the Rising. Resettlement efforts were still ongoing, like a chilling echo of Australia's colonial past. There was a whole second report on those, even longer than the documentation on the fence.

With Jack and Olivia squabbling good-naturedly in the front seat about who should control the radio, I settled deeper in my seat and kept reading.

4.

After we had been driving for four hours, Olivia had declared that it was time to break for lunch, saying, "There's no point in seeing Australia entirely from the car. That won't give you any more of an idea of who we are here than looking at a bunch of pictures, and you could do that anyway." Before I could protest, she had turned off the highway and driven us deep into a eucalyptus grove, where miraculously, there was a small parking area and an assortment of picnic tables. Jack hopped out as soon as Olivia stopped the engine, heading for the nearest table.

Olivia herself was more casual about things, moving at a frankly sedate pace. I eyed her as she removed the cooler from the car. "You planned this. I cannot believe that Australia is riddled with secret picnic areas, just in case a native needs a teaching moment for a visitor."

"Of course I planned this," she said, looking affronted. Somehow, her blue hair just added to the surrealism of the moment; she was standing outdoors with no visible protective gear, looking at me reproachfully from beneath a blueberry-colored fringe. "I'm a Newsie. We plan everything. You should know that. Now come on, Jack's going to worry about us."

"Jack's probably off wrangling a zombie kangaroo to give me another bloody teaching moment," I muttered, and got out of the car.

Jack was actually checking the ground around the picnic tables when we approached. He looked up, smiled, and said, "No fresh tracks. We should be safe here for a little bit. Just try not to shout or set anything on fire, all right, mate?"

"I will keep my pyromania firmly in check," I said, uneasily taking a seat at the table. I only realized after I sat that I had positioned myself to have a clear line of sight on the car, making it easier for me to run. It's not that I'm a coward; I believe my professional accomplishments speak to my bravery. It's that, unlike the people I was traveling with, I am not bog-stupid about safety.

"Good," said Olivia, and began unpacking cold sandwiches, crisps, and baggies of rectangular, chocolate-covered biscuits from her cooler. Once these were set out in front of us, she produced a self-heating thermos and broke the seal, triggering its thermal progression. "Tea should be ready in a minute."

"There are some small blessings to this excursion," I muttered.

Jack sighed. "Look, boss, this isn't just about making you uncomfortable."

"Could have fooled me, but I'm listening," I said.

"You need to be able to deal with the outside when we tell you that it's safe," he said. "We don't have hermetically sealed environments here the way you do in London. People come and go in the outside here. If you can't adjust to that, the fence is going to be a real problem for you, since the whole thing is exposed."

"We're used to nature trying to kill us here," said Olivia, with obscene good cheer. "It's been doing that for centuries, and we refuse to let it, mostly because we want to piss it off by surviving. It's the Australian way, Mahir. Piss off nature. Show that natural world who's boss."

"Don't red kangaroos weigh something on the order of ninety-one kilograms?" I asked, still not reaching for a sandwich. "I'm reasonably sure, in the matter of me versus Australia's natural world, that I am not the boss. The massive, infected creatures that can gut me with a kick are the boss. I'm in the mail room at best."

Jack laughed. "You're funny. I never realized that from your reports."

"Yes, well. My humor is a brand best experienced live." The top of the thermos turned red, signaling that the tea was done. I leaned over and removed the cap. Olivia passed me a cup. "Thank you."

"No worries," she said, and took a sandwich.

We didn't talk much after that, being preoccupied with the simple biological necessities of eating. Jack and Olivia were nonchalant about the whole matter, remaining relaxed even as we sat in an utterly exposed position, surrounded by the Australian countryside. I found it somewhat more difficult to keep myself from jumping every time a twig snapped or a leaf rustled—both things that happened with remarkable frequency, thanks to the high number of birds that had been attracted by our lunch.

Jack caught me eyeing with suspicion a huge black and white bird that looked like a half-bleached raven. The bird was eyeing me back, looking profoundly unimpressed. "That's an Australian magpie," said Jack. "It's trying to figure out whether it can knock you over and take your food. No offense intended, but I think it would have a good shot of winning."

"Yes, especially since I would be locking myself back in the car if it so much as twitched in my direction." I shook my head. "Are all Australian birds this bold?"

"Yeah," said Jack. "Even the emus, and those are birds the size of kangaroos. You haven't learned to really appreciate fried chicken until the first time you've faced down an angry emu that wants to bite your fingers off."

"Then why do you put up with them?"

"Two reasons," said Olivia, opening the biscuits. "First off, we're back to that pesky 'conservation' thing that we're so fond of here in Australia. The birds have as much of a right to their home continent as we do, so we try to work things out with them when we can. Doesn't mean we don't occasionally shoot them—"

"And eat them," added Jack helpfully.

"—but it does mean that when they're just bopping about the wilderness, being birds, we mostly leave them alone." Olivia took three biscuits and passed the package down. "The other reason we 'put up' with them? Early-warning system. We won't necessarily hear an infected animal or human coming, but the birds will. They're *very* good about knowing when something nasty is on its way, and we can use them to tell us when we need to leave. That's worth a few sandwich-related muggings."

My ears burned. I ducked my head, considering the bird with new respect. "I'd never considered it that way."

"Most foreigners don't," said Jack, and tossed a biscuit to the magpie, which snatched it up and took off, piebald wings flapping hard. "Don't worry, we won't hold it against you. I'm sure we'll be just as out of place when we come to London."

"Is that in the cards, then?"

"Someday, maybe. When we're better established here, and I can sign on for a few global reports." Jack grinned. "I'd love to do a march across some of the abandoned bits of Russia, see what's been going on out there while no one was looking."

"I just want to see the British Museum," said Olivia, a dreamy look spreading across her face. "It's the only place in the world where you can still come face-to-face with real mummies."

"Well, then, we'll just have to make sure that this works out, won't we?" I asked, and smiled, waiting for them to smile back.

They didn't. Instead, Jack tensed, his gaze flicking to the trees around us. As if she was picking up some unspoken signal, Olivia began packing the remains of our lunch back into the cooler, moving fast enough that it was clear she was in a hurry. I wanted to ask them what was going on. Instead, I forced myself to stay quiet and listen.

There was nothing. The squawks, trills, and screeches of the Australian birds had stopped sometime in the past thirty seconds, replaced by an ominous silence. My friend Maggie is fond of horror movies, and this was the sort of moment that every one of those films would have matched with an ominous soundtrack. I never understood why. That silence was the most frightening thing I had encountered in a long time.

Then Jack's hand was on my arm. I somehow managed not to jump as I looked up into his broad, worried face.

"Come on, mate," he said. "It's time for us to go."

"There are some things I don't need to hear twice," I said, and rose, and followed him back to the car. Olivia was already there, a rifle in her hands, scanning the surrounding landscape. It should have been a comic scene—the curvy, blue-haired woman with the high-powered hunting rifle—but instead, it seemed to fit perfectly with everything I'd come to know about Australia. She stayed where she was, a silent sentry, until Jack and I were in the car. Then she got in and closed the door, and we roared off down the road, leaving the silence of the birds behind us.

5.

We were half a mile down the road before Jack said, without turning, "I'm betting wombat. It's the only way it could have gotten that close without scaring off the magpies."

"I say koala," said Olivia. "They move pretty slow, and magpies don't always notice them."

"Are you trying to sort out what was coming to eat us back there?" I asked. "We could have just stayed where we were and gotten a firsthand view."

"Ah, but remember, conservation laws," said Jack.

"We could've shot it if it was a wombat," said Olivia. "They're endangered as all get-out, but they're still legal to kill, because they're too damn dangerous for even the most hard-nosed conservationists to worry about."

"What makes them worse than anything else around here?" I asked. I was picturing a monster, something the size of a bear but with the venomous fangs that every other creature in Australia seemed to come equipped with. "How big are they?"

"Barely over the amplification limit, but they're built like concrete wrapped in fur—even an uninfected wombat can be dangerous as hell, if you hit one with your car. They have incredibly slow metabolisms. That makes them ambush hunters. They'll kill and eat a man, and then just sit there for a month or more, digesting, not setting off any alarms." Olivia shook her head. "They're a menace. It's a pity, too; they're quite cute, when they're not trying to chew your face off."

"If we were anywhere else on the bloody planet, I would think that you were having me on right now," I said, peering out the window as I scanned the side of the road for signs of the dreaded wombat. I thought I saw something about the size of a small dog, but it was mostly obscured by the brush, and before I could point it out, we were past it and barreling onward down the highway.

"Welcome to Australia," said Jack, with altogether too much good cheer.

"Yes, I feel a little more welcome every time you remind me how likely it is that I'm going to die here," I grumbled, and sank lower in my seat, reaching for my laptop.

It took only a few minutes for me to locate a strong local wireless signal—a little odd, given that we were apparently in the middle of nowhere, but Australia had made great strides in connectivity since the Rising cut them off from the rest of the world. It was a very "fool me once, shame on you, fool me twice, shame on me" ideology, and I approved, especially when it allowed me to establish an Internet connection.

Checking in on the forums and downloading the latest batch of pictures that Nandini had sent of Sanjukta helped my mood a little. Toddlers are remarkable creatures, unaware of the dangers that the world will hold for them as they grow, utterly convinced of their own immortality. They're like tiny Irwins, and every morning I woke up glad that Sanjukta was so effortlessly fearless, even as I worried that this would be the day when she finally learned to be afraid. Judging by her latest exploits, which included clonking the cat with a toy truck and attempting to roll off her mother's lap onto the floor, she was nowhere near that transition.

Olivia and Jack seemed content to be quiet and watch the road unfold. I twisted around until I found a position that allowed me to comfortably rest my laptop on my legs and opened the interface to my personal blog. It was time to update my followers on my impressions of Australia.

It can be difficult sometimes, juggling the formats demanded by a personal, or "op-ed" blog, and a formal, factual blog. Not everyone manages it, and we don't require it from the Newsies anymore; we haven't since Georgia Mason was running the site. She believed that the only way to keep spin out of the news was by putting it in a bucket of its own, clearly labeled to prevent confusion. Not that it ever worked as well as she wanted it to, but then, no one saw the world in black and white like Georgia Mason did. She was unique. That's probably a good thing. Humanity thrives on shades of gray, and if you stripped us all back to black and white, I doubt most of us would be as well meaning and idealistic as Georgia Carolyn Mason. May she rest in peace and live happily ever after at the same time.

It's a bit ironic that someone who was so dedicated to black and white had an ending that was so distinctly gray—but then, irony has always gone hand in hand with the news.

I summarized my flight in as few words as I could manage without slandering the airline that would be conveying me home and then began describing Australia, allowing myself all the "I felt" and "I thought" qualifiers that the more formal reports would eventually deny me. It was pleasant, soothing, and almost entirely automatic. I even found myself waxing a little romantic about the pleasures of a continent where there were still open spaces, where birds replaced klaxons as an early-warning system, and people understood that perhaps humanity was not the end-all and be-all of life on this planet.

It took perhaps an hour to compose the post and another twenty minutes to edit it down to my satisfaction, trimming anything that read as overly romanticizing the nation. Finally, I hit the key to submit and leaned back against the seat, rubbing my hands together as I tried to get the tension out of my fingers.

"Feel better?" asked Olivia. I raised my head to find her watching me over the back of the seat, a surprising degree of understanding in her round, friendly face.

I nodded. "I do, yes. Sometimes, a little time with my thoughts is all I need to center myself."

"I understand that but good. I got the bug when I was still in school. The other kids would tease me for this or that, and I'd go sit in the library and write these long, angst-ridden blog posts about how no one would ever understand me, and how Australia was a benighted hellhole filled with barbarians and bastards." Olivia's grin was sudden, and broad enough for me to see that one of her incisors was slightly chipped. "It's all still out there, although I was posting under a closed pseudonym back then, thank God. Australia's very strict about preserving the Internet anonymity of minors, and I was never one of those girls who felt the need to drop clues about who she really was. I went online to get *away* from who I really was, not encourage the horrible kids at my school to track me down and give me hell."

"So what made you get into the news?" I asked. "Forgive me if this seems overly personal, but that's the sort of background I expect from a Fictional, not a Newsie."

"I know, right? Trouble is, I can't make shit up to save my life. I'm the worst liar you'll ever meet. But telling the truth, see, that's something I'm pretty good at. I was just finishing college when After the End Times went online, with this head Newsie who everyone agreed was just mad as a cut snake about the truth. If it even smelled of a lie, she didn't want it anywhere near her. I looked at her and said that's it. That's who I want to grow up to be. All I had to do from there was sort myself out so's I'd be good enough to get the shot." Olivia smiled again, more subdued this time. "I really do wish I'd had the chance to meet her. Georgia Mason, God. What was she like?"

I hesitated. There were a lot of easy answers to that question. I knew them all; I'd written most of them, one resentfully given interview at a time. It can be hard to see one of your closest friends go from person to icon to ideal over the course of your lifetime—not to mention her own. She became an icon when she died for the news. She became a strange platonic ideal of herself when she came back, whether or not she had anything to do with that eventual return. But Olivia was a member of the team, even if she'd joined up after Georgia, and she deserved something better than an easy answer.

She deserved the truth.

"Georgia Mason was the single most headstrong person I ever met in my entire life," I said seriously. "Once she got an idea in her head, she wasn't going to be happy until she'd run it to ground and, if necessary, beaten it to death. I once had to talk her out of doing a six-week series on irregularities in the manufacturing standards for energy drinks. Not because they were dangerous, not because they were going to get anyone killed. Just because they didn't match up to the rules. She mellowed out about that somewhat once she got her teeth into some real stories, but when she didn't have something to be focused on, she'd try to focus on the entire world, all at once, and she was always astonished when it didn't work."

"Was she a good friend?"

"The best," I said, without thinking about it. "We never met face-to-face—I never met the original, anyway, and the clone that the United States government created, while perfectly pleasant in her own right, was never the same person. Chalk it up to the trauma of dying, if you're one of those people who believe that clones share the souls of the people that they're cloned from. Both versions of her were passionate in their defense of the people that they allowed to get close to them, and they'd stop at nothing to help a friend. Having Georgia on your side was like... it was like knowing that you were somehow privileged to be on a first-name basis with a natural disaster. You knew that one day it was going to rage out of control and destroy everything in its path, and until that day arrived, you didn't have to worry about a damn thing. You were the one with the tornado in your corner."

"I've heard you talk about her before," said Jack casually. "I think everyone has, if they've listened to more than one of your interviews. But I've never heard you talk about her like *that.* I think Australia's getting to you, mate. You're starting to look out the window and tell yourself stories."

"If I can't tell myself stories here, where can I?" I shrugged. "Besides, Georgia would have wanted me to be straight with you. You're part of the site. That means you're family, even if you're distant cousins. Family deserves the truth whenever possible."

"You always talk about her in the past tense," said Jack. "Isn't she alive right now? It's confusing. Dead people are supposed to stay dead."

"Georgia Mason had too much indignation for a single lifetime," I said. "She had to come back, if only so she could correct the accounts of her death. I refer to her in the past tense because she died. My friend died. That she came back was a miracle. She did not come back the same person, and in a way, that's a very good thing."

"Why's that?" asked Olivia.

"Because the original Georgia Mason could never have gone quietly off to live a life that no one was ever going to write down," I said. "The woman that the CDC made with her face...she's a friend, too, and a good one, and I miss her, but I don't begrudge her the life she's chosen, even as I am fully aware that it is a life that would have driven the original Georgia summarily insane."

Olivia laughed. "I think I like this version of original-recipe Georgia better than the saintly one you normally talk about in interviews."

I smiled. "Yes. Me, too."

Part III

Small Planes, Large Fences, and a Rather Daunting Number of Zombie Kangaroos, Because That Is Exactly What This Day Needed

Every kind of Irwin wants you to think they have the most dangerous possible environment. Urban Irwins sneer at wilderness Irwins and so on down the line. I have Australia. I win.

—Jack Ward

I was unaware that Darwinism was a race.

—Mahir Gowda

1.

We talked for a while longer about the early days of After the End Times—that brief, beautiful period between the beginning of Peter Ryman's campaign to become President of the United States and the point at which people started actively trying to kill us—before Jack and Olivia seemed to be satisfied by my answers. They quieted, and I turned back to my typing.

Running a site the size of After the End Times means there's always something to do, even if it's just checking moderator forums and clearing out spam filters. Sometimes it also means admitting that you're several time zones away from home, and that there's a reason you have a staff. I yawned, closed my laptop, and put my head against the window, and that was the last that I knew of the world for several hours.

When I awoke, Olivia was shaking my arm, an amused expression on her face. "Does everyone from England go to sleep the minute you load them into a car, or is that something that's uniquely you?" she asked. "Because I have to say, I don't think much of it as a survival mechanism."

"Jet lag is a cruel mistress," I said piously, before yawning and stretching as best I could while still strapped into my seat. "Where are we?"

"Adelaide," said Olivia. "Welcome to the Gretchen Monroe Memorial Airfield." Seeing the confusion written wide across my face, she added, "Gretchen Monroe was the manager here when the Rising started. She kept the gates open and the fuel pumps live long enough to get twenty-three planes into the air—virtually every craft they could find that was capable of flight—before the infected swarmed and she went down. She was a hero."

"She certainly sounds like one," I said, making a private note to look up her information once we were finished with the fence. A few articles on the Australian Rising wouldn't be a bad idea, and stories like Gretchen's were always good for page hits. People like to read about heroism, especially when it happened very far away and there's no chance that they'll be called upon to do the same.

"Come on, you lazy bastards," called Jack. I looked toward his voice, finally registering our surroundings: We were parked in a small fenced lot, outside a low, tin-roofed building that looked like it had been lifted straight from a picture book. Beyond it stretched a wide swath of concrete, glimmering slightly with heat haze in the late-afternoon sun. "We've got to get into the air if we're going to make it to Nullarbor tonight."

"We're coming," Olivia shouted back, and reached past me to grab a backpack from the seat well. "Come on, boss. We need to move before Jack spontaneously combusts."

"I'd like to see that," I said, and followed her.

The land around the airfield was flat, cleared of the trees that I had come to associate with everything outside the cities in Australia. Brightly colored birds hopped and twittered in the fields, but nothing larger moved there. It should have been peaceful. Instead, it was unnerving, like the pause that comes directly before a storm.

Jack was the first one to the door, naturally, although he waited until we had reached the porch before he slapped his hand down on a blood testing unit. A few seconds passed, and a light above the doorframe turned green. There was a click. The door slid open.

"See you in a minute," said Jack, and let himself inside.

"Cheeky," said Olivia, not disapprovingly. "You next, Mahir. I'll cover the rear."

"Thanks," I said, and approached the blood-testing unit, taking a moment to consider its structure before I pressed my hand against the contact plate. It was a larger testing surface than I normally saw back in London, but that didn't make it old-fashioned or less than functional; judging by the sturdiness of the construction, this unit was as big as it was because it was military-grade. Australia might go out of its way to seem laid-back about the threat of Kellis-Amberlee and the infected, but when you looked beneath the superficial calm, their protections had teeth.

The green light turned on for me as well, and I stepped through the newly opened door into a room that looked even more old-fashioned than its exterior. A long wooden desk split the space into two halves, and a large oil painting of a young woman with green-tipped hair and a classic "fuck the world" stare stood on an easel, with a plaque identifying her as "Our Founder." Corkboards festooned with maps and paper notices lined the walls. Jack was leaning against the desk, flirting amiably with a redheaded man in mechanic's overalls. They both looked around at the sound of the door closing behind me. Jack grinned.

"Mahir Gowda, meet George Maxwell, airfield general manager. Max, meet Mahir Gowda, my boss."

"Pleased to meet you," said Max, running the words together so that they became virtually one. "Heading for Nullarbor, aren't you?"

"To refuel, yes," I said. "From there, we're heading for..." I stopped, looking hopelessly at Jack.

"Dongara," he said. "We'll be catching a car from there to the fence."

"Long trip for a foreign boy," said Max. "You could save yourself some trouble, buy a few postcards of the fence and head on home."

"Thank you, but I'd like to actually see it for myself," I said politely.

Jack laughed. "I told you he wouldn't go for it, didn't I?" he said. "You owe me five dollars. Pay up."

"I'm not sure whether I should be offended or not," I said, as Max dug out his wallet, scowling, and slapped a five-dollar bill into Jack's hand.

"Be flattered," said Olivia, stepping up behind me. "Most of the time when we have tourists, Jack's betting on how long it'll take them to change their tickets so they can get back to a 'civilized' country a little sooner."

"They can't actually be *saying* that they're leaving because Australia isn't 'civilized,'" I said, unable to keep myself from sounding appalled.

"Welcome to Murderland," said Olivia bitterly. She turned to Max. "Who's our pilot?"

"Juliet," said Max. "Where's my fee?"

"Here you go." She walked past us to set a small cooler on the counter. "Zane's special brownies and some of Hotaru's vanilla shortbread. Zane says hello, Hotaru says you're an arsehole."

"Sounds about right," said Max, as he made the cooler vanish under the counter. Turning, he bellowed, "Oi, Juliet! Your fare's here!"

"I do love the civility and refinement of this establishment, don't you, Jack?" said Olivia mildly.

"It's a real treat," Jack agreed.

I shook my head, leaving them to their banter, and turned to better study the office, looking for signs that might indicate how good the security was. After my second scan of the corners, I found them: a thin wire ran along the edge of the wall, almost obscured by the general clutter. Tracing it with my eyes, I saw that it vanished beneath the corkboard and that more wires were concealed behind the other boards. We were in the center of a very well-monitored web of sensors, and while they might all be air quality and sound-based, that wouldn't make a difference if someone infected managed to get into the building. There's more than one way of detecting an outbreak.

"Why are you trying so hard to look unsafe?" I asked, as I considered the near-invisible outline of a blast shutter, painted to appear like it was just another part of the wall. "Is it because you want to discourage tourism, or is there a deeper reason?" I turned back to Max. He was gaping at me.

Several seconds passed with nothing being said.

"Well?" I prompted finally.

"I'm sure I don't know what you mean," he said.

"Those wires." I pointed. "There's no reason for that distribution unless you're filtering the air looking for signs of Kellis-Amberlee infection. It's a good way of avoiding any local regulations about security cameras, although I can't imagine why you'd have those out here, but it's not the sort of thing that goes with your 'we're too wild and carefree to worry about security' image. So why are you trying so hard?"

"He's got you, Maxie," said Jack, sounding amused. "You'd best tell him, or you'll become his new pet project, and that's never a fun place to be."

"I think I should be offended by that statement, but I'm not," I said. "Well?"

Max scowled at me before saying, "Look. Lots of tourists who want to see 'the real Australia' make it this far, or as far as places like this one, and they say they want to 'go bush,' which they think is a real thing that people really say, because they're all mental. They're looking for theme park adventure, and if they make it past me, that's not what they're going to get. They're going to get real pain, real danger, and very possibly, real death. Tourist deaths are bad for business. So those of us who stand at the border between 'exciting but safe' and 'you'll get your damn fool arse killed' sometimes have to make a little show of how dangerous things really are."

"That makes perfect sense," I said. "I'll be sure to include a comment about how terrifying this place was when I write the posts about this part of my trip."

Max looked relieved. "Really? Thanks, mate. You're a lifesaver."

"No, you are. I'm simply a man who sees the wisdom in leaving the support structures in place." In an odd way, the false advertising at the airfield was a quick, almost iconic means of telling the truth. After all, "go any further than this and you'll probably be killed" isn't an easy message to sell most people on, and if this made it easier to believe, then it was a necessary masquerade. "I do, however, want to get to the fence before my tourist visa expires. You said something about a pilot . . . ?"

"He meant me," said a stern female voice whose thick Canadian accent was almost shocking in its foreignness. I turned. A tall, rail-thin woman with deeply tanned skin and a short bristle of bleach-white hair was standing in the doorway. She was wearing khaki overalls, and had prescription-grade sunglasses covering her eyes. "Juliet Seghers-Ward, at your service. I understand I'm taking you worthless scumbags to Dongara?"

"By way of Nullarbor," confirmed Jack. "Juliet, this is our boss, Mahir Gowda."

"A pleasure," I said.

She turned toward me, and although I couldn't see her eyes, I had the distinct, uncomfortable feeling that she was taking my measure. "You ever been in a Cessna before, Mr. Gowda?" she asked.

"No," I said. "I've been in privately owned planes, but nothing quite so—"

"It was a yes or no question. You can stop talking." She crossed her arms. "My bird's small and fast, but she's also loud as a motherfucker. She's going to shake. She's going to rattle. She might even do some rolling, depending on the weather and what's going up once we get off the ground. You'll need to wear ear protection, stay in your seat at all times, and do your praying without distracting me. Got any questions?"

"Ah, yes," I said. "Are these sincere warnings, or do you share the general air of theatrics that seems to pervade this airfield? I ask only because he"—I indicated Max—"wanted me to view this place as a sort of portal into Dante's Inferno, and while I'm more than happy to play along, I want to know whether or not I ought to be wetting myself in terror right now."

There was a pause before Juliet smiled. There was something unnerving about the expression, and it took all my self-control not to step backward.

"Oh," she said. "You're one of *those*. Well, won't this be fun."

2.

It was not fun.

While I am sure that there are people for whom an evening flight in a Cessna is a lovely experience—the sort of thing they yearn to share with friends and loved ones—it took only the first ninety seconds in the small, cramped plane for me to realize that I was not one of those people. It didn't help that I was crammed into the back with Jack, while Olivia sat up front with Juliet. This wasn't as arbitrary as it seemed: Olivia had taken some flight classes as part of her journalism licensing, while Jack had opted for first aid and additional weapons certifications. Australia might be deadly to the unprepared, but Australia's regulations tried to guarantee that the local journalists would never fall into that category.

The roar of the small plane's engines was loud enough to make my ears ring, even through the protective headphones that had been shoved into my hands during the loading process. Most of our possessions had been left in Jack's truck. The few bags that were making the trip with us had been stowed in the hold, save for a single cooler that contained our dinner—as if anyone could eat while traveling in a shaking, rattling, roaring metal tube that was being hurled through the air at speeds that hadn't seemed nearly this unsafe when I was in a jumbo jet. Jack grinned, flashing me a thumbs-up. I shuddered and looked away.

If I threw up, I'd be riding the rest of the way with the smell, assuming Juliet didn't toss me out in midair to punish me for befouling her beloved plane. The thought didn't do much to settle my stomach.

Jack's hand touched my arm. I looked back and found him watching me sympathetically. "You okay?" he mouthed exaggeratedly, accompanying it with the appropriate hand gestures.

I shook my head no.

He laughed. I couldn't hear it, but there was no mistaking his expression. "Sorry," he mouthed, before folding his hands and putting them against the side of his head, clearly suggesting that I get some sleep.

Since there was no possible world in which *that* was going to happen, I stared at him blankly for a few seconds before shaking my head and turning to look out the one small round window that was available to me. The sun was setting as we flew, casting the land below us into deepening darkness. There were swaths of lights coming on, identifying the cities, but so much of the land remained black that it almost took my breath away. This was a land that had not been fully industrialized before the Rising came, and certainly hadn't been industrialized afterward.

There are wild places in Europe and the Americas; there are places where mankind has surrendered whatever had been built to the wilderness, choosing to withdraw rather than fight the monster that we created in our labs and through our carelessness. But those places lacked the quiet grandeur of the Australian countryside, which was dark not because the lights had gone out or because the landscape had been too hostile to allow the people who lived there to build. It was dark because they had, quite sensibly, left it all alone, allowing Australia to find its own equilibrium.

I didn't know what that equilibrium was going to look like, but I was starting to believe that whatever it was, it would be magnificent.

3.

Contrary to all logical outcomes of our flight, I fell asleep somewhere between Adelaide and Nullarbor, with my cheek pressed up against the cold surface of the window and Jack no doubt laughing at me from the other side of the cabin. The plane jumped and shuddered as it touched down on the runway, and I jerked awake, grabbing for something that would keep me from toppling out of my seat.

Now I could *see* Jack laughing at me. "You're wearing a seat belt, mate," he shouted, and either the plane's engines were quieter now that we were on the ground or he had decided that this particular bit of mockery was important enough to be worth scraping his throat over. "I don't know how they work in England, but here in Australia, they keep you in your seat even when we attack the runway."

"You boys okay back there?" Olivia's shout was followed by her blue-topped head appearing around the side of the copilot's seat, a wide grin on her face. "Hey, it doesn't even smell like sick! Gold star for both of you."

"Yes, it's truly a banner day when I can be applauded for not vomiting all over everything," I said dryly, pushing my hair away from my eyes. My campaign to sleep my way across Australia wasn't making me any less tired, but it was certainly making me more irritable. "What happens now?"

"Refueling stop," said Olivia. "Juliet hooks the plane up to a pump while we run inside for coffee—or tea, since you're incurably British—and sandwiches. And a facilities break. Mustn't burst our bladders between here and Dongara. After all, we might need them later."

"Oh, God, I really am in Hell," I moaned, and rubbed my face. Still, the prospect of tea was enough to make me check my clothes to be sure that they were presentable, and when Juliet finally killed the engine, I was ready to go.

"Safe to take your belt off now," Jack said, unfastening his own seat belt and stretching as much as the plane's cramped quarters allowed. He didn't try to stand. I undid the buckle but stayed where I was, assuming that he must have some reason for his immobility.

That reason emerged from the cockpit a moment later, as Juliet unfolded her long limbs and crawled around the back of her seat like an outsized spider, her sunglass-covered gaze flicking first to Jack and then to me. Her lips firmed into a disapproving line.

"At least you had the sense to stay seated until I told you otherwise," she sniffed. "You are now free to deplane."

"Cheers, Julie," said Jack, and rose, following her out of the plane.

I remained where I was until Olivia climbed into the back. She gave me a curious look.

"You all right, boss?"

"I'm fine. I just wanted to ask you something about our esteemed pilot, and it seemed best to avoid attracting her attention if possible."

"Ah, you're wondering about her"—Olivia made a tapping motion on the air in front of her eye—"aren't you?"

"Yes, and now I'm also wondering why you didn't want to say the word."

"More fun this way." Olivia shrugged, continuing toward the open door. "She has retinal Kellis-Amberlee. Bright lights hurt her eyes. She takes the glasses off when she's actually flying the plane, unless it's daylight, and then she keeps them on."

"I wasn't aware that people with retinal Kellis-Amberlee could have pilot's licenses."

"Maybe not where you're from, but this is Australia." For a brief moment, Olivia's gaze turned disapproving. "Stop trying to judge us based on what you know, and try judging on what's actually around you. You might be surprised by how many things we don't do the way you'd expect but that turn out to work just fine all the same. Think about it, won't you?"

Then she was gone out the open door of the plane, leaving me to either follow her or sit alone in the dark with my thoughts. I followed her.

The Dongara airfield was slightly larger than the field we'd left from, which made sense; I wasn't sure airfields could get much smaller than the one in Adelaide. Jack was already most of the way to a long, brightly lit building at the edge of the tarmac, and Olivia was running after him. Neither of them seemed particularly interested in waiting for me. I slung my laptop bag over my shoulder and trudged after them, taking my time about things, trying to get a new view on this place that I was struggling to figure out.

It wasn't that Australia wasn't England: I'd been expecting that. It was that Australia prided itself so aggressively on being *Australian*, but there wasn't a book of rules or a checklist that would tell me exactly what that *meant*. Did it mean allowing women with potentially severe vision problems to pilot aircraft? Did it mean open-air picnics and penalizing people for shooting infected wildlife? Because if those things signified "Australian," then I was having a very Australian day.

The sky above me was black, peppered with unfamiliar stars. I was out of my home hemisphere, and I was increasingly coming to feel like I was out of my depth—and we hadn't even managed to reach the fence yet. Who knew how bad things were going to get once we actually made it to our destination?

In the distance behind me, Juliet was swearing loudly and enthusiastically at the fuel pump she had connected to our plane. I smiled a little and picked up the pace. Maybe the trouble was that I was looking too hard for definitions. After all, certain danger, stupid risks, and window dressing were very familiar to me, back in *my* native habitat: the news. As long as I remembered that, maybe I'd be fine.

Jack and Olivia were inside the brightly lit building, swiping their credit cards through vending machines and filling their pockets with crisps and sandwiches. Olivia looked over and grinned when the door opened.

"Hey," she said. "We got you a tea and a packet of dreadful-looking crisps that said they were authentic London-style, and you'll have to tell us whether that means anything beyond 'they've put an echidna on the package.' It's on the counter there."

"Thank you," I said, and walked over to the indicated counter. "That's not an echidna. It's a hedgehog."

"Ah. They sound more British already." Olivia turned back to the vending machine that she'd been looting one candy bar at a time. "Drink up and hit the head if you need it. We'll only be on the ground for about twenty minutes, and then it's off to our final destination."

"Ready to see the fence?" asked Jack.

"Honestly, I'm just hoping that I'll be able to stay *awake* when we get to the fence." My tea was hot, strong, and cheap, which was an acceptable set of modifiers. I dumped in a packet of powdered creamer, stirred it twice with the swizzle stick, and took a gulp before saying, "This may seem like a foolish question, but honestly, I've reached the point of assuming nothing. Are we staying in a hotel, or with some local friends of yours, when we get to the fence?"

"Fuck, no," said Jack. "We're camping."

There was a momentary silence in the building, broken only by the low buzz of the vending machines. Then, as if they had synchronized their watches before the conversation started, Jack and Olivia burst out laughing.

"Oh, *man*," said Jack. "I wish you could have seen your *face*. That was fantastic. Olive, did you get that on camera? Please tell me you got that on camera."

"I got that on camera," said Olivia serenely, as she reached up to peel what I'd taken for a round plastic sticker off the front of the vending machine. She tucked it into her pocket as she turned back to me, an almost feral smile on her lips. "Nothing like photographic proof of the terror that is Australia to really spice up a report, eh?"

"I hate you both and hope that you are devoured by whatever nasty form of native wildlife is endemic to this area," I said without rancor, taking another sip of my tea. Working with journalists for as long as I have has left me rather inured to pranks. You can't get too upset when they pull this sort of thing; it only encourages them. Some people will take any degree of encouragement as justification for launching an all-out war, which is why I simply stood there and drank my tea like a grown-up, rather than throwing my crisps at them.

Jack looked disappointed. "You could at least pretend to play along," he said in a chastising tone.

"Not to belittle your fabulous pranking skills—good incorporation of my expectations and your regional knowledge, by the way; if you were being graded, I'd give you extra marks for that—but I used to get pranked by Dave Novakowski and Buffy Meissonier. You'd need to work on my weak spots literally for years before you could break through the mental scar tissue they left behind them." Buffy had been an original member of After the End Times, and Dave had come on not long after the site launched. I missed them both desperately, and spending time with Jack and Olivia was actually making me miss them more. They weren't the same people, of course—not even close—but there were similarities.

"I'll get you somehow," said Jack. "Just you wait and see."

"I look forward to that," I said, and finished off my tea before tucking the crisps into my pocket and moving to make my own examination of the vending machines. My little spat with Olivia seemed to have been forgotten, or at least forgiven; she smiled at me and stepped to the side, allowing me to study the assortment of candy bars and crisps, all of them local brands. I didn't recognize any of them, although the components were familiar—I suppose chocolate and caramel are the same all over the world. I swiped my credit card and selected five numbers at random from the menu. Whatever I got, it would be interesting if nothing else.

We were stuffing our pockets with our heavily preserved goodies when the clack of boot heels on the linoleum caused us to straighten and turn. Juliet was standing just inside the door, sunglasses firmly in place, disapproving frown turned in our direction.

"We're fueled and ready to fly," she said. "Take care of your business and be back in the plane in five minutes, or we leave without you." This said, she turned, pushed the door open and went striding across the tarmac.

"Oh, yeah," drawled Olivia broadly. "She's *totally* forgiven you for the divorce, Jacky-Jack. That is a woman with no issues whatsoever."

Jack snorted.

4.

A little prying while we used the bathroom and hustled back to the plane revealed the rest of the story, or at least the bones of it: Jack and Juliet had been married for five years, long enough for her to become an Australian citizen and no longer need to worry about deportation. She felt that one of them having a suicidally dangerous job was sufficient and wanted him to retire from blogging, preferably before something ate him. He had married her in part because he liked having a wife who was as much of a thrill seeker as he was. They parted amicably, but with some resentment, mostly on her side.

"And we're riding about the country in a plane that she's flying because...?" I asked, as we approached the Cessna. Juliet was like a ghost flitting through the dark around the plane, verifying that everything was in the proper position for our impending takeoff.

"No one better in the sky," said Jack, with an almost wistful grin. He put on a burst of speed, moving himself out of conversational range.

"I'll never understand monogamous people," said Olivia cheerfully. "It's so much easier to settle a debate when you have someone to mediate."

"I yield to your superior experience," I said.

We had reached the Cessna. Juliet shot me a disapproving look—not really a surprise, as that seemed to be her default facial expression—and moved to climb into the pilot's seat, leaving the rest of us with no real choice but to follow. This time, Jack took the copilot's seat, leaving Olivia in the back with me. I wasn't sure whether that was a good thing or not. I didn't have the chance to ask; the engine roared to life, and any chance of a normal discussion died in the ensuing din. We all clapped our headphones on to save our hearing, dulling the sound of the engines to a bearable roar. In a matter of minutes, we were thundering down the runway like we were making a bet with God: takeoff or death.

This time, the laws of physics voted in our favor, and we rose, only jerking slightly, into the waiting nighttime sky.

The noise in the plane didn't go down by much just because we were in the air. I glanced to Olivia and saw that she had produced a pair of noise-canceling headphones substantially more sophisticated than the plane's default equipment, clamping them over her ears to block out the sound of the engines.

Conversation was out. There wasn't much to do, beyond going back to sleep or finishing my reading, and so I voted for the option that came with less unconsciousness.

The fence allowed a détente between the people who would happily have slaughtered every living thing in Australia for the sake of saving human lives and the people who were responsible for the "shoot a koala, go to jail" legislation that had so puzzled me earlier. Locking the infected animals behind the fence allowed them to live without becoming a danger to humanity. My documentation included several pages listing the circumstances under which it was acceptable to shoot or tranquilize an infected animal contained by the fence; these included things like "there were too many of them and they posed a structural danger," "we needed to cull the big males from the mob," and "breeding."

That last one stopped me for a moment. I ran a search on the document, finally finding a half page of text that detailed the ongoing efforts to maintain the kangaroo population through controlled breeding. Infected males were likely to kill females, rather than breeding with them, and joeys were constantly in danger from infected individuals of both sexes—although female kangaroos had proven surprisingly unwilling to eat joeys who were still in the pouch, possibly because their mental acuity had dwindled to the point where they could no longer tell their infants apart from their own bodies. Even the infected did not indulge in auto-cannibalism. So instead of trusting everything to nature, the Australian Wildlife Department would sometimes go to the fence, tranquilize male kangaroos, and take sperm samples for later use.

"This continent," I said, shaking my head, and continued to read.

The fence was paid for on both a national and local level: Taxes handled most of the maintenance, while the towns that remained along its length took care of any unexpected expenses. Surprisingly, no one seemed to begrudge the cost, or at least no one had openly complained; the official records listed the entire project as having a 97% approval rate, and the 3% who disapproved did so only because they felt that the fence needed to be larger in some way, either height, length, or both. No one said, "Stop taking our money." A small but measurable percentage said, "Take more of it."

There had been five deaths connected to animals which were supposedly contained by the fence since it was completed. Four of them had been ruled the result of human error, either people intentionally antagonizing the infected creatures or getting too close to the fence itself, believing that its protection would somehow render them invulnerable. It didn't. Only one of those five deaths had led to an actual outbreak in the human population, and I was almost expecting to read that the outbreak had been handled by shuttling the infected humans into the preserve on the other side of the fence. Thankfully for my ability to cope with Australia, that wasn't the case. The infected humans had been mercifully shot, just like they were everywhere else in the world, save for a few who had already gone on record as being willing to donate their bodies to science. All told, fewer than fifty people were involved in the outbreak.

It was a safety record that would have been impressive in a business park, and was virtually unbelievable when applied to a multimile construction project that seemed to have so many points of possible failure. Something was very strange here.

I was still pondering that strangeness, and what it might mean, when jet lag claimed me for the final time, and the world slipped away.

5.

"You *do* sleep like it's your only real hobby." Olivia's voice was cheerful, loud, and most of all, undistorted by the roar of the plane's engines: We were back on the ground. I opened my eyes to discover that we were virtually nose to nose. She grinned. "You slept through landing. I was a little bit afraid that you had actually shuffled off this mortal coil in midair, and we were going to have to try explaining that to the rest of the site."

"If Australia frightened me to death that easily, you would certainly have something new to add to your national mystique," I said dryly, and yawned, stretching. "Where are we now?"

"Dongara," said Jack. "We're here."

Those three words were like a slap to the face. I sat up straight, feeling more awake than I had since crossing the Pacific Ocean. "We're here?"

"Well, we're here for a generous definition of 'here,' since we've got about an hour's drive between us and the rabbit-proof fence, but yeah, we're here." Jack slipped past me and out the Cessna's open door. "Come on, mate. This is not a drill, and it's time we got this story started."

"Maybe it'll be enough to keep you awake, and won't that be a nice change?" Olivia patted me on the shoulder as she exited the plane, her bag and the cooler we had carried all the way from Melbourne in her hands. I hastily unbuckled my belt and followed her out to the tarmac.

Dongara by night looked much like everything else I'd seen since the sun set on Australia: large, ringed in unfamiliar trees, and very, very dark. The sky seemed to hold more stars than our galaxy could possibly contain, the lack of light pollution causing them to stand out like brands against the sky. I stepped clear of the plane door and tilted my head back, openly gawking at the unfamiliar brush-stroke gleam of the Milky Way. Almost as an afterthought, I pulled out my camera and took a few quick pictures. They wouldn't be studio quality, but they'd be enough to carry the impression of this incredible sky, which might as well have hung above a world where humanity had never existed at all.

"Jack?" said Olivia.

"Getting the car," the amiable Irwin replied, and went jogging away across the pavement, heading toward another of those long, low buildings that seemed to be standard issue for the local airfields. This one wasn't lit, which probably accounted at least a little for that incredible sky.

"Unmanned field," said Olivia, following the direction of my gaze. "Most of our little airfields have staff to keep the tourists from doing anything stupid, like trying to go bush, but this is Dongara. There's a proper airport to draw away the lookie-loos, and they actually encourage tourists to come see the fence. The safe stretches of it, that is."

"There are safe stretches?"

"Well, there are *safer* stretches," she said with a shrug. "No trees, no cover for whatever's on the other side of the fence, terrain the roos don't like as much. Still not a good idea to be sticking your fingers through or anything, but you're not as likely to get munched there."

"That's not where we're going, is it?"

Olivia grinned. "Nowhere close."

There was a rattle from the direction of the plane as Juliet hopped down, followed by the slam of the Cessna's door. I turned to see her stalking toward us, a clipboard in her hand. She thrust it at Olivia, ignoring me completely. Olivia, who had apparently been through this drill before, took the clipboard, produced a pen from somewhere inside her shirt, and began signing various places on the paperwork.

Speaking of which... "Physical paperwork?" I asked, directing my question toward Juliet. "What's the reasoning behind that? Every airfield I know of in Europe and North America has gone completely paperless."

"You're not in Europe or North America," said Juliet, biting off each word like it had somehow personally offended her. "Paper survives a crash, as long as it doesn't catch fire. I lock the flight info and the passenger manifests in a special box before takeoff. They stay there until we're on the ground. Anything goes wrong, the paper can tell authorities who was on the plane, where I took them, and where the outbreak may have started."

"But the plane's systems—"

"Crash hard enough, maybe they don't make it. I've got a black box. I'm not stupid. I just believe in backups." Juliet took the clipboard briskly back from Olivia. "I'll be back to pick you up in three days, assuming you idiots are still alive. If you're not, I'll bill your estate."

"Zane will be thrilled to pay you after he finishes organizing my memorial," said Olivia. She sounded like she meant it. "Where are you overnighting?"

"Jack said he'd give me a ride into town." Juliet somehow managed to make it sound like an imposition. "I have a room at the hotel, same as you."

"Then we'll see you at breakfast," said Olivia.

This was sounding increasingly like a bad idea. I just couldn't think of a polite way to suggest that perhaps inviting the irritable pilot who was supposed to get us home would be a bad idea.

Jack's return saved me from needing to put much thought into dissuading Juliet. He came rolling down the tarmac in an open-top Jeep of the variety popular with Irwins all over the world, waving enthusiastically as he drew closer. The vehicle would provide us with no protection during an outbreak, but it was fast, and it could handle any terrain that we were likely to throw at it. "Hey, you lot," he shouted, as he pulled up beside us and killed the engine. "Who wants to get to the hotel and take a shower?"

"Everyone," said Olivia, and swung herself up into the front passenger seat before I could say anything about seating arrangements.

"Er..." I began, and turned to see Juliet eyeing me, expression unreadable. I sighed. "Right," I said, and climbed into the back of the Jeep. Juliet clambered in next to me, compacting herself with the ease of long practice. It took me a little more time to get settled. Jack didn't wait; as soon as our butts hit the seats, he was off and rolling, and I got to enjoy the unnerving sensation of riding in a moving Jeep without having a seat belt on.

"Are you trying to kill us?" I asked, fumbling my belt into place. "I ask mostly out of curiosity, but also from a small measure of, 'What the bloody hell do you think you're doing?' "

"Relax," Jack called back. "We're perfectly safe." He hit the gas, cutting off further discussion as we accelerated, replacing human voices with the sound of the wind.

The airfield terminated in a familiar sight: a vehicular airlock. Jack pulled up in front of it and leaned out of the car far enough to address the nearby speaker.

"Four," he said. "Travel permits originating in Adelaide."

There was a beeping sound, and the airlock's interior door slid open. Jack tapped the gas. We rolled forward into the chamber, where he stopped the Jeep again. I twisted to look over my shoulder, watching the door close behind us. We were trapped in a chain-link cage, and unless we passed the test that was about to be offered to us, we would die in here. I took note of the construction: Unlike some more sophisticated airlocks, which could isolate passengers, this one took the classic "all or nothing" approach. We would all pass, or none of us would.

There was something comforting about that, and I chuckled to myself as the test units rose out of the ground to the sides of the car, one for each of us, their familiar stainless-steel faces gleaming in the back-wash from our headlights. Olivia looked over her shoulder and blinked at me as she slapped her hand down on the nearest unit.

"Something funny?"

"Just thinking about how much easier it would have been to travel with the Masons if this had been the American standard while I was over there." I pressed my palm down against my own designated unit. "They always hated being tested separately."

"There are airfields that offer that as an option, but I'm not much for survivor's guilt," said Jack. "If someone's going to turn, they can take me with them. Leave one last awesome report for the site, get a few rating points after I die."

It took everything I had to swallow my first response. Jack was an Irwin; they have a certain innate cockiness that is necessary to do the job properly, and part of that is laughing at death. From what I remembered about his file, he had never lost anyone particularly close to him. A few acquaintances and friends among the Irwin community, but that sort of attrition came with the territory. He didn't understand what he was saying, because he *couldn't* understand what he was saying. He had no frame of reference.

That didn't stop me from wanting to shout at him about how dying was never that simple, and how sometimes in our line of work, survivor's guilt is not only inevitable, it's one of the best outcomes you can hope for. I swallowed my anger and waited until the light on the side of my test unit turned green, signaling that I had once again evaded infection. It wasn't a surprise—there had been no real opportunities for exposure between Adelaide and Dongara—but it was still nice to have the confirmation. I withdrew my hand and waited.

Jack and Olivia both got clean results within seconds of me. Juliet took longer, which was normal; most standard test units are confused by reservoir conditions, which represent a colony of live Kellis-Amberlee inside what is otherwise an uninfected host. Juliet was medically already a little bit zombie, and would be every day of her life.

It sounded scarier than it was. Reservoir conditions might well hold the key to eventually defeating our ongoing zombie apocalypse. They were the result of the immune system figuring out a method of dealing with the Kellis-Amberlee virus, and under the right circumstances, they could result in spontaneous remission of amplification—in short, they could enable someone who had become a zombie to recover and become human again. The science of it all was beyond me, but I had spoken to quite a few doctors and researchers, and they all said the same thing: Eventually, reservoir conditions were going to save the world. In the meantime, people who had them would have to deal with recalcitrant testing units and the occasional unpleasant side effect, like Juliet's sunglasses.

Finally, the light on her unit flashed green, and she pulled her hand away. The door at the front of the airlock unlatched, sliding open with a surprising speed. It was like the airfield wanted us to leave before we could possibly require another blood test. Jack obliged, slamming his foot down on the gas so hard that the Jeep practically leapt forward and onto the road outside the airlock. Olivia whooped. Juliet looked disapproving. I groaned, confident that the wind would whip the sound away.

The road we were rocketing down at a frankly unsafe speed was about as wide as the roads back home in England, which made it a footpath by American standards. Trees encroached on all sides, mostly eucalyptus, but some that I couldn't identify before we had blazed past them. Given the darkness and the fact that I barely knew what anything in Australia was, I probably couldn't have identified them if we'd stopped and taken our time.

Eyes would occasionally appear in the tree line, reflecting back the headlights and causing my pulse to race. It didn't matter that everyone who actually lived here had assured me that nothing large enough to be dangerous was going to loom out of the dark and attack the vehicle. Humans are infinitely adaptable organisms, but *people* are products of their environments, and I was a child of London, of safe, narrow streets and no animals larger than stray cats and the occasional fox. We were *outside.* Outside, where the *animals* lived. No matter how open-minded I tried to be, no matter how much I tried to fit myself into my environment, there was nothing that could get me past that reality.

Sharing the backseat with Juliet didn't help, sadly. I turned to her, looking for some reassurance that we weren't all about to die, and found her staring fixedly forward, only the wind-whipped cloud of her hair betraying the fact that she was actually in a moving vehicle. I might as well have been riding next to a mannequin, one that had been sculpted to look like it was annoyed by everything around it. She didn't seem to be frozen in fear—which was a reaction I would entirely have understood. She just had better things to do than interacting with the people around her.

It was hard to believe that she and Jack had ever been married, or that the marriage could ever have been more than one of immigration and convenience. The world never loses the capacity to surprise me.

I was starting to relax, purely because it's impossible to maintain a state of constant terror forever, when the Jeep came screeching to a halt. I caught myself against the back of Jack's seat. Juliet didn't move.

"Look!" Olivia sounded excited, like she was offering me an opportunity beyond all measure. "In the road!"

Australia might be scaring the sense out of me, but I was still a Newsie, and when someone told me to look, my first instinct was to see what could possibly be so interesting. I leaned forward enough to see around the seats.

A small kangaroo was standing in the middle of the road. Its head was up, and its large, cupped ears were swiveling as it analyzed the sounds of the night around it, trying to make a decision about where it was going to go next. I froze, quite unable to speak. I'd seen pictures, of course, but pictures never quite capture the full reality of a thing.

In pictures, kangaroos were ridiculous animals. Their feet were too large and their forelimbs were too small, their ears were out of proportion with everything, and their tails made sense from an engineering standpoint, but not from any other perspective. In reality, they were something else altogether. The animal in front of us was as elegantly designed as any other creature, and its uniqueness made that elegance all the harder to ignore.

Finally, the kangaroo came to a conclusion about the Jeep. It shook its head, ears flapping, and hopped off into the dark by the side of the road. Jack started the engine back up.

"Swamp wallaby," he said. "Cheeky buggers, especially around here. They don't have anything to be afraid of, except maybe for becoming roadkill, and a wallaby that's been killed on the highway never gets to go home and pass the fear on to its friends and relatives."

I frowned, sinking back into my seat as we resumed rolling down the road. "I thought that was a kangaroo."

"Wallabies are kangaroos, and kangaroos are wallabies," said Juliet, surprising me. I hadn't been expecting her to speak to us again, now that we weren't her passengers. "The European explorers who 'discovered' Australia—because obviously no one who lived here ever noticed that they had a continent under their feet—didn't realize how many shapes and sizes kangaroos could come in, and so they split them into two different types of animal. Biology didn't give a fuck what the explorers thought, and when science eventually caught up to the rest of the program, we realized what the Australian natives had already known and started classifying them all as kangaroos."

"But it's hard to get people to change what they call something, hence that being a swamp wallaby even though everyone here knew that it was a kangaroo," said Olivia. "Even you. Your eyes said 'kangaroo,' and so you identified it correctly."

"We usually split them by size, for convenience' sake," said Jack, who apparently felt that he was being left out of the Australian nature hour. "Small ones are wallabies, medium ones are wallaroos, and big ones are kangaroos."

"Because this wasn't complicated enough to start with," I grumbled.

Jack laughed and sped up, although I was relieved to see that he didn't resume his previous breakneck hurtle down the road. Seeing a swamp wallaby had been interesting and a little magical, like I was glimpsing something impossible. I didn't feel like going through a full decontamination cycle because that same impossible thing had been splattered across the front bumper.

It was dark enough on the road between the airfield and the small town that had sprung up next to the fence that it was almost shocking when we came around a curve in the road and found ourselves confronted with a streetlight. It was positioned just outside a closed gate, and three people wearing not remotely enough protective gear were standing in the circle of its light with rifles in their hands, chatting amiably among themselves. There was a small guard station, which was presumably where these three were meant to be sitting, keeping an eye on the road. One of them was smoking a cigarette, calling to mind countless headlines about wildfires in Australia. None of them seemed perturbed by our approach. They didn't even break out of their conversational huddle until Jack pulled up in front of the fence and cut the engine.

"Four for the fence," he called toward the guards. "Anytime would be great, we'd like to get there before the roos stop their assault for the night."

I winced. Being rude to guards is never a good idea where I come from. These four seemed to take it in stride, however, or maybe they were just bored and appreciated having something to do other than stand around waiting for the continent to eat them. The one with the cigarette dropped it on the pavement, grinding it out with the heel of her boot before casually walking over to the Jeep. She eyed us with practiced blandness.

"Travel visas and photo IDs," she said.

"Here you go." Jack handed her a folder, indicating me and Olivia. "This should cover the three of us. Jules, you got your travel clearance for the nice woman with the very large gun?"

"I'm not an idiot," said Juliet, and produced a laminated folder from inside her shirt, offering it to the guard, who took it without a word. She tucked our paperwork and Juliet's under her arm as she turned and walked back to the guard station. The other three guards on duty looked at us with mild curiosity, like they weren't sure whether to hope we'd do something interesting, or whether to hope that we'd go away fast.

"What happens if our paperwork isn't in order?" I asked.

"They shoot us and throw our bodies over the fence," said Juliet flatly. "The infected wildlife has to eat *something*."

I turned to stare at her in open horror... and stopped, frowning. The corner of her mouth was twitching. It wasn't much, but one doesn't spend years associating with Georgia Mason, one of the most undemonstrative people on this planet, and not learn how to read subtle facial expressions.

"Interesting," I said. "Tell me, when did your infected adapt to eating meat that had been killed more than a few minutes previous? Or will they be shooting to wound and then throwing us over the fence while we're still bleeding out? That would make more sense. Seems a bit hard on the tourist trade, but I suppose a few deaths every now and then would be good for the 'welcome to Murderland' reputation you've worked so hard to build for yourselves."

Now it was Juliet's turn to stare at me. I raised an eyebrow—a trick I learned from Georgia Mason herself, back when I first started turning her dry sense of humor back on her.

"Well?" I asked. "I mean, I *am* a visiting journalist. Surely you wouldn't be making jokes in such incredibly poor taste, which means you must have been telling the truth, and I'm truly interested in understanding the methodology of my potential demise."

Juliet stared at me for a few more seconds before turning to Jack and asking, "Is he for real?"

"I haven't known him in realspace for that much longer than you have, but he's always like this online, so I'm going to guess that yeah, he's for real." Jack grinned. "I told you this was my boss. Did you think I was having you on?"

"I'm just pleased to see that you have a sense of humor," I said.

Juliet's head turned back toward me like it was on a swivel. "Really?" she said. "How do you know that I wasn't serious?"

"Australia still has a tourist trade," I replied.

Any further awkward banter was cut short by the return of the guard from before, now carrying a metal basket containing four blood testing units. "Your papers check out," she said. "Give me a clean blood test and you're good to head on through. If one of you fails, we'll hold the others for an hour to see whether they've been infected and then pass any clean survivors through."

"That's a surprisingly sensible approach to security," I said, taking a testing unit. "I'm very impressed, and whoever makes your policy should be commended."

The guard nodded. She looked faintly pleased, which was nice. It's always good to make the people with the rifles happy with you. "I'll pass that along to my commanding officer," she said. "Your travel papers said that your point of origin was London?"

"Heathrow," I confirmed, as she walked around the Jeep passing out testing units. "I'm here to do a story on the rabbit-proof fence."

"We're part of fence security here," she said, indicating her companions, who were once again mostly ignoring us. "If there's any problem, we're the ones who get mobilized to come in and take care of it."

"That must be a really interesting job," I said. "Would it be all right if I came back here and talked with you about it after we finished getting ourselves situated?"

The guard looked pleased. "Sure thing," she said. "If I've gone off duty, just ask for Rachel, and someone will come and shake me out of whatever tree I've crawled into."

"She's half koala," shouted one of the other guards. Maybe they'd been paying more attention than I thought. Relaxed and exposed as this station was, it was still an integral part of the security system protecting the longest contiguous fence in the world. They couldn't afford to have any weak links in their protection or the whole thing could come tumbling down.

Rachel shot a quick glare at her coworker before holding out her basket. I looked at her blankly, and she nodded toward the test unit I was holding. "You're clean," she said. "I need that back so I can file it."

I looked down. The unit had indeed lit up green, reacting to the blood sample it had taken from my finger. I didn't even remember breaking the seal.

"Bloody jet lag," I muttered, and dropped the test into the basket. "Thank you."

"Welcome to the fence," she replied, and repeated her circuit around the car, collecting the used test units from the rest of the group. All of them showed clean, which was unsurprising; unless swamp wallabies were infection vectors unmatched in the rest of the world, we hadn't been exposed.

The thought sobered me, and I was quiet as Rachel waved good-bye and signaled for one of the other guards to open the gate and let us through. Australia was geographically isolated enough that it did not yet have to worry about the genetically engineered mosquitoes created by the CDC as new vectors for the Kellis-Amberlee infection. They would probably get here eventually; mosquitoes are notoriously tricky when it comes to finding ways to invade new habitats. Only the fact that any plane that contained one of the tiny insect hitchhikers had a tendency to crash following the amplification of its passengers and crew had kept Australia safe so far.

This was a perfect climate for the modified mosquitoes, and unlike North America, which had its brutal winters to help it fight against the invasive pests, Australia would be virtually unprotected when that dreadful day arrived. I barely noticed when Jack restarted the engine and we drove forward, heading toward the fence at last.

The road curved, and as we came around it and the rabbit-proof fence came into view, I lost any ability to remain detached—or objective.

The road ran through a small town that wouldn't have been out of place in a photograph taken fifty years ago, if not for the metal shutters on the windows and the chain-link fences that surrounded each individual building. They were easily eight feet high, which would be enough to dissuade even the most persistent of human infected. All of them had double gates, and every gate I could see was standing open, as if an outbreak were less of a concern than not being able to go anywhere you wanted without hesitation. There were cars parked in front of the houses, and a few people stood on the sidewalks, talking about whatever it was that people who chose to live in an isolated part of Australia next to the world's largest zombie holding pen had to worry about.

I took all this in in an instant, making sweeping judgments that I was sure to regret later, as my journalist's mind insisted on sketching out the scene. We might have to flee at any moment, after all, when this ludicrous excuse for a secure fence came toppling over on our heads. If we were lucky, we might be able to make it out of the zone of infection before we became names on the Wall that commemorates all those who have died due to the Kellis-Amberlee virus.

The rabbit-proof fence was at least eighteen feet tall, topped in a triplicate row of electrified wire, with razor wire surrounding the base on both the interior and exterior sides. Floodlights illuminated the entire thing, bringing out every detail that I could possibly have wanted and quite a few that I didn't. Thick posts were driven into the ground every eight feet, and the chain link was doubled, with thick sheets of clear Plexiglas sandwiched between the layers. No fluid transfer could get through that fence, and any impact against the chain link would bend it against the Plexiglas, rather than causing it to bow inward on empty space. It was a marvel of engineering. It was a monument to human ingenuity both during and following the Rising. And it was currently under siege by a mob of at least twenty infected kangaroos.

The kangaroos moaned in an unearthly key that made the hair on the back of my neck stand on end, even as it threatened to turn my bowels to water. Every bite of food I'd eaten since arriving in Australia was threatening to make a return appearance. My questions about the coordination of zombie kangaroos were being answered as I watched: The great beasts were clearly infected, and it wasn't slowing them down a bit. In small groups, they pulled back from the fence and then bounded forward, their tails bobbing in an instinctive search for balance, before leaping into the air and flinging themselves against the chain link. Each time, they fell back to the ground, picked themselves up, and tried again.

Several humans stood inside the fence with rifles, watching the kangaroos attack, but none of them seemed particularly concerned. Even the man in the nearest sniper tower looked more interested in our car than he was in the mob of infected animals.

Jack stopped the car in the middle of the street, where we had an excellent view of the scene that was unfolding in front of us. "Well, here it is," he said, "the famous Australian rabbit-proof fence. Is it everything that you'd hoped that it would be?"

In that moment, I couldn't answer him. The words simply refused to come.

Part IV

In Which There Are Kangaroos Absolutely Everywhere, and No One Is Properly Upset About the Situation

Everyone belongs somewhere. Some of us are just lucky enough to figure out where it is while there's still time for us to find a way to get there. And once we arrive, we will never, ever leave.

—Juliet Seghers-Ward

There is nothing in this world as determined, or as terrifying, as an exile in search of a country.

—Mahir Gowda

1.

Our hotel, if you could call it that, was located on the very edge of the town. The room I was going to be sharing with Jack had a clear view of the fence and of the infected kangaroos that were still hurling themselves with mindless dedication against the barrier. The window was sound-proof glass, which was a small mercy; I would never have been able to sleep with their moans echoing in my ears.

The town had no name, according to both Olivia and the man who took my name and credit card at the hotel desk; it was part military out-post and part curiosity, and "the place by the fence" did more than enough to describe the place to anyone who had any business coming here. The only roads that actually connected the place to anything beyond the air-field were government controlled and strictly regulated.

"It's not that we don't approve of rooking tourists out of every dollar they're willing to dump into the local economy" was what Jack had said as he and I toted our equipment up the stairs to our room. "It's just that this part of the fence isn't a tourist attraction, you follow? It's a place you go when you have questions that need to be answered. No one should be posing for duck-lipped selfies with the plaque of the dead. It wouldn't be right."

"So why are we here?" I'd asked. I'd been asking myself that same question since we'd first come around the curve in the road and I'd seen, firsthand, that all those stories about Australia were not exaggerations. If anything, they had all been understating the case somewhat.

"Because you said you thought it would be interesting—and because it's about time that someone who doesn't *come* from here started to understand what's really *happening* out here. Not everything important happens in Europe or North America, mate. There's an awful lot of world that most people never seem to bother with."

Then he'd clapped me on the shoulder and gone off to help Juliet and Olivia with the last of the gear, leaving me standing in front of the window and watching the eerily silent spectacle of zombie kangaroos throwing themselves eternally against an unyielding obstacle.

"This is madness," I muttered. One of the kangaroos was struggling to get back to its feet; it appeared to have broken something in its latest impact, and it couldn't recover its balance. Another kangaroo kicked it as it bounded past on its own way to the fence. The downed kangaroo snapped its teeth at the retreating tail of the moving kangaroo. The motion was so characteristic to those infected with the Kellis-Amberlee virus that I didn't need to be on top of the action to recognize it.

Movement in the sniper tower drew my attention. A second man had joined the man already stationed there, and they were pointing to the fallen kangaroo, apparently deep in discussion about something. The first man raised his rifle to his shoulder. There was a faint jerk as the rifle's recoil traveled down his arm. I glanced back toward the fallen kangaroo. It wasn't trying to get up anymore. It wasn't doing anything anymore, just lying there motionless. I couldn't see the bullet hole, but I knew that it must have been a headshot that killed the beast. With the infected, nothing else is a guarantee.

"Oi!" Jack's voice came from the doorway behind me. I turned to see him standing there, one hand raised in a beckoning gesture. "Come on, then, the show's about to start, you wouldn't want to miss it. Your journalistic integrity would never forgive you."

"Show . . . ?" I asked, walking toward him.

"You see that big buck go down?" Jack raised one hand in a shooting gesture, sending an imaginary bullet at the wall before he turned and started down the stairs, clearly trusting me to follow. "They can't have it next to the fence. It's unsanitary, and it's not safe. Don't want anything giving the others the extra height, right? It's a tall fence, but a little teamwork or leverage and *bang-bang*, we're looking at a hot time in the old town tonight."

"Yes, thank you for that charming imagery, I've slept quite enough since arriving in Australia," I said, suppressing a shudder. "What are they going to do?"

"That's the show!" We had reached the bottom of the stairs. It was somehow no surprise to find Olivia and Juliet waiting for us in the closet-sized square that was supposedly the lobby. Jack brushed past them, apparently determined to lead the way.

I fell into step next to Olivia. "Would you please explain to me what's going on?"

"Kangaroos are protected by the Australian Wildlife Conservation Act of 2019," said Olivia. "They used to be so endemic that they were considered pests in some areas, but these days, they're on the verge of extinction almost everywhere outside the fence, even though it's against the law to shoot them for anything other than self-preservation, and even that can turn sketchy if there's no one to back up your claims."

"All right," I said slowly. "What does that have to do with anything?"

"A proper grounding in the subject is necessary for proper appreciation of the facts," said Olivia, with a lilting cruelty that I recognized quite well, having heard it at one point or another from virtually every Newsie that I had ever met. "Look, that big buck was injured when he fell. He was never going to get back up, and he presented a clear and present danger to both the town and the rest of his mob—his body created higher ground, and that's one thing we don't want the kangaroos to have. That meant the guards were within their rights to nullify the threat by shooting him. That *doesn't* mean that they can open fire on the rest of the mob."

The pieces finally came together in a single burst of glorious illogic. "They're going to draw the kangaroos away from the fence somehow? But *how*?"

Olivia beamed. "That's the show. Come on."

2.

Jack wasn't the only one who'd been excited by the promise of a little action: What seemed like it must be the entire population of the tiny nameless town had turned out for the event, lining the fence for at least fifty yards in all directions. Jack grabbed my hand and plowed into the crowd, shouting, "Journalists coming through! Visiting journalist coming through! Very important, make a hole!" Much to my surprise, people actually made a hole. Then again, they had presumably seen this before.

We wound up standing less than two feet from the fence, with Olivia and Juliet pressed up right behind us. This close, I could see every feature of the kangaroos as they attacked the chain link. Some had broken jaws or forelimbs, the bones shattered by their impacts with the unyielding metal. One had a gash across its chest that was teeming with maggots, presumably feeding on some deeper vein of infection. My stomach turned over. I wasn't particularly fond of large animals, but I couldn't understand how this type of existence was any kinder than killing them all.

A rumble from somewhere off to the right pulled my attention toward it, although the kangaroos didn't react. The infected only hunt by sound when they don't have a choice; sight and smell are much preferred, as they provide a clearer impression of the prey. Squinting, I could just make out what appeared to be a section of fence swinging into view. Then I realized what that meant, and I felt my blood go cold.

Someone was opening a gate in the rabbit-proof fence.

We were too far away to see the exact mechanics of the gate-opening process, but that proved not to matter as Olivia shoved herself forward, pressing close enough that I could hear her when she said, "They open the interior layer of the fence and insert extenders to allow them to form a small corral. Then the Plexiglas is withdrawn across just that segment, and the exterior layer of the fence opens. There's about a five-second period during which the security of the fence itself is compromised, before the interior and exterior layers connect and lock into place. The infected kangaroos have a response time of approximately eight seconds."

"And how did you find this out?" I asked, still staring at the moving parts of the fence.

"The process used to take ten seconds." Olivia shrugged, her shoulder brushing against mine. "They sped it up."

"I see." A second gate opened, this one extending from the chain-link corral that had been constructed inside the fence proper. Five small, wooly lumps that looked like dirty clouds were thrust through before the gate closed again behind them.

"What in the world—"

"Those would be sheep, mate," said Jack. "They've got the Plexiglas back into position now. They can't close the corral until after the slaughter, but they're allowed to shoot anything that makes it inside. Everybody hopes they won't have to."

"Not everyone," spat a man I didn't know as he directed a brief, poisonous look at Jack. I frowned, making note of his face. I might need to track him down later to question him about the opinions of the rabbit-proof fence here in town. Stories are always better when they're not completely one-sided.

The sheep were far enough away that I couldn't hear them bleating. The kangaroos had no such limitations. One by one, the members of the mob stopped flinging themselves against the chain link and straightened to their full height, turning their heads toward what was about to be their dinner. They began to moan. That was all the warning we received before they hopped away, moving with daunting speed across the flat terrain. The sheep, sensing their impending doom, scattered. The kangaroos pursued. In a matter of seconds, the only kangaroo remaining at our stretch of fence was the big buck that had been gunned down by the snipers.

"Look to your right," murmured Olivia. I turned.

Another section of fence was opening.

This one was smaller, about the width of our Jeep. That seemed less important than the fact that it was closer, less than twenty yards away. A team of people swaddled in protective gear stepped through, their faces obscured by the helmets that they wore. Half of them were visibly armed. The other half carried an oversized stretcher.

"What are those idiots *doing*?" The words were judgmental and dangerously censorious of the local culture. They were also mine, escaping my lips before I could think better of them.

Olivia smirked in my direction. "It's nice to see that in the real world, you get spun up just like the rest of us. Those idiots, as you so kindly call them, are extracting the dead kangaroo from where it fell. They'll take it back to the research center—we have an appointment there tomorrow—for a necropsy, so that they can find out if there was anything really interesting about it before it died. Then they'll burn the remains to eliminate the risk of infection. Good stuff, don't you think?"

"They're *inside* the fence," I said. My mouth was so dry that it felt like I was at risk of amplification, and my heart was hammering against my ribs. The door they'd used to access the interior was still open. Sure, the kangaroo mob was distracted with the sheep, but how was that going to stop a solitary from realizing that there was another source of potential prey in their territory? It wasn't. All it would take was one moment of distraction...

That moment didn't come. Two of the guards stayed by the open door with their guns at the ready, waiting for something to come from deeper inside the fence and try for the opening. The others walked along the fence line until they came to the fallen kangaroo. Then, moving with the quick efficiency that comes only from long practice, they began the process of transferring the body onto the stretcher they had brought with them.

We were close enough to where the kangaroo had fallen that I could see every detail of the transfer process, even though the faces of the guards were barely blurs behind their protective masks. I glanced off to the left. The kangaroos were still pursuing the sheep, apparently single-minded enough that they hadn't bothered to look behind themselves since they bounded off. The guards inside the fence were working hard to minimize the amount of noise they made, and I realized with something like relief that the crowd I was a part of actually served a purpose: By standing outside the fence and generating the natural white noise of a group of uninfected humans, we were helping to mask the sound made by the guards.

Then one of them moved too quickly, and the butt end of the rifle strapped to his or her back scraped against the fence, making a horrible screeching noise. The guard straightened almost immediately, cutting the sound off, but it was too little, too late; several of the closer kangaroos had stopped bounding after the surviving sheep and were standing straight up, oversized ears swiveling madly as they strained toward the sound of prey.

"This should be interesting," said Jack. He didn't sound very concerned. I shot him a quick look and saw the lie in the corners of his eyes, where the skin was suddenly carved into deep wrinkles by the musculature beneath. He was as frightened of what was coming next as I was.

Three large kangaroos apparently decided that the sound was worth investigation. They turned fully and began to hop toward the group of guards, moving more slowly than they had when they ran after the sheep, but still fast enough that it would be only a matter of moments before they were on top of the small retrieval team. The guards had guns, and presumably they were authorized to use them under circumstances like this one. That didn't change the fact that gunfire would draw more kangaroos, and would turn a bad situation even worse.

"We're all going to die," I said philosophically. "The kangaroos are going to run roughshod over those poor guards, and then they're going to come charging straight through the open gate and strip the flesh off our bones. I'm going to die in Australia. My mother will be so... well, not proud—she won't be proud at all—but she'll certainly have something to tell everyone at my funeral."

"Calm down," said Jack. "We have protocols for situations like this one."

A gunshot rang out, sharp and dismayingly loud. One of the kangaroos that had been heading toward the guards toppled over, making a horrible keening noise that was both like and unlike the normal moans of the infected. It hurt to hear. The other kangaroos seemed to agree, because they stopped their pursuit of the men, falling on their wounded relation instead. What followed was a moment of horrible carnage that left blood splattered along the Plexiglas for at least eight feet of fence. The injured kangaroo kept keening almost until the end.

"Look!" Olivia elbowed me, pointing off to the right. I followed her finger to the gate in the fence, which was now securely closed. The guards were back on our side, carrying the dead kangaroo off toward the biological containment facility.

"They'll have to go in again later for the fresh one, but that can wait a bit," said Jack, sounding perplexed.

I paused, assessing his tone and comparing it to the scene that was still fresh in my mind. Then I glanced to both the nearest sniper towers, finding them empty. That was the final piece I needed to complete a most unpleasant puzzle, one which left me with a question I didn't want to ask, but needed to have answered:

"None of the guards fired that shot," I said. "Who did?"

Jack and Olivia exchanged a look across me, and then shook their heads in semi-unison.

"Your guess is as good as mine," said Jack.

3.

It was late, and we had all had a long day. After the crowd dispersed and the guards retook their places in the sniper towers, the four of us returned to our respective hotel rooms to try and get some sleep before the sun rose and brought a whole new host of problems with it. Jack was asleep virtually as soon as his head hit the pillow, filling our shared room with the deep, mellow sound of his snoring.

Unfortunately for me, I couldn't bring myself to join him in dreamland. Hours upon hours of jet lag–induced napping were finally catching up with me, and I found myself wide awake when I most wanted to be unconscious. The hotel had a decent wireless signal, and so I occupied myself for the better part of an hour with the inevitable daily business of the site. When I found myself deleting spam from the public forums—something that was normally reserved for junior moderators, and was certainly outside my job description—I closed my laptop and pushed it firmly away. If I wasn't going to get any sleep, I could find something better to do with myself.

Like look at the fence where the temporary corral had been constructed. That had to be an interesting piece of engineering, especially since the locals had been so calm about the whole process. Everyone I knew would have been far more upset about seeing their only protection from a mob of zombie kangaroos being breached. These people had treated it like a show, something to be enjoyed while it was happening and forgotten afterward. That mode of thought was alien to me. I needed to learn more.

Quietly, so as not to wake Jack, I retrieved my coat from the back of the door and shrugged it on before slipping out of the room and heading down the stairs to the empty lobby. There was a desk, but it was unmanned, and had been since our arrival; our keys had been waiting for us in an envelope beneath the blotter. I stepped outside, pausing to give my eyes a moment to adjust. There were streetlights, but they were brightest near the rabbit-proof fence, presumably to allow the locals to get some sleep.

The second kangaroo was gone, I noted, and the mob that had been attacking earlier had scattered, leaving the land on the other side of the fence deceptively calm and empty. I walked cautiously toward it, waiting for something to loom out of the tall grass and attack. Nothing moved.

I stopped when I was a few feet from the fence, studying the Plexiglas as I looked for the bloodstains that would mark the spot of the earlier attack. I couldn't find them. Whoever had removed the dead kangaroo's remains had taken the time to hose down the fence itself. I looked up at the nearest sniper tower and was somewhat relieved to see that it was currently manned by a pair of guards with rifles. I was less relieved to realize that one of them was watching me, and while he didn't have his rifle trained on me, there was something about his posture that implied he *could* be aiming at me with very little effort on his part.

"You shouldn't stare at the snipers," said Juliet blandly. "They're allowed to shoot humans with minimal paperwork, and some of them do."

"That's charming. Yes, I like this place better already." I turned. Our pilot was standing behind me, still fully clothed, sunglasses firmly in place over her eyes. "How do they keep those towers manned? I saw two of them empty earlier."

She shrugged. "They don't, always. Only one tower in three is manned most hours, and they rotate which it is."

I stared at her for a moment before pinching the bridge of my nose. "Of course. This is Australia. It would make too much sense for the towers to be manned all the time. Let's move on. What are you doing out here?"

"I don't sleep well when I'm this close to the fence," said Juliet. "Never have, never will. I know it's not dangerous—not the way all my training tells me it is—but that doesn't change the part where I'm sitting next to the world's largest zombie holding pen. It makes my flesh crawl."

"Ah." I glanced back to the fence, and the empty land beyond it, before returning my attention to Juliet. "You're from Canada, right?"

"I am," she said, with a nod. "My family's from Newfoundland, and I was born in Toronto, since they had to evacuate with everyone else during the Rising. I never liked the city much, and I didn't have the drive for the news or the social skills for the armed forces. So I went into aviation. Used to fly supply planes across Canada while I looked for something better."

"Australia was your 'something better'?"

For the first time since I'd met her, a small smile creased Juliet's lips. "Still is," she said. "This is the country I've been dreaming of since I was six years old. It's a lot like the stories my grandfather used to tell about Newfoundland."

What little I knew about Newfoundland described a frozen, rain-drenched stretch of land that had been abandoned during the Rising partially because the infrastructure to defend it simply wasn't there anymore. I looked at Juliet dubiously.

She shook her head. "I know, the climates are nothing alike, but I was going on stories, not real experience. A land so wild that it could swallow you up in an instant, and a sea that was like a story no one ever finished telling. That's what Granddad always said about Newfoundland. That no one could ever go there without saying, 'Oh, how green this land, oh, how blue this sea; I must have lived a very good life to be allowed to come to such a paradise.'" The faint smile slipped from her lips as she continued, "I signed up for a dating service that was meant to connect Australians with foreigners interested in immigration the day after he died."

"I'm sorry."

"Don't be. He missed his home, and I like to think that he made it back there in some form after he died." Juliet turned her attention to the fence. "One of our friends is back."

"Hmm?" I scanned the land behind the chain link, looking in vain for something that wasn't a clump of grass or scrubby tree. I was starting to think that Juliet had simply been trying to change the subject when what I had taken for a small hill took a single cautious hop forward. "Well, would you look at that."

"Immature red kangaroo," said Juliet. "Probably too small to have amplified yet, although it's hard to tell at this sort of distance."

"Are they afraid of people before they amplify?"

"I'm not the one to ask," she said. "I avoid them as much as I can, and they return the favor when I see them outside the fence. The noninfected tend to be skittish, and the infected... well, you can see why I'd try to keep out of their way."

"Yes," I agreed, and watched as the kangaroo made its way to the fence, where it bent forward and started digging in the grass with its forepaws. "They're herbivores, aren't they?"

"They are. I've done feeding runs past the fence a few times—fly out, dump a payload of fodder, fly back. It's safe as houses, but it still makes me nervous, so I only do it when I really need the money."

"Or when you're trying to convince yourself that you don't need any more excitement in your life," said Olivia. Somehow I wasn't surprised to hear her voice. She walked over and stood beside me. She was wearing a long blue nightgown with purple lace around the neckline, and no shoes. It was warm enough that she wasn't even shivering as she directed a grin across me to Juliet. "He misses you, you know. I bet you crazy kids could patch things up, especially since you've still got his name on your license and ID. He's the sort of bloke who takes that as a statement of undying love."

"Because I want to go through that whole stupid circus again? No, thank you." Juliet scowled at Olivia. "I have my plane, I have my work, and he has my blessing to go off and do whatever dumb-arse thing he wants to."

I couldn't help myself: I burst out laughing. Both women slowly turned to face me, Olivia openly staring, Juliet's lips narrowing into a hard line that probably meant she was trying to kill me with her eyes. That didn't stop the laughter. If anything, it made me laugh harder, bending almost double and clutching my stomach as I tried to make it stop.

"What's so funny?" asked Juliet.

"It's just... oh, God." I managed to get myself back under control and straightened, removing my glasses with one hand and wiping my eyes with the other. As I scrubbed the lenses against my shirt, I said, "You reminded me so much of some friends of mine just now that I felt like I was falling backward through time, that's all. Shaun and Georgia used to have arguments just like that about whether or not Georgia belonged in the field. I'm sorry. I didn't mean to insult you."

"Apology accepted," said Juliet, in a stiff tone that implied the exact opposite. She turned to Olivia. "He's your tourist. You keep an eye on him. I'm going back to bed." She spun on her heel and stalked away, heading back toward our hotel.

"Well, that went splendidly," I said, any urge to keep laughing dying. "Do you think she'll push me out of the plane while it's in flight, or will she land somewhere and abandon me to the native wildlife? I suppose either option would be fatal, so it's mostly a question of how merciful she wants to be."

"Aw, don't mind Julie," said Olivia. "She's just having a rough patch. She and Jack will sort things out before we're done here, you'll see."

I raised an eyebrow. "How can you be so sure?"

"She's not the only pilot who does this run is how," she said. "If Juliet didn't want to see her ex, she wouldn't have taken the charter."

"Ah." I looked back toward the fence. Our friend the kangaroo was still there, scrubbing about in the dirt. "How did they get the second kangaroo out?"

"Not a clue. Weren't we going to visit the biological containment facility tomorrow? They'll be able to answer any questions you ha—"

She was cut off midsyllable by the sound of a gunshot ringing out of nowhere. I flinched, looking to the sniper tower, and froze as I realized that they looked as confused and dismayed as I felt. They hadn't been responsible for firing that shot. I turned toward the other visible tower and saw the same confusion reflected in the body language of the distant guards. I didn't need to see their faces to know that they were not the shooters.

"Mahir, look," said Olivia, sounding horrified.

I turned, already half suspecting what I was about to see. The young kangaroo was no longer grubbing for roots among the grass near the fence. Instead, it was puddled in a heap of limp muscle and grayish fur, eyes still open and staring at nothing. There was a wound in the side of its neck, blood soaking through the fur and grass. The poor thing wouldn't be reviving from the Kellis-Amberlee virus. Not even a disease that raises the dead can get reanimate a body that hasn't got any blood in it.

The snipers hadn't been responsible for shooting the second kangaroo earlier, either. Someone was killing the kangaroos inside the fence, and although I was coming to understand Australia more with every moment that passed, I had no earthly idea *why*.

4.

The snipers eventually dispatched a guard to check me and Olivia for weapons—we were both armed, of course, but neither of us had fired a gun within the past twenty-four hours, something which a simple residue swab quickly confirmed—before sending us back to our hotel with strict instructions to stay indoors until the sun came up.

There was a time when I would have stormed back to my room,

prepared to write a scathing editorial about mismanagement of natural resources and poor security. Time has been kind to my temper, and has given me the ability to see when patience is the best possible answer to a bad situation. I went to my bed, crawled beneath the covers, and forced myself to be still. Given enough time, stillness would deepen into sleep, no matter how awake I was.

I don't know how long it took for that miraculous transition to occur, but my dreams were filled with kangaroos hurling themselves endlessly at a fence, and it was impossible to know in the dream whether the kangaroos were sick and trying to break down the fence to reach their prey, or whether they were fleeing from some greater danger. It was almost a relief when the sunlight struck my face and brought me, gasping and only half rested, back into the waking world.

Jack was standing over me, the curtain still grasped in the hand he had used to wrench it open. "Up you get, Sleeping Beauty," he said. "You must not have many hobbies, given how much time you spend passed out."

"I have a small child," I said, sitting up and yawning. "Sleep is a precious thing and should not be spurned when it's available to you. What time is it?"

"A little past eight," he said. "I've been up for an hour. Had my jog, had my shower, and the girls are getting breakfast on the table for us at the café down the block."

I frowned, reaching for my glasses. "You lost me somewhere in the middle of that sentence. Did they take over the kitchen of the café?"

"No, they're just putting in orders for all four of us. Juliet and I are going back to the airfield so I can help her with maintenance and refueling, and Olivia said that the two of you are going to visit the biological containment facility, which sounds like it should be nicely nonhazardous." Jack beamed beatifically. "I couldn't leave if there was a chance that you were going to do something exciting in my absence."

"Of course not," I said dryly. "Where's the shower?"

"Down the hall."

"Lovely. And where's the café?"

"Down the block. If you turn left when you step out the door, you can't possibly miss it."

"Even lovelier. I'll be there in fifteen minutes."

"Good on you. I'd be fast if I were you—there's a good chance I'll eat your potatoes if you're not there before I get bored." Jack winked before he turned and left the room.

"Irwins," I muttered, and moved to dig around in my suitcase. It's bad to make general statements about groups of people—there are always exceptions, and those exceptions are likely to be offended if they hear you generalizing about them—but every Irwin I'd ever met had been gifted with a tendency toward overacting even when the cameras were off, just in case someone was spying on them while they were going about their daily lives. Shaun Mason was the same way. So was Becks. It made sense, especially given their place in the blogging world, but it could get tiring.

The shower was unoccupied, which was a blessing, and the hot water was plentiful, which made up for the hotel soap, which seemed determined to remove the top three layers of my skin before I was finished bathing. To my surprise, there was no bleach cycle—just water. Feeling clean but slightly contaminated, I pulled my clothes on and made my way down the stairs to the still-empty lobby. There was no sign that anyone had been through there since our arrival. I paused to frown at the desk. It was starting to feel like we were being put up in a false hotel, rather than a real one; there should have been an irritated clerk, at the very least, someone to glower at us when we came and went at odd hours, and to demand clean blood tests before allowing us to have any extra towels.

"Now who's trying to turn Australia into a theme park?" I muttered, chuckling to myself as I stepped out of the hotel and got my first view of the nameless little town in the daylight.

It wasn't much more impressive than it had been at night—darkness doesn't change details like size very much, not when it's beaten back by streetlights and crowds—but the overall maintenance of the place was much more apparent. The buildings were painted in neutral colors not because the paint had faded from something brighter, but because neutrals had been chosen from the beginning. The individually fenced yards were still somewhat jarring, and yet they were offset by more visibly secure front doors, and by what looked like self-latching hinge mechanisms on the gates. One press of a button and those houses could lock down as tight as anything else in the world.

The sidewalks were mostly deserted, although a few people wandered by as I studied my surroundings. They were split roughly down the middle between civilians and guards. Only the guards openly carried rifles, although some of the civilians had small handguns or pistols. In the event of an uprising, the civilian population would inevitably lose.

With this cheering thought in mind, I turned, following Jack's directions halfway down the block, at which point the smell of freshly baked croissants made directions unnecessary. I followed my nose the rest of the way to a small café that would not have looked out of place in London. The door was standing open, and the voices of my traveling companions carried out into the street: Olivia, laughing, voice half garbled by a mouthful of something; Jack, louder and more boisterous, trying to prove something, if his tone was anything to go by; and Juliet, quiet, audible only because her words somehow fell into the space between his. I couldn't understand a thing they were saying, and I didn't need to. The sound of them was quite enough.

I paused at the door, smiling a small, private smile. It wasn't meant to be shared, because it would have required too much explanation. I hadn't traveled with a team since the last time I went to North America—the last time I saw Shaun Mason in the flesh. I'd forgotten how much I enjoyed it.

"Did you save me *anything*?" I asked, finally stepping inside.

"He lives!" Jack thrust his hands into the air, grinning ear to ear. "There's pancakes and toast and oatmeal and fried egg and fried tomato and fried mushroom and croissant with cheese. Sit down and stuff your face."

"What Jack means to say is that he tried *really hard*, but not even he could conquer my ability to keep ordering more food," said Olivia. "We did save you a seat, though, even if the food is mostly here because Jack is a failure at life."

"Well, thank you all," I said, and moved to sit. "Is there tea?"

"There's tea," confirmed Juliet, and pushed the pot over to me.

"Then this morning is truly perfect." I busied myself with preparing a plate. The table was set family-style, with bowls and platters of food, rather than individual servings. As I reached for the mushrooms, I glanced to Olivia and asked, "What time is our appointment for the biological containment center?"

"Half an hour," she said. "If you hadn't shown up when you did, I would have come looking for you with a go-box. Have you got a recorder on you?"

"I never leave my bed without one."

Olivia nodded, looking satisfied. "Good."

"Meanwhile, we're going to be making sure that our escape route is still fully intact and ready to fly our handsome butts out of here," said Jack, making an airplane gesture with one hand. "You'll call if anything really interesting happens, yeah?"

"Yeah," confirmed Olivia. "You can play grease monkey with impunity."

"Don't worry," said Juliet. "I intend to work the stupid out of him." She stood and walked toward the door without looking back or saying good-bye.

Jack laughed, pushing his own chair away from the table. "I recognize a hint when I hear one. See you lot later."

"Bye, Jack," said Olivia cheerfully.

"See you soon," I said, and reached for my fork. With only half an hour before I needed to be fed, presentable, and professional, I intended to eat as fast as I could. A man must have his priorities, after all.

5.

The biological containment facility—helpfully identified by a large sign reading RABBIT-PROOF FENCE BIOLOGICAL CONTAINMENT #17—was an attractive, white-walled facility that could easily have been repurposed as a museum, had the need ever arisen. Only the four men standing outside the door with rifles at the ready disrupted the illusion that we were on our way to a day of education and enlightenment. Which was perhaps not such an illusion after all, once I stopped to think about it.

"ID?" said the first of the guards.

Olivia produced her photo ID. I did the same. The guard took them both before pulling a small scanner out of his pocket and running it over our names. He squinted at the screen. I maintained a carefully casual posture, wondering what would happen if he didn't like the results. Something unpleasant, no doubt.

"Here you go." He handed back our IDs. "You're on today's list. Will you be entering the airlock separately or together?"

"Together," said Olivia, before I could formulate a response. "We haven't done anything that could have resulted in an infection."

That seemed to be the right answer. "On you go, and have a nice visit," said the guard.

"Cheers," said Olivia.

"Thank you," I said, and followed her through the facility door into the airlock on the other side. It was a fairly standard design, with three testing units arrayed against the glass wall in front of us. As I watched, yellow lights came on above two of the test units, while the third remained dark. Olivia walked calmly to the unit on my right. I moved to take my position in front of the other one.

"I hate these high-security places," she said, slapping her hand down on the test panel. "It's such a waste of time."

"If we were anywhere else in the world, this would be our sixth blood test today," I said, mimicking her gesture.

Olivia wrinkled her nose. "Everywhere else in the world wastes an unconscionable amount of time."

"You know, I actually cannot argue with that." The light above my testing panel blinked green, and a lock disengaged somewhere in the glass wall with a soft hiss. A second later, the same thing happened with Olivia's testing panel. This time, the hiss of the lock letting go was followed by the entire glass wall sliding open, allowing us to finally step unencumbered into the lobby of the biological containment facility.

Olivia walked to the middle of the room and stopped. Lacking any better idea of the protocol, I did the same. She looked to me and smiled. "Rey should be here in a moment," she said. "He's going to take us on a tour of the necropsy lab, the specimen storage unit, and the viewing lounge. That should give you a solid grounding in what they do here."

"Rey is a doctor? A scientist? A government employee?"

"All of the above, but he was my boyfriend before he was any of those things, so I still get to abuse him mercilessly," said Olivia. She brightened, suddenly focusing on something past my head. "And there he is now."

I turned. Rey was a tall man of apparently Pacific Islander descent, with long, dark hair pulled into a ponytail and dangling over one shoulder. He was wearing a lab coat, tan slacks, and a black button-down shirt, and he looked surprisingly relaxed for someone working in the most secure facility I had thus far encountered in Australia.

"You must be Mahir Gowda," he said, walking toward me and extending his hand. "I'm Dr. Reynaldo Fajardo. Olivia's told me quite a bit about you, all of it remarkably positive. I was starting to think you were the boss version of 'my girlfriend who lives in Sydney.'"

"Is that like 'my girlfriend who lives in Ireland'?" I asked, shaking his hand.

"Or Canada," agreed Rey amiably. "So how much has Liv told you about our work here?"

"Virtually nothing," I said.

"I wanted him to get the story without my biases," piped up Olivia.

Rey smiled. "Same old Liv," he said. "Are you coming on the tour, at least?"

"If you don't mind."

"I don't." He turned, motioning for us to follow. "As I'm sure you gathered from the sign outside, this is research post seventeen on the fence line. There are thirty-one stations, all told. Most are manned. The unmanned ones are checked on three times a week, to be sure the cameras are in working order and that there's nothing we need to investigate further within their designated territory. Each station is responsible for between four and twelve kilometers of fence monitoring. That includes the visible land inside the fence."

"Are there research stations inside the fence line?" I asked.

"Yes, but none of them have permanent staff. Everyone who works there goes on a voluntary basis and receives hazard pay. They're very picky about who can volunteer. No one with children, no one with dependent parents, and no one who is currently in a serious relationship."

"That's why we broke up," added Olivia.

Rey nodded, mouth twisting a little. "I wanted to do deep research. Can't do that with a girl waiting for you back at port. It might split your attention when it needs to be singular, and you're not the only one who'll get killed in a situation like that one."

"I see," I said. "Are you enlisted?"

"No; we're employed by the government, but the researchers are not technically part of the armed forces, since we're studying the structure of the virus, and any breakthroughs we have could be considered an attempt to weaponize Kellis-Amberlee if we were part of the army." Rey's mouth twisted further. "It's remarkable the hoops you have to jump through if you want to do proper medical science without joining the World Health Organization."

"At least WHO wasn't involved in the CDC conspiracy," I offered.

"Doesn't change the part where I'd murder for their resources." Rey stopped in front of a door and produced a key card from inside his lab coat, swiping it through the reader next to the doorknob. "Please do not lick anything past this point. Do not touch anything that looks like it might be dangerous, which really means 'don't touch anything at all,' and try not to scream if something jumps out at you." On that encouraging note, he pulled the door open and motioned for us to step inside.

"Yes, thank you, that's quite terrifying," I said, and went where I was bid.

The next room was actually more like a viewing area, roughly the size of a stretched-out closet with a solid glass wall separating us from a second, larger room, in which the two kangaroos from the night before were laid out on tables, their bodies split down the middle by tidy incisions before being pinned open like frogs in biology class. Three figures in hazmat suits moved between them, taking notes, extracting organs, and making measurements.

Rey stepped up beside me, the door swinging closed behind him. "The necropsies began immediately, and continued through the night," he said. "They'll be finished sometime around noon, when we're positive that there's nothing left to learn from these bodies. At that point, the remains will be cremated and put into storage. We've been arguing for years that the ashes should be used to fertilize the land on the other side of the fence, since we're removing bodies that would otherwise enrich the soil, but there are some silly buggers in Parliament who believe that it would be a health hazard."

"They don't think it would be a health hazard," said Olivia. "They think it would upset people unduly, and they're happy to keep buying fertilizer if it comes with a little peace."

"But they continue to sell it as a health hazard, which means people continue to believe that cremains are somehow capable of passing along the Kellis-Amberlee virus," said Rey, with the air of an argument that had been going on since long before I arrived on the scene and would be continuing long after I was gone.

"Can you learn anything from the stored remains?" I asked, before the discussion could go any further. It was an interesting local news angle, but "Australian scientists argue for dispersing powdered kangaroo into the atmosphere" would just start a public panic, no matter how hard I worked to add context.

"Most of what we learn comes from the biological samples we take *before* we burn things, since cremains are essentially biologically inert," said Rey, with a faintly aggravated air that didn't seem to be aimed at me, precisely, so much as aimed at his ongoing argument with Olivia. "Look." He pointed to the glass. "Susan's taking brain tissue samples from both of the specimens. She's already done that twice by this stage in the examination, but since the Kellis-Amberlee virus continues to work after death, sometimes for days, we need to see the tissue at different stages of reanimation in order to properly assess the effect of the virus on the body."

"How do you store your samples?"

"Some are flash frozen, others are preserved the old-fashioned way, in formaldehyde. They don't pose an immediate danger, if that's what you're asking; there's never been an outbreak traced back to the specimens we collect in these research stations."

"That's reassuring," I said.

Rey nodded. "I tend to think so as well, since I live here. Come on. There's something else I want you to see." He turned, walking to a door at the far end of the narrow room. He unlocked it with a swipe of his key card and stepped through, holding it open for us to follow.

The next room was as narrow and confined as the first, with one unpleasant difference: There were no lights, and when Olivia stepped in after me and closed the door, it became completely dark.

"Everyone in?" asked Rey. "Good."

He must have done something—flipped a switch or pressed a button—but of course, I couldn't see whatever it was he did. All I saw was a window slowly opening, filling the same amount of space as the previous room's glass wall, but showing an entirely different scene. This window looked out, not on a lab full of working scientists, but on a tangled forest enclosure that wouldn't have looked out of place in a zoo. It was dark inside, with infrared lights providing sufficient illumination for our weak human eyes to see what was in front of us. Something moved in the brush. I managed, somehow, not to jump. It still felt as if my skin separated an inch or so from my body before settling back down into its normal configuration.

"This is where we keep the swamp wallabies that we've recovered from the fence line," said Rey. "They get stepped on by the larger kangaroos, but the injuries are very rarely fatal, so we're able to bring them inside for observation."

"Are they infected?" I asked.

"They're too small to amplify, but they can be carriers; since they've been inside the fence, they can't be released outside of it, for fear that they'll somehow carry the infection to an unprepared population." Rey snorted. "As if there were any unprepared populations left on this continent. Regardless, we can learn a lot about the ecology inside the fence by observing them while they recover, and once they're healthy enough that they can evade the bigger fellows, we put them back where we found them. Usually a few miles in, that is—we don't want to drop them right on the fence line. That would just be cruel of us."

I peered into the darkened enclosure, studying the flickers of motion until they resolved themselves into gray-furred, kangaroo-shaped creatures like the one we'd seen on the road during our drive in. Some of them looked toward the glass; others ignored us completely, choosing to focus their attention on chewing bits of greenery or grooming one another. "Can they see us?"

"Some of them can, yes," said Rey. "That's the other thing that keeps us from releasing them outside the fence line. They're too small to amplify, but anything mammalian *has* the Kellis-Amberlee virus. It's why no one has to get chemotherapy for their cats anymore."

"Did people really do that?" I asked distractedly, watching as one of the larger swamp wallabies bounded across the floor of the enclosure.

"Oh, yeah. It was a big market, cancer treatments for pets. Anyway, everything mammalian is infected now, which sort of stopped that. And about half the wallabies we're retrieving from inside the fence have reservoir conditions. Mostly retinal, probably because that gives them a survival edge, so the ones who go retinal live longer."

I turned to stare at him. The darkness obscured most of his face, but I got the distinct impression from his tone that he was enjoying this.

The impression only strengthened when he said, "Come on, then. Next up's the nursery, and that's *always* a hit with the tourists."

"You mean it makes them wet themselves in terror," chided Olivia.

"Same difference," said Rey. "Follow me."

6.

The nursery reminded me uncomfortably of a pre-Rising thriller that Maggie had forced me to watch while we were staying at the Agora in Seattle: a dinosaur adventure called *Jurassic Park*, in which scientists with more brains than sense cloned enormous prehistoric predators just because they could. Maybe that's an oversimplification of the movie's premise, but really, who looks at a three-ton thunder lizard and thinks, "I should get one of those for the back garden"?

Rey had led us through another unmarked door, this time into a hallway that managed to be substantially wider than either of the rooms that came before it, and then down the hall to a door labeled QUIET PLEASE! BABIES COULD BE SLEEPING! He'd pressed a button, and a few moments later, a cheerful-looking woman with improbably red hair had opened the door.

"Just in time," she'd said. "I've put out their lunch." Then she'd stepped to the side and ushered us into hell.

The nursery was a large, open room, with no sharp edges anywhere in sight. The furniture was all padded in a way I recognized from Nandini's attempts to baby-proof our flat after Sanjukta was born. Some of the corner guards looked suspiciously identical to the ones we had at home. Large, colorful blocks and foam structures were scattered everywhere, and the floor was covered in a spongy mat that sank down beneath our feet, yielding easily. It would take effort to hurt yourself in this room.

Perhaps none of that seems overly nightmarish, but nightmares take many forms, and the redheaded woman had, after all, just put down lunch for the "babies." Easily a dozen small kangaroos were clustered around bowls on the floor, heads down as they focused on the important business of eating. Several half-sized koalas were hanging nearby in an artificial tree, watching us as they systematically shoved clumps of eucalyptus into their mouths. Something spiny that looked like a horribly mutated hedgehog was bumbling around the edges of the room, looking for whatever it is that mutant hedgehogs are interested in. I had never been near this many unconfined animals in my life, and the urge to turn and run was virtually overwhelming.

"We have seventeen joeys here, from three different types of kangaroo," said the redheaded woman, with all indications of pride. "All were retrieved from mothers who died at the fence line."

"So... these are the babies of infected mothers?" I couldn't keep the horror from my voice, much as I tried.

"Many female kangaroos are infected during mating season," said the woman. "They still gestate and give birth, in part because marsupial reproduction is a faster process. They seem strangely disinclined to eat their own infants while they remain in the pouch—we're doing several research studies into exactly what causes that aversion. It isn't shared by nonmarsupial mammals, but if we could somehow reproduce it—"

"What she's trying to say is that these joeys aren't any more infected than you or I, and you shouldn't be unfairly prejudiced against them," said Olivia. With no more warning than that, she scooped a passing joey off the floor and dropped it into my hands. I instinctively pulled it closer to my body, holding it the way I would have held Sanjukta. The tiny kangaroo responded by beginning to investigate my shirtfront with its clever paws, apparently checking me for treats.

"I am not comfortable with this," I announced.

"But look at that," said Olivia. "He likes you."

"We don't need to worry about them losing their fear of humans," said Rey. "If they reach adulthood, they'll learn to be afraid of everything, and if they become infected, they'll lose their fear of humans regardless of their early experiences. So we keep them comfortable, and we work to remind ourselves that these creatures aren't just terrifying monsters on the other side of a chain-link wall."

The joey was now tugging on the front of my shirt in a way that was either adorable or terrifying, depending on how I allowed myself to think about it. "That's an admirable goal," I said.

Olivia leaned forward and took the joey away from me. I breathed what I hoped would be a largely unnoticed sigh of relief. "No point in making you wet yourself," she said. "You're still my boss, and I'm sure that would show up poorly on my performance review."

"Yes, it would," I said. I pointed to the bumbling spiny thing. "What is that?"

"That's an echidna," said Rey.

"Ah," I said. "I see why you thought the hedgehog was one of those."

Olivia laughed.

"Come on," said Rey. "This is a nice place to spend a little time, but there's more to see."

"Isn't there always?" I asked rhetorically, and moved to follow him.

Part V

In Which Everyone Is Very Relaxed about the Probable End of the World, and a Reporter Is Cast into Mortal Danger for No Good Reason

Science is a powerful force, but it will never be stronger than mankind's capacity to be afraid of what we do not yet fully understand.

—Dr. Reynaldo Fajardo

As long as science keeps building better fences, I'm glad to go along with things, at least for the moment.

—Mahir Gowda

1.

It was well past noon by the time we emerged from the biological containment facility. Olivia was chattering a mile a minute as we stepped through the front doors. Most of her words were directed at Rey, who was joining us for lunch before he went back to work. I had tuned her out, choosing to devote my energy to contemplating the structure we'd just been walked through. Unless the government of Australia had structured their fence stations to conceal the true nature of their research into the Kellis-Amberlee virus, I was willing to accept that the rabbit-proof fence served exactly the purpose that had been advertised: It was a way of keeping Australia's wildlife from eating the human population without resorting to bullets and extinction events. I even found myself considering ways that similar programs could be enacted in parts of the United States and Canada. There was enough open, empty land there; maybe the surviving native wildlife could be herded into a specific geographic region, and—

My thoughts derailed as Olivia put a hand on my arm, stopping me in midstep. I turned to blink at her before finally looking up and registering our surroundings.

"...Ah," I said. "Is this normal?"

"No," said Olivia. "It's not."

What looked like the entire population of the nameless little town was assembled on the lawn of the biological containment facility. A line of guards stood between us and them, all with their guns at the ready. I recognized Rachel from the night before, and somehow, that just made the situation more worrisome. If they were calling in the checkpoint staff, this had to be something bad.

"Rey?" said Olivia.

"I don't know," he said.

"Well, then, let's find out," I said, and started walking again, heading rapidly toward Rachel's position. When I was close enough to talk without shouting, I said, "Rachel? It's Mahir, from last night. Would you mind telling us what's going on?"

"What's going on is some damn fools trying to have a riot on government property," she said.

"It's not government property!" shouted someone from the edge of the crowd. "It's our home!"

"Your home is built on government property," Rachel shouted back. "And don't think I don't recognize you, Nicole Long, residential housing block B-3."

"Because that's not going to make people feel threatened," I muttered. Louder, I asked, "Why, precisely, are people trying to have a riot? Aren't we rather uncomfortably close to the fence for rioting? I feel like there should be a nice bus to take us somewhere safer to riot."

"We live here, why should we go elsewhere to make our issues known?" demanded a man.

I was starting to feel uncomfortably like I was inciting both sides of the conflict, which could easily leave me standing in the middle when they opened fire. "All right, I can see that everyone here has a very good reason for what they're doing right now, but as a foreigner, I have no idea what any of those good reasons are. Can someone please explain to me, in a quick, sound-bite-ready format, why there's a large group of angry people being held off by the local military?"

A red-faced woman whose eyes were puffy from recent tears shoved her way forward, shouting, "Those bastards pretend we're secure, but we're not! They pretend nothing can get through the fence, but they're wrong! Then they go threatening legal action because somebody finally did what we've all been dreaming of doing for years, and where were they with their legal actions when my Paul was disappearing, huh? Where were they then?"

"Oh, Lord," said Rey, covering his face with one hand.

I glanced quickly in his direction. "Care to explain?"

"That's Karen Langmore. She's a local—very local. Her family lived out here before the Rising, and they've never considered moving anywhere else. She thinks a kangaroo came over the fence and stole her son a year ago."

"I don't think!" the woman—Karen—shouted. "I *know*! Your fence isn't keeping them out, it's keeping us stupid and snowed, so that we don't move out of range!"

"If that's true, why hasn't anyone else been attacked?" asked Rachel. She had the Irwin trick of pitching her voice from the back of her throat down cold: She didn't seem to be shouting, but everyone could hear her. "Why haven't we been dealing with outbreaks on a monthly basis? There's no way those animals are getting past the fence! All you're doing is whipping folks into a useless panic, and people are going to get hurt!"

"If you won't protect us from the infected, we'll have to protect ourselves!" shouted a man.

Rachel turned toward him, eyes narrowed. "Are you making threats toward the local wildlife? Because that's against the law."

"I'm not threatening anyone," the man snapped. "I'm saying that sometimes, people have to matter more than animals, no matter how 'endangered' those animals are."

The guards were starting to mutter mutinously. If this didn't break up soon, it was going to turn ugly for everyone.

Newsies are supposed to stay above the story whenever possible, but I knew from bitter experience that "staying above the story" wouldn't keep the bullets from flying in my direction. "If I may?" I said, stepping forward so that I was between Rachel and the crowd. "Hello. I don't know how many of you know me, but my name is Mahir Gowda. I'm a journalist from England, and I've come to see the rabbit-proof fence."

The crowd grumbled and glared, but no one shouted, and no one shot at me. For the moment, I was willing to take that as a victory.

"I *will* be reporting fairly and honestly on what I see here. The Australian government has no authority over me once I leave your country, and I'm too well known to simply 'disappear.' I assure you, if I find that your concerns are founded, I will be trumpeting them to the heavens before anyone realizes that they should be devoting resources to stopping me."

"They'll just buy you off like they do everyone else!"

"My integrity is not for sale," I said witheringly. "If there is a problem—if my research confirms that there is a problem—then I will report on it. Of that, you have my word."

"He's not the only one," said Olivia, stepping forward to stand beside me. "But this isn't the right way to make us want to tell your stories. You're going to get us all shot, and then who's going to tell the truth? Nobody. You'll bury your lede in a hail of bullets, and no one will care enough to dig it up."

"Not only that, but if you do not disperse within the next thirty seconds, I'm having you all arrested for forming an infection hazard near the fence," said Rachel. I glanced her way, startled. She wasn't looking at me, or at Olivia; all her attention was on the crowd. "Go *home.* Don't do this again. Next time, you won't have a bunch of idiot journalists looking to sniff out a scandal just standing by. Next time, somebody's getting hurt."

"It won't be who you think," snapped Karen . . . but there was no heat in it. The wind had been stolen from her sails by logic and by danger, and she was just shouting for the sake of hearing herself. Someone in the crowd put an arm around her shoulders, tugging her away, and she went without a fight.

The rest of the crowd dispersed quickly after that, although not without more than a few glares and muttered expletives. Rachel and the other guards remained exactly where they were, none of them moving so much as a muscle until the last of the prospective rioters had moved out of view. I breathed out, relieved, only to choke on my own exhale as Rachel grabbed the front of my shirt and hauled me toward her.

"What in the blue suffering *fuck* was that?" she demanded. "Are you an idiot, or are you just too convinced of your own invincibility to see when you're risking your life for absolutely bloody nothing?"

"I would find it much easier to answer your questions if you weren't physically threatening me," I said. My voice came out surprisingly level. "Please let go."

To my relief, Rachel did. "Those people are all noise and no action. You had no reason to step up like that. You could have actually triggered the damn riot."

"I've never seen them this bad before," said Rey.

I blinked as I glanced his way. In all the excitement, I'd almost forgotten that he was there. "You mean this has happened before?" I asked.

"About once a week since Karen decided that it was kangaroos that were to blame for her Paul disappearing," said Rachel grimly. "She gets everyone worked up over the injustice, and then someone remembers that we keep live specimens in the biological containment facility, and there's a march on the place, like we won't be standing in the way with guns in our hands. Maybe they're hoping to eventually wear us down, convince us that we should 'forget' to show up where we're supposed to be. I don't know, and honestly, I don't care. She's a grieving woman. That doesn't give her the freedom to disrupt the peace."

"Please don't take this as me siding with her, but...is there *any* chance she's correct? Any chance at all?"

Rachel sighed, giving me a weary look. "Well, I don't know. Which do you think is more likely: A zombie kangaroo somehow found a hole in the fence, snuck through without attracting any attention from its fellows, made its way through the town without being seen, ignored multiple easy, delicious targets, and finally stole a toddler from inside his bedroom? Or something else happened? I don't know what that something else might be. Maybe the kid's father came back. Maybe it was a stranger abduction. We looked into it and we didn't find anything, but if it was an infected kangaroo, it was the smartest damn zombie I've ever heard of, and we should just start evacuating the continent now. Humans are finished in Australia if the zombie kangaroos are learning how to open windows."

I nodded. "I think you're probably right about that. So what set them off today?"

"I can answer that," said Rey. We all turned to look at him. He shrugged. "We retrieved two bullets from the second downed kangaroo that we brought in last night. Neither of them was from one of the guns issued to our staff, or to the guards responsible for maintaining the fence line. Which means—"

"Someone inside the fence is shooting at the kangaroos?" Olivia sounded utterly horrified, like this was a rejection of the natural order. "But how can they even line up a shot? They don't have access to the sniper towers."

"There are rooftops. Trees. And maybe they do have access to a sniper tower. Not everyone in the deployment is happy about how wildlife is prioritized out here. Somebody might bribe one of the shifts to let them up into a tower that isn't scheduled to be manned during that period. It'd be easy enough to sneak out again, after you were done getting out your aggressions on the local kangaroos."

"Why would someone who didn't like the law live out here?" I asked. "Wouldn't it be easier to move into the city, where there's less risk of surprise zombie kangaroos?"

"This is their home," said Rachel. "People like Karen, they've been out here for generations. They don't want to move to 'civilization,' they want civilization to piss off and let them have their land back. But since the fence isn't going to move, unless it's to expand, that's not going to happen."

"Ten years ago, the fence line was two hundred yards farther that way," said Rey, indicating the land beyond the fence. "The kangaroo population went up, and the fence was shifted. Eventually, they'll have to move the whole outpost in order to give the mobs room to move without stepping on each other."

I stared at him for a moment. Then, slowly, I shook my head. "Only in Australia," I said.

Olivia grinned. "Got that right."

2.

Jack and Juliet returned from the airfield about an hour later. Olivia filled them in on the events of the afternoon while I transcribed my notes, trying to get the order of events straight in my head even as I mirrored a backup to the main After the End Times server. I wasn't going to lose this information, even if I somehow lost my life out in this terrifying last frontier.

When I was done typing, I began the slightly less mechanical task of researching. A search of the public Australian government databases turned up no fewer than two hundred seventeen documents relating to the post-Rising rabbit-proof fence. Everything from the material requirements for extensions to the rules enforced within a quarter mile of the fence line was there, thoroughly documented and ready for review. As I read, I found myself more and more impressed with the sheer audacity of the situation. According to the law—the law which had been voted on and approved by the majority of the Australian population—anyone who was shot by a licensed fence guard within the zone that had been legally defined as "on the fence line" would be charged after the fact with disorderly conduct. You must have done *something* wrong, after all, if one of the guards had felt the need to shoot you to make it stop.

There were rather stringent rules governing the behavior of the guards themselves, and they were rotated regularly between postings, presumably to keep corruption at a minimum. That didn't change the fact that, had Rachel opened fire into the crowd and mowed down every single man, woman, and child who lived in the nameless little town, she would not have been at fault, while every single one of them would have been charged with posthumous offenses.

It seemed draconian. But the more I read about the process of expanding and maintaining the fence, the more I realized that it was actually surprisingly liberal. No one was required to live in the fence line encampments; many of the biological containment facilities were staffed purely by the guards, scientists, and researchers who had chosen to devote their lives to the Kellis-Amberlee infection. Towns like the one where we were staying were a rarity, occupied by people who refused to let anything as minor as a zombie infection change their ways of life. Australia allowed these people to stay in their homes—or close to their homes; sometimes the original homes had ended up behind the fence, due to unstoppable outbreaks—and asked only that they follow the rules for safety near the fence. Given the country's track record with indigenous peoples and running them off their land, this was far more enlightened than they had any real reason to be, or history of being.

The conflict came from the natural point of friction: the interaction of the human population with the native wildlife, which was protected by more laws than I would have believed possible. Not everyone shared Jack and Olivia's matter-of-fact "we're easier to replace" attitude, and some people were downright resentful of the fact that an infected kangaroo was considered more valuable than an uninfected human. It *was* an unusual perspective, but one which made more sense the more I read about the restructuring of Australia after the Rising. The people who survived the outbreaks didn't want to lose the things that made their country unique just because they'd shared a zombie apocalypse with the rest of the world. That meant conservation; that meant looking for answers. And yes, that meant allowing infected kangaroos to occasionally break loose and eat the citizenry.

More people were satisfied with the current regime than I would have thought possible. That said something interesting about the people of Australia—and it raised the question of what, exactly, would happen if the tide of public opinion ever happened to turn.

3.

We ate dinner at the small café where we'd had breakfast. Jack and Juliet seemed to have come to a new understanding, or maybe it was just another iteration of an old understanding; they ate while gazing at each other, neither of them contributing to the conversation. Olivia took up the slack, chattering a mile a minute, until I could barely keep up with her rapid changes of subject and apparent mood. After I finished my meal—a passable mushroom and vegetable pie, made somewhat unusual by the inclusion of chunks of baked pumpkin alongside the more customary turnip and potato—I excused myself and walked back to the hotel to make an early night of things.

The lobby was still deserted. Except for the four of us, I hadn't seen a single sign of life inside the hotel proper. On the street outside, yes, but inside, no. I shook my head, chuckling a little at the haunted house ridiculousness of it all as I walked up the stairs.

Had I been paying more attention, I might have noticed that the door to Olivia and Juliet's room was standing slightly ajar, enough that an observer would have a clear view of the hallway as I walked toward my own room. I might have seen the subtle signs that someone had come this way: the indentations in the carpet, the disturbance in the air. I was wrapped up in my thoughts, however, and the first indication that I was not alone came when the hand reached out from behind me, pressing a curiously scented cloth over my mouth and nose.

Chloroform, you idiot, I thought, and then my eyes were closed, and the world was an unimportant distraction, and I thought nothing past that point.

4.

I returned to consciousness to find myself being jarred viciously by the motion of a vehicle which had not, if I was any judge of such things, been maintained properly, or indeed, maintained at all. Keeping my eyes shut, I attempted to move my arms, and found, to my delight, that they responded easily and normally to my commands. I didn't know who was around me or how many other passengers this hell-bound conveyance might have, but I needed to know my options. I slid my hand carefully to my hip, verifying the presence of a buckled seat belt. Whoever had abducted me wasn't intending to kill me accidentally, then. That should probably have been reassuring. In the moment, however, it merely made me tired.

"Are you awake, or are you just getting ready to do some sleep masturbation?" asked Olivia, close enough that she might as well have been leaning over my shoulder.

Relief flooded over me. Clearly, my would-be attacker had been interrupted by my traveling companions, and we were fleeing for the airfield. "Olivia?" I turned toward her voice, opening my eyes at the same time. "Did you . . . see . . ."

We were not driving toward the airfield, unless the airfield had moved and was now located in a large, empty stretch of grass, with no road or streetlights anywhere in sight. Olivia, who was strapped in next to me in the back of what appeared to be a fortified military Jeep, offered me a wan smile, only barely visible in the glow coming from the instrument panel in the front seat. There were at least two more people riding with us—the driver, and a third passenger in the seat next to him. I could see the backs of their heads, but not their faces.

"I did see who attacked you, yeah," Olivia said. "He helped us get you out to the car. I'm really sorry about this. There wasn't any other good way to convince you that we needed to break about a dozen—"

"Two dozen," said the driver: Rey.

"—sorry, two dozen laws about travel beyond the fence." Olivia shrugged. "This way, you can legitimately say that it wasn't your choice if you decide to bring us up on charges."

"Assuming you live that long," said Juliet from the front passenger seat.

"Well, I see the gang's all here," I said, with surprising steadiness.

Apparently, my terror was translating into bland annoyance. "How did you convince Jack to stay behind while you were drugging and abducting me?"

"Oh, we didn't," said Olivia. "He's on the roof with a gun in case anything decides to flip the Jeep while we're out here."

Words failed me. I stared at her, hoping that my expression would convey all the things my voice was refusing to let me say. Much to my irritation, she laughed. I scowled. Apparently, silence and staring were not the way to get my point across.

"Don't be so *British*, Mahir," she said. "We're perfectly safe."

"No we're not," said Juliet. "We're driving across open terrain inside the rabbit-proof, kangaroo-proof, *zombie*-proof fence, which is there for a reason, and it's not an aesthetic one. We're in a ludicrous amount of danger. We would be in a ludicrous amount of danger even if we weren't in Australia, where even the things that aren't infected want to kill us all. There's no point in lying to the man. He's not an idiot."

I turned to stare at the back of Juliet's head. She twisted in her seat to meet my gaze. She wasn't wearing her sunglasses anymore—the lack of light on this side of the fence must have made them unnecessary, and her night vision would make her an invaluable lookout. Looking into her eyes was like trying to stare down a shark, implacable and ageless.

"Don't get me wrong, Mr. Reporter. I know how dangerous what we're doing right now really is, and I wouldn't be going along with it if Jack hadn't asked me to. But that doesn't mean I'm on your side in this. You're going to see what we came out here to see, whether you like it or not."

"Why are you people all assuming I wouldn't have liked it?" I demanded, aggravation bringing my voice back from wherever it had fled. "Did any of you think to *ask* me before you drugged me and loaded me into the back of your car? I might have agreed to do this openly!"

"Ah, but then you'd be legally liable for trespassing beyond the fence line," said Olivia. "This way, if we're caught, you'll have plausible deniability, and the traces of chloroform in your system to back it up. You'll be deported instead of being imprisoned. Everybody wins."

"Everybody but us," said Juliet. "We'll go to jail. For a long, long time." She twisted back around in her seat. "So you'd better appreciate this."

"How can I appreciate this when I don't even know what it *is*?" I demanded.

"It's an answer," said Olivia. "We're still not completely sure what the question was, but it's an answer, and that gives us a place to start. Rey?"

"I've been observing unusual infection patterns in the kangaroos that cluster around the fence for the last five years," he said. He sounded as calm as if he were delivering a lecture in a nice, safe classroom, not driving a Jeep across an open field where we might be attacked at any moment. "I'd looked at the reservoir conditions, of course—everyone has at some point—but then I'd dismissed them, because all the information coming out of the big organizations said that they were anomalous, and actually analyzing that data takes years of targeted study. Then things got bad in North America, and your team released the reservoir condition data."

We hadn't released all of it. We'd never shared the information on spontaneous remission, for one thing, or the statistics on parent/child or sexually transmitted immunity. There's telling the truth, and then there's blowing up the monkey house without having anywhere to put the monkeys. "So?" I said cautiously.

"So I started looking at the data in a new way," said Rey. The landscape was becoming less uniform; we were driving toward a clump of what I started to recognize as eucalyptus trees. "The thing about marsupials that's really interesting—I don't know if you thought about this earlier today, when we made a point of showing you the nursery—but the thing that's really interesting is how infected mothers can continue to nurse uninfected infants. A kangaroo joey is incredibly far below the amplification threshold, and it lives purely on its mother's milk. They're getting a viral load that could cause the entire population of Sydney to amplify, and they're getting it every hour of the day."

"Meaning what?"

"Meaning reservoir conditions along the fence line are sky-high. Half the babies you saw today have them, or have the beginnings of them. Some show signs of developing two or even three reservoir conditions. And here's the really interesting part: Only about half the juveniles we raise and release show up in the infected mobs. The rest never seem to get sick."

"How interesting," I said, keeping my voice as neutral as I could.

"It's more interesting than you think," said Rey. "*Their* offspring? The ones with one parent—sometimes even two—with a reservoir condition? They never amplify at all. They seem to be immune."

"Which means what?" I asked. "Human zombies can't breastfeed."

Olivia shuddered. "It says something about my friends that I keep hearing that sentence," she said. "It never gets any less disgusting."

"Maybe not," said Rey. He steered our Jeep into the shadow of the trees and turned off the engine. The sudden silence was deafening. "But this is a chance to learn more about the structure of the virus and the way that it behaves when a population is allowed to find equilibrium. We have to protect the kangaroos."

I stared at the back of his head. "That's why we're here?"

"You wanted to see the real Australia, mate," said Jack, as he slid off the roof and landed lightly next to the car. "Doesn't get any more real than this. Now come on. It's time for you to meet the locals."

5.

We walked in a diamond-shaped formation through the trees. Jack took the front and Juliet took the rear, with the rest of us sandwiched between them like an unruly school group. Rey moved almost as quietly as Jack and Juliet did, his careful footsteps and obvious awareness of the terrain speaking to his knowledge of the area. Olivia and I blundered along, her good-naturedly, me with the growing conviction that we were about to be eaten.

Nothing but us moved within the shadow of the trees. Nothing that I saw, anyway; Jack paused at one point, turning to shine his flashlight toward something in the distance. It reflected off two round eyes, low to the ground and utterly chilling.

"Wombat," he said, with an air of satisfaction.

"Is it infected?" I asked.

"Doesn't matter. If it is, it's too slow to catch up with us. We'll just need to keep an eye out when we come back. If it's not, it's not going to mess with us. Uninfected wombats are pretty chill little dudes."

"I am firing you when I get back to my computer."

Jack's grin was a white slash cut through the darkness. "No you're not. If nothing else, tonight's little party game proves that I'm absolutely the best Irwin you've got on the roster. You can fire Olivia if you'd like."

"Shut up, you," said Olivia.

Jack laughed, and we started walking again.

"Why did we park so far from where we're going?"

"Noise," said Rey. "You should probably stop talking. We're going to look at a nonaggressive mob, but your voice could still spook them."

"I thought you didn't worry about them losing their fear of humans," I said, dropping my voice to just above a whisper.

"Yes, well, that's the other concern," said Rey, who didn't sound nearly concerned enough for my tastes.

I stopped talking.

The rest of the walk through the forest was an exercise in silent terror. No one spoke, but Jack swept his flashlight constantly across the underbrush, drawing glints of light from more pairs of eyes that I would really have been happier not seeing. He didn't shoot at any of them, and so I told myself that they weren't a concern. I wasn't really listening to me by that point. All my energy was wrapped up in sheer, heart-stopping fear.

Jack stopped when we reached the edge of the trees. He turned, a small smile on his face, and motioned me forward. "Well, come on," he said, very softly. "We kidnapped you so that you could see this. You may as well see it."

Common sense told me to stay exactly where I was until someone agreed to escort me back to the Jeep. Curiosity told me he was right: There was no point in my having come all this way if I wasn't willing to see what was in front of me.

I stepped forward.

Jack's flashlight illuminated a mob of maybe two dozen adult kangaroos. Some were grubbing at the ground, digging up sprouts and tender roots for their supper. Others lazed on the ground like oversized housecats, sprawled in a manner that was so undignified that it drew a smile unbidden to my lips. Joeys darted between the adults like tiny race cars, their tails lifted high and their ears pushed forward to catch the slightest sound. They were the same species as the kangaroos I'd seen at the fence, but they looked like they had come from an entirely different world. They were alert, aware, *alive* in a way that the other kangaroos hadn't been.

Rey leaned close enough to whisper, "Every adult here is either infected with a reservoir condition or is the grown offspring of one or more parents with a reservoir condition. They monitor each other. If an adult shows signs of amplification, the other adults move the joeys away until the danger is past."

The kangaroos seemed to have developed a more enlightened system of dealing with the Kellis-Amberlee infection than humanity had. I continued to stare. The research we'd recovered from the CDC had proven that reservoir conditions were the first step to coexistence with the virus, but this was... it was real. It was really happening, in front of me, and it made my heart ache in a way that I couldn't put into words. I'd been a journalist for years. Words were my livelihood. But in that place, in that moment, there was nothing.

I was so wrapped up in watching the kangaroos that I initially missed the change in Jack's posture. He stiffened, changing the angle of his flashlight beam so as to illuminate a previously ignored corner of the field. "We should go," he said, not bothering to pitch his voice low.

Some of the kangaroos were starting to raise their heads, and one of the larger males scrambled back to his feet. Slowly, I realized that whatever it was that had their attention, it wasn't us: Not a single kangaroo was turning to look in our direction. I followed the beam of Jack's flashlight and saw the eyes in the distance—eyes too high off the ground to belong to the wombat we'd seen before. Eyes that were getting rapidly closer.

Juliet grabbed my arm. "Come on, tourist," she snapped. I didn't resist as she turned me around. I just followed her as we ran back through the forest. We weren't trying to be quiet this time, and our footfalls seemed too loud for the night around us. The moaning of the infected kangaroos finally became audible as they closed in on the mob we'd come to see.

We kept on running.

6.

The trouble with running through a dark forest in the middle of the night while being pursued by a mob of zombie kangaroos is all the damn trees. Juliet did a surprisingly good job of dodging around them, and as long as she kept her grip on my wrist, I wasn't overly worried about slamming into anything. Jack had his flashlight, and he was urging Rey and Olivia along behind us. The moans were still audible in the distance. They should have faded out by now, and the fact that they hadn't meant that at least one of the infected kangaroos had followed us into the forest, probably assuming that we'd be easy prey. They were right about that much. If we didn't make it back to the Jeep before they caught up with us, we were as good as dead.

"Great idea, Jack!" shouted Juliet as we ran. Apparently, keeping quiet was no longer much of a concern. "Let's go past the fence and look at kangaroos so that Mahir will understand the importance of the research that's happening here! Oh, and by the way, let's get eaten while we're out there!"

"That's exactly what I was thinking!" called Jack. The bastard was laughing. I very rarely wanted to punch anyone as much as I wanted to punch him in that moment.

"Less banter, more run," shouted Olivia.

We ran.

We ran until my legs felt like they'd been replaced with jelly and my lungs felt like they'd been replaced with something even squishier. The moans behind us continued, and I felt a surge of gratitude for the trees. If we'd been on open ground, the kangaroos would already have been on top of us. As it was, they couldn't get up to full speed in the space they had available, and their disease-addled brains weren't allowing them to realize that they could just go around.

The Jeep couldn't be much farther. I held fast to that thought as I forced myself to keep moving. Once we were at the Jeep, we'd have an engine on our side, not to mention the structural support of the frame. We'd be able to drive away from this hellish adventure, and never look back. We'd—

Juliet stopped running so abruptly that I slammed into her. She put out her free arm, preventing me from toppling over. "We have a problem," she said, voice suddenly pitched low.

I followed her gaze to the Jeep, which was undisturbed, no kangaroos in evidence. Then I realized that something was moaning, something much closer than the mob that was even now trying to shamble its way through the woods. I looked down.

My first impression of the fuzzy round creature staggering slowly toward us was one of near-overwhelming cuteness: It was like one of Sanjukta's plush toys had somehow come alive and shown up for the zombie adventure. It was round, all of it, from its round little nose to its round little body, with stubby legs and tiny triangular ears. It also seemed remarkably solid for something so small; I got the distinct feeling that it weighed more than I could possibly guess just by looking at it.

Jack and the others ran up behind us, and Jack swore. "The fucking *wombat*. How—"

"Not sure that matters," said Olivia. "It's between us and the car."

"Well, I can't lead it away," snapped Jack. "Wombats are too damn slow, and they know it. It'll stay where it is and try to pin us down."

"We're being menaced by a teddy bear," I said, barely able to believe the situation. "We're going to die because no one can decide what we should do about the teddy bear."

"We're not licensed to shoot a wombat," said Rey.

"Oh, for fuck's sake." Juliet released my arm and whirled, grabbing the gun out of Jack's hands. I saw his eyes widen. In that moment, I think we all knew what she was going to do. No one moved to stop her. Juliet turned back around and shot the wombat three times in the head, grouping her bullets so that the entire top of the plump little creature's skull was blown away.

No one said anything as she turned and handed the gun back to Jack. The kangaroos continued moaning in the distance.

"Come on," she said. "Let's go home."

"Marry me," said Jack.

Juliet smiled a little. "You can visit me in prison," she said.

7.

We were in the Jeep and driving back toward the fence long before the kangaroos reached our position. I watched out of the rear window as they hopped out of the forest, pausing to nose at the fallen wombat. A few of the sicker-looking ones stopped there, satisfying the demands of the virus that had overtaken their normally herbivorous bodies. The rest followed us for a while, but quickly fell behind.

"Almost there," said Rey. The Jeep felt like it was going to shake apart around us. He was doing a remarkably good job of keeping it under control—and then I saw the lights of the fence up ahead of us, and stopped giving much of a damn about the Jeep. As long as we reached that beautiful fence line, everything was going to be all right.

"We're going to take a pounding tonight," said Olivia.

"Do you mean us, specifically, or the fence?" I asked.

"Both," she said. "Look." She pointed to the fence. I squinted and realized that I could see guards through the glare. They seemed to be lined up, waiting for us.

I groaned. "I'm getting deported."

"Look at it this way," she said. "It'll make a great story."

Rey continued driving straight for the fence, stopping with the bumper only a foot or so away. He cranked down his window, leaned out, and shouted, "Open the gate! This is an official research vehicle!"

"There are no research trips scheduled for tonight, sir," shouted a voice—Rachel. She sounded bloody pissed. I couldn't quite find it in myself to blame her.

"Come on, Rachel, open the gate," shouted Jack. "There's a mob behind us!"

"You could be infected, then," she said. "It seems like a huge risk."

"Rachel, *please*," said Rey.

"You are all arseholes," she snapped, following it with: "Open the gate! Guns ready! This is not a drill!"

Slowly—too slowly for my liking—the section of fence in front of us slid up, until Rey was able to drive the Jeep through the opening. The guards moved to surround us, keeping their guns trained on the break in the fence until the gate had closed again. Then they turned to train their guns on us instead. Much more reassuring.

Guards walked up with blood testing units in their hands. "Very slowly, without letting your hands slip out of view at any point, I want you to each exit the vehicle and take a blood test," said Rachel. "If any of you test positive, you're all going into quarantine."

"Same old Rachel," said Olivia amiably, and slid out of the car. The rest of us followed her.

It was almost reassuring to be going through the old familiar "take test, prick finger, wait for the lights to stop flashing" routine. The infected kangaroos arrived about halfway through the process, beginning to fling themselves against the fence. None of the people I was with paid them any mind, and so neither did I, although it took actual effort on my part. One by one, our tests came back clean and were placed into the waiting biohazard bags.

The last to get a clean test result was Juliet, whose reservoir condition doubtless confused things a bit. When her lights finally turned green, she dropped her unit into its bag before extending her hands in front of her, wrists together.

The nearest guard promptly handcuffed her. "Juliet Seghers-Ward, you are under arrest for poaching," he said. "Please come with me."

"See you at the arraignment," she said.

"See you at the wedding," Jack said, and leaned in quick, stealing a kiss.

Juliet was still laughing as she was led away. It seemed like there was nothing else she could do. The rest of us stood there, the kangaroos attacking the fence behind us, and watched her being taken.

8.

"Let me get this straight," I said slowly, struggling to keep my temper in check. "Because Juliet was the only one to harm an animal, she's the only one who's actually in legal trouble, but she could be deported?"

"Assuming a convenient Australia natural doesn't somehow find his way into her cell and marry her, thus renewing her citizenship, yes," said Rachel.

I paused, my temper dimming as I perceived the overall shape of her plan. "Ah," I said.

"Naturally, I would need to be distracted for that to happen."

"Naturally," I agreed. "Olivia is waiting outside. Would you care to walk with me?"

"Since you've proven yourself to be a dangerously seditious element, yes, I believe I would," said Rachel. She stood, walking around her desk, and moved to open the door. "Is your life always this exciting?"

"Only when I'm very, very unlucky," I said, and stepped outside... only to find myself facing what appeared to be another incipient riot. I groaned. "Such as now."

Rachel stepped out behind me. "Again?"

"Funny, that's just what I was thinking." I trotted the few steps to where Olivia was standing. "Now what?"

She turned to face me. "They're saying the kangaroos attacked last night. That Juliet's missing because the kangaroos got her."

"But that's just *stupid*," I said.

Olivia rolled her eyes. "Try telling them that."

I paused. "All right," I said finally. "I will."

"Wait, Mahir, I didn't mean—"

But I was already striding toward the crowd. When I reached the edge, I clapped my hands. Most of them ignored me. I clapped my hands again before cupping them and shouting, "May I please have your attention?"

The noise around me stopped. A few heads turned. No one looked terribly impressed. I lowered my hands.

"Er, hello," I said, suddenly self-conscious. "My name is Mahir Gowda. I'm a visiting journalist with After the End Times. I came to learn more about your fence. It's a marvel, really. I never dreamed that there could be anything like it. I've also learned quite a bit about your country. And one of the things I've learned is that you're all being bloody idiots right now."

That got a bit more attention. Irritated grumbles ran through the crowd.

"I mean it! You have more freedom than anywhere else on the planet. You can be *outside*! In the sun, in the grass, where there are birds and weird little mammals and—and no one else gets that anymore, do you understand me? People who've chosen to abandon the cities, maybe, but they have no government support. They have no guards or soldiers to support them. They have no fences. You've got the best of both worlds. You're free enough to get bored and make up stories about danger, while everyone else on this planet is legitimately terrified. The kangaroos can't get through the fence! We'd all be dead if they could, but they can't, and you know it. That's why you feel safe making a big deal of 'what if.' You know what happens when you make too much of 'what if'?"

"No, what?" shouted someone belligerently. I couldn't see who... but it sounded suspiciously like Rey.

"Someone believes you," I said. The grumbles stopped. "Someone believes you, and that's when the real fences come. That's when the gates get locked, and the testing panels go in above every door. That's when you start trading in your freedom for feeling safe. But you'll never feel safe, not all the way, because every time you narrow the cracks that danger can come in through, the cracks that remain will seem just that much wider. Is it worth it? Is it worth looking at one of the last free places in the world, and giving it all away?"

No one said anything. I looked at them, and they looked back at me, and somehow, no one needed to say anything. We all knew what the answer had to be.

Part VI

Going Home

Australia is a wild place, full of dangers that the rest of the world has forgotten. Australia is a tame place, full of people who live ordinary lives, lives that any among us would recognize. It is passionate and strange, it is boring and mundane, and it is beautiful. I dare any person in this world to stand upon Australia's soil and not think, "Oh, how green this land, oh, how blue this sea; I must have been very good to have been allowed to come here."

I must have been very good indeed.

—Mahir Gowda

1.

"You're sure you'll be all right?"

"I'll be in the very capable hands of Virgin Atlantic," I said. "If they can't get me home safely, no one can."

Olivia smiled. "I'm sorry Jack and Juliet couldn't be here."

"Honeymoons and court cases take priority," I said. "Hotaru's shortbread is consolation enough."

"Thanks again for coming. It was...nice to work with you." Olivia hesitated before flinging her arms around me. Voice muffled by my shoulder, she added, "I'll miss you."

"Oh, I'll come again," I said, returning her embrace. "Can't let you have all the fun, now can I? And I look forward to seeing your follow-up reports." We never did find out who'd been taking shots at the local kangaroos. My money was on Karen, who was happier believing that an impartial force had taken her child than the more realistic possibility of a human kidnapper. As a father, I couldn't blame her for that.

"You mean it?" Olivia asked, pulling away.

"I do. Although I may wait until Sanjukta is a little older." The image of her running freely through the tall Australian grass, unafraid of infection, was almost intoxicating. I wouldn't want her to grow up here, but I wanted her to see it. Just once. Just long enough to understand. I smiled at Olivia. "Everyone should have the opportunity to see the world without a fence in the way, don't you think?"

"Yeah," she said. She wiped her eye with the back of her hand. "Safe flight."

"I'll do my best," I said, and turned to walk toward the line for security. I had seen a different world, and I would never forget that, but some things, no matter where you go, will remain the same. Thank God for that. It is our similarities that make the differences matter, even when those differences include a fence extending as far as the eye can see, cutting a razor line across the horizon. Maybe, in the end, especially then.

The Day the Dead Came to Show and Tell

Introduction

Oh, Foxy.

One of the things I have a bad habit of doing is treating side characters like they're secretly the protagonists: like the story would be all about them if we could just change the direction of the cameras slightly, focusing on something other than the foreground. I can give you full histories for spear-carriers and torchbearers, and will, if given the slightest opportunity.

Enter Foxy. She was introduced in *Blackout* as part of the Monkey's crew, a manic pixie nightmare girl with a knife in one hand and a submachine gun in the other. She was part deconstruction of the trope and part broken bird, and I loved her on sight. Which meant that, inevitably, I was going to want to backtrack and explain how someone like her could come to be, what combination of trial and trauma went into her creation.

This is probably the novella that resulted in the most whimpers of protest from my internal proofing pool. It's definitely the one that most closely follows the traditional "zombie fiction" model. It's the story of an elementary school teacher: Elaine Oldenberg, who just wanted to keep the children in her care safe. As far as I'm concerned, she's a hero. She should be remembered that way. It's really too bad that she spends most of her time wishing she didn't have to remember anything at all.

(Fun fact: It's an open secret around here that many of my characters are based on my dearest friends. Not direct Tuckerizations, where they share names, physical descriptions, and occupations, but close cognates. Elaine was inspired by, and largely based on, my best friend in the world, Michelle "Vixy" Dockrey. This is how I show my love. Distressingly.)

The Day the Dead Came to Show and Tell

The changes brought on by the Rising echoed through every layer of American society in the years immediately following the event, and have continued to echo ever since, inexorably changing the way in which we live. Some of the changes were immediate and obvious—the relaxation of gun control laws, the cessation of the "war on drugs" that had done so much to swell the American prison population in the early years of the twenty-first century, the dramatic increase in the minimum wage necessitated by the country's sudden economic transformation—while others were more subtle, and were, in some cases, not fully understood for years. Other changes are ongoing, and will no doubt continue indefinitely. That which has been transformed does not revert to its original state just because the illusion—or reality—of danger has passed.

Perhaps the most transformed of the so-called American institutions has been the primary education system.

While the majority of college-level students have proven more than happy to turn to a wholly virtual educational experience (excepting those students entering hazardous, hands-on fields such as medicine, biology, and food preparation), concerns regarding the social skills and overall development of younger children have kept the elementary and middle-grade schools open, despite legitimate concerns about the safety of those facilities. As the events of the 2036 tragedy at Seattle's Evergreen Elementary demonstrated, those concerns should not have been left unaddressed.

—from *Unspoken Tragedies of the American School System* by Alaric Kwong, March 19, 2044

>> AKWONG: HEY BOSS?

>> AKWONG: I THINK I FOUND HER . . .

—internal communication from Alaric Kwong to Mahir Gowda, After the End Times private server, March 16, 2044

Wednesday, March 19, 2036, 7:16 A.M.

If there was any nicer place to be a schoolteacher than Seattle, Elaine was sure she didn't want to know about it. Knowledge might lead to the desire to see if the rumors were true, and that was a path that could lead to poor decisions and winding up stranded a few hundred miles from home, packed into some Idaho or Montana classroom and dreaming of the evergreens. No, it was better to accept the blessing that was her homeland for what it was: a paradise of gray skies, emerald hills, and the deep blue wonder of the Sound, which could be seen from the back of the blacktop on clear days. There were more of those than people from outside Seattle would have ever dreamt, even if there weren't as many as she remembered from her time in Southern California, where it seemed like the sun only went away at night, and then only grudgingly.

Too much sun was bad for the heart, in Elaine's opinion. It made it harder to enjoy the rain, whereas a surplus of rain just made the sun all the more precious. Maybe it was a Hallmark card way of looking at the world, but honestly, what was the point in keeping things sunny and sanitized all the time? Let a little rain in.

The alarm pad next to her classroom door was flashing on and off when she entered. She propped the door before entering the code and taking her second state-mandated blood test of the day. The first had been required to get her through the front door, and more would happen at both regular and irregular intervals until the final bell rang and signaled the return of her precious first-grade charges to their parents, older siblings, and nannies. Blood tests for students were thankfully less common; while the government needed to know that the children she taught were not in the process of converting, there was also a general understanding that forcing five- and six-year-olds to prick their fingers repeatedly throughout the day was a good way to make them afraid of school and resistant toward additional blood tests.

There was a bill up before the state senate that would grant teachers the power to request their students provide a clean blood sample whenever there was "reasonable suspicion" of conversion. Elaine was sure the bill would pass without any major opposition. Bills that traded on the words "student safety" and "think about the children" generally did, especially now that the Rising was far enough in the past that people were starting to acquire a vague sense of perspective.

The classroom's fluorescent overheads revealed small, sturdy desks scarred with pencil marks and ink stains, the plastic seats worn smooth by a decade of buttocks. It was almost possible to ignore the restraints built into the legs of the chairs, and the manacles tucked away under the edges of the desktops. She generally tried not to think about those things, or about the set of military-grade Kevlar gloves stored in the top drawer of her own desk, waiting for the day that they would be needed. She'd gone through the R&R training like every other teacher in her class—how to react when a student started showing signs of conversion, how to remain calm during the process of restraining and securing them—but after eight years on the job, she had never needed to put on the gloves for anything more severe than a skinned knee.

Not all the teachers she'd graduated with had been so lucky. Betsy Emkey had been teaching a class of third graders when one of her larger boys had managed to slink off to the back of the room and amplify. Betsy had been able to get him restrained, but not without suffering multiple bites to the arms and torso. Her school's vice principal had been the one to shoot her, after getting her students out of the room and into the care of the school nurse, who had performed blood tests on all twenty-one of the remaining students, and who had been forced to administer lethal injections to the three who came up positive. Betsy's memorial service had been small, private, and filled with people who couldn't meet each other's eyes. "There but for the grace of God" was the first thought on every teacher's mind when one of those articles showed up in the news feeds, when one of those unavoidable tragedies sparked a moment of silence from the President and a whole new round of legislation aimed at getting kids out of classrooms and into bubbles, where they could grow up safe and secure and unsocialized.

"They can learn math and reading and history anywhere, but we're the ones who have to teach them how to be a part of the human race" had been one of Betsy's favorite sayings, right after "The early bird catches the worm" and "Bless your uncultured heart." Elaine had always thought Betsy was on to something—although maybe not so much with the thing about the birds. Humanity, though, that was a thing that needed teaching. Her first graders came to her every year, standing in the doorway and looking terrified of the prospect of spending a year in Miss Oldenburg's class, which seemed so grown up and structured and strange from the perspective of their limited experiences. And every year, she gathered them close and she lifted them up, showing them the bright sun of human society, the joy of friends who didn't just exist on a computer screen, and the virtue of spending time playing in the summer air and splashing in mud puddles.

The dead might walk, and the world might be a dangerous place, but as far as Elaine Oldenburg was concerned, that was no reason to live your life in fear. Joy was the only thing that would really make the future better.

She was walking around the room, checking the supplies of construction paper, crayons, pencils, and zip ties, when a knock on the door alerted her to the fact that she was no longer alone. She turned to see the school's night custodian, Guy, standing and watching her, a smile on his broad, bearded face. His ever-present black leather cap was tilted back on his head, concealing his bald spot without hiding his eyes. The children didn't like it when they couldn't see people's eyes. Too many horror movies and news reports focusing on the ocular effects of a full-blown Kellis-Amberlee conversion, making it harder for people whose eyes were naturally black or who had developed retinal KA through no fault of their own.

"Morning, Miss Oldenburg," he said with a tip of that same cap. "Any trouble on the grounds?"

Elaine couldn't help but smile. He started every day with the same question, as regular as the blood tests at the toll booth between her house and the school. She didn't know what she would do when he reached retirement age at the end of the year—something that had been lowered to fifty for people who worked directly with children, including teachers, administrative staff, and yes, school janitors. The higher your chances of suffering a heart attack or something similar while you were at work, the sooner you would find yourself shuffled off to pasture. There were always positions teaching with the virtual schools, and hospitals were more than happy to absorb the support staff that the schools were legally required to dismiss, but still. Guy was part of the school, as much a fixture as the water fountains or lockers, and it wouldn't be the same without him.

"My next door neighbor still won't cancel his newspaper, even though he only brings it in once a week; the rest of the time, it's just an expensive eyesore announcing to the world that he's too hip to get his news online like the rest of the world," she reported dutifully. "How about you, Guy? Any trouble on the grounds?"

"Not as such, and I can't complain," he said, with a sunny smile that showed off his dentures. "Everything's shipshape and ready for the students. Do you have an exciting lesson planned for today?"

"I was thinking we might read a little, maybe learn some American history, maybe have a snack." Elaine shrugged. "I'm playing it mostly by ear."

"You always do," Guy said and laughed. Elaine laughed with him. "You have a nice day, Miss Oldenburg, and call me if you need anything. My shift doesn't end until nine."

"I'll do that, Guy, thank you," said Elaine. She watched as the janitor turned and continued on to the next classroom, where another version of their daily talk would no doubt play out. She knew that some of the teachers found him less endearing than she did, but as far as she was concerned, it was best to know and be friendly with as much of the staff as possible. It would make it easier to tell if something was wrong with them.

The clock above her whiteboard made a small chiming noise as the display turned from 7:29 to 7:30. Half an hour before she had to go out to the front of the school to collect her students and escort them back to the classroom, settling each one with a coloring sheet and a handful of colored pencils before going back to get the next. Once, that sort of arrangement would have been an invitation to chaos—leaving a classroom full of first graders alone not just once, but multiple times, was like dangling a carrot in front of a hungry rabbit and expecting it not to jump. The restraints in the legs of the desks had taken care of a lot of the problems. Students couldn't get up and race around the room; students couldn't get up at all. There would be no physical bullying while the teacher was out of the room. That was, as far as Elaine was concerned, the only small blessing to the arrangement.

There was still teasing, of course, and bullying of the verbal kind; Elaine couldn't prevent that, and the laws regarding constant surveillance in the classroom were stalled in committee as lawmakers argued an endless loop of student privacy versus public safety. Even the teachers were divided on the topic. Privately, Elaine thought the cameras couldn't come fast enough. As far as she was concerned, anything she did on school grounds was fair game for the bureaucrats. Getting qualified teachers was hard enough that she wasn't going to get fired over something as small as swearing when she jammed her finger in the door or snapping at a student who ran a little too fast in the hallway, and having those videos might make the antibullying statutes easier to enforce.

In the meantime, she walked her students one by one into the classroom, and she watched them like a hawk throughout the year, quashing bullying wherever it reared its ugly head. Everyone on campus knew that Miss Oldenburg ran a tight ship, something that very few parents would have guessed during orientation, when they were confronted with a red-haired slip of a woman in a flowered dress, who looked like she could be one of the school's student teachers, not the leader of a whole first-grade class.

There was a time when those parents would have been thrilled to meet a teacher like Elaine Oldenburg, who was still bright and vivacious and engaged after eight years in what was widely regarded as one of the toughest jobs in the world. That time was before the Rising had come along and changed all the rules. First grade was a tricky year, filled with kids who might not fully understand the importance of sterile conditions and avoiding contact with classmates who suffered from bloody noses or skinned knees. By second grade, the students generally understood the dangers they would face in their adult lives, at least academically, but first graders were still carefree and immortal, unable to accept that there was anything in the world more powerful than Mommy and Daddy and Teacher. Even that wouldn't have been such a big problem—kindergarteners were worse, so confident in their own indestructability that it was a rare month without at least one full decontamination cycle in the kindergarten wing—except for the small and immutable factor of age.

First grade was the year when the top fifty percent of students crossed the forty-pound threshold, growing into amplification range. A blood-soaked kindergartener was a walking biohazard, but it was a *safe* one, inasmuch as any biohazard can be considered "safe." The affected child wouldn't amplify. Once you hit first grade, that was no longer a guarantee. First grade was where teachers were lost.

Elaine Oldenburg smiled as she gave her classroom one last assessing look, checking to be absolutely sure that everything was in its proper place. Then she smoothed her skirt, checked to be sure that her pistol was properly holstered at her waist, and went to begin bringing in the students.

Classroom sizes reached their peak in the last years before the Rising, with as many as forty students per teacher in lower-income areas. This teacher/student disparity would later be blamed for the high fatality rates in those same schools: with too few adult authority figures to tell the students what to do, every exposure became an immediate crisis. Many great educators met their deaths in the chaos, and far too few of them managed to save the students they were fighting for. By the end of the Rising, America's educational policy was shifting toward an attitude of self-preservation over self-sacrifice: an infected student could not do as much damage as an infected teacher. It was thus the duty of those adults to shoot first, in order to save themselves and avoid becoming a threat.

The standard class size at Evergreen Elementary was eighteen. Eighteen students to each teacher, not counting student teachers and college-level aides, who—when distributed across the school—brought the actual adult/child ratio to something closer to one adult for every eleven children. When secured to their desks during the morning loading phase or during an unavoidable teacher absence from the classroom, the students were unable to reach one another. The desks were bolted to the floor to guarantee that there would be no unsupervised physical contact of any kind.

When we look at the events of that terrible day only eight years in our past, it is important to remember that the teachers of Evergreen Elementary did everything they could: they took every precaution and followed every rule. If there were any justice in the world, they would have been rewarded with long lives, successful careers, and eventual retirement to the virtual education system, where they could have continued to teach until they chose to retire. There would have been no need for them to be lauded as heroes. They would have been forgotten by the march of history, quietly wiped from the memories of all save for the students they mentored, taught, and freed into their own beautiful futures.

There is no justice in the world. There never has been.

—FROM *UNSPOKEN TRAGEDIES OF THE AMERICAN SCHOOL SYSTEM* BY ALARIC KWONG, MARCH 19, 2044

Wednesday, March 19, 2036, 8:52 A.M.

It had been a surprisingly quick, smooth load-in process, especially for a Wednesday. Monday and Tuesday, the children were too tired from the weekend to fight. Thursday and Friday, they were too excited that it was almost the weekend again to want to risk getting into trouble. That left Wednesday as the day for troublemakers and tantrums—but all seventeen students had walked through their blood tests and escort as smooth as silk. Miss Oldenburg glanced at the clock as she closed the classroom door. It wasn't even nine A.M. yet! This was going to be a wonderful day. She could already tell.

Normally, her class would have consisted of nineteen students, but Amelia's parents had pulled her out of school to visit a grandparent in Vancouver before the expected laws governing transport of minors across the Canadian border were passed, and Billy had been out sick for most of the week. He'd be allowed to come back once his parents supplied a letter from his doctor certifying that he had been symptom-free for at least five days. Kellis-Amberlee had cured "the common cold," that vast and intricate web of virtually identical diseases that had been the bane of educators since the first schoolroom was constructed, but not even Kellis-Amberlee could stop the flu, or the lingering strains of pertussis still circulating in the Pacific Northwest, thanks to the efforts of the pre-Rising antivaccination movement. With students increasingly sensitized to anything that smacked of illness, sick children were no longer allowed anywhere near campus, and were shunted to virtual classrooms as soon as their symptoms began.

It was too bad, really, thought Miss Oldenburg, as she walked around the classroom collecting the coloring sheets she'd used to distract her students as they were bolted to their desks. Billy was one of those rare students who really *loved* coming to class, despite all the fuss and bother it entailed. She knew full well that some of her kids would drop out of the face-to-face system by fourth grade, choosing the sterile security of a computer screen and a teacher they would never meet over the fleshy dangers of actually attending school. Every teacher in the face-to-face system dreamt of having their students stay on physical campuses all the way to graduation, choosing risk and reward over safety, but none of them had any illusions about how likely that was.

The elementary schools were relatively full, because kids that young—especially kids too young to amplify—were essentially fearless, unable to really understand why their parents worried so much when they walked out the door. They enjoyed the freedom of recess, and they tolerated the intrusion of the blood tests and the random infection drills. But bit by bit, that bravery would be worn away by the world around them, until most of those same students became as petrified and paranoid as their parents. It was a seemingly unavoidable cycle, and all Miss Oldenburg wanted to do was break it for as many of her students as she could. She wanted to give them a better future. It was the same thing every teacher had wanted since time began, but none of those other teachers had been striving for it against the backdrop of the zombie apocalypse.

Sometimes she wondered whether it had been as hard for them. And then she thought back on what her own teachers had said, when she was struggling through classrooms still shell-shocked and disrupted by the Rising, and she knew that it had always been this hard. It was just the nature of the obstacles that had changed, and would keep changing, for as long as there were students to be taught.

Miss Oldenburg picked up the last of the coloring sheets and walked to the front of the room, silent, back straight, sensible shoes tapping on the tile like a metronome. She could feel her students watching her, waiting for the moment when their day would officially begin. She put the sheets down on the blotter—an outdated piece of classroom equipment if there had ever been one—and picked up the remote that controlled their desk restraints. Turning back to face the room, she smiled brightly and clicked the "release" button. The desk restraints snapped open with a soft pneumatic sigh, sliding back and out of the way. Seventeen first graders giggled and stretched, reveling in their newly restored freedom, even if none of them tried to get up. This was part of the morning ritual, just as much as the long solo walk with the teacher down the mostly empty hall, passing other teacher/student pairs, before the classroom door finally loomed safe and secure in front of them. Miss Oldenburg's students weren't kindergarten babies anymore, but they still understood the power of ritual.

Ritual kept you safe. As long as you followed it, close as close can, nothing could ever hurt you.

"Good morning, class," said Miss Oldenburg. "How was everyone's evening?"

Hands were thrust into the air as the students raced to be the first to tell her about the hours between the final bell and bedtime. Glorious hours, free from adult structure and adult rules—although they were, Miss Oldenburg noted sadly, more confined than even her own first-grade hours had been. She had been seven when the Rising began, and thanks to the timing of her birthday, she had been preparing to start second grade. She remembered first grade as the last good time before everything had fallen apart. Long afternoons spent racing around the cul-de-sac where her family lived, playing tag and hide-and-seek and house with the other kids, most of whom had not survived the Rising. Long evenings lying on the grass in the backyard with her father, trying to name the stars, aware that he was just trying to keep her from spending all her time sitting in front of the television or playing video games, and yet not quite able to bring herself to care.

First grade had been the best year of her life. Maybe, if the Rising hadn't started when it did, she would have forgotten that good year in favor of remembering other, even better years... but the Rising hadn't wanted to wait for her to form more good memories. It had happened when it wanted to happen, and Elaine Oldenburg had been left thinking of first grade as an earthly paradise. Part of her still did, and always would, no matter how many fights she broke up, how many bruises she reported to the authorities, or how many times she had to call for decontamination after a nosebleed. First grade was where things still had the potential to go *right*. Everything after that...

Everything after that was all downhill.

Mikey's father had finally allowed him to have a Quest Realm account of his very own, on a child-safe server, and he was playing a Pixie Ranger with a dire wolf companion whose mouth had *so many* teeth. Mikey spread out his hands and waggled his fingers on the words "so many," like he was trying to illustrate a mathematical concept too large to be expressed in simple numbers. Jenna's rat had had her babies, and now Jenna had eleven rats—two grown-ups and nine pups—and she was going to keep them all, and she would never be lonely, not ever. Sharon and Emily were going to have a sleepover on the weekend, and they had spent most of the previous afternoon instant-messaging each other about it, and they were both so excited that they were finishing one another's sentences, words tumbling over each other like kittens at play. Scott had spent the evening adding samples to his rock collection, which was almost big enough to take up a whole shelf.

This sharing time was a normal part of Wednesday mornings, as normal as the lockdown and the coloring sheets and the way Mikey sometimes ate the red crayons—but only the red ones, making it a relatively easy problem to solve, as long as Miss Oldenburg could remember to give him greens and blues and browns instead, which she didn't always, not in the rush to get all her students safely inside. She listened patiently to their stories, nodding when it seemed appropriate, asking questions when she could see that they were holding back details out of shyness or out of uncertainty whether their share was somehow dull or stupid or otherwise not worth finishing. One by one, all seventeen of her students spoke, setting their private worlds in front of her to be judged, and she didn't find a single one of them wanting.

The clock struck 9:30 just as Brian was finishing his tale of the epic battle between his father and a bookshelf from IKEA that had resisted all efforts to put it together. Miss Oldenburg clapped her hands together, beaming. "Those were some wonderful stories," she said. "You all had the very best evening, and I wish I could have been there with you, because it sounds like I would have had a lot more fun than I did sitting here and grading your math papers."

A groan swept through the class, which was much more interested in the story of Brian's bookshelf than in the thought of getting their math papers back.

"Now, come on," said Miss Oldenburg. "You don't even know how you did yet! Maybe you all did fabulously. You'll only find out if you look at your papers." She twisted to pick up the folder from her desk, stuffed with slightly wrinkled sheets of paper and bristling with gold stars. "We're going to have a math review, we're going to discuss all of our answers, and then we're going to have the ten o'clock recess slot. How does that sound to everyone?"

This time she was met with cheers instead of groaning. Miss Oldenburg smiled brighter than ever.

"That's what I thought. Who wants to help me hand back these papers?"

>> MGOWDA: WHAT MAKES YOU THINK THIS "ELAINE OLDENBURG" IS OUR TARGET?

>> AKWONG: FACIAL RECOGNITION COMES UP TO ABOUT 80%, WHICH IS PRETTY GOOD, GIVEN SIX YEARS + PROBABLE PLASTIC SURGERY. ADD HAIR DYE, DIFFERENCE IN DEMEANOR... I NEVER SAW THE WOMAN, BUT I THINK THIS IS HER. WAS HER. SHIT, BOSS, HOW DO YOU GO FROM POINT A TO POINT B?

>> MGOWDA: YOU FOUND HER. YOU FIGURE IT OUT.

—internal communication between Alaric Kwong and Mahir Gowda, After the End Times private server, March 16, 2044

Wednesday, March 19, 2036, 9:57 A.M.

Walking seventeen squirmy first graders through a basic math review wasn't Elaine's favorite activity, but it was still rewarding to see them light up when they got an answer right, something that happened more and more frequently as they worked their way through the test. Everyone had passed, which helped, and they each wound up with two or even three gold stars adorning their shirts and sleeves. Most of the stars would wind up stuck to desks, walls, or the floor by the end of the day, and then Elaine would collect them all and stick them to her folder, which slowly grew from plain paper to a galaxy over the course of each year. She knew this was how things were going to go, just as surely as she knew that after recess they would come back to the classroom for spelling and vocabulary, which would carry them all the way to lunch. Her day was a series of small, predictable routines, cut into child-sized pieces, and that was the way she liked it to be. Surprises were for other people. First grade was for learning, and for knowing every morning how the rest of the day was going to go.

"All right, class, that's our last answer. You all did very well. Give yourselves a hand." She clapped, and the class dutifully echoed her, filling the room with the sound of palms striking together. Miss Oldenburg beamed. "Now it's time for our favorite part of the day. Who knows what that is?"

"Recess!" everyone crowed, in delighted if uneven unison. The recess assignments changed every week, to make sure that no class got a permanent claim on the nicest parts of the day. But even when recess happened immediately after load-in, spilling students out onto the blacktop while the air was still chilly from the night before, it remained everyone's favorite part of the classroom routine. Fresh air, open skies, green grass... it was magical.

"That's right," said Miss Oldenburg. She picked up her coat—ankle-length, with Kevlar panels carefully concealed beneath the thick wool—and slipped it on. She'd need to switch to her summer coat in another month or so, which was much more obviously a form of armor, with its thin nylon fabric molding itself to the Kevlar that protected her limbs and joints. "What are the rules of recess?"

"Eyes and ears open, watch for danger, run for a teacher if anything seems strange," chorused the class. They were more unified this time. The rules of recess were more familiar to them than the Pledge of Allegiance, and stood a better chance of keeping them all alive. As they got older, they would replace the word "teacher" with "policeman" or "safe room," but the rest of the rules would be with them for life.

The bell rang once, signaling the end of the previous recess period. Miss Oldenburg clapped her hands again. "Everyone up, out of your seat, jackets on, and get ready to go," she said brightly.

The students obliged, forming a quick, straight line in front of the door. There was no pushing or shoving; no one got out of first grade without learning just how quickly their recess privileges could be taken away—in some cases permanently. Everyone knew about the no-recess classes, the ones where instead of twenty minutes of freedom under the sky, they got twenty minutes to read or play with handheld games, always seated, always under the watchful eye of their teacher. Freedom was important. Too important to risk on the brief pleasure of misbehaving when being good for just a few minutes more would mean getting outside, where misbehavior was ever so much easier.

All the teachers knew that there was a certain amount of pushing and squabbling on the playground. The cameras caught it all, and it was reviewed every night by campus security, who flagged anything troublesome straight to the appropriate teacher's inbox. Students who regularly picked fights or bullied classmates would find themselves being watched more closely, or even pulled into parent-teacher conferences where their behavior would be discussed, and options would be put on the table, many of them pharmaceutical. Elaine wasn't in favor of using drugs on students who didn't have genuine medical reasons for them—Mikey had ADHD and was a much happier boy when he was taking his Ritalin; one of her students the year before had had childhood-onset OCD and had needed a complicated cocktail of pills just to get through the day without panicking over pencil shavings on the floor—but it was really between the parents and their doctor, and more and more chose sedation over the risk of a playground injury leading to exposure with every year that passed. Someday, she was sure, her classes would no longer care about recess; they would be medicated into calm acceptance of their place indoors, and the blacktops would lie empty and unneeded until they were torn up to build new, secure classrooms.

That day wasn't here yet. The bell rang again, signaling that the halls were empty, and Miss Oldenburg opened the door.

The recess system used by Evergreen Elementary, and by other schools in the district, was revolutionary for its time, and even now, eight years after the 2036 incident, experts have been unable to find any fault with the design. The issue, it can be argued, was not with the system itself, but with the simple fact that no system, however idealized, can be expected to behave with perfect predictability once a human element has been introduced. In short, the issue was not with the school itself, nor with any of the checkpoints installed to prevent incidents such as the one which unfolded on that chilly March morning. The issue was, and will always be, with us.

Elaine Oldenburg led her students down the empty hall to the rear door leading to their quarter of the blacktop. A security official was waiting there with a blood-testing station. As each student tested clean, they entered an airlock, waiting there until the entire class, and their teacher, had been cleared. Only then did the airlock open. The school playground had been divided into four sections, each containing a portion of blacktop, a portion of lawn, and a play structure. These sections were sterilized throughout the day, with a ten-minute break between recess sessions, and plans in place for closing individual sections as needed in the case of greater contamination. Walls separated them. Only sound could travel from one section to another.

The sound of laughter. The sound of screams.

—FROM *UNSPOKEN TRAGEDIES OF THE AMERICAN SCHOOL SYSTEM* BY ALARIC KWONG, MARCH 19, 2044

Wednesday, March 19, 2036, 10:05 A.M.

Seventeen first graders poured out of the back door of Evergreen Elementary and onto the playground. They had been assigned the coveted leftmost section for this week's recess, with one wall that actually bordered on the forest. The forest! The big, dark forest, full of mysteries and monsters! Half the class ran to claim space for kickball on the grass nearest the wall, where they could feel brave and clever for standing so close to the forbidden outside world. The other half took refuge on the play structure at the center of the blacktop, some of them grabbing red balls from the available basket, others swarming up the monkey bars with the ease of long practice.

It was still a little chilly, and Elaine smiled and wrapped her arms around herself as she watched her charges storm the battlements of childhood, their shrieks and laughter drifting back to her like the sweetest music ever composed. They would learn to be afraid soon enough, she knew; she had done substitute playground duty for third and fourth graders when her name came up in the rotation, had watched their sea of dismayed faces as they jockeyed for spots on the blacktop nearest the school doors, where they could flee back to safety at a moment's notice. Fear really crept in during the summer between first and second grade, she felt; that was when the world became too big and loud to be overlooked, when the fact that it could touch you became unavoidable. This was their last truly carefree time, and she was blessed to be one of its custodians.

It was a little harder to hang on to that feeling of being blessed when things got messy, as they inevitably did. "Miss Oldenburg!" wailed Sharon, running over from the strip of green, her legs pumping wildly as they ate up the distance. "Mikey pushed Emily down and said girls can't play kickball and you have to come tell him he's in trouble now! He should be in trouble! He pushed her *down*!" Sharon mimed a pushing motion, just in case her teacher didn't understand.

Elaine sighed, dropping her arms to her sides and pulling the mantle of "teacher" back over herself like a cloak of assumed authority and vague disapproval. "All right, Sharon, take me to him."

They hustled across the playground, not quite as fast as Sharon's angry run of the moment before, but faster than Miss Oldenburg's usual calm stroll. All the students who saw them pass knew that someone was about to be in trouble, and a few of them fell in behind the pair, ready to watch punishments rain down. It was a rare treat, really, at least for the students who knew they weren't the ones in trouble.

Scott watched his teacher and classmate hustle past and jumped to his feet, abandoning the piece of grass he'd been slowly shredding as he seized this rare opportunity and ran for the base of the slide. The playground equipment was all mounted on a soft, spongy material made from recycled tires and guaranteed to minimize accidents; it wasn't quite like falling on a trampoline, but it was softer than the pavement and more hygienic than sand, and it didn't rip up student knees and elbows like tanbark did. It was the perfect solution in a world where blood was the enemy, but where little kids still needed the freedom to run off their excess energy.

There was just one problem with this wonderful material: it was made of rubber, and like all things that were made of rubber, it could rip.

Scott's rock collection was the center of his world. He was a quiet, inquisitive child who enjoyed spending time in his room, playing with his toys, and liked his solitary activities. He didn't have many friends, and he didn't feel like he was missing anything. But oh, how he wanted a piece of his playground. He understood dimly, from listening to his mother and father at the dinner table, that there were adults who wanted to take the playground away; they thought that it was dangerous to have children running around outside like wild things, no matter how closely supervised they were, and would replace all outdoor play areas with enclosed, padded, *safe* equivalents, ones where there was no sky, or grass...or rocks. Scott thought this was just about the dumbest thing he'd ever heard. He also knew that no one was going to listen to him. People barely listened to him about things that were facts, like how many kinds of quartz there were or why you shouldn't play with mercury. They sure weren't going to listen to him about things that were *opinions*, like "Skies and grass and rocks are important, and you should let us keep having them."

If the playground was going to go away, he was going to save a piece of it first, so that he could look at it forever, even when everything else was gone. He'd spent months trying to figure out how he could steal a piece of playground. It was solid around the edges, fresh and square and not given to breaking off when someone tried to bend it. He couldn't bring a hammer or anything like that to school; he'd get caught and he'd get stopped and then Miss Oldenburg would take whatever he'd brought away from him. Then—worst of all, worse than anything else in the world—she would look at him sadly, shake her head, and say, "I'm disappointed in you, Scott. I thought better of you."

No. That wouldn't work. But there were other ways, and after searching all the way up into November, he'd finally found one: the plastic under the slide was starting to crack. It was good, strong stuff, but it wasn't meant to last forever in the Seattle weather, and the rain was weakening it just enough that it was breaking around the posts that anchored the slide to the ground. He'd started out by digging his fingers into the cracks, peeling back the rubber until—o, wonder!—he could see the equally cracked surface of the blacktop beneath. The new blacktop had been poured in a hurry, to meet the sudden need for higher safety standards. They hadn't installed the playground equipment on the dirt, but had bolted it straight to the blacktop.

It had taken Scott three whole months, not counting the days when snow had kept them all inside, but he had managed to work a large enough chunk of rubber loose, and now he could get his whole hand into the hole he'd created. Since then, he'd been wiggling the broken pieces of blacktop, shifting them a little bit at a time, like he was working a puzzle. They were getting looser all the time. He could feel it, measuring his progress in the increased give and lessening resistance of the artificial stone. Soon, he'd be able to pull a piece out to keep forever, and then he could stop keeping secrets from Miss Oldenburg, who was very strict about things like digging in the dirt and messing with the play structures. Technically, he was doing both at the same time, which meant she would be doubly strict, and probably doubly disappointed if she ever found out.

Some of the other kids knew about his digging—it was impossible to keep anything *completely* secret when you spent so much time with the same sixteen people, all of them bored and scared and poking their noses into your business—but they all thought it was one of those weird but harmless things that everybody had. Nobody tattled about *those* things. Someone who told on how Scott liked to dig when the teacher wasn't looking might get told on in turn, and their thing might be bigger and worse than a little dirt. There were nose pickers and butt sniffers and hair lickers in the class, all of them trying their best not to get caught, which meant not setting anyone else up to get caught, either.

Elaine Oldenburg's class was a complicated web of social connections and uneasy alliances, all of them watching each other with the wary suspicion of a Cold War American military, none of them willing to strike the first blow. All of which led, inexorably, to Scott Ribar digging in the rubber surfacing under the slide, unremarked upon and unbetrayed by his classmates, who weren't willing to put themselves into the line of fire.

Scott was so intent on working at his chunks of blacktop that he didn't notice when John—probably his closest friend in the class, which wasn't saying much, since they were both tagged "the weird kid" and left mostly to their own devices—loomed up behind him and asked, brightly, "How's it coming?"

"Shh!" Scott yanked his hand out of the hole so fast that he scraped the side of his wrist on the edge of the hole. Bright blood immediately beaded up along the line of torn skin. His eyes widened when he saw it. "Shit. *Shit.*" Saying the forbidden word made him feel a little better, but not much. He knew that blood was bad. Blood meant no more classes for the rest of the day, and not in the fun way, like when they went to the chocolate factory to watch the machines or when there was an assembly and everyone watched movies on the big screen that stretched the length of the gymnasium wall. This would be the kind of no-more-classes that meant needles, and quarantine, and interrogation, and being weighed a dozen times to make sure he hadn't magically gained ten pounds between the start of the day and the moment when he'd started bleeding. Blood was the *worst* thing.

John didn't move away. He actually leaned a little closer. "Whoa, you're bleeding," he said. "Does it hurt?" He sounded only academically interested, not frightened in the least.

"A little," admitted Scott.

Something in his tone told John what he was worried about. It was a common enough scenario, triggered by every skinned knee and bloody nose since they were kindergarten babies. John paused. This was an opportunity to take Scott from being an almost-maybe friend to a real friend, someone who would be nice to him because there were debts between them, spaces filled with secrets and unspoken oaths. "You don't have to get caught," he said.

Scott froze. "Wh-what?"

"It's on your wrist. You have a long-sleeve jacket, and it looks real absorbent inside. Just pull it down over the tops of your hands, and tell Miss Oldenburg you're cold when we go back inside. She won't make you take it off. She'd have to keep the classroom warmer if she started making kids take their coats off."

Scott was quiet for a moment, considering the scope of the monumental deceit that John was suggesting. It would mean *lying.* Not only that, it would mean *lying to a teacher.* He was almost never cold. His mom always said that he was a little furnace on legs. But if he would just *lie to a teacher*, he might not have to go through quarantine and needle jabs and people asking him questions he didn't want to answer—and most important of all, they might not find out what he'd been doing under the slide and fill in the hole before he could finish getting what he needed.

"Okay," he said. "Let's do it."

When the bell for the end of recess rang and Miss Oldenburg's first-grade class lined up to head back into the building, no one noticed that Scott Ribar was wearing his coat pulled all the way down over the tops of his hands. They had other things to worry about, and he was a weird kid, and besides, when he got his finger stuck at the airlock, his test results came back clean and uninfected, just like the rest of them. There was no danger. There was no reason to think that anything was out of the ordinary.

One teacher and seventeen students walked back into the building.

Twelve of those students would never walk out again.

>> AKWONG: DON'T HOLD DINNER FOR ME TONIGHT. I'M TRYING TO FINISH THIS REPORT BEFORE THE BOSS DECIDES TO HAVE ME THROWN TO THE WOLVES.

>> AKWONG: POSSIBLY LITERAL WOLVES, I MEAN. IF I DON'T NAIL THIS ONE, HE'S LIKELY TO DECIDE THAT I SHOULD BE THE ONE TO HEAD UP TO CANADA AND LOOK FOR S&G, AND KNOWING THEM, THEY PROBABLY HAVE A TAME PACK OF TIMBER WOLVES PROTECTING THEIR HIDDEN, HEAVILY BOOBY-TRAPPED CABIN.

>> MGARCIA: SO WHAT I'M HEARING IS "PLEASE MAKE SPAGHETTI, SINCE IT REHEATS EASILY, AND BE PREPARED TO OFFER SEX AND SYMPATHY WHEN I FINISH WORKING AND DEIGN TO COME DOWNSTAIRS."

>> AKWONG: YOU ARE THE PERFECT WOMAN.

>> MGARCIA: DON'T I KNOW IT.

—internal communication between Alaric Kwong and Maggie Kwong-Garcia, After the End Times private server, March 16, 2044

Wednesday, March 19, 2036, 10:40 A.M.

The recess period after Miss Oldenburg's class had gone to a fourth-grade classroom this week. The actual assignment of recess periods was random, but the smaller students were often followed on the playground by larger ones, and vice versa, in the theory that it would reduce potential contamination vectors. First graders got into different things than fourth graders did, and so on. This was an innately flawed way of thinking. Sadly, the flaws were not fully understood until the events at Evergreen Elementary. Because of this, no better system had yet been proposed.

The fourth graders poured out onto the blacktop, following a somewhat different pattern than their first-grade schoolmates. They sauntered, some of them looking intentionally relaxed, like they weren't bothered at all by being outdoors. A few went to lounge on the play equipment—not using it, of course, since that would have been *so* uncool, but sitting on it, dangling their feet off the edges of it, and pretending as hard as they could that they were still comfortable without a ceiling above their heads. A few of the girls wandered over to the grass and sat down, choosing bravery in order to get the privacy they so desperately craved.

There were twelve students in the class. None of them would survive to the end of the school day. But they didn't know that, not then, not with the fresh, cool air filling their lungs and the sky glimmering blue through the cracks in the clouds. They went about their business like this wasn't the last day of their lives. For Nathan Patterson and Joseph Lee, this meant waiting until their teacher was distracted and then ducking into the space beneath the slide, where they could browse the contents of Joseph's phone in peace. Joseph was a whiz with computers—there were already three private high schools jockeying for him to come to them, once he graduated from middle school—and he had been able to bypass the parental controls installed by his father with an ease that approached unreal. As a consequence, he was the only kid in class whose data plan came with all the pornography the Internet had to offer.

Joseph and Nathan sat down under the slide, staring wide-eyed at the various naked women, all of them striking poses that looked uncomfortable but somehow enticing, like there was an important component sitting just outside of their reach.

"Dude, look at her *boobs*," said Nathan.

"I'm looking," confirmed Joseph. He was less enthralled by his companion: after all, the magical fountain of breasts and butts and other parts went home with him at night, where he could look until his eyes were hot and his mouth was dry. He tried to have fresh things every day, though, just to keep Nathan from getting too jealous. So far, Nate—who was a good guy, if a little slow—hadn't realized just how inequitable their friendship was. Joseph didn't want to start getting asked to jailbreak his friends' phones. It would begin with one person, but it never stayed that way, and if the teacher found out...

Joseph didn't have to be a genius to know what the consequences of unlocking the phones of everyone in class would be. Being a genius just made the images clearer and harder to ignore. He didn't like getting in trouble. This would be trouble on a *nuclear* scale.

There was a certain irony that neither boy would have appreciated, had it been pointed out to them then or later. Because Joseph Lee didn't want to get in trouble, he and Nathan hid what they were doing from their teacher. Because Scott Ribar hadn't wanted to get in trouble, he had hidden his injury from his teacher, and from the guards who performed his blood test at the school gates. Had school security known that a student had been bleeding on the playground, they would have closed it down for the rest of the day, bringing out the canisters of bleach and the black lights and the bloodstain detection equipment. The fourth grade would have missed their recess. Everyone would have missed recess the next day. But no one would have been hurt.

Scott Ribar was too small to amplify, and had little to fear from biological contamination. He could have touched infected blood a hundred times and never risked anything more than a lecture and a thorough decontamination. That didn't mean the Kellis-Amberlee virus had spared him. It lived all throughout his body, protecting him from the little trials that had haunted childhoods for a thousand years. He had never suffered from a cold, he had never wasted a beautiful day throwing up or sniffling and being forbidden to go outside. Thanks to Kellis-Amberlee and his yearly flu shots, he had never been really sick a day in his life.

But Kellis-Amberlee was patient. It knew, in its slow, virological way, that one day Scott would become a viable host, and so it continued to replicate inside his body... right up until the moment when he bled on the ground near the slide. Then, the blood that was no longer truly a part of Scott began to change. Kellis-Amberlee was designed to have two states: one active, one inert. Separated from the electrical currents that kept it calm and inactive, the Kellis-Amberlee in Scott's blood had become active and infectious. The area under the slide was a hot zone, ready to infect anyone who came into contact with it.

The bell rang. Nathan and Joseph looked up. Nathan scowled and thrust the phone at Joseph, taking the hand he'd been using to brace himself and wiping it harshly across his mouth before he said, "That's bull. We should get more time than this."

"Yeah," agreed Joseph, slipping the phone back into his pocket as he stood. Then he offered Nathan his hand. Nathan scowled at it for a moment, still upset by the loss of the phone. Finally, he took it and allowed Joseph to pull him to his feet.

Nathan's palm was moist, and gritty with gravel from the blacktop. Joseph resisted the urge to wipe his hand clean on the seat of his pants. He didn't want to pick a fight. He could always wash his hands later—although even as he had the thought he knew he wouldn't go through with the action. He never did. "Washing your hands later" was for sissies and babies and people who had touched poop, not sweaty palms. Sweaty palms were part of becoming a man, and there was nothing wrong with that.

The pair emerged from under the slide, walking as casually as was possible, and joined the line preparing to be processed back into the school. Their teacher, Mr. O'Toole, was coming up on retirement age; he looked at them indulgently, having some small idea of what two boys who chose to hide during recess were likely to be discussing. He didn't see the harm in it, not really. Biology had been messed up a bit by Kellis-Amberlee, but he hadn't survived the Rising and become a teacher to say that the natural order of things was canceled forever. That meant allowing for a bit of good old-fashioned pubescent naughtiness.

Nathan Patterson felt perfectly fine as he approached the airlock. The virus he had wiped across his lips was still hanging there, untasted, waiting for its opportunity to travel one scant inch further and invade the sanctity of his skin. His blood test came back clean, and why shouldn't it? He hadn't been exposed yet, not really. Not to anything except the

Kellis-Amberlee already inside his body and patiently waiting for its chance to change.

As he stepped through the door into the hall he remembered the woman on Joseph's phone, the one with her back arched and her eyes slanted toward the camera, like she was remembering something secret. He licked his lips. The airlock closed behind him, and the guards recorded another successful recess, no casualties, no infections.

Those would come later.

The speed with which a body reacts to a live Kellis-Amberlee infection is impressive, even within the scientific world. As the body is already saturated with the inert virus, introducing the active, or "live" virus to the system will trigger a rapid chain reaction, beginning the conversion process in a matter of seconds. While it can take up to several hours for large, otherwise healthy individuals to fully amplify, the body already knows that it is sick. Blood tests will already betray the ongoing spread of Kellis-Amberlee. Neurological exams performed by the EIS on individuals who had not yet begun showing symptoms have shown that some higher brain functions will already be compromised, beginning the process of sliding into the unthinking "zombie" state manifested by the sick.

The source of the Evergreen Elementary outbreak was later traced to a piece of playground equipment that had become contaminated during an earlier recess session. We know that the virus was carried into the school by Nathan Patterson, age 10. He was a student in Mr. O'Toole's fourth-grade class. He weighed 78 lbs., putting him well above the Kellis-Amberlee amplification threshold. He was not infected when he passed the checkpoint protecting the classrooms.

Hand swabs and sterilization would be introduced in the state of Washington in 2037 as a direct result of the events at Evergreen. Since then, these procedures have saved an unknown number of lives. There have been no further Evergreens.

I doubt this is any comfort to the parents of the students who died. It would certainly not have been a comfort to me.

—FROM *UNSPOKEN TRAGEDIES OF THE AMERICAN SCHOOL SYSTEM* BY ALARIC KWONG, MARCH 19, 2044

Wednesday, March 19, 2036, 11:23 A.M.

Elaine Oldenburg's class was deeply involved in reviewing their vocabulary lists when the windows locked down.

It was a small sound, intentionally calibrated to cause as little dismay or panic as possible: just a clunk from the base of the window as the small bolts that usually hung suspended above the metal frame suddenly descended, forming an effectively unbreakable seal. Elaine looked up, eyes widening briefly. That was the only sign of surprise that she allowed herself to show. For a teacher, keeping her students from panicking always had to be her top priority. If she betrayed any dismay over the situation, they would pick it up, and she would risk losing control. That was something she couldn't afford.

"Everyone, heads down and read quietly," she said, pushing away from her desk. "I need to make a quick call to the office."

The students grumbled but did as they were told. Those who sat close enough to the window to have heard the locks deploy assumed that it was a drill; why else would their desks still be open? They bent their heads like all the others, pulling out their readers and focusing on the text.

Elaine Oldenburg walked briskly to the corner where the phone hung, old-fashioned and obscurely menacing in this world of cell phones and wireless headsets. The school phone wouldn't have looked out of place twenty years ago, with its big, heavy buttons and curly brown cord. She plucked the receiver off the wall and brought it to her ear.

She didn't need to dial. The school's basic emergency broadcast was already playing, and she paled as it washed over her: "—repeat, do not panic. We are investigating the reported outbreak. Please remain in your classrooms. Please do not allow any students to leave the classroom. Please do not inform the students that there is a problem. We repeat, do not panic. We are investigating—"

Elaine carefully set the phone back in its cradle and turned to look around the room at her students. They were reading, or at least pretending to read; some of them were no doubt just staring at the pages, wishing that the confusing jumble of numbers and letters would resolve itself into words. All of her students were reading at the required grade level, but it was harder for some than it was for others. Just like it had always been. *The Rising couldn't change everything, I suppose,* she thought, and reddened a little, annoyed by her own flippancy. There was an outbreak on school grounds, or at least there might be. That was what she should have been thinking about, not how well her students were or were not reading.

Keeping her movement as calm and casual as possible, she walked over to the door and tried the knob. To her surprise, it turned easily, and the door—designed to open from the inside and not the outside, no matter how hard the knob was twisted—came open when she tugged. She took a deep breath before sticking her head out into the hall, looking both ways for signs that anything was wrong.

The airlock at the end of the hall was deserted, the guards no doubt elsewhere on campus, investigating the reported outbreak. The blacktop was a charcoal blur through the thick safety glass, but she saw no movement there; if there had been a class at recess when the infection was detected, they had already been recalled and returned to the safety of their classroom.

Well. The desks weren't locked, and the door wasn't locked; whatever was going on, it couldn't be all that bad. Elaine Oldenburg pulled her head back inside and closed the door, turning to find herself watched by seventeen pairs of solemn, staring eyes. She forced herself to smile. It felt artificial, but she had practiced the expression over and over, until she knew that it would seem real to anyone viewing it from outside. That was part of her job. She was a teacher. She had to reassure her students.

"They're testing the locks," she lied smoothly. "I was just following instructions and making sure that all the doors were correctly shut."

Sharon put her hand up. "Miss Oldenburg, I need to go to the bathroom," she said. A few of the other students snickered. Sharon, who was remarkably good at ignoring teasing over things that everyone did—had, in fact, done an irritated book presentation on *Everybody Poops* after some of the boys teased her for being a girl who went to the potty—ignored them, focusing on her teacher.

"I'm sorry, Sharon, but the bathrooms are off-limits right now," said Elaine apologetically. "It's not an emergency, is it?"

Sharon's cheeks reddened, and she lowered her hand. "No, Miss Oldenburg." An emergency—a real emergency—during a lockdown would mean using the bucket in the supply cabinet. Sharon might be bold about her need to occasionally leave the room, but no first grader ever was going to be happy about peeing in a bucket with only a thin door between them and their classmates.

"All right," said Elaine. "They should end the test soon, and when they do, we'll be able to go to the bathroom. Anyone who needs to." She walked back over to her desk, taking her usual place against the front of it, wishing that she dared to open the top drawer and withdraw her service pistol. She didn't like wearing it around the students most of the time, and she wasn't allowed to have it out when there wasn't an emergency: teachers weren't allowed to carry openly except during load-in and load-out until fifth grade, when it was assumed that their students were both a potential danger and smart enough not to grab for a loaded weapon. But oh, she wanted it. With an unspecified potential outbreak somewhere on campus, and seventeen little souls trusting her to keep them safe, she wanted it more than words could say.

"All right, where were we?" she asked. "Jenna, I think it was your turn."

" 'Tremble,' " read Jenna. "T-R—"

Class continued normally, with Elaine—now firmly Miss Oldenburg once more, pulling the mantle of her position around herself as if it would somehow protect her from the natural terror that was clawing at the back of her throat—leading the discussion. The windows were still locked. The windows were still locked, but the doors were open, and there had been no alarm. This didn't match any emergency procedure she knew, and she was quite reasonably afraid. She also knew that she couldn't share her fear with her students.

It was almost a relief when the alarm began to ring. It was a series of descending tones, designed to be impossible to ignore but not to incite panic, since it sounded more like a video game fail sound than a fire alarm or police siren. That was the idea, anyway. The children had heard it before, during drills and student orientation, and they knew that it meant something was wrong. When added to the locked windows and their teacher's obvious discomfort, it was clear to all of them that something was *very* wrong.

The desk restraints locked shut a few seconds later—or tried to. Less than a third of the clasps intended to hold the students in their seats actually deployed; eleven students found themselves partially restrained, with one leg connected to the desk while the other remained free. Several of the students who had been locked down began to cry. So did several of the students who hadn't been. They knew something was wrong.

Scott Ribar put his hands over his face. Emily, who sat next to him, glanced in his direction and started screaming.

Panic is a strange beast. It comes quickly when called, and leaves slowly, if it ever leaves at all. Adding Emily's shrill, terrified screams to the tears and confusion already filling the room had panic clawing at the door in a matter of seconds. Miss Oldenburg moved faster than any of them had ever seen her move, pushing away from the desk and running down the aisle of desks and half-contained students until she reached Emily. Emily was still too small to convert, and so Miss Oldenburg made a judgment call, grabbing the girl by the shoulders and pulling her around to face her teacher.

"What is it, Emily?" she demanded. "What's wrong?"

"*Blood!*" wailed Emily. "Blood, blood, he's all over blood!" In her terror and confusion her vocabulary was deserting her, leaving her with the simplistic syntax of a younger child—but even young children can get their points across when they really need to.

Miss Oldenburg's head whipped around, attention suddenly focusing on Scott, who had dropped his hands and was hiding them in his lap as he cringed away from her. He might even have gotten out of the chair in his effort to move away, if not for the single clasp that had closed around his left ankle. "Scott? What is Emily talking about?"

Scott shook his head, his mouth a thin, terrified line.

With the word "blood" still hanging in the room like a condemnation, Miss Oldenburg straightened and took a step toward his desk, demanding, "Let me see your hands." If he refused... she didn't know what she would do if he refused. She couldn't grab him. If there was any chance of contamination, touching him would be a quick way to make the situation even worse.

Thankfully, this was her classroom, and in her classroom her authority was absolute, even when it didn't have to be. Scott slowly pulled his hands out from under his desk and held them toward her, letting her see.

There was a thin brown stain at the very top of his left palm. It seemed to extend upward. "Pull your sleeve up," she instructed. He did, revealing the scrape that ran along the side of his wrist. There wasn't a *lot* of blood.

There didn't have to be.

"Scott, did you hurt yourself at recess?" It was a struggle to keep her voice level. He nodded, not meeting her eyes. "Scott, did you know that you were supposed to tell me if you got hurt? That I needed to know if you were hurt?" Again, the nod, and the lack of eye contact. Miss Oldenburg swallowed bile, resisting the urge to move as far away from him as the confines of her classroom would allow. "Scott, this is very important. Did you get blood on anything else? Did you bleed anywhere?"

"Just the ground a little, under the slide where nobody goes but me." The words were slow and halting, and filled with shame. Even if Scott was too small to amplify and hence too small to fully understand the scope of what he'd done—because he hadn't been taught yet, because there was no point in terrifying the children when you didn't have to—he knew that bleeding and then hiding it was one of the worst crimes he was capable of committing at his young age. He *knew*. But he had done it anyway. "I didn't get blood on anybody or the floor or anything. I soaked it all up in my jacket, see?" He thrust his arm toward her, like the absorbent lining of his jacket would serve as an apology all by itself.

Elaine recoiled, stopping when her hips hit the desk behind her. The students stared in wide-eyed silence, unable to fully process the sight of their normally calm, collected teacher reacting with such obvious terror. She took a deep breath, forcing the veil of Miss Oldenburg down over herself again, and said, "Don't take your coat off, Scott. Don't touch *anyone*. Especially don't touch me. I'm too big. Your blood would... your blood would hurt me."

Scott's eyes went round and bright with terror. "I don't want to hurt you, Miss Oldenburg! I don't want to hurt anybody! I just wanted a little piece of blacktop for my rock collection! I'm sorry! I'm sorry!" Then, to her shame and dismay, he started to cry.

Her classes on crowd psychology and maintaining order in the classroom told her to soothe him. Her classes in virology and outbreak containment told her to stay as far away from him as she possibly could. To her shame and her relief, safety won. "Stay in your seat, Scott," she said, and turned and walked back to the front of the class, where she moved behind her desk and unlocked the top drawer.

For some teachers, putting on the Kevlar gloves and strapping their service pistol to their waist would have brought a feeling of security, like they had finally put the world back in order. For Elaine Oldenburg, it felt like a declaration of failure. Whatever was happening on campus may well have started in her class. There was going to be an inquisition, a review; she could lose her license. Maybe that would be for the best. She loved teaching, but the feeling of cold dread now gathering under her breastbone was painful enough that it would be a long, long time before she could forget it. Maybe it would be best if she wound up going to the virtual schools early, where she would never need to feel like this again.

She knew that the memory of the fear would pass by the time she stood before the review board. All she had to do was get her students through this day, and everything would be all right, one way or another. She walked to the hook where she had hung her coat, with its sturdy Kevlar panels and protective cloth folds. Any little bit of armor between her and the disaster would be welcome.

As for her class, they watched with wide, silent eyes as she went through each step of the process. Some of them understood what she was doing. Others, who had managed to stay just a little bit more sheltered than their classmates, had no idea.

When she was finished, she turned to them, clapped her hands together—the sound muffled by the gloves—and said, "I don't know why the desk restraints aren't working, but I need you all to stay good and quiet in your seats until I tell you that you can get up. Do you understand?"

"Yes, Miss Oldenburg," they chorused, ragged and out of synch with one another.

"Good. Thank you, class." She turned and walked over to the class phone, picking it up. As expected, it was still playing the emergency announcement. She pressed "0" to get to the office. Nothing happened. She pressed "0" again. Still nothing happened. The cold feeling under her breastbone grew stronger.

Hanging up the phone, she walked back to the door and pressed her ear against it. No sounds came from the hall. She tried the knob. In the case of a real outbreak, it should have already locked, keeping them safely isolated. It wasn't locked.

"I will be right back," she said, turning to look at the class. "Do not get out of your seats."

And then, Elaine Oldenburg made what would prove to be her only mistake during the 2036 outbreak at Evergreen Elementary: a mistake that came very close to ending her life and preventing the heroic actions that she had yet to undertake.

She left the classroom.

Many of the security systems put in place in this country's elementary and middle schools were installed at the behest of "security experts" who had done their time with the TSA before the Rising, and were now being hailed, due to political connections and expert handling of the media, as masters of the safer world. They owned the companies that constructed desk restraints, magnetic window locks, and school-wide door controls systems. They recommended their machines to Congress and to the individual states. They put blueprints in front of anxious parents and said, "These things, and only these things, will keep your children safe."

There is nothing more desperate for reassurance than a parent. I have no children of my own, but as I work to raise my little sister, I find that more and more, I can be drawn in by the clever men with the elaborate blueprints who say, "This will protect her" and "This will guarantee her safety." "Guarantee" is a big word, isn't it? It's a word that says your trust is not unfounded.

As the exploratory committees formed after the Evergreen incident would prove, our trust was very much unfounded. The men and women who sold us the security of our children knew less about their jobs than many parents did. Those parents had survived the Rising on the ground, after all, and had done it despite the many dangers the world placed in front of them. The "security experts" had seen the darkest days from the safety of protected government rooms. Perhaps it was inevitable that they, and the systems they worked so hard to sell, would fail us. The tragedy is that in so doing, they also failed our children.

—FROM *UNSPOKEN TRAGEDIES OF THE AMERICAN SCHOOL SYSTEM* BY ALARIC KWONG, MARCH 19, 2044

Wednesday, March 19, 2036, 11:58 A.M.

The hall was empty. Elaine Oldenburg walked slowly and carefully down the exact center, following the red line painted on the tile. Here, no one could reach out of an unlocked classroom or stumble out of the bathrooms to grab her. Here, she would have time to react before anything happened.

Of course, walking that line, she felt so terribly, terribly exposed. She wanted to run to the wall, to let it provide her with the safety she so craved. She knew that "safety" in an outbreak situation was an illusion, and that the best way to stay safe was to tread the line without failure or deviation—but this wasn't really an outbreak situation, was it? There was an alarm, sure, but the doors weren't locking and the desks weren't following the written procedure. This had to be a misunderstanding, potentially triggered by Scott and the biohazard now soaking through the lining of his coat. She would notify the principal, and he and his staff would take care of it. She might get disciplined. She might not.

In that moment, walking down the center of the empty, echoing hall, she really didn't care either way. All she cared about was reaching the office, where there would be people. People meant safety. People meant she could stop being responsible for everything in isolation, and could start following orders again.

She had forgotten the small and simple reality that people also meant danger; people meant a place for the Kellis-Amberlee infection to gather and spread, converting innocents into instruments of destruction.

Perhaps most damning of all, she had forgotten—or maybe never really stopped to think about—the fact that while countless improvements had been made to the school layout and security since the Rising, some ideas were too institutionally embedded to change easily. School nurses had been all but phased out before the dead began to walk, viewed as a liability and a drain on limited resources. After the Rising, medical care became a priority in schools again. Nurses and trauma kits were installed in elementary schools everywhere. Unfortunately, no one really stopped to consider the standard location of the nurse's office, tucked away as it was with the rest of the school's administration. At Evergreen Elementary, to get to the nurse, you first had to pass through the main office, which was connected to both the principal and the vice principal's office. All the people responsible for making decisions about the school and how it would fare in an outbreak were right there, sharing a single common room... and the interior doors were almost never closed.

The exterior door was a different story. Elaine sped up when she spotted it. She was almost at her goal. Soon, everything would be different; soon, the hard knot of panic in her chest would let go, and she would be able to return to her class. She reached for the doorknob.

Something moved behind the frosted glass.

She froze.

One of the stranger tests teachers were required to pass involved watching shadows on a wall. Some of them moved fluidly, like healthy, uninjured humans. Others limped or shuffled along, but did it in a specific manner: people walking with canes, people walking with leg braces. *Human* ways to walk. Others shambled and stumbled, not using any sort of artificial assistance, but not walking normally, either. Those were the ones she had been trained to watch for, and while it took a few seconds for her conscious mind to catch up, her subconscious remembered what it had been taught. Her arm seized up, refusing to move any closer to the door, and to damnation.

"No," she half-whispered, and then clapped a hand over her mouth, realizing her error. The office door was solid, but almost its entire upper half was frosted glass...and none of the doors were locked. The button that controlled the doors was inside the office. If the outbreak started there, no one would have been thinking about saving the rest of the school. They would all have been thinking about saving their own skins.

The shadow that had shambled by the window stopped. It shuffled back a step, and stopped again, head canted very slightly to the side. She couldn't see anything more than an outline, but she knew that the shadow's owner was listening, waiting for another sound. In that moment, she would have stopped her own ceaselessly hammering heart, if she could have; anything to make herself less living, less visible, less endangered.

The shadow didn't move again. Elaine began to hope that she hadn't been noticed. Then, as if her hope was an invitation all by itself, the shadow behind the glass stepped closer and began to moan.

Elaine Oldenburg turned and ran.

>> MGOWDA: HOW IS IT COMING?

>> AKWONG: IF MAGGIE AND I EVER HAVE CHILDREN, WE ARE HOMESCHOOLING THEM. MAYBE HIRING PRIVATE TUTORS. ANYTHING BUT ALLOWING THEM TO ENTER THE PUBLIC SCHOOL SYSTEM.

>> MGOWDA: THAT GOOD, HUH?

>> AKWONG: 40% OF AMERICAN SCHOOLS STILL ALLOW THE NURSE'S OFFICE TO SHARE A CONNECTING DOOR WITH THE ADMINISTRATIVE

OFFICES, WHERE THE SECURITY BACKUP CONTROLS ARE LOCATED. 63% OF AMERICAN SCHOOLS ARE USING SECURITY SYSTEMS THAT DON'T HAVE THE POWER TO OVERRIDE THEIR OWN CONTROLS. SO IF THE BUTTON IN THE OFFICE THAT WOULD ALERT THE LOCAL POLICE IS DAMAGED OR MALFUNCTIONING, HITTING THE SAME BUTTON IN THE ACTUAL SECURITY CENTER DOES NOTHING.

>> MGOWDA: CHARMING. HAVE FUN TRYING TO SLEEP TONIGHT.

>> AKWONG: I HATE YOU.

—internal communication between Alaric Kwong and Mahir Gowda, After the End Times private server, March 16, 2044

Wednesday, March 19, 2036, 12:06 P.M.

Elaine Oldenburg's class looked up in terror when the door slammed open. Emily screamed. Several students began to cry. Miss Oldenburg half ran, half stumbled into the room, slamming the door behind her. Nothing had chased her down the hall. Nothing had needed to. She knew what the moaning from the office meant.

She looked around the classroom, taking in the terrified faces and the tear-filled eyes, and knew that she had a choice to make. She could try to calm them, she could try to keep them under control . . . or she could run. Her return to the classroom had been automatic, training and habit cutting through the thin veil of panic and forcing her back to the one place she knew she could be safe. The halls had still been empty when she ran along them, and zombies weren't good with doorknobs; even if her dimly sensed presence led the inhabitants of the office to break down the door, it would take them time. She could still run. She could step back out of the classroom, and she could run.

Emily was hiccupping now, her terror transitioning into misery. Mikey and Jenna were both crying, her silently, he in great whooping gasps that echoed through the otherwise silent classroom like a heartbeat. Half of them were still manacled to their chairs, sitting ducks for whatever might come through that door.

Elaine Oldenburg could have run. But in the end, she was a teacher before she was a survivor, and so all she did was step away from the door, fix a smile on her face, and say, "We're going to have an adventure. Won't that be fun?"

Her students—children of the post-Rising world, who knew that adults never said things like "We're going to have an adventure" in reality, only on the television, where everything was safe and nothing ever lunged out of the dark to rip and rend and tear—looked at her mistrustfully. Mikey stopped crying. That was a small relief.

"All right, everyone. I need you to sit quietly and leave each other alone. And I need someone to volunteer for a very big help."

Several hands went up. Elaine beamed.

"Excellent." She walked over to her desk and picked up her roll sheet, looking down the column that gave her students' estimated weights. It was intrusive, and she would have hated having her own weight listed for her teacher to see when she was in school, but at moments like this one, she not only understood the reasoning, she embraced the necessity.

Brian was the smallest boy in the class by three pounds. She looked up. His hand was raised. Thank God. She wouldn't have wanted to force this on someone who didn't want to help. It felt... wrong, somehow, to be asking her students to expose themselves to a potential biohazard, but she didn't really have a choice. It wasn't something she could do herself, not if she wanted to stay with the class, rather than trying to eat them.

"Brian, you're going to help me take care of Scott," she said. She opened the top drawer of her desk and produced a screwdriver. The students looked at it warily. Sharp-edged metal objects had been forbidden at school for their entire lives, except in the hands of teachers. Someone could get *hurt*. Someone could *bleed*.

But someone was already bleeding, and despite Miss Oldenburg's attempts to keep things as calm as possible, they were all beginning to realize that something was very wrong in their normally quiet classroom.

"Yes, Miss Oldenburg," said Brian dutifully. He started to slide out of his seat, and then froze, unsure as to whether he was supposed to be getting up.

Elaine nodded enthusiastically, beckoning him toward her as she walked toward Scott's seat, the screwdriver loose and somehow menacing in her hand. "Yes, that's right; come over here," she said. "We need to get Scott out of his seat, first off, and I can't touch him. Have you ever used a screwdriver before?"

"I helped my daddy—uh, I helped my dad put together a bookshelf last month," said Brian, his cheeks flaming red at the babyish slip. No one laughed, though. A bunch of the other kids would normally have laughed at him for using the word "daddy," and not one of them did. They were all scared. They all wanted their parents. In that moment, "daddy" was probably second only to "mommy" on most of their minds.

"Okay, good." Miss Oldenburg held out the screwdriver, clearly waiting for him to take it. Finally, fingers shaking, Brian did exactly that. She crouched down and pointed to the restraints holding Scott in place. It would have been difficult to miss the way she positioned herself, far enough back that Scott couldn't have kicked or scratched her if he'd been trying. It was... it was scary. Added on top of everything else that was going on, it was *terrifying*. "Do you see how the restraints are connected to the leg of the desk with little screws? If you can undo those, you can let Scott up."

"I want up, too!" wailed Emily. Her announcement was followed by a string of similar declarations, some of them angry, others mangled by tears and phlegm.

Miss Oldenburg stood up straight and clapped her hands. The class went instantly silent, staring at her with wide, wary eyes. "All of you need to be quiet and sit still," she said, in the tone she normally reserved for bad behavior and inattention. "Brian is going to let Scott up. We are going to take Scott to the closet, and we are going to decontaminate his hands and arms. Does anyone know what that means?"

Sharon put her hand up. Miss Oldenburg nodded to her, and she said, primly, "It means you're going to use bleach and wipe all the bad stuff away."

"That's right," said Miss Oldenburg. "Right now, Scott is a biohazard. That means that if I touch him, I might have to go away, and then there wouldn't be any teacher here to help you. So Scott has to come first. Do you understand?"

Normally, the idea of no teacher would have been a fascinating one, carrying the promise of mischief and excitement. Now, with the alarm still going and Miss Oldenburg wearing her recess coat and long gloves inside the classroom, the idea was terrifying. Several more students began to cry. The rest shook their heads in mute, anxious negation.

"Are you saying you don't understand, or that you don't want me to leave?"

"Please don't leave," whispered Jenna. The students around her nodded.

"I don't want to, Jenna. That's why Brian has to help me with Scott before we let anybody else up. Brian?" Miss Oldenburg crouched down again. "It's okay. You can start taking out the screws now."

"But I don't wanna touch a biohazard," whimpered Brian.

Miss Oldenburg swallowed her sigh. She couldn't push too hard, not if she wanted him to actually follow instructions. "He isn't dangerous to you, Brian. You don't weigh enough for him to be dangerous to you. That's why I asked you to be the one to do this very important thing. Because he can't hurt you, not until you weigh much more than you do right now." Not *that* much more, but there was no point in frightening the boy further. Not when he was already looking at the screwdriver in his hands like it was a venomous snake.

"Don't wanna," repeated Brian.

"Do you want us to leave Scott here while the rest of us go to safety?" She regretted the words almost immediately, but she was committed now: she couldn't take them back. "I have another screwdriver. I can let everyone else in this class go free, but I can't touch Scott, not until he's been decontaminated. Is that what you want?"

"No," whispered Brian.

"Are you sure?"

This time, Brian didn't say anything at all. He just nodded miserably, looking at the screwdriver in his hands.

"Then please. Let him out of the chair."

"Okay," whispered Brian, and scooted closer to Scott, who hadn't said a word during the entire exchange. The bigger boy just stared at his desk, not moving or speaking while Brian laboriously undid the screws holding the ankle restraints in place.

There were some people—mostly in equipment manufacturing, who stood to make money from the change—who wanted the simpler restraints, with their external hinges, removed from classrooms. Their nightmare scenario was the one that was being played out, with a potentially contaminated student being released by a well-meaning teacher with access to a screwdriver. But Scott wasn't the only student being held down by a restraint that couldn't save him, and even the most sophisticated models still had misfires. As long as the technology possessed any capacity for failure, there would need to be some sort of manual release. The nightmare of the administration didn't come close to the nightmares of the parents, who could all too easily picture their children, trapped, being left behind when the release switch for the classroom restraints was somewhere out of reach.

Brain was small and didn't have much upper body strength, but he was also determined, and had used a screwdriver before. After only a few minutes, all four screws were on the floor, and Scott was free. He stood shakily, and stopped as Miss Oldenburg held out her hands, palms first, warding him away.

"Scott, Brian, I need you to go to the closet," she said. "Scott, do not touch *anything*. Brian will open the door for you. Do you understand?"

The two boys, looking terrified, nodded but did as they were told. Miss Oldenburg followed them, pausing when she reached her desk to look back at the rest of the class.

"All of you stay quiet and in your seats, and do not open the door for *any reason*," she said. "Do you understand me?"

The class nodded, ragged and out of synch with one another. Miss Oldenburg looked at them for a moment, trying to decide whether or not to believe them. In the end, she decided that it didn't really matter either way; she had to do this.

"I'll be right back," she said, and followed Brian and Scott into the closet.

It was a small, claustrophobic space. The shelves were packed with basic school supplies: paper, crayons, extra ammunition, formalin, bleach. Miss Oldenburg gestured for Brian to close the door as she took down one of the sterilization bins from the shelf and set it on the floor in front of Scott. Then she got down the bottle of bleach, and the face masks. She got one. So did Brian. Scott did not.

"I am very sorry, Scott," she said gently, and began pouring bleach into the bin.

It was hard not to reflect, as the bleach fumes filled the enclosed space and the clear liquid lapped against the plastic walls of the bin, on the strange irony of the situation. There was a time when a teacher who forced a student to bathe in bleach would have been fired, for good reason, and charged with child abuse. Bleach was a caustic chemical. It could burn sensitive skin. And that didn't really matter just now, because bleach was the only thing stable enough to store in a classroom, and this was an emergency—and while she didn't want to burn Scott, she didn't want to leave him for dead, either.

Elaine Oldenburg gasped, just a little, behind her mask. Before that moment, she hadn't fully realized that she was planning to leave the classroom.

It was a risk. The classroom, for all its faults—no water, no restrooms, large, if locked, windows taking up much of one wall—was at least familiar and semisecure. They could stay inside and ride out whatever was happening on the rest of the campus, and while the alarm would probably start upsetting the children soon, there were things they could do. Quiet things, things that wouldn't attract any monsters that happened to be wandering the halls.

But there *were* no monsters wandering the halls just yet: the halls were echoing and empty, and completely free of dangers, at least for as long as the office door held. If they moved *now*, they could get to the airlock and get outside. They'd be able to run. There would still be a quarantine, of course, and all the students would need to be thoroughly tested for traces of live Kellis-Amberlee, but they would live. She could save them if they moved fast and moved smart, and didn't stand around waiting for rescue... because rescue wasn't going to come. The very flaw in the school security that would allow them to escape was going to delay any sort of rescue effort, and could make things a lot worse.

The doors hadn't locked. The doors were supposed to have locked—and whenever a live outbreak was happening in an enclosed space, like a school, any door that wasn't locked was considered an infection risk. Even building barricades to keep the infected out wouldn't make any difference; barricades could be broken, barricades didn't have the weight of a securely locked door. Everyone on campus was infected now, legally speaking, and anyone who came onto campus was likely to come on shooting. It didn't matter that the victims were children. It didn't matter that many of them were too small to have amplified. The school had failed to lock down properly, and while their parents would mourn them, the safety of the city was more important than a few little lives.

Sometimes Elaine thought the most unfair thing of all was that she had to live in this day and age, where children were collateral damage. But then, before there were the walking dead there had been school shootings, and those had been much easier to get rid of, hadn't they? Ban the assault rifles, make the background checks tighter... save lives. And none of that had happened, until the dead rose and people found something better to shoot at than kindergarteners and cafeteria workers. So maybe every day and age was bad, in its own way.

"Please take off your clothes and get in the bin, Scott," she said, and handed a sponge to Brian. "We need to wash him all over. I know it's hard. But we have to do it, or we could get sick."

Brian was crying. So was Scott. So was she. But they had to do it, or there was no way she could justify taking Scott with them when they left—and they had to leave. They had to get out alive. They had to try.

The Evergreen incident raised several questions. How had the security systems been allowed to fail? How was it that human error—the guards at the airlock first missing the blood on Scott Ribar's hand, and then missing the live viral particles on Nathan Patterson's lip—had been compounded by computer error, leaving the doors unlocked and the alarms that would have notified the authorities unsounded? Why did none of the teachers have the ability to contact the police or, better yet, the CDC? Why were there no clear evacuation plans in place for incidents of this nature, and how could they be put in place for the future?

What very few people bothered to question were the rolls of the dead. Name after name, student after student, all of them killed by a cascading combination of failures that should never have been permitted to happen. Some would try to place the blame on Elaine Oldenburg, after review of the school security records proved conclusively that one of her students had been the flashpoint for the outbreak. Others would wave their hands and say that it was a regrettable but ultimately blameless combination of factors, one to learn from and prevent. The teachers unions began petitioning for more and better weaponry. The school board began petitioning for more and better security.

The parents of the students who had died at Evergreen Elementary were virtually forgotten. The few who bothered to sue the school district for damages were paid off quickly and quietly. The lucky families whose children had stayed home that day said nothing, perhaps feeling that their good fortune would be taken from them if they dared to flaunt it. Who can blame them for a little nervousness, given the circumstances?

None of the students who survived have ever spoken to the media. We reached out to them, to ask whether they would break their silence and speak to us. There have been no replies. Whatever happened in the halls of Evergreen Elementary has been lost to posterity, save for those fragments captured on the school's security cameras . . . and given the horrors that those fragments imply, perhaps it is better that way.

Perhaps there are some truths better left forgotten.

—FROM *UNSPOKEN TRAGEDIES OF THE AMERICAN SCHOOL SYSTEM* BY ALARIC KWONG, MARCH 19, 2044

Wednesday, March 19, 2036, 12:01 P.M.

Elaine Oldenburg's class was one of five in the first grade. The school extended from kindergarten through fifth grade, although there were only three fifth-grade classes; many students were withdrawn from the physical school system after fourth grade, or transferred to a middle school where they would be less likely to endanger smaller children through their mere presence. All told, thirty-three classes were in session when the alarm began to sound. It was too much to ask for that many students to remain calm and collected, especially when the restraints failed to activate correctly, resulting in fewer than half the students being locked into their desks.

Nathan Patterson had started feeling unwell fifteen minutes after the end of recess, and had been sent to the nurse's office for observation and blood tests. Mr. O'Toole had followed school policy and not asked Nathan to take a blood test before leaving the classroom. If it had come back positive—which it couldn't, there was simply no way Nathan had been exposed; it was a ridiculous idea—the door would have locked, and the safety shutters on the windows would have descended, containing the infection, yes, but also containing the entire class. Blood tests were only requested in the case of student illness when the student could not be safely transported from the classroom to the office.

Joseph Lee, who sat next to Nathan, kept casting anxious glances at his friend's empty desk. Nathan should have been back by now. But instead, the alarm was sounding, and Mr. O'Toole couldn't get the office on the phone. Something was seriously wrong. And why wasn't Mr. O'Toole calling for help? Someone needed to tell the police that something was going on at the school.

Cell phones were forbidden during class, but with Mr. O'Toole pacing back and forth in front of the whiteboard and half the class distracted by crying, or sitting very still and trying *not* to cry, Joseph decided he could risk it. He slipped his phone out of his pocket, swiping his thumb across the screen to unlock it. The familiar glow of his background sprang into view. Habit made him fold himself around the screen, trying to keep from attracting Mr. O'Toole's attention. He needn't have bothered. In that moment, his teacher wouldn't have noticed the students beginning to dance on their desks and sing the national anthem. His mind was miles away, following a trail that would have been familiar to everyone in the room: like the rest of them, Mr. O'Toole was trying frantically to convince himself that this wasn't what it looked like.

It wasn't an outbreak.

It couldn't be an outbreak.

Joseph brought up his keypad and considered it for a moment, waffling between calling home and telling his dad what was going on, and calling 911 and letting the authorities know what was going on—although he wasn't really sure what he'd say in the second instance. Like, was it prank calling if you told the police that the alarms at school wouldn't stop ringing, and the desks weren't locking right, and the doors weren't locking at all? It seemed like something that somebody ought to know.

Finally, he decided that he should call his father. Dad could take care of the difficult part, like deciding whether or not to contact the police. Joseph brought up his father's number and pressed "call."

Nothing happened. Joseph frowned at the phone. The display said he had five full bars of service, so why wasn't the call going through? He tried again, this time dialing his mother's cell, and got the same result: nothing. Fear began to gather in the space behind his eyes, swelling and twisting until it filled the entire world.

Mr. O'Toole was still pacing back and forth, paying virtually no attention to his class. Joseph worried his lip between his teeth, trying to decide where the line was between "reacting normally to a crisis" and "losing your shit." He was pretty sure Mr. O'Toole was on the wrong side of the line. He was just terrified of slipping and joining his teacher there.

Joseph wiped his mouth dry with the palm of his hand before he resumed worrying his lip between his teeth. The small abrasions this created were perfect for the fomite specks of Kellis-Amberlee that he had picked up from Nathan's hand when they were sitting under the slide—Nathan, who had touched the ground where Scott Ribar had scraped himself. The virus was invisible to the naked eye, but not to Joseph's immune system, which promptly launched an all-out defense against the invaders. This defense included the boy's own store of Kellis-Amberlee virus, which recognized its brethren, even in their new, strangely folded configuration, and began to refold itself in viral sympathy. The cascade was beginning.

Joseph was unaware of all this; Joseph would not begin to feel unwell for another five minutes, by which time it would be far too late to take any precautions or attempt any quarantine. In many ways, fomite transmission was more dangerous than the flashier and easily detected bite or splatter transmissions, because it was so quiet, so easy. Touch a contaminated surface, touch your mouth, nose, or eyes, and wait for the virus to do what comes naturally. Joseph had become an incubator for Kellis-Amberlee.

Hands shaking—with nerves, nothing more; not yet—he raised his phone a third time and dialed 911. Again, the call did not go through. Fear fully bloomed in his chest, setting his heart hammering against his ribs and speeding the infection through his body. The faster the blood circulated, the more quickly the live-state Kellis-Amberlee would be able to convert the slumbering stockpile in his veins. "Mr. O'Toole?" he said, thrusting his hand into the air.

Mr. O'Toole stopped pacing and turned, frowning blearily at the room for a moment before his attention finally focused on Joseph. "I cannot approve any trips to the restroom while the alarm is sounding," he said stiffly.

"It's not about the bathroom," protested Joseph, cheeks flaming red as uneasy giggles broke out around the rest of the room. Unlike Sharon in Miss Oldenburg's class, Joseph didn't ask to go to the bathroom very often. He found the idea of broadcasting his bodily functions to his classmates faintly mortifying. "I tried to call my dad and the call didn't go through."

Mr. O'Toole's frown deepened. "No cell phones in class," he said. He started down the aisle between the desks, heading toward Joseph. "Hand it over."

Joseph pulled his phone back, out of his teacher's reach. "You don't understand," he said, hating the thin whine that was beginning to appear in his voice. "I tried to call my dad, and my mom, and the *police*, and none of the calls went through. Their numbers didn't even ring. Something's wrong with the phone."

"It's not the phone," said Mr. O'Toole. "If you had asked me before you decided to panic yourself and your fellow students, I could have explained that you would be unable to get a call out. When the alarm starts ringing, the cell blockers in the school's communication network activate. None of us can make calls out right now."

Joseph stared at him, slack-jawed. His tongue was dry, probably from panic, so he swallowed hard to moisten it before asking, "Why would they do that? Who thinks that's a good idea?" Murmurs rose from the classroom around him, echoing the sentiment.

Mr. O'Toole pressed a hand to his temple, like it hurt, and thrust his hand out again. "The phone, Joseph, please."

"But I didn't even make a call!"

"The rules are still very clear about cell phones in class." Mr. O'Toole gave his hand an admonishing shake. "You can have it back after the end of the day."

"This is so unfair," said Joseph, and slapped the phone—now thoroughly contaminated by fomite traces—into Mr. O'Toole's hand.

"Life is unfair," said Mr. O'Toole. "As for who thought blocking cell communications from the campus was a good idea, it was recommended by our state's governor when he approved the current security plans used by this campus, and our sister schools. It prevents local law enforcement from being swamped by calls from students—like yourself—when the alarm goes off. If there is any need for law enforcement, they will be contacted by the office. It helps keeps things under control. It prevents a panic."

"But you can't get the office on the phone," said Joseph, looking more concerned than ever. "What happens to us if the office doesn't call the police?"

Mr. O'Toole—who was five minutes away from wiping his eye with one contaminated hand, and who would not need to worry about complicated issues like cell phones and law enforcement for very much longer—didn't have an answer. "Everyone, take out your history books and turn to chapter twenty-three," he said, turning and walking back toward the front of the room. "If we're going to be stuck in here, we're going to use our time productively."

The groan that rose from the collected students was briefly louder than the persistently ringing alarm, and could almost have been mistaken for a moan.

When asked why he had approved legislation that included the installation of cellular and wireless communication blocks in all elementary and middle schools, Governor Wilson (D) replied, "This system was recommended by some of the top minds in private and military security. I am shocked and ashamed by the manner in which it has failed our schools. It has failed our students. I have failed our students. We will be auditing the entire security structure of our schools, and there will not be another Evergreen. Not on my watch. Not in Washington."

Governor Wilson did not complete his review of the school security systems before the next election, when he was defeated by his opponent, Heather Benson (R), the mother of Emily Benson, who had died while under the care of Miss Elaine Oldenburg. Despite running for office on a school security and personal tragedy platform, Governor Benson did not change any of the previous governor's policies. As of this writing, fifty-seven Washington elementary and middle schools are still designed to block all outgoing cellular or wireless transmissions during an emergency situation.

Thus far, Governor Wilson has been correct: there has not been another Evergreen. It is less clear whether his words will remain true as the years go by, or whether they will become one more lie in the tapestry of untruths that has defined the educational system in this country.

—FROM *UNSPOKEN TRAGEDIES OF THE AMERICAN SCHOOL SYSTEM* BY ALARIC KWONG, MARCH 19, 2044

Wednesday, March 19, 2036, 12:35 P.M.

Scott wept steadily but silently as Miss Oldenburg helped him into a pair of clean trousers and a button-up flannel shirt, both taken from the supply of emergency clothes at the back of the closet. It was always best to keep a few things on hand in case of "accidents," and many of the children had borrowed a shirt or a pair of underpants from the general supply at least once. They teased each other about it when they thought she couldn't hear, she knew, and she allowed a certain amount of it, stepping in only when it became actively cruel.

Brian had been pressed against the closet door since the bleach wash was finished, an expression of mixed terror and fascination on his face. It was like he was interested in the process despite himself, and wanted nothing more than to pretend that interest didn't really exist; it was a trick of the light, maybe, or some sort of temporary psychosis brought on by the steadily beeping alarm—which, Elaine readily admitted to herself, was becoming unsettling. The alarm was never supposed to ring for this long. It was meant to sound, get everyone's attention, and then be turned off, allowing teachers to communicate with students without an annoying buzz underscoring everything they said.

More important, it was meant to leave silence in its wake. Silence was a powerful weapon when you might be dealing with an outbreak. Without silence, how were you supposed to hear things coming? The infected could be on top of you and moaning before you knew that they were there in the first place.

The thought made Elaine shudder, which caused Scott to raise his head and stare at her, clearly terrified. She pasted a practiced Miss Oldenburg smile across her face and buttoned the last button on his borrowed shirt. "There you are, all better," she said. "You're ready to rejoin the class."

"Okay," he mumbled, and moved as if to pick up his coat from the floor.

Moving with a speed no one would have suspected she possessed—including herself—Elaine Oldenburg lashed out and grabbed his wrist before he could complete his reach. Scott froze. Brian froze. For a moment, stillness reigned.

Then, in a very small voice, Scott said, "Miss Oldenburg, you're hurting me."

She was squeezing too hard, she *knew* that she was squeezing too hard, but she couldn't force herself to loosen her grip. "Scott, I don't think you understand the situation," she said, and it was a struggle to keep her voice level. She didn't want to start yelling at him. If she started yelling, she was never going to stop, and it didn't matter how much he deserved it—these kids started learning never to hide blood before they were out of diapers, and he'd turned *her* classroom into a biohazard zone because he didn't want a time-out—it would frighten the rest of the children, and she couldn't afford that. Not now, not with the alarm ringing steadily in the background and her control over the classroom eroding with every deviation from the norm.

Scott stared at her, eyes wide and glossy with tears. That should have been enough to make her let go, but she still couldn't.

"Scott, if you touch your coat, you could get exposed again, and then we'll have to bleach you again," she said, slowly and calmly. "But because bleach is hard on your skin, if we do that, you could start bleeding more, and then we'd have to leave you here. We can't take you out into the classroom if you present a danger to the other students. Do you understand?"

"Yes, Miss Oldenburg," he whispered.

Finally, wonderfully, she was able to make herself let go. Her fingers ached from squeezing so hard. There was a livid red mark on Scott's wrist. She supposed she should feel bad about that. She would later, of that she had no doubt, but later was very far away; later came after they were all safe, and off school grounds, and she was explaining to a disciplinary committee why she had felt the need to squeeze a student until she could feel his bones, thin and fragile, beneath the blanket of his skin.

Elaine Oldenburg had never expected to be excited by the prospect of facing a disciplinary committee, but now she realized that if she faced that committee, that would mean they had survived. Survival was something she very much wanted to experience. "All right," she said, and stepped back, and opened the door.

Brian immediately fled back to the safety of his seat, throwing himself into the chair so hard that the desk would have rocked if it hadn't been bolted to the floor. He folded his arms and dropped his head into the hollow they created, clearly putting himself on time-out. Miss Oldenburg followed more decorously, her hand resting on Scott's shoulder as she herded the sniffling, teary-eyed boy back into the company of his peers. Fifteen pairs of eyes fixed on him before shifting to Miss Oldenburg, waiting to hear her pass sentence. The fact that she was touching him meant that the danger had to be past, didn't it? She wouldn't have done that if he had still been a biohazard. That meant that they were safe now, didn't it? Didn't it?

"Take Amelia's desk, Scott," said Miss Oldenburg, giving him a small push in the appropriate direction. "Your desk isn't safe." His desk would need to be doused in formalin, and even then, the administration would probably elect to remove it completely and replace it with a new desk, one where a small boy had not sat, bleeding, for the better part of a class period. It was easier to destroy than it was to decontaminate. That was how the world had always worked, and the rising of the dead hadn't done anything to change that.

Scott sat. The class looked to her, all save for Brian, whose head remained firmly down on his desk. Some of them looked wary, like they were afraid that she would pull them into the closet next. But even under the wariness, there was a level of trust. Trust that she would get them out of this; that she understood what she needed to do and would make sure that it happened, no matter what. She was their teacher, and this was their classroom, and no one could defeat her. Not here, not in the place of her power.

Elaine—who was having increasing trouble holding on to the veil of Miss Oldenburg, who seemed more and more like a dream with every minute that passed, that alarm still chiming in the background—looked out on her classroom and knew, just knew, that she was going to disappoint them. There was nothing else she could possibly do. And if that was the only possible outcome, there was no sense in wasting time standing around and waiting to know what she was supposed to do. She was supposed to try to save them. If that attempt came with failure, well, so be it. At least she would have tried.

"Everyone, we're having a very special drill today," she said, and upon hearing the words spoken aloud, she found that she could very nearly believe them. There was power in the teacher voice, and even she was not immune. "I want everyone to gather up your things very quickly and quietly, all right? If you have a coat, put it on. If you brought mittens or a hat with you today, put those on, too. I know you're not normally supposed to wear them when you're inside, but the rules are different today."

"Because of the special drill?" asked Sharon cautiously.

Elaine nodded. "Yes, exactly. During special drills, some of the rules are different, because that way we can practice doing things under unusual circumstances. If you're not fastened to your desk, you can get up if you need to. I'm going to help everyone else out of their seats." She picked up the clean screwdriver, the one she hadn't given Brian to help Scott out of his desk, and began moving around the classroom, undoing screws and loosening restraints until, one by one, her students were able to pull themselves free.

As for the students who were not confined, they scurried to grab their bags from their cubbyholes and their coats from the coat hooks near the door, all of them returning to their seats without needing to be told. Once seated, they watched Miss Oldenburg making her circuit of the room. Some of them were crying. Others were dry-eyed and patient, waiting for the moment when she would snap her fingers and everything would make sense again. They knew that the moment was coming. All they had to do was be patient, and she would fix the world. She was the teacher. That was what she was supposed to do.

Finally, the last of Miss Oldenburg's first graders was free. She walked back to her desk and started to put the screwdriver down, only to pause and slip it into the pocket of her coat. Anything that might be a weapon was going to be useful in the hours ahead. She couldn't have said how she knew that; she just did, as surely as she knew that this was the last time she would see her class assembled like this, all of them trusting in her to see them safely through the day.

"All right, class," she said. "I want everyone to line up by the door. Find a partner. Take your partner's hand, and don't let go. Do you understand me? Don't let go *no matter what.* We're going to use the buddy system as we walk down the hall, and I'm going to trust you to stay together, because I need to be able to scout ahead."

"Miss Oldenburg?" Jenna thrust her hand into the air, not waiting to be called on before she continued, "Where are we going? It's not time for lunch."

It was, actually, and bellies were beginning to grumble all around the room. But the fear was stronger. They were catching it from their instructor like a virus, and it told them each that hunger mattered less than survival. Survival was the only thing worth having. "We're going on a little field trip," said Miss Oldenburg. "We're going to go see the parking lot. Won't that be fun?"

"We've *seen* the parking lot before," said Jenna crossly. "That's not a field trip."

"That's still where we're going," said Miss Oldenburg. She sounded strained. "Get your things and join the line."

Jenna, taken aback by Miss Oldenburg's tone, did as she was told. Once she had joined the line, Miss Oldenburg walked along it one last time, checking to see that everyone had someone else by the hand. Jenna—who had been late to join the line, and wasn't the best-liked student in the class under normal circumstances—had no buddy, and so Miss Oldenburg took her by the hand, and opened the classroom door, and led them out into the hall, away from the illusion of safety, and hopefully toward the reality of it.

>> AKWONG: IT'S DEFINITELY HER. THE RESULTS JUST CAME BACK FROM THE FACIAL RECOGNITION SOFTWARE. THE HAIR WAS THROWING OFF OUR RESULTS—I THINK MAYBE THAT'S WHY SHE CHOSE THAT COMBINATION OF COLORS.

>> MGOWDA: HOW SO?

>> AKWONG: ELAINE OLDENBURG ALWAYS LOOKED YOUNG FOR HER AGE. SHE TENDED TO GET FALSE POSITIVES WHEN AGE REVIEW SOFTWARE SCANNED HER TO SEE IF SHE WAS PRESENTING A FAKE ID TO BUY WINE OR CIGARETTES. BUT SHE HAS THE COLLAGEN DECAY AND EYE MUSCULATURE STRAIN OF SOMEONE HER ACTUAL AGE. BY DYEING THE BOTTOM LEVEL OF HER HAIR WHITE, SHE CONFUSES THE SOFTWARE EVEN MORE. IT STARTS THROWING BACK INCORRECT RESULTS.

>> MGOWDA: BUT IT'S DEFINITELY HER.

>> AKWONG: YES. ELAINE OLDENBURG IS—OR WAS, I GUESS—THE WOMAN YOU MET AT THE MONKEY'S HOUSE. I FOUND HER. I FOUND FOXY.

—internal communication between Alaric Kwong and Mahir Gowda, After the End Times private server, March 16, 2044

Wednesday, March 19, 2036, 1:14 P.M.

The hallway was empty when Elaine Oldenburg's first-grade class emerged and stood, blinking, in the fluorescent light. Elaine looked around uneasily. Surely her door couldn't be the only one that had failed to lock, and with an unlocked classroom, surely she wasn't the only teacher who had thought to take her students and get out. Something seemed very wrong about the absolute stillness of the hall, although she couldn't have said exactly what it was if pressed, and with seventeen first graders looking to her for leadership, she couldn't take the time to figure out what her instincts were telling her.

The airlock door leading to the blacktop was slightly closer, but that was just another, slightly larger trap, and one that was even less secure than their unlocked classroom. They needed to go for the airlock past the office, the one that would grant them access to the parking lot and put her outside the reach of the school's cell blockers. She could call for the police then, and explain that the office was contaminated and the classroom doors weren't locking. They'd bring the CDC, and the school would be properly quarantined. It might take hours—or even days—to clear all the classrooms and get the unaffected students back to their parents. In the meantime, her students would be free and clear and safe at home. That was what she needed to focus on. Safety.

"This way," she murmured. "Everyone stay together, and don't talk unless you absolutely have to. Silence is golden."

"But—" began Mikey.

"Shhh," said Miss Oldenburg. He shushed, and the group of eighteen began walking slowly, cautiously, down the hall.

Sharon—who had buddied off with Emily, as she was always inclined to do when she had her choice of partners—lagged until the two of them were at the back of the group. Emily gave her friend a sidelong look, trying to question without saying anything. She knew that Sharon was the leader; that was how things had always worked between them, ever since they met in day care. She didn't mind so much. Sharon had good ideas, and she knew how to make them become real things, while Emily mostly just had ideas about how to sneak snacks into her room for them to enjoy during their sleepovers. She was, and had always been, content to follow.

Sharon lagged more. Now there was two, three, four feet of space between them and the pair ahead of them. Dropping her voice to a whisper that Emily had to strain to overhear, Sharon said, "I still need to pee."

"Can't you pee after we get where we're going?" Emily asked nervously, and promptly hated herself for the question. She knew that it was her nervousness that cemented Sharon as their leader. If Emily had been a less nervous person, she could have called the shots. She *could.*

"No," said Sharon, looking at Emily with scorn. "There's no bathroom in the parking lot. I'd have to go in the bushes. Boys might look. I wouldn't be able to wash my hands. I'm not going to do it."

"Oh," said Emily, beginning to understand. The hallway would take them right past the bathrooms. If they lagged far enough back, maybe Miss Oldenburg wouldn't even notice when they slipped away. Sharon always peed superfast, especially when she really had to go. They could catch up easy, and no one would ever know that they'd snuck away.

"C'mon." Sharon tugged Emily with her as she sidled toward the wall. The girls' bathroom was only about ten feet up ahead, so close that she could almost feel the relief already. She needed to pee, and she wasn't going to do it in a bush, and she wasn't going to do it in a bucket. If Miss Oldenburg was too nasty to understand why a good girl didn't want to use those things, why, Sharon wasn't going to let that make *her* nasty, too.

The bathroom door was just ahead, inviting them in. Swallowing her giggles, Sharon gripped Emily's hand tighter and pulled her buddy with her into the open doorway.

The bathroom had been designed to minimize unnecessary contact with surfaces, on the theory that small children weren't always the best at washing their hands. The doorway led to a small "hallway" created by extending a false wall across the actual bathroom. Everything was tiled in blue, easy to care for and clean. Sharon walked primly down the hallway, turning the corner into the bathroom proper. Then she stopped, frowning, unable to immediately process the scene in front of her.

There were five stalls in this bathroom, and five sinks on the wall across from them. All the stalls had open doors, but one of them was occupied; someone was lying on their back inside the stall furthest from the door, their feet poking out and pointed at the ceiling. That would have been strange enough, but they weren't the only person lying down inside the bathroom. One of the teacher's aides was huddled in a ball in the middle of the floor, and the tile around her was red, like someone had spilled a bottle of paint. But why would anyone be painting in the bathroom? It didn't make any sense.

Someone in the middle stall moaned.

Emily tried to pull her hand out of Sharon's, but the other girl, who she had always considered to be far braver than herself, had gone rigid with terror. Her fingers were locked on Emily's, and no matter how hard Emily pulled, she couldn't break free.

The moan came again, and then another of the teacher's aides shambled into view. He had red all around his mouth, like he'd been putting on lipstick without a mirror. His eyes were all black, swallowed up by his pupils. He rocked back and forth, head shaking almost bonelessly, before his eyes settled on the two girls.

He moaned a third time. Sharon moaned, too, a small, terrified sound that nonetheless seemed to come all the way up from her toes. Something warm and wet covered her legs, and she knew that she was peeing herself. That was even nastier than a bucket or a bush, but she couldn't make it stop, and she couldn't make her feet work.

"Sharon, let go," whimpered Emily, fighting against her friend's grip.

Sharon couldn't make herself do that, either. All she could do was stand rooted to the floor, Emily fighting against her, as the teacher's aide shambled closer.

Then there was nothing but teeth, and pain, and redness, and the dim, disappointed feeling that there should have been more than this; that *she* should have been more than this, somehow. Only she wasn't.

By the time her limp hand fell away from Emily's, it was too late. For either of them.

The security cameras at Evergreen Elementary were old. They had been installed during the construction of the school, and they had never been upgraded. The money was always being channeled into "improvements." New scanners, better locks on the windows, more automation. Ironically, because of this lack of "improvements" to the camera system, it was the only thing that did not fail at some point during the outbreak. It had been installed by people who not only knew what they were doing, but who had no political agenda to push. All they wanted to do was monitor the school, and they accomplished that goal.

The deaths of Sharon Winchell (7) and Emily Benson (6) were recorded in detail. I have not chosen to view those tapes; I will not be describing their deaths for you. They have earned more decency than that from me, and from anyone who reads this.

—FROM *UNSPOKEN TRAGEDIES OF THE AMERICAN SCHOOL SYSTEM* BY ALARIC KWONG, MARCH 19, 2044

Wednesday, March 19, 2036, 1:20 P.M.

The screams came from behind them, high and shrill and utterly agonized. The fifteen remaining students whirled around, eyes going wide and glossy with fear. Then, unified by their terror, they did the only thing that made any sense to them: they mobbed their teacher, clustering around her skirted legs like chicks trying to nestle under the winged safety of a mother hen. Elaine did not let go of Jenna's hand. That seemed like the most important thing, somehow: that she continue to demonstrate the buddy system for her students, even as they abandoned it in favor of hiding behind her.

Her free hand shook as she drew her service weapon, releasing the safety with a flick of her thumb. Somehow, the tiny sound of the safety snapping back was what made everything real. Not the screams, not the alarm, but the reality of holding a gun in her hand, ready to fire, with students all around her.

"Miss Oldenburg, where are Sharon and Emily?" She didn't know who asked the question; the students had become an undifferentiated mass around her. The only one whose identity she was sure of was Jenna, and that only because she was holding Jenna's hand.

"Move."

The students looked at her blankly—the ones who weren't crying or staring fixedly back toward the sound of screaming, which was beginning to taper off, losing strength and volume with every second that passed. They didn't have much time left. That was the most important thing. Safety was now a span measured in screams, and the screams were ending.

"*Move*," she snapped, and—pulling Jenna with her—she turned and began walking rapidly toward the airlock door that had been their destination all along. There was definitely an outbreak in the school. The screams confirmed it. They needed to get off campus, and they needed to get off campus *now*, before things got any worse.

One teacher and fifteen students ran down the hall, some faster than others, but all managing to stay loosely grouped together. Terror made anything else unthinkable.

"Where's Sharon?" whimpered one of the girls, her face obscured by the bodies all around her. "Where's Emily? Why are we leaving them? We have to go back. We have to go back for them."

"Hush, we're almost there," said Miss Oldenburg, and kept walking. She wasn't quite running—her legs were much longer than the legs of her students, and she knew that if she broke into a full-out run, she would leave them behind. Part of her silently screamed that she should be doing exactly that: saving herself. Let the children find their own way off campus. She was at risk of amplification, and all they were at risk of was dying.

But that was exactly the reason she couldn't run. She was their teacher. She had made them a promise, however unspoken: she had promised to do her best to keep them safe, and that meant she couldn't run away and leave them, not even to save herself. She had to get them off campus. She had to get them back to their parents.

They ran past the office door. Elaine couldn't resist glancing toward it to reassure herself that it was still securely closed, and she very nearly tripped over her own feet when she saw that it was standing ajar. There was something sticky-looking on the doorknob that could have been jam or finger paint. She knew that it wasn't either.

Nothing was moving in the narrow slice of office that she could see as they ran by, but that didn't necessarily mean anything. The infected were surprisingly good at lying in wait when they weren't actively hungry, waiting until their prey was cornered or close before they made a move. Stillness could be a trap as easily as it could be safety. There was only one thing she knew for sure: that whatever had been contained in the office was contained no longer.

The airlock was so close that she could practically taste the outside air on her tongue, feel the rain falling on her face—all the little signifiers of freedom in Seattle, of being somewhere other than these closed, dimly lit hallways where the dead were walking. Miss Oldenburg moved a little faster, hauling Jenna with her, the rest of her class trailing along like so many ducklings.

They were less than three feet from the airlock door when the heavy steel gratings designed to isolate and seal the school in the event of an outbreak slammed down, blocking their view of the parking lot and reducing the light in the hallway by more than half. Miss Oldenburg skidded to a stop, staring in disbelief. The students stopped as well, some of them panting from the exertion, others in tears as they clustered around her skirts once more. They trusted her to get them through this safely.

They had no idea how wrong they were. As Elaine Oldenburg stared at the featureless steel barrier between them and safety, she thought that she was only just beginning to understand herself.

The security lockdown at Evergreen Elementary was triggered by Ashley Smith (10), a student in Mr. O'Toole's class. She had witnessed the amplification of her teacher, and had been saved from his initial, insatiable hunger by two small accidents of circumstance: she was seated toward the rear of the classroom, and her desk was one of those that had failed to lock properly upon receiving the signal from the school's central computer.

Based on the analysis of the remains in Mr. O'Toole's room, as well as the partial feed from one of the playground cameras covering the area nearest Mr. O'Toole's window, Ashley was able to wiggle free of the single desk restraint that had deployed. She had been wearing two pairs of socks, as well as a pair of thick flannel pants. By pulling up her pant leg and removing her shoe, she loosened her bonds enough to let her yank her foot loose and run for the window, which she broke with the classroom's rear fire extinguisher.

Ashley Smith was halfway out of the room when she was dragged back by the hands of her already-amplified classmates. This caused a sufficient amount of contaminated material to touch the sensors, and a full lockdown of the campus was initiated. This still did not lock the internal doors, which were operated on a separate system.

In short, with one small act of self-preservation, Ashley Smith managed, entirely by accident, to transform Evergreen Elementary into a killing field. It's difficult to blame her for wanting to survive. But it's also difficult, knowing what we know about the incident, not to wish that she had made her break for freedom a scant five minutes later.

—FROM *UNSPOKEN TRAGEDIES OF THE AMERICAN SCHOOL SYSTEM* BY ALARIC KWONG, MARCH 19, 2044

Wednesday, March 19, 2036, 1:35 P.M.

The children were sniffling. One of them had started to make little gasping noises, like an asthma attack was on the horizon. Elaine knew that if they didn't move, she was going to lose them—and she also knew that returning to the classroom would be worse than futile. There was something in the bathroom: Sharon and Emily's disappearance confirmed it. The office door was open. There was nowhere to go but forward.

In cases where the internal doors failed to lock, all individuals were to be treated as infected. That was basic policy. First graders were large enough that the media wouldn't linger overly long on their deaths—but kindergarteners? Even the most hardened of CDC field doctors wouldn't be able to authorize gassing a room full of kindergarteners without thinking twice about it.

"This way," she said, giving Jenna's hand a squeeze, and started down the corridor to their left.

The occupants of Ms. Teeter's kindergarten class were quietly occupied with their coloring sheets, music playing to cover the sound of the alarm, when someone knocked on their door. Ms. Teeter, who had been sitting ramrod-straight at her desk with her gun hidden in her lap, got laboriously to her feet and walked toward the door. It wasn't locked. The damn locks had failed to deploy. She'd been part of the committee arguing against taking the ability to manually lock the doors away from the teachers. The bureaucrats who said that it was for their own safety had never been put into a position like this one, of that she was sure.

She was just glad she'd had the presence of mind to close the shades after the windows locked. The sound of the steel plating dropping to block any chance of escape had been loud enough to attract some attention from her students, but they hadn't seen the glass go blank, or realized—yet—that there was no way out of the school. Once that happened, the tears would begin. She wanted to avoid that for as long as possible.

The knock came again. A few of the children had looked up toward the sound, interested but not alarmed. She had worked very hard to keep them calm, and the last thing she needed was for some panicky little twit to come charging in and upset everything.

At the same time, she had been a kindergarten teacher for long enough that she was running up against mandatory retirement age, and one doesn't spend that much time with small children without retaining at least a sliver of softness in the heart. "Who is it?" she called. Zombies didn't knock, and whoever it was, they weren't pounding; she had the time to be polite.

"Elaine Oldenburg! First grade!"

There was a note of panic in the younger teacher's voice that she didn't like; no, she didn't like it at all. Panic had a tendency to spread, especially when it was offered to the younger children as an option. "I'm sorry, Miss Oldenburg, but we're in the middle of class right now."

"Please, let us in."

Ms. Teeter's eyes widened slightly behind the lenses of her spectacles. Was the woman roaming the halls with her entire first-grade class? Didn't she understand the situation? "Go back to your own classroom," she suggested, trying to keep her voice from shaking. "I think you'll find that to be a much more comfortable arrangement."

"We can't," hissed Miss Oldenburg, dropping her voice so low that Ms. Teeter had to strain to hear it. "There are... problems... between here and my classroom. Let us *in*, unless you'd rather have fifteen students on your conscience."

Miss Oldenburg clearly knew something she did not. Ms. Teeter spared a glance for her own nineteen charges, most of whom were still sitting and coloring quietly. A few had put down their crayons and were watching her to see how she would answer this stranger's request. None of them seemed frightened. She was direly afraid that that was about to change.

"I'm opening the door," she said quietly, and turned the knob, pulling it inward to reveal a red-haired woman wearing a Kevlar jacket over a flowered dress. She looked too young to be in charge of anything, much less an entire class of first graders, but they clustered around her like she was the only port left in a storm. Ms. Teeter looked at Miss Oldenburg solemnly, scanning her for blood or signs of injury. Miss Oldenburg looked back, just as solemnly, and didn't say anything.

Finally, with a sigh, Ms. Teeter stepped to the side. "Please don't make me regret this," she said. "The children don't know what's happening."

"Neither do my children, not really," said Miss Oldenburg. She let go of the little girl whose hand she had been holding and shooed her inside. The rest of the class quickly followed, some of them even heading for the shelves where the picture books and quiet toys were stored, like they had just been waiting for the chance to return to more familiar environs.

Ms. Teeter was not entirely surprised when one of the smaller boys veered away from his classmates and hugged her leg, burying his face against her trousers. She looked down at his tousled brown hair, and guessed, "Brian Elkins?"

The boy nodded, not pulling his face from her leg.

"Why, look at how big you've gotten! We've missed you, you know. The class isn't the same without you." It was all automatic, the reassurance, the comfort: all part of her training as a kindergarten teacher. But the child seemed to relax, and that was all she'd been hoping for.

The door shut with a click. Ms. Teeter looked up, eyes narrowed, to see that Miss Oldenburg was now inside the classroom, along with the last of her students. Miss Oldenburg held out her gloved hands, showing that they were free of blood or other contaminants.

"The blast doors are sealed," she said quietly, trying to keep her voice soft enough that Ms. Teeter's class wouldn't hear. She would have preferred not to let her *own* class hear, but they already knew, didn't they? They had been there with her when the shutters came down. "The interior doors are not. That's how we got out of the classroom."

"You should have stayed there," said Ms. Teeter coldly.

To her surprise, Miss Oldenburg shook her head. "We only left after I had gone down to the office to see why the alarm kept ringing. There's been... we have..." She stopped for a moment, looking lost. Ms. Teeter felt a cold surge of alarm race through her veins, chilling her completely. She might not appreciate this woman's invasion of her classroom, but she did respect her as a fellow teacher; while they had little direct interaction, they'd been in the same staff meetings, the same union Skype calls late at night when the school was closed and they were all safely tucked away in their own homes. Miss Oldenburg ran a tight ship. Everyone agreed that she did. So why was she standing here, in Ms. Teeter's private kingdom, looking like that?

Miss Oldenburg suddenly smiled, dropping down into a crouch and putting a hand on Brian's shoulder. "Hey, buddy, why don't you go see how your classmates are doing? We're going to be here for a little while, and I don't want to hear about anybody fighting with the younger kids, or pushing them around. We need to set a good example. Can you go make sure that's happening? For me?"

Brian looked uncertain, and glanced up to Ms. Teeter, as if checking in with his old teacher. The chill in her veins deepened.

"That would be wonderful," she said. "I would really appreciate the help."

"Okay," he said, and hesitated, looking between the two teachers as if he was unsure which of them he should be treating as the ultimate authority. Finally, he hugged Ms. Teeter's leg a second time, and then fled deeper into the classroom.

Miss Oldenburg stepped closer to the kindergarten teacher, pitching her voice even lower as she said, "There's an actual outbreak. This isn't a security glitch or an unannounced drill."

"How can you—"

"It started in the office. I heard the moaning. That's why the alarms have been ringing all this time with no announcements, no calls. We should have cartoons playing on every screen in this school, but we don't, because there's no one left to activate the cable. We're on our own. And I..." She paused, taking a deep breath, before she said, "I lost two students getting here. I think they split off from the group to use the bathroom, and one of the infected was lurking inside. They were both too small to amplify, thank God. That's the last thing we need."

Ms. Teeter was simultaneously stunned and amazed by the other woman's coldness. "You lost two students, and all you can say is 'they were too small to amplify'? My God, that's—"

"The office door was open when we passed it," said Miss Oldenburg. She sounded calm, almost serene, like she had decided this was a problem best viewed from a distance. "There's something in the bathroom, and the office door was open. I don't know how many infected we're dealing with. I just know that the doors aren't locking, and as long as the doors are unlocked, any emergency personnel who respond to the outbreak will be fully justified in going in guns blazing. Legally, we're all infected."

Ms. Teeter took a step backward. "That's why you're here," she said wonderingly. "You know my students are too small to amplify."

"That makes this room the best chance *my* students have," said Miss Oldenburg. "Killing kindergarteners is bad public relations. If there are any students that will be treated like they're still human, it's going to be the kindergarteners."

"You're endangering my children!"

Several of the kindergarteners looked up from their coloring sheets. Ms. Teeter fought the urge to clap a hand over her mouth. She hadn't intended to speak that loudly, or that boldly. Keeping the students calm had to remain her first priority.

Miss Oldenburg waited until the students had returned their attention to their work before she said, calmly, "Report me to the union. I don't care. I'm going to get my kids through this alive—and they don't present any danger to your students. Most of them are too small to amplify, and I haven't been exposed. I can help you keep the class under control. *Both* of our classes under control."

"You don't understand what you're asking me to do." Ms. Teeter saw the logic of what Miss Oldenburg was proposing. She also saw that putting fifteen more students into her classroom would only exacerbate the problems she knew were already coming. Would the first grade agree to naptime, or would they call it "babyish" and cause a revolt? How could the graham crackers and juice boxes stretch to cover fifteen additional mouths? And the noise—would the noise the class was inevitably going to make draw the infected right to their door? It didn't lock. It opened inward. If enough bodies piled against it, it was *going* to come open, and she couldn't build a barricade without panicking the students.

"We have nowhere else to go."

And that was the problem. Miss Oldenburg and her students had nowhere else that they could go—and wasn't kindergarten all about learning how to share?

Ms. Teeter sighed. "All right," she said. "You can stay. But this is *my* classroom. We're following *my* rules. Do you understand?"

Miss Oldenburg smiled brightly. "I do."

As with all recorded outbreaks, once things began to go wrong at Evergreen Elementary, the cascade became inevitable. Each infected individual represented the potential for countless more—and worse, with so many students below the amplification threshold, there was no need for the usual infect/consume pattern. Students below the threshold were meat to feed the virus, and students above the threshold were targets for infection.

When Mr. O'Toole's class spilled out into the hallway, they spilled out alongside five other classrooms, and proceeded to consume or convert all students and teachers inside of twenty minutes. The exponential process had begun.

Meanwhile, outside the campus, no one was aware that anything was wrong until a passing patrolman drove by the school and saw the closed steel shutters covering every window and door. He called his precinct immediately, and they notified the CDC that something appeared to be going on at Evergreen. The call went out at 1:20 P.M., ten minutes before the first parents arrived to collect their kindergarteners at the end of what they all believed to have been a normal school day.

They had never been so wrong.

—FROM *UNSPOKEN TRAGEDIES OF THE AMERICAN SCHOOL SYSTEM* BY ALARIC KWONG, MARCH 19, 2044

Wednesday, March 19, 2036, 4:16 P.M.

As the hours trickled by, Ms. Teeter slowly admitted that she'd been wrong about letting Miss Oldenburg and her students into the classroom: it hadn't been a bad idea at all. The first graders had all been shaken by their time in the halls. Whether that alone was enough to shock them into good behavior, she didn't know; she just knew that they were playing nicely with each other and with the younger children, many of whom were wide-eyed with wonder over the "big kids" choosing to play blocks or color with them. It was a sort of peace that could never have been sustained for more than a day, but as a temporary thing, it was a miracle. Adding the extra students had made her own class easier to control, not harder.

Miss Oldenburg herself was clearly a well-trained individual who knew the students in her care very well; she never seemed to raise her voice or lose her patience as she dealt with little squabbles and petty disagreements between the kids. It was almost like having a teacher's aide, but one with actual authority, one the children listened to and cared about. The cookies and granola bars had stretched further than expected.

Even naptime had been successful, as the first graders were exhausted and ready for a little quiet time.

Ms. Teeter was starting to think that they might actually weather this storm successfully when something slammed, hard, against the classroom door, causing the wood to bow slightly inward. Everyone jumped. Several students—from both classes—began crying, although the kindergarteners seemed to be crying out of surprise, while the first graders were crying out of fear.

"Everyone!" Miss Oldenburg was on her feet before Ms. Teeter could begin to really react. The younger teacher clapped her hands, and the students flocked to her, all of them clustering around her skirts as if she could somehow lead them into safety. Miss Oldenburg looked over their heads to Ms. Teeter. "The closet. How big is it?"

Ms. Teeter understood immediately. "Big enough, if we throw the nap pads and supply bins out into the room."

"Okay." Miss Oldenburg did not walk—she ran to the closet door, wrenching it open, and said, "Everyone, help me make this as empty as you can. First one to hit the wall wins!"

"Do we have to pick up and put down careful?" asked one of the kindergarteners warily, looking for the trick.

Miss Oldenburg shook her head. "As long as you don't hit anyone, you can *throw things*," she said, in a tone that implied she was granting them a great favor.

In a way, she was. The students exchanged wide-eyed looks and then swarmed into the closet, cramming as many little bodies into the space as they could. As nap pads and boxes of old toys and reams of paper came flying out the open door, more space was created inside, and more kids pushed their way in to join the fun.

Something hit the classroom door again. Harder this time; it shifted on its hinges. Ms. Teeter looked at it, and then began calmly moving debris away from the closet door. From what she could see, it was emptying quickly, leaving only the skeleton shapes of empty shelves pushed against the walls. The more frightened students were taking refuge on those shelves without being told, a natural human response that nonetheless came with the convenient side effect of creating more space in the closet as a whole.

The final box of plush toys hit the classroom floor, and Miss

Oldenburg ushered the last two students into the closet. There was a little room left inside. Just enough for a small adult.

There was not enough room for two.

Ms. Teeter and Miss Oldenburg looked at the available space and then looked at each other, trying to block out the horrible sound of hands hammering on the classroom door as they struggled with the grim decision at hand.

"You should go," said Miss Oldenburg. "My students trust you. Your students barely know me."

"You're faster, and better equipped," said Ms. Teeter. "I haven't fired a gun outside of the range in years. You'll keep them alive better than I will."

"If I climb the shelves—"

"You'll bring them down on the students. Only one of us will fit in there. You know it as well as I do." Ms. Teeter smiled a little. "I was near retirement anyway. I suppose this is just a way of getting there early."

"Please—"

"Get them out. Do whatever you have to do, and get them out." Ms. Teeter gave Miss Oldenburg a brisk backward shove, sending the other woman stumbling toward the closet. "Get them out, or I'll find a way to come back and haunt you, I swear that I will."

Elaine Oldenburg was a pragmatist in many ways; she understood as well as Ms. Teeter did that there was only room for one of them in the closet. If she was relieved that the choice had been taken out of her hands, well, that was only natural; no one really wants to die, when the cards are down and the chance to flee is gone. "I will do my very best," she said, and stepped into the closet, and pulled the door shut behind her.

The closet became very dark. There was a pause as the students attempted to adjust to this new reality; then, as had become almost the norm, someone started to cry.

She had to get control over the combined classes now, or she was going to lose it forever. "Everyone close your eyes," said Miss Oldenburg. The crying stopped, briefly suspended by the need to listen to directions. Good; that was a start. "We're playing a game of hide-and-seek, and the only way for us to win is to be very, very quiet. No one make a sound, okay? No matter what you think you hear."

"Where's Ms. Teeter?" asked a small voice.

Dammit, I don't know their names, thought Miss Oldenburg, and said, "She's going to stay in the classroom and make some noises to confuse the people who are trying to find us. She wants to help us win. We should let her help us, and that means we should be just as quiet as quiet can be, okay? Everyone, cover your mouth and keep your eyes closed, and let's be quiet!"

The students, blessedly, did as they were told. That sort of obedience might have been odd before the Rising, but these were the children of Kellis-Amberlee: they had learned, sometimes directly, sometimes through osmosis, that when adults told them to do strange but seemingly harmless things, it was best to listen. Even if they didn't understand that those strange things could easily be matters of life or death, they knew that they mattered to the adults, and that failure to obey could come with hefty consequences.

Outside the closet, Ms. Teeter had been waiting for the sound of voices and whispering to stop. She knew that the infected used sound to hunt when they couldn't use sight. Calmly, she walked to the "record player"—a specially designed mount for her MP3 player, which slotted neatly into the front—and turned up the volume until it couldn't go any louder. That wouldn't block the gunshots entirely, she knew, but it might take the edge off. It would be better if they didn't have to hear her die.

The hammering on the door was getting steadier. Something must have attracted them. It had been long enough since Miss Oldenburg and her students arrived that Ms. Teeter couldn't quite bring herself to blame the other teacher, convenient as it would have been. Sometimes things just happened.

Calmly, she leaned against the edge of the desk and pointed her gun at the door. When the hammering eventually tore it from its hinges and sent it crashing to the floor, she began to fire. She only had six bullets, and she wasn't practiced enough to get a head shot every time. Of the swarm of teacher's aides, security staff, and teachers that shoved into her room, only three went down and didn't get back up.

Only when the chamber clicked empty did she realize that she should have kept a bullet back for herself. She swore that she wasn't going to scream.

It was a promise she did not keep. But in the end, who could really blame her?

>> AKWONG: THIS IS THE WORST THING I HAVE EVER WRITTEN.

>> MGOWDA: WORST IN THE SENSE OF "POORLY DONE," OR THE SENSE OF "WHY AM I FORCING MYSELF TO RECORD THESE THINGS"?

>> AKWONG: THE SECOND.

>> MGOWDA: GOOD. THAT MEANS YOU'RE LIVING UP TO GEORGIA'S STANDARDS. YOU'RE TELLING THE TRUTH.

>> AKWONG: DOES THE TRUTH ALWAYS HAVE TO HURT THIS MUCH?

>> MGOWDA: SOMETIMES I THINK THAT'S THE ONLY WAY WE EVER REALLY KNOW IT'S TRUE.

—internal communication between Alaric Kwong and Mahir Gowda, After the End Times private server, March 16, 2044

Wednesday, March 19, 2036, 4:25 P.M.

The screams cut through the closet door like knives. Several of the children whimpered, and Miss Oldenburg hurried to hush them, groping blindly through the dark to pat heads and stroke shoulders in a vain effort to lend comfort where there could be none. In the end, perhaps the true miracle of the day was that none of the children began to scream. A single scream would have spelled the end of every single soul crammed into that too-small supply closet: they were trapped, with no easy means of escape, and the classroom on the other side of the door was alive with the infected.

Ms. Teeter did not die quickly, but neither did she keep screaming after the initial pain had passed. She moved quickly into the dark, agonizing place where only death can bring salvation, and once there, she quickly passed away. The mob—which included several teachers, larger students, and teacher's aides—did not need to expand, and so they ripped her limb from limb and feasted on her remains, creating a mess that was morbidly akin to the finger paintings that her students had been doing for the duration of her career.

When Ms. Teeter was no longer alive to scream and squirm, and the easy pickings had been stripped from her bones, the mob moved on. It wasn't an instantaneous process; each of them moved at their own speed and with their own agendas now that there was no hunt to unify them. Some turned and walked back out into the hall almost as if they had rejoined the living, moving quickly and with purpose. Others shambled, limping on broken ankles or clutching at wounds that would have been fatal, were it not for the increased clotting factor that accompanied Kellis-Amberlee.

In the closet, Elaine Oldenburg pressed her ear against the door and held her breath, straining to hear every motion from the classroom outside. The students sniffled and shifted around her, but all of them were keeping quiet thus far. She had never been more proud of her class. She could hear them shushing the kindergarteners, helping the younger children endure their seemingly senseless time in the dark.

Finally, when several minutes had gone by without any sounds loud enough to be heard over the still-blasting MP3 player, Elaine dared to feel around on the wall until she found the light switch. "Everyone, cover your eyes," she whispered, trusting the relative quiet to magnify her words. Then she turned the lights on.

The glow revealed shelves packed tight with tiny bodies, and a floor crammed full of the same. Most of them were hugging one or more of their classmates; only a few had climbed as far as the third or fourth shelves and were huddled there, isolated and afraid. Many of them were crying. She looked at them all, and they all looked to her, waiting for her to tell them what they should do next. Even the kindergarteners had an expression of painfully absolute trust in their eyes, like they knew that she would steer them safely through whatever dangers were ahead of them. She was their teacher. Of course she would know what to do.

Try telling that to Sharon and Emily, she thought bitterly. Outwardly, she just smiled, trying to look as encouraging as possible, and said quietly, "We're going to keep being very still, and very silent, all right?"

"Where's Ms. Teeter?" asked one of the kindergarteners. He didn't bother to keep his voice down. Elaine winced, her hand starting to twitch upward as if to slap the volume out of him. Then she froze, recognizing the impulse for what it was and rejecting it in the same instant. She couldn't hit a child, no matter how much that child was endangering them. She just couldn't.

"Ms. Teeter had to stay out in the classroom to make sure that we could be safe," she said, forcing her voice to remain level. "Part of being safe is being very, very quiet right now. I need you to be very, very quiet. All right? Raise your hands if you understand."

One by one, all of the students raised their hands—even the boy who had spoken before, although he still looked dubious, like he wasn't sure that this intruder who had somehow replaced his teacher could possibly have their best interests at heart.

Elaine Oldenburg wasn't completely sure herself, but she was at least going to try. She turned in a slow circle, careful not to kick or step on any of the children surrounding her, and considered the closet. It was small, tight, and windowless; she couldn't see the walls for the shelves, which had been bolted in place, probably due to some pre-Rising safety regulation or other. Kellis-Amberlee getting out of the lab hadn't done away with the need for earthquake compliance or childproofing in the lower grades; it had just added another level of complexity to the whole situation. She tilted her head back. The ceiling was reasonably low, only a foot or so above the highest shelf, and covered with the large square tiles that made up most of the classroom ceilings. It was easy to take down and replace the individual tiles.

That was what she had to count on. "All right, everyone. I want you to stay very still while I check on something." The students continued to watch her silently as she worked her way through the press of bodies to the nearest shelf. She gave it a small, experimental shake, and determined that the bolts would hold. With this accomplished, she began to climb.

Being a first-grade teacher meant a certain amount of exertion was unavoidable. Students would always need to be fished down from desks or off of the monkey bars at the end of recess; that was just the nature of childhood. Shelf by shelf, Elaine pulled herself higher, until finally, she could reach up and push against the first of the ceiling tiles. It resisted.

She pushed again, harder, and felt it shift. A thin trickle of dust dribbled down, running along the side of her face and dirtying her hair. She ignored that as she gave the tile a third push, even harder this time.

It lifted entirely out of its setting. Elaine swallowed the cheer that threatened to burst from her throat. Instead, she nudged the tile to the side, reached up, and pulled herself up through the opening she had created.

The school had been constructed with a drop ceiling, allowing for attic storage and additional insulation in the classrooms. That was the idea, anyway. Then the Rising had come, and the funds for finishing the roof area had been channeled into security and better isolated systems. The school was heated and cooled by the same centralized controls, and the space above the tiles had never been filled with fiberglass foam, leaving it empty and perfect for her needs. The tiles creaked a little beneath her, but seemed capable of holding her weight, as long as she was careful to keep it distributed over several of them at once. Her students were all smaller than she was—if she could safely be in this space, so could they. There was even light up here, motion activated and installed for reasons she couldn't fathom and honestly didn't care about. She wouldn't be trying to coerce a group of children into a dark, unknown space. They would be having an adventure.

There was still a chance.

Elaine was smiling as she climbed back down from the ceiling. The students—who had been inching ever closer to panic after her disappearance—visibly relaxed when she stepped off the bottom shelf and onto the floor. A few of them even clapped their hands, the normally small sounds seeming impossibly loud in the enclosed space. Elaine didn't chastise them. She had more important things to take care of.

"All right, everyone, we're going to have an *adventure*," she said. She smiled brightly, trying to conceal her own nerves behind an expression of serene good cheer. If she started to crack, she would take the children with her, and they would all die. "Who here has wondered about what's above the ceiling tiles?"

Almost every hand in the room went up. They were, after all, still children, and even in a bad situation, they were canny enough to recognize the opportunity to explore a normally forbidden place when it was offered to them. The hands that hadn't been raised belonged mostly to the smallest children—and, Elaine was dismayed to realize, to Brian and Scott, both of whom were huddled miserably on single shelves, with no other children to keep them company.

She would have to deal with that problem before it got any worse. For the moment, however, her priority was getting these kids out of harm's way. "All right, I need two class monitors. Who wants to volunteer?" Again, a sea of hands presented itself. She placed a finger on her chin, looking thoughtful, and finally said, "Jenna and Mikey, you're going to be our monitors. Here's what you're going to do..."

The next several minutes were spent arranging a human chain, with Jenna at the bottom boosting students up the shelves, and Mikey at the top, pulling them through the hole in the ceiling. She felt awkward sending them into the crawl space without her—she should have been supervising them at all steps, not letting them out of her sight during an actual outbreak—but there were matters she needed to take care of on the ground level.

Once half the students had gone up the shelves, leaving her with space to maneuver, she crossed the closet to Brian and Scott, who were stacked, one above the other, on an otherwise empty bookshelf. She crouched down, putting herself on a level with Brian and just above Scott. "I know this is hard," she said quietly, "but we have to keep moving. It's the only way we're going to keep everybody safe. Don't you want to be safe?"

"I want to go home," whispered Brian, his words almost drowned out by the sound of feet scuffling on shelves and hands fumbling for purchase. He didn't look up or let go of his knees, which he was hugging in a death grip against his chest.

Her heart went out to him, it truly did, but she didn't have time to be as patient as he needed her to be. "This is how you get to go home," she said, injecting a trace of steel into her tone. "If you want to leave this closet, you need to climb. You need to do what I say."

"And then I can go home?"

Elaine Oldenburg was becoming increasingly sure that none of them were going to be leaving the campus ever again. No matter what she did, it wasn't going to be enough, and they were all going to die. That didn't stop her from nodding firmly as she said, "Yes. Then you can go home.

But you have to move, Brian. You, too, Scott. We can't stay here any longer. It's time for us to go."

The two boys were silent for a moment, making her wonder if she was going to need to put hands on them and physically make them move. If it came to that, she wasn't sure she *could* put her hands on Scott. He had been a walking biohazard not very long before. He might still be infectious, on some level. Even if she was growing convinced that none of them were going to walk away, she wasn't quite prepared for suicide. But could she bring herself to leave him behind, if it came to that?

Then, slowly, Scott came out of his curl. "Okay," he said, and slid off the shelf. Brian followed.

Elaine heaved a sigh of relief and straightened, preparing for her own climb up the shelf and into the roof. Maybe she couldn't save them all. Maybe she couldn't save any of them. But she could damn well keep on trying.

Like most elementary schools in the Pacific Northwest, Evergreen Elementary maintained strict parental access protocols at the time of the outbreak. Kindergarten classes began letting out at 1:35 P.M.*; parents were not allowed to line up in front of the school prior to 1:30* P.M. *and were only permitted to assemble in groups of ten, corresponding with the children who had been flagged for first release. Each week brought with it a new order for student dismissal, e-mailed by the school at the end of day on Friday. Parents who were late collecting their children without first notifying the school were fined heavily, and the impacted students were rendered ineligible for first release for a period of eight weeks. It was a good system. It managed to reduce traffic and prevent gridlocks, even when multiple grades were released at the same time.*

On the day of the Evergreen outbreak, it all broke down. No amount of preparation could have braced the school for a steadily arriving stream of concerned parents—parents who, once it became clear that their children would not be, could *not be released, began to panic in earnest. Cars clogged the parking lot, driveway, and surrounding streets, making it more difficult for emergency personnel to get through.*

The death toll of the outbreak cannot be pinned on the parents, who were after all following the rules that they had been told would protect them, and did nothing wrong. But neither can we afford to downplay the impact their growing mob mentality had on both containment and emergency response.

In the end, there is plenty of blame to go around.

—FROM *UNSPOKEN TRAGEDIES OF THE AMERICAN SCHOOL SYSTEM* BY ALARIC KWONG, MARCH 19, 2044

Wednesday, March 19, 2036, 4:52 P.M.

The tiles had, thus far, continued to hold, although they creaked alarmingly if the students held still for too long. Miss Oldenburg continued to ease her charges along, murmuring words of encouragement and cajoling when necessary. Several of the younger children were crying, and had been since they realized that they weren't going back to their classroom. Since none of them had yet progressed to full-on bawling, she hadn't been forced to find a way to make them stop. If they really started wailing...

Well, that was a problem she would deal with when it presented itself, and not a second more. Borrowing trouble seemed like a bad idea when they already had so much of it readily at hand.

They were moving toward the side of the school, at least if her vague idea of how the ceiling divisions matched up to the halls and classrooms below could be trusted. They had been forced to stop twice now by screaming from below, marking an ongoing—and ultimately futile—battle between the infected and their prey. Each time, the screaming had stopped, replaced by low, unsteady moaning. Each time, she had commanded the students with quick, unyielding gestures to be still and keep silent. They had seen enough news programs about the infected to know what those moans meant, and had frozen like so many scared rabbits until the sounds faded and Miss Oldenburg had started coaxing them forward again.

It had been a little harder to get the group moving each time. She wasn't sure how long she could keep them under control—but then again, maybe she wouldn't have to do it for much longer. If they reached the wall, they would reach the air filtration shaft. She remembered Guy pointing it out so proudly, like he'd been the one to design the school and install the big air pipe.

"It's technically a weakness, on account of how it connects to the school roof without any bars or electrical fencing or whatever," he'd said. "But zombies can't climb, and we don't have any dead people crawling around the attic. It's safe as houses. If there was ever an outbreak on the property, this is where I'd go. Right here. This is what would get me out."

As she crawled along, she wondered belatedly whether he'd already been thinking of this very scenario, and had been trying to give her a way out in case it ever came to pass. He was a smart man, and he'd always liked her. Maybe he was somewhere up here in the roof with them, crawling along, heading for his own salvation. That thought lead to another, more unnerving one: he'd said that there were no dead people crawling around in the attic, but that didn't mean there was no one who'd been bitten and not yet amplified. Someone who was already infected could be lurking just around the next corner, waiting to lunge.

A small hand caught her sleeve. Elaine nearly screamed, stopping herself and swallowing the sound at the last moment. She turned to see a little boy from Ms. Teeter's class tugging on her dress, a solemn expression on his face.

"Yes?" she said, keeping her voice low.

"I need to go," he said.

That simple, mundane admission sparked a chorus of similar statements from all sides. Elaine winced. "We can't stop at the bathroom right now, honey," she said. "Can't you hold it just a little longer?"

The boy shook his head.

Elaine grimaced as she cast a panicked look around the crawl space. If any part of it was being used for storage, that part wasn't currently lit; the light only extended for five or so feet past the leading edge of the children, and the motion sensors were sensitive enough that the lights had already turned off again behind them. That was good—the motion sensors being sensitive meant that it was less likely that anyone could be up there with the class—but it was also bad. If there were buckets or boxes or other helpful, containerlike objects up in the roof, she wasn't going to be able to find them in time.

"All right," she said, keeping her voice as steady as she could. "Do you need to go number one or number two?"

Cheeks burning with the sheer mortification of discussing such a thing with an adult who was neither his mother nor his teacher, the boy said, "Number one."

"That's good. All right. I know this... I know this isn't the usual way, but I want you to go over there"—she gestured toward the nearest low divider, some ten feet of crawl space away—"and pee on the floor."

The boy looked horrified, as did the other children close enough to have heard her terrible proposal. "I can't do that!" he said. "That's *dirty*. I can't."

"Then you'll have to hold it," she said firmly. "We can't go down to the bathroom right now. There are..." She stopped herself before she could tell him exactly what was in the school that prevented their descent. Many of the children probably knew. Those same children were clearly repressing the information, choosing temporary ignorance over the strain of knowing. She wished she could do the same. "We have to keep playing this game until we win. You want to win, don't you?"

Looking puzzled, the little boy nodded.

"Then if you have to go, you have to go up here in the roof. I'm sorry. It's the way things are right now." It was a terrible excuse. She knew it, and so did the children, who looked at her with mingled expressions of doubt and confusion, like they couldn't believe that those words were actually leaving her mouth. But she stood by them. She had to. There wasn't any other choice.

Finally, still looking confused—and like he might start to cry at any moment—the little boy crawled off to the place she had indicated to take care of his business. Elaine rubbed her forehead with one hand, allowing herself to close her eyes and take a few quick, stabilizing breaths. This was all so much harder than she had ever imagined it could be.

Then again, she hadn't had any idea, when her day began, that she would be dealing with an on-campus outbreak before the day was done. If she'd known, she would have called in sick, or at least worn trousers. At least being above the classrooms meant that the alarm wasn't as loud. At least most of her students were still alive.

At least zombies couldn't climb.

More than a minute slithered by before a hand tugged on her sleeve. She opened her eyes and turned to see the little boy from before kneeling next to her. His cheeks were so red that she worried briefly that he was going to pass out. "I couldn't wash my hands," he said miserably.

"It's all right," she assured him. "Once we finish the game, we're all going to get a nice hot bath." The CDC would scrub them so clean that one little tinkle without soap and water at the end would seem like nothing. All they had to do was get there.

Raising her voice just a little—just enough that it would carry—she said, "All right, everyone. We need to move." She crawled forward, trying to spur them into action.

The ceiling gave way beneath her.

It wasn't an immediate thing. It might have been better if it had been. A quick drop would have slammed her into the classroom floor below, and might have meant that less of the ceiling would have caved in along with her. She would never know what had weakened the tiles at that precise point. Maybe it was the long hesitation of the group putting slow but constant stress on them. Maybe it was old water damage weakening the connection between the individual tiles and the thin frame that had been designed to hold them in place. Whatever the reason, the ceiling first lurched, sinking down, and then—before she could do more than catch her breath and try to wish away what was about to happen—collapsed completely.

Elaine Oldenburg fell. Roughly two-thirds of the students in her care fell with her, and like the tiles, they tumbled gradually. Some were on the piece of ceiling that collapsed, and they plummeted down at the same time as she did, pinwheeling in a cloud of tile fragments and broken supports. Others managed to grab the edges of the hole her fall had created, only to fall a few seconds later as their underdeveloped upper bodies failed to give them the purchase that they needed. In less than thirty seconds, only four students remained in the roof: two of the kindergarteners, and Scott and Brian from Miss Oldenburg's class.

The lucky four peered through the hole in horror, looking down on an empty fourth-grade classroom. Some of the other kids had landed on desks or slammed into the floor so hard that blood was coming out of their mouths or noses. A few of them didn't seem to be breathing. And in the midst of the shattered throng sprawled Miss Oldenburg, her limbs splayed, her eyes closed.

"Miss Oldenburg?" whispered Scott. The teacher didn't respond. A few of the other kids stirred and groaned, but they were living groans, I-don't-wanna groans, not the pained exhalations of the dead. He *knew* what infected people sounded like, even if no one wanted to believe that he could know something like that. Suzy down the street's grandpa had died and come back again while her mom was babysitting for him. Scott had heard the dead old man moaning through the door. He'd never forget that sound.

"Miss Oldenburg?" he whispered again, louder. The classroom door was open. That seemed suddenly very important, and very scary. Why, if the classroom door was open, just about *anything* could come through. "You have to wake up now. Please?" One of the kindergarten babies up in the roof with him started to cry. Scott glared at her, which just made her cry harder.

She wasn't the only one. Some of the kids down on the floor were awake now, and they were almost all of them crying, rubbing at their eyes and elbows and knees while they made little gasping, sobbing sounds, like they just couldn't keep it inside anymore. The kids who weren't crying weren't moving, either. They were just lying there, and some of them were bleeding, from their ears or mouths. One kindergartener had blood soaking slowly through the left leg of his pants, turning the corduroy fabric from green to a dark, unpleasant shade of brown.

Miss Oldenburg wasn't moving. She wasn't bleeding either, so maybe it was okay, but she wasn't moving, and the classroom door was open, and this wasn't okay, this wasn't okay at *all*.

Scott's cheeks were wet. Dimly, he realized that he was crying like a little baby. For once, he didn't care. All he cared about was his teacher, lying silent and motionless on the floor below, not telling them what to do next.

"Miss Oldenburg?"

>> AKWONG: I'M ALMOST DONE. I NEED A SHOWER, AND MAYBE A STIFF DRINK.

>> MGOWDA: YOU DON'T DRINK.

>> AKWONG: RIGHT NOW, I FEEL LIKE I'M READY TO START. HAVE YOU EVER LOOKED AT SOMETHING AND FELT LIKE YOU WERE NEVER GOING TO BE CLEAN AGAIN?

>> MGOWDA: I WAS AT GEORGIA'S FUNERAL. I SPENT SIX HOURS IN THE BATH AT MY HOTEL, AND I STILL FELT FILTHY WHEN I WAS DONE. TO BE QUITE HONEST, PART OF ME STAYED DIRTY UNTIL YOU TOLD ME SHE WAS BACK AMONG THE LIVING.

>> AKWONG: DOES IT GET BETTER?

>> MGOWDA: THAT'S WHAT THE ALCOHOL IS FOR.

—internal communication between Alaric Kwong and Mahir Gowda, After the End Times private server, March 16, 2044

Wednesday, March 19, 2036, 5:03 P.M.

Elaine Oldenburg woke to the soft, brittle sound of children crying all around her. The back of her skull felt like it had been split open and then glued back together by careless surgeons, and when she forced herself—slowly, so slowly—to sit up, bits of tile and shattered roof dug into her hips and side. Her back ached from the impact. At least nothing felt like it was broken; she had landed incredibly well, considering the circumstances. And at least she hadn't landed on any of the children.

The children! She looked frantically from side to side, only wincing a little at the pain the motion sent lancing through her head. Students littered the floor to either side of her, some of them sitting up and hugging themselves as they cried, others still flat on their backs, unmoving. Worst of all, the classroom door was open. Depending on how much noise they had made as they fell...

"Miss Oldenburg?"

Scott's voice was barely above a whisper. Elaine looked up, and saw his pale, worried face peeking over the edge of the hole in the ceiling. The distance between them seemed insurmountable, and made it even more miraculous that she had fallen as far as she had without injuring herself. "Scott, move away from the edge," she said, keeping her voice as low as she dared. "You don't want to fall."

"Miss Oldenburg, how are we supposed to get *down*?"

Elaine hesitated before she said, "You're not. It's not safe down here. I want you to go around the hole. Keep heading for the wall. You'll find a hatch there. Open it, and slide down the chute on the other side."

"But—"

"If you do it, you'll come out on the lawn. You'll get *out*, Scott. Take whoever's still up there with you, and get out." Elaine's expression hardened marginally. "You owe them."

And Scott—who knew the part he might have played in today's events, even if he didn't fully understand it yet, and wouldn't for years—nodded. "Okay. Will we see you outside?"

"Yes," lied Elaine. "You will."

His head vanished from the edge of the hole. Elaine watched for a few seconds to be sure that he wasn't going to come back. Then she turned her attention to the children around her, the ones who were still in her care . . . the ones who had fallen.

Not all of them had survived. Mikey was nearby, his eyes open and his head twisted hard to the side. He was never going to log back onto his treasured Quest Realm account. Distantly, that hurt her more than the reality of his death. Elaine knew she was separating from the situation, turning it into something abstract and endurable, and she let it happen, because *endurable* was what she needed. It was what her students needed.

A low moan drifted through the open classroom door. Elaine stiffened. "Quiet!" she hissed, pressing herself lower to the floor in an effort to keep from being seen by anyone—anything—that shuffled by in the hall. "Everyone, quiet."

Most of the students obeyed, freezing as their own terror overrode their fear. One, a kindergartener whose corduroy pants had gone virtually black with blood, kept sobbing. It was a small, tinny sound, but that would be enough; any infected person who was still roving the school would be able to home in on it like a bloodhound. Elaine scooted closer to the student.

"Please, sweetie, please, you have to be quiet," she whispered.

The little boy looked at her with wide, tear-filled eyes, and continued to sob. It had all been too much, the fear, the pain: he couldn't stop, no matter how much he wanted to do as he was told.

"Please," she whispered again. This time he shook his head. It was a tiny gesture, accompanied by an even louder sob. His pupils almost obscured his irises, dilated by shock.

Biting her lip, Elaine let herself really *look* at the boy's leg for the first time. The shape of it was off, somehow, like the bones no longer formed the straight lines they were supposed to. There was a lot of blood, not only soaking into the fabric, but pooling on the tile floor. The moaning from the hall was getting louder, and his sobs weren't stopping. They weren't going to, not unless he bled out, and they didn't have time to wait.

"I'm so sorry," she said, and put her hands on either side of his head, like she'd been shown in her self-defense classes, the ones that were supposed to let you keep fighting even after you'd run out of ammunition. All her lessons had focused on two things: minimizing blood splatter and preventing reanimation. It was very clinical. She'd been a very good student.

She was distancing again. It was better than the alternatives, which were all very close and very immediate. No matter how much she tried, she couldn't distance herself enough. When she thought about it later—which she would do as little as she possibly could, because some things simply don't bear thinking about—she would always know what sanity sounded like when it finally broke. It would sound like the small, delicate bones of a kindergartener's neck, snapping.

The other children didn't make a sound as she carefully eased her hands away from the boy's neck, leaving him to lay limply, staring at the ceiling with unseeing eyes. She pressed a finger to her lips and made a gesture with her free hand, indicating that they should get as low to the floor as possible. Shock, or maybe terror, made them follow her directions. She flattened herself down with them, and waited.

The moan from the hall came again, louder still. Out of the corner of her eye, she saw something shuffle past the open door. Then something else, and something else, until a stream of infected bodies was shambling past, claiming the school eternally as their own. Elaine stayed flat against the floor, praying silently that none of her charges would panic and start to scream, praying that the infected would shamble on past them.

If there had been fewer dead bodies in the school, less blood and offal scattered about, things might have gone very differently. But the infected had stopped trying to turn the students they came across, and had started using the bodies to satisfy their insatiable hunger instead. When the lead members of the pack smelled the blood and other bodily fluids in the classroom, they kept going, assuming that there was nothing through that door worth finding. In a matter of minutes, the only sound was the soft shuffle of feet moving away down the hall, leaving Elaine Oldenburg and her surviving students behind.

The children didn't move. Tears rolled silently down their cheeks, but their tiny bodies were frozen with fear. Normally, Elaine would have tried to coax them out of their terror, encouraging them to let it go and return to her. For the moment, however, their inability to move was exactly what she needed. She pushed herself away from the floor, remaining hunched over to make herself look small, and cautiously inched across the classroom toward the open door. She was almost there when something moaned in the hall outside. She didn't think: she just reacted, flinging herself to the side and toward the shelter of the teacher's desk, blocking her view of the door—and the door's view of her.

She was focusing so hard on landing without making a sound that it took her a moment to realize that there was someone behind the desk with her. Elaine clapped a hand over her mouth to keep her gasp from escaping, and stared into the blank, empty eyes of one of the fourth-grade teachers, a gentle, pleasant man named Mr. Kapur. He wouldn't be leading his class on his annual butterfly-spotting expedition this spring: his throat had been ripped neatly out, and chunks of flesh were missing from his arms and shoulders. His attackers had kindly spared his face, making him all too recognizable.

Elaine swallowed several times in an effort to keep herself from vomiting, and listened as the straggling moaner shuffled by in the hall. All the while, Mr. Kapur stared at her, seeming almost reproachful in his blankness. This was her fault, his empty eyes implied. She should have watched her students more carefully; she should have seen that Scott was bleeding, and called for an immediate lockdown of the blacktop. That she hadn't done so only proved that whatever came next, she deserved it. But he hadn't, and neither had the children. This was all on her.

Silence reigned once more. As quickly as she dared, Elaine pushed herself away from the body of Mr. Kapur and stood unsteadily, too scared and off balance to trust herself in a crouch. She would fall over if she tried to keep herself low to the ground, and then the zombies would surely return to finish what they had started. How many more bodies were strewn around the classroom, she didn't know, and didn't want to know. The hole in the roof was starting to seem well-placed to her. They could have all landed on the desks. They could have landed in a pile of bodies. Instead, most of them had landed on the floor, which, while unforgiving, was at least unobstructed.

Part of her wanted to protest that a pile of bodies would have been softer, that maybe one of Ms. Teeter's students who was now dead would still be alive if they had fallen through a slightly different spot, but she forced that part firmly aside. If she allowed herself to think about the dead kindergartener, she would have to think about *how* the boy had died, and she couldn't do that. Not yet. Maybe not ever.

Still cautious, moving as slowly as she could, Elaine picked her way along the wall behind the desk to the supply cabinet, and tried the door. It was locked. A thin mewl of dismay escaped her lips before she could stop it. Of *course* it was locked. The lower grades could be mostly trusted—they couldn't reach the higher shelves, where the bleach and ammunition was stored—but once students reached amplification size, it was standard policy to lock the closet doors. Mr. Kapur might have the key, or it might have been lost somewhere in the chaos that had overtaken his classroom. The only way she'd know was by searching his corpse.

Elaine Oldenburg was a woman on the verge of breaking. She had been pushed further and harder than she had ever imagined possible, and it took everything she had left to turn and walk back to the body of her colleague. Carefully, she knelt down and searched through his pockets. There were no keys. She bit her lip almost hard enough to draw blood as she straightened up and began easing his desk drawers open. The keys had to be here somewhere. Falling was bad, yes, but being on the ground with the infected was even worse. If she found the keys, she could get them into the closet; get them back into the crawl space. They could still get out of this death trap. They could still—

She had been so focused on what she was doing that she had forgotten one very important part of her situation: the children, whose shock was wearing off, and not all of whom were accustomed to following her orders. Three of the surviving kindergarteners scrambled to their feet, almost as if they were executing a prearranged plan, and sprinted for the door, ignoring their surroundings as they gave in to the burning need to be *away*. *Away* was the only thing that mattered. Not the muffled cries of their classmates, not the teacher who whirled, staring, at the sound of their footsteps on the floor: *away* was everything.

In the blink of an eye, the three kindergarteners were out of the classroom and running down the hall, unsupervised, seemingly unaware of the dangers that awaited them. Elaine only had a moment to reach a decision. Keep looking for the keys, or run after the children?

There was a third option, and terrible as it was, it seemed like the only one worth taking. She stepped out from behind the desk, beckoning the children who had not run to come and stand around her. Then she waited.

She didn't have to wait for long. The three children had run after what they presumed to be the sound of rescue, and was actually the sound of their destruction. The screams started less than half a minute after they left the room. Elaine grabbed the hands of the two nearest children, hissed, "No matter what, *do not make a sound*," and ran. The students, trained to obedience and lines, and motivated by their fear, followed her.

The screams from the far end of the hall were still echoing as Elaine and her students raced along, skidding around a corner and throwing themselves into the unknown. Classroom doors gaped at them like toothless, broken mouths, granting them glimpses of the horrors within. Elaine scanned the walls as well as she could without slowing down, looking for construction paper decorations and cubbyholes. They needed a kindergarten, or a first-grade or even a second-grade class; someplace where the students would have been too small to reanimate and the closets would have been left unlocked. Something where she wouldn't have to rummage through a dead man's pockets before she boosted her students to safety.

Then she whirled around a corner and found herself looking down the barrel of a shotgun, held in the shaking, blood-covered hands of the school's night janitor. Guy should have been gone hours since, but here he was, still in his overalls and janitor's cap, with blood soaked so deeply into the fabric that it could almost be excused as an unusual sort of dye. Only the still-blue fabric around his collar betrayed just how much blood had been spilled, and how guaranteed his amplification had become.

"Guy," she gasped. The screams from behind them had stopped. That wasn't a good thing. It meant that the infected were no longer preoccupied with their latest kill, and would be looking for something else to hunt—soon. She couldn't stand here in the open with her remaining children. That would be suicide. "I didn't know you were still here."

"Miss Oldenburg." The janitor's voice was unsteady, shaking like his hands. At least his eyes were clear, displaying none of the pupillary dilation that would signal final amplification. "You shouldn't be in the halls. The alarm—"

"—has been ringing for hours. Guy, we need to go past you. Please, let us go past you."

Slowly, he frowned, looking puzzled. Elaine's heart gave a lurch. If he was too far gone to understand speech, she didn't know what she was going to do. Amplification changed the way a person's thoughts worked, gumming them up until they couldn't move quickly, or sometimes at all. It was part of the process that reduced a living, thinking human being to a mechanism for spreading the Kellis-Amberlee virus more effectively. Since it happened differently with every victim, spreading through their bodies and minds at varying rates, there was no real way of knowing whether Guy had minutes or hours left before he started trying to kill them all.

Well. It probably wasn't hours.

"There's nothing past me, Miss Oldenburg," he said. "Everyone's dead. You can't go back that way."

"We have to," she said. "The halls behind us are full of the infected." Jenna was crying, pressing her face against Elaine's hip and burying her free hand in the fabric of Elaine's skirt. Elaine couldn't allow herself to be distracted, not now, not under the circumstances. She kept her eyes locked on Guy, begging him to understand—begging him to still be human enough to let her go.

"Don't know how the damn things got inside," muttered Guy. He glanced past Elaine and the children, looking down the hall. The corner blocked the mob of the infected from his view. "Thought we had protection."

That was always the problem, wasn't it? People thought of the infected as things that could be kept out, and didn't think of them as the virus that was already there, just waiting for the opportunity to stir and open its eyes. Kellis-Amberlee hadn't managed to "get inside." It had just found a way to wake.

"Guy, please, focus," Elaine said. "We need to go past you. We're trying to find a way out of the school."

"Oh, yeah?" For the first time, he looked interested; the barrel of the shotgun dipped slightly. "But you won't be taking me, will you? I'm just a janitor. Not good enough for your little escape plan."

"You're already infected." The words were harsh. Elaine pressed on anyway. "I can't take you with me, or they'll shoot us all as soon as they see us. They might shoot me anyway. I'm over the amplification threshold."

"But none of your students are." Guy hesitated before asking, "Roof?"

"If we can get there." There was no sense in lying to him: he was the one who'd told her about the vents, and more, he was the one with the shotgun. If he didn't want her to make it any further, she wouldn't. "The infected can't climb."

"Not once they're fully amplified," he said. "What will you do if there's already something up there, waiting for you?"

"Die." More of the students started crying. She could feel her control over them wavering. It was a miracle that they'd been able to keep calm for as long they had. Once she lost them... it would be the three kindergarteners running down the hall all over again. She'd never get them back. "This is our only chance. Now please, let us pass."

"I don't know—"

He didn't get the chance to finish his statement. A low groan echoed from one of the nearby classrooms, followed by a chorus of answering moans. The children instantly clustered around their teacher, clutching her dress and casting terrified looks at the open door.

"We have to go," implored Elaine.

Guy—who was close, yes, to full amplification, but whose ability to think was still intact, if somewhat slowed by the infection raging through his veins—took a deep breath, forcing down the thoughts of blood and skin crushed between his teeth that were starting to overtake him. "Go," he said.

Elaine looked at him and nodded. Then: "Children! Come with me!" She took off at a run. The surviving students of her class and Ms. Teeter's kindergarten took off with her, keeping up as best they could.

They had almost reached the end of the hall when Guy's shotgun blared, the sound echoing through the school like a beacon to the remaining dead. Elaine kept her head down and kept running, pulling Jenna along with one hand, trusting the others to keep up.

A door, already half-open, slammed all the way open as they ran past it. Arms emerged, questing arms attached to blood-drenched bodies and hungry, relentless teeth. Three of the kindergarteners were ensnared and dragged, screaming, into the classroom, where their bodies were quickly obscured by the teeming sea of hands.

The infected hadn't been hungry before. Elaine understood that dimly, even as she kept running, and kept urging the remaining students to stay with her, to run, to not look back or slow down for any reason. She had been able to travel the halls in relative safety before because the infection had just been getting started, and later, because the infected were satiated, their bellies stuffed tight with the flesh of their teachers and classmates. But zombies burnt through calories so fast that it was inevitable that they would have become hungry again, and started reacting faster to anything that seemed like it might be food. Anything, like the sound of footsteps that were just a little too swift, just a little too steady, to belong to the living dead.

If they hadn't fallen through the roof, Elaine and her students might have all made it out of the school alive, because the infected hadn't been actively hunting. But now they were, and all the remaining children and their teacher could do was run.

The rioting outside reached a fever pitch at approximately 4:57 P.M., two minutes after Elaine Oldenburg and most of the students in her care fell through the ceiling into Mr. Kapur's classroom. The parents engaged in shouting at emergency personnel and—however unintentionally—delaying the CDC breaching of the school did not know of Elaine's travails, or what her students were being forced to endure in the name of finding freedom. If they had known, perhaps they would have fallen back and allowed the police to clear the area; perhaps they would have given the CDC open access to the campus, before it was too late for the small number of surviving children trapped inside. Perhaps not. This is the realm of speculation, after all, and while we can ascribe motive and logic to the events of that long-past March afternoon, we are not in the business of writing fiction. Even opinion, in this context, must be subservient to the news.

The first arrests were made at 5:02 P.M., one minute before—based on the information recovered from the hallway security cameras and student reports to the police—Elaine Oldenburg regained consciousness. The arrests continued for another eight minutes, by which time Elaine and her charges had left the classroom and were running through the school, hurtling themselves toward an uncertain fate.

We, who have the privilege of perspective, can look back and say that there were a hundred things she could have done to keep her students alive, that she passed up a thousand opportunities in her headlong flight. But Elaine Oldenburg did not have perspective on that day. What she had was a riot raging outside the school doors, preventing help from arriving. What she had was a campus designed by the lowest bidder, which locked down in ways that all but guaranteed lives would be lost.

We forget sometimes how easy it is for the survivors to look back on history and judge those who came before. It's simpler when there is a villain, when there is a reason for things to have gone so terribly, terribly wrong. But sadly, sometimes all there is to find is a little boy with a scraped-up hand, and a patient virus, and a teacher who did the best she could against unspeakable odds.

Sometimes, there is no reason for things to go wrong. They just do.

—FROM *UNSPOKEN TRAGEDIES OF THE AMERICAN SCHOOL SYSTEM* BY ALARIC KWONG, MARCH 19, 2044

Wednesday, March 19, 2036, 5:14 P.M.

Three more students had been lost by the time Elaine and her remaining charges—only four; how did it ever get to be only four? There should have been seventeen in her class alone, not three—turned another corner and found themselves facing something that might have been salvation. Elaine slid to a stop. The four students did the same. The surviving kindergartener wailed as she grabbed hold of Elaine's knees, panting and shaking from the effort of running. Elaine patted the little girl's head with her free hand before carefully easing her gun out of its holster.

The sound of the shots would bring any remaining zombies running. That, more than anything, was why she had chosen flight at every opportunity: better to run and live than to make a heroic stand and die when the bullets ran out and the entire school descended, hands outstretched and hungry. Unfortunately, she didn't see another avenue. There, straight ahead of them, was the door to her classroom, where she knew the closet was unlocked. They would be able to get back to the roof. They would be able to get *out*.

And there, standing between them and the all-essential door, was Mr. O'Toole.

He seemed to be alone, which wasn't unusual for a member of a mob that had been confined in an enclosed space: sometimes they would split up to shamble into new areas, looking for food. When they began to moan, it would attract the others, allowing each individual to become a whole new potential food source. It was practical in a way that was almost unnerving.

The former teacher was looking squarely at her, his mouth hanging very slightly open. He hadn't started to moan yet, but she knew that it was just a matter of time; any second now, he would realize that he was in the presence of good, untainted flesh, and he would begin to moan. That, or the zombies they had left behind them would catch up. Either way, she had seconds to decide what she would do.

"I'm so sorry," she said, and put three bullets in his head.

The children—who had remained almost preternaturally calm throughout their long ordeal, understanding on some level that calm was the only thing that had any potential to save them—all began to scream. Not in unison, which would have been disturbing but not as disorienting; they screamed on four different pitches, in four different speeds. Jenna, who had been almost stoic, sobbed as she screamed, breaking up her wails into small, shattered gasps.

"Almost there," said Elaine. She holstered her gun and scooped the kindergartener into her arms, bracing the little girl against her shoulder as she ran for her classroom. The other three followed, too stunned and scared to do anything else. She was their teacher. She would protect them. In that moment, the children she had already failed to save were the furthest thing from the thoughts of her small, scared survivors.

They weren't far from Elaine's thoughts. Those children were all she could think of as she barricaded the classroom door with her own desk—the only piece of furniture not bolted to the floor. As she led the survivors to the closet and helped them, once more, up into the empty dark of the crawl space.

They moved quickly this time, the teacher and her four charges: they moved without hesitation or lingering long enough to let the tiles grow weak beneath them. When they finally reached the far wall, they found the grate that should have covered the air shaft hanging askew.

"Class dismissed," said Elaine weakly, and boosted the first of her students into the dark tunnel to freedom.

>> AKWONG: IT'S DONE.

>> AKWONG: I AM LOGGING OFF.

>> MGOWDA: YOU DID GOOD WORK TODAY. THANK YOU.

>> AKWONG: I TOLD THE TRUTH.

>> MGOWDA: I KNOW. GEORGIA WOULD BE PROUD.

>> AKWONG: I HOPE SO. IS THIS WHAT IT ALWAYS FEELS LIKE WHEN YOU TURN OVER A ROCK AND SHOW THINGS THAT WEREN'T MEANT TO BE SEEN?

>> MGOWDA: YOU LEARN TO WASH THE STING AWAY.

—internal communication between Alaric Kwong and Mahir Gowda, After the End Times private server, March 16, 2044

Friday, March 28, 2036, 8:03 A.M.

The public defender assigned to represent Elaine Oldenburg in the initial hearings to determine her culpability in the deaths of twelve of the students in her care stood in front of the courthouse, glancing anxiously at his watch. Elaine was three minutes late. Not a horrible offense, not yet, but one that was worrisome in light of the charges that might be brought against her if this inquiry found her to have been at fault. She clearly didn't understand the depth of the trouble she was in. He would have to explain it more clearly when she arrived.

When nine o'clock came and went with no Elaine, he notified the police.

At her apartment, they found all her personal possessions . . . even her identification and teacher's certification, which she was meant to have taken with her to the courthouse. There was no note. There was no indication that she had gone anywhere. Elaine Oldenburg had simply disappeared into the night, leaving everything behind—everything but the contents of her savings account, which she had drained the night before. She was gone.

Maybe it was better that way. It gave the school system a scapegoat and prevented the parents of the survivors from being forced to endure a lengthy trial, arguing against the compelling stories that could so easily have been theirs, if their children had been slightly slower, slightly differently placed in the order of events. Elaine Oldenburg vanished, and she took so much of the blame with her. People looked for her, of course, but not long enough, and not in the right places.

Where she went when that long, terrible school day ended was anybody's guess. The only person who knew for sure was Elaine Oldenburg . . . and she wasn't saying.

Please Do Not Taunt the Octopus

Introduction

Dr. Shannon Abbey is possibly one of my favorite characters in the entire Newsflesh setting. She's practical, pragmatic, and pissed off, which makes her a joy to write; she's not so much a mad scientist as she is a highly annoyed scientist, which makes her a useful plot device. But that doesn't mean she sits around all the time waiting for the opportunity to be useful. She does things. Sometimes they're unpleasant things. Sometimes they're morally questionable things. But she never stops *doing* things.

This story was written to bridge two of the ongoing story lines and to give two of my favorite characters the opportunity to combine their unique outlooks on the world. It's a companion piece to *The Day the Dead Came to Show and Tell*, exploring the effects of trauma and the ways individuals choose to cope with it. Foxy made her choices. Dr. Abbey is trying to do the same. She's also trying to survive. Not always the easiest task in the post-Rising world.

Everything about this story was a delight. If it seems like I don't have much to say, it's because "oh boy oh boy oh boy" gets old.

Please do not taunt the octopus.

Please Do Not Taunt the Octopus

Chapter 1

Relative Perspectives

I hate the term "mad scientist." Shit yeah, I'm angry. I have every reason in the world to be angry. But what right do you have to call me insane?

—Dr. Shannon Abbey

Dr. Shannon Abbey is one of the more dedicated, driven individuals it has been my pleasure to know. Considering the company I have been known to keep, this is both high praise and a dire warning.

—Mahir Gowda

1.

My day started like any other: with the sound of screaming from the next lab over, followed by one of the interns—Dana or Daisy or something like that—running past my door, her hands flung up over her head and her mouth open in an ongoing howl. She wasn't on fire or covered in blood, so I figured it couldn't be that big of a deal. I put my head back down and resumed studying the quarter's expense reports.

It would be easy to think that running a semisecret underground virology lab wouldn't come with any of the normal paperwork. It would also be incorrect. Contractors and supply companies don't donate their time and wares just because a lab happens to operate outside the usual boundaries. If anything, they're likely to charge *more*, since there's always the chance that this month's order will be the last. They have to get their dues in where they can. It used to piss me off, but there was nothing to be done about it, and besides, the more I paid, the more I could count upon their discretion. A bribed bastard never tells.

Thank God for the American Affordable Care Act. It was passed in a limited form right before the Rising began, despite the opposition of one hell of a lot of people who thought that providing health care to their fellow citizens was somehow, I don't know, inappropriate. Honestly, it was a miracle the thing passed at all, considering that we're talking about the era of vaccine denial and homeopathic cures for everything from autism to erectile dysfunction. If the Rising hadn't come along when it did, most of the United States would probably have died of whooping cough before 2020, leaving the middle part of the continent ripe for Canadian invasion.

But resistance to public health aside, the ACA *did* pass, and after the Rising made the consequences of ignoring one's fellow man blazingly apparent, it was strengthened and improved until the United States had one of the best health care systems in the world. My interns might be officially unemployed and not drawing a salary, but at least I didn't have to worry about paying their medical insurance.

The intern—I was pretty sure her name was Daisy; I seemed to remember her saying something about flowers, or *The Great Gatsby*, or something equally inane—ran past again, still screaming, still not on fire. I narrowed my eyes and dropped my stylus on the desk before pushing back my chair. Joe, my black English Mastiff, raised his head and made a bewildered ruffing noise deep in his throat. I leaned down to stroke his ears.

"Good boy, Joe," I said. "You guard the desk. I'm going to go cut a few strips out of my new intern. Maybe I can make you some jerky. Would you like that, Joe? Would you like some nice intern jerky?"

Joe made another ruffing noise, all but indicating that he very much *would* like some nice intern jerky. I stroked his ears again.

"Good boy," I repeated, and made my way out of the office, pausing only to grab my lab coat from the hook next to the door.

There's something powerful about a lab coat, no matter how dirty or threadbare it may become. I was never going to get the bloodstains out of this one, and even if I had, I'd spilled a glass of ruby port on my right sleeve the week before. That's the sort of stain that *nothing* will remove, not even hydrofluoric acid. Although acid would remove the fabric, so technically, it would also remove the stain.

But yes: power. A person who wears a lab coat is a person who knows what's up: a person who can change the world, for either good or ill, through the studied application of science. A person who understands the way things are done. And in *my* lab, when *I* wear a lab coat, it means that some serious shit is about to go down.

The screaming intern wasn't screaming anymore by the time I stepped into the wet lab three doors down from my office. She was crying instead, her hands clasped over her face in what seemed to me to be an excessively theatrical manner. Three more of the interns were clustered around her, varying expressions of shock and dismay on their faces. The tank behind them was empty. I sighed.

"All right, where the fuck's the octopus?"

One of the interns pointed up. I followed the line of his finger to the light fixture at the center of the ceiling. A large white mass was clinging there, three of its legs slapped flat against the plaster. The rest of its legs were twined around the light fixture itself, holding it in place.

"Barney, dammit." I crossed my arms. "You know you're not supposed to be up there. How are we supposed to take cell samples if you're sticking to the damn ceiling all the time?"

"Eh-eh-it grabbed my *face*!" wailed probably-Daisy. Her voice was distorted by her hands, which was possibly the most annoying thing she'd done since the screaming began.

"Of course he grabbed your face," I said. "If you give Barney the opportunity to grab your face, he'll grab your face. Everyone knows that. Grabbing faces is his one true joy in life, since we won't let him stick to the ceiling all the time, and he's never going to get laid." Octopuses died shortly after they mated. It was a biological kill switch that all my tinkering hadn't been able to remove, which made hormone depressants and celibacy the only real solution. I needed my test subjects to live until I was done with them. Barney had been with us for ten years now, and I was planning to keep him for ten more, no matter how cranky he got.

Probably-Daisy finally lowered her hands and stared at me. I looked impassively back at her, raising an eyebrow for emphasis. If she was going to work in my lab, she was going to need to learn to deal with the fact that sometimes, things were going to get messy. She was honestly lucky that she'd just had her face grabbed by an angry octopus. Worse things had happened to my staff in the past, and not all of them had survived.

"Does anyone have a stick?" I asked. "We need to get Barney off the ceiling and back into his tank. Preferably today. I can't authorize feeding the rest of the cephalopods while he's still hanging around out here, and I don't want an army of angry, hungry octopuses rampaging through the place."

"Sorry, Dr. Abbey," said Tom. He'd been with me longer than most of the research staff, a distinction he bore with dignity, grace, and a whole lot of marijuana. As long as he didn't try to do delicate work while he was stoned, I really didn't care. Besides, the more interested he got in hydroponics, the better everyone else's food became. It was a win-win situation. Especially for me, since as long as I looked the other way when he lit up, he didn't leave me for a more legitimate, less murderously dangerous workplace.

"It was an accident," said Jill. She hadn't been with me as long as Tom, but she'd survived two outbreaks in her time, one by removing her prosthetic leg and using it as a club. She was also one of the only researchers in my lab that we hadn't recruited. She'd just shown up one day, like a particularly tall, gawky, Canadian puppy with a fondness for bioluminescence.

Between the two of them, I had managed to create the perfect intern-hazing machine. Tom was lackadaisical enough that no one ever expected him to move quickly or act cruelly, and Jill was a safety valve on his occasionally dangerous impulses, turning what could have been harmful pranks into octopus antics and the occasional sewage line backup. Maybe it was cruel of me to put that sort of pressure on the new kids, but to be honest, I didn't really give a fuck about whether I was being cruel. My interns either broke while they were brand-new and still under warranty, or they proved themselves capable of surviving under laboratory conditions.

Really, what one person saw as cruelty, another person would probably see as a mercy. There was no way of knowing who could and couldn't hack it before they'd been put into a position to try, and the consequences for failure weren't pretty.

Probably-Daisy looked from Tom to Jill and back again before finally turning to me, her tears stopping in the face of her confusion. "Wait," she said. "Why are you acting like this is normal?"

"Because it *is* normal," I said. Tom handed me a stick. I took it, and began gently prodding at the legs Barney had wrapped around the light fixture. "Didn't you see the signs? The ones that say 'don't taunt the octopus'?"

"Yes, but... that was also the e-mail address you used when you offered me this job," said probably-Daisy. She picked herself up from the floor, only wobbling a little. Her tears were by now completely forgotten, washed away by everything that was happening around her. That was good. It showed flexibility, assuming she wasn't on the verge of a complete nervous breakdown.

If she was, I was going to owe Tom another bag of fertilizer for his ganja garden. He had been betting against her since day one, when she'd worn high heels to the pharm lab. Jill thought—and I was inclined to agree with her, although I would never have said so—that Tom didn't understand what it was to be a woman coming into an established workplace. We didn't care about those conventions here: As long as my employees wore shoes they could run in, and took their chemical showers on time, I could give a shit how they chose to present themselves. But the CDC didn't work like that. The CDC might never work like that, not even now that the EIS was rebuilding their command structure. And probably-Daisy was just the latest in a long line of prettily gift-wrapped, beautifully disloyal CDC spies.

The sooner she figured out that I knew what she was, and didn't care, the better off she was going to be. In the meantime, she had to survive her first week.

"I use that as my e-mail address in part because it's a really basic aspect of lab safety," I said. "The octopus has eight arms, incredibly good eyesight, and enough brains to hold a grudge against anyone who pisses it off. So when I say, 'Do not taunt the octopus,' what I'm actually saying is, 'Have a sliver of self-preservation in that rotten walnut you persist in calling a brain.'" I poked Barney again with the stick. Barney took the stick away and poked me back.

Probably-Daisy looked to Tom and Jill, seeking moral support. They both shook their heads, and didn't say anything. They knew when their input was not needed.

"What's your name, anyway?" I tried to grab the stick back from Barney. He used it to whack me upside the head.

"Zelda," said probably-Daisy.

"Wow, okay. I was way off." I grabbed the stick again. This time, Barney let me have it. I tossed it aside and held my arms out, and he let go of the ceiling, falling like so much dead weight. The impact of him slamming into my elbows made me stagger a little. He curled his legs around me, and I pulled him close to my chest, providing the comfort and security that a healthy octopus needs. "Don't let him grab your face again. Jill, Tom, don't let the interns feed Barney if they're going to freak out when he behaves in a totally reasonable manner."

"Yes, Dr. Abbey," they chorused dutifully.

"Good. Now go the fuck back to work." I walked out of the room,

Barney nestled comfortably in my arms and slowly turned a deep shade of orange as he adjusted his chromatophores to match my shirt.

Sometimes it's good to be in charge.

2.

It was generally pretty easy to get Barney to go into the recreation tank. It was wide and shallow and usually contained other octopuses, or sometimes an interesting crab or toy that he could take apart. This time, he clung to my arms and chest like he was afraid I was going to drop him, even going so far as to wrap the tip of one tentacle around the back of my head. The feeling of suckers trying to find purchase on my hair was bizarre, and made me glad all over again that I had abandoned the professional vanity of my youth in favor of the practical buzz cut of my... non-youth. Middle age.

"Just call me mature for my years, and don't ask for my birthday," I said to Barney, who responded, in typical fashion, by reaching up and trying to wrap his arms around my face. I sighed, pushing him away as I waded into the water. It was cold enough to chill my ankles and calves immediately, and my shoes were going to need some serious time in the dryer, but whatever. If it got Barney to let me go, it was worth the sacrifice.

"You need to let go now," I said, bending forward until the back of his mantle touched the water. Barney lessened his grip, but didn't release me completely. I moved my hands so that they were tucked under his central arms, rather than supporting his body, and began gently pushing him away.

Like most octopuses, Barney was smart enough to be a problem and alien enough to human modes of thought that he didn't really subscribe to mammalian notions of right, wrong, and "I shouldn't stick to that." Still, he had been my lab animal since he had first emerged from his tiny, translucent egg sac and into a thick solution of protein, mutagenic agents, and Kellis-Amberlee. He was the first Giant Pacific Octopus I had failed to infect, and he was still at the forefront of my cephalopod studies. And after years of working with me—voluntarily or not—he knew when he was pushing his luck. With what I could only describe as a disgruntled pulse of his chromatophores, he released me and sank down into the pool, settling on the smooth, sandy bottom.

"Thanks," I said, reaching down and pressing one hand flat against the surface of the water. He reached up and twined the tip of one arm briefly around my wrist before letting me go and ambulating off to look for something to play with.

It must have been nice, being an octopus. I couldn't even say that the lack of sex was a deterrent, since I myself hadn't gotten laid in more than two years. "Mate or die" might not be built into the human genome, but the need to actually form an emotional connection with someone is, chemically speaking, and running an underground virology lab leaves very little opportunity for dating.

I waded back to the edge of the pond and stepped out, grimacing at the way my shoes squelched on the tile. The two researchers currently responsible for maintaining the pool looked at me from the other side of the room, their expressions making it clear that they wanted, desperately, to ask why I had decided to take my octopus for a walk. I lifted my eyebrows and waited until they looked away. Then, smirking, I turned and walked back toward my office.

To say that this is not the future my parents envisioned for me when I said I wanted to become a virologist would be an understatement. They pictured a life of scientific accomplishment and research performed in perfectly clean, brilliantly white rooms, with no fewer than five layers of security between me and the things I worked on. They pictured marriage, a family, and above all else, safety. Their daughter was going to be a doctor. Their daughter was going to find the cure for Kellis-Amberlee. Their daughter was going to save the world.

They were sort of right. For a while, I'd thrived in just the sort of environment they'd imagined for me. I had gone from Health Canada to the Canadian branch of the CDC, an organization established after the Rising for the purpose of keeping things on a relatively even, zombie-free keel. I'd met a good man, gotten married, and started thinking about children. There are people who say that it's immoral to bring kids into the world we have today. Most of those people aren't really thinking about the long-term consequences of their words. If everyone stopped having kids, the human race would die out. Maybe not directly because of Kellis-Amberlee, but does that really matter? We'd still be dying out due to the zombie apocalypse. Screw that.

Then came the outbreak at Simon Fraser University. My husband, Joseph Abbey, was on campus, giving a lecture to a class of future software engineers. Someone got sick, someone died, the dead began to walk, and rather than sending in a team of soldiers to save the healthy, the people at the switch decided to cut their losses and burn the whole thing to the ground. It was the first major firebombing on Canadian soil since the end of the Rising. There were no survivors. Including my husband. Including, once I had managed to beg, borrow, and steal my way into accessing the few shreds of footage that had managed to survive the "accidental" purge that followed the bombs, my professional career.

They—Health Canada, the CDC, the governments of their respective countries—were lying to me, and had been lying to me since the day I said, "I think I want to go to medical school." They weren't keeping us safe. They weren't searching for a cure, or even for a solution. They were just writing us off as acceptable losses. After Simon Fraser, I couldn't believe that any losses were acceptable. Not unless I saw them with my own eyes.

I'd handed in my resignation the day after the funeral. The CDC had refused it. They had also refused the second one I handed them. I don't know if they bothered to refuse the third. I was gone before anyone could come looking for me. I've been gone ever since.

Technicians walked past me in the hall, and if any of them found the wet splotches on my shirt, or the fact that I was soaked to the knees, to be a little bit strange, they were smart enough not to say anything about it. It's always nice to have confirmation that I hire intelligent people—sometimes brains are the only things that stand between a living person and a gruesome death. Or maybe brains and Kevlar.

Joe lifted his head when I opened my office door, looking perplexed as only a large canine can. I offered him a smile and closed the door behind myself, heading for the closet on the other side of my desk. "It's okay, Joe," I said. "Barney just gave me a few hugs too many, and now I need a fresh shirt."

Joe's tail thumped the floor hopefully. I sighed.

"No, not right now. Sorry, buddy, but I really do need to finish these expense reports before Joey calls me up and wants to know what happened to all that human growth hormone he shipped my way last quarter. I'll make it up to you later, all right?"

Joe's tail hit the floor one more time before my "no" processed. Looking sad, he put his head down on his paws and heaved a sigh deep enough that it seemed to have deflated his entire body. I grinned. I couldn't help myself. There was just something about an overly dramatic dog that amused the hell out of me—a direct contradiction of my reaction to overly dramatic interns, who were generally sent packing at the first opportunity. One nice thing about running my own private, illegal lab: *Everything* is work for hire.

Our current facility was one of the nicer ones we'd had for a while, and we'd been there for coming on three years. That was a record for my little operation, which normally got driven out of each new facility within eleven months. I blamed the changes in the status quo that had accompanied our relocation to Shady Cove, Oregon. All my previous labs had operated in a climate where the CDC was the enemy—no question, no quarter—and the government was actively working against research into Kellis-Amberlee reservoir conditions. Thanks to some dangerous houseguests of mine, there had been what I could only describe as an ideological climate change. I wasn't coming back to the fold of "legitimate medicine" any time soon, but the new world we were moving into was a lot better for people like me.

If I was being honest with myself, I had to admit that "legitimate medicine" wanted to deal with me about as much as I wanted to deal with it. Joey knew exactly where I was located these days. So did Dr. Danika Kimberley, an EIS researcher who had managed to worm her way into the upper echelons of the restructured CDC. Either one of them could have set the wolves on me at any time, and they didn't, because they knew the work I was doing was as important as it was impossible for them to do. No ethics committees for me. No oversight. Just a bunch of skilled technicians, a lot of animals, and the knowledge that someone should have started years before I had.

It was nice, still being in Shady Cove. I had told Joey that we'd be cutting our losses and running, during the final showdown between the old CDC and the branch of the EIS that would go on to become the new one. He had cautioned me to wait a little while, to be patient, and for once in my life, I had actually listened, maybe because Dr. Joseph Shoji was one of my only old colleagues who had never, not for a second, tried to write me off as deluded or insane. He had always understood that there was a difference between anger and loss of faculties, and he didn't throw around ableist terms like "mad" just because it made him look better. So when he'd asked me to stay, I'd given him the benefit of the doubt.

My reward was the Shady Cove Forestry Center. It had been the site of the single largest massacre my team had ever experienced, when a CDC spy who had managed to worm her way into my interns decided that she could exterminate a whole lot of problems with one pair of lock cutters. She'd been torn apart by the test subjects she released, before they went on to kill eleven more of my people. *Eleven.* I had never lost that many team members in a single day, and if the infected hadn't killed her, I would have done it myself.

I had always known that the CDC was watching me. They would have been stupid not to be, and while the CDC was many things—corrupt, cowardly, morally bankrupt in a way that all the "mad science" in the world would never be able to match—they weren't stupid. They never had been. I'd even rooted out a few of their previous spies, many of whom were still with me in one capacity or another. It was amazing how quickly exposure to the real world would deprogram the little darlings, many of whom had never seen unredacted infection data in their lives. My IT department was excellent, and backstopped by the latest technology from the antisurveillance teams working in their own part of the modern underground. One of the past moles had admitted, after he changed sides, that the CDC called my lab "the roach motel." Data got in, but it didn't get out.

"Once I managed to get hired, I was supposed to keep my head down and wait for you to trust me enough to send me on a supply run," he'd said, looking just chagrined enough that I hadn't wanted to belt him upside the head with a stapler. "Then I could transmit a signal back to the CDC with everything I'd managed to learn."

"Did you?" That had been my only question, and when I'd asked it, he had shaken his head.

"Never got the chance," he'd said. "Can I stay?"

"Sure, Tom; you can stay." And then he'd shaken my hand and gone back to hydroponics, where he had proceeded to test the rumors that people could die from marijuana overdose. Since he'd survived, I was pretty sure those rumors were just that—rumors, and no more true than the one about the human clone living somewhere in Canada, off the grid and out of the public eye.

Well. Maybe that one had a little grain of truth to it.

The Shady Cove facility had everything we'd ever needed and a few things we hadn't considered, such as the octopus wading pool and the sizable living quarters that had been provided for the rangers and college interns who had originally ruled the forestry center. For the first time in a long time, my people were comfortable, no one was worried about using up the last of the hot water, and we were even starting to make acquaintances within the local black market, rather than just going for the mutual exploitation model.

It was a pretty sweet gig. I had all faith that it was going to come to a terrible end, and very soon, because that's what happens to pretty sweet gigs. And in the meanwhile, no matter how much I tried to delay or deny it, there was still paperwork to be done.

I produced a dry shirt, pants, and socks from the stock in my closet, kicked off my shoes, and tossed my wet clothes onto the floor to be dealt with later. It only took a few minutes for me to get myself re-dressed, and no elves or CPAs or other mythological creatures appeared to do my paperwork in the interim.

Sometimes, it's not so good to be the boss after all. I sat back down, picked up my pen, and bent forward. This time, the sound of screams did not come to save me.

3.

After two hours of paperwork, broken up by three cups of coffee, a banana-mango smoothie, and the corresponding trips to the bathroom, I was done. Virtually anything would have been better than filling out one more itemized list, and that included dealing with another outbreak in my own living room. "Life was easier when assholes tried to kill us on the regular, Joe," I said. Joe replied by lifting his head and thumping his tail against the floor again, eternally hopeful.

Might as well reward him for his patience. "Come on, buddy," I said, and stood. "Let's go on an inspection."

Joe was immediately on his feet, tail wagging so hard that his entire massive body shook. This time, I left my lab coat on the hook as I opened the door and stepped out into the hall, Joe pacing along beside me. Together, we filled all the available space, forming an impassable wall of scientist and dog. I liked it that way. It was good to remind people that when something needed to move, it wasn't going to be me.

Again, some of the psychology that went into my lab design and behavior could be seen as cruel, but there was always a good reason for it. I wasn't here to foster a loving workplace environment or encourage my people to be the best that they could be. I was here to save the world, and to hopefully do it with a minimum of casualties. That meant, among other things, that I needed people to remember the chain of command, and to not think that they were somehow above it because they had feelings, needs, and opinions of their own. Surprisingly enough, wandering around with a carnivore the size of a small pony helped me get my point across.

The lab where Barney had performed his classic face-hugging stunt was empty, and I was pleased to see that the floor and ceiling had both been dried off. Two of the smaller octopuses were in the tank, one of them clinging to a rocky outcropping high in the corner, and the other lazily wandering around the bottom. Joe pressed his nose against the glass and made a little wuffing noise. I pulled him back.

"Don't bark at the octopuses," I scolded mildly, wiping the wet spot his nose had left on the glass away with my sleeve. "You know they hold grudges."

Joe looked at me dolefully. I ruffled his ears and pulled him away from the tank, stepping back out into the hall. The air smelled of bleach and artificial citrus: The cleaning crew had been through recently. I nodded to myself, satisfied with their work, but kept studying the walls and floor as I led Joe through the facility. Part of being the head of an underground lab is knowing that no one is responsible for your survival but you. I didn't have *a* job—I had *all* the jobs, from making the mac and cheese on Tuesdays to scrubbing out the octopus enclosures. The fact that I outsourced them from time to time didn't make them any less my own, and it wouldn't save me from the consequences if they were done poorly.

Joe sniffed the ground as we walked, his tail waving wide and creating a dangerous barrier behind us. A dog that big, with a tail that long, can leave bruises just by being happy to see you. The various interns we passed all gave Joe a wide berth, until we reached the lobby of the forestry center. Out of all the rooms in the building, this was the one we had changed the least. It was too big and too oddly shaped to be of use for much beyond storage and socialization, and we already had several storage rooms. Consequently, the lobby was where couches and chairs from the rest of the building went to die. They were shoved up against walls and curved into conversation pits, some of which were currently in use. I waved but didn't approach. My people, no matter how much they liked me and appreciated my leadership, weren't here to be my friends. All I'd do by approaching was make them uncomfortable.

Heavy is the head that wears the crown. If you ask me—and why wouldn't you ask me? I'm a genius—heavier yet are the shoulders that wear the lab coat. Everyone in this facility depended on me to keep them alive. If that meant I wasn't invited to the Friday movie nights, well, so be it.

Sometimes I really missed the days when Shaun Mason and his little band of fools had been in and out every time I turned around. Shaun had never been afraid of me. He'd been suffering from PTSD and obsessed with getting revenge for his dead sister, and most of his people should probably have quit and come to work for me, since at least I don't hit, but he'd been *fun*. He'd been trying to make a place for himself in a world that doesn't yield easily to people like us, and he'd been doing it while knowing exactly how broken he really was.

I missed them all, honestly. Mahir and his frustrations, Alaric and his confusion, Becks—God, poor Becks—with her grudges and her resentments and her infinite potential. Even Maggie and Kelly had been interesting to talk to, in their own privileged ways. But I missed Shaun most of all. He'd been the one who reminded me most of myself, back in the early days, when there was nothing left for me but rage.

I swiped my card at the reader next to the front door. It buzzed softly, a small tone that would also sound at each of our security stations. Then the door unlocked, and I let myself out into the sweet green loveliness of the Oregon afternoon.

Mammals are pretty Johnny-come-lately in the natural world. Compared to plants and insects, we've been here for fifteen minutes, and we're already fucking shit up. Removing the large mammals from the forests surrounding Shady Cove hadn't done anything to hurt them. If anything, it had allowed the underbrush to achieve a level of lush health that the forest hadn't known in centuries. We still got squirrels, rabbits, rats, and pre-amplification raccoons, as well as the occasional possum. One of the interns swore that she'd seen a bear, but until I saw some proof, I wasn't going to worry about it. With as many cameras as we had around the edges of the building, "Pics or it didn't happen" was a totally fair request.

Joe's nose immediately went to the ground, drinking in the scent of the day. I walked with him to the edge of the parking lot, where the woods began. Then I gave him a pat on the shoulder and tugged once on the back of his collar, re-creating the degree of pressure that would have accompanied unclipping a leash. Joe's head came up, eyes bright with sudden excitement.

"That's right, good boy," I said. "You're off-leash. Go ahead and run around a little bit."

He didn't need to be told twice. Tail wagging and ears pressed flat in canine excitement, Joe went bounding into the underbrush. The greenery rustled once, twice, three times, and he was gone, returning to the wilds that had created his ancestors.

I stayed where I was, in the open space where the paving still held dominance and the forest had not yet taken back its original territory. We'd been at the forestry center long enough that we'd cleared out all the mobs in the area, stacking up infected humans, deer, and raccoons like cordwood. I'd been sending my people farther and farther to collect test subjects, because we just couldn't find them near the lab. But none of that made me feel like taking the risk of going out into the green.

A gunshot sounded from straight ahead of me, followed by a strangled yelp from—"Joe!" I didn't pause to think about what I was doing. I just charged forward, racing into the woods with my head down and my heart pounding wildly. My own pistol was strapped at my hip. It wouldn't help me against, say, a zombie bear, but a zombie bear wouldn't be shooting at my dog.

I broke through a wall of green into a small clearing, formed by a collusion of tree roots ripping up the ground and making it inhospitable to further growth. The surrounding brush was dense and tangled, pulling at my clothing even as I tried to shake it off. Joe was standing in the middle of the clearing, legs set in a wide-splayed "guard" position, a growl resonating up through his massive chest. His ears were completely flat, making him look more like a small bear than a large dog. It would have been a heart-stopping sight if he hadn't been my dog, and if my heart hadn't already been struggling to recover from the shock of hearing that gun go off.

He was growling at a large tree, his eyes fixed on its branches. I looked up, trying to see what had him so upset. It was probably human. Joe sometimes got excited about squirrels and bunny rabbits—I tried to stay out of the way when that happened, since no amount of scientific detachment could make the sight of a mastiff crunching on a rabbit's skull pleasant—but those didn't usually carry guns.

"What do you have, boy?" I asked, trying to estimate the lines of sight from the tree to where I was standing. "Did you startle a trespasser? Is that what you did, boy? Did you come out of the bushes and scare some poor local kid who was just looking for something they could eat? Or did you find yourself a looter? The difference between a looter and a trespasser is about eight bullets, by the way." I raised my voice, abandoning the pretense that I was talking to my dog. "We don't mind people passing through, but I assure you, we're not that easy to rob."

Big words for a woman in jeans and a T-shirt. Whoever was in that tree didn't have to know that, and Joe definitely helped me present a terrifying public front. Most people aren't accustomed to dogs anymore. When your family pet can turn you into the walking dead with a single bite, most people decide to go with goldfish.

"That's a *dog*." The voice was female, and ageless in that way some women have, a combination of innocence and experience that could have come out of a throat aged anywhere from seventeen to seventy. She sounded affronted, like Joe's existence was somehow an insult to her ideas about the world. "You have a *dog*."

"Yes," I said, tracking the sound of her voice until my eyes lit on a spot high in the tree. She was there. She was hidden by branches, and might not have a clear line of sight on me—but then again, she might. It was hard to say, without being able to see her hands, and the way she was holding her gun. "You shot at my dog."

"He came up out of the bushes at me! He was going *ow-ow-ow-ow*!" Her onomatopoeia for the sound of Joe's bark was shallow, restricted by the span of her rib cage, but it was surprisingly good: I would have recognized that bark anywhere.

"Yeah, he does that when he's running around his own backyard. It means he's happy." I didn't move. "I know you have a gun. I know you took a shot at my dog. Do you have any more bullets? Because if you take another shot at my dog, I will have to return fire."

"Is he a good dog, or a bad, bitey dog? I don't think I should have to leave bad, bitey dogs alone." The woman in the tree sounded genuinely curious. She also sounded somehow off, like she was working harder to speak than she should have needed to.

Joe hadn't bitten her: I knew that. With the size of his jaws, if he'd been able to catch any part of her body, one of them would have died. Either the woman, from blood loss, or Joe, from lead poisoning. Whatever was wrong with her, it predated her encounter with my dog.

"Whether he's a good dog or a biting dog depends entirely on your relationship with me," I said. "Joe follows instructions. Do you have any bullets left?"

"Yes, but not so many," said the woman. "I've been running out of bullets. Running out of pills, too. So I said, wait, I said, maybe there's a somebody who could make both of those things better. So I asked some questions, and maybe used a few more bullets—definitely used a few knives—and found out where there was a somebody. I don't want to hurt you. You seem like a nice lady, and like I said, I've been running out of bullets. You're a nice lady with a really big dog. The dog is probably better than bullets in a lot of situations, huh? I bet when you have a dog that big, nobody messes with you."

"We're getting off the topic, my unseen friend, and that topic is whether or not we're both walking away from here under our own power," I said. "You say you're low on bullets. You say you don't want to hurt me. Well, you're on my land. If you're not here to hurt me, what are you here for?"

"I'm looking for someone." The feeling that something was wrong came through even more strongly in her brief, blunt statement. It was like she'd been drawing strength from her run-on sentences, using them to keep herself together. I'd heard that sort of thing before, from exhausted interns who were sure they could solve the zombie apocalypse if they just gave up sleep and learned to live entirely on coffee and adrenaline.

It always ended in a crash.

"Who?"

The tree rustled. "Will your doggy hurt me if I come down?"

"Not unless you draw first. Joe? Heel."

Joe's massive head swung around to me, and he leveled the most reproachful look I had ever received in my direction. He *had* the person, he seemed to say; they were *right there.* Why would I pull him away from someone, when he *had* them?

"Heel," I said again, and with a deep, long-suffering sigh, Joe turned and trotted over to sit down by my feet. He was still tense and alert, his body thrumming with the need to leap back into action. I placed my free hand atop his head, feeling the tension run upward through my fingers, until it filled my body the way that it was filling his.

"All right," I said. "You can come down now. You don't threaten us, and we won't threaten you."

There was no verbal answer from the tree. But the branches rustled, and something scraped against the trunk. And then, with no further fanfare, a woman dropped down to the ground in front of me.

She was short, and for a moment, I thought she was just a kid. It would have gone with that voice of hers, half Disney princess, half prom queen. Then she straightened up, unbending her knees and lifting her head, and I knew that whoever she was, wherever she had come from, she was older than that—mid-thirties at the least, and maybe even a well-preserved early forties. There were fine lines around her eyes, which were an unprepossessing shade of slate blue, and deeper lines around the corners of her mouth. Her hair looked like it hadn't been brushed in weeks. It was bundled into a thick ponytail that was going to hurt like hell when she finally tried to wash and style it again. It looked like it was a dark reddish brown, but it was honestly hard to tell, with all the dirt.

Her clothes fit her size: She could have raided the Juniors section at the local Target for them, if there had been a local Target. There were holes in the knees of her overalls, and her long-sleeved rainbow shirt was as dirty as the rest of her. She wasn't really showing any skin apart from her face and hands, but I didn't need to see her flesh to know that she was shockingly thin, bordering on emaciated. There are people whose bodies function best without an extra ounce on them. This girl wasn't one of those people.

She looked at me with the wary unease of someone who had seen the worst the world has to offer, only to discover that they didn't deserve anything better. "I'm looking for someone," she said again. "I'm running out of pills, and I'm looking for someone."

"From those two statements, I'd guess you're looking for a doctor," I said.

She nodded, biting her lower lip.

"Who are you looking for?"

"I... the person who said I should come here said Dr. Abbey, and I was sort of coming this way anyway, already I mean, so I came here to see if I could find him. Dr. Shannon Abbey. Please. I can pay. I don't have money, but I can pay. I'm running out of pills. Please." She held out her empty hands. They were shaking, I noted impassively, probably from a combination of hunger and withdrawal: Whatever pills she was looking for, their absence was hitting her hard.

"Please," she repeated, and collapsed.

I waited several minutes. She didn't get back up.

"Well, shit," I said with a sigh. "Looks like we have a houseguest. Come on, Joe. Let's go get somebody who can help us haul her bony ass inside."

Joe gave the stranger one last suspicious look. Then, with an amiable wuffing noise, he turned and followed me back toward the lab.

Chapter 2

Coming In Fom the Cold

Science is a cruel mistress. That means you should always have a safe word before you try to change the world. Otherwise, how will science know when to let you go?

—Dr. Shannon Abbey

Coincidence doesn't really exist. We see connections where there are none, and ignore all the connections that were never made. The story sounds so much better when we only talk about the miracles that happen.

—Georgia Mason

1.

"You don't usually come back from walking the dog with women who look like they just escaped from *The Care Bears Meet Mad Max*," said Tom dubiously, peering through the small glass window in the office door at the unconscious girl now sprawled on one of our guest cots. Locking her in until she woke up had seemed like a reasonable precaution. Jill had suggested that we also handcuff our guest to something—possibly Joe—but we had all agreed that this would have been overkill. People don't usually react well when they wake up and find themselves fastened to things.

"To be fair, that's less a statement of the sort of things I'm likely to find interesting, and more a critique of the available resources. If the woods gave me more *Mad Max* refugees, I would definitely bring them home," I said, and sipped my cocoa. Chocolate always settled my nerves after a bad run-in in the woods. Unlike Joe, who had forgotten the gunshots as soon as I filled his food bowl, I still had the ghosts of adrenaline running rampant in my blood. The thought of losing him was going to keep me up for days.

Fortunately for me, the same woman who had caused me such terror had also presented me with a charming mystery to preoccupy my racing mind. I just needed her to wake up and let me start trying to solve her.

"I'm not comfortable with this," pressed Tom. He turned away from the door, focusing on me instead. "It could be a trap."

"What, you think the CDC is so desperate for information that they're willing to starve one of their own people to the point of collapse—she's undergone severe muscular wasting because she's so hungry, did you notice that? She's lucky she was able to climb that tree in the first place, and she's luckier that she didn't break a hip getting down—just to get past our cheerfully lackadaisical screening process? You're cute, but no. Zelda is their latest attempt to trick us into spilling things we don't want to have spilled, and she's about as effective as a hamster in a python cage."

Tom blinked several times. If it hadn't been for the clarity of his eyes, I would have suspected him of hitting his stash before coming to talk to me. "Zelda? The new intern?"

"Yes, Zelda, or as I prefer to call her, 'not-Daisy.' " He looked blank. I shook my head. "You need to read more. Anyway, yes, she's a CDC plant. I confirmed that the same day that her application hit my desk."

"But how—?"

"The same way I confirm all our CDC plants: I did a deep background check." More accurately, I paid a woman in Canada to do a deep background check. Tessa Markowski was competent, affordable, and discreet. That combination put her miles above most of her contemporaries, who would sell you out as soon as look at you—and like many of the people in our cheerfully anarchistic underworld of secret virology labs, hackers, survivalists, and folks who really liked owning big dogs, she hated the CDC with a passion. It was a match made in heaven, assuming you believed in places like that.

I didn't, really. But I believed in Quebec, and that was where I sent her money. In exchange, I got all the information I could want on any name I happened to throw her way. It was a good deal all the way around.

Tom frowned. "I'm so sorry," he said. "I thought her credentials checked out. I thought she was a good fit. I—"

"You're getting off the subject," I said. "If we didn't hire CDC plants, we wouldn't have any staff at all. It's all part of my master plan."

"You have a master plan?"

"I'm a mad scientist, aren't I? We all have master plans. Without them, we'd just be faintly disgruntled scientists who think we really ought to form a committee to discuss our grievances." I turned back to the door. Our mystery woman was still dead to the world—although she was not, I noted, actually deceased. Her attenuated thinness made every rise and fall of her chest painfully obvious. I could almost count the ridges on her sternum through the tattered fabric of her shirt. If we didn't get some food and fluids into her soon, she was probably going to die.

No, the CDC wasn't responsible for her tracking me down. Whoever she was, she came here for her own reasons, and following her own agenda.

"Someone sent her to us," I said quietly.

"What?"

"Nothing." I glanced at Tom as I turned away from the door. "I want you to head for the kitchen, let Patrick know that we need a full meal of soft foods. Mashed potatoes, buttered noodles, plain white rice, and some clear chicken broth. Jell-O would also be good. Probably cherry, almost everyone likes cherry Jell-O. It's the universal donor of hospital desserts."

Tom, who was too young for the concept of "universal donors" ever to have held any meaning for him, continued to look at me blankly. I swallowed the urge to sigh. Sometimes it can be easy to forget that I don't really work with anyone my own age. Except on the rare occasions where Joey or Danika decide to call me up for a chat, I am the lone adult in a sea of children, like Captain Hook finally taking full responsibility for the Lost Boys after getting rid of that loser Pan.

"Guess that makes Joe Tinker Bell," I said, and smiled to myself. "Never mind, Tom: just ignore everything I said after 'full meal of soft foods.' Patrick can take care of the rest, and he'll design a better menu than either of us ever could. I'm going to go check with my sources, see if anyone knows who our mystery guest might be."

"We can't just leave her here alone," said Tom, sounding horrified. "What if she gets out?"

I managed, somehow, not to roll my eyes. If there had been any justice in the world, I would have received a medal for that. "That room was designed to hold a fully amplified adult male for up to a week before he had to be cycled out, and the only reason we'd need to move a specimen is so we could hose down the walls. I don't think a girl who doesn't weigh eighty pounds soaking wet could break down that door."

"No, but she might be able to unscrew the hinges," he said. "Zombies aren't known for their problem-solving capabilities. People are."

I paused. "All right, you have a point," I said, after taking a moment to absorb what he was saying. "I'll send not-Daisy down here to keep an eye on today's surprise guest. It'll be one more in her undoubtedly long line of learning experiences. First she gets hugged by an octopus, and now she gets to watch an unnerving feral woman sleep. Funtimes!"

I turned and walked out of the room before Tom could offer another objection. Reasonable as he was being, I didn't have the patience for him, and I didn't want to yell. Never yell in the middle of a mystery. It distracts people from the core issues—those being "What the fuck is going on?" and "How do we all get through this alive?"

Hopefully, I'd have answers to both very soon. In the meanwhile, not-Daisy was going to learn why the CDC had to *keep* sending plants into my facility, despite the fact that almost all of them made it back alive.

I was smiling as I walked down the hall. Really, this was proving to be a much better day than I'd expected when I sat down to do my paperwork.

2.

Not-Daisy wasn't thrilled about her new assignment, which just made my awesome day even better. Nothing said "Mad science: you're doing it right" like pissing off the people who didn't want to work for me in the first place. After putting in a quick call to Jill and asking her to take a security team out and sweep the woods, I sat down at my computer, shoving my now deprioritized paperwork aside with one hand. I'd probably regret that later, but oh, it felt good in the here and now.

There are a lot of ways to contact people over the Internet, some of them more subtle than others. I accessed a Lego trading forum that I had belonged to since long before my current status as a scientific outlaw became a thing, dropped by the "Antiques and Oddities" section, and posted a request for Unikitty figures from *The Lego Movie*, one of the last computer-animated films released before the Rising had come along and shut down theatrical productions for several years. Then I sat back to wait.

Tessa Markowski was an odd duck in a barnyard full of odd ducks. If there's a norm for hackers and computer experts, I've never encountered it: All the members of their clade that I've known have been idiosyncratic to the point of seeming like they took a class in not fitting in with the other children. Whether it's a routine or a reality has never seemed to matter much, although I'm sure there's a great research paper lurking there for a mad sociologist to exhume one day. As a mad virologist, I've had to focus my attention on what they can do for me, and what they can do is make my life one hell of a lot easier... as long as I'm willing to play by their rules.

Five minutes after I posted my request to the Lego forum, my computer beeped, signaling that I had received a private message. I clicked the little red flag at the top of my screen.

HOW MUCH?

It wasn't personal, and it didn't invite chatter, but then, I didn't need it to. I smiled as I tapped out my reply: $500 FOR LOOKING, $1,500 IF YOU FIND ME SOMETHING I LIKE. HAVE A MYSTERY FOR YOU. ALSO HAVE BOX OF MOVIE-BRANDED LEGO BLIND BAGS. NONE OPENED. I HAVE COUNTED THEM. ALL FIGURES ACCOUNTED FOR, ALTHOUGH I CAN'T GUARANTEE SOMEONE DIDN'T REPLACE SOME OF THE ORIGINAL PACKETS WITH PACKETS FROM A DIFFERENT BOX.

Again, Tessa was a unique sort of woman. Based on what little I'd been able to glean from our conversations, she was a single mother, utterly devoted to her son, and one of their great shared joys was pre-Rising Lego, which had been a lot more creative and free-form than post-Rising Lego. All the modern build sets focused on killing zombies, constructing impenetrable safe houses, and staying alive—useful things, sure, but all part of daily life. When Tessa built with her son, they constructed pirate ships and castles, robots and highways, and she was *always* looking for minifigs, the tiny plastic people who inhabited the Lego world.

Her reply was almost immediate.

PICS OR IT DIDN'T HAPPEN.

I attached a picture and sent it to her, leaning back in my seat to wait. I counted quietly as I did. I had just reached thirty when my computer beeped, telling me that I had an incoming call from an unlisted number. I smiled, and answered.

The window that popped up framed Tessa's fine-boned, pretty face almost perfectly. She had curly green hair, two rings in her left nostril, and looked like she was about nineteen, despite being only a few years younger than I was. Good genes. Good thing she had a sharp mind to go with them. Over the years, I'd been able to patch together most of her story: Internet bride from Russia who came to Canada looking for a better life and found herself married to a man who worshipped the ground she walked on. He was the one who'd insisted she get a college education, sending her to school for a Computer Science degree. I didn't know his name, or what had happened to him. I just knew that somewhere between her graduation and the birth of their only son, he had died and left her a widow with limited job skills in a country thousands of miles from the one where she'd been born.

Lucky for Tessa, she had her degree to fall back on, as well as his life insurance, and a surprisingly large library of books on computer crime—both how to do it and how to do it without getting caught. So when the Canadian government came and said that she had six months to get out of the country or demonstrate that she had a skill that made her worth keeping, she demonstrated how good she was at disappearing into the rabbit warren of underground services and hidden people.

Sometimes I wondered if she was anywhere near where the Masons had ended up. Then I dismissed the thought. Wondering where they were was dangerous. For them, and for me. Georgia Mason might forgive me if I set someone on their trail—she was the kinder, gentler model—but Shaun? We'd been friends. Still were, no doubt, in his mind; I had every faith that one day there would be a knock on my door, and I'd open it to find Shaun standing there, as carefree as if no time at all had passed. He was also the one who wouldn't hesitate to put a bullet between my eyes if he thought I was a danger to Georgia. No matter how much he liked me, she was his entire world, and no one smiles at the monster that's come to end the world.

"You really have these things?" demanded Tessa without preamble. Her accent was a fascinating mix of Russian and Quebecois, with vowels borrowed at random from both regions. Her son had to have the most amazing vocabulary. I didn't know for sure. I'd never seen him, knew of his existence only through rumor and Tessa's insatiable desire for Lego. For all I knew, he was as dead as the husband, and she was building pirate ships with a tiny, undemanding ghost. As long as she kept doing what I paid her for, I didn't care.

"I do," I said. "One of my people found them at a swap meet." That was a bit of an untruth—I had found them myself, while I was vaccinating kids from the local survivalist community. But my stall *had* been set up at the local swap meet, and I'd been paid in trade for my services.

"The bags haven't been opened?"

"I checked the glue myself."

Tessa worried her lip between her teeth for a moment, clearly thinking it over—or pretending to, anyway. The money I was offering her wasn't great, but the expense of smuggling a box of Lego figures through the back channels our little underground had developed would be at least twice her fee. I was offering her a fair deal. She just didn't know what I was offering her a fair deal *for*. "What's the situation?"

"I found someone on my property today."

"Everyone finds people on their property. If they're not dead when you find them, they are shortly after. What's the problem?"

"Well, first problem is that I didn't find a zombie, I found a *person*. She was lucid and capable of coherent speech. We've done a base-level blood test on her—she came back as clean as you or me. I'm doing full blood work, naturally, but I don't expect it to show me anything different."

Tessa smirked. "When you say that 'you' are doing full blood work, you mean the many attractive young people who labor in your nasty laboratory are doing full blood work, yes?"

"What's the point of having many attractive young people working for me if I can't make them miserable from time to time?" I shrugged. "It's part of my job as a mad scientist to turn them against the world through whatever means necessary. But we're getting off the subject. She showed up looking for me."

"What?" Tessa sat up a little straighter. "She knew you were there, and she didn't run like a person with a shred of survival instinct? I like you, Doc. You pay on time and you send the bonuses you promise. But I ever found myself sharing space with you, I'd get the fuck out."

"I'm flattered, truly," I said dryly. "She thought I was a man, which tells me she was going on reputation and not any real data. Can't stop people from talking unless you use a rifle, and that gets messy. Hard to maintain a business when you kill everyone who knows who you are."

"Fair, but that still doesn't explain what she was doing there," said Tessa. "Not too many people go looking for you on purpose. Fewer who don't know that they're looking for a woman from the land of the traffic cones."

"My fashion sense is not up for debate," I said. "I have pictures. She's in pretty bad shape, and she's lost enough weight that she's in danger of organ failure, but you should be able to start facial recognition based on what I can give you. Five hundred if you can tell me who she is, fifteen hundred if you can tell me who sent her and how deep I should bury the body. You get the Legos either way."

"Five hundred for a name, a thousand for a background, and fifteen hundred if I get you the rest," countered Tessa. Her smile was wide enough to show the silver cap on one of her teeth, glittering in the light from her monitor. "A girl has got to eat, and growing boys need to eat even more."

"Fair," I agreed. I hadn't expected to get away with any less, but that was the thing about dealing with Tessa: If I didn't bargain, at least a little, she felt cheated. We all have our little quirks. "How fast can you get started?"

"For you, Doc, and for those Lego figures, I can start right away. Transmit whatever you've got to my usual drop box, and I'll get to work. Pleasure doing business with you." The picture blinked out, leaving me looking at my desktop background.

I smiled. The game, as some old dead dude once said, was definitely afoot.

3.

"Report." I crossed my arms and leaned against the doorframe, trying not to look impatient. It was harder than I expected, maybe because I *was* impatient. I wanted answers—not out of fear that our guest would hurt me or my employees somehow, but because she was the most interesting thing that had happened since the Masons left. Mad science may be a little more fun and fancy-free than the boring mainstream kind, but that doesn't make it exciting on a day-to-day basis. If anything, mad science steals the excitement from a lot of things that *should* be exciting, like surprise fires, stabbing people with needles, and the occasional ceiling octopus.

"I'm not sure why our guest isn't dead," said Jill, looking up from her computer. "If you told me that this was all a joke, and that you'd given me a faked-up blood sample to see whether I was paying attention, I would believe you. I'm just saying." She paused, watching me expectantly.

I raised my eyebrows and waited.

Jill's face fell. It was a complicated expression, beginning with the muscles around her eyes and finishing when her chin dipped slightly forward, almost hitting her chest. "My God, you're serious," she said. "This is a living person's blood."

"Now you're getting it," I said. "Report. Now. Before I lose patience."

"Um, right. Okay. Her iron levels are ridiculously low—if she's not normally anemic, she definitely is now. She's malnourished. I don't think she's had a decent meal in weeks, which is probably how she's been able to medicate herself this far."

I raised my eyebrows for a second time. "Medicate herself...?" I prompted.

"You said she came here looking for pills, right? Well, there's a reason for that. This girl is drugged to the gills, and some of the shit she's taking I've never seen on the open market. I mean, she has the usual assortment of psychotropic drugs—there's some LSD, some magic mushrooms, all those fun things you don't want your sister doing—but there's also a couple of synthetic cannabinoids that I don't even *recognize*. She came back positive for JWH-018, and that hasn't been on the drug circuit in years. It's mostly used for therapy and pain management in people who are so sick that they don't need to be lucid anymore."

Jill stopped to take a breath. I didn't say anything. I had the feeling she was just getting warmed up.

I was right. She continued, "The worst of it—apart from traces of what I think is probably cocaine, and the Ecstasy, and did I mention the PCP? Because she's also on PCP—is the synthetic ergine. Someone went to the trouble of coming up with a new derivative of shit that already fucks you up so bad that you can't tell up from down, and then they pumped this poor girl full of it. Why? I don't know. Maybe they just wanted to see what would happen. But I can tell you this: If you wanted to take the trip of a lifetime, all you'd need to do is lick one of her blood panels."

"Since you're recommending that I lick her blood panels, I'm assuming she doesn't have hepatitis or anything fun like that?"

"Nope, no fun diseases, except for the omnipresent Kellis-Amberlee," said Jill, far too cheerfully. "I'm running immunity panels on our last samples now, but as she shows no signs of a reservoir condition, I don't think she's going to be another Shaun Mason. Sorry about that."

"He was one of a kind," I said.

Jill snorted.

Calling Shaun Mason—or more appropriately, Shaun Mason's immunity to the fully amplified form of the Kellis-Amberlee virus—"one of a kind" was a bit inaccurate. He had been exposed at great and intimate length to someone whose body generated antigens, due to the presence of a live-state viral reservoir condition. As a consequence, his own body had learnt how to fight the virus, and did just that when he was exposed. It was a neat trick, and probably one that could be replicated by hundreds, if not thousands of people and large mammals around the globe. I just didn't have access to any of them, and my banked supply of Shaun's blood was running low.

Kellis-Amberlee was the reason that Jill wasn't serious when she told me to lick our guest's blood panels. Everyone on the planet is infected, including our mystery woman, and as soon as her blood had been removed from her body, the virus that slumbered there had woken up and started going about its business. It was a surprisingly good preservative, maybe because the blood was never allowed to fully "die." It was also a biological hot agent rivaled by very few naturally occurring diseases. One drop and we'd all lose our minds in the most literal and permanent of fashions.

"Will she live?"

Jill bit her lip, worrying it for a moment between her teeth before she said, "I'll be honest: I don't know. We've got her set up on a saline drip for the dehydration, and we can set up a feeding tube if she doesn't wake up soon, but if she doesn't get some body mass back, she's not going to pull through. Even if she does... the withdrawal from the drugs she's been taking would be hard on someone twice her size. As skinny and malnourished as she is, they could easily kill her."

Well, crap. "Can we synthesize something that will take the edge off? I don't mind playing methadone clinic if it gets us a healthy person at the other end."

"Why?" Jill frowned. "I know you like a mystery, but there's such a thing as going too far. We didn't invite her here. Make her comfortable, provide palliative care, and if she dies, she dies. She didn't become our responsibility just because she collapsed in front of you. If you'd taken Joe out an hour later, she would have died and risen, and you wouldn't be trying to save her. And did you forget the part where she tried to shoot your dog? Shit. You'd fire half the staff for raising their voices to Joe. Why do you want to save someone who tried to hurt him?"

"I'd fire the staff—including you, Jill—for raising their voices to an animal that they know is friendly, well-trained, and not a threat," I said. "This woman didn't know any of those things. A giant carnivore came bounding through the woods, and she reacted like someone who enjoyed being among the living. I can't fault people for trying to stay alive. Not when everything we teach them is focused on survival. As for the rest... I was a doctor before I became anything else. The first rule we were taught in medical school was 'Do no harm.'"

That wasn't quite true. The first rule we were taught in medical school was "A cadaver is not a toy." Even though the bodies we used for practice were pickled and sterilized to the point of becoming virtually useless for any fine diagnostic work, they had still started out as living people, and they deserved our respect. That was what separated us from the zombies. We could still show respect for the things that shared our world. Even if sometimes that respect took the form of a clean death.

"So?"

"So if we let her die just because we didn't invite her over for popcorn and a movie, we're doing harm. This is an opportunity to practice medicine. Not mad science, not virology research, just medicine. The old-fashioned kind, where you start off with someone who's sick, and you finish up with someone who's well."

Jill's eyes narrowed. "Sorry, boss, but I know you too well to believe this degree of altruism. What's the real deal?"

"The real deal is, she found us somehow. Someone told her that we were here to find, and that if she wanted drugs, she should come looking." I felt my expression harden. I made no effort to soften it. Jill had seen me at my worst, and she hadn't run screaming into the night. She wasn't going to run now. "I need her alive, and I need her lucid enough to tell me what brought her to our doorstep, because whatever it is, it's not going to happen again. Do you understand? Now, keep running those blood tests, and whatever sort of methadone clinic we have to become, that's what we're going to be. We're going to save her life if it kills her."

"Yes, ma'am," said Jill, and twisted back around to her computer. The conversation was over. I had my information, and she had her orders. Now all we had to do was save a life.

4.

Mystery girl was still unconscious when I returned to the viewing area, Joe sticking by my side like a happy, tail-wagging shadow. Not-Daisy jumped at the sound of my footsteps, and jumped again when she saw Joe. I frowned at her.

"You may want to think about taking up yoga," I said. "It's very calming, and if you're going to flinch every time I come into a room, you need some calm. You can also talk to Tom about the many restorative benefits of marijuana. As long as you're not stoned when you're supposed to be working, I don't care. This isn't the CDC."

The shadow of her guilt moved across her face so fast that I wouldn't have seen it if I hadn't already been watching for it. Not-Daisy wasn't going to be one of my long-term employees; I could already tell, just from the way she reacted to things—or didn't react to them. It was for the best, really. People as high-strung as she was didn't do well in a lab like mine, where losing control for a minute could result in your life coming to a swift, sticky end. She'd be better off with the CDC, where she would do her research from behind six layers of security, and never need to see how the sausage was made.

"I just didn't expect you, is all, Dr. Abbey," she said. "I'm sorry I'm so jumpy. The octopus thing this morning really threw me off."

"Barney does what Barney wants," I said. "Just wait until what he wants is to sneak into your quarters in the middle of the night and turn the light on and off for an hour. He's a big adventure in tolerance. What's the situation with our guest?"

"No change," said not-Daisy. She sounded relieved to be back on something that resembled familiar ground. She knew how to watch an unconscious woman remain unconscious. That was fairly normal CDC fare.

"Good." I motioned for her to get up. "Go on. Back to whatever you were doing when I had you pulled for this duty. Scrub something, or culture something, or whatever it is they have you assigned to this week. I can watch her sleep."

Not-Daisy stood—a little too quickly—and started for the door. I let her get halfway there before I cleared my throat. She froze. Smart girl.

"I don't recommend trying to send any e-mail right now, however. We're on high alert, thanks to this woman's presence, and it's entirely possible that an innocent e-mail to a friend or family member could get flagged as something that it wasn't. A coded transmission to the CDC, for example. I know they'd be very interested in our guest. And I know I'd be very interested in finding out what someone could have said that would activate that flag. Do you understand?"

"Yes, ma'am," she said, barely above a whisper.

"Good. Because while I don't pay enough for absolute loyalty, I am very, very dedicated to security. It's what separates us from the animals. Enjoy your assignments, Zelda. We're glad to have you working with us here."

"Yes, ma'am," she repeated, and scurried out of the room without looking back.

"She isn't going to last the month, Joe," I said, settling into the seat she had so recently vacated. The one-way window into the observation room gave me a perfect view of the bed where our mystery woman slept. An IV was connected to her right arm, held in place with pieces of surgical tape. The needle was the size we always used, but she was emaciated enough that it looked like it was going all the way through her arm. I didn't envy whoever Tom had deputized to get her IV started—although knowing Tom, he had probably done it himself. He didn't like leaving things to chance.

A catheter snaked out from under the blanket. As her body was rehydrated, involuntary urination became a risk, and no one wanted to clean that up. Luckily, she was starved enough that there was no need to really worry about other waste products. Can't shit if you don't eat. And other inspirational proverbs that were never going to catch on.

She looked peaceful, lying there on her back with her eyes closed. Someone had wiped most of the dirt from her face, revealing pale skin with an almost purplish undertone. There were freckles on the bridge of her nose. That seemed incredibly sad to me, for some reason. Whoever she was, whoever she had been before she stumbled, half starved, to my doorstep, she was the sort of person who freckled when she went out in the sun, and must have spent her life drowning in SPF-40. The fact that she wasn't burnt now told me that she had traveled mostly at night; she'd been filthy enough when I found her that she definitely hadn't been keeping up any sort of skin care regimen.

"So who are you, strange girl?" I asked. "Why are you here? Why did you come looking for me?"

She didn't answer. She just slept on.

Chapter 3

Please Do Not Taunt the Octopus

There are people who will tell you that the ends justify the means, right up until they're talking about their own ends. Then, suddenly, morals and ethics matter. Funny thing, that.

—Dr. Shannon Abbey

Good morning, class. Who's ready to learn?

—Elaine Oldenburg

1.

"Dr. Abbey?" Not-Daisy's voice was soft, almost hesitant, like she was afraid that I was going to sic Joe on her for daring to come near my office. For a moment I entertained the fantasy of doing precisely that: unleashing my faithful hound and shutting her up before she found a way to tell the CDC about our mystery guest. I'd always been fairly relaxed about the presence of spies and infiltrators. No matter how often I moved the lab, being connected to the supply chain meant being vulnerable to discovery: The CDC was always going to find me, and having found me, they were always going to send their people in to try to learn what I knew.

Most of the time, what I knew either wasn't worth reporting, or wasn't worth protecting, or was hidden behind closed doors and managed by my more loyal staffers. But something like our mystery woman had been vulnerable to discovery from the start. How do you hide a stranger who falls out of the forest and virtually lands on your head? The answer was sadly simple. You didn't. Mystery girl had been sleeping for two days, and we'd managed to block all of not-Daisy's attempts to message her government masters in that period. But we weren't going to be able to stay on high alert forever. Eventually, either not-Daisy was going to get something past us, or we were going to have to make a decision about her probable retirement situation.

"Yes, Zelda?" I asked, looking up and away from my computer. If I was thinking about having her killed for security reasons, it seemed only polite to use her name, at least to her face. She was always going to be "not-Daisy" to me.

"Um, you said that we should notify you if there was any change in, um, our visitor's status? And there's been a change."

I stood, knocking my chair backward in the process. "What kind of change?"

Not-Daisy's eyes were sad and resigned. She understood what she was saying. That was the moment when I realized that she knew she'd been set up by her employers. They weren't showing faith in her by sending her to me: They were saying that she was, on some level, essentially expendable. "She's awake."

"That's certainly a change," I said, trying to keep the excitement out of my voice. I stepped around the desk. Joe rose to follow me, and I shook my head, accompanying the motion with the hand gesture that meant, "Stay." "No, Joe. I'm sorry, buddy, but you need to stay here."

Joe's butt hit the ground while his face was still composing itself into a look of pure bewilderment. I was going somewhere. I was his person. If I was going somewhere, he was supposed to be going somewhere with me. That was the way the world *worked*. But I was telling him to stay, and when I told him to do a thing, it had to be done. That was also the way the world worked.

"I know, buddy," I said, and scratched his ears. "Stay. Guard. We'll do something fun later, okay?"

Joe slowly sank back to the floor, resting his head on his massive forepaws. He looked at me so reproachfully that I almost went back on my decision and told him to come along. But the last time our mystery woman had been awake, she'd taken a shot at Joe. She didn't have any of her weapons anymore. That didn't mean I wanted to tempt her. I shot one last apologetic look at my dog and turned to head for the doorway, where not-Daisy was waiting for me.

We fell into step together as we walked down the hall toward the observation room, not-Daisy shooting sidelong glances in my direction like she expected me to attack her at any moment. I tried to keep my eyes forward, and to resist the urge to whirl and shout "Boo!" at the poor terrified thing. No matter what she thought of me, I wasn't a monster, and I wasn't going to let her turn me into one. Even though it would have been fun to watch her jump out of her skin.

Jill and Tom were both waiting in the observation room when we arrived. Jill was seated at the monitoring station while Tom leaned against the wall and chewed a piece of peppermint gum, probably to cover the lingering smell of pot that hung around him like a shroud. "What's the situation?" I asked, stepping inside.

Not-Daisy stopped in the hall, staying a foot outside the doorway. She knew this wasn't her project, and more, she knew that she wasn't really welcome. I respected that, even as I wondered whether she knew just how unwelcome she actually was.

"She woke up fifteen minutes ago," said Jill. "Sat up, looked around, looked at the IV, and then lay back down. I thought she was asleep again, until I realized that her heart rate was elevated. She's waiting for something."

"We thought it was best that we call you," said Tom. "We can gas the room, knock her out again—"

"Let's not," I said. "We want to talk to her, right? And she's not ripping out the tubes. That implies that she's at least somewhat lucid, and understands that we're trying to help her with all this stuff, not hurt her. So let's assume that she can be reasoned with."

"You're not going to go in there by yourself, are you?" asked Jill, sounding faintly horrified—but not, I noted, even remotely surprised. My people were used to me. Jill had been with me for the infamous "Shaun Mason gets exposed to Kellis-Amberlee and fails to seroconvert" incident, and had watched me walk into a room with a man who should by all rights have been a zombie. There wasn't anything I could do that would surprise her anymore.

That didn't mean I needed to be stupid just to keep my people on their toes. "Fuck, no," I said. "Tom, you're with me. Bring the tranq gun; we don't want to kill her, but if she so much as looks funny in my direction, you're going to send her off to play with the magical pastel bunnies in the Shouldn't-Have-Fucking-Done-That Meadow."

"Got it, boss," said Tom, and saluted only half jokingly before he took the tranquilizer gun down from the wall.

I turned to Jill. "Stay here; monitor everything. If her heart rate spikes or you get an odd reading, notify us immediately, and we'll get out of there. If you get a bad feeling about something, notify us immediately, and we'll get out of there. If you just don't like the look on her face..."

"Notify you immediately, and you'll get out of there," said Jill.

"Good girl." I turned and walked out of the room, past not-Daisy, who was still hovering in the hall like she thought that this would all start making sense if she just waited long enough. Poor kid. CDC plant or not, she was going to come to learn that the world was under no obligation to make sense either now or ever. Logic was a story we told ourselves to keep from going completely insane in the face of all the impossible things reality threw at us on a daily basis.

The door to the room where our mystery woman was being kept was only a few feet down the hall. I pressed my thumb to the panel next to the doorknob, only grimacing a little as a needle lanced out and sampled my blood. My lab contained less than half the recommended number of blood testing units for a facility of this size, and most of them were external; once you were inside, we figured we'd be able to tell if you were infected. But some doors needed to be locked, and some tests needed to be run. If someone was going into one of the isolation rooms, it was important to be absolutely sure of their amplification status.

The light above the door flashed twice before turning green, and the dead bolt released. "Tom, stay close," I said, and opened the door. If we'd been a more formal facility, he would have needed to take a blood test as well. I didn't see the point in that. He was already behind me. If he was infected, it was way too late to start worrying.

The mystery woman was still in the position she'd been in when I looked through the window: arms flat at her sides, feet together, face turned toward the ceiling. Really, if I hadn't had so much experience with recalcitrant patients, I probably wouldn't have been able to tell that her eyes were cracked just enough to let her see me through her lashes.

"Good morning." I pulled a plastic chair away from the wall and moved it a few feet closer to her bed, creating space for Tom to stand behind me without holding the door open. I sat, putting my hands on my knees so that she could see I was unarmed. Tom wasn't, of course, but I was showing trust. Now it was up to her to show me the same. "My name is Dr. Shannon Abbey. You're in my lab. You've been asleep for the last two days. I know you've noticed the IV, and I assume you've also noticed the catheter, since those are fairly hard to miss. I'm sorry we had to put those in without your consent, but you weren't waking up, and I figured you'd rather be surprised than dead. Feel free to correct me if I'm wrong. I have plenty of bullets, and I'm always happy to fix my own mistakes. It seems cleaner that way. Less like I'm trying to avoid blame for my actions. I always take responsibility for the things I do."

The mystery woman didn't respond. Her eyelashes fluttered slightly; she was still awake, and she was paying close enough attention that she had allowed her rigid muscular control to slip for a moment. I glanced to the two-way mirror on the wall. Jill would have told me if our guest's vital signs were showing tension or other indications that she was getting ready to attack.

"We provided medical care in part because it was the right thing to do, but I admit, we also did it because we wanted you to survive long enough to wake up and explain yourself. This is a secure facility. We operate under a veil of strict secrecy, and we do not encourage or invite visitors. So I'm really curious as to how you found us." Tessa was still working, still running facial-recognition programs and trying to trace our mystery woman to some distant point of origin. The fact that it had taken her two days already, with no success in sight, told me that someone very, very good had gone to great lengths to scrub this woman from the world. Deleting an identity that thoroughly was hard as hell, and not something that anyone would do on a whim.

Still the mystery woman didn't respond. Her eyelashes didn't even flutter this time. I was either losing her interest or I was back on ground that she'd expected me to cover. I wasn't sure what was worse—and I realized I didn't know how long she had *really* been awake. Someone who looked at surprise IVs this calmly might well have held her peace for a long time before she even sat up to see what they were. I needed to proceed with caution.

"You're in slightly better shape now than you were when I found you. Your body was starting to digest itself; you'd gone into a state of what's called 'ketosis,' meaning that you were basically fueling everything you did by burning your own muscle tissue. You're going to need a lot of rehab to get back to anything resembling fighting shape, and I suppose that what I'm really offering you here is a chance. Not a choice—that comes later—but a chance. If you can tell me why you showed up on my doorstep, why you were looking for me, I'll consider letting you stay here long enough to recover a little bit of that lost muscle mass. You might have a chance in hell of keeping yourself alive when I finally toss you out. Or you can keep playing silent treatment, and I can throw you out just like you are now. I told my people that my Hippocratic Oath was part of why I let you stay—that whole 'above all else, do no harm' routine—but

I've patched you up. I've given you the thinnest sliver of a prayer that you'll survive. My conscience will be clear if I have to throw you out into the forest to die."

"I wasn't looking for you." Her voice was dry and raspy, the voice of someone who hadn't spoken in days. Her eyelids relaxed, settling into a closed position. "I was looking for your husband, or your brother, or whoever it is who owns this place. Somebody told me he was out here. They said he could get me what I needed, and all I had to do was find his front door."

"Hasn't anybody ever told you that you can't get something for nothing? Any doctor you could find in a place like this would charge dearly for whatever he—or she—gave you. It usually isn't going to be worth it."

Her laugh was small, and utterly devoid of mirth. It was the laugh of someone who had been broken, more than once, and put back together in increasingly foreign combinations, until she had less in common with whoever she had once been than a jellyfish had with a juniper tree. I knew that laugh. I heard it coming from myself, some days. "I knew I'd have to pay. You always have to pay, and the more you need a thing, the more it costs. That's why we have things to bargain and to barter with."

"My people searched you. You were telling the truth when you said that you didn't have any money. You're low on bullets, and the only recreational pharmaceuticals we found on you were in your bloodstream. There's nothing you could pay with."

"I have a body. I have my training. I can kill people. I'm real good at killing people." She giggled, a high, discordant sound that grated on my nerves. It didn't seem like it had come from the same throat that had offered the dry, quiet laughter we'd heard before. I glanced back at Tom, and saw that he looked just as unnerved as I felt. That was something, at least. I wasn't the only one who heard the fault lines in her giggles. "It's probably what I'm best at. Everybody says so, and everybody needs *somebody* dead. Goods and services, it's all goods and services."

"We don't need anybody killed," I said firmly. "We never outsource our assassinations."

"Dr. Abbey will," she said. "If you let me see him, I'm sure that he will."

"That's going to be a problem, because I *am* Dr. Abbey," I said. I couldn't keep my irritation out of my voice any longer. "My name is

Shannon Abbey. This is my lab. It is very large. I have been giving you my patience. It is very small, and growing smaller by the minute."

The mystery woman was silent for a few seconds. Then, finally, she opened her eyes, blinking rapidly as they adjusted to the light, and turned her head to look at me. She was frowning, lips pursed in what was virtually a pout. The expression was far too young for her, and looked learned rather than instinctual. Whoever had taught her that shrill, nerve-racking giggle had probably taught her the pout at the same time. It made my flesh crawl.

"You're Dr. Abbey?" she said, uncertainly.

"Have been for years and years," I said. "No brother. No husband. Just me. This is my lab: I'm the one you came here looking for."

"You have to help me!" She sat up, nearly dislodging her IV in the process, and tried to reach for me. The catheter pulled her up short. She glanced down, clearly unsure what she should do. There was a small click from behind me as Tom brought the tranquilizer gun into position. She looked up again and went very still, her eyes narrowing with a shrewd, calculating intelligence that didn't fit with anything she'd displayed so far. Our mystery woman might be awake and talking to us, but she was still a mystery, and she was going to remain that way for as long as it took to get her to start making sense. Which meant she might be a mystery forever.

"Why don't you stay where you are, not making any hostile moves, and try telling me what it is you want me to do for you?" I gestured behind myself, indicating Tom and the gun in his hands. "This is Tom. He works for me. If you're looking for drugs, it's possible that whoever you spoke to was thinking of him. Tom grows some of the best marijuana you'll find in this part of the Pacific Northwest, and we trade a lot of it on the black market for things that we need. Is that why you're here? Did you need some of Tom's drugs?"

"No," she said firmly, shaking her head as she settled back on the cot. At least she was trying to play by the rules. Even if she was only doing it to avoid being shot, it showed a degree of understanding about what was going on around her. I liked that. It might mean we wouldn't have to kill her. "No, and no, and no again. I ran out of cookies, and then I ran out of pills, so I asked some people some questions. Most of them didn't want to give me answers. I made them. I asked again and again, until I knew what I needed to know."

Fear writhed in my chest like a fistful of maggots. "Did you kill the people you asked for answers? Did you kill people in order to find me?" My connections on the black market were good, but no one's connections were good enough to survive something like that. If this little slip of an assassin had carved her way through the local drug dealers and information brokers in her quest to find me, the repercussions were going to be devastating.

"Only one, and he asked for it." Her eyes flashed. "He liked his hands. He liked putting them on people who hadn't asked to have his hands on them. He put them on me, after he'd said he didn't know what I needed to know. So I took them off, and then there was *so* much blood, and then the people who lived there with him came in, and they said they'd been waiting for this to happen, they said it had been coming for a long time, and they told me to leave, but they weren't angry. They just didn't want me there while I was all over covered in his blood."

"Ah." I had actually heard something about this, from one of my contacts near Portland. They'd had an incident in one of the way stations with a transient girl and a veterinarian who, yes, had a reputation for putting his hands where they didn't belong. People had been trying to catch him in the act for years. The women he got grabby with had a tendency to either vanish or refuse to talk, claiming that nothing had really happened. Way I heard it, he'd grabbed for the transient, she'd cut his hands off with his own bone saw, and nobody had done anything to stop her from leaving.

If she'd been dropping my name by that point, none of the survivors had heard it. Interesting. "Who told you about me?" I asked. "Who first said, 'You should look for Dr. Abbey'?"

"Don't remember," said the woman, shaking her head defiantly. "I was just looking for someone who could give me more pills. I need my pills. They make the world look the way that it's supposed to look, and not the way it wants to look when the pills run out."

She had to be talking about the synthetic cannabinoids Jill had found in her blood. Those were the only drugs strong enough and nonstandard enough to both change her perceptions of the world *and* be difficult to replace. "I'm not a pharmacist," I said. "This is a research facility. This isn't a place people come for pills."

The woman looked at me blankly for a moment. "You should have been a pharmacist," she said. "You could have said 'Hello, sir' and 'Gosh that's a nice hat, ma'am,' and filled little bottles with littler pills, and given lollipops to kids who behaved." She rolled back into her original position, staring up at the ceiling. 'Be good boys and girls, and you'll have all the good things in the world, and none of the bad things, ever again, forever after, amen.' "

"Look, I'd like to help you," I said. "I'm not what you were looking for, but you're here now, and I know you've been through a lot. Can you tell me your name? Where you came from? Anything that would make it easier for me and my friends to help you?"

"I am a raven who used to be a writing desk, and there aren't going to be any more cookies ever again, because Kitty did a bad thing, and when kitty cats do bad things, they have to go down the well." The woman closed her eyes. A single tear escaped and ran down her cheek. "I don't think she made it out of the house. I'm almost certain that she didn't, and I can't really be sorry, because it was her fault that everything went wrong, but she was still my Kitty, and I loved her. She shouldn't have done the bad thing and I don't want to *know* I don't want to *know* what she did, I need my *pills*!" She balled her hands into fists, punching the sides of the bed so fast and so fiercely that Tom and I both jumped.

It was honestly a miracle that Tom's trigger discipline was so good he didn't shoot her with a tranq dart right then and there. She stopped punching the bed and said, in a suddenly toneless voice, "I'm tired now. I think I'm going to sleep some more. Thank you for the saline, and for letting me sleep here. If you kill me while I'm sleeping, that's okay. It's what I deserve. I won't be mad."

"What's your name?" I asked again.

She didn't answer.

2.

Jill met us outside the door. "She's asleep," she said, voice tight and somewhat agitated. "She literally went to sleep the second she stopped talking. This is someone who's had training for that sort of thing."

"Ex-military?" I asked.

"Not unless she was Black Ops and got herself deleted from the system," said Jill. "Your hacker would have found her by now if she was in the military databases. That's one of the first places anyone with a lick of training goes to look for someone like this."

"Fair," I allowed. "All right, keep an eye on our guest, and if she wakes up again, call me. I'm going to go see if anything else has come to light. You." I turned, looking past Jill to not-Daisy, who was still standing in the spot she'd been in when we entered the observation room. "Go feed the lab animals, make sure everyone is still doing their jobs. We need to be operating at top capacity."

"Why?" asked not-Daisy, blinking at me. She looked like a sheep, easily led and even more easily confused. My hands itched to slap the stupid off her face. I tucked them into my lab coat pockets. I don't hit my staff, no matter how much they might sometimes aggravate me. There are lines that should not be crossed. They separate reputable underground establishments, like mine, from the black market free clinics, where, sure, you might get your vaccinations, but you also might get to become an uncredited and unwilling part of someone else's experimental testing pool.

It's a hard world these days, and no matter how hard we try, it just keeps on getting harder. "Because life goes on, even when there's a mystery to be solved. Maybe especially when there's a mystery to be solved. And because you work for me, and I just told you to do it. So unless you're interested in exploring other employment opportunities, you'll scoot."

Not-Daisy's eyes went very wide in her wan face. She nodded, quickly, and scurried away down the hall, leaving me standing alone with Jill and Tom. I turned to face them.

"Jill, I need you to go over all the personnel records for people whose origins we have not absolutely confirmed, and check them again," I said. "Zelda there may be our only current CDC plant, but it's possible she's not our only potential mole, and there's something about this situation that doesn't smell right to me. I want to be sure that whatever happens next, it's because we fucked up, not because somebody fucked us."

"I love the conviction that we're about to get fucked," said Jill. "It's real comforting."

"There are three constants in this world, Jill," I said. "One, you don't know everything. Two, what you don't know can absolutely hurt you. And three, someone's getting fucked. The only question is, who's wearing the strap-on? Tom, while Jill is going over our records, I want you to look at those synthetic cannabinoids she isolated from our mystery woman's blood. I don't expect you to be able to replicate them exactly, but if you can come up with a way to synthesize something similar, that could be an enormous help. I don't think she's going to talk to us until we start offering her what she wants, and what she wants are those pills."

"We don't know what those drugs *do*, and there isn't time to do proper testing if I'm just trying to synthesize a batch based on what we already have," Tom said. "We could be giving her just about anything. Those chemicals aren't toys."

"No, but neither is a woman who somehow got my name and had the resources to track us down without leaving a trail," I said. "Our location isn't a state secret, but we're pretty good about not saying, 'Here we are, come rob us blind.' Depending on the quality of the places she's been asking around, however..."

"You're afraid she's the precursor to a raid?" Jill couldn't quite keep the disbelief out of her tone. "*Her?* I don't care how much she wants to offer to kill people for aspirin, she's not someone's advance spy. No one sends somebody in that poor of physical condition to scout for them. There's no guarantee you'll get your scout *back* when you starve them half to death."

"I don't think she's a scout." I glanced over my shoulder at the closed door. "She's too disjointed, for one thing. Whether it's the drugs or whatever she's been taking them to treat, she needs help. I think she's a distraction, and a tracking dog. Sometimes when I need to flush out specimens, I'll send Joe into the woods with the retrieval team. He likes running into groups of the infected and starting to make a ruckus. I know they can't hurt him more than he can hurt them, so it's a good way to collect zombies for my research. Do you understand what I mean?"

"You're saying that when you want to find a doctor, you send in a sick person," said Tom slowly. "One that you're not too concerned about losing."

"Exactly." I turned back to the pair. "We need to know where she came from, we need to know how she got here, and we need to know who pointed her in our direction. Until we know all that, we can't afford to trust that everyone who's here has our best interests at heart. Remember what happened last time?"

Tom and Jill exchanged a look. "We remember," said Jill. "We're on it."

"Good," I said. "Report back in an hour, just so I know where we stand—and call me if she wakes up again. I'll be in my office." I turned and started down the hall before they could ask any more questions. Sometimes I think the worst part of being in charge is all the questions. They never end, and somehow, I'm always expected to be the one who has all the answers.

Joe was still on the floor with his head on his paws, sulking, when I made it back to the office. I started counting silently as I walked to my desk, and made it to twenty-three before his delight overwhelmed him and his tail started wagging. "You're no good at sulking, Joe," I scolded. "If you want me to really *believe* in your suffering, you need to suffer for at least thirty full seconds. I'd recommend trying for an entire minute. Just for realism."

His tail continued to wag as his head came up off his paws. I wasn't just back in the room, I was back in the room and *talking* to him. Truly, this was a banner day. I sighed.

"You're a good dog, Joe, but you're a terrible negotiator. You could have held out for anything you wanted, and instead I've been forgiven with a tail wag and a goofy smile. You need to learn to look out for your own interests." I opened the top drawer of my desk, pulled out a dog biscuit, and tossed it to him. He caught it out of the air and began the ecstatic process of reducing it to so many gooey crumbs on the carpet.

Crunching sounds accompanied me as I turned back to my computer, typed in my password, and sent Tessa a chat request. She was better about allowing those through normal channels when she was actively on a job: there was only so much cloak-and-dagger that either one of us could handle as a part of our daily lives. I had no way of knowing whether or not she was at her computer, so I opened one of the files Jill had e-mailed to me and began reading about the drug cocktails isolated from our guest.

I was on page three, and was beginning to really agree with the "if you told me she was dead, I wouldn't argue with you" diagnosis, when my chat client beeped to signal an incoming call. I minimized the file and opened the chat window, revealing Tessa's face. She was wearing a surprising amount of glitter smeared around her eyes, and she wasn't smiling.

"Tell me you got me something to work with, because I still got nothing," she said.

"Nice to see you, too," I said. "She woke up for a little bit. She didn't tell us her name, but she talked, and I have video. Will that help?"

"Speech patterns and accent might let me start narrowing in on an origin, and an origin would help me figure out her identity, so yes, that'll help." Tessa shook her head, curls bouncing. "This is starting to haunt my *dreams*. I've never had a missing person this determined to stay that way who hadn't been intentionally scrubbed from the Internet."

"Sending the file over now." I opened the drive where our feeds from the isolation room were stored, selecting the twenty-minute segment that included my conversation with the mystery woman and dropping it onto the chat box. A small status bar immediately appeared, displaying the status of the transfer. "She's still not too lucid. Part of it's probably the drugs, and part of it's probably withdrawal from the drugs. I have Tom working on synthesizing something to help her through the next few days. That'll give us something to bargain with, even if it doesn't do anything else."

"What did she say?"

"Well, she offered to kill people for me. And that 'Kitty did a bad thing,' but that she didn't think Kitty had made it out of the house. I don't know whether she was talking about a pet or a person, but—" I stopped talking. Tessa was sitting suddenly ramrod straight, her eyes gone wide in their circles of club makeup, her mouth gone suddenly slack with something that might be shock, or might be plain and simple fear. "Tessa? You want to tell me what you just figured out? Because honestly, I'm getting a little tired of not knowing what's going on."

"You're sure she said 'Kitty.' She didn't use some other word, or a proper name."

"No, she said 'Kitty.' She said it multiple times, she was very clear." The status bar turned blue and then disappeared. "See for yourself, you should have the file now."

"Hang on." Tessa bent her head and started to type. I heard my own voice through her computer speakers, distorted by distance and compression. We always sound strange to ourselves when heard in playback. This was especially strange. I might not have recognized myself, if not for the mystery woman's voice speaking a second later, answering me, confirming the provenance of the file. Tessa began shaking her head. "No," she said. "Nyet. No."

"What?" I tapped on my computer screen, hoping the noise and motion together would be enough to catch her attention. "Tessa, *what?* You can't freak out without inviting me to your 'everything is ruined forever' party. It's not nice, and it's not productive. What's wrong? Why are you trying to refute reality? Refuting reality never works out in the long run, trust me."

"This woman... I may know who she is." Tessa looked up, shaking her head again. "I think she used to work with the competition. A man from Seattle, who did the kind of work I do, but I will be honest: He was better than I will ever be. I have more patience for legwork, I am happier to look for missing people and use the skills I have, but this man? He could wipe you from the world if you told him where to start. He could build an identity out of nothing, put a person in cracks that no one even realized were there until they might as well have existed all along. He was an artist."

"What happened to him?"

"What happens to all the artists in this world? He died." She kept typing, her eyes fixed at a point below the level of her webcam. I could see the roots of her hair, dark brown showing through her carefully cultivated blonde. "The community was in an uproar for months. Some people even said it was a hoax, that he was doing the ultimate ID scrub and scrubbing himself right out of reality. Nobody knows for sure. I've seen the autopsy reports. They look legit to me, but what do I know? I'm no doctor."

"Besides, they could have autopsied a clone." Tessa's head snapped up, eyes even wider this time. I shrugged. "What? I did physiological examinations of the second Georgia Mason, remember? Clone tech is more advanced than we like to think it is, especially when you don't need your clone to do anything but die. Let me tell you, that doesn't take any special skills." Anybody could die. It was almost the only thing that every person on Earth had been designed to do with equal proficiency.

"I didn't even think of that." She bowed her head as she resumed typing. "They called him 'the Monkey.' If he had a real name, he scrubbed it years ago—maybe before he did anything else. The best always experiment on themselves, you know? Means you have time to be sure that whatever it is you're doing really *works*, that it's not just chance. He had the resources to get himself a clone, if he really wanted one. If he needed to disappear."

"This is all fascinating, but what does it have to do with my mystery woman?" I asked.

"He always lived with at least two women. They were... let's call them his 'public relations team.' That's what you call your lovers who sometimes kill people for you, right?" Tessa's scowl was visible only in the way her cheeks distorted, tightening and pulling at the sides of her face. "A friend of mine worked for him for a while. He deleted her whole original identity, just wrote her out of the world and wrote her back in as part of his private menagerie. He called her 'the Wolf,' and when she fell out of favor, he deleted that identity, too. We've never found her body. I don't think we ever will." She was still typing, more fiercely now, like she thought she could bring her friend back from the dead through sheer force of anger.

"So what? You think our guest was one of the Monkey's girls?"

"The last two recorded members of his little zoo were 'the Cat' and 'the Fox.' A hacker and a killer, according to all reports." Tessa glanced up. "The Cat's body was recovered at the same time as the Monkey's. The Fox's body never was."

I paused. "I know why I've heard that name before. The Masons went to the Monkey. He was supposed to get them new identities. Instead, he fucked around and nearly got them all killed. Shaun really hated that guy." Had he mentioned women working for the Monkey? I felt as if he had, at least once, at least in passing. He'd been a little distracted by the time he and the others made it back down the coast to me—something about finding his dead sister reborn in a CDC holding facility had taken his mind off things he would have once considered to be of the utmost importance.

"Well, your Shaun may have had good reason. This woman seems really fixated on the idea that someone she calls Kitty 'did a bad thing.' If that bad thing involved your friends, that could explain why things went so sour at the Monkey's place."

"That would make the woman I have the Fox, correct?" When Tessa nodded, so did I. "All right, keep digging, and if you find *anything*, I want to know about it. I'm going to drop a line to the folks I still know at After the End Times, and see if any of them can confirm your ID."

"If they do, let me know, okay? Finding the last of the Monkey's girls would be a pretty big deal in the circles I move in." I must have made a face, because Tessa put her hands up, and said, "I wouldn't tell anyone where she was until after she's not with you, I swear. I value your business, and I value you not sending people to close my mouth permanently. I'm not going to go spilling your secrets all over the Internet just because I want to look cool for my friends."

"I pay you for secrecy," I said coldly. "Just remember that." Then I killed the connection, before she could make any more excuses. If there was any chance at all that our guest was worth something to someone, getting a confirmed ID had just become even more important. And now I had to do it before Tessa did.

"I hate subcontractors," I muttered, and reached for the phone.

3.

It's possible to maintain a landline in today's day and age, and there are even reasons that it can be considered superior to having a cell phone, if you do it right. Old phone cables run through the entire North American continent, laced through earth and stone like veins through the human body. Most of them haven't been used, or consistently monitored, in decades. One person with a decent understanding of how they work and a few skills picked up from an old telephone company repair manual can set up safe, secure, off-the-grid communications. It's kind of funny, in a sideways sort of way: People used to go for burner phones and cell blockers, thinking that they were keeping themselves secure, and now those same people would kill their own mothers for a black market landline and the tech to keep it clean.

I held the receiver between my cheek and shoulder as I typed, listening to the ringing. Finally, the line clicked, and an amiable female voice announced, "Kwong-Garcia residence, Maggie speaking."

"Tick tock says the clock, when the watch runs down," I said.

There was a pause. "I don't really like this cloak-and-dagger bullshit, okay? I've got a scrambler on the line, courtesy of Daddy, so if you're calling for Alaric or whatever, you can stop with the weird code phrases and the pretending that this sounds even remotely normal. It doesn't. Anyone who happens to be in the room with me would know something was up if I gave you the countersign, so how about we just don't?"

"When did your father get you a scrambler good enough to trust?" I asked.

"It was a wedding gift," said Maggie. "Dr. Abbey? Is that you?"

"It's me," I confirmed. "Congratulations on that, by the way. I'm sorry I wasn't able to attend. You know how it is. Underground virologist, fugitive from the law, all that."

"We really liked the KitchenAid you sent," said Maggie. "I would've sent you a thank-you note, but we didn't so much have a mailing address."

"I was thanked in spirit," I said. "Is Alaric around? I need to ask him some questions."

"He's working right now, but I can get him if it's important." Maggie paused. "What am I saying? You *picked up a phone.* This isn't just important, it's cause for a ticker tape parade."

"I don't think they have those anymore," I said dryly. "As to the rest, I take your point, and will try to be in touch more often, if only so you don't decide to mount some sort of expedition to my place of work and take me out. Now, can you please put Alaric on the phone?"

"Just a second." There was a soft click as she put the phone on mute. That was something I actually missed from working at the Canadian branch of the CDC. We had all used heavy handset phones, holdovers from the pre-Rising world that could be hit with a hammer and still function. With those, putting down the phone would invariably make a loud clunking sound, keeping everyone aware of what was happening around them. I didn't trust phones that could be put on mute. They created too much opportunity for plotting.

A few seconds passed before the line beeped, and Alaric's familiar voice said, "Dr. Abbey? Is that really you?"

"You should learn to trust your wife," I said. "She said it was me. Ergo, it was me. Why is that so difficult to believe?"

"Because you never call. You write sometimes, but you never, ever call. Not even when we got married. You sent a fancy blender via courier. It would've been nice to hear your voice."

"You're hearing it now, and all you're doing is complaining about it." I sighed. "It's nice to talk to you, too, Alaric. Now, what can you tell me about the Monkey and his girls?"

"What?" Alaric sounded genuinely baffled for a moment. His tone turned quickly wary as he continued, asking, "Why do you want to know? Why are you calling me?"

"Because I can't call Mahir—it's too difficult to synchronize time zones, and even voice over IP is risky when you're bouncing it between continents. No one has a number for the Masons. Becks is dead. That leaves you."

"No, not just me. Hold on." There was a soft scuffing sound; he hadn't put the phone on mute, he had put his hand over the receiver. "Maggie! Come in here, and bring the splitter." The scuffing sound was repeated, and his voice was suddenly back in my ear. "Maggie's getting the headphone splitter. You need to talk to both of us. Her because she has data, me because I'm not going to sit here eavesdropping in my own home."

"I love how suddenly my actions are being dictated to me," I said sourly. "Why am I talking to Maggie, and not to you? You're the Newsie. She writes smut for a living."

"I write excellent, extremely literate erotica, thank you very much," said Maggie primly, her voice coming through as clearly as her husband's. "It pays more of the bills than his reporting ever will, so you should respect the pornography."

"Your father pays all your bills," I said, without rancor. "Since Alaric says I should be talking to you, what can you tell me about the Monkey and his girls?"

"He was a controlling narcissist who didn't allow for any resistance or deviation from the relatively narrow roles he dictated for the women who came into his orbit," said Maggie without hesitation. "He'd had extensive plastic surgery at some point: *No one* looks that generic unless they've designed themselves to look that way. I wish I'd been able to get the number for his surgeon. That work was amazing."

"You're perfect just the way you are," said Alaric. "You don't need a plastic surgeon."

"Maybe I don't right now, but it's always good to have a few numbers on file," said Maggie serenely. "I may want to cover the scars on my stomach someday. Pancake makeup and concealer are good for a lot, and yet sometimes I'd like to be able to hot tub without tinting the water beige."

"This is a fascinating conversation, and I'm just thrilled beyond words to be able to be an unwilling participant, but can we please get back on track?" I asked. "I need to know about the Monkey's girls. I understand that he had two. Can either of you describe them for me?"

"The Cat was tall, thin, brown hair, cold eyes. She did a lot of the grunt work for him. I get the feeling she was a computer genius, but I didn't get details," said Maggie.

"Her name was Jane," said Alaric. His voice was much more subdued. "We dated for a while back in college. She was always a little cold, but I figured that was just the sort of person she was, you know? Not everyone is physically demonstrative."

"The sex was apparently amazing," said Maggie. "Seriously transcendent. I *did* get details about that, but to be fair, I asked for them. The woman should've written a book on fucking, instead of going into the business of fucking people over."

"I am thrilled to be learning more about the intricacies of your marriage, and will send you my therapy bills," I said flatly.

"I'm good for them," said Maggie.

"Yes, I know," I said. "So that's the Cat. Jane. I've heard reports that she didn't make it out of the Monkey's compound alive." Even if she had, she wasn't the woman in my observation room. My guest could have been a natural brunette, and she could have had cold eyes when she wasn't drugged to the gills, but no one, however charitable, was ever going to call her "tall." I'd met taller teenagers. "There was another woman, though. Tell me about her."

"You mean Foxy?" asked Maggie. "She was little. Red hair. Blue eyes. Violent as all hell. She seemed like she was only really *happy* when she was hurting something—although she was the one who really got upset when we found out that the Cat had betrayed us. The Monkey was angry when he found out. But the Fox was sad. She was disappointed. It was sort of like she was a little kid in some ways, and she didn't want to believe that the people who were important to her could actually do anything that was really wrong."

"There's more." Alaric's interjection was soft enough that I almost missed it.

Good thing I have good ears. "What do you mean, there's more?"

"I mean... do you keep up with the site at all? The articles, I mean, not the op-ed columns or the updates from the Masons."

"Not as much as I should," I admitted. "Running a lab is a full-time job, even when you can do it legitimately. Under these conditions, it's a full-time job for three people, and there's only one of me. My reading for pleasure has sort of fallen by the wayside."

"Okay. I wrote an article a few months ago that I really think you should read. Send me a currently valid e-mail address, and I'll send it over to you." Alaric sounded hesitant—more hesitant than normal. "It'll explain a lot about the Fox."

"Okay," I said. "Can I show you a picture?"

"Sure," said Maggie. "Send it to my submissions account. We both have access."

"On it." Cradling the phone between my cheek and shoulder again, I pulled up the video of our mystery guest—who was growing less mysterious by the second—and clipped a single frame that showed her face in cool, silent repose. The lighting was good, highlighting the pallor of her skin and the purple shadows under her eyes. I attached it to an e-mail, sent it off, and waited. The connection was good. I didn't have to wait for long.

"Mother of God," said Maggie.

Alaric, who had spent more time in my lab than she had and knew exactly where that room was in the facility, was less restrained. "Dr. Abbey, what the fuck is the Fox doing in your observation room?"

"So you're both identifying her as the woman from the Monkey's compound?" I asked. "Please be clear in your answers. I need to be sure."

"If it's not her, she has a twin sister," said Maggie. "That's not okay."

"It's her," said Alaric.

"Okay. That's what I needed to confirm."

"Dr. Abbey, I don't think you understand." Alaric was sounding more alarmed by the minute. "She's a killer. That's what she does. It's what she *lives* for. She may have been upset when the Cat broke the rules, but that wasn't going to stop her from putting a bullet in anyone who got in her way. You need to get her out of there. You're not safe while she's with you."

"I'll take that under advisement. In the meantime, Alaric, send that article over; I need all the help I can get in dealing with this situation, so if you've got something you think will help, I want it. Both of you, congratulations again on your wedding—I hope you'll be very happy together. Give everyone my best, and don't call back." I hung up without saying good-bye. Farewells weren't really my style, and hadn't been since my husband died. Maybe it was a silly superstition, but I live in a world where the dead walk: I can be superstitious if I want to.

Alaric's e-mail had already arrived, shunted though a dozen layers of increasingly sophisticated software to reach my inbox, where it waited for me to open it. I clicked. I opened. I read. And somewhere in the middle of his report, titled "Unspoken Tragedies of the American School System," I began to cry. Thankfully, there was no one in the room with me but Joe, and Joe was loyal. Joe would never tell.

4.

"Is she awake?"

"You asked us to notify you as soon as she woke up. I have not notified you. I value my position here in this lab, rather than outside in the wilds with no weapons and no references to show the next evil lab that I want to work for. Ergo, she has not woken up." Jill didn't look away from her computer as she spoke. Apparently, even being her boss didn't put me above blood test results in her estimation. That was actually heartening. I signed her paychecks, but science was her real employer. That was exactly as things were meant to be.

"The lab isn't evil, it's ethically challenged," I said. "We do good things."

"I bet Frankenstein told himself the same thing," said Jill, still typing. "She's asleep, but she's not *deeply* asleep. You could probably wake her up, if you wanted to go another five rounds with Sleeping Beauty: the horror movie edition."

"Were you always this rude and disrespectful?" I asked.

"Not until my boss told me that talking back would help me on my annual reviews," said Jill. She finally turned to look at me. "Do you want me to call Tom to come and play backup? He's just down in his lab, playing with cannabis. You know, like he does every day."

"Yes, but this time he's doing it because I asked him to," I said. "I'll be fine. I don't think she's here to hurt me. I think she's genuinely here because she needs help, and because the last person she trusted to help her used her instead. Used her hard, and put her away broken."

"We're not the Island of Misfit Toys," protested Jill. "We can't be responsible for every broken doll you come across."

"Why not?" I asked, amiably enough. "I decided to be responsible for you."

Jill didn't have an answer for that, and so I turned away and walked out of the room, heading the few feet down the hall to the observation room where our mystery woman—who was becoming less mysterious with every moment that passed, even if she was becoming somewhat sadder at the same time—was waiting for me.

She didn't stir as I opened the door and stepped inside. I shut the door behind me, walking calmly to the seat I'd been occupying earlier. Routine was important when dealing with people who had every reason to be suspicious of you: It both made you predictable, which could be comforting, and it lulled them into a false sense of security. It was amazing how many people took "doesn't deviate" to mean "*can't* deviate." If I could build that assumption in her mind, however subtly, I would put myself in a much better position.

"Elaine," I said. "Wake up. I need to talk to you."

The woman on the cot flinched. That was all I needed to know that she was awake, and more importantly, that I was right. She was the Monkey's faithful killer, the one he called "the Fox," but before that, she had been a schoolteacher from Seattle named Elaine Oldenburg.

"I could sell your location to a lot of people. There are still warrants out for your arrest, thanks to the things that happened at your old school. None of the parents of the surviving students want to press charges, but you know how parents are. They're always looking for someone to blame. The way you disappeared sure did make you a person of interest." I leaned back in my seat. "I *could* sell your location, and I'm not. That should be enough to earn me a little conversation, don't you think? Stop pretending to sleep, and talk to me."

"Nothing here is worth saying," said the woman. Her voice was very small, and it lacked the lilting edge that it had held before: Now it was filled with a deep resignation, like this was the ending that she had always expected but had somehow been holding out hope would be avoided. "I was, I wasn't, and now you're telling me that I am again. It's not fair. When I took the cup and sword, he promised me I'd never have to be again. That was the deal. Give myself over to service, and never be anyone I didn't want to be ever again, no matter what happened, forever and ever, amen. That was the *deal*." Her voice took on a plaintive edge that cut through the air like the whine of a bone saw slicing through flesh. "He wasn't supposed to leave me."

"Do you mean the Monkey?" I asked, trying to keep my own voice as neutral as possible. All those drugs that she was on . . . some of them could be used to induce a dissociative state. If Elaine had gone to him because she had heard that he could supply her with drugs that would do that, then his death could have seemed like the greatest betrayal of all. "I'm sorry. I don't know if you know this, but the Monkey is dead. He died in Seattle."

"I know he's dead." Now she sounded almost dismissive. I was giving her old information, and she didn't have time for that. "I saw him die. I didn't shoot him, if that's what you're asking. I could have done it, but I didn't do it. I wasn't mad at him. Everyone is just as they're made, that's all, and he made himself into what he was one inch at a time."

"I don't understand what you mean," I said.

"I mean he made me with drugs and promises, and he made himself with drugs and surgery and blood and women who would do whatever he wanted them to do. His only mistake was the Cat. She was a hunter. He didn't want hunters. He wanted killers. They're not the same thing, you know." She smiled beatifically, her eyes still closed. "They never have been."

"He died two years ago," I said. "A lot of people thought that you had died, too. How did you not run out of drugs until now?" Because that should have happened a long time ago. There was no way she could have been maintaining the levels of chemical modification that Jill had found in her bloodstream. Some of those compounds had short shelf lives; they broke down too quickly for her to have been traveling with any kind of a supply. Others were just hard to make, and dangerous to carry. The only way our girl had made it through the past two years was by finding another supplier—and that didn't fill in any of the gaps that were starting to open around her. She wasn't telling her story. The story I'd been able to uncover had some holes.

"The Monkey always used to say, 'If something happens to me, go here,'" she said, and finally turned her head toward me, opening her eyes. They were fathomless and cold. I could have fallen forever into those eyes. "He gave me names. Addresses. Safe houses I could run to. But some of them weren't as safe as others. Some of them had problems that had to be solved with fire, and with screaming." She shrugged a little. "It's a living."

"So these safe houses, they gave you the drugs that you needed? How did they know what you needed?"

"Monkey told them. He always knew he might die someday. Dying someday came with the job, like getting cavities comes with eating too much sugar, or breaking toes comes with dancing ballet." She sounded so calm, like she wasn't talking about her own life. "So he gave the safe houses lists of what I was on, and told them that they could have me if they'd keep me nice and gone. I trusted him. I believed he wouldn't give me to bad people."

"Did he give you a copy of that list?"

Now she sighed, shaking her head. "He said knowing what I needed would just make me unhappy, because then I'd be able to see just how broken I really was. I guess he was trying to protect me again. He loved me best, you know. Out of all his girls, he loved me best."

"Is that so?" I asked, as neutrally as I could. I didn't recognize what she was describing as love, but I had been around long enough to understand that sometimes love doesn't look like anything you would expect. Sometimes love is a spider hiding in the corner of the room, dark and brooding and terrible to anyone who doesn't experience love in the exact same way. That's what makes love so dangerous, and so impossible to destroy. You can't kill what you can't see.

"Oh, yes," she said. "I wasn't the first, but I was the best, and all I had to do was spend most of my time not being anyone at all. That was what I wanted most, and he gave it to me. He let me not be anyone at all." Her face fell. "I'm becoming someone again. I don't like it."

It was hard not to get frustrated with her. It was half like talking to a child and half like talking to one of the fragile attempts at artificial intelligence that people like Tessa periodically pushed out onto the greater Internet, hoping that the sheer flow of data would transform them from particularly well-designed Chinese rooms into actual people. But getting mad at those programs didn't make them function any better, and neither would getting mad at her. "Why don't you like it? You were a person before the Monkey got his hands on you."

"I was a *bad* person," said the woman. I couldn't decide what to call her. She wasn't the Fox anymore—and it wasn't like I would have ever used such a stupid name for a flesh-and-blood person; even at my most understanding, I have my limits—but she hadn't turned back into Elaine yet. Assuming she ever could. Some of those drugs had permanent, long-term effects, and those were just the compounds I had heard of before. The experimental cannabinoids, who knew? "I was supposed to keep the children safe, and I didn't. Why would I want to be her ever again? All she was good for was losing. The Monkey made me stronger. The Monkey took all that pain away, and he gave me laughter and happiness instead. I miss him."

I didn't say anything. I wanted to yell at her. I wanted to tell her that she'd been used by a man who got her addicted to synthetic narcotics and then given her to his friends when he died. But none of that would have done any good. Love is a spider, and spiders weave webs. "I'm sorry for your loss, but look. I need to know how you found us. I need to know what you're doing here. I need to know what you *want*, aside from the drugs."

"Can you give me drugs?" She pushed herself up onto her elbows, showing more animation than she previously had. "I need my pills. I don't like feeling this way."

"What way?"

"Any way." She shook her head fiercely. "I don't like *feeling*. Everything is supposed to be calm and smooth and fun, and yeah, sometimes it's all irrationally violent, but that's okay, because the drugs take the scary out of it. I didn't ask for this. I didn't ask to be the one who had to survive and keep on going. Can you make it go away?"

"None of us asked to be the ones who survived; we just got lucky." Or unlucky, depending on how you wanted to look at it. "Yes, we can provide you with a certain amount of pharmaceutical support. How much we provide will depend on what you can tell me."

"I'll tell you anything you want," said the woman. Her voice was eager, almost pleading. "I'll kill anyone, or do anything, or whatever. Just please, please, give me the pills."

"How did you find us?"

She pulled back slightly, eyes darting to the side. "I asked people where I could go for drugs. They said to come here. They said this was the place to go."

"Who did you ask? Who told you that this was the place to go?"

"People. Please." She looked at me pleadingly. "Please, just give me the drugs. I don't have that much time. Please, you have to help me. They promised you could help me."

Something about her stance was setting off alarm bells in the back of my head. The trouble with mysteries was that they always came with the urge to *solve* them. They were like shiny baubles to bat at, and they were *distracting*. She had distracted me from the moment she dropped out of the tree, too thin and too sick and too far gone to have made it all the way into the woods without help. Someone had broken her—and while the Monkey might have done some digging on her fault lines, it couldn't possibly have been enough to leave her the way I'd found her. She'd been strong enough to survive for two years without him. Someone else had broken her down. Someone else had left her at my doorstep.

"You're a trap, aren't you?" I sounded more weary than anything else, even to my own ears. I knew Jill was listening in, and I raised my voice as I demanded, "Who left you here?"

"Please," she moaned. "Please, just give me the drugs I need. They can't make them for me. They can't, they never could, that's why I had to come here. You have a lab, they said. Food, they said. I didn't want to, but the pills ran out, and I need my pills."

"Who can't make your drugs for you? Who sent you here? Elaine, you have to tell me. If you want your pills, if you want me to help you, you have to tell me *who sent you here*?" I stood, not quite towering over her. I'm short. She was shorter, and lying in the bed besides. For once in my life, I got to be the imposing figure in the room.

The Fox—Elaine, she had to be Elaine, because anything else was too stupid to be tolerated—rolled onto her back and closed her eyes, pointing her face toward the ceiling. She looked pale and wan and fragile; so fragile that I could break her with a look, with a touch, with anything at all.

"Clive," she said.

I swore. I couldn't help it. "Stay here, stay *right here*, and don't you move. If you move, my staff will fill this room with formalin, and we'll watch the video of you melting at the company Christmas party every year from here until the death of time. Got it? Actually, I don't care if you've got it, you're fucked up on drugs and I'm in charge. Stay where you are." Then I turned and stormed out of the room, moving as fast as I dared without starting a panic.

Clive had sent her. May whatever God or gods exist have mercy on us all.

Chapter 4

When Your Back's Against the Wall

All I ask is that people leave me alone to pursue my private perversions of science. Why is that so difficult to understand? Why do I have to keep buying bullets in bulk to get my point across?

—Dr. Shannon Abbey

The fortunate among us do not live their lives haunted by the ghosts of their better selves. Very few of us are truly fortunate.

—Mahir Gowda

1.

Nothing exists in a vacuum. That's physics, but it's also human nature. If you take a single person and isolate them, they will find ways to start warping the world to conform to their needs and expectations. When I left the CDC, I was a single woman with a medical degree, a chip on my shoulder, and my husband's not inconsiderable life insurance payout. I didn't have a lab, or a staff, or the resources to defend myself: All those things came later. I did have some connections within the various health organizations that effectively governed our world, and even the friends who were no longer willing to be seen with me were sometimes willing to sneak me a few hours of computer access or let me have off-the-books access to their research facilities, but that was about it. Everything I'd built since then, I had built on my own, one brick at a time. And yeah, in the process, I may have racked up a few debts . . . and made a couple of enemies.

Because nothing exists in a vacuum, any time you set up a society that has to operate off the radar and out of sight, you're going to get your share of con men, grifters, and petty despots who think that the way to control everyone around them is with an iron fist—skip the velvet glove. Every black market on the West Coast had its own tin king or pasteboard queen. Gangs controlled some of the supply chains, and could have been a serious problem if not for the fact that they knew I controlled most of the painkillers and vaccines in this part of the country. If they didn't want to die of measles or deal with the consequences of their own insistence on riding motorcycles down poorly maintained roads, they didn't fuck with me.

And then there was Clive.

For every wanna-be boss man and petty little comptroller with more bullets than sense, it seemed like there was someone in the shadows: someone smarter than they were, someone who understood how to bide their time and plan for a future that was coming faster than any of those amateurs could dream. Some of those potential overlords found better things to do with their time. Others found themselves on the receiving end of a coup before they could properly get started. And then there was Clive.

Clive, who controlled most of the narcotics trade from Vancouver down to Redding, spanning two countries and hundreds of miles. Clive, whose detractors tended to disappear, only to show up later in the zombie-baiting pits or roaming wild on the highways, mindless, infected, and good only for research and dissection in labs like mine. Clive, who had offered more than once to buy me out, smiling through his perfectly straight, perfectly white teeth and saying things like "cooperation is a virtue," and "if you scratch my back, I can scratch yours."

The only venture he'd ever undertaken that hadn't been successful had been an attempt to control the zombie traffic along his narcotic routes. He'd believed that he could single-handedly take back territory that had been ceded by two governments, and when he'd failed, he had executed all the mercenaries and scientists who had been working for him, doing everything he could to wipe the proof that he wasn't infallible from the face of the planet. He might have succeeded, too, if it weren't for the fact that the underground scientific community is very small, and we gossip like academics. Some of my staff had been a part of that doomed project before they had realized just how doomed they were, and disappeared into the night.

Clive knew where my lab was. Of course Clive knew—nothing as big as the Shady Cove facility could have remained completely off his radar, especially not with the supplies we purchased on a monthly basis from the surrounding communities. We generated our own power and fed it back into the under-grid, using that excess to pay for some of the things we couldn't create for ourselves. No matter how many solar panels we concealed on the structure or hydroponic-food bays we created, we were always going to be dependent on the outside for some things, and that meant that people like Clive would always know how to find us.

But that didn't mean he knew how to get inside, or where our weak spots were. If he wanted to learn *that*, he would need to get someone past our fences. Someone small and light, who he could monitor the entire time. Oh, she didn't have a tracker on her—my people were nothing if not efficient, and any chips or devices attached to her clothing would have been microwaved into uselessness two seconds after it was discovered—but visual surveillance will always have its place, no matter how advanced the world becomes. Clive could have watched her work her way past our outer defenses, and then watched as I took her into the building. If he claimed her as one of his people, he could even convince the court of public opinion that he'd been mounting a rescue mission to get her back. Everyone knew that I was a mad scientist. They were happy enough with that reputation when they needed vaccines or had questions about food and water safety, but as soon as someone mentioned body snatching or raising the dead, those same people were happy to turn on me. It was part of the job.

No one liked Clive, but they feared and respected him. Tell them the right story, and they'd take it as the gospel truth, just to keep his knives away from their throats. Clive didn't like me, because I represented something uncontrollable, incomprehensible, and heavily armed that didn't pay him the "taxes" he was so fond of demanding. He'd wanted my people and my resources for years. Now it looked like he was finally making his play.

I skidded to a stop in the doorway of the control room, where Jill was still staring in horrified silence at the window to the observation room. Elaine hadn't moved since I left. I guess she felt like she'd worked hard enough for one day. "Did you hear that?" I demanded.

"Shit," said Jill, turning slowly to face me. "Fuck. Damn. Shit-fuck-damn."

"Since you're not taking a correspondence course in profanity, I'm taking that as a yes," I said. "Call back anyone we have in the field or visiting the local encampments. I want this place locked down tighter than a CDC administrator's sense of whimsy. Grab as many security people as you think you'll need, and have everyone searched for bugs or bombs on their way back in. Have you finished running deep backgrounds on everyone we have on staff?"

"No," said Jill. "I'm maybe sixty percent of the way there. I've flagged five people who might be feeding data back to corporate or private health concerns. No one else from the CDC yet. We do have Amal from the EIS down in research, but since she gave us a copy of her résumé, with references, including your friend Danika, I didn't have to look very hard for her."

"Amal's fine, Danika vouched for her," I said, waving my hand dismissively. "Tell her to keep doing the security checks, and to notify you if she finds anything. Pull those five people and lock them up until this is settled. Tell them we're doing isolation tests if they give you any trouble." They wouldn't give her any trouble. Spies expected to be caught, and spies who had been caught expected to be shot if they caused any problems. If our five were loyal to someone else, they'd be relieved to be facing nothing more serious than short-term incarceration.

"What do you want us to do about Zelda?" Jill stood, wobbling a little as the servos in her prosthetic leg reoriented themselves to the level of the floor. "I can't give her a gun. She hasn't passed any of our marksmanship tests, and I don't think the CDC prepped her for anything more strenuous than doing lab work when they sent her out here."

"I swear I'm going to contact Joey and tell him that while I don't mind him sending spies over here to do my chores, I need a slightly better class of infiltrator," I said. "All right, we're blowing her cover. I'll do it, I can't help lock down the lab without getting in the way. If there's anyone else here who's serving two masters, find them, and tell them that they're quitting one of their jobs today. I don't care whether they decide to work for me or decide to be locked up until it's safe to throw them out—just make sure we're not going to have anyone trying to hold our lines while they're thinking about how they're going to type this up for their bosses."

"On it," said Jill. She leaned forward and punched a few keys on her keyboard. The lights in the observation room flickered almost imperceptibly. "She's locked down. Your keycard will still open the door. So will mine, Tom's, or anyone's who has full security access. You're sure no one with full access is on someone else's payroll?"

"If they are, we're going to find out real fucking fast," I said. "Now, move."

She moved. So did I. I ran one way down the hall and she ran the other, outpacing me with ease. Jill might not do much fieldwork, but she'd been a runner before the accident that claimed her original leg, and her prosthetic had been designed to let her keep as much of her old life as possible. She could have graced any lab in the world, if they hadn't been so small-minded about what constituted physical health. As it was, I got lucky, and she got to squat in an abandoned forestry center, trying to unsnarl the structure of Kellis-Amberlee one twist at a time.

There were no alarms or blaring lights to signal the moment when Jill got to Tom and told him to put the lab into a state of high alert. A few doors locked themselves. A few banks of fluorescents changed shade, going from a cool white to a more artificial, less relaxing yellow. That was all my people needed to know that we had a problem, and the staff members who hadn't been with us for long enough to know what an emergency looked like could take their cues from the people around them.

All except for our darling not-Daisy, who was about to get a hard lesson in exactly how little she was valued by the people who had sent her to me. The CDC might be getting better about their human rights violations—might actually be learning that you can't feed your best and brightest through a meat grinder year upon year and still expect to have a competent, reliable staff that wasn't completely corrupt—but real change takes time. Danika and Joey could rebuild the organization from the ground up, and they'd still have to deal with people like the ones they had replaced.

Some ways of thinking are seductive. They tell you "one person doesn't matter as much as a world," and while that's technically true, there's a big difference between choosing to burn a single population center in order to save a province, and deciding to bomb a school because there are a few live infections among an otherwise healthy student body. To choose a completely random example, not in any way influenced by my own life or experiences. Not-Daisy was the product of the old system, and she was going to have to deal with what that meant.

I found her in one of the smaller labs. They were supposed to have been closed off for the moment—we weren't doing any research in epigenetics or botanical treatments for Kellis-Amberlee, and hadn't been since Shaun Mason had arrived and brought us all his lovely biological data on sexually transmitted immunity and the role of reservoir conditions. The blood I'd been able to extract from the man before he fucked off to the wilds of Canada with the clone of his dead sister had changed everything, and had closed several avenues of fruitless inquiry.

We were going to repurpose those labs eventually. But when I came down the hall, I saw that one of the banks of lights was on and that the door, which should have been tightly closed, was cracked open just enough to let the room's occupant hear if anyone was coming.

That was the idea, anyway. In practice, most people aren't that good at paying attention to their surroundings when they're already nervous, and my experience with corporate espionage told me that not-Daisy would be plenty nervous, especially if she was trying to get around our firewall without getting herself caught. There was no question that she, or someone very much like her, was in the lab. My people knew better than to open closed doors just so they could smoke a joint or have a little illicit hanky-panky: They learned that early and they learned it hard, usually when Joe came bounding into the room barking his canine heart out. The ones who didn't learn it from Joe had a tendency to learn it at the end of a Taser.

I paused outside the door, considering my options. I could take it slow and easy, without frightening the woman... but had she really *earned* that sort of consideration? And more importantly, was I really feeling generous enough to give it to her?

"Fuck, no," I murmured, and kicked the door open.

The effect was immediate, and highly gratifying. There was a loud clatter from the other side of the lab, accompanied by the familiar sound of someone typing as fast as their little hands allowed, trying desperately to get their data out before the authorities shut them down. Of course, normally it was *my* people trying to get their info transmitted ahead of someone with actual legal power. My power was all situational. I had no legal authority, but hey, who needs legal authority when you have the ability to strand someone in the middle of a zombie-infested forest without backup or weaponry? Everything is relative. And relatively speaking, I was the most powerful person for miles—at least until Clive made his appearance.

"You can stop typing now," I said calmly, still standing in the doorway of the lab. "Jill has already shut down all outgoing transmissions, so you're not going to get your data to whomever it is that you actually work for. Who *do* you work for? I know you're with the CDC, but I'm really curious to know who arranged to have you assigned here. Did you piss somebody off? Refuse some inappropriate sexual advances? Oh, they say that sort of thing doesn't happen anymore, but we're both women, we've both worked for those assholes. The truth is somewhere between the party line and the bottom line, and it's moving all the goddamn time."

"Dr. Abbey?" Not-Daisy's voice was timid, filled with a fear that was too believable to be anything but genuine. She stood up, her face a dim mask lit by the glow from her computer screen. "I-I'm sorry. I didn't know I wasn't supposed to be in here. I just thought this was a good place to... to sit and review my notes. I mean, there's so much to learn here..."

"It's okay, Zelda. I know." I sounded exhausted. That was almost a surprise to me. I usually relished these confrontations, which either ended with an expulsion or a change of sides. Under the circumstances, however, all I could really feel was tired. "Zelda Roland. Top of your class at Stanford, recruited by the CDC before you even picked up your diploma. You were supposed to be fighting the good fight, and yet somehow you ended up here instead. So who did you cross? Who did you offend? Or are you one of the idealists—do you really think that all research should belong to the CDC, even if that means you have to sneak into an independent lab and steal it? Time's short, Zelda, and your answer will determine what happens next. So talk."

She took a breath, clearly preparing another protest... and then she stopped, and straightened, the mask of the frightened intern dropping away like a coat she didn't need to wear any longer. She was still scared; she would have been a fool not to be. Whether she trusted the people who had sent her to me or not, she was embedded in what part of her must have viewed as enemy territory, and I was between her and all the exits. Even if she'd been able to make it to the exit, she would have been stranded in the forest. We patrolled regularly. Shady Cove was safer than, say, Santa Cruz. It was still abandoned territory, and it belonged to the infected.

"In the event that my cover is breached, I have been instructed to remind you that I am an employee of the United States government. As such, any retaliation against my person will be considered a federal crime, and will be prosecuted accordingly."

"Nice," I said agreeably. "Succinct, yet threatening. This is where I remind you that I'm a Canadian citizen, and that if I were arrested, the Canadian government would demand that I be returned to them to stand trial." My own government would be harsher on me than the feds could ever be. To the feds, I was a mad scientist and a valuable nuisance, tolerated because of the things I might yet discover. My friends in the CDC and medical-research community even considered me an asset. After all, I vaccinated the underground population, preventing an outbreak of whooping cough or measles from adding a whole new frisson of despair to life after the zombie apocalypse. But to the Canadian government...

To them, I was a traitor and a disappointment and a stain upon an otherwise pristine record of loyal patriots slaving away for the greater good. People who say Canadians are the politest people on the planet have never been on the receiving end of a disappointed military official's anger. I'd die before I let them ship me back to my home country.

Sadly, sometimes that meant other people had to die in my stead. "Well?" I prompted. "Are you going to tell me what you did to get yourself sent here? Or did you volunteer?"

"I refused to run some human-serotype trials," she said. Her tone was flat. The fear was still there, but it was buried under old shame and older disillusionment. "I said that it was against my moral and religious beliefs. It was... it was shameful, what they wanted done. My supervisor said that I was violating my contract, that I had agreed to do whatever the CDC required. Then he said that if I wanted to redeem myself, I could take a field assignment. And then he sent me here."

Serotyping is most commonly used to distinguish types of bacteria. The only way it could have been part of a test that Zelda would refer to as "shameful" was if it had been being used for organ transplant typing. Organ transplants weren't easy before the Rising, and they've only gotten more complicated, and more expensive, since then. You can't carve bits out of dead people and drop them into live ones anymore, not unless you want your live people to undergo explosive amplification and start trying to eat your surgeons. I briefly considered the implications, and then dismissed them as irrelevant to the issues at hand: staying alive, and neutralizing the threat of the CDC stepping in. "I'm going to want the names of the people you were working for. Dr. Kimberley is going to be very interested in knowing who's doing that sort of study." Zelda's eyes widened. I sighed. "They really didn't brief you, did they? I tolerate spies for a reason. Part of that reason is that I know the CDC isn't really out to get me, since your new director is one of my old lab mates. She's also fucking weird, but we try not to hold that against her. She's cleaning house right now, and people like you give me the information she needs to know about whose research she should be reviewing more closely."

"But that's... that's... that's treason!" Zelda stared at me like I had just told her Santa Claus was a myth and the Easter Bunny had undergone amplification.

"Everyone has their own definitions," I said. "Zelda Roland, do you admit that you are in the employ of the Centers for Disease Control, and that you have entered my lab under false pretenses, to collect information on my staff and our research for your actual employers?"

Her eyes darted from side to side, making one last pointless bid for freedom. She didn't find it. There were no exits aside from the one where I was standing, and she wasn't quite desperate enough to charge straight at me. Finally, her shoulders sagged. "Yes," she admitted.

"Great. Please return to your quarters. We're going to give you a gun and lock you in." Her eyes widened, and I sighed. "No, we don't expect you to kill yourself. What kind of monsters do you take us for? Signs point to an attack on this facility sometime in the very near future, and since I can't trust you, I can't have you on the front line, but I won't leave you defenseless either. After all this is over, we can discuss your future employment prospects, and who you're going to be working for. Oh, don't look so confused. You have to know that I've welcomed a few defectors from the CDC. We'd be happy to make you one of them. You're good. Cocky and green and way too easily manipulated, but good. You can talk to Tom about what we require if you want to change employers."

"You... you'd let me stay here?" She paused. "You *knew*? You didn't just find out?"

"Mad science is not forgiving of stupidity or willful blindness, Miss Roland," I said. "You were too good and too easy to recruit. There's no way you hadn't already been picked up by an acronym agency. If it had been WHO or USAMRIID, we would have told you thanks but no thanks. They play too roughly with their toys. The CDC we can usually get along with. Now, will you please remove yourself quietly to your quarters, before I have to make you go?"

"Yes, Dr. Abbey," she said. "Thank you, Dr. Abbey." She picked up a notepad from next to the workstation she'd been using and half ran toward me, only stopping at the last moment, when it became apparent that I wasn't going to get out of her way.

I smiled sweetly. "Just to be clear: If I find out that you went anywhere but back to your quarters, I will add you to my list of enemies. You won't enjoy that list. You won't be on it for very long, either. No one ever is. Clear?"

"Clear," she said. "I'm going to my quarters now."

"Excellent," I said, and stepped aside. She rushed past me, careful to avoid actual physical contact, and broke into a run as soon as she hit the hall. I stayed where I was for a silent count of twenty, letting her get away. She needed time to think, and I? I needed time to find a way to keep my people—including Zelda and Elaine—alive.

It was time to call Tessa.

2.

Joe pushed his head into my lap as I sat down at my computer, his finely honed canine instincts picking up on my distress. He was big enough that he made typing difficult. He also made me feel safe, and so I let him stay as I sent Tessa a chat request. Just to make sure she understood the urgency of my situation, I sent her three more in rapid succession. Childish and annoying? Maybe. But it was oh, so soothing, and I needed a little soothing just then.

People rushed by in the hall outside my open office door. None of them stopped to ask me for instructions or tell me what was going on. I had trained them well, and they all knew that a mad scientist who was working peacefully at her desk was a mad scientist who wasn't going to react well to being interrupted. They'd call if they actually needed me for something. If everything went well, they wouldn't need me for anything at all.

I was preparing to send another chat request when a window popped up on my screen, framing Tessa's harried, exhausted face. "What is it?" she demanded. "We didn't have an update scheduled until tomorrow, and I have found nothing new."

"Clive dumped her on my doorstep," I said, skipping the introductory material and going straight for the advanced course. "I need to know how many people he's rolling toward me, when they got moving, and whether they have any heavy artillery. I'm assuming he wants to take the building in one piece, so if he's smart, he won't have brought a tank, but when's the last time Clive went for 'smart' over 'showy'?"

"This wasn't part of our original deal," said Tessa—but it was just for show. Her hands were already starting to dance across the keyboard, performing a hacker's ballet for one soloist and an audience of me. "I could hang up on you right now and it wouldn't damage my reputation one little bit."

"Except for the part where Elaine Oldenburg is in my observation room, and before she came to me, she was with Clive. He used her the way hunters used to use real foxes: He set her loose to see which way she'd run, and now he's chasing her." I shook my head. "I hired you to find everything you could on her, and you never found out that Clive had sent her. If I told people, it would ruin you. That makes this a part of the original deal. He's coming after her. He's coming for me."

"And if anyone asks why he went up against a neutral party, he can say you kidnapped one of his people to experiment on," said Tessa. "I'd be impressed if you weren't so screwed. As it is, I'm just glad I'm a couple of thousand miles away. Can you courier my Lego before he shoots you in the head? I'm asking for my boy, you understand, not for myself."

"I sent them off two days ago."

Tessa smiled briefly as she continued typing. She wasn't looking at her webcam anymore. She probably didn't even realize that it was still on. Then her fingers stilled and her eyes grew wide. "Okay. I've got chatter about Clive putting together a big party, lots of calls for caterers and cooks—looks like he has a force of about sixty men, three explosive experts, and six virologists with him. Why would he need to bring his own virologists?"

"Because he's planning to kill me, scare my staff into agreeing to work for him, and put his own people in charge," I said blithely. "It's what I'd do in his place. No tanks or air support, huh? Just bodies on the ground, and his firm belief that the sheer size of his balls will be enough to make us lay down our arms and surrender. Asshole."

"What does he want with your lab?"

"We have vaccines, medicines, all the equipment and supplies he'd need to cook biofuel and meth—hell, what *doesn't* he want with my lab? If it weren't already mine, I'd want to come and take it away from me. Can you get a read on his location? Is he on the move, or did we catch this early enough to cut it off at the pass?" *Please, he's still in his man cave, fantasizing about how fun it's going to be to put a bullet through my skull,* I thought. *Please, we caught this while it was latent, and not once the infection had become systemic.*

It was almost funny how quickly I defaulted to putting things in medical terms, and it wasn't funny at all, because that was how I coped with situations I didn't have a better way to handle: I turned them into cases, things to be studied and taken carefully apart, one quivering chunk at a time, until they were quiescent and couldn't hurt me anymore. Looked at in that way, my reaction wasn't funny at all.

"Give me a second." Tessa's fingers resumed their ballet, performing arabesques and leaps at a speed that my own more mundane typing never even approached. She frowned, worrying her lower lip between her teeth. Then her face fell. I didn't really need to hear her answer: not once I'd seen her expression. But she looked up all the same, and said quietly, "He's been on the move since yesterday morning. His people will be tripping your perimeter sensors within the hour."

"Got it." I sighed. "Well, this isn't how I was planning to spend my afternoon. I'll pay you before I go to get myself slaughtered by a megalomaniac. Your Legos should be there in a few weeks. I hope you enjoy the shit out of them."

"I'm sure I will," said Tessa gravely. "It's been a pleasure working with you, Dr. Abbey. I hope you'll be able to kick his hiney all the way back to the hole that he crawled out of. E-mail me if you do. I will watch the news until I hear from you." And then her picture was gone, replaced by the blank face of my monitor.

I looked at my reflection in the glass and sighed. I looked sad, and why shouldn't I? My facility was about to be under attack, Jill was still looking for infiltrators who weren't as civic-minded as Zelda from the CDC, and maybe worst of all, Tessa had just confirmed—with a single, casual comment—that her son was no longer among the living. She would enjoy the Legos for him. He was beyond enjoying anything at all.

Some days I think the world as it is was invented just to fuck with us. And then I realize that doesn't make any sense at all, because it assumes a childish, vengeful God. If there is a God, He or She isn't a child. God is a scientist, and all this shit we're wading in is our agar. It's the only growth medium we're ever going to get.

"Fuck my life," I muttered. "Come on, Joe. Let's go get ourselves killed." I rose, pushing Joe's head off of my lap in the process. He followed me out of the room.

3.

Tom was in his lab when I arrived. His own little swarm of interns and technicians was gone, all of them probably helping lock down the facility, but he was still bent over his compounding station, adding a pinch of this and a drop of that to a vial, like he was making the world's most complicated brownie recipe. I stopped in the doorway and cleared my throat, not wanting to startle him. Tom rarely worked in things that could actually explode, but I didn't need to take any chances today.

"Hi, Dr. Abbey," he said, without looking away from his station. "Give me just a second, I'm almost ready for you."

"Should I ask what you're doing, or is this one of those things that's better for me not to know?" I asked. "In case you missed the announcement, Clive is on his way, and he's bringing an army. All hands are supposed to be getting ready for war, not making whatever that is."

"It's a blend of synthetic cannabinoids," said Tom. He added another drop to his vial. "It's not precisely a match to the cocktail Jill extracted from our guest, but it's close enough that the effects should be extremely similar—maybe even better. I went for long-term impact instead of short-term potency. She drinks this, she'll be talking to space lobsters for days."

"...and since she's been hanging with the space lobsters for years, she'll be fully functional while she's doing it," I said slowly. "Tom, you're a genius. How much of this stuff do you have?"

"Just the vial," he said. "I can make as much as we need, but there could be some nasty side effects if she takes this for much longer. I'm surprised she isn't already experiencing permanent psychological damage."

I thought of Elaine, so confused and erratic as she lay there in her bed. "Maybe she is," I said. "I just don't think she cares at this point. The space lobsters matter more to her than a few brain cells. Call it the opposite of antipsychotics and move on."

"Right." Tom added one more drop, swirled the clear contents of the vial gently, and put in the stopper before he turned to hold it out toward me. "I present you a single dose of space lobster bait. To be taken orally, and only if you're really, really sure you don't like the reality the rest of us are living in."

"You're a miracle worker." I took the vial gingerly. "Now, get your guns and get to the wall. Your people are going to need you there to back them up, and I don't feel like explaining why my leads were all hiding in their labs while Clive shot all the interns."

"Because we're smart enough not to go where the people who are shooting at us are. This obvious genius is why you made us leads in the first place." Tom turned back to his work desk as he spoke to me, his hands beginning to move in quick, confident arcs as he put all his perishable and dangerous supplies away. It was probably best not to leave a bunch of synthetic cannabinoids sitting around without supervision, although the idea of hitting Clive's men with water balloons full of space-lobster juice was oddly tempting. See how *he* liked dealing with a bunch of stoners where he was expecting an army.

"Genius or not, find your spot and hold it," I said. "Trouble is en route, and if we want to be able to continue saying that we work here, we need to cut it off at the pass." I started to turn away.

"Dr. Abbey?"

Tom wasn't a man who was given to uncertainty; even when he was higher than a kite, he tended to speak in calm, assured sentences, sounding like he was holding forth all the wisdom of the universe. Hearing his voice quaver, even a little bit, was enough to make me stop and turn back toward him, a frown upon my face. Joe paced me, willing, in his implacable canine way, to follow me forever, no matter how many times I changed my mind about where I was going.

"What is it, Tom?"

He looked at me earnestly, and asked, "Do you have a plan? Is it a good plan? Or should we be running for the hills right now? We'd have to leave a lot of our equipment behind, but I think we could make it. Give him the facility. We've rebuilt before. We can rebuild again."

"Ah." I bought myself a few seconds by looking around the lab. Tom had been in this room since we arrived in Shady Cove: had holed up here with his staff when one of our periodic CDC infiltrators had tried to kill Shaun Mason and his crew by letting our experimental subjects out of their cages. A lot of good people had died that day. Maybe it should have made this space feel haunted, but somehow, it had done the opposite: Their blood on the walls had felt like a cleansing, like it was giving us permission to finally lay down roots. Tom was right that we had rebuilt before. We had moved so many times that I had sometimes joked that our permanent address was "return to sender." But this space, this place, this had become our home. It wasn't perfect. Maybe it wasn't even good. But it was *ours*, and I'd be damned before I'd let Clive chase us away from what we had worked so hard to make.

"We have too many experiments in progress, and too many people who've never dealt with a teardown, much less an actual relocation," I said. "We stand our ground. If it looks like we're losing, we reassess. But we both know that if we run, we'll suffer just as many casualties as if we stand, and I don't want to be the reason for that many graves. Understood?"

"Understood," said Tom. "I'll see you on the Wall, if I don't see you before."

"Honey, one day we're all going to see each other on the Wall," I said. "Get to your post." And then I turned and walked away, a vial of volatile chemicals in my hand and a big black dog pacing at my side. What I was going to do next might be unforgivable in the annals of the world... but Clive had forced my hand, and I wasn't sorry. Maybe that's really what makes me a mad scientist; maybe it's what has always put me on the path to becoming a monster.

I'm never sorry.

4.

Elaine was awake when I returned to the observation room. She was lying perfectly still on the bed, but her eyes were fixed on the ceiling, and they darted toward me when the door opened. She stiffened a little as she caught sight of Joe. Joe, who clearly remembered her, tensed and slicked back his ears, jowls lifting just enough to serve as a reminder that he had a great many fine, sharp teeth just longing for a leg to be buried in.

"Down, boy," I said, tapping the top of his head. "We're not eating our guest today. We're here to offer her a trade." I turned my attention to

Elaine. "How are you feeling, Miss Oldenburg? Awake and peppy? Ready for your new master to sweep in and carry you away?"

"Please don't call me that," she said quietly. She sounded more resigned than anything else. The minute traces of drugs remaining in her system were starting to clear out; soon, she'd be fully sober, maybe for the first time in years. "That hasn't been my name since Evergreen."

"I know. It was a neat trick, disappearing from your life and then disappearing from your own mind. The Monkey helped a lot with that, didn't he? All those chemicals he mixed for you, to help you hide yourself. I'm sorry you felt the need to do that. We've all had to do things that weren't necessarily good for us, just so we could stay alive."

Elaine chuckled. It was a brittle, brutal sound, filled with ghosts I'd never seen but whose names she clearly knew. She probably called roll for them every morning before she opened her eyes, counting off the children who didn't make it out of the school. "You have no idea. Whatever it is you think you've done, whatever crimes you think you've committed... you have no idea."

"Maybe I do and maybe I don't, but either way, I'm here to offer you a deal." I looked at her flatly. "You don't work for Clive. You were doing what he told you to do because you thought it would get you what you needed, but you've been a free agent since you left the Monkey, haven't you? No one's been able to keep you in the pharmaceutical style to which you had become accustomed."

Elaine's brow wrinkled as she looked at me. "You're getting at something. I'd appreciate it if you didn't take such a long way around."

"Time is short, but that's no excuse to be shoddy. Are you a free agent? Yes or no. I need to know if you're loyal to Clive and staying strapped to this bed, or whether I can make a deal with you."

"I wouldn't trust me," said Elaine. She smiled slightly, although the tension didn't leave her eyes. "Everyone knows I'm crazy."

"And everyone knows I'm a mad scientist. It's amazing what everyone knows, isn't it? Usually what everyone knows is insulting and sort of ableist, because the people who know everything always seem to think of themselves as being perfectly normal. But that's neither here nor there. Are you a free agent? Yes or no. I'd say I could keep asking all day. I won't insult your intelligence like that. As soon as the shooting starts, I'm gone."

Elaine sighed deeply, sinking back into the bed. "Yes. Yes, I'm a free agent, yes, I came here because Clive said that this was where the drugs were, yes, I knew he would probably follow me and use me as a distraction, yes, I was all right with that, because he has people who would know how to synthesize more drugs if they could get their hands on samples from here. As long as I was willing to become *his* attack dog, he'd take care of me. That's how it is for me. I go with the ones who'll give me what I need."

"How loyal are you?"

She shrugged. "How far under can you put me? Because that's all I want. I just don't want to be Elaine Oldenburg ever, ever again. The Monkey understood that. He made sure I didn't have to know the woman in the mirror. He made sure I forgot their names."

I didn't have to ask her which names she meant. No matter how many people she might have killed since she'd become the Fox, none of them were ever going to matter as much as the students in her first-grade class back at Evergreen Elementary. There are some losses that don't get easier with time, and some costs that you never stop paying. She and I had that much in common. Maybe that was why I was willing to take a chance on her capacity for loyalty.

Or maybe I was a mad scientist after all. I withdrew the vial Tom had given me from my pocket, holding it up so that she could see. "One of my people was able to extract and analyze some really interesting chemical compounds from your blood. And then, because he's an overachiever, he synthesized them for me. This is one dose of pure bye-bye logic, and it should be enough to keep you flying for a few days. Long enough for us to toss Clive out on his ear, and for my people to break down the structure a little further, give you something that burns cleaner for longer and without as many negative side effects." Given that kind of time, and knowing where she came from, I might be able to find the Monkey's original supplier. None of the information on him said that he was a drug dealer. Whatever he'd been feeding Elaine, he'd been getting it from outside his little compound, and that meant that I might be able to get my hands on her original brand.

We'd still make our improvements, of course. If she wanted to chemically divorce reality, I wasn't going to judge, but that didn't mean I had to help her melt her own liver.

"Give it to me." She tried to lunge forward. The wrist straps holding her to the bed stopped her. She was scrappy, though: She kept trying, straining against her restraints like she thought she could dissolve them with the sheer force of her need.

"Not quite yet. See, you may be a drug-addicted killer, but there's nothing on you, in either of your identities, that implies you don't keep your word. So here's the deal. I want you to work for me. I want you to kill for *me.* I want the gun in your hand to be pointed where I aim it, and I want your word that you don't hurt anyone who's on our side. I'll give you what I have if you agree to my terms. If you don't want to stay after Clive's people have been driven back, we can talk about it. I'm not keeping you against your will. But first, I want your word that you'll help us."

She frowned. "Why do you want me?"

"Because we're scientists. We know our way around a gun, and we can hold our own, but we're not killers. We're not you. And because I don't really care yet whether you live or die, and I have the feeling you don't either, as long as you die flying." I gave the vial a little shake. "I can get you off the ground. All you have to do is work for me."

"I didn't used to be a killer, you know," she said. "I was a schoolteacher. I wore dresses with little flowers on them, and I hated that they made me carry a gun. But they taught me how to use it. I was top of my class in all the marksmanship rankings. I passed self-defense with flying colors. It was like the universe was getting me ready to turn into someone else."

"Is that a yes or a no?" I asked.

"Give me the vial, give me a pair of good, stompy boots, give me a gun, and you've got yourself a killer," she said.

I smiled.

Chapter 5

Can't Stop the Slaughter

Weapons of mass destruction are not, in and of themselves, evil. The evil comes from what you use them to accomplish—and how much collateral damage they do.

—Dr. Shannon Abbey

I don't gotta do anything you tell me, mister guy. All I gotta do is sing a little song, dance a little dance, and make a little murder.

—Foxy

1.

The Shady Cove Forestry Center was designed with the tourist experience in mind, intended to be open and airy and welcoming to the classes of schoolchildren and buses of retirees that were destined to come pouring through its doors. I'm sure all those people had a grand old time before the Rising came along and shut down casual woodland excursions forever. Since the Rising also shut down Shady Cove forever, the locals probably had better things to worry about than what was going to happen to their forestry center. They had left it open and abandoned, with all those lovely windows glittering in the sun, and all those big, echoing rooms just waiting for something to come along and fill them up. That had been the condition of the place when we first rolled in, following an old map and a bunch of rumors. *Indiana Jones and the Middle of Fucking Nowhere*, coming never to a theater near you.

So far as I was aware, while Clive might have spoken to people who had been inside my lab, he had never been inside himself. That meant that he was probably still picturing that old center, on some level: the big, empty spaces, the even bigger, even more vulnerable windows. And to be fair, if we'd still been trying to stay off the CDC's radar like we used to before the change in administrations, he would have been at least superficially correct. We used to make our modifications with an eye toward the satellites passing overhead, trying to minimize the visible changes to the landscape. Once Danika and Joey took over my former place of employment, all of that went out the window. Secrecy was replaced by security.

It had taken us a little while to adjust. It's hard to throw out the lessons of years, and we were never going to flaunt our presence. But if Clive had been looking for an easy kill, he should've shown up years ago.

The big picture windows were gone, not boarded over, but entirely replaced by metal plates and armored hatches that were too high for any normal infected to reach. The roof was a sea of solar panels, sucking in sunlight and producing electricity—the only way to cut us off was to block out the sun, and that was beyond the military capabilities of any small-time black-market king. And while we might have cleared the grounds to such an extent that it was now possible to move both vehicles and troops in closer than I liked, those same grounds concealed a wide assortment of defenses. No land mines, sadly. Land mines don't really differentiate friend from foe, and we had animals. We also had damn near everything else that could safely be planted in a garden, from radio-triggered barbed-wire caches to retractable spikes.

Give me a group of easily bored scientists and engineers, and give me a couple of undisturbed years, and I can build a stronghold that will never be breached. At least that was the hope. We were about to see just how secure my little modifications had really made us.

Scientists, engineers, and interns lined the interior of the metal "windows," their guns pointed out the hatchways and their faces as protected as possible. More of my people were in the trees and hides outside, although they wouldn't be shooting. They'd be operating the remote defenses and trying to stay out of sight for as long as possible. Jill was on one of the catwalks, shouting instructions and making violent hand gestures whenever people didn't move quickly enough. For the most part, they moved quickly enough. Jill worked for me, and I wouldn't have wanted to cross her when she was in this mode.

Joe paced by my side, a deep, sonorous growl resonating up from his chest and shaking his entire body. He knew something was wrong, and while he may not have fully understood what it was, he was prepared to protect me until his last breath. Loyalty like that is rare and precious, and I hated that I was having to abuse it by taking him toward a confrontation that could require him to make good on his promises. Good dogs should never be asked to prove that they're good dogs. If there's anything in this world that we should take on faith, it's good dogs.

"Dr. Abbey, they're coming." The call came from one of the engineers, a balding redhead I couldn't name on sight. That wasn't important. What mattered was the situation.

"How close?"

"Quarter mile out. They just passed Liza's hide. She managed to trigger two of the camera drones, and then she dropped off the radio." The redhead's voice was grim. He knew as well as I did what Liza's sudden silence was likely to mean. We'd go out later, after the shooting stopped, to check on her. If she was alive—unlikely but still possible—we'd offer whatever medical care she needed. If she wasn't alive, we'd make an effort to recover her body, if she hadn't already risen. It wasn't much of a retirement plan, I'll admit, but it was the best that we could offer.

"Got it. Keep your positions. Where's Tom?"

"He's at the lookout."

"Got it," I said again, and kept on walking.

The designated lookout point was halfway around the forestry center lobby, situated above what had once been the front doors, before we boarded them over and plastered the seams with fast-drying concrete. They were still one of our weakest points if someone came along with, say, a tank, but they were no longer a day-to-day risk. A metal ladder leaned against the sealed doors. Tom was standing at the top, a pair of binoculars held up to his eyes, staring out at our euphemistically named "lawn."

"Situation?" I asked.

"Bad," he replied. He looked over his shoulder and down, shaking his head. "Clive's actually marching on us. He's actually marching on us, with actual men carrying actual guns. What is this, the Rising?"

"It's that or it's the wild, wild West," I said. "Hold the wall as long as you can, Tom. That's all I can really ask you to do."

"What are you going to do?"

"I'm going to negotiate," I said, gesturing over my shoulder toward the PA system. It would broadcast from the speakers outside the building, drawing the attention of every living creature—infected or not—within half a mile. If Clive and his people didn't take us out, the zombies I was about to attract just might. "Well, that, and I'm going to pray that we're getting a miracle today."

"Do people like us get miracles?" asked Tom dubiously.

I thought of a gaunt, dead-eyed woman with oddly dyed hair, lying in my observation room and holding a vial of clear liquid like it was the most precious thing in the universe. "We might," I said, and moved toward my station. It was time to talk to the bogeyman, for all the good that it was going to do.

2.

Clive's people marched right out into the open, as cocky as you please. They stopped at the edge of the trees, too far out for us to shoot and too close for us to ignore. They weren't *that* cocky, then: not cocky enough to believe that we would have left ourselves undefended. As I watched on the monitor next to the PA, three of Clive's men began setting up portable workstations that would no doubt allow them to perform full magnetic resonance scans on the ground. Soon they'd know about every trap, underground cable, and earthworm within a hundred yards. Once that happened...

"Screwed" was a word. So was "totally and completely thunder-fucked," although that may have been more of a phrase. It was time to stop sitting around waiting for a miracle, and start doing something.

I flicked the PA on.

"Hello, Robin Hood and your Merry Men, this is the lab of Dr. Shannon Abbey regretfully informing you that the free vaccination clinic is closed this week. Please take your guns and your grim-looking mercenaries and head on home. We'd be happy to treat whatever STIs you've picked up during your adventures next month, when we open our doors to the public at half-past never o'clock in the afternoon."

There was a brief scramble at the front of the mob, and then Clive himself stepped into view.

He was good-looking, in a tough, "tattooed to the point of losing all individual images" sort of a way: like a children's coloring book that walked, talked, shaved its head, and scowled at anyone who happened to cross its path. He was wearing tactical gear that he somehow managed to keep from looking silly through the sheer dint of being six and a half feet tall. It's amazing how much you can forgive with height.

He was carrying a whiteboard. He scrawled something on it, and held it out for me to see: the number of a common radio frequency. So that was how he wanted to play it, huh? Well, I could play along.

"I've got a radio right here, Clive, and I'm tuning it to your station. Now, how about you call in and tell me what's on that portable black hole you call a mind?" I fiddled with the radio next to my transmitter as I spoke, flipping through half a dozen channels of static and the local number station before settling on his chosen frequency. Then I took my finger off the "send" button, and I waited.

It wasn't a long wait. One of Clive's men brought him what looked like a tricked-out walkie-talkie. He brought it to his mouth, and a moment later his deep, surprisingly smooth voice boomed out of the radio: "We demand your immediate surrender, Dr. Abbey. If you open the doors and let us in, we won't even feel the need to shoot you. Make us wait, and . . ." He clicked his tongue, saying wordlessly what would happen to anyone who resisted.

I depressed the "send" button. "That's a very kind offer, Clive, but I'm afraid I'm going to have to refuse. You see, I have some very delicate experiments going on here, and while it would be super fun to find myself kneeling in front of you with a pistol in my mouth, it would make it hard to chart the data. Go home. We're not letting you in."

"I have more guns, better men, and more ammo," said the radio. "What can you possibly have that could stand against me?"

"Well gosh, I dunno, but there's a lot of walls, and a big black dog, and did you know there was an octopus? Because there's an *octopus*. I haven't seen one of those in *years*." The voice was female, and absolutely giddy with delight. It was also a little higher pitched than I expected, like its owner had somehow slid backward through time, to a simpler age—fourteen or fifteen, young enough not to really care about consequences or costs. I turned.

Elaine Oldenburg wasn't standing behind me: Elaine Oldenburg had left the building, possibly forever, courtesy of Tom's space lobster juice. Instead, I was looking at the Fox, last of the Monkey's girls and pure killing machine in hospital scrubs and pigtails. She was grinning from ear to ear, the face of a woman whose connection to reality was no longer quite strong enough to serve as any kind of tether. She had managed to find half a dozen guns somewhere and had them tucked into the elastic waistband of her pants like this wasn't an incredibly dangerous thing to do. She was holding a scalpel in each hand.

I wasn't sure which to be more impressed by: her transformation into a character out of a pre-Rising comic book, or the fact that she'd managed to do it without setting off any alarms or triggering a panic among my staff. "The octopus is named Barney; I'll introduce you to him later," I said. "Did you kill anyone?"

"Not yet," she said. "But the day is young, and there's always time for a party."

"Right," I said. People around the room were turning to stare at us—more at her than at me, admittedly, since I was nowhere near as exciting, visually speaking, as a relative stranger with a whole lot of guns. "So you know, killing anyone who works for me will not constitute a party. It may, however, get you thrown out. Do we have an understanding?"

"I'm not stupid, Dr. Abbey. Don't ever, ever make the mistake of thinking that I am. Kitty made that mistake. She didn't make too many after." The Fox beamed first at me, and then at Joe. "Hello, doggy! I'm sorry I tried to shoot you before. You were scary, and I was confused. I won't try to shoot you anymore."

Joe looked at her, ears cocked, and made the small *boof* sound that meant he was confused but curious, and willing to explore the situation further. The Fox beamed.

"This is adorable and all, but Clive is at our gates, so I need to get back to negotiating with the megalomaniac now," I said. "The man on top of the ladder is Tom. He's in charge of making sure we all come through this alive. Check in with him, and then do whatever you can to bring us through this alive."

Something hardened in the back of her eyes, turning reptilian and cold. "Are those your orders?" she asked. "Do whatever I can to bring us through this alive, and try not to kill anyone who's currently inside?"

I nodded. "Those are my orders. Do you understand them?"

"That's the second time you've asked me that. Slow pupils don't make it to the head of the class, but they do get gold stars for participation." She was still too thin, this wild-eyed woman with the guns shoved into her pants and a raging case of bedhead. She looked like she could be broken over a larger person's knee with a minimum of effort. And she was somehow, despite all that, still scary as hell. "I understand your orders. Better make sure everyone else understands them, too. Where's the back door?"

The question was enough of a left turn that I paused for a moment before turning to the nearest group of armed interns and snapping, "Carlton! Take our guest to the back door, unlock it, and let her out."

The Fox smiled. "Better. See you soon, Dr. Abbey. Remember, I'm *your* dog now. Woof." Then she was gone, running fleetly over to Carlton, who looked like he couldn't decide whether he was being rescued from the shootout to come or sentenced to something even worse. She grabbed his arm, pulling him away from the others, and together they ran to the back of the room and disappeared.

The radio squawked as Clive began transmitting again. "Abbey? I hope you don't think that you can improve my temper by ignoring me. You're actually accomplishing just the opposite. I don't take kindly to being left hanging in front of my men."

"Sorry, Clive, just dealing with some personnel issues here inside my lab. Note the possessive. This is *my* lab, and these are *my* people, and while I appreciate your interest, I really am going to have to decline."

"Your call, Abbey. A pity. I really thought you cared about their lives."

The transmission ended. The gunfire began.

3.

Firefights are never as clean as they appear in the movies, where even a shot to the throat never seems to coat the surrounding areas with blood the way that they really ought to. Before the Rising, it was because no one wanted to offend the delicate sensibilities of the women and children that people assumed were flocking to *Buckets of Blood III: The Bucketing* because of its complex themes of abandonment and human nature. After the Rising, it became a matter of public safety. People who saw that much blood were likely to lose their tempers, their lunches, and their sense of proportion, in that order.

Clive was not playing by MPAA rules. His men unleashed a barrage of gunfire on the front of the forestry center, shooting through the weak points in the wood and sending bullets lancing through the room. Someone cried out. Someone hit the floor. I heard Tom shout, "Return fire!" and then there were guns going off in the enclosed lobby, their reports sounding out loud and angry over the cries and screams of my people.

Joe barked, adding even more chaos to the scene. I grabbed his collar before he could start trying to bite bullets out of the air. He wasn't fast enough—he was an experimental subject, not a miracle—but that wouldn't stop him from trying, if he got offended enough by what was going on.

"Stay," I hissed, hunching down. Clive and his men were still visible on the monitor. I wasn't the only one with a view on the outside: As I watched, three of his people went down, targeted by my security. One of the shooters fell off her platform immediately afterward, targeted by someone who had been able to analyze her position based on the trajectory of her shot. Her head split when she struck the floor. Three more of my people were immediately there, one of them putting a bullet in her forehead while the other two were pouring bleach on the resulting hot zone.

Gunfights before the Rising only killed you one way. Now they get you coming and going, as the dead rise up and make the situation even worse. That might explain Clive's bullet-spraying tactics. If he shot enough of us, we'd have an outbreak on our hands. Then he could just walk away and come back later to clean up whatever was left.

We'd weathered outbreaks before. Whatever Clive thought of us, we were tougher than he knew. But it was sort of hard to focus on that with bullets passing overhead and people screaming all around me.

There was a flash of motion on the monitor. I tracked it with my eyes, and clapped a hand over my mouth to cover my gasp as it resolved into the Fox, still barefoot and dressed in borrowed surgical scrubs, with a scalpel clutched firmly in each hand. She was approaching from the side, in Clive's blind spot—even if he'd had people watching that zone before the shooting started, they were all preoccupied now, trying to take us out before we could do the same to them. That explained why she wasn't shooting. Gunshots would have attracted attention.

She caught the first of Clive's hired guns before he had a chance to realize that he was in danger. The scalpel sliced across his throat with almost surgical precision, and then she was gone again, vanishing into the underbrush, leaving him to drop his gun and clutch helplessly at his throat. It wasn't going to do him any good. He was a dead man walking now, a dead man stumbling back toward his own people and grasping for them, grasping for *anything* that would let him hold on to life for just a little bit longer. Human beings don't die easy. If we did, the Rising would have been a lot shorter, and would have had a very different ending.

One of the other mercenaries shouted something as her wounded comrade stumbled into her, coating her in a layer of blood that was surely hot with live Kellis-Amberlee. She fired twice, and the man the Fox had wounded collapsed. The woman had barely a second to breathe before one of the other mercenaries turned and shot at her, sending her toppling after him. She'd been exposed. They couldn't risk it.

"Goddammit, Abbey, what sort of bullshit do you think you're pulling?" demanded the radio. Clive sounded angrier than I'd ever heard him. It was almost comic, in a way. He was the one attacking us, yet we were the ones refusing to play along with whatever narrative he had crafted in his power-addled little mind. How dare we not just roll over and die? It was so unreasonable of us.

I've always been unreasonable like that. I pressed the button on the PA, and said, "Well, I don't know. I tend to file this sort of bullshit under 'defending my home.' Take your people and leave, Clive. You don't have enough men to storm this castle."

"I'll be back, Abbey," said Clive. "I'll be—"

"No, you won't," said the Fox, her voice coming through the radio so clearly that for a moment, I thought she had somehow gotten back inside. A thick gurgling noise followed her announcement. I turned to the monitor to see her standing behind Clive, the tip of her scalpel protruding through the front of his throat.

He gurgled again before he fell, collapsing like a sack of wet laundry. The Fox beamed, waving enthusiastically toward the forestry center.

That's when one of his remaining men shot her.

Chapter 6

Sterilizing the Lab

We can raise the dead. We can cure cancer. We can make the world better in every possible way, save one: No matter how hard we try, we just can't cure stupid.

—Dr. Shannon Abbey

Everyone's living in a fantasy world these days. The only thing that matters is whether your fantasy is hurting anybody else. If it's not, then who am I to judge?

—Tatiana Markowski

1.

"Dr. Abbey?"

I was sitting on the edge of the wading pool with Barney's tentacles wrapped around my forearms, sharing a content moment with my resident troublemaker. Joe was on the floor nearby, head on his paws, silently judging me for loving a boneless squishy thing more than I loved him. Judge on, big guy, judge on. I turned at the sound of my name. Jill was standing in the doorway, a cast on her left arm and a line of stitches on her forehead. It was going to heal without a scar. Most of the wounds we'd suffered were.

Most, not all. Three of my staff were dead; the main lobby was still closed off for decontamination and repair. We'd burnt six of Clive's people, as well as Clive himself, after we had pumped enough lead into them that they weren't going to get up again. Not all wounds heal easy. Not all wounds should.

"What is it?" I asked.

"She's awake."

2.

The Fox—Elaine—whatever the hell she wanted to be called—was back on her bed in the observation room, staring up at the ceiling. She turned her head toward me when I came in, and her eyes were just unfocused enough that I knew I was going to be speaking to the killer, not to the tender of children. That was fine by me. I've never really known how to talk to people who chose to spend a lot of time around kids. Bullets and blood, those are things I'm more familiar with.

"The bullet nicked your liver and perforated your intestine," I said, skipping "hello" in favor of a status update. "We were able to repair most of the damage laparoscopically. We didn't even have to sedate you, thanks to all the drugs you're on. Thanks for saving us the trouble."

"Am I going to die?" she asked. She sounded almost hopeful.

"Not this time."

"Oh." She frowned before looking at me mistrustfully and asking, "Are you here to throw me out?"

"Why the hell would I do that? This is where you go when you get broken. I'm a scientist. I fix the toys that other people throw away." Toys like Zelda, who was still trying to figure out whether she was staying with me or heading back to the CDC. Toys like Tessa, who might not be trustworthy but deserved to be trusted all the same. Everyone's a toy to somebody.

The Fox—Elaine—whatever—blinked at me, uncomprehending.

Then, slowly, she smiled.

All the Pretty Little Horses

Introduction

This is the first of the two new stories in this volume. The odds are good that many of you have skipped straight here. Welcome. I hope you will enjoy what was one of the most difficult, emotionally challenging pieces I've sat down to write.

Every story has multiple sides.

This, for the first time, is Stacy and Michael Mason's side of the story.

Hush-a-bye, don't you cry, go to sleep, you little baby.
When you wake you shall have all the pretty little horses
Dapples and grays, pintos and bays,
All the pretty little horses.

Hush-a-bye, don't you cry, go to sleep, you little baby.
When you wake you shall have all the pretty little horses.

—TRADITIONAL PRE-RISING LULLABY

All the Pretty Little Horses

Chapter 1

What We Lost

It is the finding of this court that Stacy Mason is innocent. She did not murder her son. She acted in self-defense, and for the good of the community, and we are sorry for her loss.

—Judge Vernon, California Supreme Court,
January 9, 2018

Oggie?

—Phillip Mason

1.

The cleanup crews provided by the state of California were almost done with the city of Berkeley. They had been hauling away truckloads of bricks and broken boards and makeshift barriers for the past week; before that, they had been devoted to biohazard removal, digging up the bodies of the mercifully dead and cleaning out the basements that had been turned into makeshift morgues when nothing else was available. They were interchangeable in their orange biohazard suits, faceless behind their sheltering faceplates.

"I heard that a crew in Petaluma stumbled on a nest of zombies yesterday," said Michael Mason, twitching the curtain aside as he watched the orange figures move across a neighbor's yard. "They lost four people before the gunners could get to them, and two more from infection. It's not a very well-organized program."

He kept his voice light, conversational, like he was talking about the weather and not a major biohazard cleanup operation. He waited several minutes. There was no response.

With a sigh, Michael turned away from the window. There was a lump in the bed he shared with his wife—a lump of approximately her size, or at least the size she'd been when Judge Vernon had passed judgment on her case. Stacy Mason was not a murderess in the eyes of the law, or in the eyes of those who had survived the Rising. Everyone had a story like theirs, it seemed, decorated with the bodies of the loved and lost. Not many were mothers who had shot their only sons. Not many were women who had insisted that they be taken into custody and tried for what they'd done. In those regards, as in so many others, Stacy was special.

She had crawled into bed the day that she was found innocent, and she hadn't emerged since, except to use the bathroom. She ate when he brought her food. She answered direct questions, when she couldn't see a way around them. She was leaving him alone, and try as he might, Michael couldn't find the way to bring her back.

"Stacy?"

There was no response from the bed. Michael sighed again before he walked over to sit down on the edge of the mattress, on his side of the bed. The space between them was a chasm filled with screaming, and with the wide-eyed face of a little boy who had died twice, once of a terrible virus, and once when his mother put a bullet through his brain. Phillip had deserved better. *They* had deserved better. Michael only hoped that they still did.

"Stacy, sweetheart, you're going to have to get up soon. I've pulled as many strings as I could, but the cleanup crew is doing our side of the street tomorrow. We can't stay here while they're checking for contamination." They shouldn't have been allowed to stay for as long as they had. Michael had called in favors with the school administration, the mayor, and even the governor, who regarded the Masons as genuine heroes of the Rising.

The Masons had fortified their Berkeley neighborhood, turning it into a safe haven for survivors. The Masons had run complicated rescue operations that fanned out across Berkeley, Albany, and even Oakland, saving literally hundreds of survivors before the infected became too prevalent to allow for further attempts. The Masons had kept the lights on and the stomachs of their people full, thanks to good resource allocation and knowing how to work within their means. Out of all the small survivors' enclaves found when the government was actually able to start stepping in and saving people, theirs had been among the largest, the most functional, and the least chaotic.

Through it all, Michael's voice had been going out to the world every night, first over the Internet, and then over the radio, when the local ISPs went down. He had spoken to the city, and to anyone outside the city with a good enough antenna. He had promised them that they were stronger than this crisis. He had told them what to do. Stacy had been too busy during those dark days to do her own broadcasts, but he had included a segment called "Stacy's Survival Suggestions" in every other show. The number of people who had come up to him since the barricades came down, to tell him that those survival suggestions had genuinely saved their lives...

It was staggering. Thousands of people were still alive because of him, and because of his brilliant wife, who had proven to be a genius where surviving the living dead was concerned. At least until the day the tanks and military convoys had rolled into Berkeley, and they had been ordered to stand down.

He would never forget watching Stacy take the reports from her scouts, who had been following the movement of their rescuers through the city. She had looked so confident then, square shouldered and tan under the cruel midwinter sun. Phillip had been in the ground for three years, buried deep, but never forgotten. Michael had looked at his wife, and then at the soldiers who were fanning out over the street, and thought, *We did it. We survived.*

Three months later, he was no longer quite so sure. Stacy's strength had been the strength of a thing under immense pressure, so compacted that it could no longer show the cracks. When the pressure had been removed, she had fallen apart.

"Stacy, sweetheart, I need you to wake up now." He reached over and touched her shoulder. "The car will be here to take us to our hotel in an hour. We're staying at the Claremont. They cleared it out last week. Some of the rooms are off-limits, but the structure is sound. You always wanted to stay there." They had even joked, during the early weeks of the Rising, about abandoning their comfortable encampment to take back the grand old resort hotel. It had been Stacy who eventually rejected the idea, saying "No one wants to wait out the end of the world in the Overlook Hotel." She'd always been a fan of popular literature, and it was hard to get much more popular than Stephen King.

"Leave me here," Stacy said. Her voice was thin from disuse. It still sent a wave of relief washing over Michael. She was *listening.* She might be doing a poor job of responding, but at least she was listening. "I can help them find the bodies."

"Stacy..." Michael left his hand resting on his wife's shoulder. He needed the contact more than she did, he suspected. "Stacy, the bodies aren't here anymore. *He's* not here. His body was removed weeks ago, remember? They took him away while your trial was going on. They wanted to see if your accounting of what had happened had been accurate."

It hadn't been, of course. As soon as the apocalypse was... not over, exactly, but no longer occupying the entire world, Stacy had fallen apart and started calling herself a murderer. She had killed her son, according to her; she had been startled by him playing a game, and had pulled the trigger without thinking about it. She needed to be punished.

Michael would never stop thinking about the day they'd buried Phillip. It had been so early in the crisis. They hadn't known yet that they needed to be careful with the animals. They had wrapped his little body in some of their precious plastic sheeting and buried him deep, where nothing could dig him up again. Three years in the ground without embalming wasn't kind to anyone, but Phillip had been so lovingly prepared for his burial that the technicians who examined him had been able to take the samples that they needed. They had been able to find the marks of Marigold's teeth, and the Kellis-Amberlee virus still slumbering in his flesh.

Stacy Mason had been found innocent in every court except the court of her own mind. That was where she was being found guilty every hour of every day, and might be for the rest of her life.

"He's not here anymore, Stacy," Michael whispered, leaning a little closer. "I'm so sorry. I miss him so much. But he's not here, and it's time for us to go."

"Go where?" Stacy rolled over. Any elation he might have felt died when he saw the blankness in her eyes. It was like looking into the eyes of a corpse. "We have nowhere to go. This is where we fought. This is where we failed him. We should stay here."

"They'll arrest us if we're not off the property by tomorrow morning," said Michael. "This is vital work. They need us not to be standing in the way." Anything that lit up under their scanners would be removed, and destroyed. Michael didn't like to think about how many of their possessions—how many of *Phillip's* possessions—were going to be gone when they came back, assuming the whole house wasn't burned down as a possible infection hazard.

In some perverse way, he hoped it would all be destroyed. Maybe then they could start over clean. They had hazard money from the state, rewards for staying and fighting and not clogging up the overtaxed, overpopulated "safe zones." Considering how low property values had become in any urban area, Michael had faith that he could find them a new house, one that wasn't filled with ghosts, without much effort. It might be good for Stacy. Maybe if she wasn't living in a haunting, she'd be able to remember who she was.

"I don't want to go."

It was a small, straightforward admission, and it broke Michael's heart. He touched the back of his fingers to his wife's cheek, and said, "I know. But we have to. It's time to start moving on. I've already packed our things, and I'm sure I missed something. Do you want to check and see if there's anything you want to take?" Anything they removed from the house would be scanned, of course, but the scans would be less broad, and more targeted. They'd overlook things like sweat and semen—things that could easily wind up on a favorite blanket, for example—and allow them to be kept. The government was trying to protect their people, not punish them for surviving.

"No," said Stacy, sitting up and swinging her feet around to the floor. "I'll do it, though. You were always terrible about remembering to pack enough underwear."

Michael watched as she crossed to the dresser, and wished with all his heart that he could believe this was the beginning of her recovery.

2.

"All right, Stacy and Michael... Mason." The desk clerk looked up from her screen in surprise. She was young, barely out of her teens, with two-tone hair and gauges in her ears. She would never have been able to get a job at the Claremont before the Rising. Maybe that was a good thing about the zombie apocalypse: Old, unnecessary societal standards were falling, replaced by a new normal that seemed far more reasonable. "Um. I'm sorry, this may be inappropriate of me, but are you *the* Michael and Stacy Mason? From the radio?"

"Yes, we are," said Michael. Stacy didn't say anything. She was leaning listlessly against the counter, looking around the refurbished lobby with vague disinterest.

The new owners of the Claremont had spared no expense in getting things "back to normal." The chandeliers sparkled, the hardwood floors gleamed, and the whole room looked like a throwback to an earlier time, as long as you ignored the bars on the windows and the armed guards standing next to the doors. This, too, was the new normal. All the elegance, with a slightly higher cost of upkeep.

"Oh, wow. Um. I didn't know that you'd be—are you in one of the cleanup zones?" The clerk reddened. "That was rude of me. I'm sorry. Can you wait here while I get my manager? I'll be right back." And then she was gone, vanishing with surprising speed through a door marked PRIVATE.

"What was that all about, do you think?" asked Michael.

"She probably doesn't want to give a room to a pair of criminals," said Stacy.

Michael blinked. This was the first time she'd called *him* a criminal. "What do you mean, sweetheart?"

"I mean I'm a killer, and you're my accomplice. She's going to get her manager so he can tell us that we can't stay here." Stacy finally turned to look at him, and the intensity in her eyes was hard to bear. "We'll have to pay for what we've done eventually. We may as well start now, don't you think?"

"Sweetheart..." Michael stopped. He honestly didn't know what to say. She needed help. She needed a therapist, someone who knew how to talk her through her grief. But all the therapists who'd survived were currently being deployed by FEMA as part of an effort to rebuild a shattered population, and it would be months, if not years, before they were allowed to settle and reopen their practices. Stacy had refused to apply for government assistance, saying that her mental health was not the business of anyone but her and her family. There was no one to help her but him, and he was entirely unequipped for the job.

The desk clerk, breathless now, burst out of the door she'd vanished through, with a thin, well-groomed older woman behind her. Michael could see the signs of the Rising written clearly on the manager's skin: the deep lines that no amount of foundation makeup would conceal, the short, blunt nails, to keep her from hurting herself when the nightmares came. Survivors learned how to recognize one another. Their scars were always different, but in some ways, they were always the same.

"Thank you for waiting," said the clerk, staccato as a burst of gunfire. She didn't retake her position at the monitor. Her manager did that, swiping a card quickly across the built-in reader as she updated the security restrictions on the machine.

"The Claremont is honored to have you with us, Mr. and Ms. Mason," said the manager. "I'm Cynthia Norskog, and you saved my life several times over the last few years, although you've never met me before. I was holed up all by myself. If it hadn't been for your broadcasts, I don't think I would have made it." Her fingers flew across the keyboard, selecting and updating. "You're heroes. I feel so privileged to be able to meet you and thank you for everything that you've done."

Stacy straightened a little as Cynthia praised her, tilting toward the other woman like a flower moving toward the sun. "Really? We really saved you?"

"I don't know what I would have done without the sound of another human voice, a *living* human voice, coming into my apartment each night," said Cynthia. "I was lucky. I lived above a bakery that had its doors locked and covered in metal sheeting when things got bad. We never lost power. I lived on crepes and lemon zest for three years. But really, I lived on a voice from the radio, and I practiced every technique you had him relay to us up on my roof. Just me, and my homemade spear, and the need to see this crisis to an end."

Her machine beeped. She withdrew two key cards and held them out toward the Masons.

"Thank you," said Cynthia. "This isn't enough. Nothing I could do would ever be enough. But as long as I'm manager here, you'll stay free at the Claremont, even when your house isn't undergoing a government cleansing."

"You're welcome, and thank you," said Stacy, taking the keys. It was the most animation Michael had seen out of her since the trial.

He watched her thoughtfully as she took a picture with the manager and clerk, and as she held the camera for his picture with the excited duo. Whatever spark she'd found lasted as they crossed the lobby to the elevator, and rode up to the very top of the building, where their keys unlocked a palatial suite larger than their first apartment. Enormous sliding glass doors made up almost half of one wall, looking out over the entire city of Berkeley.

"My God, the view," he breathed.

Stacy didn't answer. He turned to see her heading toward the bedroom, her shoulders beginning to slump again. Michael sighed. He knew how this ended: with her crawling into the bed, her clothes still on, and returning to the fugue state that seemed to consume most of her time these days. It hurt to see her like that, in ways he could never have imagined before everything had become so complicated.

But he'd seen a way out. He'd seen her break that shell and come back to the world of the living, even if it wasn't quite as the woman she'd been before. He loved her with all his heart, no matter who she had to be in order to live with herself, and he more than half suspected that the original Stacy—the Stacy who'd danced with him on the college quad the night he asked her to marry him, the Stacy who'd been a mother to Phillip and a member of two local book clubs—was gone forever, another casualty of the Rising. He could live with that.

They lived in a world where the dead could walk, after all.

3.

True to his suspicions, Stacy had gone to bed without even removing her shoes. He had done that for her several hours later, when he finished making his phone calls and calling in his favors. The equipment was delivered to their room at seven the next morning.

"Stacy." He sat down on the edge of the bed, putting a hand on her shoulder and shaking lightly. "Sweetheart, I know you need your rest, but I need you to wake up, please."

"What?" Stacy opened her eyes. For a moment—just a moment—she looked like the woman she'd always been, and he felt his heart swell with love for her. Then she blinked, and the blankness came back, and the moment passed. "Michael, go away. Let me sleep."

"I wish I could, but if you go back to sleep, we'll miss the truck."

Stacy frowned, waking up a little more as she peered at him. "What truck? Michael, what are you *talking* about?"

"I spoke to some friends of mine last night. The CDC is going to be cleaning out the Oakland Zoo today, and I thought it would be good to go along with them. Take some pictures, document the process of reclaiming our city—and do it in a place where most of the damage will have been to nonhuman subjects."

For a moment, Stacy was silent, and Michael was afraid that he had misread the situation. Maybe the answer was keeping her far away from the zombie menace, insulating her until she could pretend that the world hadn't changed... but if the world hadn't changed, then she was a murderess, a mother who had killed her own son. He didn't think she could live with herself, in that world. No, she needed to be part of a world where what she had done was justified and right, and the only choice she could possibly have made. She needed to be part of *this* world, even if he had to drag her into it.

Then, slowly, Stacy nodded. "All right," she said. "Did you pack my camera?"

Michael smiled.

An hour later, when the CDC van pulled up at the Claremont Hotel gates, Michael and Stacy Mason were waiting outside. He had an MP3 recorder and a portable charging station, in case he wound up needing more juice. She had a camera slung around her neck, like a photojournalist getting ready to venture out into the jungle for the first time. The van's driver looked them up and down before saying something to his passenger, who nodded and opened his door, hopping out.

"Morning, folks," he said. "I'm Lieutenant Collins. Under the circumstances, and as you're outside the chain of command, you can call me 'Bernie.' I'd prefer that. It tells me that the screaming is coming from someone whose death I wouldn't have to explain to the brass. Do you understand what it is we're doing today?"

"The CDC is cleaning out the Oakland Zoo," said Michael. "We're coming with you as observers, and to document the process. The Rising is going to be our generation's defining event. We need to get as many pictures and firsthand accounts as we can."

"You need to not get your asses chewed off by a zombie bear because somebody over my head thinks you're cute," said Bernie. "If one of my people says jump, you say 'how high?' If one of my people says freeze, you stop where you are, and you do not move. If you are bitten, we will shoot you. If you are scratched, we will shoot you. If you touch a bloodstain and then touch your mouth, nose, or eyes, we will shoot you. Do I make myself clear?"

"Perfectly," said Stacy, and there was a crisp alertness in her voice that made Michael's heart sing. "Do you have Kevlar that we can borrow, or were you just planning to let us flush out the zombies with our soft, delicious bodies? We can roll with either option, but the latter gets you a slightly less positive report."

Lieutenant Collins frowned at her. Stacy smiled genially back. Finally, he looked away.

"Kevlar's in back, along with the rebreathers we'll be using in enclosed areas."

"Why?" asked Michael. "Kellis-Amberlee isn't airborne in its negative state."

"Breathing the air in a monkey house that's been closed up for three years may not kill you, but you'll sure as shit wish it had," said the lieutenant grimly. "Now, all aboard that's coming aboard. We have a lot of work to do before the sun goes down."

"Yes, sir," said Stacy. She opened the van's side door, revealing three surprised-looking CDC operatives, and climbed in. Michael was close behind her. Lieutenant Collins shut the door behind them. They heard his door shut a few seconds later. The van started, and they were off.

The main body of the van had no windows, making it impossible to see how close they were to the zoo. Michael watched Stacy instead. She chatted and politely flirted with the operatives, asking them questions they probably shouldn't answer and then charming responses out of them. It was like traveling back in time to the days when she'd done similar things at his faculty parties, only now the targets of her attention had guns instead of gradebooks. Yes. He had made the right decision. This was where she belonged now, in a setting so patently divorced from who she'd been before that she could be herself again.

The van pulled to a stop with a jerk. Stacy sat up a little straighter. "Are we here?" she asked. "Why did we stop?"

The door slid open, revealing the desolate sweep of the parking lot at the Oakland Zoo. "We're here," said Lieutenant Collins, unwittingly answering Stacy's question. "Everyone, move out, find your assigned group. Masons, you're wherever you want to be. Personally, I'd recommend wanting to be in the van for as long as possible, but as you're civilians, that's not my call."

"Damn right it's not," said Stacy. She stood, as much as the van's low ceiling allowed, and walked over to where Lieutenant Collins waited, offering him her hand. He took it automatically, and she used his arm to help herself down. Then she smiled at him, as dazzlingly as if he had been the one to offer. "Isn't this exciting?" she asked, and removed the lens cap from her camera.

Michael followed more slowly, letting the three men from the CDC get out first. He was gathering his thoughts, trying to prepare himself. He was fairly sure that wasn't possible.

He was right.

Three groups of soldiers had assembled in the zoo parking lot, each of them standing near a troop carrier. The three CDC observers had broken up and gone to their respective stations, their yellow biohazard suits standing out among the olive green. Michael raised his recorder.

"Domestic cleanup crews are in orange, zoo cleanup crew is in yellow. Are there other colors? Do they have a deeper meaning? Can the extent of local infection be ascertained by looking at the cleanup crews? Find out."

"Michael!" He lowered his recorder and turned toward the sound of his name. Stacy was waving to him from some fifteen yards away, her camera in her free hand. She looked so *natural* in her Kevlar vest and hiking boots, like this was who she'd always been intended to be. It made his heart ache a little for her. How could it have taken him so long to see her clearly? "Come see what I found!"

"Coming," he called back, and trotted over to her, feeling the disapproving eyes of Lieutenant Collins on the back of his neck as he moved. He'd have to find a way to flatter the man's ego before the end of the day, or he'd never be able to get himself and Stacy onto another cleanup job. And he already knew that he wanted to get Stacy, at the bare minimum, onto another cleanup job. She was... lighter, in a way that he hadn't seen for a very long time. It was almost like seeing his wife again.

Stacy had found a ball of garter snakes, tucked under the back wheels of an abandoned car. There must have been two or three hundred of the striped serpents there, all of them twisted together like an impossible macramé of slithering sides and flickering tongues.

"I've never seen one this big," said Stacy, and took a picture. "What do you think happened?"

"Zombies aren't particular about what they eat, but they tend to go for mammals first; the virus knows it won't gain any traction with other creatures." Thank God for that. Michael had spent half the Rising waiting for the first confirmed zombie eagle to swoop in and end what remained of the world. "Bears, coyotes—anything large enough to convert would have done a number on the small dogs and house cats. They removed most of the natural predators for these snakes, and the snakes thanked them by having a population explosion."

"The ecosystem is recovering. It's just changing at the same time." Stacy snapped a few more pictures before turning to look at the zoo gates. The CDC crews were walking toward that distant entrance, moving slowly, methodically, like they had all the time in the world. "Can we go in?"

"Yes, if we stay with the cleanup crews and don't get in the way. That's what we're here for."

Stacy's smile was sudden and electric, and took Michael's breath away. "Then let's go."

They walked back to the others side by side, catching up with the CDC's people about five yards outside the entrance. Stacy took pictures of everything: the gates, the bloodstained ticket booth, even a backpack that had somehow remained pressed up against the fence for who knows how long, bleached by the sun and battered by the rain. A piece of paper with the owner's name written on it had been wedged under a little clear plastic "window" at the top of the bag, and it was still legible, even though Molly was never going to be coming back to collect her things.

Michael glanced at Stacy anxiously when he saw her photographing the backpack, waiting for the reality of another dead child to send her crashing into a fugue state. It didn't happen. She moved straight to capturing pictures of the CDC troops as they cut the locks off the zoo gates, and he began, almost unwillingly, to relax.

The zoo was no longer a slaughterhouse—it had been too long since the initial outbreaks—but the signs remained, scribed in dried blood and bits of bone. Michael had seen enough zombie attacks to be able to read the story written in the stains. It was not a pretty one.

The three teams separated once inside, heading for different sections of the zoo. Michael hung back, waiting for Stacy to choose a direction, and then followed the group she was with, periodically raising his recorder to capture a few thoughts on the scene around them. It was eerie in its devastated stillness—not as eerie as the deserted streets of Berkeley, perhaps, but worse at the same time, because this was a setting he had never pictured in this manner. The zoo was supposed to be a place of education and joy, preserving animal life for future generations. Instead, it had become the same as everyplace else. It had become a graveyard.

They passed open-air enclosures meant to house the great herbivores, the antelope and zebras and giraffes. Some of them had been pulled apart on their artificial grasslands, bones scattered and bleaching in the sun. Others told a different story: Their bones were intact, pressed up against fences or collapsed at the bottom of protective moats. Somehow, Kellis-Amberlee had gotten to them, turning them into killers of their own kind, until starvation had finally taken over.

Birds picked through the ruined habitats, crows with their casual strut, pigeons with their bobbing heads, and more types of duck than Michael had ever seen in one place. A flash of white flew by, and a heron landed atop the desiccated corpse of a black bear. It preened the feathers of its breast before striking a classic pose, neck bent, one foot drawn up against its body. Michael heard a click as Stacy's camera went off.

"We're going to have to burn the whole place to the ground," said one of the men in green. "There's blood everywhere."

It wasn't inaccurate. The blood had dried long since, and some of it had been worn away by the wind and the weather, but the traces still remained, marking the pathways of infection. It was a striking image. Michael captured it with his recorder, describing it in careful detail.

The day unfolded from there, bitterly predictable and viciously surprising at the same time. There was movement in the monkey house: The spider monkeys had an enclosure that featured plants they had been known to eat and enjoy in the wild, and somehow two dauntless monkeys had managed to turn this into survival. There were tooth marks on the bones that littered the floor. They had eaten each other not out of virus-induced hunger, but simply because they needed to stay alive. The monkeys were skeletons clothed in fur that rushed the glass when they saw the humans, shrieking and pleading with their high-pitched simian voices. The keepers had returned. The days of peace and plenty were sure to follow.

Michael averted his eyes as the soldiers went around to the back of the enclosure and put the monkeys out of their misery. The click of Stacy's camera followed on the heels of the gunshots, punctuating the scene.

There was more motion near the reptile house. Michael watched in awe as the big alligator that had been hiding in its moat surfaced, blinked its reptilian eyes, and opened its mouth in what was either a greeting or a threat display. It was impossible to tell without getting closer, and none of them wanted to do that.

"How the fuck is that thing still alive, Lieutenant?" asked one of the men, looking shaken. "I signed up for zombies, not crocodiles."

"It's an alligator," said another man. "They're everywhere in Florida. We're pretty sure they could survive a nuclear holocaust. They might glow, but they'd still eat your cat."

"Alligators are reptiles; they can't be infected," said Michael. The big gator closed its jaws, watching them warily. It knew humans were a source of food, but maybe it also knew that humans were the reason it was here, in this cramped, stinking enclosure, instead of roaming free through the Everglades and ignoring the zombie apocalypse with the rest of its species. "Is there any way we can remove it before the zoo burns?"

"I'll put it in my report," said Lieutenant Collins. "I believe there's going to be a second team that comes through and removes anything we've flagged as salvageable. They may not have a place to keep an alligator."

Everyone was briefly quiet, looking at the big reptile wallowing in his moat. The alligator, having decided that he wasn't going to be fed, sunk back below the surface of the water.

"We really fucked everything up, didn't we?" asked Lieutenant Collins. The question didn't seem to be directed at anyone specific: It was more asked of the open air, and the silence. Michael looked at him thoughtfully, and didn't say anything.

The mission moved on.

There were more signs of life in the reptile house, although not many: Most of the snakes, lizards, and terrapins had long since surrendered to hunger and the elements. But a few had managed to survive, feeding on whatever they could find. The king cobra enclosure was smashed in. There was no dead snake inside. They left the reptile house quickly after that, all of them glancing into corners with the jittery unease of humans who had just been reminded how closely related to monkeys they were—how closely related to prey.

The last stop of the day was the zoo gift shop, which had been deemed the most likely place for infected to have taken shelter and potentially survived. It was connected to the outside; a broken window would have made it possible to den there while also leaving to hunt.

Stacy, naturally, was eager to get started. So when Lieutenant Collins barked, "Civilians outside until I give the all clear!" she sulked. Quite literally sulked, folding her arms and leaning against a clean patch of wall as she glared at the men now streaming into the gift shop.

"We should be in there," she said, looking at Michael. "They're going to knock everything over and mess everything up, and we're not going to be able to get any good pictures."

"I think they'll be more careful than that," said Michael. "Have you been able to get some good shots today?"

"Hundreds," said Stacy. She stroked her camera the way she used to stroke their son's hair. "It's amazing. Some of these pictures... I never really wanted to be a journalist, but I think I could have won a Pulitzer if I'd taken pictures like this before everything got weird."

Stacy's pictures were generally amateurish in composition and framing, more family snapshot than striking vista, but Michael nodded all the same. The subject matter transcended the technique. "I was thinking I might write an article about all this. I've been taking notes all day, and if we combine them with your pictures..."

"Who would publish it?" Stacy shook her head. "I don't think the newspaper is going to be a thing for a long time."

"Maybe not ever," said Michael. "I was thinking I could publish it myself. The Internet is getting more stable by the day, and I know how to put together a decent site. All the old blogging sites are pretty well overrun, so I'd have to do the HTML by hand until I can find a better client, but—"

"Do you think people would read it?"

"People listened to my broadcasts for all these years," said Michael. "They're more interested than anyone realizes. We all sunk into our own heads during the Rising. We had ourselves and the other survivors around us, if we were lucky. Now people want to expand again. They want to know about things they haven't seen with their own eyes."

Stacy pushed away from the wall. "Then we need to get them the full story," she said, and went striding toward the gift shop, where the shadows of the soldiers moved against the windows.

Michael hesitated. Then he followed her. If this was where she needed to lead, he would follow.

He would follow her to the ends of the earth if that was what she needed.

Chapter 2

What We Found

BlogLife is proud to announce that we will be bringing you exclusive reports from everyone's favorite duo, Michael and Stacy Mason, every Friday. You can't get this anywhere else, folks! Learn about your new and reborn world through their practiced and trustworthy eyes.

—PATRICE SUMMERS, BLOGLIFE LTD., MARCH 15, 2018

Stacy, I'm scared. I can't leave my house. I think...I think this is good-bye.

—CAROLYN SHIELDS

1.

"BlogLife just announced the partnership," said Stacy. She sounded almost pleased, almost like she thought that something mattered. "We should start getting paid by the end of the month. I'll be able to buy a new camera."

"That's excellent, sweetheart," said Michael, looking up from his laptop. He was writing an article about their recent trip to the Shattuck shopping district. It contained so many historic buildings that no one had been willing to approve its burning, especially not with all the nearby houses empty and sealed off while the city was rebuilt; instead, the contaminated parts of the district were being replaced, one at a time, a shining new neighborhood rising out of the old.

Privately, he thought it was a waste of time and money. The new normal was not going to include outdoor shopping promenades and cafés with open-air seating. The new normal needed more fences, more overt signs of security. But it was a good image, the old world being torn away and then rebuilt, just like the people of Berkeley. His article would read closer to the official story than to his actual beliefs. There was no point in upsetting people. Not now. Not when they needed comfort more than ever.

"I'm still amazed that so many people want to read these articles," said Stacy. "I mean, TV's coming back, they're even talking about reopening the movie theaters, and people are sitting at home, staring at screens full of words and pictures."

"Both the words and pictures are improving steadily," said Michael.

He had been writing academically for most of his adult life. He was learning how to inject more humor and compassion, to edit the truth when necessary to make the story more palatable for an injured but healing world. Stacy's photos were simplistically staged, but powerful all the same. How could they help being powerful, with the subject material she had to work with? And she, too, was getting better, thanks to practice and tutorials. One day, she might even be good.

"Do you think this trend is going to last?"

Michael paused, really thinking about his words before he answered. Finally, he said, "Yes, I do. The last thing the media taught us in the old world was that we couldn't trust them. If it hadn't been for me telling my students, and you e-mailing your friends, we would have lost even more people than we did. Where were the educational programs when everything was falling apart? Where was the trustworthy, mellow-voiced newscaster telling people to aim for the head? The government tried so hard to keep people from realizing what was going on that they broke everyone's trust. People want something new to trust. They're turning to the bloggers who somehow kept posting during the dark days, the ones who were in places with reliable wireless all the way to the end. They're turning to the YouTube stars. And they're turning to people like us. It's a brave new world. We're on the ground floor."

"I'd like to try video," said Stacy, and while she was trying to sound disinterested, Michael could hear the yearning in her words. "I think it would be good to show people in a little more detail what's going on. Maybe I could go for a walk around campus."

"The campus hasn't been cleared for human habitation yet."

Stacy's smile was feral. "I know," she said. "There's no telling what I might find there."

She was *doing* something. She *wanted* to do something. Michael held fast to that idea as he took a breath and said, "I'll talk to the administration and see if I can get you a spot on the next survey team."

"Thank you," said Stacy. She leaned across the couch where they had both been working all morning—the new showroom model couch they'd bought to replace the one the cleanup crew had burnt—and pressed a kiss to his cheek. Then she returned to sorting through her pictures, as if the conversation hadn't happened at all.

Michael got up to find his phone.

2.

Stacy had been allowed to accompany the survey team into the heart of the UC Berkeley campus. Michael had not. There was only room for one civilian, according to the dean who had approved his request; two would be a safety risk, both to themselves and to the team. Michael wondered if part of it might be the fact that he was still officially on the faculty, and him dying on campus would look very bad for the school when it came time to reopen. It hadn't been worth fighting. If he had pressed the issue, they might have refused to let Stacy go, and she had been buzzing with delight for days by the time the Jeep finally pulled up in front of the house and carried her away.

She had returned home muddy, bruised, and with a camera full of what she called "primo footage." She had thrust it into Michael's hands, asking him to upload the raw data onto her computer while she took a shower and doused herself in bleach. And then she had passed out on the bed, wrapped in a towel, arms splayed, like a puppet whose strings had been unexpectedly cut. With no one to tell him not to, and no previous instructions on the matter, Michael had done what came naturally:

He had settled down to watch her footage.

The videos were jerky, moving quickly with Stacy's attention. It was something like watching *The Blair Witch Project*, only shot in full daylight, and with no prankish filmmakers shaking the tents to create a sense of terror. All the fear in these images came from the knowledge that whatever was hiding in the bushes could be the last thing you ever saw. UC Berkeley had always been a green campus. Now, after three years of neglect, it was a jungle of tangled underbrush and towering trees, making it difficult to see more than ten yards in any direction.

The first five-minute clip showed them hacking their way onto campus via the entrance near the Life Sciences Building. Some students had been trapped there during the early stages of the Rising, he remembered; he had communicated with them via radio for weeks, before all transmission finally stopped. He'd tried not to think about what might have happened to them.

The second clip had been recorded inside the Life Sciences Building. Stacy's camera played unflinchingly over the scattered bones and bloodstains, answering the question of their survival once and for all. Michael winced, but didn't close his eyes. There had always been a raw power in Stacy's photographs, a necessity that transcended her often-amateurish technique. That power was present in the video, but amplified tenfold. She didn't need to compose every frame perfectly, not when they melted together to form an inescapable whole.

Stacy Mason had finally found her calling.

The videos went on. There were dozens of them, sweeping through halls and classrooms that he remembered all too well. Michael realized he was crying, and pressed on anyway. If this footage was powerful enough to make *him* cry, when he knew what was coming... "Stacy, darling, you've hit the jackpot," he murmured.

He was on the fifteenth video when the reasons for the mud on her clothes became clear. The survey team had been crossing the quad when something moved, and four infected burst out of the bushes. They were fresh, painfully so, and Michael had the presence of mind to think about writing an article on the dangers of complacency in newly repopulated zones before the infected were charging the team—before they were charging his *wife*.

The sound of automatic gunfire drifted out of the speakers, as well as the sound of moaning and shouts from the survey team. The camera focus danced back, and Michael realized that Stacy had to be running backward, trying to capture every possible moment. "Oh, God," he breathed.

He should kill the sound. He knew that. Even a recording of a zombie's moan could attract others, and he didn't know whether the neighborhood was *completely* clear. He couldn't bring himself to move. He just focused on that constantly moving image, the camera shifting, the zombies running, and Stacy—Stacy was *laughing*. Stacy was running backward while the men with guns tried to stay between her and the zombies, and she was laughing.

Then she fell.

It was abrupt, so abrupt that for a moment, he couldn't tell what had happened, just that she was shouting and the camera was rolling, literally rolling end over end. There was a splash. He realized that she had run backward straight into the narrow creek that cut across the campus, and was now lying at the bottom of it.

The camera swung around to focus on Stacy's face. She was grinning, showing the mud on her teeth. She hadn't looked so happy, so *alive*, since before Phillip was bitten. Michael's heart seemed to be caught in his throat, making it difficult to breathe.

"Wasn't that fun?" she asked the camera. "Come on. Let's go do it again."

The clip ended after she had successfully scrambled back up the creek bank to solid ground, whooped, and started trotting toward the survey team. Michael didn't press "play" on the next one. He just sat there, eyes turned toward the ceiling, and thought about what he could do to make this better. She was still in there, his Stacy; he'd just seen her, laughing at him from the video screen.

He just needed to find a way to make her stay.

3.

Stacy's videos, spliced together with a basic suite of home editing tools so that they formed three fifteen-minute "reports," were an instant hit. More than a hit: a phenomenon. They blew up the BlogLife servers twice, and were promptly mirrored all over the world. They weren't the first videos to come out of the post-Rising world, but there was something about them that caught and held the public eye.

Stacy was reading reviews three days after the videos posted when she suddenly laughed, drawing Michael's attention. "Listen to this," she said, and read, " 'It's like watching Steve Irwin's spiritual successor try to get cozy with the dead.' I think I'm flattered? I think that was intended to be flattering."

"It was," said Michael wonderingly. There it was: the missing ingredient. Stacy was having *fun*. Stacy was happiest when she was in motion, forgetting the things that had happened to them, the things that she had been forced by circumstance to do. The pain didn't come through in the videos. Only the joy, and joy was something that was in short supply these days.

"Well, then, I'll be sure to wear a khaki shirt next time I decide to go out and film myself."

That was the opening he'd been waiting for. "Actually, if you're looking for another opportunity to film—"

This time, it was Stacy's head that snapped up, her eyes widening in hopeful anticipation. "Did you find us a cleanup crew to shadow?"

"Better," he said. "There's going to be an expedition to Santa Cruz, to see how the town fared and clear out any survivors. It's virgin ground. They just reopened the highways, and there are still sincere concerns about zombie deer in the wooded areas. We'd be riding with a mixed CDC and Army detachment, and meeting up with the Coast Guard in Santa Cruz proper—unless, of course, you wanted to meet up with the Coast Guard in San Francisco, and approach Santa Cruz with *them*."

"San Francisco..." said Stacy thoughtfully. "Wouldn't that mean there would be a chance of zombie sea lions interfering with the mission?"

"Yes," said Michael.

"So it's sea lions on one end, and deer on the other." Stacy paused before asking, in a voice full of hope, "Could we ride *in* with the Coast Guard, and back with the CDC?"

Michael had been assuming that would be her answer, and had made the arrangements accordingly. Still, he smiled, and said, "I'm pretty sure that would be doable."

Stacy all but flew across the room to kiss him, and he had never been more proud of his ability to plan ahead.

That night, when she reached for him in the dark, he began to feel like this was going to work: like the path he was charting would carry them safely out of her trauma and into the warm world that was waiting on the other side. She was coming back to him, one video at a time, and as long as he could keep things moving forward, they had a chance.

The next three days passed in a rush of preparations. Stacy had to buy new batteries for her camcorder, a trip that somehow resulted in her coming home with the tiniest video camera he'd ever seen, a little square of lens and LED that clipped to the collar of her blouse and recorded the entire world in Stacy's-eye perspective. Michael had to call the appropriate authorities to confirm that they'd be allowed to both enter and leave Santa Cruz. Blood tests would be required on both ends, he was told, since they planned to be transporting survivors out of the area; everyone would need to check out as clean. Michael was fairly sure that blood tests were going to be a daily part of life before much longer, and had agreed to the stipulation without pause.

That was another report he should write, he thought; something on the efficacy and necessity of blood testing for the live Kellis-Amberlee virus. He wasn't sure he liked the idea of the government building a database of what was in his veins, but he could see the writing on the wall, and it was always best to seem like a visionary when possible. He didn't have Stacy's sheer joy at the work they were spending an increasing amount of their time doing. That meant he would need something else to sell him to the public, and integrity seemed like the best plan.

The irony of turning integrity into something he could sell had not escaped him. But Stacy *needed* this, right down to the center of her bones: she needed the cameras on her, and the excuse they offered for going out into the world and challenging it to do its worst. She was still damaged from what they'd been through—might always be damaged; Michael was no expert, but he knew how to do his research, and she was showing a lot of the signs of PTSD when the cameras weren't on. It was just that rather than flinching away from the sound of gunfire, she craved it, because when the guns were firing, she was back in the place where what she had done could be forgiven. She yearned for the simplicity of the Rising. The cameras gave her that. He didn't want to lose her. That meant he needed to find a way to stay on camera next to her.

Watching her strap on her Kevlar and check her battery packs, he rather thought that he'd move the world, if it meant he got to stay with her. If it meant he could convince her to stay with him.

There was a knock at the door. Michael stood, crossing the room and peering briefly out the peephole before he undid the dead bolt and swung the door open, revealing Lieutenant Collins. Michael raised an eyebrow.

"Are you our designated babysitter, then?" he asked.

Lieutenant Collins shrugged. "This is my territory and I don't have an issue with the two of you coming along, provided you keep making us look good. Hello, Stacy."

"Bernie!" Stacy was all smiles as she walked over to kiss the lieutenant's cheek. "How's Nathan? Has he called you?"

"He's doing well," said Bernie. He was married to a man who worked for FEMA, and was currently on assignment somewhere in central California, trying to get the country's food production back online. "He said to tell you that he really enjoyed that last cleanup report you posted. He thought I looked suitably heroic."

"Well, just let him know that if he needs more pictures of you, I'm the girl to call," said Stacy. "I have a lot more than I can use."

"You're going to regret telling me that," said Bernie. He turned to Michael, and suddenly he was Lieutenant Collins again: a subtle shift of posture that meant it was time to get down to business. "I'm going to be riding in with you on the Coast Guard vessel. Most of my team is already en route via Highway 17, but as they're expecting to encounter some difficulties, we may beat them to Santa Cruz. In the event that we do, we will be remaining on the boat until such time as they arrive and we can continue safely. Do you have any questions about what we're going to be doing today?"

"Yes," said Stacy. "I know we're looking for survivors—or you're looking for survivors, really, and we're looking for footage of you being awesome while you do it. Do you have any reason to think that we'll *find* survivors in Santa Cruz? Or is this some sort of public relations 'look, we tried' maneuver?"

"Santa Cruz was hit hard, early; we lost touch with them before we lost touch with Berkeley," said Lieutenant Collins. "To be honest, we didn't expect to find survivors *here*. The fact that we did means we can't afford to write off anyplace that isn't a smoking crater. Apart from that, Mr. Mason's little radio show got us thinking, and we started checking local bands. We've picked up a distress call out of Santa Cruz twice, both within the last three weeks. So while there are no guarantees, it seems like we have an obligation to go in."

"Is the timing in any way connected to the rumor I heard from the governor's office, about an official 'hazard zone' system being put in place?" asked Michael. "Santa Cruz sounds like it would be deemed pretty hazardous, and that might complicate further rescue missions."

"I'm not at liberty to comment on federal regulations that may or may not be in the works," said Lieutenant Collins. "We get in, we look for survivors, the two of you try not to get yourselves killed, we get out. Am I clear?"

"Perfectly," said Stacy, and smiled like it was Christmas morning.

After that, there was nothing Michael could do but go along with it.

4.

The drive to San Francisco was smooth, even pleasant. The roads had been clear for weeks, the wrecks and abandoned cars having been reclaimed by the cleanup crews. Some of them—the ones with less biological contamination—might be repaired and used as emergency vehicles. After three years sitting in the elements, often with doors and windows open, Michael doubted the numbers would be very high. The rest would be recycled, reduced to their component materials and then used to construct things that were needed more. Like blood testing units.

The thought of checking his viral load using something that had originally been a Prius was funny enough to make him snort, once. That earned him an odd look from one of the soldiers they were riding with, and he did his best not to do it again.

San Francisco was magnificent in vista without the smog of industry surrounding it. Stacy leaned out the window to take pictures of the bridge, which had been rebuilt less than a year before the Rising, and had somehow managed to endure without maintenance or repair for the duration of the crisis. It was still probably unsafe to drive there, and Michael tensed until they turned off onto solid ground.

A vessel—Michael couldn't remember if it was considered a boat or a ship when it was big enough to hold fifty men and crewed by the Coast Guard; "vessel" seemed safely generic—was waiting for them at the dock, a line of men in naval blue standing at the rail, their guns at the ready. Lieutenant Collins hopped out of the front passenger seat while the transport was still rolling to a stop. His men were close behind him, rising and filing out with the sort of practiced military precision that it was best not to get in front of. Michael and Stacy remained where they were, waiting for the crush to pass before they grabbed their gear and followed.

The wind blowing off the sea was cool, and tasted faintly of decay. Michael started toward the dock, and stopped as one of the soldiers put out an arm, blocking him.

"Sir, no sir," said the soldier. "We are to wait here until given clearance to approach."

"I just wanted to see what's making that smell," said Michael.

"Sea lions," said a woman in naval blue, strolling up to the pair. "We shot thirty yesterday, when we prepped the landing for your arrival, and another fifteen this morning. They seem to be attracted by the smell of their own dead. Poor bastards keep coming back to what they know, even though they don't belong here anymore."

Michael shuddered. "Sea lions, naturally. They used to be a tourist attraction."

"And now they're attracted to tourists, because they're hungry as hell." The woman's smile was a razor-blade slash across her raw-boned face. "There was a time when shooting these blubbery fuckers would've brought a hundred animal rights groups down on our heads, and now it's just part of the daily routine. You Mason?"

"Michael Mason, yes." He gestured to Stacy, who was about ten feet away and taking a picture of the broken pavement of the parking lot. He was sure she had a reason, something deeply symbolic that would get them another hundred readers. Honestly, as long as she was happy, he didn't care. "My wife, Stacy. We're accompanying the Santa Cruz mission for the purpose of documentation."

"Oh, I know why you're here," said the woman. "I'm Commander Huff. This is my vessel. You're going to be my guests for the duration of the trip. You will follow directions from my crew. You will not touch any part of the ship that you are not given permission to touch. You will not photograph the ship's controls. You will not photograph any crew member who does not grant you explicit permission to do so. You with me so far?"

"I am," said Michael. "I'll tell my wife. If I may ask, however, your uniform . . . is everyone on this vessel a commander?"

"Good catch," said Huff. "I was a field commission. Lots of people got turned or eaten during the Rising, and the ranks had to be filled. I'll get a pretty uniform that says 'hey, hey, the chick's in charge' to outsiders once there's time to schedule a fitting. Cool by you?"

"Absolutely," said Michael. "We are your guests."

The commander looked pleased and faintly disappointed at the same time, as if she had been looking forward to the argument she had been sure was coming. "Well, all right, then," she said. "Welcome aboard."

Commander Huff turned and walked back toward her vessel, where Lieutenant Collins was waiting. The pair saluted each other, following whatever rules of military conduct covered encounters such as this one—Michael made a mental note to do some research before he wrote up the experience—and then walked, side by side, onto the deck. The men who had come in the troop transport followed. Michael and Stacy brought up the rear, Stacy taking pictures of the approach, the water below, and yes, the piles of dead sea lions littering the shore.

Then they were all aboard, and the vessel was casting off, starting the long, cold trek toward Santa Cruz.

If he had been asked later what the best part of the day had been—sincerely asked, in private, not publicly asked by one of his fans, who got much more sanitized, less personal answers—he would have said the trip from San Francisco to Santa Cruz, with the ocean below them and the sky overhead, and nothing to force him to think about the dead. At least not until Stacy sat down next to him and started happily burbling on about how the harpoon guns were intended to be used if a zombie whale attempted to take out the vessel, and that was perfect, too, because it meant that she was just as happy as he was. They were both out in the world, both enjoying it for what it was, and they were together. This was how things should always be. He would move heaven and earth if he had to, to keep it like this.

The smell of smoke presaged their arrival in Santa Cruz. They sailed around a curve in the coastline and there it was, college town and jewel of the Pacific, burning. Not all of it: just the eucalyptus trees above one of the beaches. But they burned so bright, and with such ferocity, that for a moment Michael believed the entire city was aflame.

"We weren't planning to make land there anyway," said one of the soldiers, and another laughed nervously, while Stacy aimed her camcorder at the burning trees. There were dark specks on the beach, writhing toward the water. Seals, Michael realized, with a sort of horrified fascination. They were seals—infected seals, from the way that they were moving—fleeing from the fire.

"Commander says we're going to swing a little further up the coast, park at the marina," said another man, this one wearing blue. "Most of the boats are gone. People either tried to sail for safety, or they abandoned them and then the weather took care of the rest."

"This is so exciting," said Stacy, turning to beam at Michael.

"Yes," he said. He couldn't quite stop his stomach from churning. They were heading toward the unknown, and while this had seemed like an excellent idea when he was safe at home, it was seeming less clever by the minute. Stacy was alive here, in the field, but what about him? "Exciting."

They arrived at the marina fifteen minutes later. As the sailor had predicted, most of the boats that had once harbored there were long since gone, leaving empty, half-collapsed docks behind them. The Coast Guard vessel seemed immense when compared to those narrow wooden paths across the water. It sailed straight and true for the shore, paying no heed to the lines of the collapsed docks. Wood vanished beneath the prow, and was spat out again in the white foam of their wake.

"All right, men, listen up." Commander Huff appeared at the rail as the vessel stopped moving forward. "We can't trust the docks, so we're going ashore in the RIBs—that's 'rigid-hulled inflatable boats,' for our guests." Laughter broke out as the sailors and soldiers turned to look at Michael and Stacy. "Ten to a boat; we're sending our best gunners first, then medics, then we start going through ranks. Those of you who are not going ashore will assist with monitoring from the water. If we need to do a rapid evacuation, you *will* be the ones responsible for saving our asses, and you *will* be explaining it to the brass if we all die mysteriously. If it shambles, shoot it. I don't care what it's wearing."

Michael raised his recorder and murmured, "Note to self, report on impossibility of 'friendly fire' in a situation where loyalty changes with a single drop of blood."

Commander Huff shot him a look, apparently preparing to yell at him for defaming the military before she realized what he had actually said. Her face softened, and she nodded, once. Then she turned back to her crew.

"We will be fast. We will be stealthy. We will be without mercy to the infected, and we will be angels to the living. Are there any questions?"

"Ma'am, no, ma'am!" exclaimed the crew, in perfect, practiced unison. Michael saw Stacy's smile widen, and knew that she had managed to capture that moment on her camera, preserving it to stitch into her report. She didn't have permission; she could get it later, if the shot was iconic enough. And it would be. He had to wonder how real the moment had actually been. Commander Huff had been expecting them, after all; she would have had plenty of time to script her speech to the crew, to find the best angle to hold her head for the morning light to find her features, making her look like something out of a recruiting video.

Even as he wondered, he realized that it was all academic: He didn't really care. If Commander Huff wanted to craft her own truth, and preserve it forever on Stacy's video camera, that was between the two of them. More and more, he was coming to see the truth as a moving flag, something malleable and self-made. Outright lies were wrong—the number of deaths that could have been avoided during the Rising was a testament to that—but sometimes truth was better when it was subjective.

He would rather be a happily married man with a wife who was recovering, for instance, than whatever he would become if he stripped the little white lies and careful constructions away.

Reality was all about what you had in the camera's viewfinder when you pressed "record" and allowed everything that wasn't in the frame to be forgotten. That was what mattered. That was the truth that would be preserved.

"Mr. Mason?"

Michael didn't recognize the sailor who had materialized at his elbow. He forced himself to smile anyway, trying to look wise and professorly, when really, he was just tired.

"Sorry about that," he said. "I was just taking a moment to woolgather before we left the ship. Better to do it now than later, don't you think?"

"Yes, sir," said the sailor, who, from his expression, thought it would be better to do it never. This was a dangerous world, after all; it didn't forgive the people who stopped to stare off into space, and it wasn't likely to start anytime soon.

Michael followed the sailor to the RIB that would be transporting them to shore. Stacy was already seated, her camera aimed at the distant shoreline. He knew she had an excellent zoom function on that thing; he had looked over the specs more than once, after all. Could she already see the infected through her lens, watching them shamble around the world that had once been theirs, and was now forevermore beyond them? He wanted to ask. He didn't want to know.

"Hello, sweetheart," he said as he settled beside her. He pressed a quick kiss to her cheek. She smiled, but didn't look away from the shore.

"We're having an *adventure*," she said, not bothering to conceal her glee.

"Yes, indeed we are," he said, and the RIB dropped away from the ship, down onto the surprisingly hard surface of the sea, and it was too late to turn back, even if he'd wanted to. It had been too late to turn back for years.

5.

Santa Cruz was a city of ghosts.

The Rising had been too long to leave the buildings unscathed, and too short to have worn them fully into neglect and decay. Weather-treated flags still snapped from the tops of flagpoles; houses still wore their last coats of paint as if they hoped that maybe somehow a miracle would happen and their owners would come home. There were potholes in the roads, but the ongoing droughts had prevented them from becoming chasms. Santa Cruz had been a lovely, charming, tourist-oriented town before Kellis-Amberlee. Now it looked like a seaside dive, a place that had been largely forgotten by everyone except for its inhabitants, but which might still thrive under the right circumstances.

Nothing was thriving in Santa Cruz save for feral cats, seagulls, and the dead.

They had encountered their first zombies as they trudged up the beach toward the parking lot beyond. Three former college students had come shambling out of a copse of eucalyptus trees, their mouths slack. They hadn't started moaning yet; Michael wasn't even sure they'd had the time to realize that they were sharing their beach with the living. The sound of the waves was good cover for the sound of footsteps in the sand, and the wind was blowing out to sea. Regardless, the infected hadn't had the opportunity to sound the alarm. The soldiers had drawn silenced rifles, shooting straight and clean, and all three of the former students had crumpled to the ground.

The expedition had given the spreading red patch around the fallen zombies a wide berth. It was better to avoid hot zones whenever possible—even when walking into a zone that was much larger and more dangerous than a little blood could ever be.

The parking lot at the head of the beach was still studded with cars, all of them showing the effects of having been parked in the sea air for years. It also contained a detachment of soldiers in Army green. Commander Huff saluted. Lieutenant Collins did the same. The woman at the head of the group returned their salutes, eyes flicking across the people gathered behind them. Her eyes narrowed slightly when she saw the Masons. She dropped her hand.

"Lieutenant Lambert," she said. "Any trouble?"

"A few hostiles on the beach; nothing we couldn't handle," said Lieutenant Collins. "You?"

"We've been mowing them down like wheat since we got here," she said. "Welcome to hell."

"Any signs of the civilians we're here to recover?" asked Commander Huff.

Lieutenant Lambert fixed her with a cold eye. "I have seen nothing living that doesn't have wings or claws to defend itself. That SOS was a ghost."

"Where have you been?"

Lieutenant Lambert began running down the list of places her men had cleared, or tried to clear. They hadn't had any fatalities as yet, but part of that was on their movements: They had stuck to the outskirts, using silencers and air-propelled projectiles to cut down any hostiles they encountered. Zombies were drawn to noise. They didn't fully understand that the death of one of their own meant that there were probably living people near.

"We need to press on, toward the university," said Lieutenant Lambert. "We've just been waiting for you mooks to show up and give us the extra manpower to make it possible that we might survive."

"Wait."

It took Michael a moment to realize that Stacy had been the one to speak. Slowly, he turned to look at her. The soldiers were already staring at the civilian who had dared to open her mouth.

"Is there a problem, Ms. Mason?" asked Lieutenant Lambert. She stressed the "Ms." just hard enough to make it clear, in a single syllable, how little she approved of the civilian presence on this mission. Whether it was because she had been hoping to keep whatever glory it produced to herself or because she was genuinely concerned about their safety, Michael couldn't have said. He didn't care to speculate, either. Fear clenched his stomach, cold and cruel and unforgiving.

Please don't let them arrest us, he thought. All the ground Stacy had gained would be undone if she wound up in a jail cell: He knew that, even as he knew that their position had become suddenly precarious. One syllable and everything was changing.

"No problem, ma'am," said Stacy. Her tone was suitably deferential. The magnitude of the situation wasn't escaping her, and Michael was glad. She continued: "I just don't think pushing on toward campus will do us any good. Look, Berkeley was more urban, more defensible, and Berkeley *fell.* All the survivors were off campus, because the school itself became a killing jar. UC Santa Cruz isn't going to be any better. It's almost certainly going to be worse. If you're looking for survivors, you shouldn't be looking on campus. That's just going to rile up the locals and lose a bunch of good people in the process."

"Where do you think we should be looking?" asked Lieutenant Lambert. "My apologies for not consulting you before. I was unaware that you were a Santa Cruz native."

"I'm not," said Stacy, who was smart enough to see when she was being baited. "But I'm a faculty wife in the UC system, and more importantly, I'm a mother. We used to come out to Santa Cruz all the time. I know where there's a radio, a relatively secure facility, and a low human population. Assuming they could survive the deer, they'd be well positioned to come through the Rising alive."

"Where?" asked Commander Huff, before her counterpart could speak.

Michael wished that he were the one holding the video camera as Stacy turned to look at Commander Huff. The sun was shining behind her, catching highlights off her hair, and her expression was grave, the face of a woman who saw an impossible task ahead of her and couldn't wait to get started.

"Natural Bridges State Park," said Stacy. "They have a full ranger station there. They'd have a radio, and they would have people who knew how to use it."

Commander Huff nodded slowly. "We'll start there."

Lieutenant Lambert didn't say anything at all.

Later, Michael would remember the trip across Santa Cruz like something out of a terrible dream. The two squads had merged until he no longer knew which soldiers had been on the boat and which had been patrolling the city with Lieutenant Lambert. No vehicles were quiet enough to use without attracting the attention of the infected, and so they had traveled on foot, sticking to the outskirts, cutting down zombies whenever they appeared. The science of killing the dead had advanced since the start of the Rising. After twenty zombies had appeared and fallen, there had been no fatalities among the team members.

Michael was beginning to think that they might make it through this unscathed when they reached the mouth of the Natural Bridges State Park. It was the site of the annual monarch migration, when thousands of black-and-orange butterflies would descend from the heavens and turn the eucalyptus groves into a living cathedral of fanning wings and fluttering bodies before they continued on their way. A ranger station had been built there to monitor the butterflies. There was also a small educational center filled with souvenirs and snacks for the children. He remembered taking Phillip there once, before things had gone so terribly wrong. He had looked forward to coming back every year until his son was too old to enjoy that sort of day trip with his parents.

Phillip was gone now, and Michael was finally back at Natural Bridges. There were no zombies in evidence as the squad made its way carefully up the path leading to the educational center. The soldiers on the edges of the group watched the woods as they walked. Human zombies were less of a concern than infected animals this close to a wooded area. An infected human could do a lot of damage, but it couldn't bite through Kevlar. An infected dog, on the other hand, could potentially rip off limbs.

"Michael, look." Stacy's voice was hushed. He followed the angle of her hand as she pointed.

There was a line of Christmas lights on the roof of the educational center.

It was too high to be noticed by casually roving zombies, and there had been no indications that they were attracted by light: They weren't moths. The fact that it was still lit up meant that there was electricity inside, and more, that someone wanted people to know that they were still inside.

"I see it," said Commander Huff, and motioned for her people to split up and surround the building. Lieutenants Collins and Lambert did the same. Michael and Stacy tried to keep moving, remaining protected without interfering with the operation.

Commander Huff was the first to reach the door. She knocked twice, quick, sharp sounds. Michael winced. He winced again as she called, loudly enough to be heard by the people inside, "This is the United States Coast Guard. We understand that you folks were hoping for a rescue."

The door opened. The barrel of a shotgun appeared. All around the Masons, safeties clicked off and rifles swung up, ready to fire. The shotgun's owner remained out of sight, obscured by the wall of the educational center.

"Good tactical thinking," murmured Stacy. Michael could only nod in agreement.

"Prove it," said a high, terrified voice—the voice of a teenage girl who had been suddenly cast into an unwanted, unbearable position of authority. Assuming she wasn't alone in there, which she very well might have been. Michael tried to remember what he knew about the interior of the building: how it was laid out, how many rooms there were. Mostly what he remembered was a small kitchenette area, supplied with the sort of snacks that tired children would whine for, an assortment of teas, and a hot water canteen. Not enough to keep many people alive during a zombie apocalypse. Really, it was a miracle that it had been enough to save the girl.

Commander Huff waved for her people to lower their weapons. "My name is Fiona Huff," she said, in a voice that was softer and gentler than anything Michael had heard from her thus far. "I'm a commander with the Coast Guard, and I am very much hoping that we can find a way to get you out of there without anyone else being hurt. Now, I know that you're smart enough to know that the infected don't talk. Why don't you open that door a little wider, and you can see that I'm not injured?"

"What if you're here to raid us?"

On the word "us" Stacy glanced to Michael, her eyes wide and alight with the possibilities that had suddenly opened in front of them. Maybe the teenager had been a better protector than any of them had guessed. Maybe she still had a child or two alive in there with her, and what could have been just another tragedy was about to become a beautiful story of hope and perseverance in the face of adversity.

"I assure you, we are not here to raid you," said Commander Huff. "We are here to offer aid and get you out of this place. The choice is yours. You can open the door and find out whether I'm telling you the truth, or you can close it, and we can go."

There was a long pause, pregnant with fear and uncertainty, all of it radiating from the girl on the other side of the door. Michael couldn't imagine what she'd been through. Keeping even one child alive for three years must have been a nightmare that consumed her every waking moment, and now that rescue was at hand, it was too much for her to let herself believe.

He had experienced similar feelings when he'd watched the drab-olive troop carriers come rolling up their street, spilling out soldiers in tactical body armor, their weapons cocked and ready to put the infected down. It had been too much to believe, and so he—and all the others—had simply turned their faces away. After you'd been ground down for long enough, hope ceased to be the thing that got you through the day. Hope became the thing that got you killed.

Finally, a hand snaked around the opening in the door, just below the barrel of the shotgun, and pulled it cautiously open.

The girl on the other side was somewhere in her mid to late teens. It was difficult to say just how old, as short and skinny as she was, and Michael realized with a start that her growth would almost certainly have been stunted by three years of isolation and poor nutrition. His little enclave in suburban Berkeley had been lucky on so many levels that none of them had been in a position to recognize until it was all over... assuming it would ever really be over.

She was dark-skinned and wary, with her hair cut close to her scalp and curling softly upward in a natural puff. It was the only soft thing about her. Her clavicle showed clearly through her skin, which was stretched as tight across her skeleton as the head of a drum.

"Do you have any ID?" she asked, in a voice that was filled with cautious prayer.

Commander Huff touched the name tag on her breast. "I'm afraid I don't have my wallet with me," she said.

The girl's eyes began to fill with tears. "You really came." She lowered her gun. Then, to the surprise and confusion of the people who were watching her, she looked over Commander Huff's head to the trees, and called, "Stand down!"

A series of clicks sounded from the direction of the tangled wood behind the troops. A few of the men looked wildly around. Then one of them pointed.

"There!" he exclaimed.

Michael turned in time to see a wiry teenage boy unbuckle the belt he'd been using as a stabilizer and drop out of the trees. The boy recovered quickly from his controlled fall and ran for the educational center, weaving through the massed soldiers like they weren't even there. He slid past Commander Huff and took up a position behind the girl, watching everyone around him warily.

Two more teens appeared a few seconds later: a boy and a girl, both with short-cropped black hair and matching, rounded features. This pair stopped at the edge of the building, balancing on the balls of their feet, ready to run.

All three were carrying long-barreled rifles.

"I see you've been doing all right for yourselves," said Commander Huff. "We received your distress signals."

"All right?" said the first boy, eyes going wide. "You think we've been all right? We've been dying out here, and you didn't come. We thought you were going to come. My parents—"

He started to take a step forward. The first girl's arm across his chest stopped him where he was. "Stuart, *no*," she said firmly. "They're here now." She looked to Commander Huff. "Are you here to take us home?"

"I am here to take you someplace safe," said Commander Huff, sidestepping the question of "home." For these kids, if they were from Santa Cruz, home didn't exist anymore. Until their names and identities were confirmed, there was no way of knowing whether they had families to go back to.

"So we're done?" The girl's voice was beginning to thicken with tears. "We're finished? We're off duty, and we can go?"

Commander Huff frowned. Stacy gasped. It was a small sound, but enough to pull the attention of the group to her. Commander Huff's frown deepened.

"Ms. Mason?"

"I'm sorry, Commander, I know we're supposed to be observing, not interfering, but I couldn't—I mean, I—" Stacy took a step forward, suddenly radiating motherly concern. Her attention switched to the girl. "You don't know me, but I know this place. I brought my son here once. How many of them have you been taking care of?"

That was the trigger; that was the phrase that finally broke the girl who'd been willing to face down the Coast Guard with nothing but her shotgun and her snipers. Tears rolling down her cheeks as she silently sobbed, she pushed the door all the way open.

Michael and the others gazed in dismay at the children who were clustered behind them, their day camp counselor turned den mother. *It's like Peter Pan and Wendy,* he thought, only half nonsensically.

That night, when he was safe in his home, with the walls between him and the wolves of the world, he would sit at his keyboard and tease out that thought into the first of a series of essays on the children he called "orphans of the Rising." It was an off-the-cuff label, but it would stick, as would the images of hollow-cheeked, huge-eyed children clustered in the shadows of the educational center, waiting for the return of parents who had left them behind three years previously, and who had never made it back to them.

"Fifteen," whispered the girl, and cried, garnering surprised, concerned looks from her teenage lieutenants.

One of the children stepped forward: a little girl, no more than six years old. She looked at the guns without fear, finally focusing on Stacy, and asked, in a sweet, faintly lisping voice, "Did you bring food?"

Stacy's laughter was heavy with tears. She produced a granola bar from inside her vest, and the children—who were alive, gloriously alive—swarmed over her like the infected adults that they had been hiding from for the past three years.

6.

Fifteen children and four teenagers had been loaded onto the boat for the return ride to San Francisco. It would get them back to civilization, and to proper medical care, sooner than the caravan through the Santa Cruz Mountains. Michael and Stacy had watched as the kids were given their first-ever blood tests, the lights on the units switching one by one from red to green. It was no real surprise. Only the teens were above amplification weight, and even that was questionable: They were skin and bones and sinew, worn down by the world until there was almost nothing left.

But they had held the line. All four teens had been weeping unreservedly by the time they reached the water, so relieved by the release of their burdens that they didn't even seem to realize that they were being rescued, too. The children would survive. The four day-camp assistants who had been on duty the day that the world changed forever would be able to start the long, slow process of moving on.

"Imagine what they must have been through," said Michael, taking his seat next to Stacy on the truck that would carry them back down the mountain, out of the danger zone. Half of the troops would be staying to continue searching the city for survivors. This would be the dirty, gritty side of the job, and the fact that what they had already done was regarded as the "clean" part meant that Michael had no regrets about leaving.

"Hmm?" Stacy looked up from her camera's viewport. Footage from the educational center flickered there, bright and silent. Even though there had been no infected in the woods—something that concerned Michael a little; how had the children been able to hold the line for so long, in what should have been a perfect hunting ground?—it was still safest to review any exterior recordings with the sound off. "I'm sorry, sweetheart, I wasn't listening. Do you think I sounded maternal enough when we found out about the children? I wish you had a camera of your own. It would have been so nice to have some second-person footage to splice in."

"...that's true," said Michael, after a pause. "I was just saying that they must have been through a lot."

"I can't believe they survived. They must have been living on blackberries and frogs." At Michael's blank look, Stacy shook her head, and explained, "There's a little swamp not thirty yards away from that building. Frogs can't carry the virus. If they went hunting for amphibians, they could have kept some protein in their diets without getting sick. Protein is important for growing children. Do you think Lieutenant Collins could arrange for me to interview the counselors, once they've had time to be medically cleared? I could potentially help them find their families, by publicizing their situation..."

"Stacy." Michael put a hand on her knee. She turned to look at him, eyes wide and filled with the scars of old wounds. "I don't think we should push these kids. They've been through a lot."

"Everyone's been through a lot, Michael. If their families are still out there, there's no guarantee the government knows where they *are*. And if their families didn't make it through the Rising, a little positive media attention could make the difference between languishing in one of the facilities the state has been setting up, and finding a new home. A *real* home, with people who will love them, and take care of them, and not push them away because they're a little bit broken." Stacy's eyes had drifted back to her viewfinder while she spoke. On the tiny screen, the rescued children poured out of the educational center, throwing their arms around the legs of soldiers, stuffing their faces with whatever snacks the troops had concealed in their vests.

Sounding distant now, she said, "There are a lot of kids whose parents didn't make it through the Rising. A lot of kids who aren't ever going to get to go home. I know it seems self-serving, and maybe it is, a little bit. Maybe I can't be anything *but* self-serving anymore. And I don't care. If I can help one child—just one—find their way to a home, it'll be worth it. I'll take it."

Michael said nothing. He just squeezed her knee and settled back in his seat, watching the trees scroll by outside the window.

The wheels were already starting to turn deep in his mind, although they wouldn't reach their inevitable conclusion for some time. Perhaps it would have been better if the universe had interrupted him; perhaps it would have been kinder if he'd been jarred from his contemplation by an infected deer bounding from the shadows, or a tire going flat. But none of that happened.

The cars rolled on, and Michael Mason thought about the future.

Chapter 3

What We Gave Away

I have found the Masons to be trustworthy, reliable, and eager to carve out a place in our changed and changing world. Given their history, I still cannot endorse this course of action. I do not believe it will be healthy for any of the parties involved.

—Lieutenant Bernard Collins, August 6, 2018

We were only supposed to be in charge for a little while. There were adults in the beginning. They went to get help. They never came back.

—Smita Gupta

1.

"Did you get the viewership numbers for the weekend?" Stacy didn't look up from her tablet. She was stirring something on the stove, something red and sticky that smelled like spaghetti sauce and herbs, and Michael was struck all over again by how beautiful she was. How beautiful, and how fragile, for all that she was the stronger of the pair of them. He was just better at keeping her from seeing where the breaks were.

Maybe that was what marriage was really all about, he mused, as he walked over to the island at the center of the kitchen and set down his computer. It was about being able to break in different ways, so that someone was always covering the weak spots. She had covered for him during the Rising. He was happy to cover for her now. No, not happy—honored. It meant she still needed him.

"I haven't had time," he said.

Stacy looked up from her sauce, a line forming between her eyebrows as she looked at him in confusion. "What do you mean, you haven't had time?" she asked. "I know you weren't on campus all morning. I got the alert when you passed through security."

"That's the stupidest of the many stupid security systems I've seen recently," he said. "How are people supposed to react to e-mail telling them that so-and-so has just cleared a blood test, when they're getting that e-mail six and eight times a day? It becomes white noise. White noise is how things get missed."

"You should do a report on that, and tell your wife what you meant by 'I haven't had time,'" said Stacy firmly. She was like a dog with a bone sometimes. It was what made her such a good... whatever it was that they were becoming. Some people had started calling them "journalists." They were even getting imitators, as their videos and articles spread wider and wider. It felt good. If people were copying you, that meant that you were doing something right.

"I'm sorry, dear," he said, apologetically enough that Stacy's shoulders unlocked a bit. "I've been talking to Lieutenant Collins."

Now her demeanor changed completely, becoming sunny and open. It was like looking back in time to the woman she'd been before the Rising, and he wanted nothing more in the world than to make her stay like this. "How is Bernie? What's he been up to?"

"He's been running rescue and recovery missions all up and down the coast. Lots of children hiding out in attics and basements. They even got a couple off of a yacht anchored in the middle of a reservoir. No one's sure how those kids survived. He says it would be a miracle, if they weren't all being loaded into a system that's already overtaxed to the point of breaking down. As it stands, it's just one more tragedy." Michael looked at her levelly, hoping she would come to the conclusion he was trying so hard to lead her to. "They're opening an orphanage just up the highway, in Sacramento."

"Didn't they already open one in Dublin last week?" asked Stacy.

Michael nodded. "Lots of kids, Stace. Lots of parents who didn't come home after they locked the doors."

Stacy's smile faded, replaced by a sad, stricken look. She leaned back against the counter. "Those poor kids," she said. "I always thought... I thought we were going to be a world of parents in mourning. Not a world of orphans."

"They're expanding the foster care system. Loosening the background check requirements—not that we could have performed them with any accuracy. Too many records got deleted during the early days, when online activist groups decided to 'balance the scales' by wiping out people's prison records." Prison records, and the sex offenders registry, and a remarkable number of bank accounts, since apparently "balancing the scales" also meant "lining your pockets in whatever ways you possibly can."

A lot of the records that had been lost had been related to small things, unfair things, like felony convictions for marijuana possession, or disproportionate jail terms that had been summarily canceled when the prisons began burning down. But there were still killers, and rapists, and hardened criminals now walking the world with no records to tie them to their past lives, and not all of them were going to take this second chance as a reason to change their ways.

"Oh," said Stacy softly.

"Lieutenant Collins has agreed to let us come and do a feature on the orphanages. I reminded him of what you did for those kids from Santa Cruz. They all have homes now, you know." All but two had been orphans, as it turned out: Their parents were buried in unmarked graves, or still shambling with the infected in the forests and deserted streets of Santa Cruz and Gilroy. But there had been people who were willing to open their homes after they saw those children's faces.

Maybe it could be done again, on a slightly wider scale. Stranger things had happened, after all, in a world where the supposedly dead could get up and walk.

"That's very kind of him," said Stacy. Her voice had taken on that distant, almost mechanical tone that meant that she was thinking.

Hopefully, she was thinking the same things he was—or would be able to adjust her thinking once she saw the children. "It would be a day at each facility, with travel passes to allow us to drive ourselves, and then a third day for any follow-up interviews or footage we felt we needed. What do you say, Stacy? Want to help some kids?"

Stacy looked at her husband, struggling not to frown. He would take it as a rejection of him, and his idea: She'd been married to the man long enough to know that, just like she knew that he had some ulterior motive for arranging this story. Maybe it was about their ratings. The folks at BlogLife were still trying to figure out how to measure traffic and merchandise sales in a single quantifiable way, and she lived in constant fear that they would refine their math only to decide that the Masons weren't worth the cost of their insurance.

She didn't know what she would do if someone took her camera away from her. It was still a relatively new part of her life, and yet she increasingly felt naked and isolated without it in her hands. She needed the news, the sensationalism and spectacle of it all, to keep herself from losing her grasp on the world.

"Do you think it would be good for ratings?" she asked, finally.

Michael nodded.

"All right." Stacy took a deep breath before forcing a smile. "Let's help some orphans."

2.

Dublin was the closer of the two centers, being only about an hour up the road. It would have been a longer drive once, before the state increased the speed limits on the highways and cracked down on the need for travel permits outside the cities. Michael kept his hands on the wheel and raced down the road, trying to pretend that the armored cars parked every two miles or so weren't intimidating, and that he wasn't afraid of the potential that something might shamble out of the ruins of Lafayette or Moraga and fill its stomach with his flesh.

Stacy squealed like a much younger woman and pointed out the window, calling, "Michael, look! Wild turkeys! A whole flock of them! They must be having an amazing surge in their population, with the reduction in traffic."

"And coyotes," he said. "Not so many of those around these days." The interchange for Walnut Creek was coming up ahead. Once there, they would go through a military checkpoint that would test their blood and review their travel passes. Michael was almost looking forward to that. He hadn't been through a checkpoint without Lieutenant Collins in weeks, and it would be nice to see how the current security procedures were applied to the common traveler.

"Do you think the ecosystem will recover from losing the big predators?"

"I think we've introduced something new and much larger to take their place," said Michael. "Infected dogs, bears, even people—they'll all be happy to play the role the coyotes have played until now. The feral cat population is exploding in some places."

Stacy, who had encountered the sharp end of more than a few formerly pampered felines, grimaced. "You don't have to remind me," she said. "I never knew Persians could be so vicious."

"We never domesticated the cat. We just convinced it to stop attacking us when we started feeding it regularly," said Michael. "We stopped feeding the cats, they stopped keeping up their side of the bargain."

"I never want another pet," said Stacy.

Michael said nothing.

They passed through the security checkpoint with a minimum of trouble. The guards on duty didn't even question why Stacy was filming them the whole time, allowing Michael to do the majority of the talking. Recording the police had been legal since well before the release of Kellis-Amberlee, and everyone had their own way of coping with the ways in which the world had changed. A video camera and a little silence was nothing compared to some of the things Michael had seen since the Rising.

They were passing the Dublin city limits when Stacy said, very softly, "I feel like this is some sort of ploy on your part, and I don't really know what it is. Are you hoping to make me see that we're better off without kids to hold us back?"

Michael nearly lost control of the car. If there had been anyone else on the road, he would probably have caused an accident; as it was, he looked around frantically once he had them back in their own lane, waiting for a police car to come zooming out of nowhere and demand a second blood test. Loss of motor control was an early sign of conversion. When no such interception appeared, he reduced speed and pulled over, leaving the hazard lights flashing like a bloody reminder that there were people here, living people; don't shoot, don't stop, just drive on by. The age of the Good Samaritan was, at long last, most conclusively over.

"I would never try to make you see that, because it's not true," he said at last, twisting in his seat to face his wife. She was still so beautiful, but it had never just been about her beauty; beauty faded, tarnished, *changed* based on what happened around it. It had always been about the person behind the beauty, the smiling, laughing, brilliant woman who had somehow been tricked into marrying him. He could see her still, a little frayed around the edges, a little damaged, but present and aware and not too far away from him. Not yet.

Stacy looked at him gravely. He leaned over and grabbed her free hand in his, and she didn't pull away. She didn't put down the camera, either. He honestly couldn't have said whether or not that was a good thing.

"I miss him every day, Stacy; *every day.* I keep expecting him to come barreling around a corner, shouting about the monsters under his bed and how much he wants to go to the park. He was our *son*, Stacy. Our *son*." The depth of longing in the word surprised even Michael. It hung between them like a stone dropped into thick tar, not falling, not fading, but preserved and terrible, forever.

"So what are we doing here?" asked Stacy. "What's your game?"

"It's not a game," said Michael. "It's our life. In Santa Cruz, when you saw those kids, and after, when you were interviewing them—it was like you were awake again. Your camera brought you halfway back to me. Those children brought you the rest of the way." She'd been so animated, so alert, so *Stacy*—it had been like looking back through time to a moment before the Rising, when he had believed that the world could be fair.

Stacy's eyes widened as his meaning sunk in. Then, violently, she began to shake her head.

"No," she said. "No, Michael, no, you can't be serious. You can't *mean* that. I'm in no condition to take care of a child. I've been a mother once. I'm never going to be a mother again. You know that."

"Maybe these children don't need a mother," said Michael. "Maybe they just need an adult who'll care enough to teach them how to stay alive. The orphanages are overloaded, and getting worse every day. Can you honestly say that being with us would be worse than being part of a system that doesn't even know how it operates yet?"

"Yes," whispered Stacy. "Yes, I can."

Michael sighed. "Sweetheart, I promise you, we are not going to do *anything* that you don't want to do. I haven't committed us to anything. This is the sort of decision that everyone needs to have a say in. You, me—"

"And the child," said Stacy. "How would we tell a kid that they were living with a murderess? It's better if we don't have to."

"You're not a murderess," said Michael. "The courts cleared you."

That was the wrong thing to say. Stacy's expression twisted, crumpling in on itself, until she finally looked away from him, choosing to look instead at the camera in her hands. She turned it over once, until she was facing the lens: a confessional, a moment taken in isolation and held up as the whole of the situation.

"The courts can clear me a hundred times, if they want to," she said. There was a light, almost reflective quality to her voice. "It doesn't matter. They can't force me to clear myself. That's what would need to happen before it would mean anything. And I know what I did, Michael. I held the gun. I pulled the trigger. I watched my little boy die, and I didn't even... I couldn't even hold him. I wrapped his body in plastic, and I didn't kiss him good night, and I didn't tuck him in. I buried him like he was *garbage*." Her lip twisted as she spat the last word into the car, condemning herself with her own voice.

"You saved the people who were depending on you," said Michael. "Stacy... you love the documentation of the world as it is, but you've never cared about the science. That's always been my job. Don't you think I read all the studies I could get my hands on, the second that the CDC declassified them? Don't you think I've been following all the research, private and public and fringe? Phillip was *gone*. He was gone the second that damn dog bit him. You didn't kill our son. You set him free."

Stacy turned away from her camera and stared, instead, at her husband. Michael nodded very slightly.

Stacy dropped the camera.

No police came along as the two of them clung to each other and sobbed. That was for the best. Michael wasn't sure how he would have explained the situation, or even whether he would have been able to find words. In that moment, in that time, there was nothing but Stacy's arms around him, and the tears burning down his cheeks, cleansing and confining them both forevermore.

3.

The orphanage system was still too new to be keeping very precise time. The Masons pulled up in front of the old office park gates thirty minutes after their appointment, only to be waved through by the haggard-looking guards after a quick, perfunctory blood test. Stacy, who was still trying to repair the damage her tears had done to her makeup, barely noticed.

Michael parked in front of the main office—a small, dismayingly glass-fronted structure that had once been the business park's convenience store, judging by the ghosts of old signage that clung to the stonework like pale reminders of a world now gone and buried. A cursory effort had been made to shore up the glass, making it more difficult for an infected hand to burst through, but in the end, it was just that: cursory. The small, poorly defended building wouldn't last twenty minutes in a real outbreak. The only surprising thing about it was that all the glass appeared to be pre-Rising, having somehow come through the tragedy intact.

There was a single woman sitting inside, bent over her computer and typing with anxious rapidity. Stacy paused long enough to take a few seconds of footage, showing the woman through the glass as if to punctuate just how dangerous the whole setup was. Then she pushed the door open.

A bell rang. Not looking up, the woman said, "There was no one here during the Rising. The owners were smart enough to run while the running was good. We actually managed to track them down and pay them for the building, believe it or not. And zombies are stupid. They didn't think to break the glass when there wasn't anything inside that they wanted." She finally raised her head, offering us a wan smile. "You must be Stacy and Michael Mason. Welcome to the East Bay Children's Center."

She had smooth, medium brown skin, with a spray of freckles across her nose, and a blue streak had been dyed down the right side of her naturally dark hair. Michael placed her accent as Southern California, and her ancestry as a mix of European and Chinese. All useless information now, when all anyone could ever really say they had come from was "before." Before the dead rose; before half the world was devoured. Everything else seemed a little less important than it would have been, once upon a time.

"Director Song?" asked Michael.

The woman nodded. "No one else would sit here, believe me. You can call me Edie. Please, come in, sit down, try to pretend that you're not surrounded by towering piles of paperwork that may collapse and bury us all forever."

"I thought most offices were paperless," said Stacy. She looked at the papers around her, not disapprovingly, but with the sort of vague confusion that she sometimes got when things refused to add up. "Why so many files?"

"Is that thing on?" Edie gestured toward the camera. When Stacy nodded, she said, "Go ahead and start shooting. I only want to explain this once, if I get a vote."

Stacy frowned but raised the camera, tinkering with the focus until she had just the angle she wanted. Then she said, a little more slowly and a little more clearly, "With the push toward greener business and reducing waste, why are there so many paper files here? Are you trying to save money on insulation?"

"Well, you may not have been aware, but there's been a lot of pulling back on the 'Green California' initiative since the zombie apocalypse," said Edie. She sounded perfectly cheerful, like this was the only logical consequence. "Something about how we'd reduced greenhouse gas emissions by dying in droves. Anyway..." She sobered. It was an artful transformation. Michael began to realize that her appointment to the job might have been about more than her failure to run away fast enough.

In times like this, sometimes what you needed more than someone who knew how to do the job was someone who knew how to sell it. Edie leaned forward, resting her hands on the desk. In that moment, she transformed herself from a slightly dizzy woman who looked just like the interchangeable TAs who had once thronged in the halls of UC Berkeley into a serious, trustworthy administrator. The sort of person who could be trusted to want what was best for the children under her care, no matter how many of them there were.

"Because of the way the children come to us—found in abandoned buildings, trapped in shopping malls—it's not always possible to know for sure what their status is. In order to verify that they are orphans and wards of the state, not just misplaced, we have to find everything we can about them. What you see here is all the documentation that we have been able to dig up on our kids. Birth certificates. Medical records. School files. We don't have all the material we want on all of them, but we have enough on many of them to conclusively link them to their families."

"How many of the children you have here have been confirmed as orphans of the Rising?" Stacy's question was calm. The phrase that Michael had coined and that had gained so quickly in popularity sounded only natural tripping off her tongue, especially here, in this little, glass-walled chamber packed with the last notes of a lost world.

Edie looked at her levelly. "There are four hundred and seventeen children in this facility alone, ranging in age from somewhere under a year to fifteen years of age. Children aged sixteen and up have been emancipated as a matter of necessity. We just don't have the space to keep them."

"That wasn't—" began Stacy.

Edie kept on talking. "Of those four hundred and seventeen children, we have been able to find files confirming the identities of approximately two hundred and nine. Technically, that puts us one child over fifty percent. And all two hundred and nine of those children are unquestionably orphans. We have confirmed the death of one or both parents. In the cases where only one parent's death could be confirmed, we have found sufficient evidence to show that the missing parent was eaten, frequently by the one we *could* find. As of the emergency session of the United States Congress which concluded last week, in cases where one parent is dead and the other is missing, all parental rights will be voided following our investigation, rendering any and all adoptions fully legal."

"Don't you think that's a little harsh?" asked Michael. "Some people may still be in hiding, or trapped in infection zones."

"That's possible, yes," said Edie. "It's also staggeringly unlikely. I have over four hundred children here. Children in need of homes. Children who cannot stay in this facility forever. We're not trying to create a Dickensian horror using American kids as the plucky orphans. We want these children to find homes and families, families who will help them through the trauma of surviving a *zombie apocalypse*. If that means we remove a few people's parental rights, that's a price that we're willing to pay."

"Would the parents be willing to pay it?" asked Stacy.

Edie sighed. "Honestly, I think most of them already have. If you've been separated from your children, under circumstances like these, you're not going to think that they're still out there waiting for you. We've found at least three people who, when offered the chance to be reunited with their children, replied, 'My child is dead' and shut the door. People are moving on. People are trying to put the Rising behind them. They want it not to have happened. Part of that is burying the dead. Part of that is letting what's gone stay gone."

Michael glanced at Stacy, afraid of what he might see reflected in her face. His breath caught in his throat, choking and collaring him.

All he saw in her eyes was longing.

Edie's smile was as sudden as a winter sunrise, and twice as filled with shadows. "Our kids are happy, healthy, and have no strings attached. The choice to rescind the rights of any surviving parents was made as much for the protection of the children as anyone else. We're not going to have a bunch of people come sashaying in saying, 'Right, thanks for dealing with the nightmares and the trauma and the therapy bills and the malnutrition and the neglect, we'll have our kids back now, and if you try to say no, we'll sue.' These kids need stability. They need to know that the people they go to sleep loving will still be there when they wake up in the morning. If that means 'finders keepers, losers weepers' is suddenly a phrase that can be applied to children, well. I'll be more than happy to let that be my legacy. It's better than any of the other options on the table."

Edie Song had survived the Rising, just like everyone else who still counted themselves among the living. She seemed friendly enough—amiable even, the sort of woman who couldn't possibly have cut her way out of a horde of the infected during the worst of the conflicts. Some people had been lucky: They had been able to make it to government safe houses or private compounds before things got bad, and had weathered the Rising in relative peace and safety. But there was something in the way she smiled that made Michael suspect that her story hadn't been that straightforward, or that kind.

"Can we see the children?" Stacy's voice was soft, and filled with a plea that Michael couldn't quite identify. Was she hoping for a yes, or for a no?

This time, Edie's smile had no shadows in it at all.

4.

The security separating the administrative office from the main orphanage was top-notch, as befitted a state-sponsored facility. Michael studied the blood test panels—state-of-the-art, fresh off the assembly lines in Silicon Valley, where the computer assembly rooms had found themselves quickly converted for medical equipment manufacture—and the men who stood near them, guns at the ready. It was all very impressive, there was no question about that.

But there *were* questions that needed to be asked. Questions like "Who will pay for the upgrades, when this is no longer the best we have to offer?" and "How long will these children stay in the public eye, rather than becoming one more thing we don't want to talk about?" The human race had paid a great deal to survive through the dark days of the Rising. A few children wouldn't be that much more to lose.

We can't let that happen, he thought, as he pressed his hand against a flat-screen panel, and felt the needle bite into his palm. *Whatever it takes, we can't let that happen.*

The light flashed green, and the final door unlocked. Together, the three of them stepped into what had once been a telephone company's regional office, and was now the home of over four hundred wards of the state of California.

The walls had been painted a cheery shade of green, shading to blue toward the tops. The floor—originally industrial tile, if the rest of the architecture was an accurate gauge—was covered in a cheery yellow carpet. It was surprisingly pristine. Edie saw Michael squinting at it, and grinned.

"Stain-resistant, water-resistant, even flame-resistant. You could set this carpet on fire and it would blow itself out in a matter of seconds. It was judged too expensive for the post-Rising home owner, and so the company that makes it donated it to us as a sort of 'here you go, please give us some good publicity' move," she said.

"I want some," said Stacy.

"I can give you their card." Edie continued across the lobby, heading for the elevators. As she walked, she gestured to the overstuffed couches and armchairs that filled the right half of the echoing room. "This is our visiting section. When people have come to consider a specific child for fosterage or adoption, but aren't quite ready to commit, we set up the meetings here."

"Supervision?" ventured Stacy.

Edie sobered. "Controlling their hopes. The children, I mean, not the prospective parents. These are kids who've already seen more than their fair share. They've lost their birth families. Some of them had to put down parents or older siblings during the bad days. We have children who have no interest in being adopted, ever, because this is the first stable home they've had since the dead began to walk. We have others who want out of here desperately, because they can't even pretend that the world is back to normal until they have beds and houses of their own. This place isn't perfect—not by a long shot. We have problems with the older children picking on the younger ones when no one's looking, and with behavioral issues that could be handled just fine one on one, but which become difficult to treat and manage in an institutional setting.

And then we have the adults who stroll in here, and say they want to see the kids, but what they really want is to reassure themselves that they're making the right choice by not being in charge of another living thing."

They had reached the elevators. Edie pressed the call button with a quick, vicious jab of her finger. The motion was so angry, so filled with futile rage, that it said more about the situation than any number of pre-rehearsed speeches. Michael glanced to Stacy, who nodded quickly. She'd been filming. She was still filming.

"I saw your reports on the situation in Santa Cruz," said Edie, more quietly, like she was rethinking the wisdom of her words even as she spoke them. "That was some good work. We've had three successful adoptions that we can trace back to your site. Everyone calls these kids 'orphans of the Rising' now. Having a label like that to hang on them... it's helping. It humanizes them, and that can make all the difference in the world. That's part of why you have the access you do. I just have one request."

"What's that?" asked Stacy.

"Don't toy with them. Don't make promises you can't keep. Don't pretend that you're considering an adoption if you're not. These are *children*. They need homes. They need families. They need to wake up every morning knowing that the people around them will still be there when the sun goes down." Edie shook her head at the stunned expressions that both their faces now wore. "I have eyes. I saw the way you looked at the kids on that video, and I know about your backgrounds. Did you really think I wouldn't have pulled your records before I allowed you to come here? Hell, your Wikipedia pages mention that you lost a child during the Rising. I can understand why you'd consider opening your home to a new one. I can also understand why you would decide that you couldn't stand it. All I am asking is that you not make any promises that you're not intending to keep. Can you do that for me? Can you do that for the kids?"

"I can," said Stacy.

Edie looked to Michael. He nodded. She smiled.

"Good," she said. The elevator doors swung open behind her, and she gestured for them both to step inside, already talking again, already back in her comfortable administrator's voice. "The elevator is state-of-the-art, with an optional blood testing panel in the wall. Adults who show any signs of disorientation or discomfort can be required to confirm their infection status before they're allowed to disembark. A staff member is always present when the elevators are in use, which helps. Anyone who does not follow staff instructions regarding blood tests and health concerns will be immediately removed from the premises."

"What about children large enough to amplify?" asked Michael. "Are they subject to the same restrictions?"

"Children of amplification weight and above have separate living quarters, and are encouraged to submit to voluntary blood tests multiple times per day," said Edie. "Many of them are on the 'do not seek adoption' list—they're close enough to adulthood that this is more of a way station than a permanent stop. We're focusing our permanent placement efforts on children ages eight and below."

Michael, who knew how difficult it had been to find homes for teenagers before the Rising, said nothing. Whatever sacrifices were being made, they had already been considered, at length, by people with more information than he had available to him. He could research the subject of teen adoptions post-Kellis-Amberlee when he was safe at home, and no longer needed to worry about ruining the narrative line of Stacy's video.

"Will we meet any of the older children?" asked Stacy.

"Only if they agree to see you," said Edie. "Because most of them have removed themselves from consideration for placement, they're no longer required to speak with adults who are not employees of the orphanage, from the government, or involved with their academic assessments. The state has granted free admission to the UC system for all of our older kids. They'll have a chance to make a life for themselves. Some of them will probably do better than the adults who are meant to be taking care of them. They won't have as much to mourn."

"No one came through the Rising unscathed," said Stacy.

The elevator beeped as they reached their destination. Edie shot her a sympathetic look before stepping through the slowly opening doors. "No. No one did."

If the lobby had been changed, the upper floors—once the purview of cubicle farms and endless meetings in glass-walled rooms—had been totally transformed. Some of the cube walls were still there, reconfigured into cubbies and private rooms along the far wall, but most were gone, replaced by tables, beanbag chairs, and freestanding shelves heavy with books and toys. Many of them looked secondhand, but that actually added to the homey atmosphere the space was trying so hard to project. "You can be safe here," said the space, and "you can be at home here," said the space, and most of all, "you can stay here for as long as you need to." Whether this was home or just a stopping point, it was safe and clean and familiar. It would do.

Four hundred children had seemed like a great number, disclosed in a glass-walled office barely big enough to hold three adults without becoming cramped. In this vast, open office, it became negligible. When all the other floors in use by the orphanage were factored in, it was suddenly understandable that Michael could count no more than forty children as he looked around the room. They were seated on beanbags or on the floor; they were standing frozen next to bookshelves and toy boxes, their hands full of whatever prizes they had been moving to claim when the elevator doors slid open. His first, dizzying thought was that all the children who had survived the Rising had somehow done it by transforming themselves into wild deer. They still *looked* human, but they were completely motionless, barely even breathing as they stared at the predators in their midst.

Then Edie stepped forward, and smiled—a new smile, a reassuring smile, the kind that a shepherd might use to reassure the flock—before she said, "Everyone, I'd like you to meet Stacy and Michael Mason. They're the ones who took all those recordings in Santa Cruz, and helped the children from the butterfly shack. They'd like to talk to you about what it's like here."

The words "Santa Cruz" seemed to break whatever spell the children had cast upon themselves. They were suddenly in motion, half swarming toward the adults while the other half hung back, creeping close enough to listen without coming near enough to put themselves in danger.

"—went to Santa Cruz? Mandy said those videos were faked—"

"—went to the Boardwalk with my parents when I was eight, I ate six hot dogs—"

"—you see any banana slugs? They're super yellow, I think they're really cool—"

"Did you see my mommy?"

The question scythed through all the noise around it, startling the other children into silence. One by one, they stepped aside, until a little girl of no more than five was looking calmly and clearly at the Masons.

She was only a baby when this started; she probably doesn't remember a world before the Rising, thought Stacy, her stomach giving a sickening lurch as the implications struck home.

Oh dear God, thought Michael.

Stacy recovered first. She knelt down a little, putting herself closer to the girl's eye level, and said, "I'm sorry, honey. We didn't see any adults while we were there." Not uninfected ones, anyway. All the adults in Santa Cruz had long since fallen prey to Kellis-Amberlee, and would not be kissing any boo-boos or making any beds. Never again.

The little girl looked at Stacy solemnly. "Did you look?"

"We did look, yes. We looked in as many places as we could, and the soldiers who were there with us looked in even more. We didn't find your mommy. I'm sorry."

The little girl nodded. "Okay. Thank you for looking."

Edie's hand fell on Stacy's shoulder like a great weight. Stacy looked up. Edie was stone-faced, more statue than woman. "I promise, Chrissy, you'll know as soon as we know anything about your mommy. But you promised me to stop asking our guests, remember?"

"I remember," said Chrissy, without a trace of shame. "You didn't say the promise would mean people who'd been to Santa Cruz. That's where my mommy was when she stopped answering her phone. You didn't say, and so I didn't know."

"You know now," said Edie.

"I do," agreed Chrissy.

Stacy stood. "I don't mind," she said.

"That's very kind of you," replied Edie. She looked at the children, and then back to the Masons. "This is our midrange group. None of them have reached amplification weight as yet, and they're all old enough to manage with minimal supervision when not in class. We have six teachers visiting the center, and we're hoping to add four more, just to keep class and study group sizes down. Most of our children are reading at or above their age level. The next floor up is for our older children, and above them, you'll find our youngest residents. Most of them are under the age of two, although we have a few three year olds who have yet to be socialized into the wider population."

It was efficient; it was effective; for all the warmth and comfort that

Edie and her staff were so clearly struggling to provide, it felt disturbingly industrial to Michael. "We'd like to see the whole facility," he said.

Edie smiled. "Right this way."

5.

The orphanage complex in Sacramento was built inside a refurbished arcade-style strip mall, with gates and razor wire blocking the entrances. It was a necessary adaptation to such an open-air facility, but it still lent the entire place an air of military grimness that struck Michael as excessive and Stacy as aesthetically distasteful. The children there were kept in the same three age groups as the children in Dublin. The oldest children were already looking into military service as a way to practical experience, medical school, and eventual enrollment with the CDC. The youngest children cooed and waved their hands in the ways of babies since the beginning of time, unaware that they were the last sons and daughters of an old world, or that they would grow up to become part of something new.

The administrator in Sacramento was a nervous-looking man named Roy who didn't seem to enjoy the position, or being anywhere near the children, even the ones who were far too small to amplify. But he knew all the guards by name, and he could tell at a glance whether the throngs of orphans that waited around every corner were complete. If there was one child missing, he knew, and would go looking. He'd been given the job for a reason, and he did it well. That didn't stop the Masons from walking away from Sacramento feeling like it could use a hand from the team that was running Dublin—but then, they were such different facilities. Who could say whether the techniques that worked at one would work at the other?

And then there was the reality of the situation to be considered. This was only the beginning: This was the shallow end of the curve. Most of the orphans of the Rising hadn't been recovered yet, and many of the ones who had were undergoing medical treatment, or waiting for their parents to be verified as dead. There would be more orphanages before any of them were closed. Many, many more.

Michael and Stacy sat in their living room, their laptops propped against their respective knees, looking at the footage she'd taken. Footage of children asking about the size of their houses and the number of guns they owned in the same sentence; footage of older children demonstrating the technique for field-stripping a rifle, sleeping with shotguns next to their beds like those were the talismans that would keep them from conversion. Michael was focusing on the interviews. Stacy was focusing on the accounts of their survival—or she was supposed to be, anyway.

The footage on her screen, looping over and over again, showed a roomful of toddlers and small babies, all of them sleeping under the soft naptime lights. Her fingers brushed a corner, touching the virtual hair of a little girl.

Michael took off his headphones, and waited.

He didn't have to wait for long.

"Yes," said Stacy. Her voice was thick with tears, heavy with regret, cold with shadows: It was a voice issuing from the unmarked grave of the woman she had been, and it drew a line of fear down her husband's spine. There were implications in that voice, dark, terrible implications, things that would never stand the light of day.

He knew, even before he spoke, that this was his once chance to stop what he had put into motion. A hint of disapproval, and she would bury that poor, sad woman again, this time forever. She would learn how to be the new Stacy, and she would do it without wearing her ghosts around her shoulders.

But he loved those ghosts. He loved her. In the end, that was all that truly mattered. "Yes, what?"

"Yes, you're right. We should adopt." Stacy smiled. Only for a moment. Then the expression faded into something more calculating—something that was sadly more familiar, since the Rising. "Boy or girl, do you think? A boy might be seen as an attempt to replace Phillip, and we're not doing that. But I don't know how to raise a little girl."

"We could get one of each," said Michael.

Stacy smiled again.

Chapter 4

What We Stole

Thank you for coming back. I promise you, you won't be sorry.

—Edie Song, Director of the East Bay Children's Center, August 7, 2018

You're doing a very good thing. You're heroes today. Don't forget that.

—Roy Baxter, Director of the Sacramento Children's Center, August 7, 2018

1.

The crowd outside the Berkeley courthouse was becoming restless. It was barely a crowd, really—eight reporters, each with a handheld recorder, and a few armed guards. It was enough.

"How's my hair?" asked Stacy. She lifted the towheaded toddler on her hip a little higher, surprising him into opening his eyes and giving her a suspicious look. She patted his head with her free hand.

"Perfect," said Michael. His own arms were full of a second toddler, this one dark-haired and clinging to his neck like she was afraid that he was going to disappear. "Are you ready?"

"The adoption's final," said Stacy. "Let's go."

Michael nodded to the guard, who pushed the door open and allowed the new family to step out into the bright light of morning. Stacy was instantly all smiles, even as the toddler in her arms eyed the shouting reporters with suspicion and dislike.

"Ms. Mason!" shouted a young blogger with a camera that probably cost more than his family's first car. "What are their names?"

"Well, Nicholas, this is Shaun," said Stacy.

"And this little bundle of shyness and sunshine is Georgia," said Michael. "Everyone, we'd like you to meet our new family."

The reporters closed in, asking questions and taking pictures, and all the while, serene as the morning, Stacy smiled.

Michael watched her out of the corner of his eye, and wondered whether he had made a mistake. Too late now: The cards were dealt.

They were going to have to play them.

Hush-a-bye, don't you cry, go to sleep, you little baby.
When you wake you shall have all the pretty little horses
Dapples and grays, pintos and bays,
All the pretty little horses.

Hush-a-bye, don't you cry, go to sleep, you little baby.
When you wake you shall have all the pretty little horses.

—TRADITIONAL PRE-RISING LULLABY

Coming to You Live

Introduction

This is what you asked for.

Coming to You Live

Book I

O Canada

Some people call what we did "running away." I call it "a strategic retreat before I started shooting motherfuckers in the head." Isn't that a nicer way to put things?

—Shaun Mason

No matter how far we get from the people who made me what I am today, I'm still not sleeping. So I guess they won after all. Bully for them.

—Georgia Mason

One

The dream was always the same: I woke up, and I was in a world gone white. White walls, white floor, white ceiling, white bulbs in the naked light fixtures. One wall had been replaced by a mirror, and when I sat up and looked at myself, I was wearing a white hospital gown. The only color left in the world was my hair—brown—my eyes—brown—and the blue ID band around my left wrist. I raised my arm to look at it.

SUBJECT 7C—DESIGNATE GEORGIA MASON

The intercom clicked to life, and Dr. Thomas's voice filled the room, cool, distant, and artificially compassionate. "Good morning, Georgia. Did you sleep well?"

"I had a dream," I said, still looking at the ID band. "I dreamt Shaun came and found me." I dreamt we'd toppled the CDC. I dreamt we'd saved the President, and lost Becks, and saved the country, if not the world. I dreamt of Canada, and the wild green fields of freedom. All those things seemed so far away now, like they had never been possible.

"That's good." Dr. Thomas sounded pleased. I tensed. It was never good when the doctors responsible for my care sounded that happy. It usually meant pain to come, and more restrictions on my already limited privileges. "We designed that dream for you, Georgia, to make you feel better about your ongoing confinement. Did he break you out of here? Did he take you away from all this? To Canada, perhaps?"

I went cold. "Yes," I admitted, having long since learned that lying to the men who kept me captive did me no good at all. The fact that I could even consider lying was a testament to what they'd done to me. The woman I'd never been but remembered being would have died before she lied, no matter what the circumstances were. The most she'd ever been willing to do was withhold information, not sharing the things she didn't consider important. That vicious dedication to honesty had been enough to get her killed, and get me created, with my greater talent for saying one thing when I meant another.

That didn't make it a fair trade. I liked being alive—it was a fun way to spend my time—but I would have given it up in an instant if it could have meant being the original Georgia Mason again, not a cheap knock-off. Shaun would have torn down the walls of the world to get back to the original. He didn't even know that I existed.

And now even my dreams weren't safe from the men who'd made me.

"That's very good," said Dr. Thomas. "We're going to be making some adjustments to your programming over the next few weeks, Georgia. It's important that you know what we're planning to do, because we need to see if awareness allows you to fight the changes. We need you to struggle. Not that it's going to do any good. You were born in this room. You're going to die here. But you knew that, didn't you? Even in your sweetest dreams, you knew that seeing the sun—seeing Shaun—was too good to be true."

I threw back the covers, intending to leap out of bed and hammer my hands against the mirror. They were probably standing right on the other side, watching me, *judging* me, measuring my reactions. Well, I'd give them a reaction. I'd give them an explosion. I'd hit that glass until it shattered, and then we'd see who was trapped here. I wasn't trapped here with them. They were trapped here with *me*.

But when I pulled the blankets off my legs, my legs weren't there. My body ended in a pair of carefully bandaged stumps. Dr. Thomas was laughing, his voice drifting through the intercom like the judgment of an angry god.

"Oh, I'm sorry," he said. "You must have been so deep in the dream that you forgot. We removed those the last time you tried to run, Georgia. You can't run anymore. You're never going to get away from here. You're never going to leave us. We'll keep you until we're done with you, and then we'll keep you in jars, sliced and sectioned for study, until you give up all your secrets—so give up, give up, give up—"

The dream always ended the same way, too: I woke screaming, clawing at the air, with the winter chill heavy on my skin and Shaun's hands pinning my shoulders to the bed, Shaun's voice cutting through my cries as he pleaded with me to—

"Breathe, George, *breathe*, they can't hurt you anymore, they're not here, and if they *were* here, I'd throw a fucking party, right after I shot them into Swiss cheese, so come on, Georgia, *breathe*."

My vision cleared and there he was, bending over me, his knees planted in the mattress and his hands holding me down, keeping me from hurting myself. I stopped flailing, giving one final kick for the sake of feeling the blankets against my heels. My body was still my own. My mind belonged to me. My *life* belonged to me—to me, and to the man who was looking down on me with such terrified concern. My best friend. My adoptive brother, weird as that past relationship was in the light of our present one. The only person I'd ever loved enough to die for.

"Better now?" asked Shaun.

"Better," I said, and forced a smile.

He watched me for a moment longer before he took his hands off my shoulders and collapsed, all but boneless, to the mattress beside me. "That dream again, huh?"

I nodded wordlessly. He didn't need me to describe the dream: He'd heard it all before, over and over again, on the nights when I woke up screaming. It wasn't as bad as it had been when the dream was new. Back then, I'd managed to claw off strips of my own skin trying to remove the tracking devices my subconscious mind believed were planted there, the ones that would inevitably lead the CDC to our position and put me back in that featureless white room. It didn't matter that the CDC as I remembered it no longer existed, subsumed as they'd been by the EIS and by the sweeping policy changes put in place by the Ryman administration. The CDC had created me, growing me from a few scraps of DNA and programming my oldest memories from a combination of the electrical patterns of the original Georgia Mason's brain and their own ideas about what sort of person I should be. I was their daughter and their masterwork, and one day, they were going to come for me.

When they did, though, Shaun was going to be ready. I could see that simple, sincere truth in his eyes, and so I allowed my own eyes to close as I nestled up against him, breathing deeply, and waited for sleep to come back and claim me again.

It was going to be a long wait. As Shaun rubbed my back, and the sound of the owls going about their business outside drifted in through the windows, I found that I was okay with that.

Two

Georgia was still asleep when I rolled out of bed and tiptoed for the door, leaving her to slowly roll into the warm spot created by my body. I stopped at the door and looked back at her, unable to stop myself from smiling. She always looked so peaceful in the mornings. Sure, it was usually because she'd exhausted herself screaming in the middle of the night, but that didn't change the fact that in the morning, when her eyes were closed and the screaming was over, she looked like this was working, like she was healing, like she was getting *better.*

It was amazing how good we were getting at lying to each other and to ourselves about the state of our respective recoveries. George slept in stages: pre-nightmare, nightmare, post-nightmare, like a marathon runner who had to punish her body before she could let it relax. I didn't sleep so much as move from one catnap to another, sometimes staying in bed for ten or twelve hours just to get half that much rest. As long as I never dipped much below the surface of my dreams, I didn't have to live with the things they would try to show me.

We had gotten lucky, Georgia and I. We had taken everything the world had thrown at us, and in the end, we'd been able to walk away together, side by side, and let everyone else keep fighting without us. If George wanted to get hung up on the fact that the woman who'd walked away from the fight wasn't exactly the same as the woman who'd signed up for it, well. I wasn't the same man either. I didn't even have the convenient excuse of having died and come back as an abomination of science. Unlike George, I'd been alive and kicking for every awful moment, even if I'd spent more than half of it out of my mind with grief and shock.

Some days I wasn't sure I had ever come back *into* my mind. George got the nightmares to tell her that everything she knew was a lie, but at least when she was awake, she believed in the world around her. She believed I was real, and that I loved her; she believed that the sky and the forest and the snow would keep us safe. She believed we'd done the right thing, even though I knew she thought—sometimes privately, sometimes aloud and with a vehemence that frightened even me—that we'd paid way too much for what we'd gotten away with. She always believed.

Me? I wasn't sure I believed in anything anymore, not even in myself. Sometimes I thought *I* was the one who'd died in Sacramento, bleeding out my life across the inside of our van, and that everything I'd experienced since putting the gun to my best friend's head and pulling the trigger was either the hallucination of a dying mind, or—even worse—the vicious work of some CDC tech. Maybe I was a brain in a jar, and George's nightmares were my subconscious trying to make me face the truth. Maybe. After everything we'd been through, it didn't seem that far out of line.

But then she'd smile at me, or rub her thumb across the corner of my mouth to try to coax me into kissing her, and I would think, nah. Nah, there's no way I could have a dream this good; there's no way my lies could ever be this perfect. Truth is stranger than fiction, and so this had to be the truth. It was just that the moments when I could believe that were few and far between, and they didn't seem to be getting any more common.

My name is Shaun Mason, and I am not okay.

I walked through the cabin, picking up pieces of my gear from tables and couches as I made for the back door. We were careful about decontamination—we had to be, until we knew whether my immunity to Kellis-Amberlee, which had been contracted from the original Georgia, had been sexually transmitted to her clone, and the mere fact that I could think that sentence with a straight face said something about how fucking weird my life had become—but we weren't always careful about where things got put away after they were certified clean. Body armor tended to wind up on the couch in the front room. Boots got piled up by the back door. And weapons went on every flat surface in the place, always loaded, always close to hand.

That part, at least, was intentional, for both of us, even if we never wanted to talk about it. George and I both knew that one day, someone was going to come looking for us. Maybe they would be a friend, a member of the EIS who just wanted to check George's vitals, since there had never been a clone who'd survived outside laboratory settings for as long as she had. Maybe they would be an enemy, an old CDC scientist come to reclaim their secret weapon and use it for evil. It didn't matter either way, because she wasn't going back. *We* weren't going back, and anyone who tried to make us had better be prepared to learn just how many bullets we could squeeze off in the space between "hello" and "good-bye."

My pistol was on the low mail table next to the door. I picked it up, checked the clip, and shoved it into my belt before I opened the door and stepped out into the fresh air of the Canadian morning. The sky was a perfect, pristine blue, save for the long tail of a jetliner high overhead. Transcontinental, if they were willing to risk cutting across abandoned territory. During the Rising, when the dead had risen from their beds and gone walking around snacking on the living, most rural and low-population areas had been declared too dangerous, impossible to defend, and evacuated. The United States had lost the state of Alaska, judged too hostile for human occupation and left for the zombie wolves and polar bears to divide between themselves. Canada had lost substantially more. Pretty much the entire middle of the country had been written off and left for the infected.

The infected, and people like us, who had nowhere else to go. Anyone who didn't want to live in the modern American surveillance state, where everything you did could and would be held against you in a court of law, wound up running for the Canadian border. It was still a largely deserted country. Our closest neighbors were fifteen miles away—a nice group of First Nations activists who refused to miss out on this opportunity to take back what the European settlers had stolen from them—and even they were only there for half the year. They moved from site to site, working them all, helping to massage this land back into something livable.

Farmers and survivalists and cultists and dog breeders and political refugees dotted the Canadian countryside like mushrooms growing after a rain, hiding in dense forest or on the banks of rivers or, as with me and George, in plain sight. Everyone who knew us expected us to be living in an underground bunker, where George could craft her manifesto and I could do pushups until my biceps exploded. That was why we had found a nice little cabin that had been sealed against the weather and clearly deserted within the past decade and claimed it as our own. Sure, the original owners might have been surprised by some of our enhancements—razor wire and pit traps and homemade land mines not being exactly standard for their brand of rustic "getting back to nature"—but under the circumstances, I didn't think they were going to question it. There had still been food in the pantry when we'd found the place. The original owners were probably long dead, eaten by their neighbors while out for a walk and leaving a perfectly good cabin for us to find.

Me, I had no interest in being eaten by the neighbors. Even more, I had no interest in *George* being eaten by the neighbors. I'd managed to survive losing her once. I'd done it by driving myself insane and rolling through the world like a wrecking ball, breaking everything I touched with the sheer force of my denial. The fact that I'd survived that period of my life was nothing short of a miracle, and I meant that literally. Only a miracle could have brought my dead sister back to me, and now that I had her, I wasn't letting her go. Not if I had to burn the entire fucking world down to keep her safe.

Branches crunched underfoot as I walked across the yard, steering well clear of the orange spikes that marked the land mines and the yellow spikes that marked the pit traps. The infected didn't pay attention to little things like lawn ornaments. There was always the vague concern that we'd kill somebody who was just coming to borrow a cup of sugar, but anyone who lived out here would know that you didn't stroll up to the front door and ask for what you wanted: You stood as far away as you could while still being heard, and you yelled. Yelling might attract the dead, but it would sure as hell make the living friendlier.

The smell of pine was a constant, perfuming the air and hiding any underlying decay. It was nice, like living inside a giant car air freshener. I allowed myself to relax as much as I ever did, falling into an easy rolling gait as I walked the edges of the property we called our own.

A couple of my traps had been triggered in the night, catching stoats, wolverines, and one red fox that was still very much alive. It bared its teeth and snarled a warning as I approached. It was lucky: It had managed to wedge itself into one of the live-catch traps I used to tag the local rabbit and feral cat populations. If it had gone for something more its size, it would have crushed its skull on an unyielding metal bar, and be good for nothing but tonight's bait.

"What are you doing in there?" I asked, pulling on my gloves and moving around to the back of the trap. The fox watched me warily, but was too confined to turn around. That was good. I liked foxes. They kept the vermin down, and since they never reached amplification weight, they couldn't become zombies, which made them decent neighbors. Best of all, they *hated* the smell of the infected, and they liked to yell at infected things. When foxes yelled at something, it sounded like a murder party getting underway. As biological early warning systems went, you couldn't do much better than foxes.

The fox growled. I unlatched the back of the trap, tilted it at an angle, and shook until the fox popped out. It didn't hang around to posture or pretend that it was bigger than it was: It just took off running, vanishing into the underbrush without leaving so much as a footprint behind. I smiled as I reset and re-baited the trap, using a bit of nicely stinky canned fish as the lure. It was always good to confirm that we still had foxes around here. The natural world was putting itself back together, one piece at a time.

Then the fox screamed. Not a pain scream: a fury scream, rage scream, "you are wrong and should not be" scream. I was very familiar with that sound. I tensed as I set the trap down and removed my gloves, trying to move fast and silently at the same time. It wasn't an easy combination. It was a combination I'd had a lot of practice at.

I drew my gun. It fit perfectly into my hand, as it always did, as it always would. No matter how bleak and confusing the world got, no matter how not okay I became, there were some things that stayed the same. A man, a gun, a world full of zombies in need of putting down. The simple things in life.

The underbrush rustled. A gray wolf stalked out into the open, legs stiff, head down, a low moan whispering from its jaws. I smiled.

"Howdy," I said, and thumbed off the safety. "I guess it's time for you to meet the neighbors."

Three

The sound of gunshots woke me, distant enough not to be alarming, close enough to be worthy of my attention. I opened one eye, trying to count the reports registered by my semiconscious mind. Three. I was relatively sure there had been three. I closed my eye again, waiting, and sure enough, there were three more. Shaun was out for his morning constitutional, which included playing with the local wildlife. Since he hadn't started setting off sticks of dynamite and wasn't screaming for backup, I figured he hadn't managed to flush out another zombie moose. That was a good thing. I hated dealing with prehistoric megafauna that refused to go extinct like the rest of the supersized land mammals before I'd had my morning caffeine.

When the gunshots didn't resume, I rolled out of bed, eyes still closed, stretched, and felt around on the floor for my bathrobe. It was crumpled up under the edge of the bed, along with three shoes, a pillow, and an empty Coke can. I shoved the can into the pocket of my robe as I slid it on, rose, and walked toward the bedroom door, all without opening my eyes.

The original Georgia Mason—the one who supplied the DNA that made all of me, and the memories that made most of me—had developed retinal Kellis-Amberlee when she was a little girl. I remembered feeling my eyes go strange on me as the muscles stopped responding and the tear ducts stopped lubricating properly, forcing me into an unending cycle of dark glasses and saline solutions. I remembered the doctors talking to her/my parents, saying things like "Acquired Kellis-Amberlee Optic Neuropathic Reservoir Condition" and "still possible to live a normal life." Most of all, I remembered learning how to do everything in the dark while I allowed my eyes to rest, because they were a limited commodity. Given enough light damage and enough time, I would go blind, which would severely interfere with my workflow.

The body I lived in now, the person I was now, had never dealt with any of that. My eyes were factory standard; my vision was just this side of perfect. The CDC's attempts to force specific reservoir conditions in their clones had resulted in amplification, which was a waste of taxpayer money. Not that cloning one mouthy dead journalist *wasn't* a waste of taxpayer money—I probably cost more than last year's corn subsidies—but there was no reason to waste more than absolutely necessary. I had been the showroom model, never intended to set foot outside the lab. The release model had been surgically altered, given blown-out pupils and degenerating retinas by a clever surgeon's knife. If *she* had been the one to walk away, then all the precautions Shaun and I still took by rote would mean something, rather than being one more way to honor the memories of a woman I had never actually been.

But did it matter which mind had formed the memories, when they were still real to me? I walked through the first steps of my day with my eyes closed because everything I was told me that was the way to do it; under normal conditions, when no one was trying to kill us, I got to have my darkness. I had long since memorized the entire cabin. I could run from one end to the other without opening my eyes. It was soothing. It was home.

The light changed around me as I stepped into the hall. I opened my eyes, enjoying the dimness as I continued on my way to the kitchen.

Neither Shaun nor I was an electrician. That had always been Buffy's job, clever as she was with anything that involved a power source. She could rewire anything to suit her, and some of the miracles she'd accomplished with a soldering iron were probably in violation of the actual laws of science. But we knew how to read, and we knew how to follow instructions, and when we had found this cabin, we had been able to set up the generator systems and get them all online before the snow came and the world went white.

Our first winter had been a hard one. We hadn't known our neighbors, such as they were, yet; when we'd needed to go looking for food or basic supplies, we had found ourselves confronted with a seemingly never-ending stream of frowning faces and suspicious questions. Who were we? Why were we here? What made us think that they would sell us their precious eggs or potatoes or apples, when we were strangers who might not care enough to stay? We couldn't have things shipped to us, not when the U.S. government was likely to be monitoring our accounts, watching for any activity that could betray our location. They'd promised to leave us alone. They'd allowed us to walk away. But there was such a thing as being too trusting, too ready to believe the people in power when they claimed they were the good guys now, and that was a mistake that neither of us had any interest in making.

We'd clawed our way through the first winter, and then the first year, one day at a time, coming out of it thinner, wiser, and all the more determined to make this work. This was our life now. It belonged to us. And we were *not* going back.

Shaun had learned how to tan and prepare hides, reading everything he could find on the subject and pushing his Kellis-Amberlee immunity to its limits. Several times he had come home from the forest shaking and feverish and refusing to let me touch him. He would lock himself in his office, holing up until the shaking stopped and there was no chance that he was still infectious. Out here, there was always a demand for safe, sterile, *clean* fur, which kept people warm better than anything else could. Shaun used the remains of the things he killed to bait the traps that brought in more, and bit by bit, we built up a rapport with our neighbors, while also cutting down the number of things that wanted to eat us.

I learned how to garden. Together, we constructed a greenhouse to compensate for the cold, and I grew tomatoes, melons, peppers, and greens, which we dutifully canned and put aside against the inevitability of winter. We bought Coke in bulk from a black market connection who also supplied Shaun's coffee, my birth control, and the occasional new pair of jeans. Our neighbors learned to trust us. We learned to trust them. A few of them even knew who we were, even though Shaun told them that his name was "Phil," that my name was "Jean," and that we were a married couple from Seattle who'd decided to drop out of society after a new iteration of Mason's Law had required us to have our beloved corgis put to sleep. It was a paper-thin cover story, obviously fake if looked at with a critical eye, and that was what made it so secure.

For the people who recognized us as Shaun and Georgia Mason, the reporters who refused to die, a pathetic cover story said "we trust you enough that we're not bothering with a convincing lie." For the people who didn't know who we were and had no idea what we were running from, that same story said "we are not good enough liars to be a threat; we're just here to live our lives in peace, same as you, same as anybody." A story that was *too* good would have painted us as possible government spies trying to infiltrate the community. The kind of people who chose to live in this little slice of the middle of nowhere weren't the sort who looked kindly on government oversight.

And that label included us, now. We were that kind of people. We didn't want to be monitored, and we didn't want to be protected, and we didn't want to be legislated. We just wanted to be left the fuck alone.

Not that we were leaving the world alone forever. The world needed our attention. Maybe that was a little self-aggrandizing, but look at the facts: The one time I'd trusted the world to get by without my input, it had gone off the rails in a big, big way. The people in power needed to be held accountable for the things they did, and Shaun and I were in the best possible position to do it. We'd already given our lives—me—and our sanity—Shaun—in the service of telling the truth. We'd given everything we had. We'd given too much. What did we have left to lose? Only each other, and we were never far enough apart for that to happen. Any attack or airstrike that took out one of us was going to take out both of us. And we were not planning to go down easy.

Our kitchen was small and surprisingly cozy, with cream-colored walls and red-and-white checked curtains on the windows. It was warm, and homey, and completely out of character for the face we'd always worked so hard to show people. This was us, relaxed. Us, safe. Us, not running away anymore. I walked to the fridge, opened it, and took a can of Coke from the door, noting as I did that the salmon we had set to marinate the night before looked like it was just about done. It was a simple dressing, sugar and vinegar and crushed cranberries, but it would still taste better than anything we'd ever eaten, because we were the ones who'd set the menu. No more focus groups or nutritionally ideal proteins, no more sponsors or captors. Just us. That was the best seasoning in the world.

My head spun as I opened the can of Coke and took my first sip. As always, it was cold enough to burn as it traveled down my throat, waking up my body just a bit more. I held the can against my temple, willing it to stop the spin. Sometimes I got disoriented in the mornings, that was all. No big deal.

Except that when you're an illegally grown and programmed clone of a dead journalist, living in the middle of nowhere with no access to medical care, since seeking medical care would mean exposing yourself to the people who made you, *everything* is a big deal. Those were the thoughts that kept me from going to sleep, as opposed to the nightmares that kept me from staying that way. If Shaun broke his leg or one of us got an impacted molar, there was no one out here to save us. We were young and healthy for now, but we both knew that wasn't going to last forever, and while living long enough to get old was a luxury we couldn't count on, the fear of getting old in the middle of the Canadian wastes was a concern we couldn't ignore.

I lowered the can and took another swig, bigger this time, trying to force caffeine into my body as fast as I could. When I pulled it away from my lips, there was blood on the rim.

I looked at it blankly for a long moment, trying to make sense of what I saw. Then I raised my other hand and touched my lip. My fingertips came away bloody. I gave them the same look I'd given the can, trying to justify the bleeding to myself. There was no good answer for it, no good reason for my blood to be fleeing from my body.

Shaun. Shaun couldn't see me this way. He'd freak out if he thought there was something wrong with me, and I needed us both calm if we were going to review our options. I turned to face the door, taking a step toward it.

Somewhere between my foot coming up and my foot coming down, I lost consciousness. I don't remember falling. I don't remember having fallen. I just remember the thought, sharp as a needle across the blackness that was taking me down:

Oh, God, no. I can't leave him again.

And then there was nothing.

Book II

Pay the Piper

It's always the ones who made the mess who talk about how cleaning it up should be a group effort—or better yet, how cleaning it up should be somebody else's problem. It's almost like the kind of people who break things for fun don't care for being held accountable.

—GEORGIA MASON

I will never get tired of the sound my fist makes when it slams into some over-entitled asshole's nose. Cartilage crunching is my jam.

—SHAUN MASON

One

Normally, George came and fished me out of the woods after an hour or two, citing things like "breakfast" as a good reason to shower and rejoin the human race. Personally, I figured she just got lonely, since her usual routine didn't involve logging on and getting to work until after lunch. Once she started, it was hard for her to *stop*. So she made it a rule to do stuff like socializing and going out in the yard before she let herself reach for the keyboard. I guess it made her feel less like she was addicted to her job. It was cool by me. I knew she was a junkie, and so did she, but we all needed our illusions to get through the days. If she wanted to pretend she wasn't hooked, that was okay.

Her lying to me made it easier for me to lie to her. We both knew recovery was a process. We both understood the necessity of taking it one day at a time, and we'd both spent our share of hours chatting with the folks at the helplines, her over one of Buffy's video chat servers, randomized and anonymized until government agencies could have blown their entire budgets trying to track her down, me over cruder but equally effective text clients. We spilled out our guts to each other, and when that didn't fix things we spilled out our guts to strangers, and none of that changed the fact that recovery was a process and we both wanted it to be over, finished and done with, and let us get back to our lives.

So George pretended she wasn't addicted to her work, and I pretended I wasn't still out of my goddamn mind, and we got by.

"She kept you up all night again, huh?" The Georgia who asked was leaning up against a nearby tree, wearing her old, familiar uniform of black and white, even down to the sunglasses covering her too-normal eyes. That was one thing my Georges had in common: They both had brown eyes, untouched by Kellis-Amberlee. The real one's eyes were like that because the scientists who built her weren't as good at playing God as they wanted to think they were. This one's eyes were like that because even at my craziest, I had been trying to remind myself that she was a hallucination.

The not-real George wasn't bothered by my lack of response. She continued, "I would never do that to you. I sleep like a baby."

I didn't say anything. George had left me alone out here for an unusually long time, hence her imaginary twin showing up to needle me, but that didn't mean she wasn't waiting for me in the cabin, ready to chase the bad dreams away with a smile and a touch of her hand. My hallucinations could seem solid sometimes. On the *really* bad days, they covered almost every sense I had. They still didn't feel as real as she did.

"You can't ignore me forever, Shaun. You can try, but you know as well as I do that I wouldn't be here if you didn't need me. You think you're healing? If you're healing, *why am I still here?*" Her voice dropped to a hiss at the end of her sentence, turning menacing. "She'll leave you. That's what she was created to do. She always leaves you. I'm the one who loves you enough to stay. I'm the one who's always going to be here. Just me. You'll see."

"I don't think I want to talk to you anymore." I closed my eyes, keeping them closed for a slow count of five before I turned toward the tree where she'd been standing, opened them, and said, "Leave."

And just like that, she wasn't there. The skin on my arms lumped itself into large, painful knots of gooseflesh, a physiological response to a psychological problem. I shivered, picked up the last of the night's catch—a wolverine that had managed to neatly decapitate itself on the bar-trap I'd set for it—and turned back toward the cabin. I needed to get out of the woods. I needed to see Georgia. I needed to hear her voice outside my head, not just in the empty, echoing space that had opened when she'd died, and still hadn't finished closing.

Hallucinatory George used to be my friend. She'd offered me advice and held my hand when I needed to sleep; she'd told me she loved me, and I had believed her. I still did. She was my projection of the woman I knew and loved best in all the world, and the one thing I'd never brought myself to doubt was Georgia's love. Our adoptive parents sort of fucked us up. They didn't know how to deal with kids who lived long enough to grow up, and while I guess they did their best, it wasn't good enough. We'd grown up starved for affection, starved for *connection*, and the only place we had known that we could find it was with each other. So we'd tangled ourselves together until sometimes I thought I could understand what family meant. The rest of the time I thought, *Shaun, dude, you are so fucked in the head that you can call this girl your sister while you're thinking about going down on her*, and that was true, too, but that was the model we had. It wasn't right. It probably wasn't healthy. It was ours.

So yeah, when I first started having conversations with my dead sister, I was pretty much okay with it. Everybody has their own coping mechanisms, and me? Well, I went crazy to stay sane. For most people, that would have been the end of it. They would have been haunted by the increasingly complex hallucinations until they either gave themselves completely over to the delusion or decided it was time to go on some heavy-duty antipsychotics and get over themselves. The trouble with me was, I got her back. Some trouble, huh? Oh poor me, I got a miracle. I became the luckiest man in the world. My prayers were answered, and it was all sunshine and good times from there on out... except that when I prayed to get her back, I had never prayed for my sanity to return. Recovery was a process, and it was taking a lot longer to heal than it had taken for me to be hurt.

Imaginary Georgia had been my mind's way of protecting itself from the crushing reality of a world that didn't have her in it anymore, and deep down, on the level of thought that I couldn't access no matter how hard I tried, I didn't believe she was going to stay. Sure, she was back among the living *now*, but that was just some sort of cosmic filing error. Somebody, somewhere, was going to realize that I didn't deserve this, this... this *mercy*, and she was going to leave me again, for good this time. If I allowed myself to fully recover before that happened, I was going to find myself alone in a world that didn't have the real George, and didn't have the fake George; a world that didn't have any George at all. That was a world I couldn't imagine living in, and so even as I curled close to the flesh-and-blood woman who shared my life, I clung to the ghost who haunted my heart. I couldn't help it.

The night's catch had been good, at least: Not counting our friend the fox, I had three wolverines, a pine marten the length of my arm, and six rabbits. Rabbit fur was always in high demand, especially among families with children. The necessity of fur was something you came to terms with when you lived in a place with winters this harsh and an infrastructure this insecure, but people who remembered the world before the Rising still liked to dress their kids in rabbit, which they remembered as a relatively low-cruelty, farmed fur.

There was no such thing as fur without cruelty. There was no such thing as *life* without cruelty. Everything a person had was something someone else didn't have. In the end, it all came down to balancing the damage that you did. My rabbits died fast and clean, and did me the favor of not leading predators too close to the cabin. They would bait my traps and pay my debts, and while killing them might have been cruel, I did my best to make sure that their lives weren't wasted.

I hung the carcasses in the curing shed, a blood-scented box of metal and concrete that would have spelled instant infection for almost anyone else. Even George hadn't been out there since we'd finished settling into the property, although I had taken video for her a couple of times, when she'd asked. We didn't have any secrets from each other.

There was a flash of dark hair out of the corner of my eye as my mind reminded me, unflinchingly, that we didn't have any secrets we could *see*.

Working with blood the way I did meant I was a walking hot zone, and made it essential for me to be careful with what I touched. That was why I'd installed a chemical shower, in its little plastic pod, right outside the shed. I stripped down, hoping George was watching from the window—it was always fun when I could give her a little show; both of us were still drunk on the idea of being allowed to love each other without social mores and disapproving looks getting in the way—and shoved my clothes into a biohazard bag before stepping into the self-sealing green box.

Even in the middle of nowhere, certain protocols have to be followed. People had taken "safety" to the level of religious mania, making it *unsafe* in their obsessive need to put it above all else. That didn't mean decontamination was optional, or make bleach anything other than the ongoing salvation of mankind. I spent the recommended time in the chemical spray, scrubbing every trace of blood, every scrap of viral fomite, from my skin and hair. I emerged smelling of citrus lotion and cleanliness, pulled on the sweatpants that hung from the interior hook of the unit, stepped into a pair of plastic slippers, and strolled, clean and damp and decontaminated, back toward the cabin.

Nothing moved in the windows. I frowned. George might still be in bed—that wasn't unheard of, especially after she'd had a bad night—but she usually got up when she heard the shower. It was rigged to set off a beeper in the kitchen when someone turned it on. We'd had a few uninvited guests, usually people who'd been driven to the wilderness rather than choosing it, show up on our property and assume they could take advantage of an unguarded opportunity to get themselves clean. That was okay, sort of; we made enough, between her vegetables and my furs, to pay for a few charity-case showers over the course of the year. The trouble was, people like that sometimes wanted more than just a bath, and that was less okay. That couldn't be allowed.

A twinge of nervousness ran down my spine, tightening my skin and making the hair on the back of my neck stand on end. I was being silly, I knew, but I still picked up my pace, walking as fast as I dared before I would have to admit that I was running. There was still no movement in the kitchen.

She's probably still in bed, I thought, and opened the back door, and stopped dead. My eyes widened until it physically hurt. Every muscle in my body seemed to be cramping at the same time, becoming nonresponsive. I couldn't move. I *had* to move. Everything hinged on my moving.

But I had hallucinations, right? I saw things that weren't there. I saw an imaginary Georgia. So maybe this was that. Maybe my cruel, cruel brain had decided to stop playing nice, and had moved on to presenting me with worst-case scenarios, intrusive thoughts that would gradually transform my life into a waking nightmare. It was a terrifying thing to contemplate, and right now I liked it a lot better than the idea that this could be really real, that this could be happening.

My hallucinations were visual, auditory, and sometimes tactile. They never included taste, and they never included smell.

I could smell the blood.

George was lying in a curved comma on the kitchen floor, the angle of her body seeming somehow outraged, like she was furious with herself for having limitations, like she was furious with gravity for enforcing them. She had dropped a nearly full can of Coke when she fell; the sticky brown liquid had spread across the floor in a fan of droplets. It was going to attract ants. That was a small, petty thing to focus on, but that was what made it so *safe*. We were going to have ants, and George was going to be furious, because she *hated* ants. At least this time I could blame her, and not one of my botched attempts to make caramel. We would laugh, and laugh, and laugh...

The sound I was making wasn't laughter. It was barely even human, and it hurt my throat. Under the circumstances, that was the least of my concerns.

The Coke had been in her hand when she fell, and had splattered away from her. The blood, though, that was all her. It surrounded her head like a corona, some asshole artist's idea of religious art. I finally remembered how to move. I rushed into the kitchen, the screen door slamming behind me, and dropped to my knees on the sticky, blood-tacky floor, reaching for her.

"George? Hey, George, can you hear me?"

She didn't respond. I rolled her halfway into my lap, feeling the limp, dead weight of her. The blood had come from her nose; there were caked-on trails leading from both nostrils, fanning out to cover her mouth and chin. She looked like a zombie, like she'd been feasting on something unspeakable. Was that possible? Could she have amplified?

Anything was possible. If she opened her eyes and they were black with virus and devoid of humanity, well, it would just be like we were finishing what we'd begun, back in Sacramento, back in the van. I was so tired. I wasn't going to fight her.

I also wasn't going to write her—or us—off that easily. I slid my arms under her body and stood, staggering a little under the weight of her. She hung limply against my chest, her head rolling to rest on my shoulder. Blood was getting everywhere. That was all right. Maybe I leaned too heavily on my immunity these days, but this was *George*. I would have risked infection for her even before we knew that the virus didn't want me.

Step by careful step, I carried her through the cabin to the bathroom and lowered her into the tub. She didn't open her eyes, not even when I braced her head against the cold tile and gingerly removed her blood-soaked robe, for fear of later contamination. Her stillness was a vote against her being infected: Zombies didn't usually sleep calmly while people treated them like giant dolls. I clung to that thought as I got a washcloth, wetted it down with warm, soapy water, and began wiping the blood from her face.

Maybe she was already dead. Maybe I was fooling myself. I didn't care. She was all I had, and I wasn't going to lose her. Not today. Not like this.

"I'll still be here for you," said the George who wasn't real, perching on the edge of the sink and smiling sweetly at me, like this wasn't exactly what she wanted. Her and me, alone against the world, the way it had been when I was at my lowest. The way it had been when she was the only thing keeping me from swallowing a bullet. "I'll never leave you."

I didn't say anything to her. I just kept my eyes on the real George, and prayed, foolish as it was, that she was going to wake up.

Two

My eyelids felt like they'd been weighted down. I struggled to open them, noting their unresponsiveness with a clinical detachment that I recognized as my own effort to stave off panic. Part of me knew, absolutely and without question, that when I *did* manage to open my eyes, I would be back in CDC custody—or worse yet, that I would never have left, because everything I'd experienced in my lifetime had been a simulation, a way for them to test how things would play out if I ever managed to escape. My nightmares were real. Canada was the dream.

If I was capable of dreaming, I was capable of thinking. If I was capable of thinking, I was capable of finding a way to make the things I'd imagined real. So it didn't matter where I was when I opened my eyes: What mattered was that I opened them. With a wrenching effort that I felt all the way down to my bones, I forced my eyelids to respond, and found myself staring at the ceiling of our bathroom in Canada.

Relief washed through me, beating panic back, at least for the moment. I was home. I hadn't been dreaming this whole time. The fact that my body felt like it was made of lead didn't matter; I could deal with that. I had dealt with worse. My freedom was the important thing. My freedom and—

"Shaun!" Adrenaline reawakened my overtaxed muscles as I sat bolt upright in the bathtub. The bathroom door banged open less than a second later, revealing Shaun standing there, wearing one of the battered pairs of sweatpants he always put on after he'd been out in the shed. His hair was standing up in uncombed spikes, and his eyes were wild with panic and fear. There was a smear of dried blood just below the line of his jaw. Given how careful he always was when he came in from the woods, I was willing to lay bets that it was mine.

"George?" His voice was shaking, filled with fear and disbelief. He took a cautious step into the bathroom, studying my eyes. "Are you... are you okay?"

With a pang, I realized that he was checking for signs of infection. "Not really," I said. "I think I passed out." I raised a hand to check my lip. My nose wasn't bleeding anymore. That was something. "I don't feel so good."

"Yeah, I think I figured that out when I came in and found you sprawled on the fucking floor, George," said Shaun. There was an edge to his voice, reminding me of how often he used words as weapons. They weren't usually aimed at me. That didn't mean they couldn't be. "How long has this been going on? Did you think I wouldn't want to know?"

"I've been dizzy for the last few days, but I thought it was my period coming on," I said. "I get anemic sometimes. You know that. Today was the first time I've started bleeding. Come on, Shaun. You *know* I wouldn't have tried to hide this from you. If nothing else, I would have wanted you to help with the decontamination."

His face fell, anger cracking and dropping away, to be replaced by raw, aching misery. "I thought you were dead," he said, taking a step toward me. "I thought you were leaving me."

"I'm not, and I'm not," I said, before tapping my jaw, mirroring the spot where he was smeared with my blood. "You've got red on you."

He stopped, blinking at me like I was speaking a foreign language, and not quoting a pre-Rising horror comedy. Then he turned to the mirror, shoulders slumping as he saw the blood. "I'll wash up," he said.

"Thank you." We each harbored our own private reservoir of Kellis-Amberlee, even when it wasn't manifesting as a proper reservoir condition. Under normal circumstances—a nosebleed, a cracked lip, a normal menstrual cycle—people didn't trigger amplification in themselves. The body remembered the blood as part of the whole, and so the virus didn't activate. There was probably some complicated scientific reason for that. I didn't know what it was, and I didn't have the medical background to figure it out. What I *did* know was that any blood that had been out of contact with my body long enough to have dried to that shade of brown was no longer a part of me, and would happily infect the blood that I had left.

Shaun turned on the water and broke the seal on a disposable sponge, beginning to scrub. That gave me the opportunity to pull myself to my feet, using the lip of the tub and then the walls to stabilize my shaking legs. My body was responding to me now, but it still felt weak and oddly gummy, like something was keeping it from fully understanding my instructions. It didn't feel like amplification. Thanks to the CDC, I may be the only human alive who actually *knows* what amplification feels like. As for what this *did* feel like...

I didn't know. And that terrified me.

The lip of the tub was too high for me to easily step over, given the way my legs were shaking. I looked at it bleakly before raising my eyes and watching Shaun's reflection meticulously scrubbing off every bit of mirrored blood. "When you're done with that, can you come over here and help me get out?"

"Sure thing," he said. His tone was light. His eyes were full of screaming. "Can you wait just a few seconds?"

"I've got nothing else to do today." That was a lie. Mahir was expecting an op-ed from me on repealing Mason's Law, and why we were doing ourselves a disservice by refusing to keep animals that were above the amplification threshold. I was focusing on the coevolution of spillover diseases, and some reports that had leaked out of Poland, of all places, describing a reduced amplification rate among black market pig farmers. It was possible that the virus, in bouncing back and forth between mammalian species, was finding a way to settle into a less aggressive form, as characterized by increased reservoir conditions. Smallpox and the milkmaids all over again, playing out in real time.

Somehow, I didn't think Mahir would mind waiting a little while if we told him that my health was on the line. He hadn't seen me since Shaun and I had run for Canada and the safety of a big country with very little monitoring or infrastructure. We still chatted sometimes, over secure relays, when I was submitting an article. It was nice to know that someone missed me who had actually met *me*, and not just the original Georgia.

Not that she'd ever had a lot of friends. She was my original, the template from which I was drawn, and she would have been just as content as I was with a world that consisted of nothing but herself, a wireless connection, and Shaun. I was living her happy ending, and Mahir was a part of that.

Shaun dropped his sponge into the biohazard bin next to the sink, dried his hands on a towel, and turned to face me. I was struck once again by how perfectly he fit into this environment. Neither of us had ever expected to be playing house like this, worrying about washing towels and doing the dishes, and yet here we were, perfectly content in our weird little world. "All better," he said.

"Here's hoping," I said, and held out my arms. He put his hands under them, cupping my ribcage, and lifted me easily.

Too easily. He frowned again. "Have you been losing weight?"

"I didn't think I had," I said, but that was a lie, too, wasn't it? I hadn't been eating much for the last week or so. My appetite was down, and I wasn't good at choking back food I didn't feel like putting in my mouth. I gave him an alarmed look. "Something's wrong."

"Yeah, it is." He didn't put me down. Instead, he swung me up into his arms, cradling me against his chest like an invalid. I would have objected to the treatment, but at the moment, it felt appropriate. "You're going back to bed."

"No, I'm not," I said, planting one hand against his chest and pushing gently. His skin was warm and smelled faintly of citrus. "This isn't going to get better just because I go back to bed, and if I get another nosebleed, I could ruin the mattress. We need to go to the kitchen, and I need my laptop."

The look he gave me was pure betrayal. "Dammit, George, you're not going to sit down and start working like nothing happened."

"No, I'm not," I said again. "I'm going to sit down and call Dr. Abbey. If anyone can tell us what's going on with me, it's her." She was also the only doctor I knew who Shaun actually trusted. If she told us we had to come to her, he'd go.

"Okay," he said, almost sullenly. He hoisted my knees—my *bare* knees—a little higher as he adjusted his grip on me.

I snorted as I suddenly thought through one more thing about my situation. "Actually, *can* we stop by the bedroom? I should probably put on a clean robe before I start calling our friendly neighborhood mad scientist. Just so she doesn't get the wrong idea about what I'm reaching out for."

Shaun's laughter was as welcome as it was unexpected. "Oh, wow. 'Hey, Dr. Abbey, you're a dedicated violator of the rules of God and man and everything, but how'd you like to come join us in the middle of the country for a threesome?' Yeah, she'd probably hang up on us."

"Or worse, she'd say 'sure,' and show up," I said. "She was married once, remember? She still has needs. We could host a mad science sex party."

"Hey, George, remember when I said I didn't know what I wanted for my birthday?"

"Yeah?"

"I want you to never say those words in that order ever again."

I laughed as he carried me down the hall to the bedroom, my head resting against his shoulder. Maybe things were going to be okay.

Three

George was not okay.

She thought she was fooling me, but even the three percent variance between her and the original Georgia couldn't make her that good of a liar. Her hands had been trembling as she was getting dressed. Not much. It was a little tremor, and I might have missed it if I hadn't been so focused on making sure she didn't fall down again. I wondered whether I might have missed it the night before, or the day before that. She'd been feeling dizzy for a few days, and I had been too distracted with my traps and my furs to notice. The thought made me sick. What if I lost her again because I didn't pay close enough attention?

A ghostly hand touched the back of my neck. I shrugged it off. This wasn't the time to let myself get distracted, especially not by something that wasn't even real.

"Okay, ready," said George, grabbing her laptop off the bedside table as she turned toward me. The sunlight was coming through the window behind her, catching all the bleached bits of her hair and turning them almost white. It was time to dye her hair again. Bartering for the stuff was pretty easy, but she didn't like to do it too often; said that her vanity shouldn't be taking food out of our bellies. What she didn't seem to understand was that her vanity was also my peace of mind. It was easier to remember that *she* was the real Georgia, and not the little voice inside my head, when her hair was the right color.

"You sure you don't want me to carry that?" I asked.

George hugged her laptop against her chest in an almost defensive gesture. "I'm sure," she said. "The day I can't even hold my own computer is probably the day they bury me."

I felt myself go blank. "Don't even say that."

Her face fell. "I'm sorry. I didn't mean—"

"I know. Just don't...don't even say that." I turned my back on her and left the room. I wanted to keep walking, to go and wait for her in the kitchen and let my sudden, panicky anger drain away, but I couldn't do it. Instead, I waited for her to come out of the room and trailed her down the hall. She didn't say anything, and so neither did I.

Silence was a common companion in our household. We'd been waiting to be alone together for most of our lives, and part of what made it so appealing was the silence. With George, I knew I didn't have to be funny, or manic, or smiling all the time. With me, she knew she didn't have to pretend to be objective. She could have thoughts and opinions that didn't fit her public image; she could wear flannel pajamas and watch kitten videos online, and not worry that someone was going to judge her less of a serious journalist because she'd done it. This silence was different. This silence was filled with things we weren't saying, concerns we didn't want to give voice to.

What if she's dying? whispered her voice in the space behind my ears, and I didn't say anything. George didn't like it when I acknowledged her phantom twin. It made her feel like an intruder, and I guess that was fair, on some level. I'd had three versions of her in my life: the original, the hallucinatory companion who showed up after she died, and now the clone. She'd only ever had me.

George sat down at the kitchen table and turned on her screen, fingers flying across the keys as she requested a connection to Dr. Abbey. I relaxed a little. Her hands weren't shaking. She was typing as fast and as sure as she ever had, her own shoulders unlocking as she eased into the rhythm of the work.

There was only one thing she needed to complete the picture of Georgia At Work, the tableau I'd been watching since we were kids. I walked to the fridge, pulled out a can of Coke, and popped the tab before setting it down next to her left hand. She glanced away from her screen long enough to flash me a quick smile, business tempered by affection. I smiled back, and just like that, things were okay between us again. Our fights usually ended like that. It wasn't a matter of arguing: It was a matter of letting the silence grow until it could encompass us both again.

The laptop beeped. George turned her attention back to the screen as a chat window popped up, framing a round, freckled face topped up by a mass of brown curls streaked with bleach spots. Dr. Abbey was frowning. That was pretty much normal, for her. If she'd ever known how to smile, she had traded that knowledge in a long time ago, for things man was never meant to know and a sweet assortment of deadly pathogens.

"Georgia?" she said, eyebrows raising as she took in George's image in the webcam. "You look like hell."

"Nice to see you, too," said George.

Dr. Abbey shrugged. "It's been three years since you bothered to call. We got the postcards, so I knew you weren't *dead*, but if you think I'm going to be all sunshine and rainbows just because you left me alone for a while, you've never met me. What happened?"

"I had a nosebleed," said George.

"I know. Your nostrils are red and irritated, which says they've been wiped a lot recently, and you wouldn't be calling me for a cold, or I would have heard from you a long time ago. How bad was it?"

"Bad enough that I found her blacked out on the kitchen floor in a pool of her own blood," I said, looming up behind George's chair. I'd told myself that I was going to let her have this conversation without my interference, but I couldn't do it. She was being too cagey. Yeah, it was her health, but she was my life.

"Huh," said Dr. Abbey. "Any other symptoms?"

George nodded. "Dizziness, some muscle weakness, a, um, burning sensation when I try to pee..."

"Wait, what?" I said. That was a new symptom to me.

Dr. Abbey and George both ignored me. "Well, we know it's not an

STI, unless you and Shaun have gotten *really* bored wherever it is you're holed up; you both had a clean bill of health the last time I saw you," said Dr. Abbey. "That could mean kidney involvement. Have you had any unusual bleeding? Apart from the nasal variety, I mean."

"I didn't have my period last month." That had been a scare. We always kept a supply of pregnancy tests on hand. Condoms could break, pills could fail to work. There was always the risk of someone deciding to relabel expired medication for the sake of making a quick buck. Any time George was even five minutes late, she was popping open a little white box and checking to make sure we hadn't fucked up. It wasn't that we were morally opposed to the idea of kids, someday. We knew we weren't actually genetically related, and our upbringing had been screwed up enough that we weren't likely to pass along any weird brother-sister socialization, even if we had more than one. We just weren't sure what bearing a child would do to a cloned body. It had never been done... or at least, it had never been done openly, legally, or outside a CDC lab, and the sort of people who would think getting a clone pregnant to see what happened was a good idea were exactly the sort of people we didn't want to talk to.

"Okay." Dr. Abbey's usual expression of mild annoyance smoothed out, replaced by a neutrality as unfamiliar as it was terrifying. "I don't want to know where you are, and I know you wouldn't tell me if I asked. But do you have a car, or some other means of transport?"

"We have our van," said George. "It's in perfect working order, and we know it's not currently bugged or transmitting any sort of signal that the people who might be looking for us are capable of picking up."

"At least not while we're in the middle of goddamn nowhere," I added, before she could offer any more reassurances. "There's every chance that there's some sort of sat-tracker on the thing that triggers if we go over the border back into the United States."

"No, there's not." Dr. Abbey dismissed my concerns with a wave of her hand. "I've had my sources looking for details on the bugs that were planted on you for years. None of them has ever mentioned a sat-tracker, or anything remotely like it. If you've cleared the bugs out of your onboard computer systems and removed any physical trackers, you're clean. Which is a good thing, because you're coming here, and I'd rather not have the entire EIS land on my doorstep looking for the opportunity to chat with the pair of you."

"Can't you diagnose me over the video link?" asked George. "Put me back to bed for a week and tell me to drink lots of orange juice. Which is superexpensive up here, by the way, so I'll wind up drinking cranberry juice instead."

"Adorable as your misguided faith in me is, no, I can't diagnose you over a video link," said Dr. Abbey. "Or, rather, I *can*, but you won't like any of the conclusions I can draw without a physical examination. You know I supported the two of you running off to play Little House on the Prairie. Nobody wants you to have a happy ending more than I do. But at the end of the day, we can't allow sentimentality to make us forget your rather, well, 'unique' origins. You're not like any other patient I've ever worked with."

"None of them were clones, you mean," said George. She made no effort to conceal her bitterness. With us, she didn't have to.

"That's exactly what I mean," said Dr. Abbey. "You're a singular case, Georgia. Maybe someday that won't be true, but right now, you're the only clone on record to have survived more than two years outside of laboratory conditions—and before you say anything, yes, that's because all the others have been cut open and harvested for their organs, or otherwise sacrificed to science. There's no reason to think they wouldn't have been able to live long and healthy lives if not for people like me who wanted to pull them apart and see what made them tick."

"There's also no reason to assume they wouldn't have fallen apart as soon as the proteins binding their muscles to their skeletons started to dissolve," said George.

"Exactly," said Dr. Abbey. "How long will it take you to drive here? I'm still in Shady Cove."

I did a double take. "The forestry center? Really? I thought you would have abandoned that place years ago." Some bad stuff had happened there, including the deaths of a whole bunch of her people. If any place was going to be haunted, it was the Shady Cove Forestry Center.

"It suits my needs, and the EIS has agreed to pretend that they don't know I'm here, if I promise not to tie any of their spies to anthills to express my displeasure," she said. "It works out. I've got a good setup. We've improved a lot since your last visit. We'll be able to figure out what's going on with you, Georgia, and get you back in fighting shape in no time."

"It'll take us about three days," said George. "Is there anything we should bring?"

"Some samples of your topsoil, groundwater, and if you have something you're using for a well, bring a sample of that, too. Do you do your own canning?"

George nodded.

Dr. Abbey snorted. "Oh, man, the Masons as domestic little farmers. I should have been making bets. I could be buying myself a brand-new car right about now with all the cash I'd be raking in. Bring a couple of cans. I want to do as much of an environmental sweep as I can."

"But you don't think this is environmental, because Shaun isn't sick," said George, in her calm, collected, "I am conducting an interview and must not get emotionally involved" voice.

"No, I don't," said Dr. Abbey. She sobered. "I think you should have called me a week ago. Better yet, I think you should have been coming to see me once a year, just to be sure everything was working properly. Now, pack your things and get over here as fast as you can. I won't leave the door unlocked, but I will leave the lights on."

The connection went dark, disconnected from her end. George sighed.

"She always did have to get the last word," she said, and closed her laptop, standing. "We need to pack."

"*I* need to pack," I said. "*You* need to sit back down and, I don't know, catch up on e-mail or something while I do the strenuous stuff."

"No," she said. She sounded surprisingly calm. "I need to pack. You need to go take those samples Dr. Abbey needs. We can't put me to bed right now. If we're going to get out of here as fast as we need to, we *both* need to be working, and we *both* need to go tell the Smiths that we're going on vacation. Otherwise, they're going to assume you buried me somewhere on the property, and that we're not coming back."

"They'd have a hell of a time getting through the automated defenses," I said. "The cabin will be fine."

"Yeah, but I sort of like the Smiths," said George. "I don't want to get a reputation for blowing up the neighbors. We need to tell them we're taking a trip and will be back soon, and we need to do it together. I will pack clothes. You will take groundwater samples. I will sit down if I feel even a little bit dizzy. I will call you if I think I'm about to pass out. We will get out of here a lot faster if we're both working on getting our stuff ready, and the first step is for you to stop arguing with me."

Her voice was calm, but her cheeks were red and her eyes were wild. I paused.

"You're scared," I said. It seemed so understandable once I said it out loud. "I'm sorry. I didn't think—"

"I know you're afraid of losing me," she said, reaching out to set her hand on my arm. Her skin was warmer than it should have been. She was probably running a fever. That didn't seem like the sort of thing that came on all at once, and I found myself wondering what Dr. Abbey would say. How long had I been overlooking symptoms? George continued, "I don't blame you. I'm terrified of losing you. But Shaun, I'm the one who's sick. I'm the one who could be . . . getting sicker. So I need to help. Okay? I can't just sit around letting you take care of me. Not when it means we get to the doctor even one minute later."

"I can't do this again," I said. My voice was soft. I couldn't make it any louder. Not without screaming. "I don't care if we have to kidnap the head of the CDC, I can't do this again. You have to be okay. You have to."

"And that's why you have to let me help," said George patiently. "We need to get moving. Okay? Can we do that?"

"Okay." I leaned in and kissed her. She kissed me back. Her lips, like her fingers, were too warm. Images of funerals danced across my mind, refusing to be pushed aside.

"Okay," she said again, pulling back. "Let's get moving." She walked toward the hallway. I watched her go before turning to the back door. I had water samples to take, and neighbors to notify, and most of all—most importantly of all—a sister to save.

Book III

Should Auld Acquaintance Be Forgot

The only way anyone ever knows what matters to them is by losing it. If losing something breaks you in a way that can never be repaired, then that was what mattered. Now you know. Congrats. Try to live with it.

—Shaun Mason

There's always time for one more draft, one more round of revisions, one more fact-check. Until there isn't. Until you realize that all this time, you've been spending the time you had on things that didn't matter at all.

—Georgia Mason

One

It had taken us years to turn our cabin from somebody else's abandoned vacation home into a place that we could consider our own. Every wall, every floor, every window sealing had something of us in it. Usually caulk, sure, but also time, and sweat, and tears. We had learned how to be adults in that cabin. We'd learned how to take care of ourselves, and figured out how to take care of each other. *Years*. And yet it only took a few minutes for the cabin to dwindle and disappear in our rearview mirror, becoming part of the past, and not necessarily part of the future.

If Dr. Abbey couldn't fix me, I was never going to walk on the creaky floorboard in the hallway, or gather eggs from our broody chickens, ever again. I was pretty sure that if that happened, Shaun wouldn't be going back either. He was still a haunted house all by himself, still playing host to the ghosts he'd gathered for his own protection when the original Georgia died. He couldn't go back to a house that was also haunted by his memories of me. That would be one ghost too many, and it would break him, if losing me hadn't broken him already.

It was funny. I wanted to live. I wanted to keep having a *life*. Georgia—the original Georgia, the one I remembered being but had never been—had spent most of her life worrying about how people saw her, chasing the next big story, and dreaming of a time when she could have what I had. She'd only ever wanted to be able to spend her days with Shaun, unjudged by the people who saw them, telling the truth as she understood it. She had died chasing the truth, and the part of me that was closest to being her still wasn't sure whether or not it had been worth it. I was pretty sure it hadn't been. I would never have existed if she'd been a little less committed to the chase, but she shouldn't have died for what she got. Her cause had needed a martyr. There was no reason it had to be her.

After the original Georgia was dead and I'd been coaxed out of the wreckage of her mind, I'd believed that I was going to live my days in the custody of the CDC. I had no allies, I had no assets, and I had no way out. But I'd found a way out, thanks to the EIS and the sheer cussed stubbornness that the original Georgia had baked into every particle of me. I had found Shaun. I had convinced him I was real. And I had finally, for the first time in two lifetimes, been in a position to do what *I* wanted to do, and not give a damn about what anybody else thought. When I wanted to kiss Shaun, I kissed him. When I wanted to be something other than perfectly dignified, I relaxed. I was free.

I liked freedom. I didn't want it to end. I definitely didn't want it to end like this, with dizziness and trembling and the constant urge to close my eyes and take a little nap. Shaun was driving, mostly because neither one of us trusted me to stay awake behind the wheel. Passing out and flipping the van somewhere in the middle of Canada wouldn't help our situation.

"You want to turn the radio on?" I asked. We couldn't use the GPS—too much chance of being tracked, especially once we plugged in "Shady Cove" as our destination—but radio was safe enough. Music made the miles go faster, or at least filled in the gaps where neither of us was saying anything, and made the silence a little less profound.

"No," said Shaun. His eyes were fixed on the windshield, and his hands were white-knuckled on the wheel. Our van's shocks were good, but we still shook from side to side as we rolled along the rocky, unpaved road. I couldn't blame him for wanting to give driving his full attention. The roads in central Canada had been as abandoned as the rest of the country, and time had had its way with them. It provided an extra layer of protection to those of us who were trying to hide out there. Sadly, that was a knife that cut both ways, and now that we were trying to leave, what normally kept us safe was slowing us down.

"Okay," I said. "Is there anything you *do* want?"

"I want you to be healthy. I want everything to stay the way it has been. I want to not feel like God is fucking with me again. 'Hey, Shaun, remember when it seemed like I was going to leave you alone and let you be happy? Ha ha, sorry buddy, I was just kidding.' " Shaun took his eyes off the road for a second, casting a pleading glance in my direction. "I want you to stay with me forever. That's all. It's not so much to ask, is it? Just don't leave me, and everything will be okay."

"Believe me, Shaun, I don't want to go," I said. I forced myself to smile. It had taken us less than a full day to pack our things and get on the road, but I knew how pale I had become in just that little stretch of time. My cheeks glowed red with hectic color, and that didn't help. I looked as bad as I felt. My guts were churning, and my head spun every time I moved it too quickly. I'd be amazed if I could stay awake long enough for us to reach a real road. "I want to stay forever. I want to get old with you. I'm really excited about the idea of hearing you start to whine when your hair falls out and your metabolism stops putting up with every damn thing you try to throw at it. Those are things I've never experienced. So I'm going to do whatever I can to stick around."

"She still talks to me, you know." The words were flat, devoid of emotion, strictly factual: They hung between us like a stone dropped into a pond, throwing out ripples that changed and distorted everything. I found it suddenly hard to breathe.

Of *course* she still talked to him. Of *course* he hadn't been able to wean himself off the best coping mechanism he'd ever had. I had always known that. I just couldn't believe he'd actually admitted it out loud. We never talked about his ghosts, or how haunted he was. But let's be honest: I wasn't a trained mental health professional. I hadn't been offering him the kind of support that would have made it *possible* for him to set his phantom Georgia aside. I'd been dealing with my own demons, screaming myself awake every night, and while I had tried to focus on him whenever I could, sometimes the only person I could see was myself.

Two broken things might be able to prop each other up for a while, masking the parts that were missing, but that didn't mean they'd been fixed. It just meant they'd found the secret to compensating for their deficiencies. Shaun and I had both been broken long before we ran away together, and there was only so much healing we could do on our own.

"I know. I've always known that," I said quietly. "She was with you for a long time after I died." It was important, with Shaun, not to acknowledge the differences between me and the original Georgia out loud. He knew about them—I'm not sure I could have stayed with him if he hadn't been able to admit, at least once, that I wasn't the woman he buried—but he didn't like to talk about them. For him, the continuity of my existence was more important than the shape that existence had taken. I knew that. I had accepted, long since, that I would always be the center of his world and the other woman simultaneously, unable to ever quite replace the two iterations of me that had come first.

"Sometimes she tells me you're going to die." His eyes stayed on the road. "She talks about how flesh is transitory but she's forever. She can follow me into the field. She can't get infected. Even if I slip up, fuck up, whatever, she won't leave me the way you will. She's never actually told me to kill you, but I think she would, if she thought she could get away with it, you know? She would be thrilled if I slit your throat while you were sleeping and just walked away."

Hearing him say those things in his calm, methodical voice was painful, but not shocking. His imaginary Georgia was the worst kind of intrusive thought, and she wasn't going to let herself be replaced just because I had a body and she didn't.

I leaned over until my head was resting against his shoulder. The dizziness faded a little. I closed my eyes. That helped even more. "Everybody dies," I said. "What matters is what we do before that happens. I'm pretty okay with everything I've done. I saved a President. Overthrew the CDC and replaced them with a different group of shadowy overlords. I learned how to fix a broken toilet. I told the truth. I loved you. So I'm going to chalk this life up as a win, and I figure whatever comes next . . . comes next." It was funny. I was the only person I knew who'd actually *died*, and I had no idea whether there was an afterlife. If Heaven existed, Georgia had gone there after her body died, which meant I didn't have those memories. For me, her life—our life—had ended with the sound of a gun going off, followed by blackness.

Maybe there was something on the other side of death, some paradise or punishment or purgatory. Maybe when I got there Georgia would be waiting, along with all the other clones, the ones I'd left to burn when the Seattle CDC exploded, and we could find a way to make peace with each other. The only version of me who wasn't going to have another shot was the one in Shaun's head—or at least that was what I tried to tell myself when I got jealous of her for existing, for taking up his time and trying to turn him against me. It was hard to deal with the idea that I could be jealous of someone who didn't exist, even if it was the most natural thing in the world.

"I don't want you to go," he said doggedly. "That's all. There's no 'what comes next.' She wants me to be with her, and not you, but she's not *real*, and you are. I've already lived like that once. I can't do it again."

"So we figure out how to fix this," I said. "Dr. Abbey is smart. She knows what she's doing, and she's going to find a solution. We just have to get to her, okay? She'll make it all better, and we'll be able to go home, and carry on like nothing happened."

Shaun was quiet for a while. Then, in a soft voice, he said, "Your nose is bleeding."

I sat up, reaching for the glove compartment, and the napkins. It was going to be a long drive.

Two

According to the old maps of Canada, our cabin was located in the province of Alberta. We'd traveled a long way from our entry point of Niagara Falls, all of it in a westward direction. I hadn't been willing to go too far north; the snows got heavier the higher you went, and we'd had no experience with real winters back then. Now, we could probably make a go of it in Alaska. Maybe I'd suggest that to George after all this was over. Sure, I liked our cabin, but we were still closer to the United States than I liked.

Then again, times like this made me glad that we'd been afraid of freezing to death. Even with the bad roads and the impassable bridges, it had only taken me two days to drive from home to Shady Cove. Two days of granola bars, cold coffee, and warm Coke; two days of watching George try to pretend that her head wasn't spinning, even as she mopped the blood off her face. Honestly, if the drive had been any longer, I would probably have gone even crazier than I already was. I wanted to help her, and there was nothing I could do.

Dr. Abbey's people had been working on the roads since the last time we'd been there. The pavement had leveled out about a mile away from the forestry center, becoming remarkably smooth, even as it continued to look, to the naked eye, like no one had been through here for decades. The trees overhung the road in carefully cultivated arcs, blocking most of the aerial view. Someone watching via a satellite or unmanned drone would find themselves with very little in the way of usable footage. Heat sensors might do them some good, but even that, I wasn't so sure of. This was Dr. Abbey we were talking about. She'd probably figured out some way to coat the leaves in a harmless chemical that blocked mammalian heat signatures, just to piss the government off.

That was the kind of person she was, and by extension, the kind of person I was about to entrust with George's care: She would flip off God for the sheer satisfaction of not letting him think he got any credit for shit he did at the beginning of creation. Dr. Abbey was probably the only person I'd ever met who would argue with the law of gravity. Not because she didn't like it, or because she didn't use it. Because she didn't feel like it should be rewarded for doing its job. In some ways, that made her an uncertain ally. Right now...

If there was anyone who would look at a clone's medical problems and go "yeah, whatever, let's break the laws of God and man a little more, just to see what happens," it was her. She would do her best. I trusted her that far. I trusted her with our lives.

The parking lot was almost jarring after the carefully curated road leading up to it. We came around a corner and then we were rolling over smooth black concrete, flawlessly maintained, obviously cleaned and re-tarred on the regular. There was no effort being made to conceal the fact that people were using this space—and maybe that had something to do with the center itself.

Half the big glass windows were gone, broken by some outside force and then boarded over. The rest were intact, and light from inside escaped to pollute the otherwise untouched twilight. The doors were closed, but there were cars outside, too new and well maintained to have been abandoned since the Rising. Dr. Abbey really had put down roots. She might be hiding the ways to reach her out of habit, or because there were other dangers to be considered; I didn't know, although I was going to do my best to find out. A mystery might be just what I needed to distract me.

Assuming I could focus on anything other than the issue at hand. I drove around to the back of the building, where the entrance to the garage was located. It seemed a little odd that Dr. Abbey would have her people park outside when there was a perfectly good garage for them to use, but she probably had her reasons, and whatever they were, she would probably explain them, loudly, possibly while rolling her eyes at how slow I'd become after a few years in the Canadian wastes. It was almost nice to be coming back into the sphere of someone who thought that exposition was a normal part of the way people talked to each other. One good thing about Dr. Abbey: You always knew where you stood.

The garage door swung open at our approach, no blood test required. I stiffened as I realized that we'd passed back into the world of blood tests and needles. I would probably be paying for George's medical care in a couple of pints, and maybe some bone marrow samples if Dr. Abbey was feeling particularly frisky. I was okay with that in principle, but it had been so long since someone had come at me with a needle that I wasn't sure how I would react when it actually happened.

There was an open space next to the employee entrance. It had originally been intended for use by the handicapped, judging by the blue lines and the faded ghost of a painted wheelchair. Someone—probably Dr. Abbey—had hung a sign on the wall in front of it: RESERVED PARKING FOR CLONES AND ASSHOLES. I snorted as I pulled in and killed the engine.

George didn't stir. I turned to her, holding my breath until I saw the slow rise and fall of her chest. She was alive. That was all I needed. As long as she was alive, there was hope, and hope was more than I had been given on several occasions.

"Hey, George." I leaned over and shook her shoulder. She made a faint noise of protest, raising one hand like she was going to bat me away. It dropped back to her lap as the motion proved to be too much trouble, and she slept on. I shook her again. "Wake up. We're here. We're in Shady Cove."

"Mmgh?" She finally opened her eyes and looked at me, disorientation and grogginess warring for control. Then she blinked, and saw me properly, and smiled. "Hey, you. I was having the weirdest dream."

"Did you dream that you were a clone having weird medical problems, and that we were taking you to see a mad scientist in the hopes that she could fix it? Because if not, I've got to say your dreams need to work harder to trump reality."

"No. I dreamt we were back at the Agora. Remember that place?"

"How could I forget?" The Agora was Seattle's haven for the ultra super scary rich, a hotel and resort that could cater to every need of its guests. It was exclusive enough that most people, George and me included, couldn't even afford to breathe its air. We had stayed there once, thanks to Maggie Garcia, our resident Fictional and stealth heiress to Garcia Pharmaceuticals. She was a great lady and a good friend, and had married one of our other coworkers, Alaric Kwong, after George and I took off for Canada.

I was still a little sorry about missing the wedding. It hadn't been safe for us to come back to the United States then. It still wasn't, if I was going to be realistic. It was just that the alternative was worse.

We'd been at the Agora when we freed George from the CDC. She had dyed her hair brown in the bathroom of my suite, turning from a stolen science experiment back into herself right in front of my eyes. She had never looked back, and neither had I. If she was talking about the Agora, where everything had started for us...

Nope. I wasn't going to think that. "Come on," I said. "We're here, and Dr. Abbey is going to get pissed if we don't come inside and say hello before she has to come out and get us."

George was in no shape to carry anything. I left our bags in the van as I walked her to the door, providing an arm for her to lean on while trying to be unobtrusive about it. I didn't want her to feel like I was hovering. At the same time, I wasn't going to let her fall. I was never going to let her fall if I could help it. That was what she had me for. To keep her on her feet.

Who's going to keep you on your feet when she dies? whispered the sticky-sweet voice of her invisible twin. At least I couldn't see her. If I could keep my hallucinations at bay, this would all go a lot more smoothly. *You need me to prop you up. You've always needed me.*

"I don't need you," I muttered, before I could catch myself. I winced. George shot me a quick glance, but there was no blame or malice in her expression. She knew what I was dealing with. My mental health was no less important to her than her physical health was to me, and that was just one more reason that I couldn't afford to lose her. She was all that was keeping me even halfway down the road to sanity.

The blood testing panels next to the door were dark and deactivated. We exchanged a look. Then George shrugged, pragmatic to the last, and knocked on the door. It swung immediately open, revealing a short, slender woman with freckles across the bridge of her nose. Her hair was pulled into pigtails, one over each shoulder, and dyed the impossible brick-red color of fox fur, save for the tips, which were bleached snowy white.

She was holding some sort of complicated rifle. Of course she was.

"Hi!" said Foxy brightly, beaming at the two of us. "Who wants me to shoot them first?"

Three

The last time I'd seen Foxy, she'd been waving from the window of a house that was about to explode. I had assumed that she'd been killed in the blast. We both had. So finding her standing in Dr. Abbey's lab was a bit jarring, to say the least.

But it was still *Dr. Abbey's* lab. I knew Shaun had been in touch with her during the trip. Sometimes he'd called in over wireless relays when he thought I was asleep or dealing with something that would keep me distracted. He hadn't wanted me to hear how worried he was about me, like he thought my own awareness of my condition was somehow veiled in self-deception. He didn't know how many symptoms I'd been able to hide from him since we'd left the cabin, and hopefully, he never would. It was a small, petty wish, but it was mine, and I was holding to it.

Dr. Abbey would have told us if it wasn't safe, or if she wasn't here. So I raised an eyebrow, and asked, "What are you shooting us with?"

"Huh? Oh, nothing, if you come with me to decontamination. Didn't I say that first?" Foxy's face scrunched up as she thought about the last few minutes. "I guess maybe I didn't. It's good to see you again! I figured for sure you'd be dead by now, but Shannon says nope, you've been alive this whole time. That's important, you know. Staying alive in a straight line. You can stop, if you have to, but it's very hard to start again."

"That's true," I said, trying not to laugh at her. We still didn't know what that gun of hers did. It looked like it might be some sort of tranquilizer delivery system, intended for use only if we refused whatever decontamination process Dr. Abbey wanted us to go through. Since Foxy was the one holding it, we could probably wind up tranquilized for sneezing. It was best to tread lightly. "Let's go get decontaminated, and then we need to unload the van. We've been living in it for the last few days, and it smells pretty ripe."

"Shannon collects dead things and doggies," said Foxy. "Nothing can smell worse than dead things and doggies. Come on." She started down the hall. We followed her, lacking anything else to do.

Shaun took my hand as we walked, lacing his fingers through mine and holding on so tightly that it hurt. I didn't mind. I still felt shaky enough that having him there to lean on was important, and if he needed to hold me to be sure that I was real, it was a service I was happy to provide. My own heart was hammering, seeming to echo through my entire body. Until we'd arrived, I hadn't really considered the part where Dr. Abbey was a *doctor.* Maybe that seems silly, but it was the truth. She didn't fall into that category in my thoughts. She was a mad scientist, an ally, a friend, a dangerous enemy, but not a *doctor.* Even when we'd been asking her to help me, she hadn't clicked over into that category.

But now here we were, and it was time for her to start doctoring. Time for the white walls and the backless gowns and the needles and the tests—

My hands spasmed, forcing themselves into fists without my willing them to do so. Shaun gasped a little as I crushed his fingers, but he didn't pull away. Instead, he pulled me closer, close enough that I could smell the sweat under his deodorant.

"Breathe," he said, in a low voice. "This isn't like before."

I shot him a grateful look. He didn't need to ask what was wrong, because he knew. He knew every part of me, the ones that were like his original Georgia and the ones that were entirely my own, forged in the strange crucible of cloning and medical experimentation and escape. He didn't judge, either. That was the best part. Whoever I was, whatever the source of my soul, he loved me all the same. I was his George. That was all he'd ever needed me to be.

"I know," I said. "I just...I guess I didn't think about what this would mean until we got here." I hadn't *allowed* myself to think about it, because thinking about it would have meant admitting that I was willingly handing myself over to a woman who had belonged to the CDC, once upon a time, even if she'd found it in herself to walk away. Dr. Abbey was our friend. She was also the face of my worst nightmare. Those two things didn't contradict each other. They existed simultaneously, informing each other, and nothing I did would change them.

"I'm going to be with you the whole time," he said. "No matter what."

"That's not quite true," chirped Foxy, turning around and walking backward as she led us down the hall. "You have to go into separate rooms for decontamination. Doctor's orders. Something about making sure that there's no confusion about what came from who."

"What are you doing here, Foxy?" Shaun sounded more weary than curious. He didn't let go of my hand. "I thought you were dead."

"Oh, don't worry," said Foxy brightly. "I'm pretty sure I *was* dead, or close enough for tax purposes. Got some real nasty shrapnel in the back when the house went boom-boom, and bled all over the place. It was a bad, bad scene. But then some of the Monkey's friends came to see what had happened, and they found me and took care of me until they didn't, and then I came here, and now Shannon takes care of me, and tries to help me remember how to be a people instead of a weapon of mass destruction, and Tom makes me my space lobster juice for when the screaming gets too loud. So it's all good. We're here, by the way."

She stopped walking between two doors. They were labeled, in quixotic fashion, "Squids" and "Mollusks." Shaun raised an eyebrow.

"Okay, I'll bite," he said. "Which one am I?"

"All gender is a construct and binary gender doubly so, but you have a hard shell and you're hard to kill, so you're probably a mollusk," said Foxy blithely. "You should get clean now. Shannon doesn't like to be kept waiting."

"Right," said Shaun. He looked toward me, expression going grave. "George..."

I let go of his hand. The gesture felt somehow terribly final. "It's fine," I said. "We're going to get clean, and then we can go tell Dr. Abbey all about my medical history. It's *fine*."

Shaun didn't look so sure. I was starting to get frustrated with his separation anxiety. Yeah, he was going to have issues if I died, but dying was the last thing on my list of things to do, right after "topple one more major world government, just for fun" and "learn how to make jam that doesn't ferment."

"I'll be right back," I said, and pushed open the door marked "Squid," stepping into the echoing white chamber on the other side.

The Shady Cove Forestry Center had been intended as half educational opportunity, half training ground for the rangers of tomorrow. During its heyday, up to fifteen junior rangers would be living there at any given time. That meant the facility came with a good number of showers, enough to keep everyone clean when they were at full occupancy. Dr. Abbey and her people inhabited the building more completely and for longer periods than those long-dead rangers had ever dreamt, and they'd taken the time to make a few modifications to the place.

The wall between the Squid and Mollusk rooms was clearly newer than the walls around it, tiled in an off-green shade that looked like it had been raided from a hotel pool. The door closed behind me as I was studying the tile, sealing itself with an ominous click.

"Hello, Georgia," said a female voice. It came through a hidden speaker and echoed off the walls until it seemed larger than the world. I clapped a hand over my mouth to keep myself from screaming.

The doctors back at the CDC had almost always used the intercom to talk to me. They didn't want to risk getting any closer. At first, that was because they weren't sure whether I was going to amplify and kill them all. Later, it was because they didn't want to deal with my endless questions and demands. They had taken away anything that could have been used as a weapon, but I still had my hands, my knees, and my teeth. Those things were more than enough, once you had nothing left to lose.

There was a click from the intercom, and the door on the other side of the room opened, revealing a short, curvy woman in a lab coat and a bright yellow T-shirt with a biohazard symbol blazoned across the breast. She looked almost apologetic, which was nearly as jarring as the voice from above. Dr. Shannon Abbey didn't *do* apologetic. She was a slave to science, and followed wherever it led, no matter how cruel those roads became.

"I'm sorry," she said, stunning me further. "I remember you talking about the intercoms back at the CDC, but I didn't think about the fact that you might not like faceless voices speaking to you. You want to come with me? Please? It's good to see you again, even though you look like shit."

"There's the sympathy I was expecting," I said. I looked around the tiled room again, and then back to Dr. Abbey. "I haven't showered yet."

"I know. The decontamination cycle is nine minutes long, and can't be canceled once it begins. That gives us time to talk before your—should I even call him your brother? Before Shaun gets involved."

"Legally, he's my brother, because we were adopted by the same people," I said, understanding washing over me. She needed to talk to me alone, and we were both smart enough to know that *that* wasn't going to happen if Shaun had anything to say about it. The choices were "trick him" or "drug him," and while the latter might have been easier, I didn't want to go there if I had any other choice. I walked toward her, my steps echoing against the tile. "Functionally, he's my best friend, and my... boyfriend seems so small. He's my Shaun."

"I know what you mean," she said, stepping aside to let me exit the room. The door slid shut behind me, and I heard the water come on. The room was decontaminating itself now that it had presumably been exposed.

Exposed... I stopped, eyes widening. "I haven't been tested," I said. "I could be an infection risk right now."

"You could," agreed Dr. Abbey. "There's also the part where you're turning into a blood fountain with very little warning, which is all kinds of fun. I can't decide whether that's a function of high blood pressure, or a weakness in your sinuses. Either way, we're going to find out. Come on. I promise, I'm a big girl, I can monitor my own infection risks."

Her logic was sound. My legs still felt like lead as I forced them to start moving again and followed her down the long white hall to a small office. Joe the mastiff was asleep on a huge cushion against one wall, his massive head down on his paws. He was snoring. I couldn't stop myself from shuddering at the sight of him. Dogs aren't common these days, since Kellis-Amberlee is the ultimate spillover disease: It moves between mammalian populations with ease, and large predators are its best delivery system.

Dr. Abbey followed my gaze and smiled, an expression that was equal parts fond and sad. "Good old Joe," she said. The dog didn't stir. She walked past him to a cabinet, opening it and beginning to take down an assortment of medical supplies—a blood pressure cuff, a package of syringes, all the basic, terrifying tools of the medical profession. "He's getting on. Big dogs don't live as long as small dogs. Their hearts give out. I don't know what I'll do when he's gone."

Having never had a pet, I didn't have anything useful to say. Instead, I stood where I was, trying not to fidget or shy away as she kept removing things from her seemingly bottomless cabinet of horrors.

"I'm not going to lie to you, Georgia; even if I wanted to, I've never been the sort of person who sugarcoats or censors things for the sake of other people's sensibilities, and I wouldn't know where to begin." Dr. Abbey began putting things on her desk, lining them up in a neat little row. "I've talked to Greg and Joey about your situation, and they agree that we're in uncharted territory here. They also say hello, and wanted me to remind you that you're allowed to contact them once in a while, just to let them know that you're still breathing."

"I always knew I was *allowed*," I said. "If they were that worried about whether I was dead or alive, they could have checked with Mahir. He still publishes my op-ed columns, when I send them in. I think he'd notice if I was dead."

But he didn't know why Shaun and I had both gone silent for the last three days, did he? Neither of us had bothered to notify him, or anyone other than our immediate neighbors. Part of it was habit: We had always been a closed loop, me and Shaun, Shaun and me, and moving to the wilds of Canada had just made that tendency even stronger. If we couldn't supply something, we went without, rather than asking someone else to help. And part of it was the knowledge, absolute and unshakable, that if I called, Mahir would come. We had been friends even before we were colleagues, and I had never questioned his loyalty. Mahir had a life now. He had a wife, and a daughter, and really good reasons never to set foot in North America again. Calling him would have been unfair.

"Mmm-hmm," said Dr. Abbey. She didn't sound convinced. I didn't feel all that convincing. "Danika is on her way."

I stiffened. "What?"

Dr. Danika Kimberley was an EIS neuroscientist who'd been undercover with the CDC during the project that had cloned the original Georgia Mason and created me. She probably understood the neural interface that had given me Georgia-prime's memories better than anyone else who was still alive. She was a good woman, and she had played a pivotal role in getting me out of the Seattle installation before it was blown to hell. And none of that meant that I wanted her anywhere near me, especially not right now, when I couldn't afford to decline medical care.

"One of two things is happening right now, Georgia. I don't know whether I can stop either one of them, but one is within my skill set, and the other is so far beyond me that it might as well be rocket science," said Dr. Abbey. She picked up a piece of tubing and a syringe. "First, we have to consider the possibility that your body is just giving up. Multiple organ failure has been observed in clones before, and none of them were as old or as unsupervised as you've been. There may have been early signs that you missed, just because you didn't register them as potentially important."

"Right," I said. That was always a risk, even with medical texts and access to the Internet. I wasn't a doctor. At the end of the day, I wasn't going to see the things that doctors saw.

"This may be difficult for you to believe, but that's actually the good option. Roll your sleeve up, please."

I rolled up my sleeve. "What's the bad option?"

"The bad option is that your neural programming is starting to go." Dr. Abbey tied the tubing around my arm, bringing the veins into stark relief. "You're a unicorn, Georgia. You're something no one had ever done before—something that ethically speaking, no one should have done in the first place—and you represent an ethical black hole. Scientifically speaking, you should have lived and died in the room where you woke up, monitored constantly, so science could learn everything about you. How have those implanted memories settled? Are they being undermined or reinforced by the memories you've formed since waking? Is the neural matrix flexible enough to deal with changes, or is it too static to adapt when confronted with data that contradicts things the original Georgia Mason believed were true? Is the matrix really stable, or is it just taking a long time to degrade? You're a walking, talking database of lost chances and unanswered questions, and ethically speaking, that's exactly what you need to be. You became a person as soon as you opened your eyes and started thinking."

Cold fear slithered along my spine, reptilian and ancient. "What would it mean if my neural programming went?"

"Honestly, Georgia?" Dr. Abbey uncapped her syringe and slid it into my arm, not even bothering to warn me about the pinch. Both of us watched as my blood flowed red and hot into the chamber. "I have no idea."

Four

The decontamination cycle was about average in length, which didn't stop me from jerking on the clean sweatpants provided and running out of the room as soon as the door unlocked. The cold air of the hallway hit me like a slap. Foxy, who had been sitting cross-legged on the floor, waiting patiently, flowed back to her feet and smiled sunnily at me.

"There you go," she said. "You smell less awful now."

"Where's George?" The light above the second decontamination chamber's door was green; there was no one in there. George should have been waiting for me.

Foxy cocked her head to the side, smile fading. "I don't think you're happy to see me," she said. "Why aren't you happy to see me? I'm happy to see *you.* You remember the Monkey and the Cat and the house where I used to live, and nobody does those things anymore. That makes us friends. Shared memory is the foundation of friendship." Her tone changed on the last sentence, becoming almost grounded as it lost the floaty, singsong quality that her voice normally contained.

I didn't have time to wonder about that. "I'm happy to see you, Foxy, okay? I thought you were dead, and it's always nice when someone you thought was dead turns out not to be. In the 'walking around and still being a people' sense, not the 'zombie infected grr' sense. I just... where's Georgia? She was supposed to be going through the same decontamination cycle I was." I was struggling not to panic. My thoughts were chasing themselves in circles, and I could virtually feel the phantom fingers on the back of my neck. Fear of losing George had brought her phantom twin to the surface. She was always there, always waiting for the chance to slip back into the place that she thought of as rightfully hers. It was getting harder to fight her. The added stress of not knowing where the real George was didn't help.

"Oh, Shannon wanted to talk to her in private. You know, girl stuff." Foxy dimpled. "Anyway, she said I should meet you when you got out of the shower and take you to them. Did you want to put a shirt on? You're all chesty and it's distracting."

"The door closed," I said.

"I can find you a shirt," said Foxy. Again, there was that unusual seriousness in her voice. It was easy to think of her as much younger than she was: Her bone structure and general muscle tone fed into that idea. But there were lines in the skin around her eyes and mouth, and it wasn't outside the realm of possibility for her to have seen the Rising firsthand. Maybe she hadn't always been this way. Maybe she was like me, broken by outside forces and told to figure out how to keep going now that she was something new. If that was the case, she had found a unique, and uniquely homicidal, method of coping.

"Okay," I said. It was never good to argue with someone who had that many guns. "But after you find me a shirt, you take me to my sister. All right?"

"Absolutely," chirped Foxy. She grabbed my hand, all childlike mania again, and dragged me down the hall.

Dr. Abbey's people had definitely settled into the forestry center. We passed rooms clogged with white-coated researchers, moving around cages full of rats or tanks of wet, squelchy things. Some of the things had suckers. Others seemed to be nothing but shapeless clouds of shadow and silt that moved through the water like smoke. Foxy never slowed down. The rooms blurred, one into the next, without revealing their details to me. On some level, I was grateful. If I'd been able to see everything that Dr. Abbey was working on, I would have had to think about it. That never ended well.

"So what are you doing here, Foxy?" I asked.

"A bad man used me as a decoy to try to make Shannon let him in, like the Big Bad Wolf blowing and blowing and blowing the house down," she said blithely. "She says he used me like a weapon, and that it was inappropriate, because people aren't weapons, they're people, and I deserve better. I think she's been locked up here so long that she's turned into an idealist, but that's why I stick around. She's going to need people who don't believe in ideals, when the sky falls down and the wolves are at the door." She slanted a glance in my direction. "Tom works in hydroponics. He makes drugs for me, so I don't have to be an idealist."

"Drugs?" I frowned. "Foxy, if they're drugging you..."

"No, no, silly boy, *they* aren't drugging me, *I'm* drugging me. I take my pills and I drink my drinks, and the people I used to be don't come to the surface." Her gaze sharpened. "You're a reporter. You work for that site. The one with the smiling man who wears the red glasses."

It took me a moment to realize she was talking about Alaric. His latest masthead picture showed him wearing a pair of red-framed glasses. "I do," I said.

"Then you must have read the things he *said* about me. He dug so deep he hit the bottom of the world, and he *said* things." She pulled open a door in the wall, revealing stacks of neatly folded sweatpants, sweatshirts, and medical scrubs. The sweats were gray. The scrubs were blue. I reached for a sweatshirt. If I showed up wearing scrubs, George would probably have a panic attack. "You should know who I used to be."

"If it was one of his big fact-finding articles, then sorry, I'm a bad coworker." The shirt was snug, but it would do. "I don't go in for the historical stuff. If it can't chew my face off or be used to shoot something that's trying to chew my face off, I'm not interested."

"Oh." Foxy blinked, her entire demeanor softening. "So you don't know."

"Honestly, Foxy, the only thing I know right now is that I want you to take me to Georgia. Please. I'm scared out of my mind, and I'm doing my best to stay cool, but I don't know how long I'm going to be able to pull this off. Will you take me to her?"

"Now that you're wearing a shirt, sure. Follow me." She turned and trotted down the hall. I followed, trying not to let my eagerness cause me to overtake her. I needed her to get me to George, and I didn't want to spend the next hour wandering around this maze masquerading as a medical facility.

Voices drifted from an open door up ahead. One of them belonged to Dr. Abbey. The other—

"George!" Now I *did* put on a burst of speed, beating Foxy to the doorway by several steps. Inside was an office, small and cozy, with a dog bed taking up most of one wall. Joe was sleeping there, and under any other circumstances, I would have spared a moment to be amazed that the old dog was still kicking. At the moment, I had better things to worry about. George was sitting in a straight-backed plastic chair, sipping what looked like orange juice. Her hair was dry. She hadn't gone through decontamination at all.

Dr. Abbey tricked me, I thought, and that wasn't important, not really, because George was turning to look at me, a weary smile on her lips. She wasn't hurt. She wasn't dead. Things were still okay.

"Hey," said George. Her smile didn't reach her eyes, which were sad and scared. "Sorry to frighten you. I like the shirt."

"What she's not saying is that she had no input in the matter," said Dr. Abbey, looking up from her computer. "I needed to talk to her without you in the room. Locking you in the shower seemed like the best solution, since I knew there was no other way I was going to get the two of you apart. Hello, Shaun. Long time no see. You're looking well. Canada agrees with you."

"That's more than I can say for a certain Canadian," I said, scowling. "You had no right to do that to us."

"Right and wrong are all about where you're standing," she said. "There used to be a thing called 'doctor-patient confidentiality,' before the CDC made your health the world's business. I wanted to talk to

Georgia about her condition, and what it could mean for her, specifically. It's up to her how much of that she passes along. I know you don't like being left out of things, but you need to accept that this is her body, and it's her choice whether she tells you everything or holds certain aspects back. There are going to be times when this needs to happen. I'd rather not trick you again. I will, if you make me."

I opened my mouth, preparing to speak—and then I stopped, closing it so hard that my teeth rattled like a Halloween prop. I took a deep breath, held it, let it out, and said, "All right."

George blinked. Dr. Abbey lifted an eyebrow.

"All right?" she echoed. "Who are you, and what have you done with Shaun Mason?"

"I'm the man whose sister is really, really sick right now, and I'm not going to get in the way of anything that could make her better," I said. "Do I want to? Yeah. I hope you've got a real zombie problem in your woods right now, Doc, because I'm going to need something to distract me from all the help I can't offer."

"You're helping," said George. "You brought me here. You're still here. Don't ever think that you're not helping." She got out of the chair. Only the way she held on to the arm, fingers clenched tight and arm suspiciously rigid, told me how much effort that was. Someone who didn't know her might not even realize that she was sick.

"I'm trying," I said, offering her my arm as I looked back to Dr. Abbey. "Do you know what's wrong with her?"

"Not yet," she said. She held up a small vial of something red. I realized, after a moment's blank staring, that it was George's blood. "But I will. You can trust me on that."

"We're already trusting you on everything else," I said, putting an arm around George's shoulders. She leaned into me, as much for support as for comfort. "What's one more thing?"

Dr. Abbey nodded, and didn't say anything. For the three of us, in that moment, there was nothing else to say.

Then Foxy stuck her head in from the hall. "Should I show them to their room?" she asked. "Because it's almost time for me to go take my pills, and I don't think I should show them anything after that. It's always hard to know whether I'm showing people a thing that *is*, or a thing that I think *ought* to be."

"In a moment, Foxy," said Dr. Abbey. Foxy beamed and withdrew again.

George's eyebrows were climbing toward her hairline. "I have so many questions right now," she said. "Did you see Alaric's report . . . ?"

"Wait, you read that?" I asked.

She punched me lightly in the chest. "You're not as disinterested as you pretend to be. Everyone here knows it."

"I still didn't read the article," I said. "You know Alaric's prose doesn't do anything for me."

Dr. Abbey snorted. "The two of you have been living alone in the wastes too long. You've forgotten how to leave room in conversations for other people—not that you were ever particularly good at it to begin with. Yes, I read Mr. Kwong's dissertation on the case of Elaine Oldenburg, and yes, I am aware that she's the woman we call 'Foxy.' She has severe depression and PTSD, and has been coping by means of pharmaceuticals for years. We're supplying her with synthetic cannabinoids, mixed by one of my assistants, and I've been working with her on cutting back. Someday I may be able to wean her off them completely. She isn't exactly keen on the idea of facing the world without filters, but she's been trying. People used that girl unconscionably. If you ever need proof that the dead aren't the real monsters, just look at her. But she's trying, and I'm trying, and she has a home here for as long as she needs one. Even if she does track unmentionable things on the carpet."

She turned on George. "As for you: I don't know what's wrong with you yet. I *do* know that you're dehydrated, and that we need to get that taken care of pronto. I'll be at your room in an hour, to set up a saline drip and to show your damn fool brother how to keep it from kinking. Now, go get cleaned up. We have work to do."

George still leaning against me for support, we went. Dr. Abbey was right.

We had work to do.

Book IV

Enemy Without, Enemy Within

I am the only person I know whose deaths can be counted on more than one finger. I don't know whether or not that's something to be proud of. I legitimately have no idea.

—Georgia Mason

I hate problems I can't punch.

—Shaun Mason

One

I was lying on the bed in what had become my usual room when Dr. Abbey looked up from her computer, said, "I'll be right back," and rose, stalking out the door. I barely had time to lift my head and blink before she was gone, leaving me alone with Joe. The big black dog was asleep again, stretched out so that he occupied most of the floor to one side of my bed. Dr. Abbey was an expert at stepping over and around him, seeming to waltz through the spaces where the dog was not, all for the sake of not needing to disturb her faithful companion. It was sweet. It was surreal—I had never lived with a dog, and her devotion to the animal was strange to me, like it belonged to somebody else, somebody who wasn't a no-nonsense mad scientist dedicated to understanding the structure of Kellis-Amberlee. But it was nice not to be alone.

"I wonder where she's going in such a hurry," I said. Joe didn't respond.

We'd been in Shady Cove for a week. I spent my days moving between the bed in the treatment room and the bed in the room I shared with Shaun. Not for fun reasons, either. On one end, I gave blood and allowed Dr. Abbey to subject me to every test she could think of, looking for the place where my body was betraying me. On the other end, I crawled under the blankets and slept, so exhausted by the effort of lying on a mattress and answering questions that I couldn't see straight. I was alive. I couldn't call what I was doing living.

Shaun wasn't handling the situation well, although he was doing his best to keep me from seeing how distressed and frightened he was.

Every morning, he walked with me to meet Dr. Abbey, and kissed me on the cheek before he left us alone together. From there, he walked to the lobby, met up with Foxy, and left the building, heading out into the woods to collect samples for Dr. Abbey's studies. He'd brought back six infected humans, three infected deer, and two dead wolves in just the last few days. It seemed to help him, and it wasn't like he needed to worry about infection. Idleness was a much bigger threat for him. It left him too much time to think about what was happening—and as we both knew, Shaun's mind was his own greatest enemy. I was aware that my phantom twin was waiting in the wings, ready to replace me the second I stepped aside. She would probably have done it before then, if she'd thought Shaun would let her get away with it.

I knew she couldn't think anything: that she was just a function of the damage my death had done to the man who loved me more than anything else in the world, and the damage he'd done to himself as he struggled to adjust to a world that didn't contain me anymore. She was a figment, a phantom, incapable of thinking anything that Shaun didn't think first. Her desire to replace me was a reflection of his deep-set fear of being left alone again. As long as he held on to her, he would never have to worry about me leaving him. I couldn't be angry at him—not for that. I understood his terror all too well. So I had to settle for being mad at someone who didn't exist for reinforcing those fears, and making him think that I was going to leave him.

Even though she might be right. It was getting harder and harder to get out of bed, and my nosebleeds were becoming more frequent. Dr. Abbey was patching the leaks as quickly as she could find them, but without knowing the underlying problem, I wasn't sure she was going to be able to do enough. I was going.

I just didn't know where.

I was staring at the ceiling, considering the virtues of getting up and finding something to drink—Dr. Abbey kept orange juice in the little fridge next to my blood samples—when someone knocked on the doorframe. I lifted my head to see a tall, Nordic-looking woman with ice-blonde hair standing there, wearing weathered blue jeans, a green cable-knit sweater, and sensible sneakers. I blinked once, my mind briefly overlaying her image with a silk blouse, red pencil skirt, and stiletto heels that would sound like gunshots whenever she took a step.

But Dr. Shaw had been an illusion, cold and bright and mirror-brittle, only intended to get the woman behind it to the finish line before the mask was dropped. Dr. Danika Kimberley was real, a warm, living, smiling human woman who walked to my side and brushed my hair away from my forehead the way I'd always imagined a mother would. "Hello there, you silly little thing," she said, voice thick with unshed tears. Her accent was Welsh: She was a long way from home. "Had to go and break yourself, didn't you just? I suppose it was a decent excuse to see me again, although really, you could have just called, and saved us both the trouble."

"I thought you'd have more fun this way," I said, and forced myself to smile.

Dr. Kimberley hadn't been a part of the team that grew me, but she'd been associated with them, close enough to the heart of the project that she'd been able to steal some of my time for her own use. She had claimed sleep studies and analysis of my brain waves, anything to keep her interventions believable while she worked to get me the hell out of there. I would be forever grateful to her for that, even as her position within the EIS guaranteed that I would never really be able to trust her.

"Well, you'll be glad to know that Shannon sent me copies of your scans to review while I was on the way over here, and there's nothing wrong with your neural integration. I'll want to run a few more tests, of course, for the sake of being thorough, but it looks as if your memories are locked in there as tight as ever." She leaned over and tapped one finger against my forehead, like she was checking a melon to see how ripe it was. "Your network is not unsnarling. Your troubles are purely physical, nothing to do with those early, implanted thoughts."

I relaxed slightly, letting out a breath I'd only been half-aware of holding. I was Georgia Mason because of the memories implanted in me during the final decanting process at the CDC: They had grown a body from the original Georgia's genetic material, but even as identical twins would grow up to be different people, I would have become someone very different if I hadn't been programmed with all the original's thought patterns and recovered memories. Maybe it was a crime that the woman I should have become had never been allowed to develop, but I didn't see it that way. I was me because of those memories. I didn't want to lose myself. I needed to be here.

"So what's the problem?" I asked. "Am I just too awesome for this world?"

"Something like that, yes." Dr. Kimberley pulled a chair over to my bedside and sat down. There was a flicker of motion from the doorway. I glanced past her. Dr. Abbey was standing there, her face drawn in an expression of silent regret. My heart seized in my chest, cramping up until I couldn't breathe. Dr. Abbey never made that face. Dr. Abbey raged and scowled and demanded that the world adhere to her standards. She didn't stand there refusing to meet my eyes while her own eyes grew over-wet with tears.

Dr. Kimberley took my hand in both of hers. I transferred my terrified gaze to her.

"I need you to remain calm," she said. "Can you do that for me, or would you like a sedative first? I have some that won't put an undue amount of pressure on your system."

I wanted to ask why she would come prepared with sedatives, but I was direly afraid that I already knew the answer; more, I didn't want to hear the careful, clinical words she would use in answering me, each chosen to convey the maximum amount of information, with the minimum possible amount of distress. Her bedside manner could be cold at times. No one was ever going to say that it was anything less than professional.

"I don't need a sedative," I said.

"All right," she said. "We need to run more tests. We need to be sure. But I believe we've found a cause."

"Tell me," I said.

She did.

Two

Foxy trotted off when we reached the forestry center door, heading for the decontamination rooms. She needed to strip off her gear and scrub herself clean as soon as possible, to avoid potential infection. I needed to decontaminate—I was a danger to others until I did—but I wasn't in any hurry. There was no way for me to catch Kellis-Amberlee, and Dr. Abbey had taken to requesting blood samples every time I showered, just in case she could catch my cells in the process of doing something interesting.

She never explained what "something interesting" meant, and to be honest, I was afraid to ask. If anyone was going to mutate me into some sort of giant green monster, it was probably going to be her.

I sauntered down the hall, waving to a few of Dr. Abbey's research assistants as they passed on the catwalks overhead. Most waved back. Some I knew by name; others were just a part of the ever-shifting landscape of the place. They were all individuals. Jill had a prosthetic leg and rolled her eyes a lot. Tom walked in a constant mild funk of pot smoke, and was always happy to share a joint in the hydroponics section—an offer I had taken him up on several times, when the pressure of worrying about George got to be too much. In the end, though, they were all the same. They were the people who were going to help Dr. Abbey find a way to save Georgia. Nothing else mattered.

The first decontamination room I came to was unlocked. I slipped inside and disrobed, shoving my soiled clothes into the hamper before I stepped into range of the showerheads. "Shaun Mason, visitor," I said clearly. "Preferred temperature: hot. Preferred scent: eucalyptus. Duration, max six minutes."

"Preferences have been noted and logged, Shaun Mason," said the bland, pleasant voice of the shower. "Did you have a productive excursion?" The water came on, blasting me from all sides.

"Caught two more zombie deer, and I think there's a bear somewhere nearby," I said. "I will forgive the oatmeal in this place if there's a bear. I haven't shot a zombie bear in *ages*."

"Wow, that's interesting," said the shower. "Dr. Abbey wishes me to remind you that you will need to submit to both a blood test and a small donation before you will be allowed to exit the chamber." I wasn't really having a conversation with the shower, of course: A.I. technology isn't that advanced. The decontamination system had a variety of preprogrammed responses and cues, which it cycled through according to the input it received. It flagged keywords at the same time; when Dr. Abbey got the report on the decon, she would also receive a memo listing my kills and the fact that I suspected a bear of living somewhere nearby.

I used to hate it when computers talked to me. After a few years in the middle of nowhere, I've gotten more resigned to the fact that it's never going to stop, and I've become more willing to talk back. At least that way I'm carrying on a conversation with something that's not in my head.

"Oh, come on," said George's voice. "The things in your head aren't so bad."

I knew I shouldn't turn around, that turning around would do nothing good for my state of mind. I turned anyway, and there she was, naked, leaning up against the shower's far wall and smiling a slow, sly smile. I had to give my hallucinations this much: They were high quality. Water beaded on her skin, and when she uncrossed her arms, I saw the flash of her ID tattoo on the inside of her wrist. The original George had had that tattoo. The current one didn't. The CDC had never prepped her for release—had never prepped her for *me*—and since she hadn't bothered to renew her license after we fled the country, neither of us had ever seen the point of seeking out an underground tattoo parlor. Tattoos were dangerous enough under rigidly controlled and sterile conditions. Vanity wasn't enough reason to get one.

"Go away," I said. "I don't need you here."

"But you do, Shaun, you *do*," she said. "When's the last time you saw your little clone up and walking around under her own power, huh? She's running down. You need to come back to me while I'm still willing to have you."

"See, that's the awful part," I said, giving her one last look before I turned my back, closing my eyes and tilting my face up into the spray. "I know you'll always be willing to have me. I'm the only thing you have. But I have a life that doesn't have to include you if I don't want it to. Go away."

"You'll always want me," she whispered, her fingers brushing the back of my neck one last time. I knew that if I turned around to look, she would be gone—for now. Because the worst part of it was, she was right. I would always want her. She was safe. She couldn't leave me. Not like the original had; not like the replacement might. The fake could never go anywhere.

I went still, letting the water run over me. Was that really how I thought of her? The "replacement"? Sure, she wasn't the first George, but she wasn't a *replacement*. She was *George*. In every way that mattered, she was *George*. There wasn't a word for the part she played in my life. She was my sister, in that I didn't have any other model for what a sister was: someone who loved me, had always loved me, would always love me, no matter what. I could chase a million rabbits down the burrows in my head, and she would still be waiting for me when I popped back out. She believed in me, even when I was too lost to believe in myself. She understood me better than I understood myself.

She was my sister because the Masons had wanted us to be family, and she was my family because there was no one else in the world who loved, wanted, and accepted me the way that she did. She wasn't a replacement. She was *George.*

The shower said pleasantly, "Please close your mouth and eyes," and the water became bleach, cold and caustic and sleeting down over me like a punishment. I stayed where I was, enduring it as my due. I deserved a little suffering for even thinking the word "replacement," even if it went unspoken. She was sick. She needed me. I couldn't let myself weaken.

But maybe it was time, after all this was over and we were getting ready to head home, for me to talk to Dr. Abbey about steps we could take to quiet the voices in my head. I had tried drugs once before, and it hadn't worked out so well—it had made me actively suicidal, which was no good—but that had been before George returned from the grave. As long as I had one of her, I could be basically okay. I just couldn't be alone, that was all. Not that big a deal. Not that unusual a thing. And if we were going home, if we were lucky enough to be going home...

I knew I was the only man in her life. It was time to make sure that she was the only woman in mine.

The bleach cycle was followed by one more rinse, and a fine citrus mist intended to keep the bleach from doing too much damage to my skin. Dr. Abbey didn't hold with blood tests every five feet or constant monitoring of where people went once they were inside, but she kept her sterilization systems fully operational. That was essential. Bleach dried people out, and dry skin could split and crack, creating an infection risk that went way beyond Kellis-Amberlee. Without lotion and citrus sprays to rehydrate people, staph infections would have run rampant, and things would have become a lot less pleasant.

Foxy was waiting in the hall outside. Like me, she was clean and dressed in fresh clothes, with the scent of strawberries and lime hanging in the air around her. She was barefoot, and kept rocking from her heels to her toes, an anxious expression on her face. I had never seen Foxy look nervous before—not like that.

My heart sank, and somewhere on the edge of hearing, phantom laughter echoed. I swallowed, trying to moisten my suddenly dry tongue. "Hi, Foxy," I said. My voice sounded high and strained, the voice of a man who was barely keeping it together. "What's going on?"

"Shannon said I was supposed to come and get you, and that I should be really normal and casual about it, because she doesn't want you to freak out," said Foxy meekly.

"I'm not going to freak out," I said, without pausing to think about whether or not I was lying to her. "Did she tell you why?"

Foxy shook her head.

"Did she tell you where you were supposed to take me?"

Foxy nodded.

"All right. Did she tell you whether Georgia was alive?" That was the real question: That was the only question that mattered. Because the first time George had died, I'd been in the position to avenge her. There had been people I could hit, people I could *blame*, and when that was over, there had been people I needed to survive for. This time...

There was no one I could hit. If Georgia was dead, Dr. Abbey hadn't killed her; Dr. Abbey had simply failed to save her, and I wasn't so far gone that I couldn't understand the difference. Dr. Abbey deserved my thanks, not my vengeance. And there was no one else. All our enemies were either dead or so nebulous that I couldn't fight them. George was the one who saw ignorance and public misunderstanding as things to battle and destroy. I needed jaws to break and noses to punch. I couldn't do this alone. If she was dead, then I was done. I was going to turn around and walk back out the door, into the green, violent world of the woods. Kellis-Amberlee couldn't kill me. Its creations still could.

The dead had always given me a reason to live. It was only fitting that my life should end with them.

Relief washed over Foxy's face. "Gosh, no," she said. "You mean your sister, right? The one who keeps having oopsies?" She fluttered her fingers near her lip, like she was miming a bloody nose. "Gosh, no, she's not dead. I mean, she's not *fine*, that would be a little untrue, since she's really sick and all, but she's not *dead*."

I moved without thinking, sweeping Foxy into an embrace that lifted her off her feet and pinned her arms to her sides. "Oh, thank God!"

She was stiff as a board against me. I realized abruptly that I had picked up another human being without asking. I looked at her face. Her eyes were wide and glittering bright, filled with a calm, still breed of terror that I normally saw only in the very young.

"Please put me down," she said. Her voice was level and steady. She sounded like every teacher I'd had in elementary school, prepared to tell me, at length, why roughhousing was never acceptable. "If you don't, I'm going to cut off your balls and your thumbs and anything else that looks like it sticks out more than it strictly needs to, and I'm not going to be sorry."

"But I'm sorry." I lowered her back to her feet and let go. She promptly scurried backward, stopping when her shoulders hit the wall. She stayed there, watching me warily. I sighed. "Foxy, I'm really sorry. I was just so relieved that I didn't . . . I shouldn't have touched you without your permission. It won't happen again."

"Shannon told me about what Georgia is to you, and what you are to Georgia." She was still using that calm, measured teacher-voice. I'd never heard her sound so lucid. Somehow, that made her seem even more frightening. "I know you're worried about her, and I know you were probably scared that something had happened. But you don't get to touch me. No one gets to touch me. I'm the Monkey's girl."

"Foxy . . . the Monkey's dead. We saw him die."

"I know. Sucks, don't it?" The corner of her mouth twitched, like she was trying to smile. "When I'm really lucid, I know I'm no one's property, especially not a dead man's, and *especially* not a dead man who used drugs to rewire my brain so that I'd have to love him. But it doesn't change things. He made me. He owns me. Just because I'm here and he's not, that doesn't make things any different. No one gets to touch me but the Monkey, and the Monkey's never going to touch me again. Now, come on. Dr. Abbey is waiting."

She turned and padded off down the hall. Still shaky from adrenaline, and sorry to have grabbed her the way I had, I followed.

The door to George's treatment room was open. I stepped into the doorway and stopped, eyebrows raising at the scene in front of me. Dr. Abbey leaned against the wall, her hand resting on Joe's head, the massive black dog leaning against her leg. A tall blonde woman sat next to the bed, talking earnestly with George—at least, she was until I entered. She stopped then, and they both turned to face me. George managed to find a smile, although it was strained, colored with pain and weariness.

Dr. Kimberley didn't bother. She just looked at me, expression neutral. She had a poker face that could have ended dynasties, and in a way, it had—it was her infiltration of the CDC that had allowed George to get out before they killed her, and without George, the EIS would never have been able to succeed in their coup.

"Shaun," she said, after a few seconds had passed in silence. "You're looking surprisingly well for someone who went to live in a place without reliable electricity. Have you lost weight?"

"A few pounds," I said. "You're looking good for a scary neuroscientist who may be working for the enemy. Dr. Abbey . . . ?"

"Danika is here as my guest, and you'd do well to remember that I have rules against murdering my guests," said Dr. Abbey. "They're even written down these days."

"That's because of me," said Foxy. I glanced to the side. She was slouched against the hallway wall, picking her fingernails with the point of a scalpel. I couldn't decide whether that was intended to be a warning or a harmless fidget. There wasn't any reason it couldn't be both.

I looked back to Dr. Abbey. "Why didn't you tell me she was coming?"

"Because I asked her not to," said George. I turned to her. She looked so tired, and so small, like that bed was in the process of swallowing her alive. "Dr. Kimberley is the only person we have who really understands my neural programming. We needed to be sure it wasn't coming undone. And if you'd known she was coming, you would have pitched a fit, and we would have wasted time trying to make you understand why this was necessary. Silence was the fastest way."

"You're getting way too good at lying to me," I said. There was no heat in my words. I couldn't be mad at her for long.

George smiled again. "Only through omission, and only when I absolutely have to. She's here because I needed her. Can't you play nice for that?"

"I can try," I said.

"You'll be glad to know that her neural programming is holding," said Dr. Kimberley. "That was one of the primary reasons I needed to be involved."

My George existed because the people who had cloned the original's body had also been able to clone her *brain*. I wasn't sure what would happen if the neural programming failed, but I was willing to bet that I wouldn't like it. "What was the other reason?"

Dr. Kimberley stood. "Why don't you sit down?" she said.

Three

Shaun stood there for a moment like the world's biggest lost kid, hands hanging slack at his sides and face trapped in that look of flummoxed confusion that usually came right before he punched something. Then he shuffled over to take the seat that Dr. Kimberley had abandoned. I reached out and took his hand, squeezing it with all the strength I possessed. My grip was still good: The problems ravaging my body weren't affecting my hands. Not yet, anyway.

"Cloning is a complicated science," said Dr. Kimberley. "Some people still think it should be impossible, for both moral and logistical reasons. It takes a human body nine months to grow in the womb, and another twenty years to finish maturing. We condense that process into the span of less than a year, using hormones and growth stimulators and yes, controlled cancerous cells. The cancer is why this sort of thing would have been impossible before Kellis-Amberlee: We need the potential and power of tumorous growth to force a cloned embryo to adulthood, but without the virus to come in and shut it down, it would result in a completely unusable outcome. That being said, there's a lot of strain on the maturing clone body. Things our bodies did over the course of years, theirs did over the course of weeks. There's no time to slow down, or recover, or adjust for weaknesses that might otherwise be missed."

"What the fuck are you talking about?" demanded Shaun. I squeezed his hand and he turned to look at me, eyes bleak with terror and despair.

"Just listen, okay?" I asked. "That's what I need you to do right now. Listen. Learn the facts, and then we can talk about them when she's done."

"I don't like this," he said.

"I don't either," I said. "We still need information before you get angry at the doctors who are trying to save me, all right?"

"All right," he said, after a long pause. He squeezed my hand, and turned his attention back to Dr. Kimberley. "I'm listening."

She smiled. Not with happiness: with resignation, and acceptance that whatever was about to be said, she was going to have to live with the consequences of having been the one to say it. I tightened my grip on Shaun's hand. His temper was sometimes impressively bad, and he didn't always have the best impulse control, especially where I was concerned. Alaric and Mahir had both had some really unpleasant stories about things he'd done while I was dead, mostly involving slamming people up against walls and occasionally breaking noses. I didn't want him to punch anybody, or anything, and so I held on tight, and kept him with me. I just wanted him with me.

"Georgia's organs were put under immense strain while she was being grown, and were further damaged by the CDC during her conditioning and preparation," said Dr. Kimberley. "I don't know if you're aware, but we removed some biological time bombs from her system shortly after we removed her from CDC custody. They were based on the venom of a creature called the 'sea wasp,' and they both put additional pressure on her organs and left some residual traces of themselves behind. She is suffering from a condition called hyperkalemia, which means the potassium in her bloodstream is elevated. Now, normally, her kidneys would be doing most of the work to fix this. Hyperkalemia can be fatal, but it doesn't usually get this advanced." She stopped, looking like she wasn't sure how to continue.

Dr. Abbey had no such qualms. "Her kidneys have basically shut down," she said flatly. "They're at maybe twenty percent function, and we're having a dialysis machine brought in. I don't have to tell you how dangerous that is."

Dialysis had been routine before Kellis-Amberlee made blood one of the most frightening substances on the planet. Filtering the toxins out of my bloodstream meant risking the activation of the virus sleeping in my veins. It was unlikely—only a very small percent of dialysis cases ever had to deal with that particular complication—but it wasn't unheard of.

Shaun bore down on my hand until it felt like the bones were about to give way. I didn't tell him to stop. This was a sharp, external pain, and compared to the things my own body had been doing to me, it was nothing. It was almost pleasant to have something else that I could focus on. "We're *not* keeping her on dialysis forever. You're right that you don't have to tell me how dangerous that is. She'll amplify. She'll die."

"And since I don't have my reservoir condition to protect me anymore, that's a bad scene," I said. "I still think I get a vote here, Shaun. You remember that, right? That I'm the one who gets to make the final call about my treatment?"

He shot me a half-alarmed look. "I do, but—you know how bad this is, don't you? This could kill you."

"Thing is, *not* doing it *will* kill me. Sometimes you have to roll the dice if you want to win the game. And she's not done." I turned back to Dr. Abbey. "You need to tell him the rest."

"You mean the part he *really* isn't going to like? Oh, sure, I had nothing better to do with my time today. Getting yelled at by your asshole boyfriend is exactly what I needed to make my life complete." Dr. Abbey paused to dig her fingers into the fur atop Joe's head, gathering her thoughts, before she looked at Shaun and said, with perfect clarity and calm, "I told you her kidneys have basically shut down. What you may not realize is that they're going to continue failing. That means that even if there were no other risks associated with dialysis, it would still be necessary to keep her breathing until we can reach the next stage of her treatment."

"Her liver has also been compromised," added Dr. Kimberley, who must have been feeling left out. "It's not as damaged as her kidneys, but that's not saying much. As to why this is all happening at once, when her kidneys started to go, they put more pressure on the rest of her system, and any weaknesses that had been waiting to show themselves began to manifest. Which is a good thing, in a way. It means there aren't likely to be any more nasty surprises lurking. It just means..." She stopped.

Dr. Abbey didn't say anything. Both of the doctors who were working to keep me alive just looked at me, and I realized that they were waiting for me to explain the next steps to Shaun. It made sense. He was less likely to be angry with me than he was with them; he loved me, and he just wanted me to be okay. Making myself the target of his distress was the safest thing for everyone. I still felt a little bit like I was being thrown to the wolves.

I pulled my hand out of his and sat up straighter in the bed, trying to look imposing, trying to look like I wasn't as upset as he was. It was hard not to resent the fact that I needed to be strong for him, even though I knew that he spent a hell of a lot of time being strong for me. "Do you remember Dr. Shoji?" I asked.

"I do," said Shaun. "He's still with the CDC, isn't he?"

"Technically, he's with the EIS; Joey quit the CDC a long time ago," said Dr. Kimberley. "More importantly, he's still a friend before he's anything else. He's your friend. He's my friend. He's the President's friend."

Ryman's term in office was nearing its conclusion, but as long as he held the White House, we could at least be sure that the United States government wasn't going to hunt us down for shits and giggles. That was a small mercy. "He's coming here."

"What?" Shaun's eyes narrowed. He turned to glare at Dr. Kimberley. "Why?"

She licked her lips nervously, eyes darting from side to side before settling on Shaun. Sounding almost apologetic, she said, "I want you to understand that this wasn't part of a nefarious plan, Shaun. This was all about the medical science, and about understanding how a simple neural map had been able to become so strong. There was the possibility that Kellis-Amberlee was bonding with people on a genetic level, through the same process that has happened throughout history, and that it might thus be absorbed and become less dangerous, and we needed test models for that..."

"That is some *Resident Evil* bullshit," said Shaun. "What did you do?"

"They didn't lose all their samples when the Seattle lab went up, and even if they had, they would have still had all the blood she"—Dr. Abbey gestured toward me—"donated at the various checkpoints and checkups between her escape and the two of you getting the fuck out of Dodge. They've been cloning Georgia ever since she ran away."

Shaun went very still. I put a hand on his arm.

"No more neural maps," I said. "No more implanted memories. None of them have been allowed to wake up." At least that was what Dr. Kimberley had told me, and I needed to believe her; I needed to let myself believe that this was a genuine rescue, and not a deal with the devil.

"Mostly, we've been working with isolated systems," said Dr. Kimberley. "Tissue analysis, infection analysis, even a few maps of the process via which a reservoir condition takes hold. We're learning a lot. We've been utterly respectful, I swear."

"Did you ask permission?" asked Shaun mildly. I recognized the danger in his tone. "I mean, did you like, e-mail her or something and say, 'Hey, can we keep playing with your genetic material, just to see what happens'? Because if you didn't, I'm not sure you can call what you did 'respectful.' True to form, maybe. You science assholes, you never care who gets hurt, do you? You just want to see what you can do. How far you can push it."

"Since she's offering to save my life, could you maybe stop with the recriminations for five minutes and *listen?*" My voice cracked. I felt bad about that. I wanted to stay strong, serene, the girl who could handle anything. But I was scared out of my wits, and I needed Shaun to focus. I needed him to be in my corner, not just on my side. "Please. I'm begging you here. Just listen."

"Sorry." Shaun rubbed his face with one hand. "I'm listening."

Dr. Kimberley took a breath to steady herself, and said, "Dr. Shoji is bringing the supplies we need for a full transplant operation. Since all cloning is done under sterile conditions, we don't need to worry about conflicting strains of Kellis-Amberlee; Georgia's infection will be the only one present, and will spread into the new tissue. There's a chance, given her previous reservoir condition, that she may develop a new reservoir condition following the transplant. She'll be monitored the entire time. She'll have three of the best doctors in the world working on her."

"Is either of you a surgeon?" Shaun demanded.

"Joey is," said Dr. Abbey. "He's fully licensed and has been practicing within the last five years. He only takes cases that interest him. People would kill to have him operate on them."

It was my turn to frown. Something wasn't adding up. "Then what were you working on with Dr. Shoji when you were both at the CDC?" I asked. "What would you need a surgeon for?" I wasn't sure I wanted to know. There was no way the truth could be worse than the things my imagination could come up with.

"I'm a virologist who works in genetic engineering," said Dr. Abbey. She was sidestepping the question: I could hear it in her voice. "Joey is also a virologist, but he specializes in the impact of the virus on the body, not in the virus in its pure state. He genuinely wants to know what a disease will do to somebody." She sounded faintly baffled, like this was an obsession that made no sense at all. "He's been a licensed surgeon for the past twenty years. If there's anyone you should trust to open up your sister, it's him."

Shaun went pale and didn't say anything. I sighed.

"I don't think he trusts *anyone* to 'open me up,'" I said. "But since it has to happen anyway, please continue."

"Joey is coming here with fresh, untaxed organs," said Dr. Abbey. "He's going to perform the surgery, stay long enough to be sure that Georgia is on the mend, and then get back to his very important work."

Sometimes Shaun was faster on the uptake than I was, generally when our lives were on the line. "Dr. Shoji is with the EIS. Dr. Kimberley is with the EIS. Both of them are working on Georgia's case. Neither of them can really afford to do this sort of charity case unless there's good publicity in it for them. Dr. Abbey, who did you *tell*?"

"She told us," said a voice from the doorway. We both turned. Mahir—older, thinner, with more gray at his temples than I remembered—offered a wan smile. "Alaric's just parking the car and negotiating a cease-fire with Foxy. He and Maggie should be right in. Hello, Shaun. Hello, Georgia. It's been a long time."

"Yeah," I said, and smiled back. I couldn't stop myself. It wasn't possible. "It has."

Book V

The Gang's All Here

None of these people understand what "good-bye, we're disappearing forever now, have a nice life" actually means.

—Shaun Mason

Friendship is a love that endures past death, but not always past living.

—Georgia Mason

One

Dr. Abbey and Dr. Kimberley had left us alone to get reacquainted—at least, that was what Dr. Kimberley said. Dr. Abbey had just snorted, said, "Well, we have a lot of shallow graves on the property," and sauntered out, following her taller, blonder friend toward someplace where a bunch of reporters weren't. Foxy had accompanied Maggie and Alaric into the room, and stayed to watch the fun. I wanted to ask her to leave. I wasn't sure how to do it without getting myself shot. I didn't say anything.

Alaric looked about the same, like he had looked at the past few years, shrugged, and decided he was going to let someone else play-test them and then get back to him after the beta. Maggie had aged more visibly. There were gray hairs mixed in with her customary blend of natural brown and bleached-blonde curls. Even without that, the dome of her belly would have made it impossible to deny at least six months of the intervening time. Despite her obvious pregnancy, she had still been delighted to see Joe the dog, giving the massive carnivore chin-scritches and belly rubs before he had lumbered to his feet and gone looking for Dr. Abbey. Now Maggie was sitting in the chair next to George's bed, hands folded in her lap, eyes wide and serious and solemn as she waited for an explanation.

That was what they all wanted: an explanation. How could we have run off and left them; how could we have let our own need for a happy ending supersede the debts we owed to our friends and to the people who loved us. And I... I didn't have an answer. I had never really thought about it before. There had always been something else that needed doing, whether it was repairing the plumbing or dealing with a wasp's nest in the eaves, and life had been simple, in part because life had been too full to become complex.

"We just don't understand why you never came back," said Maggie, with the air of someone who was asking a perfectly reasonable question and hence had every expectation of a perfectly reasonable answer. Her tone was light, with none of the shadows or recriminations I heard whenever Alaric or Mahir spoke. But then, Alaric and Mahir had always belonged to George: She had recruited them, trained them, and guaranteed their loyalty in a hundred little ways, all while I was busy with my own team. Maggie had been Buffy's, a Fictional to the core, and owed no firm allegiance to either of us. I found myself wishing, more than anything, that at least one member of my core team had survived. Dave had died getting the rest of us out of Oakland, and Becks had died getting us out of the White House. That was what Irwins did. We died.

It was my fault that I couldn't master that small, essential part of my own damn job.

"We never said we were going to come back," said George. "As I recall, we said exactly the opposite. We said we were going to vanish into the wilds of Canada, and that we were going to miss you all, but that you were never going to see us again. We *told* you. It's not our fault if you didn't believe us."

"I suppose that we felt we deserved better than a few tense IRC sessions and double-blind texts, after everything we'd been through," said Mahir. "I've tried not to be mad at you, Georgia. It's... difficult. You were my best friend."

"Shaun was mine," she said. Her words were clear, but not cruel: She wasn't trying to be hurtful. She was just doing what she had always done best of all, and telling the truth as she understood it. "I love you all. You were the most amazing team we could ever have assembled. But if we'd stayed, we would have been painting giant targets on all of you, to go with the targets we would have been painting on ourselves. Even with Ryman protecting us, we'd pissed off too many people, and we'd all be dead or in jail by now. I'd probably be in a lab somewhere, being taken apart one piece at a time..." She stopped, grimacing at the ironic nature of her words, given her current situation. "We had to go. You know that."

"You could have called," said Alaric.

"Or answered a few of the notes people had me pass to you," said Mahir.

"Or come to the wedding," said Maggie.

"And don't try to say that communication wasn't safe—you've been sending articles this whole time," said Alaric hotly. He always did have a surprising temper under those glasses and that calm expression. Most Newsies did. They were calm until they weren't, and then, look out. "If it was safe for you to write about the farming communities of the Canadian wastes, it was safe for you to send an e-mail saying 'congrats on your marriage, sorry we couldn't be there.' It was safe for you to send an e-card for Alisa when she passed her firearms safety exam. You had options. You had *choices*."

"We did," agreed George. "We chose to stay away. We chose to let the story end. Because that's what everything becomes when we're together, when we're *making* the news instead of just reporting it. I'm a clone who thinks she's a dead woman and helped to uncover a generation-spanning CDC plot. Shaun has PTSD, talks to the dead woman whose memories I have, and is the first person confirmed immune to Kellis-Amberlee amplification. You don't think people have been monitoring you all for signs that we were in direct communication, not just using dead drops for our articles? Looking for ways that we could be tracked? We walked out because we were done. We still are."

"Maybe if Buffy were still here." Everyone turned to look at me. I realized I had spoken, and shrugged, deciding to roll with it. "She could have watched the watchers, and made sure our secure lines stayed that way, and no one would have been in danger. But she's gone. She was the first to go. Y'know? Maybe if she hadn't died, we would have stayed immortal, like we were supposed to be. Reporters are supposed to live forever, or die off camera, where no one has to admit that we signed off for good. Buffy died. Becks and Dave died."

"I died," said George quietly. Alaric and Maggie both winced. Mahir just looked sad. "I know I'm not her—I know I was born in a lab—but I remember the shotgun against the back of my neck. As far as I'm concerned, it happened to me. I *died.* If I want to walk away, I should be allowed to walk away. I've earned it."

"We've earned it," I said. "Nobody gets to say that we didn't."

"We're not saying that," said Maggie fiercely. She rubbed her belly with one hand, looking down at it reflectively for a moment before she said, "It just feels like it should have been more . . . final. It should have been something we could remark on later, like 'oh, that ticker tape parade was a big clue that things were changing.' You just left, that's all. You slipped away. We thought we'd have more time."

Belatedly, I realized that Maggie was the only one in this room who hadn't been given the opportunity to say a real good-bye. She'd been recovering at the Agora while the rest of us went to Washington D.C., and by the time she'd been well enough to be released from the hospital, George and I had already been gone. We hadn't been willing to risk going all the way back across the country just to tell her how grateful we were for all her help. Alaric had promised to tell her. But it really wasn't the same thing, was it?

Maggie looked up and met my eyes, her mouth twisted into a bitter downward curve that told me her thoughts had mirrored my own. "It shouldn't take a medical emergency for you two to come home, you know. You should just . . . you should just come."

"I'm sorry," I said. "I'd promise to do better, but right now, I don't think I can make any promises that I'll actually keep."

"I can understand that," said Mahir. He pushed himself away from the wall. "Let's go impose upon Dr. Abbey's unwilling hospitality a bit more, shall we? The kitchen's still there, so far as I know, and I could murder a pot of coffee."

"I miss coffee," said George, closing her eyes.

"No caffeine?" Alaric sounded horrified and fascinated in equal measure, like the idea of an uncaffeinated Georgia was the most terrifying thing he could think of.

"No, Alaric, no caffeine." She opened one eye, shooting him an amused look. "As it turns out, when your kidneys stop working, the doctor cuts back on your unnecessary habits. Like Coke. I can't afford the filtration."

"God, get well soon," he said, and she burst out laughing. There was a pause, and then everyone else joined in—me included. She still had a sense of humor. Our friends were here, and they were still talking to us; they were willing to let us lean on them now, the way that, in a fairer world, we would have been leaning on them this whole time.

Maybe things were going to be okay.

Two

Things were not okay.

Our days had fallen into a quick, easy rhythm. Maggie and Alaric worked from the kitchen, where there were plenty of outlets and Dr. Abbey's assistants were unlikely to complain too much about having their space occupied. It helped that having Maggie around was sort of like having an infinite credit line to the black market, especially since she was pregnant; her parents had always loved spoiling her, and if she wanted to run up her credit cards smuggling chocolate and medical supplies into a not-so-secret mad science base in the middle of Oregon, they were fine with that. At least this time no one was shooting at her, and she was surrounded by some of the best doctors in the world. True, Dr. Abbey was more likely to mutate the baby than she was to improve its chances of a healthy birth, but Dr. Kimberley had worked in pediatrics, and several of Dr. Abbey's assistants had experience with pregnancy. Some of them firsthand. Maggie's appearance unlocked a certain level of access to the private lives of the people around us. At least three of the assistants had children, on-site, and brought them out to meet us as soon as "us" included someone who was about to be a mother.

Shaun still spent most of his time outside, gathering samples and specimens, but he came back earlier, and decontaminated sooner before going to catch up with the people who'd once shared every aspect of our lives. He wasn't coming to see me as much. I tried to tell myself that it was because he had missed having other people to talk to, and not because he was afraid of being there when my kidneys finally failed and I choked to death on my own blood.

I wasn't that good of a liar.

Mahir was taking up the space Shaun had vacated. He only budged from my room when he needed to sleep or eat, or when Dr. Kimberley ordered him out—something she was doing with increasing frequency as my kidney function dipped lower and we waited for Dr. Shoji to arrive with my replacement organs. She was still being cagey about how they were going to be transported without amplifying. I was afraid I already knew the answer, but I couldn't voice my concerns aloud. Not without really considering what I was willing to do for the sake of my own survival.

Mahir had no such constraints, possibly because his life wasn't the one on the line; possibly because he had been so close to the original version of me, the one who was willing to die for the sake of a story. He was sitting next to my bed three days after they had arrived, laptop on his knees, tapping away while Dr. Kimberley administered my morning medication. She murmured some vague pleasantry, some unformed comment about how well I was doing, and she was gone, rushing off to do another series of labs and gather another file of invaluable data. My situation was going to make it easier for the EIS to work with cloning technology in the future. I should have been bitter about that. Mostly, I was just so damn *tired*.

"You know he's bringing a box with him," said Mahir, closing the lid on his laptop as the door clicked shut. The two sounds blurred together, becoming one conclusive snap. "A big one, about six feet long and three feet across. Big enough for a body."

"I know." I closed my eyes. It was easier when I didn't have to look at the world, when I could pretend that all of this was just some sort of strange and unending dream. "There isn't anything else that makes sense."

"And you're . . . all right with that? I know that you don't want to die, but—"

"Why is it any different when the organs come with a body to keep them sterile and healthy?" The question even *sounded* weak. "She's never woken up. She doesn't have the neural capacity to wake up. I'm not really okay with the fact that she exists; I didn't expect to come back and hear that the EIS was continuing to work with my tissue. But if the clones are going to be out there, I may as well benefit from them. They've sure as hell benefitted from *me*."

There was a long pause before Mahir said, "I thought Canada might soften you a bit. Give you time to get some distance, find some peace. I didn't expect it to make you harder."

"Oh, no?" I opened my eyes, sitting up as much as the tubes strapped to my arms allowed, and glared at him. "This is harder? Wanting to *live*, instead of dying *again*? I can remind you all that I'm not the original Georgia as much as I want, but I still remember dying as her. Do you know what that does to a person? I close my eyes on the bad nights, and Shaun's pulling the trigger." Or I was confined to a bed, just like this one, at the mercy of the doctors who milled around me like moths around a candle. My whole world was a nightmare now. "Do I think this is a responsible use of cloning technology? Actually, yes. I think this is the *only* responsible use of cloning technology. Am I afraid that they've lied to me about how developed her brain is, and that I'll be killing someone who is in basically the same position I was, just so I can keep going? Yeah. Am I going to do it anyway? Yes. I am. You should know that."

"I do." He shook his head. "If you tried to tell me that you weren't going to do it, I'd be doing my best to talk you into it. I may not get to talk to you much these days, but that doesn't mean I'm ready to live in a world that doesn't have you in it."

I blinked at him. "So what was all this about . . . ?"

"I want to know that you've thought things through, and that you're not compromising your principles because you're afraid of leaving Shaun alone." Mahir looked at me gravely. "The two of you were always a bit, well, codependent. You function beautifully as a unit, and you fall apart when you're separated. That concerned me back when you had an outside support system. Now that you've essentially walked away from it, it terrifies me."

"I am afraid of leaving Shaun alone, because I *wouldn't* be leaving him alone," I said. "I'd be leaving him with the voices in his head—and they're getting mean. He didn't get magically better just because I came back."

"He needs to talk to Dr. Abbey about treatment."

"He is, I think. He's had long enough to figure out that he can't do this on his own, and he's ready. But if I die here, all bets are off. You know him. You know how he reacts." I laughed bitterly. "Like, you actually *know*, because you've seen it happen. If I die again, he's going to go off with the voices, and let them lead him to his doom. So no, I'm not compromising my principles for the sake of Shaun. I'm doing it because I want to live to fight another day. I *am* taking him into consideration as I approve my treatments—and I assume you're sitting here, taking notes, because you're planning to write up this ground-breaking medical case."

Mahir flushed, looking away. "Nothing like this has ever happened before, Georgia. This is all new ground, and you know that the EIS won't publish their results for anyone else to see. They'll keep it all quiet and under their control, because that's how they do things."

"Still?" I couldn't quite keep the wistfulness out of my voice. The world wasn't kind—the world had never been kind, and I knew that better than most—but I had been hoping, at least a little, that things would have changed after everything we'd done. Maybe that was egotistical of me. I didn't know. I just knew that we had paid a great deal for a new world, and now it didn't look like we were going to get it.

"They're better than they were. Haven't you been reading my articles?"

"Some," I said. "I read more of Alaric's work these days."

Mahir looked hurt. "Really?"

"Really." I shrugged. "He does human interest and history; things that have already happened. Things I could never have changed. You... you're still reporting the news. You're doing heavy digging, and you're doing it from Europe, which means you're not endangering your family in the process. I am so proud of you. But if I read your work, I'd want to help. I'd want to get into those situations, I'd want to dig for those answers, and I'm not... I'm not *ready* yet. I'm still recovering. So is Shaun. We both need more time, and that means I can't afford to let you make me start caring again."

Mahir looked at me silently for a long moment before he nodded. "That makes sense," he said. "I've had similar thoughts. I went to Australia—did you see that one? Beautiful country, just beautiful, and their approach to security is so evenhanded and sensible, it made me want to grab Nandini and Sanjukta and head straight for immigration. San's young enough that she could grow up thinking that was the way the whole world was. She could be so much less afraid than I know she's going to be, living in England, with a blood test unit on every doorway and regular contamination drills in the Underground. I could spare her, if I was just willing to walk away. I haven't gotten there yet. Some days, I feel like it's only a matter of time."

"How did you get here, anyway? You must have been on a plane the second Dr. Abbey contacted you."

"It took me a few hours, actually," said Mahir, with a short smile. "I hopped a flight from Heathrow to Hamburg, went from there to Helsinki, and finally got dropped off at an old research installation up in

Nunavut. It's supposedly fully decommissioned, although we both know how often *that's* true, especially when there's something useful to be had by keeping a place operational. A few bush pilots fly out of there, small-range planes, exorbitant fees. The site paid for my tickets, by the way. In case you were planning to question my use of the operational budget."

"Are you planning to write an article about the pilots in Nunavut?" I asked.

Mahir grinned this time, bright and lasting. "Your instincts are still good. Yes, I am. I'll be spending a few days up there before heading home. A few of the pilots have agreed to show me around, as long as I elide any identifying details that might lead the government to them."

As if the government didn't already know: As if places like that, in a world like this, hadn't long since been accepted as the cost of doing business. People still needed to move around. We had become a global economy before the Rising came, and there were always going to be reasons to travel between continents—reasons that sometimes didn't allow for the long, grueling process of going through official channels. Mahir's passport had been issued by the nation of India, a place that currently didn't technically exist. As such, he was in a better position than most to use the smaller, underground airports; he didn't need a visa to go anywhere in the world, and he couldn't be arrested for crossing international borders unless he was already a wanted criminal.

Some of the things we'd done in the process of toppling the CDC's leadership and replacing them with people from the EIS were technically illegal. All those charges had been dropped by President Ryman after we got his wife back. As long as he was careful, Mahir's freedom of movement would remain unchallenged, and he could continue to report on the ways in which the world had adapted.

"That sounds fun," I said. "I think you'll really enjoy writing that one."

"I enjoy writing all of them, even the hard ones." He was quiet for a moment before he said, "You know, Georgia, people wonder what happened to you."

"I know." There were whole forums and bulletin boards devoted to Shaun and me, groups of people who traded rumors and blurry snapshots that could have been virtually anyone like they were currency. We had become celebrities by doing the impossible—unveiling the CDC, coming back from the dead—and we had cemented our place by doing something else that should have been impossible. We had disappeared. In a world where surveillance was king and the CDC almost always knew where everyone was, we had dropped off the grid completely.

"It's a great story."

And there it was. Finally, the thing he'd been waiting to say since the day he arrived was out in the open, sitting between us like the inevitability it was. I leveled a flat gaze on him, waiting until he looked away before I asked, "Does it matter whether I want it to be written? Do I get to ask for professional courtesy, and actually believe that you're going to extend it?"

"Dammit, Georgia, don't try to make me the bad guy here."

"Why not? You and I both know that the only way you could bring yourself around to the idea that Shaun and I would want to be a human interest story is by casting us as either victims or villains somewhere in the back of your head. I'm guessing 'villains' was easy, since we walked away and left you holding the bag, until you actually saw us again, and saw how damn sick I am." I waved a hand furiously at the equipment surrounding me. Even that much motion tugged on my IV, sending a twinge of pain through my arm. I wanted to rip it out. I wanted to reject everything about the machines that were keeping me alive, and the technology that had created them.

I was the product of modern science and fringe medicine. I should never have existed. There was no one in the world who hated that fact more than I did.

"You think we want to be here? You think I want to see you look away every time I turn my head, like I might somehow not have realized that you were watching me? Newsflash, Mahir: If it were up to me, I wouldn't be in this bed. I want to live, yes, but not like this. Not in a... in a white room, where everything smells like antiseptic, and you never get to see the sky." The walls were a pale cream green, but the principle was the same. This room was a cousin of those sterile rooms at the CDC, where clever scientists had violated the laws of nature in order to prove to themselves that they could. On paper, I had been created so that they could use me as a weapon against my brother, but that was never the real reason. They made me because they could. They didn't give a crap about whether or not they should. Scientists never did.

"People want to know," said Mahir quietly. There was guilt in his tone, but there was steel there, too. I had put it there. I had taught him to pursue the story no matter what tried to get in the way, no matter how hard your target squirmed and fought. What mattered was telling the truth, writing it all down and showing it to the people who needed to know about the things they hadn't been there to witness for themselves. What mattered was the record. The person who wrote down what happened was really the one who made history, like a craftsman made a wall. One brick—one story—at a time.

"What if I don't want them to?" The question came out rawer than I'd expected. I paused, swallowing to steady myself, before I continued, "What if I want to be forgotten? I'm not really interested in being anybody's martyr. Been there, done that, got the urn with my ashes in it, sort of creeped out by that. I don't want to die, but I don't want to be a story anymore either. I want to be a person."

"What about what I want?" Mahir raised his head and met my eyes squarely for the first time since he'd arrived. He was so much older than he'd been when all this started. We all were. "You walked away, and I let you go, because I thought you'd come back. I thought we'd have time to put all this in order, arrange the narrative, figure out what sort of direction we wanted to go. And you never came back. We're here now because Dr. Abbey called us."

"Why did she?" It was the question I'd been itching to ask. She had no good reason to summon our friends and acquaintances—not unless she thought I was dying, and if that had been the case, she would have been better off sedating Shaun and finding a nice room without anything breakable in it. This made no sense.

Mahir frowned. "She said you had something to share."

"No. Not really. I missed you all—please believe me when I say that—but I never said I wanted to see you again. Sort of the opposite, really. I don't want anyone to see me like this."

"I called your friends because I was calling *my* friends, and I wanted to be sure that no one was going to get so excited by the squishy science goodness of it all that they failed to remember that you were a person," said Dr. Abbey. We both turned. She was standing in the doorway of my room, next to an Asian man in tan shorts and a Hawaiian-print shirt.

"It's always a risk, with us," said Dr. Joseph Shoji. "Hello, Georgia. You're looking awful today."

"Thanks, Doc," I said, and scowled. "You summoned everyone here because you didn't trust the people you were already calling? Doesn't that seem a little counterintuitive to you?"

"Not really." Dr. Abbey walked into the room and started fiddling with my IV, ignoring Mahir completely. "I needed the best in the world if I was going to save you, and I needed an escape plan if I wasn't going to save you. Shaun would tear this place down around my ears if he thought I'd done something to hurry you to the grave. So I called my contacts at the EIS, focused on people who already knew your medical history, and summoned my medical dream team. At the same time, I tipped off the people who love you as to your location. There's no way we could fail to give you the best possible care with this many eyes on us. It just wouldn't work."

"Huh," I said. I couldn't dispute the wisdom of her actions. They were backward and strange and not even remotely the actions of a normal person, but they made sense for *her*, and they would do what she needed them to do: They would protect her. If I didn't survive the transplant, Mahir, Alaric, and Maggie would be able to talk Shaun down. Nothing was going to make him okay at that point—nothing was even going to come close—and they were probably the only people in the world, excepting Rick, who stood a chance of reaching him.

If Rick showed up next, I was going to scream. Having the vice president of the United States swing by to see how I was doing was just too surreal, even for me.

Dr. Shoji's smile was clearly forced. The concern in his eyes was just as clearly real. "Georgia," he said. "How are you feeling?"

"Like I'm two steps short of a medically induced coma, but who's counting?" I looked at him calmly. "Did you bring what you needed?"

"I did," he said. "We can operate in the morning."

Three

George couldn't go to sleep without the sound of my breathing, and she couldn't come to me, wired up as she was to all those tubes and machines. We dozed together, me stretched on the six inches or so of mattress between her body and the edge of the bed, her squarely centered, arms at her side, like a wax dummy in a store window. I tried to pretend I wasn't scared out of my mind. She tried to pretend the same, and neither of us spoke. What would there have been to say? I couldn't beg her not to leave me; she was already trying her hardest, and implying anything else would mean implying that I thought she was going to fail.

Besides, the Georgia who didn't really exist was more than happy to fill the silence. She had talked all night long, giving voice to the thoughts that raced through my aching head, but putting her own brutal twist on them.

"She's going to die again, you know. That's what people made of meat and mad science do. They *die*. That's going to suck for you. At least you'll have a date for the funeral, huh?"

"You should give up on her right now. If you walk away, you can pretend she got better. How does that sound? You and me and the big wide world, and you get to tell yourself she's still here, furious and alive."

"You always knew it was going to end like this."

"You'll always have me."

I kept my eyes closed and swallowed my whimpers, refusing to give her the satisfaction of seeing how she was getting to me. She knew, of course. She was inside my head. But for the moment, I could still curl next to my flesh-and-blood girl, stiff and silent, and tell myself that things were going to be all right.

Morning broke and the lights in the room came on, chasing away the shadows behind my eyelids. I opened them and Dr. Abbey was there, flanked by Dr. Kimberley and Foxy, a solemn expression on her face. George was still asleep, or at least still had her eyes closed. I sat up.

"Is it time?"

Dr. Abbey nodded. "You need to leave the room now, Shaun."

"What?" I stared at her. "No. You're not going to operate on her in here, are you?"

"No. We have an operating theater prepared. You can watch if you want—I know better than to try to stop you—but I wish you wouldn't. It will probably be distressing for you."

"I'm supposed to try to convince you to come out hunting with me," said Foxy blithely. "I have grenades and a rocket launcher and I went out last night and found some big holes that probably have bears or foxes in them. We could set them on fire if you wanted. Ever seen a burning zombie bear trying to climb a tree? It's really funny."

"I can't decide whether or not that's animal cruelty." George still wasn't waking up. I frowned at her. "Hey, George? You okay?"

"She's out," said Dr. Abbey. "The sedatives in her IV put her under hours ago. We're going to be sedating her further for the surgery, but this was the best way to make sure she was fully relaxed before we went in. With the amount of work we're going to be doing, this was the best thing for her, medically."

Slowly, I turned to look at Dr. Abbey again. "She didn't tell me you were going to be doing that."

"She didn't know." The admission was calmly made, as if there was nothing wrong with drugging someone who didn't expect it. Dr. Abbey looked me in the eye as she continued, "She might have refused because she wanted to be awake to support you, and that wouldn't have been good for her overall health. You're my . . . long-term science experiment who walks like a friend. She's my patient. I have to put her first."

All those words made sense. None of them should have been put in that order. I slid off the bed, glaring daggers at Dr. Abbey and Dr. Kimberley. "This isn't right."

"This is the only thing that's right," said Dr. Kimberley. "Please, go with Foxy, and let us save your sister."

"No," I said. But I didn't stop them when they unhooked the IVs from their stands and unclamped the headboard from the wall, and rolled George—still sleeping peacefully—out of the room. I followed, with Foxy dogging my heels like an eager, murderous puppy. I wanted to tell her to back off and leave me alone. I didn't. Not only was I a little bit afraid of what she'd do if openly rejected, but there was something comforting about her presence. As long as she was there, I couldn't be left alone with the voices in my head.

And maybe she knew a little about hearing voices. I glanced at her. "Hey, uh, Foxy? Can we talk later?"

"Sure," she said. There was no smile, for once; only sympathy. I wondered how much of her "space lobster juice" she'd had today. It didn't seem to be nearly as much as usual. "You want to ask about getting hopped up on drugs, huh?"

"What?"

She shrugged expansively, the motion seeming to originate somewhere around her sternum and then spread out through her entire body, rather than being localized like a normal shrug. "You're crazy. You know that, right? I mean, Shannon says it's not a good word to use, because sometimes people who *aren't* crazy point it at people who *are* and use it like a weapon, but I figure we're both crazy, so that makes it okay."

I was painfully aware of how close Dr. Abbey and Dr. Kimberley were. They were focused on getting George's bed down the hall without bumping the equipment that was keeping her alive into anything, but they could still hear every word that we said. Maybe that was for the best. Maybe they needed to know that I had been thinking about these things.

"Yeah," I said. "I guess I'm crazy."

"Good," said Foxy, visibly relieved by my admission. "So see, here's the thing: *I'm* the kind of crazy that can't handle what it's done, and gets dangerous, so they give me drugs to make me a different kind of crazy. I'm not like this naturally. Tom makes the juice, and I drink the juice, and Elaine stays way down, below the surface, in the place where reason and rhyme and writing desks can be sort of forgotten about until we need them. She's always here. I'm always here. But she doesn't get to be in charge, and so I get to keep breathing. Your kind of crazy is... it's sadder, I think. You don't need the space lobster juice. You need something else."

"He needs antidepressants and a mild antipsychotic," said Dr. Abbey, glancing back over her shoulder. "I don't know that you're schizophrenic, Shaun, but I know that you shouldn't be hearing voices the way you do."

"She won't hurt you," said Foxy. "She just wants to help. She's helped me, and she didn't have to."

"Yes, I did," said Dr. Abbey. She sounded suddenly tired. I looked up, and saw that she and Dr. Kimberley had stopped, George between them, in front of a closed door. "Shaun, if you really want to watch this, go with Foxy; she can show you to the theater. But I wish you wouldn't."

"You know I have to," I said quietly. I turned to Foxy. "Show me?"

"Okay," she said, and pirouetted on her heel, light and graceful as she turned and led me back down the hall to another door. This one was smaller, recessed into the wall. There had been a sign affixed there once; the scars from the screws still stood out against the wood. She opened it, and I followed her mutely through, up a flight of stairs to a small room, once a projectionist's booth. It held seven chairs, pressed too closely together for comfort. Only one was open, at the very center of the row. The others were filled with faces I knew—Maggie, Alaric, Mahir—and faces I didn't know as well—Jill, Tom, and another of Dr. Abbey's assistants. The people who knew me and George as *people*, not just accidents of science, looked at me with quiet sympathy in their eyes. The people who worked for Dr. Abbey didn't look at me at all. Their attention was reserved for the glass wall in front of us, and the round, sterile room below.

Dr. Abbey's people had been rebuilding the forestry center to suit their needs for years. It shouldn't have been a surprise that their rebuilding had included a full operating theater, complete with observation room. The fact was so logical that it seemed almost silly to question it. I walked silently to the open chair and sat, folding my hands white-knuckled on my knees. Maggie put her right hand on my shoulder. I didn't turn. I knew that if I looked at her, she would be overflowing with sympathy, so concerned for my well-being that she couldn't contain it. And I would break. That would be one step too far into the darkness, and there would be no coming back.

Below me, a woman who looked exactly like my sister lay naked on an operating table, a ventilator covering her nose and mouth. I would have thought that she *was* George, if not for her hair, which had been shaved completely off—that, and her lack of scars. George didn't take the kind of risks I did, because she couldn't afford to. There was still no such thing as a risk-free life. She nicked her hands, skinned her knees, went through all the small injuries that the body was heir to, especially when that body lived in a cabin in the middle of nowhere. This girl, this... body, was pristine. She had never opened her eyes, never seen the sun, never had the memories of a dead woman used to jump-start her cloned mind into sudden self-awareness. She was an empty shell.

A shell that contained something we needed. Dr. Shoji moved around the motionless clone, checking machines, checking his tools. He barely looked up when the door opened and Dr. Abbey backed into the room, pulling George's bed. George followed, eyes closed, surrounded by the silent sentinels of her IVs. Dr. Kimberley came last.

There was a pause while all three of the doctors left the room to scrub up and get ready for what was to come. When they returned, they were gowned in green, faces and hands covered, sterile. Dr. Kimberley sprayed some sort of aerosol, decontaminating the room.

"This process used to be a lot more complicated," said one of the assistants—Jill. She sounded like she was trying to be helpful. Just the sound of her voice made me want to punch her lights out. "Sterilizing a room was difficult and time-consuming, and the risk of infection was much higher than it is now. The spray binds to particles in the air, and—"

"Not right now, okay?" interrupted Alaric. "That's our friend down there. We don't want to talk about this now."

"Oh," said Jill. "Sorry." She fell silent. The rest of us remained that way.

In the theater below, Dr. Shoji picked up a scalpel.

Four

I opened my eyes, and the world was filled with light. Too much light: It burned. I made a wordless sound of protest, clapping my hands over my eyes. The fact that I still had hands, still had eyes, was great; it spoke to survival, or at least the sort of result where I was mostly intact at the end. The fact that my eyes felt like great balls of molten lava shoved into my skull was a lot less awesome.

"Someone get me a UV blocker," snapped a voice. It had a Welsh accent. I ran through my mental catalog of voices, relieved that I still had *that*, and identified it as belonging to Dr. Kimberley. "Were none of you *thinking*?"

There was a clatter as someone rushed to get a UV blocker for her. I took a breath and tried to focus past the pain in my eyes, which was already fading. I wanted to know what else was going on with me.

First: There was no other pain. Just the eyes, and even as I thought about the absence of pain elsewhere, that pain blinked out, gone like it had never happened. I couldn't seem to feel anything below my breastbone. That realization made my breath hitch for a moment, but I caught myself, forcing the panic down. Dr. Kimberley would never have allowed them to cut off anything I was going to need later. Neither would Dr. Abbey. I didn't know Dr. Shoji well enough to trust him that completely, but the other two? I would trust them with my life. I *had* trusted them with my life. I just had to believe that I'd been right to do so.

"Here you go," said another voice—Dr. Abbey—before a hand tugged at my wrist, trying to pull it back down to my side. "You have to uncover your eyes now, Georgia. I promise, this will help."

I tried to respond. My lips wouldn't obey me, and what came out was a petulant grunt.

"The paralytics we used to keep you from moving are still working their way out of your system," she said. "Only the fact that you were hurting let you move in the first place. Now trust me, and let me work."

I stopped resisting. She pulled my hands down, first one and then the other, positioning them by my sides. The way she placed them meant that I could feel the curve of my hips, the solid swell of bone and muscle under my fingers. The sheer solidity of my own body was soothing. I stopped fighting against the drugs. They would wear off soon enough.

Something light settled on the bridge of my nose. "You can open your eyes now," said Dr. Kimberley. "I'd like if you'd try to do that for me. I need to see whether you have any voluntary muscle movement, or if it's all reflex."

Open my eyes. Right. I could do that. Maybe. I struggled to remember how the normally effortless motion was supposed to go, fighting against the thick lassitude that covered me. Finally, wrenchingly, my eyelids opened, and I was staring at the ceiling.

"There you are." Dr. Kimberley leaned over me, smiling. "You should be able to move soon. Not that you should. In fact, if you start moving too much, we'll be knocking you out again. So don't."

"Bedside manner," said Dr. Abbey. "Get one."

"Oh, as if you're one to talk?" Dr. Kimberley briefly wrinkled her nose before returning her attention to me. "All right, we're going to go over the results of your surgery in order of most to least important, and we're going to do it now, while you're still too drugged to interrupt me. Blink once if you understand."

I blinked. There was an oddly hollow quality to the light in the room, like it had been stripped of some essential, nearly intangible element.

"First, you'll be happy to know that we were able to replace your kidneys and liver with the cloned organs," she said. "All the necessary blood transfusions were conducted before the supply was contaminated. It was tight, but we managed it. You're going to be all right, Georgia. Your body is working properly again."

"Well, mostly," said Dr. Abbey.

Dr. Kimberley grimaced. "Yes," she agreed, in a reluctant tone.

"Mostly. The danger of clones has always been keeping them from spontaneously amplifying when they take their first breath of contaminated air—and all air is contaminated. There's not a safe breeze on the planet. In this case, we were able to seal and shut down a room, but we couldn't decontaminate your entire body. Doing that would have wrecked your immune system, and caused more problems than we were already struggling to solve."

"Full autoimmune collapse is not the gift that keeps on giving," said Dr. Abbey. She sounded almost . . . cheerful, like she was finally getting everything she'd ever wanted, and had only needed my near death to put the last pieces into place. "So you still have an immune system, and now you have organs that work, and still have that factory-fresh smell. They should be good for another fifty or sixty years. I *am* going to want you and Shaun in here every eighteen months, so that I can look you over and be sure that you haven't done anything perishingly stupid to yourself."

That was always a risk, especially with Shaun as my primary companion and arbiter of whether or not something was a good idea. I blinked to indicate my understanding.

"Good, good," said Dr. Kimberley. "We were able to seal your incisions almost immediately; there will be minimal scarring, and you should be up and about by the end of the day. I recommend as much bed rest as possible for the next week. No jumping jacks, marathons, or vigorous sex."

My cheeks heated. Dr. Abbey cackled. Not laughed—cackled, the gleeful sound of a wild creature in the deep woods.

"Look, her blush reflex works," she said. "I told you we replaced enough blood for normal vascular function."

"If she were equipped with a penis, I suppose you'd be suggesting direct stimulation, just to see whether she could become aroused." Dr. Kimberley sounded peevish. I decided she was my hero.

"Yes, I would," said Dr. Abbey. She leaned over so that I could see her face. "Look. We know that reservoir conditions are brought on by an interaction between the virus and the host body, and that specific host bodies will have a tropism toward specific reservoir conditions. Identical twins are more likely to develop identical conditions than strangers who have been exposed to the same root strain of Kellis-Amberlee. We don't know why it happens that way. We just know that it does. Even induced conditions, like the ones in Joe or the ones the CDC attempted to force in some of their clones, will usually break along genetic lines. I always said that if you were exposed to a concentrated enough dose of the virus, while unable to amplify for whatever reason, that you would probably develop either retinal or spinal Kellis-Amberlee. They're connected. Not sure why. But they tend to co-manifest about half the time, and—"

"You know, Shannon, sometimes I suspect you could keep talking while the building collapsed around your ears, as long as you felt you had an audience," said Dr. Kimberley mildly. "Your eyes hurt, Georgia, is that correct?"

I blinked once. After Dr. Abbey's speech, I was pretty sure I knew *why* my eyes hurt, but I still wanted to hear her say it out loud.

"I am sorry to have to say this, but judging by the viral structures building in your aqueous humor, you are in the early stages of retinal Kellis-Amberlee. We discussed removing your eyes and attempting a transplant, but we didn't want to take any such drastic steps without your consent."

The same adrenaline that had allowed me to raise my arms earlier flooded back into my system, allowing me to shake my head very slightly. It was barely more than a rocking from side to side.

It was enough. Dr. Abbey smiled. "I didn't think so," she said. She held up a syringe, and said, "We're going to put you back under for a little while, so that you can process out the worst of the drugs. You may experience some discomfort when you wake. It shouldn't be too extreme. We're going to turn the lights out, and I'll see if I can't scrounge you up some sunglasses. All right?"

I couldn't answer her—that sort of fine motor movement was still beyond me—and so I simply closed my eyes. Something pricked the skin on the inside of my elbow, and a cool, tingling sensation flowed into my veins. Sometime after that, consciousness simply slipped away.

When I woke for the second time, the room was dark; the IV lines had been removed, leaving me free to get out of the bed; and Shaun was curled up next to me like the world's biggest house cat, his head resting on my chest and his arm wrapped around my waist, holding me possessively in place.

I raised my free arm and poked him in the head. He didn't move.

"Shaun."

No reaction.

"Shaun."

No reaction.

"Shaun, if I don't get up and pee *right now*, everything is going to be awful. Everything. Let me up."

No reaction.

I sighed. "Goddammit, Shaun, don't be an asshole."

His eyes opened. Lifting his head, he gave me a smile that could have melted snow, and said, "You calling me an asshole is the sweetest sound I've ever heard."

I smiled back. I couldn't stop myself. "That's because you are one. Now let me up."

He rolled away, letting me slide out of the bed. My legs were shaky, but they held. True to Dr. Abbey's word, there was a pair of sunglasses on the bedside table. I slid them on, further darkening the room. My eyes hadn't finished changing. When they did, wearing sunglasses in the dark would become second nature again, and the lack of light wouldn't bother me at all.

When I turned, Shaun was sitting up in the bed, watching me. "Are you upset?" he asked, in a quiet tone.

I had to stop to think about it. Finally, I said, "Yes, and no. I didn't exactly miss having fucked-up eyes. We're going to have to hang so many curtains." Back to migraines and staying inside when the sun was highest; back to constant vigilance, to keep from damaging myself further. "But it's going to be nice, I guess. Having my reflection look right." It might stop some of those dreams, the ones where the *real* Georgia Mason showed up and took her life back. "Besides, think of all the lightbulbs we'll save."

Shaun laughed. "There you go," he said. "Silver lining."

"Yeah," I agreed. Because really, that was the biggest thing. My eyes had been damaged by the virus. But I got to stay. I got to stay with him, in the world.

That was all that really mattered.

Five

I was asleep by the time Georgia came back from the bathroom. I woke up to find her in my arms, sunglasses still seated firmly on her nose. She didn't stir as I extricated myself, tiptoed out of the room, and started down the hall toward the kitchenette. I needed coffee. Coffee would make everything better.

Mahir was already waiting there, his hands cupped around a mug of tea. He raised his head at the sound of footsteps, and asked, "Well?"

"She's okay." The words were like a prayer. I smiled, and repeated them: "She's okay."

"Thank God. Is she awake?"

"Not right now. They told you about the...?" I pointed to my left eye.

Mahir nodded. "Yes. I'm sure she'll adapt well. You both will."

"Yeah. About that." Maybe it was selfish to focus on myself at a time like this, but if George was going to live, I was going to stay with her. Completely with her, no matter what that required. "Before we go, I'm going to talk to Dr. Abbey about getting myself medicated. I'm tired of this."

"That sounds like a very wise idea," said Mahir. "Are you going to disappear again? Never come to see us?"

"We have to come back here every eighteen months," said George. I turned. She was standing in the kitchen doorway, sunglasses in place, and she looked so *right* that my knees went weak. "Maybe we can arrange to meet up. See each other. Debrief."

Mahir smiled. "I'd like that."

There was a pot of coffee on the hot plate. I went to pour myself a cup, finally content, all the way down to my bones. It was going to be okay. George was going to live; I was going to get better; we were going to find a way to balance our privacy with our responsibilities. It wasn't happy ever after—that doesn't happen until you're dead—but for the moment, considering the alternatives, it was more than close enough for me.

Acknowledgments

So we have reached the end. Some of you will skip this as meaningless errata; others will read it carefully, to keep the book from being over. I've been in both camps, in my day, so: If you're done, that's fine. Thank you for coming with me this far. There are no deep secrets or precious reveals past this point, and you can go, if you like. If you want to stick around for just a little while longer, though, I would appreciate it.

Thanks to Merav Hoffman, in whose dining room most of *Countdown* was written, one frantic entry at a time; I was racing the clock daily, which can't have made me the most pleasant of houseguests. She has always been understanding of the time I give to fictional friends when she's standing right there, waiting for her shot at my attention.

Thanks to Michelle Dockrey, who picked me up when I was shattered and put me back together one piece at a time. She was with me through the completion of *Feed*, and has been my greatest cheerleader through these stories—and through my life, which I can't imagine without her in it. She hears the ideas before I write them down, and she fixes them after I do.

Thanks to Brooke Abbey, who was, yes, the model for Dr. Shannon Abbey—although my post-zombie mad scientist is a little crankier than her real-life counterpart. She has fact-checked the drug use and pharmaceuticals throughout these stories, making them more accurate than they have any right to be.

Thanks to Michael Ellis, without whom this series might never have been started, much less completed; he listened to more rambling about this setting than any human being should have been expected to endure, and he did it all with goodness and with grace.

Thanks to Kate Secor and Gian-Paolo Musumeci, at whose dining room table parts of the overarching plot were broken down and built back up, all culminating in the day when I was asked a question that changed absolutely everything.

Thanks to DongWon Song, who took a chance on an urban fantasy author with a manuscript about zombies in one hand and a lot of big ideas in the other. He made this series what it is. I will forever be grateful to him.

Thanks to Diana Fox, for bringing me to DongWon in the first place, for trusting that I knew what I was talking about and would see this story to its necessary ending.

Thanks to Will Hinton, who has done his best to meet my sometimes idiosyncratic needs, and who has seen this volume from concept to completion.

Thanks to Chris Mangum, Amy McNally, Ryan Nutick, Amber Benson, Sarah Kuhn, Margaret Dunlap, Cat Valente, Patty Pace, Phil Ames, Sunil Patel, Amanda Weinstein, Talis Kimberley, Will Frank, Torrey Stenmark, Amanda Perry, Lauren Panepinto, Ellen Wright, the whole team at Orbit, and as always, to Shawn Connelly, for keeping me on an even keel. I know it can be a challenge, and I appreciate it more than you will ever know.

And thank you to you, the reader. Thank you for reading, for writing me to tell me what you thought; thank you for your fanart, for your costumes, for your fanfic (which I can't read, but I still enjoy knowing it exists somewhere out there on the big wide Internet), for everything. Thank you for making these words possible. Thank you for trusting me enough to let me lead you into these woods; thank you for trusting me to lead you out again.

I promise I will always do my best to be worthy of that trust.